Also available

The last two novels in
Antonia White's sequence of four

THE SUGAR HOUSE
and
BEYOND THE GLASS

are separately available from Fontana
in one volume.

ANTONIA WHITE

FROST IN MAY

(1)

FROST IN MAY
THE LOST TRAVELLER

FONTANA PAPERBACKS
in association with Virago

Frost in May

First published by Desmond Harmsworth 1933
First published in paperback by Virago Press Ltd 1978
First published in this edition by Fontana Paperbacks
in association with Virago Press Ltd 1982

Copyright © The Literary Executors of Antonia White 1980
Introduction copyright © Elizabeth Bowen 1948, 1973

The Lost Traveller

First published by Eyre & Spottiswoode 1950
First published in paperback by Virago Press Ltd 1979
First published in this edition by Fontana Paperbacks
in association with Virago Press Ltd 1982

Copyright © The Literary Executors of Antonia White 1980
Introduction copyright © Carmen Callil 1979

Made and printed in Great Britain by
William Collins Sons & Co. Ltd, Glasgow

Frost in May

Introduction

Frost in May is a girls' school story. It is not the only school story to be a classic; but I can think of no other that is a work of art. What, it may be wondered, is the distinction? A major classic is necessarily also a work of art. But a book may come to be recognized as a minor classic by right of virtues making for durability – vigour, wideness, kindness, manifest truth to life. Such a book gathers something more, as the years go on, from the affection that has attached to it – no question of its aesthetic value need be raised. A work of art, on the other hand, may and sometimes does show deficiency in some of the qualities of the minor classic – most often kindness. As against this, it brings into being unprecedented moments; it sets up sensation of a unique and troubling kind.

School stories may be divided and subdivided. There is the school story proper, written for school-age children; and the school novel, written for the grown-up. There is the pro-school story and the anti-school – recently almost all school novels have fallen into the latter class. *Tom Brown's Schooldays* has a host of dimmer descendants, all written to inculcate manliness and show that virtue pays. *Stalky and Co.* fits into no classification: one might call it an early gangster tale in a school setting. The Edwardian novelist's talent for glamorizing any kind of society was turned by E. F. Benson and H. A. Vachell on two of the greater English public schools. The anti-school school novel emerged when, after the First World War, intellectuals captured, and continued to hold, key positions along the front of fiction. A few, too few, show a sublime disinfectedness that makes for comedy, or at least satire. In the main, though, the hero of the anti-school novel is the sombre dissentient and the sufferer. He is in the right: the school, and the system behind it, is wrong. From the point of view of art, which should be imperturbable, such novels are marred by a fractious or plangent note. Stephen Spender's *The Backward Son*, not thus marred, is a work of art; but I should not call it strictly a school novel – primarily it is a study of temperament.

To return to the school story proper (written for young people), those for boys are infinitely better than those for girls. The curl-tossing tomboys of the Fourth at St Dithering's are manifestly and insultingly unreal to any girl child who has left the nursery; as against this, almost all young schoolgirls devour boys' school books, and young boys, apparently, do not scorn them. For my own part, I can think of only one girls' school story I read with pleasure when young, and can re-read now – Susan Coolidge's *What Katy Did at School*. As a girls' school *novel* (other than *Frost in May*) I can only think of Colette's *Claudine à l'École*.

I began by calling *Frost in May* a school story. By subsequent definition it is a school novel – that is to say, it is written for grown-ups. But – which is interesting – Antonia White has adopted the form and sublimated, without complicating, the language of the school story proper. *Frost in May* could be read with relish, interest and excitement by an intelligent child of twelve years old. The heroine, Nanda Grey, is nine when she goes to Lippington, thirteen when, catastrophically, she leaves. She is in no way the born 'victim' type – she is quick-witted, pleasing, resilient, normally rather than morbidly sensitive. Call her the high-average 'ordinary' little girl. She is not even, and is not intended to be, outstandingly sympathetic to the reader: the scales are not weighted on her behalf. We have Nanda's arrival at Lippington, first impressions, subsequent adaptations, apparent success and, finally, head-on crash. *Frost in May* deviates from the school-story formula only in not having a happy ending. We are shown the school only through Nanda's eyes – there is no scene from which she is off stage. At the same time there is no impressionistic blurring, none of the distortions of subjectivity: Lippington is presented with cool exactness. Antonia White's style as a story-teller is as precise, clear and unweighty as Jane Austen's. Without a lapse from this style Antonia White traverses passages of which the only analogy is to be found in Joyce's *Portrait of the Artist as a Young Man*.

The subject of this novel is in its title – *Frost in May*. Nanda shows, at the start, the prim, hardy pink-and-white of a young bud. What is to happen to her – and how, or why?

Of the two other girls' school books named, one is American and the other French. *Frost in May* is English – but English by right only of its author's birth and its geographic setting. Lippington is at the edge of London. But it is a convent school – of a Roman Catholic Order which Antonia White calls 'the Five Wounds'. Its climate is its own; its atmosphere is, in our parlance, international. Or, more properly, as one of the girls put it, 'Catholicism isn't a religion, it's a nationality.' A Lippington girl is a Child of the Five Wounds; she may by birth be French, German, Spanish or English, but that is secondary. Also the girls here show a sort of family likeness: they are the daughters of old, great Catholic families, the frontierless aristocracy of Europe; they have in common breeding as well as faith. From Spanish Rosario, Irish Hilary and French-German Léonie the rawness of English Protestant middle-class youth is missing. Initially, Nanda is at a twofold disadvantage, never quite overcome. Her father is a convert; she herself was received into the Catholic Church only a year before her arrival at Lippington. And, she is middle-class, her home is in Earl's Court. There is one Protestant here, but she is aristocratic; there are two other middle-class girls, but they come of Catholic stock.

Lippington is a world in itself – hermetic to a degree possible for no lay school. It contains, is contained in, and represents absolute, and absolutely conclusive, authority. Towards what aim is that authority exercised? On the eve of the holiday that is to celebrate the canonization of the foundress of the Order, the Mistress of Discipline addresses the school. '"*Some of that severity which to the world seems harshness is bound up in the school rule which you are privileged to follow . . . We work today to turn out, not accomplished young women, nor agreeable wives, but soldiers of Christ, accustomed to hardship and ridicule and ingratitude*."' What are the methods? '*As in the Jesuit Order every child was under constant observation, and the results of this observation were made known by secret weekly reports to Mother Radcliffe and the Superior . . .*' How did one child, Nanda, react to this? '*Nanda's rebelliousness, such as it was, was directed entirely against the Lippington methods. Her faith in the Catholic*

Church was not affected in the least. If anything, it became more robust.'
Nonetheless, when, at thirteen, Nanda is faced by her father with the suggestion that she should leave Lippington to receive a more workaday education elsewhere, her reaction is this: *'She was overwhelmed . . . Even now, in the shock of the revelation of her dependence, she did not realize how thoroughly Lippington had done its work. But she felt blindly she could only live in that rare, intense element; the bluff, breezy air of that "really good High School" would kill her.'* And, elsewhere: *'In its* [Lippington's] *cold, clear atmosphere everything had a sharper outline than in the comfortable, shapeless, scrambling life outside.'*

That atmosphere and that outline, their nature, and the nature of their power over one being, Nanda, are at once the stuff and the study of *Frost in May.* They are shown and felt. The result has been something intense, sensuous, troubling, semi-miraculous – a work of art. In the biting crystal air of the book the children and the nuns stand out like early morning mountains. In this frigid, authoritarian, anti-romantic Catholic climate every romantic vibration from 'character' is, in effect, trebled. *Frost in May* could, for instance, go down to time on the strength, alone, of Léonie de Wesseldorf – introduced, in parenthesis almost, but living from the first phrase, on page 78. Momentum gathers round each sequence of happenings and each event – the First Communion, the retreat, the canonization holiday, Mother Frances's death, the play for the cardinal, the measles idyll . . . Lyricism – pagan in the bonfire scene, sombre on the funeral morning – gains in its pure force from the very infrequency of its play . . . Art, at any rate in a novel, must be indissolubly linked with craft: in *Frost in May* the author's handling of time is a technical triumph – but, too, a poetic one.

The *interest* of the book is strong, though secondary; it is so strong that that it should be secondary is amazing. If you care for controversy, the matter of *Frost in May* is controversial. There exists in the mind of a number of English readers an inherited dormant violence of anti-Popery: to one type of mind *Frost in May* may seem a gift too good to be true – it is. Some passages are written with an effrontery that will make the Protestant blink – we are very naive. As a school Lippington does, of course, run counter to the whole trend of English liberal education: to the detached mind this is in itself fascinating. The child-psychologist will be outraged by the Lippington attitude to sex and class. Nanda's fate – one might almost feel, Nanda's doom – raises questions that cannot be disposed of easily or perhaps at all. This book is intimidating. Like all classics, it acquires further meaning with the passage of time. It was first published in 1933: between then and now our values, subconscious as well as conscious, have been profoundly changed. I think it not unlikely that *Frost in May* may be more comprehensible now than it was at first.

ELIZABETH BOWEN

Chapter One

Nanda was on her way to the Convent of the Five Wounds. She sat very upright on the slippery seat of the one-horse bus, her tightly-gaitered legs dangling in the straw, and her cold hands squeezed into an opossum muff. A fog screened every window, clouding the yellow light that shone on the faces of the three passengers as they jolted slowly along invisible streets.

After several sociable but unheeded coughs, the third occupant could bear the silence no longer and began to speak to Nanda's father. She wore a dusty velvet tam o' shanter and a man's tweed coat, and Nanda could tell from her voice that she was Irish. 'Excuse me, sir,' she asked, 'but could you tell me if we are anywhere near Lippington village yet?'

'I'm afraid I can't tell you,' Mr Grey answered in his rich, pleasant voice, 'all I *do* know is that we haven't got to the Convent yet, because the driver is putting us down there. The village is further on up the lane.'

'The Convent?' exclaimed the Irishwoman, 'would that be the Convent of the Five Wounds now?'

'Yes,' said Nanda's father. 'I'm just taking my little daughter to school there.'

The Irishwoman beamed.

'Now isn't that beautiful?' she said, 'you're a Catholic, then, sir?' She pronounced it 'Cartholic'.

'I am indeed,' Mr Grey assented.

'Isn't that wonderful now? To think of the three of us in this omnibus in a Protestant country and everyone of us Catholics.'

'I'm a convert,' Mr Grey explained. 'I was only received into the church a year ago.'

'To think of that!' said the Irishwoman. 'The grace of God is a glorious thing. Indeed it is. I wonder if the little lady knows what a grace has been given to her to have a father that's been called to the Faith?'

She leant over and put her face close to Nanda's.

'And so you're going to the holy nuns at the Five Wounds, my dear? Isn't it the lucky young lady you are? The saints must have watched over your cradle. There's no holier religious anywhere in the world than the nuns of the Five Wounds. I've a cousin meself . . . Mary Cassidy . . . that's one of their lay-sisters in Armagh. She'll be taking her final vows in February . . . the Feast of the Purification. Do you know when that is, my dear?'

'The second of February,' Nanda risked shyly.

The Irishwoman rolled her eyes in admiration.

'Glory be to God, did you ever hear the like?' she asked Mr Grey. 'Are you telling me that young lady's not born and bred a Catholic?'

Nanda's father looked pleased.

'No. She was received only last year, when she was eight. But she's been having instruction and learning her catechism.'

'It's wonderful, so it is,' the Irishwoman assured him, 'and it's a sign of special grace, I'll be bound. Perhaps she'll be called on to do great things in the service of God, who knows? I wouldn't be surprised if she had a vocation later on.'

'Oh, it's early days to think of that,' smiled Mr Grey.

Nanda began to feel a little uncomfortable. She had heard a good deal about vocations and she wasn't at all sure that she wanted one.

'They say God speaks to them very early,' said the Irishwoman mysteriously, 'and that they hear Him best in the innocence of their hearts. Look at St Aloysius now. And St Stanislas Kostka. And St Theresa herself that would have been a martyr for the love of God when she was but three years old. And wouldn't it be a beautiful thing now if she was to offer her life to God as a thanksgiving for the great blessing of your own conversion, sir?'

Nanda began to like the conversation less and less. She was an only child and she had taken to her new religion with a rather precocious fervour. Already she had absorbed enough of the Catholic point of view to see how very appropriate such a sacrifice would be. But although she had already privately dedicated herself to perpetual virginity, and had seriously considered devoting her life to the lepers at Molokai, she did not entirely relish the idea of cutting off her hair and living in a cell and never seeing her home again. She was relieved when the bus stopped and the driver came round and tapped at the window.

'This must be the Convent,' said Mr Grey. 'We get down here. Lippington village is a little way further on.'

'God bless you both,' said the Irishwoman. 'Goodbye, little lady. Say a prayer every morning to thank God and his saints for bringing you to the holy faith. And say a prayer sometimes for poor old Bridget Mulligan, for the prayers of children have great power with the Almighty. I'll say five decades for you this very night that you may grow up a good Catholic and a comfort to your father.'

As they passed out of the omnibus, Mr Grey pressed something into the ragged woman's hand.

'God bless you, sir,' she called after them. 'It was the holy mother of God sent you to me today. St Bridget and all the saints guard you and watch over you and your family.'

After the omnibus had lurched away into the fog, Nanda and her father waited several minutes on the Convent doorstep before the flap behind the grille blinked up and down. After much rattling of chains and bolts the door was opened and a lay-sister portress beckoned them in.

'Will you wait in the lodge, Mr Grey?' she said in a very quiet voice. 'I'll go and fetch Mother Radcliffe.'

While they waited for Mother Radcliffe, Nanda took in her surroundings. Her smarting eyes were soothed by a long stretch of whitewashed walls and red-tiled floor. At the end of the corridor stood a statue of Our Lord in white robes wearing a red, thorn-circled heart on his breast like an order. The bent head with its pale brown hair and beard was girlish and gentle; the brass halo had been polished till it winked and reflected each flicker of the little glass lamp that burned on the pedestal. Never in her life had Nanda seen anything so clean and bare as that corridor. It smelt of yellow soap and beeswax, mixed with a faint, sweetish scent that she recognized as incense.

Outside the portress's little room, which bore the notice 'No admittance for seculars', hung a printed card, punched with a double row of holes and adorned with two cribbage pegs. Over the top was written 'Mother Radcliffe'; the left-hand row of holes was headed 'Is' and the right-hand one 'Is wanted'. In the middle was a list of all the places where Mother Radcliffe might conceivably be or be wanted, such as 'at meditation', 'in the garden', 'in the school', 'with the novices', 'at the farm', 'in the parlour', and 'at recreation'. When Nanda drew her father's attention to this, he was much pleased at the ingenuity of the device.

'They're wonderfully business-like, nuns,' he told her. 'It's all nonsense about their being dreamy and unpractical and out of touch with the world. Every minute of their day is filled up with something useful. If you only learnt one thing from them, Nanda, I should be satisfied.'

'What one thing, Daddy?'

'Never to waste time, my dear.'

In spite of the ingenious card, it seemed to take the lay-sister a very long time to find Mother Radcliffe. But at last she appeared round the angle of the corridor. She came towards them with the step Nanda was to come to know so well, the characteristic walk of all the nuns of the Five Wounds, smooth and sliding, never slow, never hurried. She advanced smiling, but never quickening her pace, her hands folded in her black sleeves. Her pale face was so narrow that her goffered white bonnet sloped to a point under her chin. This bonnet scratched Nanda's face when Mother Radcliffe bent down to kiss her.

'So this is Fernanda,' she said in a kind voice. 'I am so glad to see you, dear child. Will you say goodbye to your father now, or would you like to go to the parlour for a little first?'

Nanda hesitated, but Mr Grey looked at his watch.

'What do you think, Nanda? It's late and Mother will be waiting. But I'll stay if you like.'

'It's all right, Daddy,' said Nanda mechanically. She suddenly felt lonely and frightened. A great longing came over her for small shabby rooms and coal fires and the comfortable smells of tobacco and buttered toast. But she was one of those children who cannot help behaving well.

'That's a brave girl,' said Mother Radcliffe approvingly.

Her father gave her an affectionate squeeze and tucked a bright half-crown into her muff.

'Goodbye, Nanda. Shall I tell Mother you're quite happy? We'll be down on Sunday. Only five days more.'

'Goodbye, Daddy.'

Mother Radcliffe was tactful. She seemed to understand that Nanda did not want to hear the clang of the nail-studded front door behind her father. She led her quickly along the red-tiled passage, talking all the way. Round the corner, outside an oak door, Mother Radcliffe paused in her walk, genuflected swiftly and made the sign of the cross. Nanda, with her hand clasped in the nun's, was taken by surprise, but managed to bob awkwardly. Not liking to remove her right hand from Mother Radcliffe's, she contrived to sign herself with her left, and hoped the nun would not notice. But, in spite of the jutting bonnet which hid her profile, Mother Radcliffe saw everything.

'Come, Nanda,' she said, 'that's not the way little Catholic children make the sign of the cross. It's not reverent, dear.' Nanda felt hot with shame. But the next turn of the passage provided so much interest that she forgot her lapse.

'This is the school corridor,' Mother Radcliffe explained, 'and here are some of the other children. You mustn't be shy; there are plenty of new ones this term.'

At the end of the passage hung a large oil painting of Our Lord, showing his five wounds.

'See, there is Our Lord welcoming you,' said the nun. 'If ever you feel a little bit homesick, just remember that home for a Catholic is wherever Our Lord is.'

Instead of answering, Nanda tightened her clasp of Mother Radcliffe's cool, dry hand. Thinking about religion was a secret, delicious joy, but talking about it still made her uncomfortable and self-conscious. She was a very raw convert.

To her relief, a door burst open and a red-haired, blue-bloused girl dashed out of it. Seeing the nun, she pulled up short and made a very sketchy curtsy.

'Gently, Joyce,' smiled Mother Radcliffe, 'I thought you were having deportment lessons this term.'

'Sorry, Mother,' said Joyce gruffly. Nanda liked her. She had freckles and a pleasant grin which showed very white teeth. Being two years older, she took no notice of Nanda beyond a quick, amused stare.

More doors opened and girls of all ages and complexions

came hurrying out. Nearly all wore the uniform striped blouse and dark skirt, but here and there a velvet frock, a gold chain or a head stiff with American bows marked a newcomer. Nanda was thnkful that her own home clothes were inconspicuous enough to pass without attracting attention. The older girls seemed quite alarmingly grown-up with their huge puffs and side combs. She wondered if she would ever dare to speak to such majestic creatures. Even the fourteen-year-olds looked at least twenty with their long skirts and their neat, small waists strapped in leather belts. There were curtsies all along the passage as Mother Radcliffe passed. Most were no more than quick, springy bobs, but some were deep and slow and wonderful to watch. They must be very difficult to execute, Nanda thought, sighing at her own abysmal ignorance.

A bell began to clang. Still more girls poured out from the glass-fronted doors. Two dark-skinned, graceful creatures with gold rings in their ears slid past, both talking Spanish at the tops of their voices.

Presently Mother Radcliffe stopped a tall girl with a plait reaching to her waist, and a wide blue ribbon slung across her handsome bosom.

'Madeleine,' said the nun, 'this is a new child, Fernanda Grey. Would you take her up to the Junior School?'

'Yes, Mother,' said Madeleine graciously. Keeping her long back erect, she swept a slow and admirable curtsy. The nun inclined her head.

'I shall see you in the morning, Nanda. If there's anything you want, you can always come to my room. The one marked Mistress of Discipline.'

Nanda attempted a curtsy which was not a great success, and which Madeleine's cold blue stare seemed to make still more inadequate. As soon as Mother Radcliffe's back was turned, this new guide enquired haughtily: 'Have you been to Our Lady of Perpetual Succour, yet?'

'I don't think so,' said the bewildered Nanda.

'Well, if you're not sure, you'd better come with me now,' said Madeleine, bored but resigned.

She pushed open the door of a large room filled with excited and chattering children changing into their uniforms. A harassed Irish nun pounced on Nanda and peering at her with short-sighted eyes, asked anxiously:

'Are you Nora Wiggin?'

'No, I'm Fernanda Grey.'

'Number thirty-six are you, dear child?'

'Yes, Mother.'

'There's not a uniform for you. You'll have to wear your home clothes for a few days. Now what can have happened to Nora Wiggin? She was due here at six. I hope she's not lost in the fog. You'd better leave your hat and coat on the chair, there, Fernanda. Tidily, there's a good child. And pin a piece of paper to them with your number.'

'Yes, Mother,' said Nanda, carrying out these instructions.

'There's a good girl. You'd better go up to Mother Frances now.'

'I was just taking her, Mother,' said the righteous Madeleine.

As she trotted up the stone staircase behind Madeleine, Nanda ventured to remark: 'I didn't see Our Lady of Perpetual Succour.'

'Our Lady of Perpetual Succour is the name of the room we were in just now. All the rooms at Lippington are named after a saint. Didn't you know?' Madeleine answered.

Nanda found this very confusing at first. But she was soon to get used to it. By the end of the week she could perfectly understand the situation when someone said: 'I was just rushing into St Mary Magdalene without my gloves when Mother Prisca came out of St Peter Claver and caught me.'

She had no breath now for more questions. The stone stairs stretched up flight after flight and Madeleine's long legs strode on remorselessly. Nanda's own small ones ached, as if someone had tied a tight knot behind each knee, but she dared not ask the queenly Madeleine to go more slowly. By the time they had reached a lighted door at the very top of the building, Nanda was crimson in the face and quite sick with fatigue.

'Here's a new child for you, Mother Frances,' announced Madeleine, pushing Nanda down three steps into a large room and towards a tall and very handsome nun. This nun was surrounded by a group of children of Nanda's own age, who all stared very hard at her.

'We've been expecting you,' said Mother Frances.

Having already met several nuns during her wanderings, Nanda had begun to wonder how she was ever to identify them individually. In their black habits and white crimped bonnets, they all appeared exactly alike to her untrained eye. But looking at Mother Frances, she thought: 'I certainly shan't forget *her*.' The nun returned her look with a smile at once sweet and ironical. Her three-cornered face was white and transparent as a winter flower, and the long, very bright eyes that shone between the blackest of lashes were almost the colour of harebells. Yet all this beauty seemed even to Nanda to be touched with frost. Mother Frances looked too rare, too exquisite to be quite real. During the long, amused look the nun gave her, Nanda thought to herself first: 'She's like the Snow Queen,' and then: 'I shall never be comfortable with her.' Under those remarkable eyes, her courage left her. She felt very small and hot and homesick and common.

Mother Frances laid a cool hand on Nanda's flushed cheek and tucked a strand of hair behind her ear.

'You know Marjorie Appleyard, don't you?' she asked in a voice sweet and ironical, like her smile. Marjorie smiled with distant politeness as Mother Frances mentioned her name.

She was a pretty, china-faced little girl who lived near the Greys in Earl's Court, and whom Nanda privately thought an intolerable bore. But the fact that she had already been at Lippington a whole year made her worthy of respect. Nanda noticed that the dark blue of her uniform was relieved by a pink ribbon worn like Madeleine's blue one.

'You'll have to follow in Marjorie's footsteps,' she told Nanda. 'She got her pink ribbon in her first term, and she's never lost it yet.' Mother Frances's tone implied that there was something meritorious but slightly ridiculous in possessing a pink ribbon.

'What is a pink ribbon for?' enquired another new child, a small, self-possessed foreigner in a tartan frock.

'It's a reward, Louise,' said Mother Frances. 'A reward for being almost unnaturally good for eight weeks on end.'

Some of the children tittered, but uneasily. Mother Frances swept her amused look over the group.

'I'll have to find someone to take charge of Nanda for a few days until she knows her way about,' she observed. 'Which of you would like to take charge of Nanda Grey?'

There was a chorus of 'Me, please, Mother.' One or two even held up their hands. Mother Frances surveyed these with distaste and the hands dropped like plummets.

'We don't hold up our hands at Lippington,' she said coldly. 'This is not a High School.'

She swooped on a plain, sallow child who had not volunteered for the task.

'Why, Mildred, what a wonderful chance for you,' she said in her sweetest voice, 'and what a chance for Nanda. You're the eldest in the Junior School, and you've been here longer than any of the others.'

'Yes, Mother,' admitted Mildred, wriggling unhappily.

'That's not a very good example for Nanda, is it? I want to teach her a lot of things, but I don't want to teach her to squirm when she's spoken to. Nanda will think this is the original school where they taught reeling and writhing and fainting in coils.'

'Oh, Mother Frances,' squirmed Mildred, while the others, including Nanda, laughed.

'Do you know where that comes from?' Mother Frances flashed at Nanda.

'*Alice in Wonderland*,' Nanda flashed back.

'Good child.'

It was Nanda's first triumph. But Mother Frances spoilt it by telling the others: 'You'll find Nanda's read a great deal, I expect. She's an only child and she's got a very clever father. None of you do Latin yet, but Nanda's going to do a Latin exercise every day and send it to her father. So if we can't understand any Latin in church, we'll have to get Nanda to translate it for us.'

Poor Nanda reviled the Latin which had dogged her from the age of seven. Her father believed strongly in the importance of a classical education, and his one misgiving about Lippington had been that no Greek was taught there. Nanda blushed over her parent's eccentricity and felt a wild impulse to run away from the group of grinning little girls whose fathers did not insist on teaching them Latin.

But Mother Frances had not finished with her yet. She had kept her cruellest shot for the last.

'You'll have to get up very early, Mildred, if Nanda isn't to be late for mass. You see, Nanda's father wants her to have a cold bath every morning. So she'll have to be up a quarter of an hour before the others.'

This had even more success than the Latin exercises. Nanda felt she had been branded for life. Never, never would she live down this shame. But Mother Frances, like some expert torturer, seemed to have decided that she had had enough.

'Your desk's the last one down there on the right,' she told Nanda in her sweetest voice, and gave her a smile as if they shared some delicate joke together. 'Just under the pink angel.'

Nanda gratefully accepted this dismissal. Her desk was at the end of a long line, far away from the mistress's rostrum. Between the lines stood a statue of Our Lady, supported on each side by angels with folded wings and flying girdles. Nanda felt it was a privilege to be so near this holy company. Her desk was empty but for a small picture of the Sacred Heart gummed inside the lid and a square of black lace whose use she could not guess. She examined this, wondering if by chance it belonged to another child, but her number was neatly sewn on the hem in Cash's woven letters. She was still marvelling at this and at the exquisite *ronde* handwriting on her name card, when far away in the depths of the building a bell began to clang.

She looked up to find Mildred, to whom she had already taken a mild dislike, at her elbow.

'Shut your desk,' ordered Mildred. 'Whenever a bell rings, you have to stop doing whatever you are doing. That's for supper. Get into the file, quick.'

The other children had stopped talking and fallen into line. Mildred pushed her into a vacant place and pinched her to make her stand straight. Mother Frances, holding a small wooden object like a tiny book, eyed the ranks like a bored but efficient officer. The little wooden book snapped with a loud click and the file moved forward. Down the flights of stone stairs, passing files of older children, the Junior School moved like a compact regiment. In the refectory the regiment was broken up. One or two members were allotted to each table and the complement was made up of bigger girls. Each table had a 'president' and a 'sub-president' of responsible years, whose functions were to carve, to maintain order and to see that the last scraps of abhorred fat were eaten up by their juniors. The long ranks stretched from end to end of the big refectory: a hundred and twenty children stood behind their chairs waiting for the signal for grace. Nanda absent-mindedly sat down, but rose again, covered with shame, at a pinch from the horrified Mildred. A tall girl at a centre table muttered: 'Bless us, O Lord, and these Thy gifts which we are about to receive from Thy bountiful hands, through Christ our Lord,' and there was a loud 'Amen' from the whole school. A bell tinkled; the children drew out their chairs with a noise like thunder and sat down. A few voices rang out and were instantly hushed. At last came the bell for 'talking' and babel broke out. Nanda was too bewildered to talk. She was taking in the large, long room with its peacock blue walls, its raised platform and reading desk and its various pictures. 'I never thought there were so many holy pictures in the world,' she thought to herself. Every room she had entered since she had arrived at the Convent of the Five Wounds had had its picture or statue. The refectory was especially well provided. Right across one wall sprawled a huge reproduction of Murillo's Assumption. Over the reading-desk hung a painting of the Holy Child, clad in white and yellow (the Papal colours, as Nanda proudly remembered), standing on a sunlit hill. The Child stood with outstretched arms which made a shadow behind Him like a large, black cross, and in the background was an apple tree in full blossom with a serpent coiled round its trunk.

Lastly, on a shelf above the dais was a statue of a young man in a white pleated surplice, gazing at a crucifix, whom Nanda took at first to be St Aloysius Gonzaga and later discovered to be St Stanislas Kostka.

Supper consisted of stewed meat and rice, cabbage drowned in vinegar, and sweet tea, already mixed with milk, poured from enormous white metal urns. Nanda did not feel hungry; the combination of foods sickened her, but the President of her table, the irreproachable Madeleine, was adamant. She would not even let her off the cabbage, though the sub-president, a pleasant Irish girl, pleaded for a little relaxation of discipline for a new child on her first night.

'You've got to learn to do things you don't like,' Madeleine assured her. 'You can't begin too quickly.'

And she found time to outline to Nanda all the awful consequences, temporal and eternal, which might result from Nanda's allowing herself to become self-indulgent in the matter of food.

'If you give way to yourself in little things, you'll give way to yourself in big ones later on. Perhaps one day when you are grown up, you'll be faced with a really grave temptation . . . a temptation to *mortal* sin. If you've learnt to control yourself in small ways, you'll have got the habit of saying "no" to the devil at once. The devil's a coward, you know. If you say "no" the first time, he's often too frightened to try again.'

But the more immediate consequence of Nanda's not eating her cabbage seemed to be that she might, if she were not careful, lose her 'exemption'.

'What is an exemption?' she asked, puzzled.

But no one took the trouble to enlighten her beyond saying: 'You'll see on Saturday night.'

The others had so many other and more interesting things to discuss that Nanda was content to listen fascinated to their chatter. But she realized dimly that there were such things as country houses and deer-parks and children who had ponies of their very own. She had read about such marvels in Stead's Books for the Bairns, of whose twopenny pink paper volumes she already possessed a considerable library. Now it seemed that she was actually sitting at the same table with the inhabitants of this dazzling world. Hilary, the pretty Irish sub-president, was talking of house-parties and the boredom of the summer when there was nothing to do but play tennis.

'And to think,' she sighed, 'that they'll be starting cubbing in a fortnight and I'll be in this wretched place.'

Even Madeleine smiled sympathetically, although she remembered her moral mission a moment later and reminded her sub-president of 'loyalty'.

'Daddy's promised me a hunter next Christmas, if I get my

blue ribbon next Immaculate Conception,' went on Hilary, who was flat-shouldered and narrow-waisted, with a shapely little head. It was easy to imagine her in a riding-habit, sitting that hunter to perfection.

'I wonder if you ever think of anything but horses,' smiled Madeleine.

'They're the only things worth thinking about.'

'Hilary!' said the scandalized Madeleine.

'Oh, I only meant they're more worth while than human beings,' drawled Hilary. There was something about her voice and her air that reminded Nanda of Mother Frances.

'Hilary!' insisted Madeleine, scandalized still more.

But Hilary was already deep in a technical discussion with another expert. Nanda would have given anything to have been able to slip in one remark to show that she appreciated this glorious conversation. But, though she was good at guessing, she was too unsure of her ground, and she knew that this was a sacred subject where one blunder might betray one for ever as one of the uninitiated. So she listened, wide-eyed, wishing desperately that she were quite certain of the difference between a piebald and a skewbald, and wondering what colour a strawberry roan could possibly be. No one could trip Nanda up on the difference between Corinthian and Ionic columns. Mr Grey had taught her to distinguish between these on her first visit, at the age of five, to the British Museum. How she wished that he had also or even instead, taught her to distinguish between a bay and a chestnut.

The kindly Hilary noticed Nanda's breathless attention.

'Fond of horses?'

'Oh, yes,' whispered Nanda.

'I suppose you've got a pony, haven't you?'

'Well, n-not yet,' she had the presence of mind to stammer. 'Not a pony of my *own*. But there's an old white one that I'm sometimes allowed . . .'

'White . . . I suppose you mean grey?' said Hilary, and returned to the infallible Margaret.

Nanda was crushed. But she had to admit to herself that she deserved to be. It wasn't her fault that she didn't know that only Arabs and circus horses are called 'white', but it served her right for dragging in that pony at all. For it was only a very old and fat and wheezy one that the rector sometimes lent Mr Grey to mow his croquet lawn and which had never been saddled since it was foaled. Nanda often caught herself making slight exaggerations of this kind during the years she spent at Lippington. It was not snobbishness; it seldom even was the desire to show off; it was nearly always that agonizing wish to be like everyone else, known only to children at boarding-schools, that made her soften and enlarge the outlines of her home life. When everyone else had butlers, it seemed ridiculous to have a mere parlourmaid, and she got used to referring with fine carelessness to 'our butler'. Also the cottage in Sussex grew by imperceptible degrees to 'our place in the country', though she wisely alluded to this as seldom as possible.

Madeleine let the hunting conversation have its head for a few minutes before she turned it into more edifying channels. One of the duties of a president, as laid down by the Foundress in the School Rule, is to prevent the conversation from being too emphatic, too worldly, or too much confined to certain members of the table.

'Of course, the winter holidays are very nice, with Christmas and so on,' she announced, 'but there is something very special about the long summer holidays. They give us a chance of knowing our parents, giving them pleasure by our company.'

Nanda couldn't help wondering if Madeleine's parents really did get very much pleasure from her society. There was something in Madeleine's blamelessness which reminded her of certain heroines she had read about on Sunday afternoons in her Protestant days.

'And then there are some lovely feasts,' Madeleine went on. 'The Feast of the Assumption first of all, of course. We had such a beautiful day. Father Whitby came over from Stonyhurst and celebrated mass in our own little chapel. And my little sister Philomena made her First Communion. She is only eight years old, but Father Whitby said she was *quite* ready to receive Our Lord.' Madeleine kept Nanda well in the tail of her eye during this speech to make sure that she was listening. There was a murmur of admiration from the table.

'Eight, why she's quite a baby,' said Hilary. 'Some of the

Senior School haven't made theirs yet, though they're eleven and twelve.'

'I believe the present Pope likes children to make their First Communion young,' put in a girl who had not yet spoken. 'I shouldn't be surprised if the age was lowered officially.'

'Well, perhaps His Holiness will send for you for a private audience to tell you when he does,' said Madeleine with heavy humour. 'It's not for us to guess what His Holiness will do and what he will not do,' she added, reverting to her normal tone.

The bell rang for grace. Madeleine, while crossing herself with the utmost reverence and propriety, contrived to keep an eye on the deportment of her table.

Section by section, the children filed out, the Junior School last.

Mother Frances was waiting for them in the corridor.

'As it's the first night and you're tired,' she said, 'there'll be no evening recreation tonight. You'll say your prayers and go straight to bed.'

There were a few protesting wails of 'Oh, *Mother*,' but a look from Mother Frances silenced them.

'Go upstairs quickly and quietly and fetch your veils,' she commanded, 'and then we'll go and say our night prayers in the Sacred Heart chapel.'

Nanda was glad to discover the use of the square of black lace she had found in her desk. She followed the example of the others and draped it over her head. In another corner she found a pair of dark blue lisle gloves, and thus gloved and hooded, she filed with the others along the red-tiled corridor where she had walked with Mother Radcliffe, and through the nail-studded door outside which she had disgraced herself by making the sign of the cross with her left hand.

The children clustered together in the little ante-chapel of the Sacred Heart. Through an iron screen, they could see the red sanctuary lamps of the high altar. Behind the empty tabernacle with its mother-of-pearl door rose a huge white stone carving of Our Lord revealing His Sacred Heart to Blessed Margaret Mary Alacoque. Nanda liked this chapel; it was cool to the eye after the glare and heat of the peacock blue refectory. She liked, too, the faint scent of chrysanthemums and incense that drifted through the grille from the high altar, and the newly familiar smell of beeswax given out by the small, light-coloured benches.

'Marjorie will say prayers,' Mother Frances said in a low voice. 'I think we will whisper them tonight, in case Reverend Mother is in the big chapel.'

The prayers sounded new and intimate recited like this in small, sibilant whispers. Nanda felt a wave of piety overwhelm her as she knelt very upright in her bench, her lisle-gloved hands clasped on the ledge in front of her. 'Oh dear Lord,' she said fervently in her mind, 'thank you for letting me come here. I will try to like it if You will help me. Help me to be good and make me a proper Catholic like the others.'

Marjorie was whispering the Litany of Loretto.

'*Turris Eburnea*,' she murmured.

'*Ora pro nobis*,' whispered twenty voices.

'*Turris Davidica*.'

'*Domus Aurea*.'

'*Foederis Arca*.'

'*Janua Coeli*.'

Nanda tried to put more and more of her heart into each '*Ora pro nobis*.' She was flooded with a feeling that was half passionate love of Our Lady and half delight in the beauty of the words, pronounced, not in her father's harsh English accent, but with an Italian softness.

In the last prayer the children whispered together, she could not yet join though it was soon to become as familiar as the Hail Mary itself.

'We fly to Thy protection, oh Holy Mother of God,' began Marjorie, and the others took up: 'Despise not our prayers in our necessities, but deliver us from all dangers, oh ever glorious and blessed Virgin.'

Nanda would have liked to stay on indefinitely in the quiet chapel, but there came the businesslike click of Mother Frances's 'signal'. Already she was learning to obey. She rose briskly and, with a genuflection towards the high altar, followed the others out.

The Junior School slept in the Nazareth dormitory at the very top of the house, a flight further up than their schoolroom. Nanda whose knowledge of dormitories was derived from

28

books, where they always looked terrifyingly naked and communal, was much relieved to find that each child had a tiny white-curtained cubicle to sleep in. When the curtains were drawn, there was just room for her to stand or kneel by her bed. Mildred showed her the use of the solitary chair which was there, not to be sat upon, but to hold her clothes during the night. The chair, with the clothes folded neatly and according to a definite prescription, was to be placed outside the cubicle. If she wanted a drink, she might place her glass on the chair too, and it would be filled with water by a child told off for this special duty. Stockings were ordinarily hung over the back of the chair, but Nanda found that it was a fashion among the more pious to spread them over the top of their clothes in the form of a cross.

The possession of looking-glasses was forbidden. Instead, each cubicle contained a white china picture of the Immaculate Conception and the Five Wounds and a small red flannel badge of the Sacred Heart. These, Nanda learnt, could be supplemented by private Holy pictures or the photos of very near relatives.

'You undress inside,' whispered Mildred, 'but you put on your dressing-gown and come outside to do your hair.'

By the time Nanda reappeared, hairbrush in hand, Mildred was already torturing her own lank, dark locks into a very businesslike plait.

'Aren't you going to plait yours?' Mildred asked severely through a mouthful of tape.

Nanda's hair had never been plaited in her life, but she dared not admit it. Instead she answered weakly.

'I don't know how to.'

'Baby,' said Mildred scornfully. 'I'll do it for you tonight. Turn round.'

Nanda submitted while Mildred pulled her hair back and twisted it into an agonizingly tight rope. The efficient bony fingers tied it tighter still, until Nanda's eyes felt as if they would start from her head.

A bell rang.

'Get into bed quick,' whispered Mildred, and Nanda thankfully obeyed.

Again the bell tinkled. There was a scrambling of children jumping into bed and much noisy pulling-to of curtains. Then a voice, not Mother Frances's, but an old voice with a foreign accent, said:

'Precious Blood of Our Lord Jesus Christ.' And twenty shrill voices answered from the cubicles: 'Wash away my sins.' Complete silence followed.

The gas was turned low. Nanda, huddled on her pillow, watched the huge bonneted figure of a nun move across the ceiling. After a few minutes, the shadow came near her cubicle; then stopped and vanished. The curtains parted and a nun with black glasses came in. She held something towards Nanda.

'Well, my child?' said the nun, after a pause. She was still holding out the dim object towards Nanda.

'Are you perhaps a new child?' she enquired.

'Yes, Mother,' whispered Nanda.

'This is holy water, dear child.'

Nanda stretched out two fingers, wetted them in the sponge of the little stoup and crossed herself.

'Now, lie down,' said the nun kindly, 'you were not, by any chance, crying when I came in?'

'No, Mother,' said Nanda decidedly.

'That is good. But you were lying in such a strange way. Did your mother never tell you at home to lie upon your back?'

'No, Mother.'

'But it is more becoming that you should.'

Nanda straightened herself out from her comfortable ball, turned her back and thrust her feet bravely down into the cold sheets.

'So, it is better,' said the nun gently, 'and now the hands.'

She took Nanda's hands and crossed them over her breast.

'Now, *ma petite*,' she said, 'if the dear Lord were to call you to Himself during the night, you would be ready to meet Him as a Catholic should. Good night, little one, and remember to let the holy Name of Jesus be the last word on your lips.'

She passed silently out of the cubicle.

Nanda retained her new position rigidly for a few minutes.

'I shall never get to sleep,' she thought miserably, as she

heard the outdoor clock strike eight. But even as she thought it her lids grew heavy and her crossed hands began to uncurl. She had just time to remember to whisper 'Jesus' before she was fast asleep.

Chapter Two

Nanda found it very difficult to believe when, on the next Sunday afternoon, a lay-sister told her she was wanted in the parlour, that it was only five days since she had seen her parents. She felt so immeasurably older; so much unpicked and resewn and made over to a different pattern, that, as she trotted sedately behind the lay-sister, wearing her school uniform for the first time, she even wondered if her family would recognize her in all this new dignity. Her hair, which she had learnt to twist into the regulation plait, was drawn smoothly and tightly back from her forehead without a single straying curl, and crowned with a stiff, dark blue bow. Her pinafore was laid aside and she wore the ceremonial gloves without which no Lippington child was permitted to enter parlour or chapel.

The parlour, which lay in the older main part of the house, had begun life as an eighteenth-century ballroom, and still had a faintly secular air with its pale blue walls and velvet curtains. Sallow gilt mouldings of pipes and lutes adorned the pillars, and the parquet was polished to a most conscientious slipperiness. As Nanda entered, she caught sight of her father and mother sitting in a window seat at the far end. Her primness left her and she was on the point of skating recklessly over the waxed floor to fling herself upon them, when someone laid a restraining hand on her sleeve. It was the nun in charge of the parlour. At Lippington one did not meet even one's nearest relatives without *surveillance*.

'Gently, my child,' whispered the nun. 'There are others in the room. You must make a curtsy to them. And do not forget to curtsy to your parents before you embrace them. And it is also customary, a little formality only, to curtsy to the *surveillante* also.' Nanda looked puzzled, but the nun added kindly: 'Only when I am in the parlour. You don't have to curtsy if you meet me outside. Now, go to your dear parents.'

The *surveillante*'s name was Mother Pascoe. Like Mother Frances, she was easy to recognize, but for the very different reason that she limped always on a rubber-shod stick. She was one of the few nuns whom one could imagine transplanted into the outside world; she would look, Nanda thought, just like an ordinary aunt, with a pile of greying brown hair and perhaps a black velvet band round her neck. All the same, a sort of romance clung to Mother Pascoe. The frightened look in her pleasant, faded eyes had another source besides the almost constant pain she suffered from a broken ankle clumsily set by the community doctor. It was an open secret at Lippington that Mother Pascoe had seen a ghost. Sometimes, on very special feast days, she would tell some of the privileged older children the whole story, versions of which filtered through to the horrified and delighted ears of the Junior School.

Mr Grey stood up to greet Nanda, but her mother quite spoilt her careful curtsy by pouncing on her and kissing her.

At the same time, Mrs Grey said quite loudly: 'But, darling, what have they done to your lovely hair?'

'Oh, Mother, *please*,' muttered Nanda; 'someone might hear you.'

Indeed, the military-looking father of the red-haired Joyce was actually smiling in their direction.

'But it looked so pretty the way I used to do it for you,' pursued Mrs Grey in the same ringing and unself-conscious voice. Nanda felt herself turn scarlet. This time Joyce was staring too. Nanda had been long enough at Lippington to know that personal vanity was the most contemptible of all the sins. Suppose, by some awful chance, Joyce should say to Marjorie Appleyard, whose cousin she was, that Nanda Grey thought herself good-looking?

'Shall we go in the garden?' gasped Nanda, drowning in seas of shame. Mercifully, Mrs Grey had already thought how pretty the garden looked from the windows and Nanda steered her parents out of doors without any further disasters. The three of them paced up and down on the terrace which on Sundays and

Thursdays was barricaded at either end by a notice saying 'Visitors are not allowed beyond this board.' Nanda had some difficulty in restraining her mother from darting away down various forbidden alleys, but, helped by her father, she kept her in fairly good order.

'I *never* saw a place with so many rules and regulations,' wailed Mrs Grey. 'I'm sure we waited at *least* half an hour for you, darling child, didn't we, John?'

'Several minutes, certainly,' said Mr Grey, 'but I expect Nanda was a long way away.'

'Yes,' said Nanda spotlessly, 'and I had to do my hair and put on my gloves.' She felt remote and self-possessed.

'Quite right,' approved Mr Grey. 'I like all these little formalities and traditions. I was so glad to see you make that nice curtsy when you came in, Nanda. I felt quite like a French aristocrat coming to see his beautiful young daughter.'

He gave her his rather rare smile and Nanda began to thaw into a human being. She was very fond of her father.

'Those dreadful gloves,' wailed Mrs Grey. 'They make you look as if you bit your nails or something. And you've got the sweetest little hands. Just like mine at your age.'

'The ones that bite their nails have to wear *white* gloves,' said Nanda haughtily, 'and Mildred has to wear black *bags* on her hands sometimes. She pinches, you see.'

'That nice nun . . . Mother Pascoe, isn't it? . . . tells me you've made quite a good beginning with your work and so on. I'm very pleased,' declared her father.

'I didn't lose my exemption,' said Nanda. 'But then, they say hardly anybody does the first week unless they do something really awful.'

'Exemption?' asked her mother. 'Exemption from what, darling?'

'Not from anything,' explained Nanda patiently. 'That's its name, you know. We have Exemptions on Saturday nights in here, and the whole school sits round and Reverend Mother is here and some of the school nuns. And they read out the names of the whole school two by two, and if you haven't lost your exemption . . .'

'Exemption from what?' said Mrs Grey helplessly.

But Nanda swept her aside. 'You get a little pale blue card with "Very Good" on it. And if you've got one or two bad marks, say for talking or being late, you get a dark blue card with "Good" on it. And if you've been very naughty, you get a yellow one with "Indifferent", and Reverend Mother doesn't smile at you. But if you've been really awful and done something serious, you get a sort of dirty green one marked "Bad". They're very rare of course. And Reverend Mother doesn't even hand it you; she just puts it on the table and you have to pick it up. And if anyone's done anything really frightful they don't get a card at all, but Mother Radcliffe just reads out, "So and so . . . *No Note*," and they say the person always cries. Of course, people are often expelled after they've had "No Note".'

'Now, that's very interesting,' said Mr Grey. 'I like all this order and method. I shall be very pleased if you never get anything worse than "Good", Nanda.'

But Mrs Grey, bored, was poking her umbrella into a flower-bed.

'I think it's very untidy and unmethodical to call them exemptions,' she persisted. 'Exemption means something quite different.'

'I'm sorry, Mummy,' said Nanda politely, 'but Reverend Mother is awfully particular about those beds.'

'The nuns have lovely flowers here,' said Mrs Grey romantically. 'I suppose they feel they must have *some* light and colour in their lives.' She went on poking the bed.

'We've got a Scotch gardener,' Nanda told her father. 'His name's MacAllister. Mother Frances says he gets up in the middle of the night to curl the petals of the chrysanthemums.'

The school bell began to ring.

'I must go,' sang out Nanda, with a kind of relief. 'That's for Benediction.'

'Good gracious, I nearly forgot this,' said Mr Grey, fumbling in the pocket of his overcoat and producing a parcel. 'I met Mrs Appleyard the other day, and she happened to say that it was Marjorie's birthday next week. So I thought perhaps it would be nice for you to give her a present.'

'Thank you, Daddy. Yes, I'd like to,' said Nanda, though she had certain misgivings.

The present turned out to be a rather nicely illustrated edition of *Dream Days*, a book which Nanda had not read. The pictures of castles and dragons looked exciting; she wondered whether she could somehow manage to skim through it herself before handing it on to Marjorie, who wouldn't, she was pretty sure, think much of it.

'It looks a lovely book,' she said rather sadly.

'I'll give you one in your Christmas stocking if you like,' Mr Grey promised.

'You *are* a dear, Daddy,' Nanda muttered, fervently kissing him goodbye. 'I must simply fly or I'll be late. Goodbye, Mummy.'

The others were already lined up by the time she arrived breathlessly in the Junior schoolroom; there was only just time to slip *Dream Days* into her desk and snatch up her veil before Mother Frances gave the signal to advance.

After Benediction on Sundays, the Junior School were allowed to read for an hour before supper. Their library consisted of three shelves of Lives of the Saints and Letters from Missionaries of the early nineteenth century. In a small locked case there were some more frivolous works, including several volumes of Andrew Lang's fairy tales, some Little Folks annuals, *Alice in Wonderland*, and the works of Edward Lear. But these were story-books, only doled out for an hour or two on the major holidays that occurred two or three times a term. Nanda's own choice for the week, not entirely a free one, since Mildred was the librarian, was a small red *Lives of the English Martyrs*. Being a very quick reader, she came to the end of it while there was still half an hour of 'free study' to be filled. She did not want to go over the martyrdoms again, having supped full enough of hangings and drawings and quarterings. In fact, the account of the pressing to death of the Blessed Margaret Clitheroe had nearly turned her sturdy stomach. The exciting green volume of *Dream Days* seemed to burn through her desk; she felt she *must* look at it or go mad. But on the other hand, it was quite obviously a story-book. Probably she had no right to have it in her possession at all; in any case, she ought to ask Mother Frances's permission before actually reading it. She temporized. At any rate, there could be no harm in writing Marjorie's name in it. She took the book out and wrote laboriously on the flyleaf:

'Marjorie Appleyard. With best wishes for her birthday. From Fernanda Grey.' Her desk was conveniently far from Mother Frances's table, and Mother Frances herself seemed deeply absorbed in correcting exercise books.

Nanda had sternly meant to put *Dream Days* away at once. But somehow page after page slipped over, and before she knew it she was hopelessly enmeshed. She woke with a gasp as a thin, shapely hand blotted out the page in front of her.

'Very interesting, Nanda,' said Mother Frances, smoothly. 'Is this your library book?'

'No, Mother.'

'It's a story-book, isn't it? Did your parents give it you in the parlour?'

'Yes . . . I mean no, Mother.'

'Be truthful, my good child. Which do you mean, yes or no?'

'Well, it was given me to give someone else.'

'*Oh*, indeed,' said Mother Frances very softly, opening her harebell eyes surprisingly wide. 'Hasn't Mildred told you that we don't take things in the parlour either for ourselves or for other people?'

'Yes, I did, Mother,' piped the odious Mildred, who had screwed round on her chair and was fairly goggling with curiosity. 'I did, only Nanda was so excited she didn't listen.'

'That was a pity, wasn't it, Nanda?' said Mother Frances, sweetly. 'I'm afraid perhaps I'll have to take your exemption to remind you about that. And of course, I'll have to take the book as well.' As she shut up *Dream Days* she saw the writing on the flyleaf. 'Marjorie Appleyard,' she mused. 'Let's see . . . Marjorie's not *related* to you, is she, Nanda?'

'No, Mother,' said Nanda, a little sullenly.

'Just remember, will you, that at Lippington we do not give presents, even birthday presents, except to relatives. We do not encourage particular friendships among little girls.'

Nanda was conscious of a hot sense of injustice as Mother Frances moved gracefully away with the offending book under her arm. Her eyes pricked, and she felt horribly homesick. To stop herself from crying, she tried to concentrate once more on the sufferings of Blessed Margaret. 'As she lay on the scaffold,' she read stubbornly, 'with a smile of heavenly patience on her face, the executioners lowered an heavy oaken door on to her prostrate form. On this door they piled a mass of great weights, and, to cause her still more exquisite torment, they' . . . but the rest of the passage was obscured by a fog of tears.

Two days later, Mother Frances called Nanda up to her table. In front of her lay the wretched copy of *Dream Days*.

'Look, Nanda,' she said amiably, 'I have managed to take Marjorie's name out quite well.' The flyleaf, indeed, showed only the faintest ghost of yellow letters. 'But I just wanted to say this to you. You are a new child and a convert, and you have not quite got into our ways yet. It is not for me to criticize what your father considers suitable reading matter for you . . . in the holidays, that is. This book will remain in your trunk till you go home for Christmas. But I think that you ought to know that the *tone* of this book is not at all the kind of thing we like at Lippington. Apart from its being by a non-Catholic writer, it is morbid, rather unwholesome and just a *little* vulgar.' Mother Frances gave her a chilling smile. 'That is all, dear child.' Nanda turned to fly. Her ears were red-hot.

'Oh, Nanda,' said the musical voice.

'Yes, Mother?'

'I think your stocking's coming down. The left one.'

The Junior School day was modelled on the same ritual pattern as that of the Senior School and the community itself. As soon as the Rising Bell had clanged through the cold dormitory, each child publicly dedicated the day to the service of God, in the words: 'O Jesus, wounded on the cross for me, help me to become crucified to self for love of Thee.' A basin of hot water was allowed, but it was considered more mortified and hence more in the spirit of the Order, to wash in cold. Nanda's zeal went as far as denying herself the warm water, but as the days drew on towards December, her neck was apt to look rather grey against the whiteness of her painfully starched collar. She learnt the elaborate technique of dressing according to Christian modesty so that at no time, even in the privacy of her cubicle, was she ever entirely naked. The whole day was punctuated by prayers. Besides the morning and evening devotions and the thrice-recurring Angelus, every lesson began with an invocation to the Holy Ghost and ended with a recommendation to Our

Lady. Before supper, the whole school assembled to recite five decades of the rosary, and there was usually a novena in preparation for an important feast or a special intention to add some extra petitions to the list. The day ended with prayers in the chapel, and an elaborate examination of conscience under the heading of sins against God, against one's neighbour and against oneself. The offence to which Nanda had to own herself guilty night after night was that of 'wasting time in idle daydreaming.' On Saturdays every child in the school went to confession and, in the evening, after 'Exemptions', there were special devotions in the vestibule of Our Lady of Good Success. Here stood a silver-crowned statue of Our Lady, a replica of the one which had miraculously arrived at Aberdeen in a stone boat without sail or rudder, which was honoured as the special help of students. There were always little red lamps burning before it on behalf of brothers with imminent exams. On Sundays all the children heard two masses and a sermon in the morning and went to Benediction in the afternoon.

As a result of all this, Nanda developed a nice sense of piety. She really did begin to live all day long in the presence of the court of heaven. God the Father and God the Holy Ghost remained awe-inspiring conceptions, Presences who could only be addressed in set words and with one's mind, as it were, properly gloved and veiled. But to Our Lady and the Holy Child and the saints she spoke as naturally as to her friends. She learnt to smooth a place on her pillow for her Guardian Angel to sit during the night, to promise St Anthony a creed or some pennies for his poor in return for finding her lost property, to jump out of bed at the first beat of the bell to help the Holy Souls in purgatory. She learnt, too, to recognize all round her the signs of heaven on earth. The donkey in the paddock reminded her that all donkeys have crosses on their backs since the day Our Lord rode into Jerusalem: the robin's breast was red because one of his ancestors had splashed his feathers with the precious Blood trying to peck away the crown of thorns. The clover and the shamrock were a symbol of the Blessed Trinity. The sunflower was a saint turning always towards God, the speedwell had been white till Our Lady's blue mantle brushed it as she walked in the fields of Nazareth. When Nanda heard a cock crow, it cried: '*Christus natus est*'; the cows lowed '*Ubi? Ubi?*' and the lambs down at the community farm bleated 'Be-e-thlehem.'

Among her most revered possessions was a small white bean whose brown markings, to a seeing eye, showed the rough shape of a monstrance. This had been given her by Mother Radcliffe as a reward for good conduct. It was a bean with history. During the clerical persecutions in France, a parish priest, fearing for the safety of the sacred vessels, had buried them in a bean field. But when the danger had passed and he went to dig them up again, he could not remember in which of many fields he had hidden them. When the crop was gathered in, a certain field produced beans with a curious brown mark, just like a monstrance. The field was searched and all the holy vessels discovered intact.

The great repository of stories and guardian of pious traditions was old Mother Poitier, the French nun who taught Nanda how to go to sleep like a Christian. Nanda looked forward every day to the afternoon recreation, when, instead of playing organized games under the merciless eye of Mother Frances, the Junior School trotted up and down the long alley under the plane trees, munching bread and jam and listening to Mother Poitier. Black-spectacled and comfortably shawled and goloshed, with her fingers always occupied with some grey, unspecified knitting, the gentle old nun always reminded Nanda of the sheep in *Through the Looking-glass*. Mother Poitier must have known as many stories as Scheherazade herself. There were stories of saints and angels and animals, of good children who died on the day of their First Communion, of Jews who stole the Blessed Sacrament, of atheists who were converted on their death-beds, and, most often and most impressively told of all, stories of Blessed Mother Guillemin, the foundress of the Order of the Five Wounds.

But this agreeable recreation only lasted twenty minutes. The serious playtime at midday was an hour of unmitigated penance to Nanda. She was extremely bad at games, partly from natural clumsiness, partly because Mr Grey had a scholarly hatred of any amusement which involved running about and making a noise. The daily baseball showed her up as a short-winded runner and a butter-fingered catch. Mother Frances, who caught and shied like a boy, was fond of sending her up swift, impossible balls for the fun of seeing her wince and paw the air wildly with her woolly gloves.

'*Poor* Nanda,' Mother Frances would mock. 'She's afraid of spoiling her looks. What *would* her father say if we sent her home with a dear little Roman nose?'

And Marjorie Appleyard, who played sturdily and reliably, would titter politely. Even the despicable Mildred shone at baseball; her black, spidery legs fairly twinkled from base to base. The wretched Nanda would long passionately to bring off just one sensational catch, or even to be really badly hurt so as to have a chance of being brave about it, but the next ball would invariably find her fast asleep and up would fly her treacherous hands before she had time to stop them.

After the first intolerably slow one, the weeks ran quickly. Nanda found that being good was surprisingly easy; there seemed so little time to be anything else. Before she realized it, she had won the pale blue card of 'Very Good' seven weeks running. One more would bring her a pink ribbon like Marjorie Appleyard's. She was a little excited; a pink ribbon was an enviable possession, with special privileges attached to it. Moreover, her father would be delighted if she secured it. So she began her eighth week in a spirit of the most rigid virtue.

It seemed to Nanda that Mother Frances was keeping a particularly vigilant eye on her. Evidently, she was waiting for a chance to pounce on some lapse and take Nanda's exemption. But she was determined to defy Mother Frances. Whenever she felt her mistress's sarcastic gaze on her, she behaved more exasperatingly well than ever. On Friday morning, when there was only one more day to hold out, Mother Frances called her to her desk.

'How many very goods have you had, Nanda?'

'Seven, Mother Frances.'

Mother Frances considered her, with her head on one side. Lately, she had had a very bad cough and the bright flush it had brought to her cheeks gave her an unnatural, painted look. Her eyes shone bright as glass, and the hand she put over Nanda's was dry and hot.

'And so I suppose you think you're a model little girl?'

Nanda did not answer.

'There's goodness *and* goodness, you know. I've known children who were the despair of everyone turn into real saints later on . . . all the more real because they'd had difficult natures to fight with. Look at the Saints themselves. Most of them were very far from being just bread-and-butter good when they were young. Think of St Ignatius and St Augustine and St Mary Magdalen . . . they were sinners before they were saints. The trouble with you, my dear, is that you don't seem to have any normal healthy, natural naughtiness about you. God doesn't care about namby-pamby goodness, you know; he wants the real hard goodness that comes from conquering real hard faults. I don't mean that you haven't got faults. The trouble about your faults is that they don't show. You're obstinate, you're independent, and if a child of nine can be said to have spiritual pride, spiritual pride is your ruling vice. One of these days, if you're not careful, you'll be setting up your own conceited little judgement against the wisdom of the Church, which is the wisdom of God himself.'

A few weeks ago, Nanda would have wept at such criticism, but to her own surprise, she found she was growing a hard little protective shell. She merely bit her lip and stared at Mother Frances.

Mother Frances smiled:

'Well, I suppose I can't take your exemption for spiritual pride,' she admitted, 'only don't mistake a pink ribbon for a halo, that's all.'

In spite of her outward calm, Nanda was in a tumult. Mother Frances's speech had pierced the protective shell after all. She hadn't, until the last week, even made any special effort to be good; she had merely tried to avoid being conspicuously naughty. Her father had always demanded a high standard of quietness and obedience, and these virtues had become second nature to her. But now she was faced with the horrid thought that perhaps she was one of those spineless and spiritless creatures who are incapable of anything but a sort of negative primness. After all, she had never actually proved to herself that she wasn't. She remembered her pitiful displays on the baseball field. Obviously, she must be a physical coward. Probably she was something still more contemptible . . . a moral one. She

41

must find out as quickly as possible. The pink ribbon waved before her eyes, but she sternly blinked away its inviting image. 'The very next lesson,' she vowed, 'I'll do something *really* bad.'

Her chance came. The next lesson was history, and Friday was the day for the weekly history examination. Nanda was a favourite of mild, pink-faced Mother Patterson, who took the history class, and she usually got the highest marks in the test. According to her usual custom, Mother Patterson gave Nanda a written slip with the questions and told her to copy them on to the blackboard. Very neatly and carefully, knowing that there was no copy, she tore up the written slip. Her apprehension had gone; a high, cold excitement kept her up as, slowly and deliberately, she wiped every single question off the blackboard. There was a gasp of dismay from the history class, but as Nanda examined the row of faces, she saw something new and intoxicating written on them. She went through the day on a wave of exultation. Even the yellow card marked 'Indifferent' handed her so coldly by Reverend Mother the following night and the ruined hopes of her pink ribbon could not entirely damp her sense of triumph. Her tears during the hymn to Our Lady of Good Success afterwards were quite perfunctory, the merest tribute to society. Through her fingers she could see some of the Senior School looking at her with interest. At supper, the admired Hilary talked to her quite a lot, and even let her off her cabbage.

For the first time in her life, Nanda was a success.

Towards the end of November, Nanda noticed in the chapel an elegant young lady of twenty or so, who knelt by herself at a prie-dieu at the head of the nuns' stalls. She was a source of great distraction to Nanda, for she was very pretty, with a mass of golden curls piled on the top of her small head. Her hair seemed to shine the brighter for the wisp of black net she wore as a veil and her soft dresses fitted her slim shape as Nanda had never seen dresses fit before. At night she sometimes appeared in the school corridor wearing silver shoes and a pearl necklace and a frock cut a little low round the neck. Once Nanda saw her talking to Hilary O'Byrne and plucked up the courage to ask Hilary who the lovely stranger could be.

'Oh, that's my cousin, Moira Palliser,' said Hilary carelessly. 'She was here two years ago. She's going to enter.'

'What, become a nun?' exclaimed Nanda, aghast.

'Yes, if they'll have her,' laughed Hilary. 'She's been trying on and off since she left.'

'You see, the Order has to be very careful,' explained Madeleine heavily. 'They have to be very sure that she has a true vocation. You see, her father is an earl, and she will be a countess in her own right when he dies, and all the property will come to her. If she were to enter here, the estates would pass to the Order, and it would be a great responsibility for them. Moira Palliser has some very worldly relations – Protestants – who would like to make a scandal to prove that the Five Wounds are trying to force Moira to enter in order to get the money. Whereas, of course, it is just the other way round.'

A few days later the whole school was asked to make a novena for a special intention. Nanda guessed that the intention had something to do with Moira Palliser. Soon after the novena ended, Reverend Mother told the children at Exemptions that their prayers had been answered. On the following Monday Lady Moira appeared in the chapel shorn of her soft silk frocks and wearing the hideous flannel blouse and serge skirt of a postulant. But her hair still shone through her veil in the same mass of beautifully rolled little curls. Nanda caught sight of her face; it looked gay, almost mischievous.

About a month afterwards came the ceremony of clothing. As the children filed into the chapel, the organ was playing soft, vaguely bridal music. The altar was ablaze with candles and so loaded with lilies that the air sickened with them. Two prie-dieu were set out on a red carpet in front of the altar gates, and these also were gay with candles and flowers. In the strangers' benches sat four or five very well-dressed people and a stout person in a tartan silk frock who wore a woollen shawl crossed over her chest, and an odd little cap of black net. This person alternately held a handkerchief to her eyes and recited her rosary in French in a very audible whisper. Only two postulants were to make their first vows that day: Moira Palliser and her Breton maid. There was a flutter of excitement as they came up the aisle. Lady Moira looked pale and collected; she communicated a spiritual radiance to her secular white satin and pearls. Behind her walked the short figure of the red-cheeked, black-eyed Breton girl, encased in stiff muslin that stood out all round her in a huge bell. A little fichu of white silk came down to a point between her shoulders, and instead of a veil she wore a starched lace headdress.

The sermon was preached by a lean and soldierly young Jesuit, who fidgeted all the time with the red marker of his missal.

He began, without preliminaries:

'St Theresa said one day to her nuns: "Sisters, let us go mad for the love of God." That seems to us, perhaps, a Spanish exaggeration . . . something, in any case, more appropriate to the sixteenth century than the twentieth. And yet, we are here this morning to watch a young woman, who has everything a worldly person could desire, make a renunciation that must seem to nearly all her friends an act of sheer folly. Think of the good people at this moment playing golf at the club next door. You can imagine them saying to each other: "Either the poor girl is hysterical, or, depend upon it, she has been entrapped by those wily Roman Catholics. No doubt, the Jesuits are at the bottom of it." And they will shake their heads intelligently as they drive off from the tee. The trouble is, they don't go far enough. They should have taken the next step and said: "Lady Moira Palliser is mad. Mad for the love of God."'

By the end of the sermon, Nanda wanted to stuff her fingers in her ears. Yet Father Parry was only voicing the whole spirit of Lippington when he said that a vocation was to be more ardently desired and more warmly accepted than anything in the world. A secular life, however pious, however happy, was only the wretched crust with which Catholics who were not called to the grace of religious life must nourish themselves as best they could. A vocation followed was the supreme good, a vocation rejected the supreme horror. Father Parry spoke of people who led apparently beautiful lives, yet who were devoured by the cancer of a rejected vocation which made them loathsome in the sight of heaven. He emphasized the extreme delicacy of the call . . . it was the merest whisper easily drowned in the noises of the world. It might come quite suddenly at a dance or in the middle of a game of tennis. It might be a gradually growing conviction, beginning in very early childhood. To human thought it might seem capricious; often it was withheld in spite of years of prayer, for the spirit of God blew where it listed and often hovered over the most unlikely people. But once the call had sounded, it must be immediately and implicitly obeyed in the heart, even though the actual dedication might not take place till years later. Very seldom did it sound twice; God did not force His lovers. But it was easier for a pagan steeped in sin to enter heaven than for a practising Catholic who had stopped his ears to Christ's secret invitation.

Nanda could not decide which alternative was the more frightening, the thought of being in danger of hell or the prospect of having to be a nun. For she had an uncomfortable feeling that perhaps she had a vocation. She knew from Mother Poitier that the summons was not always accompanied by a holy joy on the part of the summoned. There were nuns who had fainted with fear and horror when their vocation had been revealed to them. Sometimes she found herself bargaining with God, saying: 'I'll do *anything* else for You. I'll never marry, I'll be poor, I'll go and nurse lepers. Only let me live in the world and be *free*.' But the chilly voice inside always answered: 'The only thing that God wants is the thing you are afraid to offer.'

She listened with painful attention as Lady Moira made her vows of poverty, chastity and obedience, and shuddered when Reverend Mother led her out of the chapel with the novice's thick, white veil flung over her orange blossom and tulle.

As the chapel door closed behind her, the nuns intoned a heavily stressed, unaccompanied psalm that beat on the nerves.

'*Sicut sagitta in mánu poténtis,*' sang one side of the choir, and the other answered:

'*Ita filia excussórum.*'

Mildred nudged Nanda's elbow.

'They're cutting her hair now,' she whispered ghoulishly.

Chapter Three

Mother Poitier was very old. As a child she had been at school at the first house of the Order at Vienne and had received her blue ribbon from Blessed Mother Guillemin herself. It was she who guarded the traditions of the saint in the young English house of Lippington, and who told Junior School after Junior School the story of Blessed Marie-Joseph's life. When one of the novices was set to painting a picture for the chapel in honour of Mother Guillemin's beatification, it was Mother Poitier who stood by the easel and jealously watched every stroke of the brush.

'You are making our Mother's habit too smart, sister,' she would say. 'Have you forgotten that she always wore an old habit out of humility?'

Or again: 'You are making her hands too white. She was not a fine lady, but a peasant who worked in her father's fields before she worked in Our Blessed Lord's vineyard. Our holy habit itself is only a copy of an old burgundian peasant's dress.'

Nanda found the official life of Mother Guillemin very dull indeed. It was printed in almost illegible type and illustrated with small, scratchy engravings of Five Wounds convents in different parts of the world. And, being written by a priest, it was full of long advisory letters from Mother Guillemin's confessor and literal transcriptions of papal encyclicals. In a fit of piety, she had prayed to win the two huge crimson volumes in a raffle in aid of the Society for the Propagation of the Faith, but by the time she had struggled through the first chapter, she wished she had prayed for the phonograph instead. It was so much more amusing to hear about Mother Guillemin from Mother Poitier, walking up and down the dusty alley under the plane trees and munching thick slices of bread thinly spread with rhubarb jam.

'Our Holy Mother was so devout,' Mother Poitier would say, beaming at the twenty attentive faces in their red woollen hoods, 'that she would go into an ecstasy at her meditations. And one day I remember . . . it was very wicked of us, but we were young and naughty and only in the Junior School, as you are . . . we crept up behind her in her stall and scattered little pieces of paper all over her habit. And when we came back, two hours later, not a piece of paper had shifted. You can think how very much ashamed we were of our own distractions at our prayers.'

Another time it would be: 'Our Mother was very ill towards the end of her life, and hardly able to eat anything. The kitchen sister was always sending her little special dishes to tempt her appetite, but the food would come back almost untasted. But one day when she had sent her in a little omelette, her plate came back empty. Every scrap had been eaten. The sister was delighted. The next day she sent her in a bigger omelette. Again every scrap was eaten. The whole community was happy. The third day she added a little bacon. Again the same thing happened. But on the fourth day one of the novices went into Mother Guillemin's room while she was having her breakfast, and forgot to knock on the door. What do you think she found? There was Mother Guillemin sitting by an open window and talking to a very dirty little boy from the village. And on the window-sill was her breakfast tray and the little boy was eating Mother Guillemin's omelette and her bacon and her bread just as fast as he could. That was the secret of our saint's wonderful new appetite. Mother Guillemin was so spiritual and so mortified that it was as if her body were glorified already and she would often eat nothing all day but the wafer at Holy Communion, although she worked harder than any man of affairs. She had the greatest devotion to the Blessed Sacrament, and she used often to say to us in the words of another saint: "So great is the virtue of this Sacrament that not only the soul but the frail body also receiveth from it a great increase of strength."'

Off the parlour that had once been a ballroom lay a circular vestibule that had been turned into a Lady chapel. Mass was only said there three or four times a year on special feasts, and the tabernacle was empty. The children used it for saying their rosary and for the special devotions to the patron saints of health, St Philomena and St Roch, which took place once a month. It was a gay little room, a little drawing-room with blue velvet curtains in the bow windows, that caught all the afternoon sunlight from the terrace outside. St Roch and his plague-spot looked out of place beside the prim and dainty St Philomena with her silver anchor and Our Lady with her distaff and work-basket. This picture of Our Lady was one for which all children of the Five Wounds had a very particular affection. The original had been painted by a novice of the Order in Rome and specially blessed by the Pope. It showed the Blessed Virgin as a girl of fourteen or so, sitting in a courtyard at her work. Instead of the conventional blue robes, she wore a bright pink dress with a laced bodice and a white hood which showed her hair done in neat Victorian ringlets.

Every new child at Lippington was told the story of *Mater Admirabilis*. It was from Mother Poitier, naturally, that Nanda heard it. She was walking with the others one November afternoon, up and down the terrace, and finding some difficulty in skipping backwards in front of Mother Poitier. Nuns are like royalty and one must never deliberately turn one's back to them.

'About the middle of last century,' Mother Poitier began, 'His Holiness wished to do Our Lady a special honour. Louise, you are not to give your *goûter* to the sparrows.'

'But St Catherine of Siena gave her dinner to the little cats,' objected Louise.

'That may be. But you, my child, are not St Catherine of Siena. His Holiness, as I say, decided to add another title to Our Lady's litany.'

'May I say what it was, Mother?' asked Marjorie Appleyard. Her china face was clear as a shell in the red worsted hood.

'Well, child?'

'*Mater Admirabilis*,' gasped Marjorie, just ahead of half a dozen others.

'Yes, *Mater Admirabilis*. Well, our Holy Mother who was in our house at Rome at the time, called her community together and asked, if they were to paint a picture of Our Lady under this new title, how they should show her. And one nun thought she should be painted on her heavenly throne and another in her home in Nazareth and another at the foot of the cross, and so on. At last, Mother Guillemin asked a new, a very shy novice, who had just arrived from Ireland. Who was that novice, Josephine?'

'Mother O'Byrne, Mother.'

'Yes, a great-aunt of Hilary O'Byrne in the Senior School.'

Nanda could not help hopping on one leg and crying: 'I know Hilary O'Byrne, Mother. I'm at Hilary's table, Mother.' And was promptly shamed by Mildred's contemptuous squeak: 'Well, so does everybody know Hilary O'Byrne. Snub to you.'

But Mildred was silenced too, for Mother Poitier turned her black spectacles, positively flashing with reproof, on her.

'That is no way for an old child to speak to a new. How often have I told you that a child of Five Wounds is known by her courtesy? No more interruptions, children, or the bell will ring before I have finished. Now, Mother O'Byrne was afraid to speak at first, for she was so young and could speak very little French. But at last she said that she thought of *Mater Admirabilis* as a young girl, still of school age, a little shy, but recollected and happy with her books and her needlework. And Mother Guillemin said: "That is how I see her, too. Could you paint us such a picture?" And Mother O'Byrne was very much confused, for she had only painted little pictures of her horses and her dogs and the country round her home in Ireland, but she was bound by her obedience, and she said that, by the grace of God, she would do her best. So she began to paint her *Mater Admirabilis* on the walls of the children's study-room (it was during the long summer holiday) and the community was always coming in to see how the work was getting on. She was painting *in tempera*, and the older nuns began to laugh at her work, because the colours looked so much too crude and bright. And some of them went to our Holy Mother and said, quite scandalized: 'Sister O'Byrne is painting such a very strange picture of Our Lady. Why, she has even given her a pink dress instead of a blue one." But Mother Guillemin only smiled and she forbade anyone to criticize the picture or even to look at it till it was finished. But she asked Mother O'Byrne in private about the pink dress, and the novice told her, very humbly, that her last new dress in the world had been just such a pink one, with a bodice laced with black, and that she had been immoderately fond of it, and had even had thoughts of it after she had entered and that she hoped, by making a present of it to Our Lady, as it were, to rid herself of such sinful temptations to vanity. At last, the day came when the picture was to be shown to the community. Poor Mother O'Byrne was very unhappy, because, though she had painted it a dozen times, she could not make the expression on Our Lady's face just what she wanted. But because of her humility and her vow of obedience, she would not ask for any more time to work on it. So she waited while Mother Guillemin drew the curtain, expecting to be shamed before all the nuns. And then . . .'

Mother Poitier turned her black glasses from face to face, smiling happily and expectantly.

'And then, as the curtain dropped, the whole community fell on their knees. For on Our Lady's face there was the most beautiful, the most heavenly look. And Mother O'Byrne said to Mother Guillemin: "I did not paint it so . . . I could not paint it so." But Mother Guillemin blessed her and said: "My child, I think Our Lady finished her picture herself."'

There were sighs of satisfaction. The old ones smiled proudly at the new ones.

'There's a copy in every convent of the Five Wounds, isn't there?' asked Monica. Monica, bright-eyed and rough-haired, was the Junior School dunce. Though she was twelve, she still could not master enough of the catechism to qualify her for making her First Communion. Every time she did a paper on Christian Doctrine, she fell into the most dreadful heresies.

'My poor Monica,' Mother Frances had said to her only last Saturday, 'do you know you have fallen into the errors of the Jansenists, the Manicheans and the Albigenses all in the space of one hundred and fifty words?'

And Monica had, very naturally, burst into tears. She had only one talent, a great aptitude for drawing dogs. She could not draw anything else, but she really did draw dogs very well. Nanda thought it must be because she looked so like a Scotch terrier herself, looking up with bright, puzzled eyes through her mane of brown hair.

'But they can never quite get Our Lady's expression in the copies, can they?' insisted Marjorie.

'No,' smiled the nun, 'Our Lady might paint her own portrait for her own friends, but she is much too modest to have her photograph taken.'

There was a chatter of dismay as a tall figure ran past, a blue ribbon flying wildly behind her.

'That's Adela going to ring the bell,' said Marjorie, who never ignored the obvious. 'She's late.'

Hurrying to scramble into her place in the file, Nanda dropped her bread and jam. She had been too much excited by the story to remember to eat it. Mother Poitier stooped and picked it up; then, extracting a rusty penknife from her immense pocket, she carefully removed any actual pebbles from the bread and jam and held it up with an inviting smile. The slice still looked very dirty.

'Now, here is a nice little penance for someone,' cried Mother Poitier gaily. 'Who would like to eat this nice bread and jam? In the siege of Paris our Holy Mother and her nuns ate bread even the rats would not touch. Louise, you were wanting to imitate the saints a little while ago. Here is your chance, dear.'

Louise bit her red lip. She was the one, slim and dark as an Indian, whom Nanda had noticed on the first night. Then, with a shake of her plait that made the tiny gold rings in her ears dance, she held out her hand for the dirty bread. Her nose crinkled with disgust as she swallowed, but she said nothing.

Mother Guillemin had laid down in the school rule that, during their first years, the children were to be gently coaxed into good and pious habits by a system of small rewards. She said quite frankly in the Letter to Superiors, which was read aloud at the beginning of every term, that if small children came to associate what was morally good with what was physically pleasant, the good habits would become fixed and remain in after years, when the sweets and extra bits of amusement were no longer forthcoming. The rewards varied from pink ribbons and silver crosses to trifles as small as a sweet wrapped in bright paper. But the ones most worth gaining were known as 'Permissions'. There were permissions of every sort and kind. Permission to go down to the farm and get in the eggs, to help in the bakehouse, to have talking in the refectory during lunch, to visit the printing loft, to go to the community mass at six o'clock, to have a story-book on a week-day. The permissions were written in an exquisite round hand on cream paper, twisted into a tiny scroll and tied with pink silk. Nanda was very much shocked when, at the fair on the Feast of the Immaculate Conception, she found a stall selling permissions at sixpence apiece.

The Feast of the Immaculate Conception in December was one of the great days of the year. Preparation for it began a fortnight beforehand, and included extra devotions to Our Lady, the learning of special songs and hymns by the whole school, and a Practice. Some particular virtue was chosen and had to be practised by the whole school. Nanda's first Practice was one of Courtesy. All the children were enrolled as Knights of the Blessed Virgin and given silver cardboard shields inscribed with the motto *Noblesse Oblige*. The nuns and the blue ribbons were entitled to give good marks for outstanding examples of courtesy that they observed, and any case of really bad manners was punished by the loss of the silver shield which could only be redeemed by heroic acts of politeness. For a fortnight the air was tense with courtesy. Nanda found her bitterest enemies kindly offering to tie her plait or button her pinafore. She was terribly embarrassed when the queenly Madeleine stooped down and picked up a fork that she had dropped. Madeleine wore stays that creaked and seemed to make her condescension more fearfully regal than ever. There was a heated debate as to whether Monica's idea of giving the school cat the milk from her supper should be praised as an act of courtesy to the cat or censured as an act of discourtesy to her parents, who had provided the milk. As the wretched Monica was known to prefer cats to milk, the vote went against her. At the end of the fortnight, on the eve of the feast, there was a solemn offering to Reverend Mother of the fruits of the Practice. The name of each child, with the number of her good and bad marks, was inscribed in an illuminated book, copiously adorned with blue ribbons and silver seals. The whole school assembled in the big hall, wearing their best white uniforms and proudly holding their silver shields. Those who had lost them huddled in a miserable group at the back, wearing their every-day blue and not allowed even to join in the singing. A little stage had been put up at the back and the curtains were pulled up three times to reveal tableaux of special acts of courtesy in the lives of the saints. There was St Martin, with Hilary O'Byrne looking boyish and handsome in gilt paper armour, dividing his cloak with the beggar. There was St Wenceslas cutting the corn with his own hand to make the bread for the Blessed Sacrament. And there was a troop of angels preparing supper for the friars, because St Francis had fallen into an ecstacy and forgotten to order any food for his brothers. Nanda noticed with envy that the smallest angel, looking very angelic indeed, was Marjorie Appleyard.

Mother Frances had arranged for the Junior School to have a special offering of their own, so after the public ceremony, Reverend Mother was solemnly ushered up to the small room at the top of the house. The desks had been pushed back and a wonderful cave of brown paper and sparkling cotton-wool erected at the end of the room. In the cave was the manger with the Holy Child and St Joseph and Our Lady, and the shepherds. Each member of the Junior School was represented by a small wooden animal with her name tied round its neck. There were sheep and goats and deer and pigs. The child who had most good marks in the Practice – it was Marjorie, of course – had her animal nearest the crib; the others followed in order.

'That is a sheep for you, Marjorie,' said Mother Frances, as she selected a very blameless lamb and planted it in place, 'because you really are rather like a little sheep, aren't you? I think Louise must be a deer, because she has such long legs and runs so fast. And what shall we have for Nanda? I think a little pig, because pigs are the most obstinate animals in the world.'

With a sweet smile she planted a stout pig in the very door of the stable.

'And now, what shall we have for Monica? I'm afraid Monica's animal will be a very long way from the Holy Child. Monica, can you tell us *yet* what the Immaculate Conception means?'

Monica turned and twisted her hands in her skirt.

'It means that Our Lady was conceived immac – immaculate.'

Mother Frances was still smiling.

'Just so. And what do those long words mean exactly?'

'That Our Lady . . . that Our Lord was born without . . . was born of a virgin.'

'But that is the mystery of the Virgin Birth, not the

53

Immaculate Conception. Don't you *really* know the difference between the two?'

Poor Monica wriggled.

'Oh, I do, Mother. Really, I do. Only I can't explain exactly.'

'That's a pity, Monica, isn't it? That's like the Protestants, who can never explain exactly what *they* mean. Nanda had better tell you. Well, Nanda?'

Nanda mumbled.

'The Immaculate Conception means that Our Lady, alone of all human beings, received the grace of coming into the world without the stain of original sin.'

'Alone of all human beings,' mused Mother Frances. 'What about Adam and Eve? Didn't they come into the world without original sin?'

'Oh, yes, Mother,' piped Marjorie. 'Original sin was the sin of Adam, the father of the human race, from whom we all inherit the primal stain.'

'Just so. So, my dear Nanda, even you aren't quite a real Catholic yet. Still there's some excuse for you. But Monica comes from a good Catholic home and ought to know better. Here are we having a Practice of Courtesy in honour of Our Lady and Monica hasn't even the common politeness to Our Lady to know what the great grace of the Immaculate Conception, her proudest title, means. I am afraid that Monica must be this little black sheep that was lost on the way and never got near the crib at all.'

On the day of the feast itself there was high holiday. The corridors were hung with garlands of evergreen and the children who had distinguished themselves in the Practice were allowed to help in the pleasant business of hanging red Chinese lanterns in perilous places. In the morning there were wild games of hide and seek all over the garden. Mother Frances, tireless as an amazon, with her habit looped up over her black petticoat, led a panting, racing band up and down the alleys. She was flushed and bright-eyed with running on a frosty morning, and she coughed as she leant against the winning post. But not one of the short-skirted children could keep up with her long strides. Then came the distribution of ribbons. Hilary's name was called out, and she almost ran up to Reverend Mother's table, sucking in the corners of her mouth to keep from laughing with pleasure. Nanda knew she was thinking not of the blue ribbon but of the hunter she had lassooed with it. Very much to her surprise, Nanda received a pink ribbon herself.

In the afternoon there was a grand reunion of Old Children. Nanda found them very fascinating. There were lovely creatures, incredibly grown up, who smelt sweet and wore big hats and spotted veils and had bunches of violets pinned to their sable muffs. Some of them displayed their Child of Mary medals hung on broad white ribbons over their beautiful worldly frocks. They giggled and chattered and rustled in and out of the study-rooms, calling out, 'My *dear*' and '*Do* you remember?' and 'How *perfectly* fascinating.' And there were depressing ones who turned up year after year and who wore clothes as hideous as the postulants' flannel blouses and skirts, and of whom it was whispered: 'She's tried to enter everywhere but they won't have her, and she's leading the *most* beautiful life out in the world; the poor *love* her.'

At five o'clock came a solemn benediction, a benediction with more candles and lilies than Nanda had ever seen, and long hymns enriched by the ripe drawing-room voices of the Old Girls. The nuns' voices were thin and clear and remote, like wood wind, but the Old Girls' sounded like 'cellos played with a throbbing *vibrato*. The smell of violets and fur mixed with the smell of incense and hot wax; the air shimmered in waves of heat and sound. Out of the chapel they went two by two in their white veils, each girl carrying a lighted candle and a calico lily. They were singing the traditional hymn of the Immaculate conception, the Old Children throwing back their heads and rolling their lace-collared necks in an exstasy of reminiscence.

> '*Sancta Maria Virgo Immaculata*
> *In conceptione, Immacula-ata*
> *Immaculata, Immaculata, Ora pro nobis, Immaculata*'

they shouted together, and the contraltos, striking deep into the bass, boomed alone, '*Immaculata*'.

Two by two, shielding their candles from their neighbours' veils, they wound through the lantern-lit passages to the Lady chapel. Big baskets stood in front of the picture of *Mater Admirabilis*, and into the baskets each pair cast their calico lilies, murmuring:

'Oh, Mary, I give you the lily of my heart, be thou its guardian for ever.'

Nanda dropped her lily with awe. It stood, she knew, for some mysterious possession . . . her Purity. What Purity was she was still uncertain, being too shy to ask, but she realized it was something very important. St Aloysius Gonzaga had fainted when he heard an impure word. What could the word have been? Perhaps it was 'belly', a word so dreadful that she only whispered it in her very worst, most defiant moments. She blushed and passionately begged Our Lady's pardon for even having thought of such a word in her presence.

Before they went to bed there was a great treat for the Junior School, one of Mother Poitier's 'special stories'. The lights were put out; the children huddled together in an exquisitely shivering group on the floor at the old nun's feet. Nanda was sitting next to Monica. She felt a hot, bony hand grasp hers imploringly and gave it a reassuring squeeze. It was nice to know someone was a little more frightened than she was herself.

'Once upon a time,' came Mother Poitier's voice out of the blackness, 'a large family of children lived in an old château in France. Their father and mother were very devout and the children received the best Catholic education of all, the education of a pious home. The father and mother had one great sorrow which they never told to their younger children. Their eldest daughter, on the very day of her marriage, had disappeared and never been heard of again. She and other young people had been playing hide and seek in the big gardens of the château and she had gone off to hide alone. Night came, and they were still searching for her. Every cupboard, every cellar was searched; the well in the garden was drained dry, and the pond dragged, but there was never a trace of the bride. Finally, her poor parents gave her up for dead, and prayed for her as for a soul in purgatory. The servants and the neighbours were forbidden to tell the story, lest it should frighten the younger ones; all they were told was that their eldest sister had died and that they must remember her in their prayers.

'Many years later, it was the birthday of their youngest daughter, who was a child of the Five Wounds. As her birthday came in the long summer holiday, her parents had allowed her to ask several of the children from the convent to help her to celebrate it. On the morning of her birthday she woke up so much excited at the thought of the fun she was going to have that, good child though she was, she forgot to say her prayers. She got up very early and called the other children together.

'"What shall we play?" she asked them.

'"Oh, let us play *cache-cache* like we do on holidays at school," cried the others.

'"Very well," she said. "And I will hide first, because it is my birthday. You are to hide your eyes for five minutes and then to come and look for me."

'So she ran away to hide, full of high spirits. Below the garden there were some old underground cellars, in which the children were forbidden to play, but the little girl was so excited, thinking what a wonderful place they would be to hide in, that she forgot all her parents' commands. She crept down the old crumbling stairs that led to the cellars and at first she was frightened, it was so dark and cold down there. But she plucked up her courage and went on. She meant to go only a little way in and hide up the first turning, but it was so very black after the sunlight outside that she got nervous and lost her way. She took two or three turnings, but in the wrong direction. She could no longer see the light from the opening. She was hopelessly lost in the cold, dark cellars. For hours, it seemed to her, she wandered up and down in the dark, beating on the slimy stone walls and screaming for help, but no answer came back but the echo of her own little voice. Then, when she was nearly mad with terror, she saw something white in a corner, under a grating that let in a little greenish light from the garden above. She went towards it and saw that it was a young woman crouching down by the wall. The child spoke to her, but the young woman did not answer. She was wearing a beautiful white satin dress and a veil with flowers, but the flowers were all withered. The child went closer and touched her, and the young woman crumbled away into dust. There was nothing left but dust and some rags of silk. The little girl screamed and screamed. Then she remembered that

God is never far away from all who are in a state of grace, and she knelt down and prayed. She asked God to forgive her for having forgotten her morning prayers in her desire for pleasure, and she promised that if He would get her out of this terrible place, she would say the fifteen decades of the rosary every day of her life for the holy souls in purgatory. Then she tied her handkerchief on to the bars of the grating and prayed that the others would see it there and come to look for her. Ten minutes later she heard footsteps along the cellars and her friends found her. She was very ill with brain fever after that, and when she recovered, although she was only eleven years old, her hair was as white as snow. But from that day to this she has never forgotten her prayers.

'Now, children, let us go quietly up to dormitory, thank God for this happy holiday, and go peacefully to sleep.'

Chapter Four

In the summer term that followed her eleventh birthday, Nanda began to prepare for her First Communion. She was in the Senior School now, where life was a sterner, more responsible affair, symbolized by a black serge apron instead of a blue pinafore. She got up for mass every morning at six o'clock and stayed up until nine at night. There were all kinds of new subjects to study . . . music, history, botany, German, mathematics, deportment, and Catholic Apologetics. The old days of learning the simpler pages of the catechism and the stories of the saints were succeeded by a study of the knottier points of dogma . . . a study to which she was to devote at least an hour a day for the next few years.

Rather to her surprise, Nanda found herself put in a higher class than any of the others who had been promoted from the Junior School. Joan and Monica and Louise and Mildred, who had been the chief figures in her life, became vague shadows whom she only saw in the chapel or at recreation. Mother Frances had disappeared from the school altogether; she was in the community infirmary in the last stages of consumption. Sometimes Nanda and the others would send up a letter to tell her that they had said the fifteen decades for her. Sometimes they would club together to have a mass said. And every time Nanda handed old Father Robertson the five shillings in an envelope, he would pat her head and say:

'Now, my dear little child, remember that this money does not *buy* the mass. No one can buy the Precious Blood of Our Lord. When you go out into the world, Protestants may say to you: "But you have paid money to have this mass said." Protestants are very easily scandalized where Catholics are concerned. And they are very clever, as ignorant people so often are, at getting hold of the wrong end of the stick. This little offering you make here is just to buy the matter of the Holy Sacrifice . . . the actual bread and wine . . . and to contribute a little to the support of the priest who says the mass. Never forget that, my dear little child.'

Whenever her old children sent her word that they were praying specially for her, a little note would come back from Mother Frances, scribbled on a piece of paper neatly cut from an old exercise book. Nanda found these notes hard to associate with the Mother Frances she had known; they were so gentle and so humble. Once there was even a lace-edged picture of the Sacred Heart inscribed 'To dear little Nanda, in loving gratitude for her prayers. Frances Page, s.c.v.'

The mistress of Nanda's principal class nowadays was a nun called Mother Percival. There was a good deal of Mother Frances's old astringency about her, but not that exquisite sense of one's tenderest vanities. Mother Percival was blunt and forceful; if she bullied, it was because she believed that bullying strengthens the character. She was a firm believer in cold baths, hockey and plenty of healthy laughter at one's own and other people's failings. Had she not been a Catholic, Mother Percival might very well have been a games mistress at one of those Protestant high schools she so bitterly despised. In her own way, indeed, she was something of a Protestant and a reformer. She represented the English tradition against the French origins of Lippington. It was due to Mother Percival that Nanda and the others no longer had to have their bi-weekly baths clothed from head to foot in long, white calico cloaks. But she made no attempt to do away with the system of spying to which all the children were subjected. Every letter written by a child of the Five Wounds had to be left open for the Mistress of Discipline to read and censure. Even letters to parents were censored and sometimes destroyed without the writer's knowing what had happened. Every incoming letter or parcel was opened and examined and only given to the recipient at the Mistress of Discipline's discretion. Occasionally a letter that was considered particularly stupid or objectionable in tone was read to the whole school and publicly criticized.

The preparations for her First Communion took up much of Nanda's time, and nearly all her thought. The First Communicants were a privileged band, set apart from the others. They spent extra time in the chapel and had daily interviews with Reverend Mother, besides special religious instruction from a visiting Jesuit. They were allowed to help in picking and arranging the flowers for the altar and in looking after Father Robertson's vestments. When there were processions of the Blessed Sacrament, before the great day of *Corpus Christi* itself, they walked in white dresses in front of the monstrance, strewing rose and peony petals from silver baskets.

Nanda looked forward to her First Communion with a mixture of awe and excitement. At mass and benediction she strained every nerve to concentrate on the mystery of the Real Presence which, to a Catholic, is even more profound and beautiful than the mystery of the Incarnation. Mother Poitier had told her about a little Protestant girl who had been taken to mass by a Catholic friend and who, when her relations had told her it was wicked to believe that the bread and wine was changed into the actual body of Our Lord, had exclaimed: 'But when the bell rang I saw the priest holding up a beautiful little child.' At the elevation, Nanda would peer and peer until the candles swam before her eyes and she was almost sure she could see the outlines of a face in the white circle of the host. She listened greedily when Father Parry talked of how the Blessed Sacrament had been foretold all through the Old Testament and how even the pagan philosophers had had some dim vision of the mystery. Plato had said that if Divine Truth were ever manifested on earth, it would take the shape of a circle which symbolized eternity and the colour white, which was the sum and perfection of all colours. The day of one's First Communion was the happiest day of one's life; even the Emperor Napoleon, in the midst of his worldly triumphs, admitted that he had never known real happiness except on the morning he first received the blessed Sacrament. Saints had died of ecstasy when the host first touched their tongue, and Mother Poitier was fond of saying that God could grant no greater grace than to die at the moment of one's First Communion. Sometimes, in moments of great fervour, Nanda would pray that she might die too, and she would leave the chapel with a queer, giddy feeling that after the tenth of June she would never see Lippington any more, never grow up or get married, never even go home for the summer holidays.

But, mixed with her devotion and longing for the great day was a fearful dread that something might go wrong, that, through her own fault, she might lose all the virtues of the Sacrament and even fall into mortal sin. There was a story in a pious book by a nun of another Order that she read over and over again with fascinated terror.

'Rose made all the preparations for her First Communion with the greatest fervour. At last the great day came. Rose and her companions were dressed in their white dresses and veils and made their way along the corridors to the chapel. Someone had carelessly dropped a sweet in the passage, and without thinking, Rose picked it up and put it in her mouth. No sooner had she swallowed it, than she realized what she had done. She had broken her fast and could not now receive Our Lord. Rose struggled with her conscience, but, alas, the terrible little devil of Human Respect won. She thought of the chapel all decorated in honour of the First Communicants, of her parents who had come from far away to see her and she had not the courage to take off her wreath and veil and say humbly: "I have broken my fast and cannot make my Communion this morning." So she went into the church with the others, and when they went up to the altar to receive Our Lord, she went too, knowing that she was making a wicked mockery of the Holy Sacrament. Afterwards, she went to confession. All her days she bitterly regretted her wicked vanity and cowardice, but the tears of a lifetime could not undo the terrible fact that she had made her First Communion in mortal sin. Just think, dear children, had Rose died before she left the church that morning, she would have passed straight from God's holy table into the fires of hell.'

Still worse was the fear that at some time she might have committed a mortal sin and forgotten to include it at confession. Years ago, fired by the example of many saints, Nanda had made a vow of perpetual virginity. At eight, this vow had not been difficult to make. But now that she was ten she could not help feeling that she was quite likely to want to get married some day. Was her promise binding? She puzzled about it for a long time. Even the thought of going back on a promise to God might be a mortal sin. It took three things, she knew, to make a mortal sin: grave matter, full knowledge, and full consent. The matter was grave enough, certainly. And though she was not quite clear what virginity actually was, she knew, that with the one exception of Our Lady, one could not be a virgin and married as well. Besides, St Joseph was always spoken of as Our Lady's spouse, so probably a spouse was not the same thing as a husband. As to full consent, she had been eight when she made the vow and seven is the age of reason. At last, she summoned up courage to mention the matter to Father Robertson when she made her usual Saturday afternoon confession.

The confessional opened on to Father Robertson's little parlour behind the chapel. Through the grating she could see his old, sleepy face quite clearly, and a little table on which his tea was waiting. She noticed that he had two pink sugar cakes, and wished that they sometimes had sugar cakes for *goûter* instead of stale bread and jam.

She shut her eyes and clenched her blue-gloved hands as she whispered as usual.

'It is a week since my last confession, Father, and since then I have been guilty of distractions at prayers and being uncharitable to my neighbour, and I've told a lie twice and I've been idle and jealous and disobedient and angry and conceited, Father.'

'Very good, my child, very good,' murmured Father Robertson. Whatever one's sins were, Father Robertson always murmured 'Very good' in the same gentle sleepy voice. There was a legend that once someone had confessed:

'Father, I have committed murder,' and Father Robertson had answered:

'Very good, my child. And how many times?'

He was about to give her absolution when Nanda whispered breathlessly:

'Oh, Father, I'm afraid I've made a rash vow and I'm not sure that I really mean to keep it.'

'And what was this vow, my child?'

'Perpetual virginity, Father.'

'And how old were you when you made this vow?'

'Eight, Father.'

'And were there any witnesses of this vow?'

'No, Father.'

'Well, my child, I do not think that, in the circumstances, the dear Lord would hold you bound by it. You can reconsider the matter when you are twenty-one. Now, make a sincere act of contrition for these sins, and all the sins of your past life.' He raised his voice and groaned: 'Oh, my God.'

When Nanda had first confessed to Father Robertson she had been very much alarmed by this 'Oh, my God.' She thought the priest was exclaiming in horror at her sins. But now she knew that it was only the beginning of the act of contrition, the rest of which he muttered below his breath. Greatly relieved, Nanda bent her head to receive absolution. Hardly waiting for Father Robertson to murmur 'Bless you, my child, and pray for me,' she fairly skipped out of the confessional.

Throughout each day, Nanda watched herself with the utmost scruple. She examined her conscience minutely every night, and made passionate acts of contrition for every fault. She gave up sugar in her tea and forced herself to eat the things she hated most to the very last scrap. Even the saintly Madeleine was impressed by her zeal and smiled approvingly as she gave her a second helping of particularly nasty cabbage. Having read somewhere of a Jesuit novice who mortified one of his senses every day, she tried to imitate him. On Monday she mortified her eyes by shutting her book at the most interesting place and not reading another word. On Tuesday, she stuffed her fingers in her ears while the organ played at benediction. On Wednesday, she refused to smell flowers and made herself sniff a particularly nauseating mixture of ink and liquorice powder. On Thursday, she put salt instead of sugar on her rhubarb to mortify her sense of taste. And on Friday, after much thought, she managed to penalize her sense of touch by scraping her finger-nails against the rough serge of her apron and putting burrs against her skin under her vest.

Among the First Communicants was a girl of twelve years old named Léonie de Wesseldorf. Léonie was half French and half German by birth; she belonged to a very old and very wealthy family whose name, to Catholic ears, had something of the glamour of Medici or Gonzaga. Nanda's private image of Léonie de Wesseldorf was of a young prince, pale and weary from a day's ride, with his lovelocks carelessly tied back in a frayed ribbon. Léonie wore a black uniform instead of a blue one, being in mourning for some ambassadorial uncle, and the dusty coat she wore in the garden had the name of Paquin on its torn lining. In her unfeminine, unchildish way, she was exceedingly handsome, yet her deeply cut mouth and beautiful shallow brows seemed like the stamp of a medal rather than the changing growth of a face. Her red, unformed hands did not seem to belong to the pale, haughty head. Nanda, always reverent towards the people she liked, looked at Léonie's hands as little as possible; they embarrassed her like a deformity. Her feeling for Léonie was one of pure admiration, the feeling of page for prince, too cold and absolute to be called love. It would not have mattered if Léonie had never spoken or even looked at her, provided Nanda could bind herself to her by a private allegiance. Léonie was invincibly lazy. She would let herself be beaten in arguments or work by Nanda or others far stupider, but every now and then she would say something startling or write a sentence so shapely and mature that the nuns would find it hard to believe she was not quoting. Her mind, like her face, seemed to have been handed down to her full-grown, a blade of old, finely tempered steel, that she carried as carelessly as her shabby Paquin coat.

Nanda and Léonie studied their catechism side by side for three weeks and were bracketed top of the test in Christian

Doctrine which the First Communicants had to pass. Monica, with much difficulty, managed to obtain the necessary forty marks out of a hundred, though she was very shaky on the subject of Transubstantiation.

The day after the Christian Doctrine examination, while the band of First Communicants was walking round the inner garden, cutting flowers for the altar, Léonie dropped behind the rest and beckoned to Nanda. For a few minutes they strolled in silence, Léonie with her handsome chin in the air and her hands deep in her pockets. It was early summer, and the small, secluded garden, far away from the playgrounds, was spicy with the smell of azaleas. Nanda was glad that it was not Wednesday and that she need not stop her nose. The warmth playing on her skin made her feel quite dizzy with happiness; she wanted to tear off her thick serge and shake her hair loose from its plait. Léonie, who was always cold, huddled her smart, disreputable coat around her so tightly that its seams showed white in the sunshine.

'Well, Nanda, my child, what do you make of all this?'

'All what?'

'Oh, the Catholic Church, your First Communion, *und so weiter*.'

Léonie had a very grown-up voice; husky and rather harsh but extremely attractive. When she sang, it cleared and sweetened, and its rich, coppery ring cleaved straight to the heart of the note.

Nanda knitted her eyebrows and did not answer. Léonie helped her.

'Do you really believe all the things in the catechism, for example?'

'Why, of course.'

'You mean you want to believe them? Being a convert, you have to make an effort . . . more effort than I, for example. And so you come to believe them better than I.'

'But don't you . . .'

'Believe them? I don't know. They're too much part of me. I shall never get away from them. I don't want to, even. The Catholic Church suits me much too well. But it's fun sometimes to see what a little needle-point the whole thing rests on.'

Nanda's world was spinning round her.

'Léonie, what on earth do you mean?'

'Well, for example, there's no rational proof of the existence of God. Oh, I know there are four the Jesuits give you. But not one that would really hold water for a philosopher.'

'But, Léonie, that's sheer blasphemy,' said Nanda stoutly.

'Not necessarily. It doesn't affect the goodness of the beliefs one way or the other. After all, there's no rational proof that you exist yourself.'

This had never occurred to Nanda. For quite fifty yards she walked in deep thought. Then she burst out:

'Good heavens . . . it's quite true. There isn't. Léonie, how awful.'

'*I* think it's rather amusing,' said Léonie, beginning to whistle.

A few days before *Corpus Christi* still another First Communicant joined the band, an overgrown, shy creature who was actually twelve but looked fifteen. Theresa Leighton was the last of a family who had been Catholics for five hundred years and of whom it was proudly said that they had never made one mixed marriage since the Reformation. Theresa was preternaturally stupid and preternaturally good-natured. She would sit with her great mild brown eyes staring agonizingly at Mother Percival as she tried to follow the simplest explanation, and then say:

'Oh, Mother, it's so *assy* of me, but would you mind saying it just once more.'

Nanda was shocked to overhear Mother Percival say to another nun: 'These old families, you know, they're like royalty. Too much intermarriage. Wonderful traditions, but not very much *here*,' and she touched her black forehead band significantly.

But what Theresa Leighton lacked in intelligence, she made up in sweetness. Never was anyone so patient, so uncomplaining, so bewilderingly unselfish. She was so amazingly good that Nanda and the others were respectful, but embarrassed. In the chapel, her queer, mild face wore an extraordinary expression of ease and happiness, as if here at least she were completely at home.

When there was a tableau of the Annunciation, Theresa was naturally chosen for Our Lady, and Nanda, as the angel, was frightened by the look of strained, expectant ecstasy in Theresa's immense brown eyes.

Even when they practised receiving an unconsecrated wafer with closed eyes and outstretched tongues, it seemed to Nanda that at the moment of Communion itself, Theresa could not look more dazed with happiness.

The great day came at last. Every time she woke up during the night before, which was often, Nanda said, as she had been told to do:

'Even in the night have I desired thee, Lord. Come, Lord Jesus, come.'

Everything she put on that morning was new and white. A white prayer-book and a mother-of-pearl rosary, a gift from Reverend Mother, lay beside her new veil, and the stiff wreath of white cotton roses that every First Communicant wore. They walked into the chapel two by two, pacing slowly up the aisle like twelve brides, to the sound of soft, lacy music. In front of the altar were twelve prie-dieu covered with white muslin and flowers, with a tall candle burning in front of each. At little stools at the side knelt the children from the Poor School, who were also making their First Communion. They had no candles, and their cotton frocks looked shabby.

Nanda tried to fix her attention on the mass, but she could not. She felt light-headed and empty, unable to pray or even to think. She stole a look at Léonie, whose pale, bent face was stiff and absorbed. She tried not to be conscious of the smell of Joan Appleyard's newly-washed hair above the lilies and the incense. Theresa Leighton's head was thrown back; she had closed her prayer-book and was gazing at the altar with a rapt, avid look, her mouth a little open. Nanda was horrified at her own detachment, she tried hard to concentrate on the great moment ahead of her, but her mind was blank, in a trance she heard the bell ring for the *Domine non sum dignus*, and heard the rustle as the others got up to go to the altar rails. In terror, she thought: 'I haven't made a proper preparation. I've been distracted the whole time, today of all days. Dare I go up with them?' But almost without knowing, her body had moved with the rest, and

67

she was kneeling at the rails with the others, holding the embroidered cloth under her chin. Under her almost closed eyelids, she could see the pattern of the altar carpet, and the thin, round hosts, like honesty leaves, in the ciborium. The priest was opposite her now; she raised her head and shut her eyes tight. She felt the wafer touch her tongue and waited for some extraordinary revelation, for death even. But she felt nothing.

Back at her prie-dieu, she kept her head bowed like the others. Above the noise in her ears she could hear the choir singing softly and dreamily:

> '*Ad quem diu suspiravi,*
> *Jesu tandem habeo.*'

Over and over she told herself frantically:

'This is the greatest moment of my life. Our Lord Himself is actually present, in the flesh, inside my body. Why am I so numb and stupid? Why can't I think of anything to say?' She was relieved when the quarter of an hour's thanksgiving was over. As they filed out of the chapel she looked at the faces of the other eleven, to see if they felt as she did. But every face was gay or recollected or content. Léonie's expression was grave and courteous; in spite of her stiff white dress and wreath, she seemed like a young soldier fresh from an audience with the King. She thought of Polish nobles who stand with drawn swords during the Credo, and wished she could be as much of the blood of this ancient faith as Léonie and Theresa. With all her efforts, all her devotion, there was something wrong with her. Perhaps a convert could never ring quite true. Perhaps real Catholics were right always to mistrust and despise them a little. For weeks she had been preparing herself, laying stick on stick and coal on coal, and now, at the supreme moment, she had not caught fire. Her First Communion had been a failure.

There was an impressive breakfast laid out for the First Communicants in the big parlour, with crisp new rolls, butter patted into swan-like shapes and a huge, bridal-looking cake. Against the walls stood twelve small tables laden with presents. Nanda's looked rather bare and dismal, for it only held a missal, a new rosary and a copy of the poems of Francis Thompson. She had no Catholic relatives to load her with gold medals, crucifixes, coloured statues, alabaster plaques and Imitations of Christ bound in voluptuous Russian leather. She had received quite a good number of holy pictures however, including one from Hilary O'Byrne, as handsome as a Christmas card, inscribed: 'To dear Nanda, on the happiest day of her life, from Hilary E. de M.'

The First Communicants, reacting after their two days of silent retreat, chattered like starlings. Reverend Mother looked in, with her glasses positively twinkling with benevolence, and even condescended to examine everybody's presents and to exclaim politely over them. But after a few minutes, she put up her hand for silence.

'My very dear children,' she said, 'it is quite right and proper for you all to be gay and happy on this day of days. But not too much noise, remember. I would like you all to be quiet and recollect yourselves for just three minutes, while I tell you a little story . . . a true one that happened this very morning. I am going to tell you this because it shows what a true Catholic's spirit should be all through life . . . that nothing is more pleasing to God than suffering bravely borne for Our Lord's sake. I expect you noticed that there were some children from the Poor School making their First Communion with you this morning. You must remember that they do not come from good homes like you; they are often quite pathetically ignorant. Well, one of the nuns was helping them to put on their veils and their wreaths, and one little girl called Molly had great difficulty with hers. So Mother Poitier fastened it on with a big safety-pin, but, as you know, she does not see very well, and she unfortunately put the pin right through Molly's ear. The poor little girl was in great pain, but she thought it was part of the ceremony, and she never uttered a word of complaint. She thought of the terrible suffering of Our Lord in wearing His crown of thorns and bore it for His sake. I am sure Molly received a very wonderful grace at her First Communion and I should like to think that anyone here had such beautiful, unselfish devotion as that. She might have gone about all day with that pin through her ear, if she had not fainted just now at breakfast. Now, talk away again, children, and be as happy as you can all day long. But even in your happiness, never forget that a good Christian is always ready to take up his cross and deny himself and unite himself to the passion of Our Blessed Lord.'

There were no lessons that day. Nanda spent the morning walking about the garden with her father and mother. They could go wherever they liked, down to the farm or over to the orchard or right round the long walk that was called 'The End of the World'. Each First Communicant was surrounded by a chattering group of brothers and sisters and aunts and cousins and, not for the first time, Nanda wished that her parents had been Catholics long enough to support the tradition of having a very large family. Sometimes they would pass Léonie, pacing between a haughty-looking brother and an incredibly impressive mother, all black velvet and ermine. Léonie would wave energetically and Nanda would grin back shyly and wish her mother wouldn't talk quite so loud. For everything appeared so extremely odd to Mrs Grey.

'What is that image, dear . . . the one of the young man in the lace-edged shirt? He's got such a beautiful face, I think.'

'Not image, statue, *please*, Mother,' begged the unhappy Nanda. 'It's St Aloysius and it's not a shirt, it's a surplice.'

'And did you put those flowers there, darling?' Mrs Grey would twitter. 'I think it's such a pretty idea putting flowers in front of the images. But why must the saint be holding a skull? It's so morbid, isn't it?'

Down by the lake, half a dozen novices were playing ducks and drakes. Someone flipped a slate neatly; it bounced half a dozen times on the still water. The novice who had thrown it stood up and laughed. It was Lady Moira Palliser.

Mrs Grey gave a little shriek of pity.

'John, *isn't* that pathetic? Those poor young women. Just think, they've given up *everything*, and there they are, throwing stones like little boys.' She shifted her parasol on her shoulder, looking kindly at the nuns. Then, with an understanding smile she turned to Nanda: 'Of course, there must be a kind of happiness in their lives. No responsibilities, you know.'

Chapter Five

One night, early in her third autumn term, when the Senior School were sitting at their evening preparation in the big study-room, the faint tinkle of a bell sounded in the passage outside. Mother Percival immediately rose from her desk on the dais, snapped her wooden signal, and announced to the eighty enquiring faces:

'Children, will you all very quietly and reverently kneel down beside your desk and pray for our dear Mother Frances, who is gravely ill? Father Robertson is taking the Last Sacraments to her now.'

Nanda wrenched her mind from Boileau's *Art Poétique* which she was gabbling to herself in a whisper, and knelt down with the rest. The little bell sounded louder and louder; feet shuffled along the stone corridor; then the noise diminished, receded, was lost in the distance. Mother Percival's signal snapped again; the children resumed their seats, and Nanda tried to concentrate once more on Boileau. But the words no longer meant anything. She gave up looking at the book and shut her eyes, repeating over and over to herself the few lines she had learned, but the tiny stroke of the acolyte's bell still rang in her ears. What was happening to Mother Frances now? Were they already anointing her eyes and ears and nostrils and hands with the holy oil, symbolizing the forgiveness of sins committed by each unruly sense and member? How many blessed candles had Mother Frances collected in her life to be lit round her death-bed? Every year Nanda carefully laid by the one she received on the Feast of the Purification for this very purpose. It was distressing to think that she had only three; her eight years of unwitting heresy had robbed her of as many comforts in her last agony. Yet, after all, why should twenty blessed candles be more efficacious than one in keeping away evil spirits? It was very puzzling. She tried to imagine the scene in the community infirmary. But where was the community infirmary? Somewhere in the building, there must be, she knew, a hundred cells and a whole counterpart of the school, libraries, classrooms, study-rooms and sick-rooms, where no lay person except the nuns' doctor was allowed to set foot. Even parents might not visit a dying daughter there. But where did this house within a house lie? She knew the forbidden stairs that led to the community's quarters, but that was all. How strange it was, she thought, that living side by side with the nuns, the children knew nothing of their lives. She had never seen a nun eat or drink; she could not imagine Mother Frances, even on her death-bed, dressed otherwise than in her black and white habit. Did they wear nightgowns? Did they have looking-glasses? It must be difficult to adjust those veils and wimples without them. Yet even to imagine such things seemed to Nanda blasphemous. Someone touched her shoulder. She started, and opened her eyes to find Mother Percival standing beside her.

'Well, Nanda, is this the way you do your preparation?'

'Sorry, Mother.'

'There is still twenty minutes of your study time left. Do your work properly and offer up a good preparation for Mother Frances in her last agony. God likes a little dull duty well done better than the most elaborate prayers.'

The next morning at breakfast, before the bell rang for talking, the Mistress of Discipline told them that Mother Frances had died during the night.

'A most beautiful and Christian death,' said Mother Radcliffe, wiping her glasses on her sleeve. 'I am sure that every nun and every child of the Five Wounds may feel she has a new friend in heaven this morning. Mother Frances is to lie today and tomorrow in the Lady chapel, and, as a great privilege, all those who were in the Junior School under her may say their rosary there tonight.'

Nanda spent the day in alternate fear and excitement. She had never seen a dead person before. At last six o'clock came and she tiptoed into the chapel with the rest, feeling conspicuous in her Senior School uniform. Her nerve failed her at the last, and she closed her eyes, so that at first she was aware of nothing but the smell of lilies and melting wax. When she dared to look, there was Mother Frances lying uncoffined among trails of white flowers, looking hardly paler than in life, and still wearing her sweet, disdainful smile. Her habit and her crimped bonnet had taken on a stiff, carved look; her hands were carefully disposed, like a statue's, over the silver cross on her breast. She looked so secret, yet so defenceless, that Nanda could not help feeling it was an impertinence for them to peer at her dead face and to scatter beads of holy water on her body. The others, too, trod guiltily, as if fearing Mother Frances would wake, and she was half relieved when Monica cried out in a hysterical whisper: 'She moved . . . I saw her move,' and had to be taken out, sobbing and clinging to Mother Radcliffe's sleeve.

The morning of the funeral was wet and grey. As the whole school plodded slowly down the alleys to the cemetery, a fine rain hissed in their lighted candles and pearled the frieze of their black cloaks. The dead leaves, ankle-deep, whistled round their shoes, and the air seemed full of clammy, invisible cobwebs that clung to cheeks and hair. Across the path, Nanda watched Theresa Leighton patiently trudging; her rapt face upturned to the rain, her veil half off, and her candle out. Was that how St Theresa looked when she set off to find the Moors and martyrdom? She thought St Theresa must have looked a little more intelligent, but crushed the idea as uncharitable. Theresa would certainly become a nun, and quite possibly a saint as well. She felt a pang of conscience that she did not seek Theresa's society more often, but, as she glanced further along the line and saw Léonie de Wesseldorf in her smart, shabby coat, clutching her candle as if she were presenting arms, Nanda forgot the very existence of Theresa Leighton.

In the cemetery, school and community formed a hollow square round the grave. It was raining in good earnest now; the flowers in the banked wreaths were becoming pulpy and transparent, and the grass struck up dankly through thin-soled shoes. At last the coffin, plain as a soldier's, was carried to the graveside by Mother Frances's four tall brothers. The nuns' voices, intoning the *De Profundis*, sounded weakly through the heavy air, and even Father Robertson's rich notes had no ring in them as he prayed that all the angels and saints might come to meet the newly-arrived soul at the gates of heaven. Reverend Mother was crying a little, and Nanda felt her own eyes prick as, after long minutes of prayers, the tall young men payed out the bands and lowered the coffin into the spruce-lined pit. It was over, and the prospect of an ordinary day, however dull, seemed warm and comforting.

When midday recreation came, everyone was still rather subdued. As it was still very damp on the grass, games were abandoned in favour of walking round the garden in 'trios'. These trios were always selected by the nun in charge on the principle that, if two children were known to like each other's company, they must, at all costs, be kept apart. At no time at Lippington were any girls except sisters and first cousins allowed to walk in pairs; since, as they were frequently reminded, 'When two are together, the devil loves to make a third.' Nor were three of the same age permitted to make a trio; an older girl, usually a Child of Mary, was sent out with two juniors, in order that she might check their conversation while being wholesomely bored herself.

By some lucky oversight on the part of Mother Percival, Nanda and Léonie were put in the same trio, with Hilary O'Byrne as their chaperone. Nanda had not spoken to Hilary for many weeks. Since she had won her blue ribbon, she had a table of her own, and a dull German princess, who wore a flaxen wig and enormous shoes like leather boats was now Madeleine's vice-president. The princess had seriously upset Nanda's romantic notions of royalty, for she was plain, stupid, and addicted to violent colds in the head. All the same, she considered her an ideal table companion on account of her passionate fondness for the hateful, vinegar-soaked Lippington cabbage.

Hilary, thought Nanda, glancing up at the slender figure on which the serge uniform looked well-cut and almost elegant, would have made a much better princess. How pretty and grown-up she looked today, with her brown hair combed in a puff above a very white forehead. Even her blue ribbon and the silver chain of her Child of Mary medal had a deocorative, Secular air.

'Are you sorry you're leaving at Christmas?' Nanda asked her boldly.

Hilary smiled, curling her upper lip inwards in a way that

would have been ugly in anyone else, but was charming in Hilary, who had teeth as white as a cat's.

'Not really sorry, she said thoughtfully. 'Though I suppose I shall howl like the rest when it really comes to the point. It'll be heavenly not to miss any more hunting. And I'm going to be presented in May. Rather a bore, really, but I'm looking forward to it all the same.'

'A ghastly bore,' assented Léonie, looping a wet strand of hair ungracefully behind one ear. 'Goodness knows how many times I'll have to go through it. London and Berlin for certain, and then Papa is sure to be sent to Vienna or Madrid, and I'll have to start all over again. I shall jolly well wear the same dreary white satin dress each time, and then I shall put it away for ten years while I sow my wild oats and produce it for one final appearance when I take the veil at Lippington.'

Nanda giggled.

'I don't see you as a nun, Léonie,' said Hilary. 'You'd make a rotten, I mean a hopeless novice.'

'A rotten novice, but a first-class Reverend Mother. And as a future Mistress of Discipline, my dear Hilary, may I remind you that there is a fine of sixpence for using the word rotten?'

But Nanda was not nearly ready to abandon the subject of courts and queens.

'Mother Frances was presented, wasn't she, before she entered?' she asked. 'I wonder what she wore.'

'A bustle, I should think,' said Léonie scornfully.

'She was very beautiful,' asserted Hilary. 'My aunt, Moira's mother, said she made a tremendous sensation when she came out. I believe she had hundreds of proposals.'

This was a new light on Mother Frances. but how, Nanda wondered, could any man have the courage even to mention the subject of marriage to anyone so proud and remote?

'It wasn't only that she looked so wonderful,' went on Hilary. 'My aunt said she'd never seen a girl who rode so straight to hounds. She was absolutely fearless. And she told me that when she left home to come to Lippington she was perfectly calm when she kissed all her family goodbye, but when the carriage came round to fetch her for the last time, Mother Frances couldn't be found anywhere. So they looked in the stables, and there she was, with her arms round the neck of her favourite hunter, crying her eyes out.'

'I wonder why she entered?' said Nanda, with a shiver.

Hilary laughed.

'Oh, the usual reasons, I suppose. I've heard people say she promised to become a nun if one of her sisters whom she adored recovered from a bad accident. Her horse bolted and she was dragged half a mile over cobbles; they didn't have safety stirrups in those days, and she was terribly badly hurt.'

'And did she recover?' asked Nanda.

'Yes, quite suddenly, when the doctors had given her up. It may have been a miracle. I don't know. But I don't believe it really had anything to do with Mother Frances becoming a nun.'

'I can't imagine anything more awful than one's last night at home before one enters,' said Nanda gloomily.

'That's because you were brought up a Protestant,' Hilary explained kindly. 'Protestants always have morbid ideas about nuns. Mother Frances made a gorgeous last night of it. The Pages gave a big ball for her and she danced every dance, Aunt Patricia said, looking too lovely in white satin and pearls and a wreath of camellias. And she was awfully particular about her hair, too. She had a man down from London, though the house was in Leicestershire, and she made him do it two or three times before she was satisfied.'

'There are some things I'll never understand,' said Nanda despairingly. '*I* think vocations are terrifying.'

'You're a heretic to the backbone, young Nanda,' said Léonie in her hoarse, amused voice. 'Still, you'd better get over your childish terrors as at least twenty percent of us will certainly become nuns of one sort or another. I shall plump for the Five Wounds. At any rate, you don't have to sleep on a plank, like a Carmelite.'

'Theresa Leighton wants to be a Carmelite,' Nanda told her.

'Oh, Theresa Leighton,' said Léonie contemptuously. 'She's too holy to last. She'll marry some boring man and have fifteen strapping children. No, it's the unlikely ones like Hilary and me who end up in the community. Isn't it, dear Sister Hilary?'

But Hilary's face had taken on a cold, clouded look.

'It's fearfully chilly mooning about like this,' she said

suddenly. 'Come on, infants, I'll race you down to Our Lady of the Lake.'

Two days later, there was an outbreak of feverish colds all through the school. The infirmary was full and every classroom reeked of eucalyptus. The children who remained at work were alternately dosed with liquorice powder and cosseted with hot currant syrup, but in spite of these precautions, the sick list grew longer and longer. After three days of snuffling misery, Nanda gave in and presented herself at the infirmary. Her eyes felt like balls of lead and her cheeks scorched, though the rest of her body shivered. Mother Regan, the flustered Irish infirmarian, rolled her blue eyes despairingly as she thrust a thermometer into Nanda's mouth.

'I hope to goodness you're not running a temperature, child,' she said. 'I haven't a single free room.'

But Nanda herself devoutly hoped she *was* running a temperature, for otherwise there was no hope of the blessed peace of a day in bed. She gripped her lips tightly, in case any precious degree of heat might be lost. Long before she felt the thermometer had had a fair chance, Mother Regan snatched it from her mouth. The nun frowned at it, held it up to the hissing gas for another look, then with a distrustful glance at Nanda, as if she and the thermometer were in league with each other, she beckoned the lay-sister who acted as nurse.

'It's a great nuisance, Sister,' she said, 'but I'll have to find this child a bed somehow. Is there anyone well enough to be moved?'

'There's Miss Theresa Leighton,' said Sister Jones doubtfully. 'She's been here the longest. And she's normal today. But she's still not very well.'

'What about Miss Marjorie Appleyard?'

'She's got a temperature still. And the doctor said all the others were to stay in bed, Mother Regan.'

'Well, there's no help for it then. Theresa Leighton must go back to her dormitory tonight. Tell her she needn't get up till second rising, and she's not to go out of doors till I give her permission.'

It was a good half-hour before Sister Jones returned to say that the room was ready. Now that she was in sight of her goal,

Nanda began irrationally to feel much better. She wondered uncomfortably whether she ought not at least to make a show of refusing Theresa Leighton's bed. It had often been impressed on her that Theresa was very delicate. But supposing the offer were accepted? She doubted whether she had ever wanted anything as much as she wanted that bed, and the relief of being admittedly ill at last. She stared gloomily at the bottles of magnesia and gregory powder in the glass cupboard, quarrelling feebly with her conscience. Other snivelling victims arrived, but failing to pass the test of the thermometer, were dismissed with the cold comforts of quinine and Condy's fluid, till the bathroom next door resounded with the hollow noise of gargling. Nanda was just about to make a half-hearted protest when Mother Regan pounced on her.

'Good gracious, child. Go and fetch your things quickly. You don't think we keep a French maid here to look after your belongings, do you? Run along now. You can bring a lesson-book or two for the time when you'll be well enough to read.'

The unsuccessful candidates for the sick-room tittered. Nanda with a sullen, 'Yes, Mother,' slouched off to obey. She certainly wasn't going to be heroic and unselfish after *that*.

Feeling rather defiant, she stuffed the Francis Thompson that Léonie had given her for her First Communion into the pocket of her dressing-gown. She was rather surprised that it had not been confiscated long ago. Wrapped in brown paper, it passed for an ordinary school poetry book. Her conscience did not prick her much, for Francis Thompson was, after all, a Catholic poet, and she boldly scattered her essays with quotations from his works. She quite understood the fuss that had been made about Léonie's own copy of Shelley, for Shelley was an atheist and there might be corruption lurking in his most innocent poems. One day, Léonie had broken away from the others at recreation and strolled round the lake, reading *The Revolt of Islam* quite openly and with an air of cynical detachment. There had been a memorable scene in which Mother Percival, pink with anger, had snatched the book from Léonie, and Léonie, very politely, had taken back her Shelley and flung it into the lake, saying: 'If the book is so scandalous, that is the best place for it. It can hardly corrupt the little fishes.' Strangely enough, Léonie had not been punished.

The infirmary rooms at Lippington were bare and dismal. There was plenty of space in each for two beds at least, but in no circumstances were children allowed to share a bedroom. The walls of Nanda's were painted a dirty green, and the only decorations were a chipped plaster crucifix, a shell, with a sponge as hard as cork, that had once held holy water, and a spotty steel engraving of Leo XIII. Round the high, narrow bed ran a curtain, whose rusty rings jangled at every movement and effectively disturbed the patient's sleep. But to Nanda the shabby room, with the grim, old-fashioned dentist's chair in the corner, the spluttering gas jet and the empty grate, looked like paradise.

She slept very badly the first night, waking at every bell that rang or clock that struck. How many bells there were; she did not know the meaning of half of them. She remembered that she ought to pray for the souls in purgatory every time the clock chimed. St Theresa used to exclaim each time the hour struck: 'An hour nearer to death. An hour nearer to heaven or hell.' Curling and uncurling herself miserably on her hot, lumpy bed, Nanda began, quite naturally, to meditate on death. In the retreat given to the First Communicants in the summer there had been a colloquy on the last agony. In the afternoon silence of the sunlit chapel, with the leaves blowing across the windows and the birds cheeping outside, it had seemed too remote to be very terrible. But now in the dark, alone, feeling sick and aching, Nanda felt the words crowd back into her head with a horribly personal application. It was only a few days since they had buried Mother Frances. Her death had not made very much impression on Nanda at the time, but now it was real and terrifying as if a pain had begun to pierce the fog of an anaesthetic. Mother Frances had died, here in this house, only a week ago. She, Nanda, must die at some time, perhaps very soon. The words of Father Parry's colloquy came back as if they were printed on a gramophone record in her head. It was odd, because she had only half listened; she had been watching Léonie and trying to trace her profile with her finger on the flyleaf of her missal. 'Transport yourself,' Father Parry had said, in his quiet, convincing voice, 'to the bedside of a dying person or beside a grave ready to receive a coffin. Ask Our Lord for a salutary fear of death and the grace to be prepared for it every day.' Was she prepared for death? She had committed a sin against charity in not offering to let Theresa Leighton stay in this very room. It was not a mortal sin. But suppose Theresa had a relapse and died? It would be her fault. A good Catholic should always be ready and willing to die. Did she really love God? Would she rather go to heaven than spend the Christmas holidays with Léonie? She did not honestly feel she would.

'What is it, after all, to die?' Father Parry had said. 'It is to say goodbye to everything in this world . . . to fortune, pleasures, friends . . . a sad, irrevocable goodbye. It is to leave your house for ever and to be thrown into a narrow pit with no clothes but a shroud and no society but reptiles and worms. It is to pass in the twinkling of an eye to the unknown region called eternity, where you will hear from the mouth of God Himself in what place you are to make that great retreat that lasts for ever: whether in heaven or in the depths of hell. Think of your friends who have gone before you. Young as you are, my dear children, there must be some who have preceded you into eternity. From the grave they cry out to you into eternity. From the grave they cry out to you: "Yesterday for me and today for thee." Ever since the day of your birth you have been dying; every hour of play or study brings you a little nearer the end of your life. A good Catholic should live constantly in the spiritual presence of death. Now, my dear little sisters, I want each one of you to imagine that you are lying on your death-bed. A feeble lamp is burning; each familiar object in the room, the very chairs and tables seem to say to you: "You are leaving us for ever." You are in the throes of your last agony. At your side are the devils and the holy angels disputing for your soul. Above your own painful, suffocating breathing, you can hear the sobs of your mother, the voice of the priest saying the last prayers of the Church. "Depart, Christian soul, in the Name of God the Father Almighty Who created thee, of Jesus Christ Who suffered for thee, of the Holy Ghost Who sanctified thee." Imagine your own body at the point of dissolution, your icy feet, your rigid arms, your forehead cold with the sweat of death. Go further still, imagine your own funeral. Think of a few weeks later, of the terrible corruption of your own body after the soul has abandoned it. Think of the odour of your decayed flesh and realize that this is nothing to the odour exhaled by one sin in the nostrils of Almighty God. And think of your soul naked at the tribunal of the God whom perhaps it has never truly loved, that God now no longer a Friend but a terrible Judge.'

Nanda felt a sweat break out on her own forehead. Was it the sweat of death? She jumped out and knelt on the cold boards, praying frantically and incoherently. A little calmed, she went back to bed and fell asleep, only to dream that Theresa Leighton was lying dead in Our Lady's chapel, wearing her First Communion dress and a gilt paper crown. As she looked at her, a worm came out of Theresa's mouth and Nanda woke up shrieking.

After the first day or two, Nanda began to feel well enough to enjoy life in the infirmary. Her temperature was still a little above normal, so that there was a comfortable justification for remaining in bed, but she was allowed to read and to do some old jig-saw puzzles that were very puzzling indeed, since about a third of the pieces were missing. The infirmary library included a few books that down in the school would have been classed as story-books and the competition for these was keen. Nanda was lucky; instead of back numbers of *Stella Maris* or *The Messenger of The Sacred Heart*, Sister Jones brought her a frivolous, secular work called *St Winifred's or the World of School*. On the flyleaf of this was written in a nun's beautiful script: 'Certain pages of this book have been cut out, as the matter they contain is both vulgar and distasteful to the mind of a modest reader. Their excision does not interfere with the plot of the story.' The book had been still further censored. Several paragraphs were inked out, and wherever the word 'blackguard' appeared, a careful hand had pasted a strip of thick, but unfortunately transparent paper over it. Nanda was a voracious reader. She devoured *St Winifred's* so fast that by tea-time she had finished it. When Sister Jones appeared, bearing a tray with the unaccustomed luxury of hot buttered toast, Nanda begged for a fresh book. But Sister Jones was firm. 'You'll not get another book till tomorrow, Miss

Nanda,' she assured her, 'unless it's a lesson-book. There can't be much the matter with you if you can read that fast.'

'But, Sister,' Nanda implored her, 'it's hours before you put the lights out.'

'Then you can say your rosary, miss.'

'Will you come back later and talk to me, then? It's so awfully dull here alone.'

Sister Jones pursed her lips.

'Good gracious, child, do you think I've nothing else to do? You can say some of the prayers Mother Regan and I haven't time to say for ourselves, what with all this sickness in the house.' She shut the door so smartly that Nanda half expected to hear a key turn in the lock. It would probably be two hours before anyone came in again. How was she going to get through such an eternity of time? Sleep was impossible. And three slim bars of toast, even if she counted ten between each nibble, could hardly last more than a few minutes. Then she remembered the Francis Thompson in her dressing-gown pocket. In a few minutes she was stumbling through *The Mistress of Vision* between gulps of sugary tea.

> 'Secret was the garden,
>   Set in the pathless awe
> Where no star its breath may draw.
>   Life that is its warden
> Sits behind the fosse of death.
>   Mine eyes saw not and I saw.
> It was a mazeful wonder,
>   Thrice threefold it was enwallèd
> With an emerald
>   Sealèd so asunder,
> All its birds in middle air
>   Hung adream, their music thralled.'

She read on and on, enraptured. She could not understand half, but it excited her oddly, like words in a foreign language sung to a beautiful air. She followed the poem vaguely as she followed the Latin in her missal, guessing, inventing meanings for herself, intoxicated by the mere rush of words. And yet she felt she did understand, not with her eyes or her brain, but with some faculty she did not even know she possessed. Something was happening to her, something that had not happened when she made her First Communion. She shut the book and tried to make out what it was. But she could not think at all, she could only go on saying to herself some words that had once caught her fancy and that now seemed to have a real meaning. 'Too late have I known thee, too late have I loved thee, O Beauty ever ancient and ever new.' But she did not want to go on. She did not want to be led into prayers and aspirations. This new feeling, whatever it was, had nothing to do with God.

The unexpected entry of Mother Percival made her feel hot and foolish. She clumsily tried to hide her Francis Thompson under the sheet, but it was too late. Mother Percival directed an unusually charitable smile at Nanda, but her eyes were on the book.

'Well, and how's Nanda?' she enquired affably. 'Much better, by the look of her. Such red cheeks for an invalid.'

'Oh, I'm nearly well,' said Nanda feebly.

'Well enough to read, I see,' smiled Mother Percival, seating herself by the bed. 'A story-book, is it?'

'No, Mother,' admitted Nanda. 'It's just some poetry.'

'Just some poetry, is it? I didn't know you had such a devotion to English literature. Perhaps you're learning something by heart to surprise me when you come back to class?'

She reached out a lean, capable hand for the book.

There was a silence while she opened it and scanned a few lines. Nanda felt the blood beating in her ears.

'Francis Thompson? That's not one of your school books is it? I didn't know there was a copy in the infirmary.'

'It's my own. Léonie gave it me for my First Communion,' Nanda said boldly.

'I see. Francis Thompson was a great Catholic poet, but he did not write for little girls of eleven. How much of this do you imagine you understand?'

'Quite a lot,' said Nanda recklessly.

'That's very interesting. Let me see.' She glanced at the page.

'Now what, for instance, does "cymar" mean? Or 'effluence'? Or "vertiginous"? Or "panoply"?'

'I don't know,' Nanda admitted sullenly.

'I thought as much. Did you ever hear about the little pig that died of trying to grunt like a grown-up pig when it could really only say "wee-wee"?'

Mother Percival shut the book and laughed wholesomely.

'Now, you see, my dear child, that you're being just a little bit silly, aren't you? Some day you'll see the very wonderful religious meaning that's hidden in all this. But not yet. Francis Thompson was a mystic and no one expects little girls to understand the secrets of the saints. Not that Francis Thompson was a saint. He was not always a Catholic, you know, and there is often something a little morbid, a little hysterical in his work. But some of his poems are very simple and beautiful. I was going to let the Fifth Form learn *To a Snowdrop* for the Christmas wishing. But I think it would be better for you to let older people judge what is best for your little understanding.'

'Please let me keep the book, Mother,' she begged.

Mother Percival smiled again and turned over some pages.

'Well, perhaps there's no harm in keeping a book you so obviously don't understand. I suppose you want the others to think what a clever little person this Nanda Grey is?'

Suddenly her eye was arrested by a verse. Over her shoulder in a poem she had never looked at before, Nanda read:

'I shall never feel a girl's soft arms
Without horror of the skin.'

But she read no more. Mother Percival hastily shut the book. The geniality had gone out of her face.

'This book goes straight to your trunk, Nanda,' she said in her coldest voice. 'There are things in it which are not fit for any decent person to read. If I had my way it should be burnt.'

Nanda was trembling with indignation, but before she had time to speak, Mother Regan burst open the door.

'I'll have to move you back to your dormitory, child,' she said. 'I must have a good-sized room at once. Theresa Leighton is very ill indeed.'

Chapter Six

Nearly two years after Theresa Leighton's death came the happiest summer Nanda had ever known. The weather was perfect. Every day dawned clear and soft and unfolded through hours of sunlight to long evenings smelling of hay and lime trees. There was a kind of gaiety and relaxation in the air; hair hung more loosely and sleeves were rolled up unreproved over browning arms. Even the bells sounded less insistent; they chimed in a lazy, worldly voice like old stable clocks. It was good to come in, flushed from tennis, to the cool, sweet-smelling chapel; to sit in a weeping willow after supper surreptitiously learning *La Nuit de Mai*; to find a chestnut flower against one's skin when one undressed at night. The children spent nearly all day in the garden; lessons, like food, tasted better out of doors and even Christian Doctrine seemed to lose some of its harsher edge when one could blink up through the green meshes of a plane tree and enquire, with earnest frivolity, whether caterpillars had the rudiments of a conscience. She and Léonie were in the same class now, for Léonie, whose parents cared nothing for reports, had deliberately failed in her exams in order that Nanda should catch her up in the Lower Third.

They were both attached, Nanda passionately and Léonie with her usual cool carelessness to two divinities in the Lower First. The two divinities were also inseparables, so that Nanda who was doing the eighth book of Virgil with her father, thought of herself and Léonie as favourite pages in the train of Nisus and Euryalus. Although Nanda devotedly admired Rosario de Palencia, she was too much dazzled by her to envy Léonie her intimacy. Whenever in after-life she wanted to imagine any heroine, Juliet or Laura or Anna Karenina, she always invested her with Rosario's looks. Never, she thought, could any creature be more exquisite than this tall Spanish girl of seventeen, with her honey-coloured hair and her warm skin, that was neither white nor pink nor brown, but faintly golden. Rosario's eyes were turquoise blue, her brows black and strongly marked; her nose, the critics said, too masculine and her mouth far too wide. Her sister Elita was the recognized beauty, but Elita's morbidly white skin and brilliant dark eyes made no appeal to Nanda. Elita was a woman. Those languid eyes said too unmistakably that she was bored here among all these dull little girls. She never played games, but sat at recreation under the limes making lace, and paid no attention to any lesson but singing. Sometimes she knelt beside Nanda at benediction, and her lazy, veiled contralto would make the *O Salutaris* sound like a love-song. The nuns shrugged their shoulders and disapproved; they scolded Elita, they reasoned with her, they laughed at her. But nothing could change her. She dawdled through the school days, sleepy and secret, and spent hours, Rosario said, sitting at the window of the private room they shared, combing her dark hair that smelt of Russian leather, and talking about love. But Rosario was different. She seemed to despise her own beauty, dragging her golden hair straight back from her face and slouching like Léonie with her hands plunged in the pockets of a black woollen jacket. She played tennis fiercely, forgetting sometimes to laugh when she was beaten, and then apologizing with her charming, wide smile. She went out for riding lessons with Elita, and returned in the severest of grey habits, with her hair crushed under an unbecoming bowler. But she could never escape from her beauty; it clung to her like a mist, like a skin, so that she seemed to move in a haze of loveliness. Everything she touched, every word she used, took on this quality of grace; her very gloves and handkerchiefs were romantic.

Léonie and Rosario had known each other outside Lippington. There were Wesseldorfs and Palencias in every embassy in Europe. They had been brought down to dessert in white muslin and blue sashes at diplomatic dinners in Vienna and St Petersburg, and had grimaced at each other when eminent old gentlemen patted their heads. Once or twice a term, they would go out together to a well-chaperoned tea at the Ritz, or a polo match at Ranelagh; Rosario exquisite in a blue dress the colour of her eyes, and Lèonie incongruously arrayed in a military-looking coat chosen by herself and an absurd, daisy-trimmed hat her mother had bought in Paris.

Léonie rarely talked about her friend. Occasionally she wrote poems to her; frosty, elegant little eighteenth-century verses in which Rosario figured as Celia or Lucinda or Amaryllis. Sometimes, with a most unusual patience, she copied out music parts for their two violins or transposed a song to the compass of Rosario's voice. But if she never praised and seldom even mentioned Rosario, she would not suffer the least slight on her from anyone else. Once Marjorie Appleyard had said something contemptuous about Elita and Spaniards in general and Léonie, without a word, had shot out her fist and sent her sprawling.

There was no unearthly radiance about Clare Rockingham, but to Nanda she, too, seemed romantic. To begin with, she was a Protestant and had only managed to be sent to Lippington after incessant quarrels with her family. But after she had returned unannounced from Germany, having escaped from her governess at Basle, and had then proceeded to lame her father's best hunter by riding him without permission at a gymkhana, the Rockinghams had decided that there was something to be said for Lippington after all. They had, however, threatened to cut her off completely if she became a Catholic. This gave Clare the glamour of a secret sorrow. For days she would mock, with her wild, crowing laugh that could be heard all down the refectory, at the punctiliousness of Catholic doctrine. Then one evening she would be found in tears at benediction. She did not attend Religious Instruction, but she borrowed Rosario's catechism and read it during free study, to the delight of the whole Senior School, who were praying quite openly for her conversion. Once she even borrowed Nanda's rosary. Seeing Nanda looking a little doubtful, Clare tweaked her pigtail and asked:

'What is it, baby? Will it hurt your rosary to be used by a pagan?'

'I'll have to get it blessed again, that's all,' Nanda explained.

Clare's eyes danced. They were odd eyes, green and, like her skin, freckled with brown.

'I say, am I as wicked as all that? Do I actually put a curse on everything I touch?'

87

'Of course not,' said Nanda. 'I'd have to get it blessed again if I lent it to anyone . . . even the Pope himself. You see, a rosary's only blessed for the person it belongs to, and so if anyone else uses it they don't get the indulgences and you don't either until it's been blessed again. Mine's blessed for a happy death, so I mustn't forget to have it done.'

Clare threw up her hands and crowed with laughter. 'What a fantastic idea, darling. Does it cost anything, having your beads blessed?'

'Of course not,' said Nanda, profoundly shocked.

'Don't look so hurt, baby. I'm only a poor, enquiring heathen. But I always thought there was something called a sale of indulgences.'

'Lots of Protestants think so,' said Nanda kindly. 'But it's quite untrue. They think that three hundred days' indulgence means that you get three hundred days off purgatory. But of course, that's quite impossible, because there isn't any time in purgatory.'

'Well, what does it mean then?'

'It's rather a long explanation,' Nanda told her.

'Go on. I'm fascinated.'

'Well, it's like this. To begin with, every mortal sin has two sorts of punishment, temporal and eternal. If you die in mortal sin, you go straight to hell. But you're let off the eternal punishment if you confess your sin and get absolution.'

'Then I should just go on sinning and being forgiven as often as I liked.'

'Oh, no,' said Nanda hastily, 'because part of the condition of getting absolution at all is that you have to have a sincere intention not to commit the sin again.'

'I see,' mused Clare. 'By the way, how do I know when it *is* a mortal sin?'

'That's awfully easy. There's got to be grave matter, full knowledge and full consent. So if you kill someone by accident, it isn't a mortal sin. Unless you meant to hurt them badly, when of course it would be. Then take stealing. It's rather difficult to know just how much would constitute grave matter. But it's generally supposed to be about half-a-crown.'

'So if I stole two and fivepence, it would only be a venial sin?'

'Ye-es,' said Nanda a little doubtfully. 'But, of course, if two and fivepence was all the person had, or if they were a widow or an orphan, or if you stole it from a church box, it would be mortal.'

'And suppose it was a very dark night and I meant to steal a half-crown and it turned out to be two shillings, it would only be a venial sin?'

'Good gracious, no,' said Nanda positively. 'It would be a mortal sin because you had the *intention* of stealing half-a-crown.'

'You Catholics are wonderfully definite about everything, aren't you? It must be a great comfort to know just where one is. But go on about indulgences.'

'Sure I'm not boring you?'

'Not a bit, infant,' smiled Clare, showing very white teeth that had crinkled edges like a small child's.

'Well, you're quite clear about eternal punishment and temporal punishment, aren't you? After the eternal punishment of a mortal sin has been remitted in confession, there's still the temporal punishment to be worked off in this life or in purgatory. Venial sins carry some temporal punishment, too, but not so much.'

'I suppose there are heaps of venial sins?'

'Hundreds,' said Nanda gloomily. 'Almost everything's a venial sin, in fact. If I don't eat my cabbage, or if I have an extra helping of pudding when I'm not really hungry, or if I think my hair looks rather nice when it's just been washed . . . they're all venial sins. And then, as if one's own sins weren't enough, there are nine ways in which you can share in another person's.'

'Good Lord,' crowed Clare. 'I bet you a holy picture you don't know 'em all.'

Nanda shut her eyes and gabbled.

'By counsel, by command, by consent, by provocation, by praise or flattery, by being a partner in the sin, by silence, by defending the ill-done.'

'It's amazing. How can all you babes reel them off like that?'

'Well, I've done catechism and Christian Doctrine for two hours a day for three years.'

'Then tell me something. I was reading Rosario's catechism on Sunday, and I came across something very peculiar. It was one of the commandments . . . "Thou shalt not commit adultery," and it said it forbade fornication and all wilful pleasure in the irregular motions of the flesh. What does it mean?'

'I haven't the faintest idea,' said Nanda coldly. 'We don't do the sixth and ninth commandments. Mother Percival says they're not necessary for children. They're about some very disgusting sins, I believe, that only grown-up people commit.'

She could not understand why Clare laughed so wildly that her green eyes brimmed over with tears.

Rather offended, Nanda said:

'I think we'd better be getting back to the others. I promised Léo to play tennis. And, besides, we're not really supposed to be about in twos.'

'Nonsense, baby. Mother Percival has got us well in the tail of her stony eye. And besides, you may be converting me, who knows?'

'I shouldn't dream of trying, Clare,' asserted Nanda, still hurt. 'Catholics don't try and convert people like that. They just answer your questions and . . . and . . . pray for you.'

Clare leaned over and touched Nanda's arm with a hot quivering hand that burned through her holland sleeve.

'Do you pray for me, baby?'

'Of course,' said Nanda in a very matter-of-fact voice, but she blushed all the same. Clare's touch embarrassed and delighted her; it gave her the queerest shivering sensation in the roof of her mouth. Why was it that when everyone else seemed just face and hands, Clare always reminded one that there was a warm body under her uniform? For a minute her freckled eyes searched Nanda's, and then she laughed softly and shook her mane of wiry bronze-bright hair.

'Go on about indulgences, infant theologian.'

Nanda was just explaining that in the old days people would perform penances for three hundred days in order to remit their temporal punishment, and that an indulgenced prayer was one which, if said with the right dispositions, entitled one to the merits such a penance would have gained, when an unexpected hell began to clamour excitedly.

Children were running from all directions towards the house; a nun appeared on the terrace, waving her arms.

Nanda forgot theology and seized Clare's hand.

'Come on, come on quick,' she cried. 'It's *Deo Gratias*, the holiday bell.'

The nun on the terrace called to them as they passed: 'Into the big study-room, children. Don't bother to change your shoes. Wonderful news for you.'

Soon the whole school was assembled, panting and expectant. Scarcely had the last child scrambled into place before Reverend Mother and Mother Radcliffe came in, their faces rippling with smiles.

'Dear children,' announced Reverend Mother, as they rose from their curtsies, 'this is one of the greatest days in the history of our dear Order. I have just heard from Rome that His Holiness has consented to the canonization of our beloved foundress, Blessed Marie-Joseph Guillemin. The ceremony will take place in a fortnight's time, on our own saint's feast.'

There was a wild outbreak of cheering. Reverend Mother permitted the noise for several minutes, then, still smiling, she held up her hand for silence.

'Now, children, I want you all to join with me in singing the *Magnificat*. The rest of today will be a holiday. At five o'clock the school and the community will sing a solemn *Te Deum* in the chapel as a thanksgiving for this wonderful grace that God has bestowed upon us all.'

She raised her old voice, a mere thin shell, but true in time and tune.

'Magnificat anima mea dominus'

and the whole school answered in a shout of delight:

'Et exaltavit spiritus meus.'

Halfway through, Nanda stopped singing. In the rich web of sound she could trace two fibres, the silver softness of Rosario's voice and Léonie's coppery ring. Beside Rosario, croaking dismally, but passionately, stood Clare Rockingham, who had not the slightest ear for music but professed to adore it because she adored Rosario.

The fortnight that followed was rich with a sense of preparation. Lessons went on as usual but with an agreeable desultoriness. Nuns would appear at the door of a classroom and beckon half the inmates away to rehearse for a play, a tableau or a concert. The piano cells echoed all day with people practising part songs. Mistresses in charge of recreation stitched vigorously at secular draperies of tulle and spangles; bands of helpers were recruited to glue feathers on to angel's wings, and the Guest House filled up with 'Old Children', whose princess frocks and picture hats were a source of much distraction in the chapel.

On the eve of the great day Mother Radcliffe summoned the whole school into the big parlour. The old ones were there, too, proudly wearing their Child of Mary medals over their pearl necklaces. Some of them had fished out their former decorations, and Nanda was enchanted by the sight of a stout Portuguese lady, the mother of three children in the school, cheerfully displaying a faded pink ribbon across her Poiret frock. Mother Radcliffe's face, as she seated herself at the little baize-covered table, announced that the occasion was to be serious.

'My dear children, old and new,' she began, 'Reverend Mother has asked me to tell you something about our saint and why the Church, after years of prayer and searching for Divine guidance, has consented to raise her from the high honours of beatification to the still higher ones of canonization. Tomorrow, in St Peter's, her picture will be carried in procession, and she will be publicly proclaimed a saint by the Holy Father himself. All of you know a little of the slow and difficult process of examination to which the Church submits her candidates for sainthood. You know that the body of the servant of God, if he or she has died a natural death, must be discovered after many years perfect and uncorrupted. You know that every written word is scrutinized, every remembered utterance weighed for the least taint of heresy or worldliness. The Pope appoints an official to act as the Devil's Advocate, whose duty it is to find any trace of evil, any departure from the highest, most heroic sanctity which might nullify the Cause of Beatification. And lastly, it must be conclusively proved, with medical testimony, that the Servant of God has worked major miracles of healing either through her direct intercession or through the touch of her holy relics. I want to tell you now of the three greatest miracles of the many our dear Mother wrought, cures which the doctors attending the cases, although many of them were not Catholics, could attribute to nothing but Divine intervention.'

She proceeded to read out the details of the miraculous cures of an elderly nun, a girl of nineteen and a little boy suffering from meningitis. The nun had been at the point of death from a fibroid tumour; three novenas had been made to Our Lady and St Joseph without result. But on being touched with a little bag containing some of the hair of Mother Guillemin, she had experienced a pain of burning. The swelling immediately subsided and the next day the doctors pronounced that there was no trace of the growth which had defied treatment for months. In the second case, the girl had been operated upon for appendicitis, and not only had gangrene set in, but a sinus had formed in the intestine. The doctors had given her up for lost, when a friend brought her a piece of the saint's habit and sewed it to the dying girl's nightgown. A novena was begun to Mother Guillemin, and on the second day the sinus suddenly healed up. By the ninth day the girl was not only out of danger, but able to get up for several hours a day. The little boy of five had been actually in his last agony with a very severe attack of meningitis. His mother, who had been sitting by his bed for two days and nights, had fallen asleep. When she woke, she was surprised to see a woman in a religious habit bending over her little son. The nun touched the boy's forehead and he smiled at her, instantly stopped moaning and lay quite still. In the morning the fever had left him and in a few weeks he was back at school and in perfect health. One day his mother saw a picture of Mother Guillemin and immediately exclaimed: 'That is the face of the holy nun who cured my child.'

Mother Radcliffe put down her sheaf of notes and smiled. There was something about her smile that reminded Nanda a little of Mother Frances. It had the same sweet disdain. Her face, like Mother Frances's, was very pale and sloped down to a narrow chin, but her pallor was solid instead of being transparent, and her features handsome but rather thickly moulded. But her eyes, smallish and of a curious grey-green like lichen, searched one's face with a good deal of Mother Frances's cool penetration. 'Physical wonders like these, my dear children,' she said in her even voice, 'are the things the world wants to hear about its saints.' She had a habit of pausing between each word, as if words themselves, having been used by so many people, had a sort of uncleanness and must have the dust blown off them before they were fit for her use. 'But for us, who are nearer to her heart, it is the small things, her silences, her mortifications, the secret signs of her spiritual growth that are so infinitely more precious. Our Mother had an ardent, even a passionate nature. She was generous to a fault. But her brother, who devoted his whole life to training her soul for God, mortified her even in her virtues. He knew that such fine metal could stand great heat. And some of that severity which to the world seems harshness is bound up in the School Rule which you are privileged to follow. Francois Guillemin made our Holy Mother study long and hard without reward, without even a word of praise. Knowing that she was afraid of firearms, he would often fire revolvers in her presence to strengthen her courage. Her mother gave her a pretty shawl to wear to mass, and her brother tore it to shreds to mortify her vanity. And once, when she had lovingly embroidered him a pair of slippers for his feast day, he threw them in the fire without a word of thanks. And it is the same in the schools of the Five Wounds today. We work today to turn out, not accomplished young women, nor agreeable wives, but soldiers of Christ, accustomed to hardship and ridicule and ingratitude.'

The morning of the feast day dawned clear and dewy, with a haze over the lake that promised great heat. Nanda was already awake when the *Deo Gratias* bell clamoured down the dormitory, and the Children of Mary, dressed up in serge aprons and white table napkins to look like nuns, came trooping in for the ceremonial 'calling' with which all big holidays began.

Rosario, stately as an abbess, without one gilt hair straying under her black hood, read out the proclamation of the holiday from an enormous scroll hung with seals as big as saucers. Wherever possible, the pleasures of the day were to be related to the events of Mother Guillemin's life. Thus the present awakening represented her vocation; hide and seek during the morning, her hidden life; boats on the lake, her voyage to America; the tableaux in the afternoon, her holy visions; a concert, the heavenly music she was often permitted to hear, and the bonfire and the fireworks with which the day was to end, the warmth of her charity and the illumination of her spirit.

After mass the children went out into the sunlit garden to breakfast in classes. As a great treat, they were allowed eggs with their bread and butter, and these eggs were gaily coloured as they were on Easter Sunday. Each child also received a picture of Mother Guillemin, with the motto 'Pray that your hearts, like hers, may be made deep with humility and fiery with charity.' It was the rule of these holiday breakfasts that the mistress should entertain her class, and today Mother Percival scored an unexpected success by a series of rhymes on the character of each of her pupils.

Léonie was:

> 'Gold under fire has a special charm
> But fire under gold may lead to harm,'

and Nanda, who had expected to be ridiculed, found herself unexpectedly flattered by a whole quatrain:

> 'A rainbow swung in a morning sky
> Owes light and life to the sun on high
> So keep your eye fixed on heaven above
> And heaven and earth will give you love.'

All the same, she was a little puzzled by it. Had Mother Percival noticed that lately she had been having odd fits of melancholy? Was there a warning concealed in it that she was too apt to consider any talents she had as her own property rather than as gifts lent her by God for His own ends? She listened without much interest to the rhymes about the others, though she was too well trained not to join mechanically in the applause. What was it that so often came over her nowadays and made her so deeply and rather pleasurably sad for no particular reason? Sometimes, the melancholy began with a phrase of music or a line of poetry, but often with far less explicable things, such as the sound of cricket bats on late summer evenings or the sight of a beautiful stranger in the chapel. She was interested, as were all the literary romantics of Lippington, in the mechanics of sorrow. She starred her essays with quotations about our sweetest songs being those that tell of saddest thought, and the bitter taste of heaven's star-laden vine and the poet's crown of laurel and thorns. She longed passionately for a definite, solid grief which should give this vague melancholy dignity and reason. When Léonie occasionally looked coldly sad, she was worrying over the fact that her father was threatened with cancer. When Rosario's blue eyes filled with tears, she was thinking of her mother, who had died in the spring. When Wanda Waleska, the fierce girl from Warsaw, clenched her hands and bit her lips while Rosario played Chopin, she was grieving for the slavery of Poland. And when Clare sobbed violently in the chapel, she was sorrowing because she was torn between the Catholic Church and her own high-handed, exasperating, beloved family. Only Nanda had no decent, acknowledged injury of her own. For a time she tried to persuade herself that she bore a secret and terrible share in the death of Theresa Leighton. But her native honesty soon forced her to admit that Theresa's death had moved her far less than the death of the Duc de Reichstadt in L'Aiglon. Then she tried to make L'Aiglon himself the noble object of her melancholy. She wore a bunch of parma violets under her dress on the anniversary of his death, and, having a drop of Austrian blood in her, tried to persuade herself that one of her ancestresses had been in love with him. But even this image would grow papery and shrivelled long before her melancholy mood was exhausted.

However, today she was gloriously, irresponsibly happy. The stale rolls tasted delicious out here under the trees, the sun was warm on her hair, and a little bubble of pleasure burst in her throat every time Léonie grinned at her. Half the morning passed in long, exciting games of hide and seek; then came a heavenly hour in the hayfield. She and Léonie were pelting each other with armfuls of dried grass and meadowsweet, when Rosario came up to them. She wore an absurd white linen hat, like a plate, tilted forward over her rich hair, and her apron was kilted back over her skirt. Rosario was incapable even of making hay ungracefully; she moved in her haze of charm like Marie Antoinette playing at shepherdesses. But she was not smiling; her black eyebrows were drawn together and she looked both sad and angry.

'Have either of you seen Clare?' she asked.

Nanda and Léonie did not look at each other.

'No,' said Nanda. 'No, Rosario.'

But Léonie answered:

'Yes. About half an hour ago. On the other side of the lake. She'd got her arm in a sling.'

Rosario's golden skin paled a little, but she only said: 'I'll go and look for her,' and walked slowly away.

Nanda was hot with curiosity, but she waited for Léonie. 'They've quarrelled,' Léonie said presently. 'Clare's so frightfully sentimental. She won't let Rosario alone.'

'I think Rosario's the loveliest person I've ever seen,' said Nanda timidly.

'Yes,' said Léonie judicially. She looked at Nanda for a minute; her face was pale and damp with sweat, a blue vein standing out in the middle of her forehead made her seem more than ever like a stern, handsome young man. Then she grinned.

'I suppose you want to convert Clare?'

Nanda blushed.

'Well, not exactly. But of course I should like her to be a Catholic.'

Léonie propped her chin on her rake.

'I'd never advise anyone to *become* a Catholic,' she said. 'If you're one, you've got to be one. But you can't change people. Catholicism isn't a religion, it's a nationality.'

'It's funny, Léo,' mused Nanda. 'You say the most extraordinary things; you're awfully slack about prayers and all that, you've even got a copy of *Candide* bound up as a missal, and I believe the nuns know, and yet you get away with everything. Yet if I do the slightest thing, I'm punished.'

'Because they're not sure of you yet. You're a nicely washed and combed and baptised and confirmed little heathen, but you're a heathen all the same. But they're sure of me. In ten, twenty years I'll be exactly the same. It's in the blood. I'd as soon be a Hottentot as be anything but a Catholic. It may be nonsense, but it's the sort of nonsense I happen to like. And when I die, my great uncle Cardinal de Wesseldorf and my great-great aunt the Carmelite Abbess de Wesseldorf, who had an affair with Napoleon before she entered, will say to the recording angel: "My dear sir, you can't seriously send a Wesseldorf to hell," and into heaven I shall go.'

But Nanda's mind had wandered to Clare. What had happened? Why was her arm in a sling? Clare was the sort of person who attracted accidents. She nearly always had a bandaged ankle or a cut finger. Perhaps that was one of the reasons why one was always so conscious of her body.

The bell for the next amusement interrupted Nanda's speculation. As they sauntered slowly towards the house, Clare herself joined them, with her free arm through Rosario's. She was laughing wildly; evidently they had made it up. But Rosario seemed worried.

'You must go to the infirmary, Clare,' she imposed. 'You're being ridiculous.'

'Nonsense, darling. What's a little burn? I'm always damaging myself. Mother Regan hates the sight of me. I didn't go to the infirmary when I had rheumatism last week, and it was absolute agony.'

'But this is different,' Rosario appealed to the other two. 'Clare burnt herself badly last night, goodness knows how, when she was lighting the gas in her room. She's just bandaged it up anyhow, but she ought to have it properly looked after.'

'Well, let's see the burn,' said Léonie sensibly.

She laid her hand on the arm in the sling, and Clare drew in a sharp breath of pain.

'No, I'm perfectly all right, silly child,' she said bravely.

'I insist on looking,' said Rosario. Her soft voice sounded dangerous.

Clare looked at her queerly for a minute, then burst into one of her crows of laughter. Suddenly she tore viciously at the knot of her sling with her free hand and her teeth.

'Then look, darling.'

Her white, lightly-freckled arm was bare and unscarred.

'Just a joke, darling. I so adore to see you looking angry and worried.'

Rosario turned pale with rage for a second; then she laughed softly, but not altogether pleasantly.

Léonie caught Nanda's elbow.

'Come on. I'll race you to the house.'

On the terrace Nanda said breathlessly:

'I don't understand Clare, do you?'

'She's just hysterical,' panted Léonie. 'One of these days she'll go off her head.'

The golden day passed richly away. After the tableaux and the concert and the long benediction among a blaze of candles and azaleas, Nanda felt she could bear no more excitement. She felt tired and surfeited with the exuberance of the holiday; her head ached and her mouth was sore from eating too many sweets. At supper they served a weak, sickly wine that made her feel dizzy. It was a relief to go down to the big field by the lake and watch the bonfire and the rockets, and to know that soon there would be bed and sleep and an ordinary, blessedly dull tomorrow.

The great fire blazed and crackled; the whole school streamed round it in a wild eddy, singing and leaping. Jets of flame, hearts, scissors, tiny maps of England broke off from the main body and vanished into the clear, dark air. Faces showed red and strange, hair tossed away from ribbons, heads were flung back and mouths opened wide. Across the circle Nanda stared, fascinated, at Clare, who was dancing like a bacchante, her bronze hair flying, her face brilliant and wild, her body leaning back as if into invisible arms. Faster and faster they danced, until the strained, whirling loop broke and a dozen children fell in a heap, laughing and screaming. There was a thunder of fireworks, and the name of St Marie-Joseph Guillemin slowly uncoiled itself in scarlet letters against the sky. Nanda felt Léonie give her arm a sharp jerk. The last burst of light from the rockets carved her face out clean against a net of leaves. Pale and stern and beautiful.

'Come away,' she said quietly.

Nanda followed her without speaking to the little clearing beside the lake. In the dimness, Léonie was only a dark shape, but Nanda could make out that her hands were clasped under her chin. Feeling suddenly shy, Nanda looked away from her at the quiet water where the mist was gathering. When Léonie spoke at last, it was in a deep, troubled voice, as if she were speaking to herself:

'O Muse, spectre insatiable
Ne m'en demandez pas si long
L'homme n'ecrit rien sur le sable
A l'heure où passe l'aquilon.

J'ai vu le temps où ma jeunesse
Sur mes lèvres était sans cesse
Prête à chanter comme un oiseau –
Mais j'ai souffert un dur martyre
Et le moins que j'en pourrais dire
Si je l'essayais sur ma lyre
La briserait comme un roseau.'

Chapter Seven

At the end of June came the annual retreat. Nanda viewed the prospect of four days' complete silence with mixed feelings. She had made retreats before, but never one so long as this, and she knew that after the novelty of the first few hours wore off, they were apt to become oppressive. During a retreat, the children lived like nuns; each one was given a classroom or a piano cell to herself, in which she spent her time between the four hour-long meditations in the chapel and the silent meals and recreations. Recreation consisted of walking up and down the alleys reading pious books or reciting the rosary, and not a word was supposed to pass one's lips after the first retreat bell had sounded. Even letters were not allowed, so that the sense of being cut off from the world was complete. Nanda entered into retreat with the best intentions, determined to make the devotions as whole-heartedly as possible and to offer them up for the conversion of Clare Rockingham. The first day was pleasant. Newly confessed and wearing clean clothes, she had the sense of beginning life over again. She spent a long time arranging flowers on the little altar of her cell, polishing the brass crucifix and the candlesticks and setting a nightlight in a blue dish in front of her statue of Our Lady of Lourdes. Next, with an agreeable feeling of travelling lightly and compactly on this spiritual voyage, she set out the four books that were to be her only companions: the *Watches of the Passion*, her missal and *Imitation of Christ* and a stout new notebook with a shiny cover in which she was to write out her notes on Father Westlake's conferences and to make pious observations of her own.

Léonie and Rosario were seasoned retreatants. They went into this solitary confinement with as little fuss as old soldiers going into camp. Rosario supplied herself with a great deal of delicate needlework of a vaguely devotional nature, while Léonie announced frankly that she was going to use her notebook to compose a blank verse tragedy on the death of Socrates. But Nanda had not yet lost her fear of the voices she might hear in the darkness. Her childish dread of a vocation reasserted itself, and she was by no means comforted when Father Westlake, in the course of the very first meditation, reminded them that in the silence of a retreat God had His chance to whisper his secret call to the soul to leave all and follow Him. Suppose that, in return for the conversion of Clare Rockingham, God should demand the dedication of her own life? Would she be equal to so heroic a sacrifice? And would it be, she asked herself in a moment of unheroic common sense, altogether fair of God to expect it, since Clare's conversion would presumably be to His own advantage? On the other hand, if eternity were everything, it was only logical to spend this life as unpleasantly as possible, in order to ensure permanent happiness in the next. But why had God made this world so attractive? It was so hard to keep one's eyes fixed on heaven when even the saints could give one no idea of what heaven would be like. If they were vague about heaven, they were very definite indeed about hell. Nanda felt a great deal more positive about the conditions of life in hell than in, say, the West of Scotland or Minneapolis. It was generally admitted, when they read the *Inferno* in class, that Dante had used a good deal of poetic licence in softening the outlines of the picture.

Nanda, full of her good resolutions, used the stout notebook for its proper purpose. Every evening, after a meagre supper eaten to the accompaniment of Mother Percival's readings of the

Life of St Francis Xavier, she laboriously transcribed all that she could remember of the day's Meditations and Considerations. She did this partly for the benefit of Clare, who was not allowed to make the retreat, although she had done everything she could to persuade the nuns to let her. She had coaxed, she had wept, she had even tried to blackmail them by open rebellion, but they had remained firm. Poor Clare was forced to live through the entire school routine by herself. She attended all the usual classes as a solitary pupil, she played bumble-puppy sulkily on an empty playground, and did lonely preparations in the huge, deserted study-room. All this naturally tended to develop her mild flirtations with Catholicism into a hungry passion to be received into the Church. She read every pious book she could lay hands on, wept noisily and regularly in the chapel, and was constantly thrusting holy pictures into Nanda's missal, inscribed in her sprawling back-hand: 'Pray hard, darling, for my great Intention.'

So Nanda wrote out her notes as carefully as possible, with headings and sub-headings and neat underlinings and managed to slip the book into Clare's eager hands when she passed her in the garden.

And this is what Clare read.

NOTES ON MY RETREAT

Meditation I.

'Sink, sink into thyself and rally the good in the depths of thy soul.' Examples of retreats in the Bible. Elija in the desert. St John the Baptist. Jonah in the whale's belly. Our Lord in the wilderness. St Ignatius in the Cave of Manresa. Importance of retreats when one has gone out into the world. Devil hates them. Puts difficulties in the way; social engagements, etc. Soul's only engagement is with God. Opportunity to show courtesy to God, to return His visits as St Ignatius returned Our Lady's visits to him in visions by a pilgrimage to her shrine at Aranzazu. Opportunity to know ourselves; to discover our faults without flinching, to set right our accounts with God. Makes us realize that we are solitary beings; naked came we into the world, etc. No human friendship comparable to friendship of God. Retreat a little death, making us see time and eternity in their right proportions.

Meditation II. Sin.

Every human being tainted with original sin. Warped instincts and passions like the beasts. Baptism remits punishment due to original sin, but does not eradicate results. Limited intellect, dull comprehension of Divine things, etc. Unbaptised babies do not go to hell, but to limbo, a sort of earthly paradise. Not comparable to real paradise. One-third of angels became devils because they were too proud to accept the idea of the Incarnation. Human race will go on till vacant places in heaven are filled. Devils' sins worse than ours; sinned with full knowledge of God. Pride first and deadliest of sins. Heresies all due to pride. Setting oneself up against God's Divine revelation in the Church. Even children have difficulties about religion. Ten thousand difficulties do not make a doubt. Doubts are most apt to creep in when moral fibre has been weakened. Vanity, self-indulgence, etc., lead to doubting God's law. Hence importance of mortification. Mortal sin makes the soul loathsome in the sight of God. Saints could detect horrible stench in presence of sinners. Soul dead to God. No good work done in state of mortal sin counts, but God in His mercy may take such works into account and hasten grace of repentance. Sacrament of penance restores these lost merits. People make too light of venial sins, but they weaken the soul's health and lead to mortal sins. Venial sins punished in purgatory cannot help themselves. Only prayers on earth can shorten their sufferings. Better to be afflicted with the most appalling disease than to commit one mortal sin. Disease a faint type of sin. Mortal sins only forgiven in confession or by an act of perfect contrition, *e.g.*, act of sincere penitence from love of God alone, not from fear of punishment. Fear of hell lowest reason for repentance. Always think of having hurt God, not yourself.

Meditation III. Dangers of the World.

Worldly pleasures, business, etc., tend to interfere with spiritual life. Things not in themselves harmful may be harmful to soul. A saint said it was dangerous to walk through a beautiful wood. Tendency to regard things for their own sakes, rather than as manifestations of Creator's power, wisdom, etc. Sermons in stones. Dangers of nature-worship. Look for God in everything. Modern Pantheism. Believing everything to be God. Idea that it is better to go for country walk than attend mass. Dangerous nonsense and loose thinking. Devil responsible for part of creation after fall. Thistles, weeds, etc. Trying to upset God's scheme. Nature only beneficial to man before fall; now enemy. Even beauty often poisoned. Choose friends for solid piety, not for superficial good looks or accomplishment. Give up a friendship if it tends to hinder you in the practice of your religion. God hates exclusive personal loves. Mother love the highest of earthly loves, because essentially unselfish. Danger of idle conversation and frivolous reading. Never read books criticizing church. Priests must read them in order to refute them. Bad books do untold harm. Writer responsible for evil his books do; he shares in every sin occasioned by it. Cannot go to heaven until book has ceased to harm. Writer of bad book appeared in flames to saint. Tormented until last copy was destroyed. Oscar Wilde must now be suffering for untold evil done by his works. Books on the index. Kingsley, Macaulay, Huxley, etc. Abominable works exposed in Mayfair drawing-rooms. Zola, Anatole France, etc. Scientific works unsuitable for women. Puff up their vanity with ideas they only half understand. If science conflicts with religion, science must, by definition, be wrong. Garden of Eden a myth, perhaps; but true in essentials. Order of creation in Bible ratified even by modern scientists. Wrong to imagine Catholics not good scientists. Pasteur, Wassermann, etc. Jesuit astronomers. Read a spiritual book for every novel.

Meditation IV. Christian's Rule of Life.

Dedicate each day to God. Rise modestly, putting on clothes, remembering how much more important to clothe soul in virtue than body in fine raiment. Morning and night prayers. Mass and Communion whenever possible. When undressing, think of Christ stripped of His garments. St Theresa rose to great heights of sanctity by always thinking of the Agony in the Garden last thing at night. Opportunities of mortification occur all day long.

Pity looking-glasses were ever invented. Think how ugly you are when you look in them. Imagine old age, decay, etc. Encourage soul to look in mirror of lives of saints to learn its own defects. Christian marriage. Not for indulgence of selfish passions or even for exclusive affection. Object to provide Christian upbringing for children. Children always welcome to good Catholics. Take no thought for the morrow. God will provide. He sends little ones trooping down from heaven. Poverty does not matter. Saints came from large families. Essentials of life, Mass and the Sacraments are free to all. Wealth carries great responsibilities. Chokes spiritual growth. Rich and poor, however, a divine dispensation. Must not try to alter natural order of things. Abominations of socialism, free-masonry, etc. Trying to do God's work for Him. Women's votes unnecessary. Let her use her great influence in her own sphere. Modesty more effective than desire to shine. Our Lady had no vote and did not want one.

Meditation V. Death.

Every human being must die. Blasphemous scientist who said that death might one day be abolished by human agency. Must always be prepared for death; *e.g.*, be in a state of grace. Then it has no terrors. St Charles Borromeo, when asked what he would do if the Last Trump sounded as he was playing chess, replied that he would go on with his game, since he had undertaken it to the glory of God. Even when body unconscious, soul might still be conscious. A strong presumption, though not article of faith, that God appears at the moment of death and gives the soul one last chance to accept or reject him. No one goes to hell except through their own fault. The Sacred Heart promised to Blessed Margaret Mary Alacoque that all who went to Communion on nine consecutive first Fridays should have the grace of final perseverance. All the same, it would be presumptuous to trust to that alone. Presumption and despair both sins against the Holy Ghost.

Meditation VI. Judgement.

Soul goes straight from death-bed to tribunal of God. Two judgements; that private one and the public one at the last day, when all one's sins and virtues will be publicly proclaimed in the valley of Jehosaphat. The soul condemned to hell would suffer only in the spirit until the last day, when the resurrected body would add to its agonies. Nearly everyone must spend some time in purgatory to cleanse away the last traces of sin. Souls in purgatory suffer, but are happy, knowing that they are sure of heaven. Sight of God makes the sinner horrible in his own sight; he longs for the cleansing fire, Dream of Gerontius. 'Take me away and in the lowest deep there let me be . . . motionless and happy in my pain.' No excuses at the Judgement Seat. No frantic pleas for mercy can alter the course of Divine justice. Decision is eternal, irrevocable.

Meditation VII. Hell.

But under this heading Nanda had written nothing but Eternally, Eternally, Eternally. It was not that she had forgotten what Father Westlake had said about hell. She remembered it all too clearly; she could have written down almost word for word his cool, accurate catalogue of the punishments of the damned. But she could not bring herself to write it down. Was it because Clare was to read her notes? Or because she wanted to forget? Or that she was superstitious and felt such things were better unwritten in case they should attract the very horrors they described? But if there was no record of the meditation on hell in her notebook, there was a definite enough impression in her own mind. Body and soul were to be tormented for ever and ever, with no interruption of agony, no numbness of habit, no ray of hope. Every sense would be revolted by filth and stench and noise; every nerve exquisitely tortured by fire to which mere earthly fire was as cool as water. The damned suffered always from appalling thirst, their swollen tongues were parched and cracked. They were hungry and the devils in mockery offered them white-hot coals to eat. They suffered still more from agony of mind, from the separation of God, after Whom they now so bitterly longed. They would gladly endure ten thousand years of torment for the sake of one second of earthly life in which they might repent and be reconciled to Him. Father Westlake had quoted a long passage from Father Faber which was already sickeningly familiar to Nanda. 'With a cry that should be heard creation through the lost soul rushes upon God and it knocks itself, spirit as it is, against material terrors. It clasps the shadow of God and lo, it embraces keen flames. It runs up to Him, but it has encountered only fearful demons. It leaps the length of its chain after Him, but it has only dashed into an affrighting crowd of lost and cursed souls. Thus, it is ever writhing under the sense of being its own executioner. Thus, there is not an hour of our summer sunshine, not a moment of our sweet starlight, not a vibration of our moonlit groves, not an undulation of odorous air from our flower-beds, not a pulse of delicious sound from music or song to us, but that hapless, unpitiable soul is ever falling sick afresh of the overwhelming sense that all around it is eternal.' Even Léonie's observation that Father Faber's style had a good deal in common with Mr Pecksniff's could not quite rob the passage of its sting. It was not so much the thought of hell for herself that appalled Nanda, for after all, she knew the means of avoiding it, but she sometimes lay awake at night worrying miserably over the damned. For months she would forget all about them, then an account of a horrible accident or a sermon like this would remind her of them. She would pray frantically for them, forgetting that it was useless. In spite of this, she would go so far as to beg Our Lady to do something for them, clinging to some vague legend about their being allowed one day's respite in ten thousand years. Sometimes, she even doubted that their punishments were eternal, only to remember, horrified, that the eternity of hell was an article of faith, and that to doubt it endangered her own soul. Indeed, the eternity of hell was another proof of God's goodness, since the theologians agreed that annihilation would be a worse punishment than endless ages of fiery pain.

In spite of her good intentions, Nanda came out of retreat with a sense of relief, and a sense, too, that her four days had not been altogether a success. She had prayed and meditated as well as she knew how; she had often been rewarded by a real sense of pleasure in the spiritual company of Our Lord and Our Lady and the saints. But over and over again she encountered those arid patches where the whole of religious life seemed a monstrous and meaningless complication. The saints, who displayed, as she was always being told, so much delightful human diversity and personality in their lives, seemed all exactly alike and irritating at that. Even their early dissipations were tame, and all too soon the dreary tale of mortifications and hatred of the world would begin. She liked some of their legends and their miracles, but with the best will in the world, she could not find their attitude to ordinary life anything but depressing and repulsive. She was frankly bored by the ecstacies and the floweriness of the Little Flower, and was disgusted with St Francis, who is popular even with Protestants, when she read that he laughed heartily when Brother Juniper cut off a pig's foot out of excessive charity to a greedy sick man. She liked the robuster saints best, St Theresa and St Augustine and Blessed Thomas More, but even these impressed her for the wrong reasons. She enjoyed a sentence, a gesture, a touch of gaiety or gallantry rather than the actual mechanics of sanctity. But she was ready to admit that her own ideas were entirely due to a perverse and worldly nature. She accepted the Catholic Church wholeheartedly and tried hard to mould herself into the proper shape of a young Catholic girl. How could an institution be wrong that was so evidently divinely inspired, that had survived for nearly two thousand years in spite of persecution and slander, that stood firm through scandals, heresies and schisms? Had not her own father, whom she admired more than anyone in the world, struggled for years against conviction, and finally sacrificed his whole career for the sake of what he felt to be the truth? She was part of the Church now. She could never, she knew, break away without a sense of mutilation. In her four years at Lippington, it had grown into every fibre of her nature; she could not eat or sleep or read or play without relating every action to her secret life as a Christian and a Catholic. She rejoiced in it and rebelled against it. She tried to imagine what life would be like without it; how she would feel if she were a savage blessedly ignorant of the very existence of God. But it was as impossible as imagining death or madness or blindness. Wherever she looked, it loomed in the background, like Fuji Yama in a Japanese print, massive, terrifying, beautiful and inescapable; the fortress of God, the house on the rock.

Chapter Eight

'I've had a glorious time, but it's heaven to be back,' said Clare
Rockingham. She squeezed Rosario's arm. 'And how are you
two infants?'

It was the first night of the autumn term, and the four had not
seen each other for two months. Nanda felt shy of the others;
traces of the holidays, of other worlds, still clung to them. Clare
wore silk stockings and frivolous bronze shoes. Rosario had
pearls in her ears; a wilted white bow drooped on Léonie's hair.
She would not feel completely happy until tomorrow when they
would all be subdued to the comforting impersonality of
uniform.

'I did such heaps of things in Leipzig that I hardly scribbled a
syllable even to Rosario,' chattered Clare, her brown eyes more
feverishly bright, more restless than ever. 'I went to drawing
classes for one thing. No one knows anything about art over
here. I'm never going to draw one of Mother Roscoe's idiotic
old plaster casts again. Do you know what a life class is? I never
told my dismal chaperone, or she'd have had a fit. The models
are quite naked; don't be shocked, Rosario darling. It's so
fascinating drawing them that you forget all about that.
Wouldn't it be fun to have a life class in Lippington? And
wouldn't Nanda make the sweetest little nude?'

'Oh, shut up, Clare,' said Nanda, blushing so much that her
skin felt as if it would crack.

'Well, I'll tell you something edifying. I went to mass every
single Sunday, and I fairly brandished my rosary in my
chaperone's face. She was so busy writing home to my family
about my shocking behaviour that she forgot to keep her eye on
me half the time. You see, they sent me to Leipzig in the hopes
that I'd forget all about this Catholic business.'

'If they're so afraid of your becoming a papist, why don't they
take you away from Lippington?' asked Léonie sensibly.

'Well, I've been to three schools before and run away from all of them. And they certainly don't want me at home yet.

'You see, they're trying to marry off Isabel. That's my eldest sister, and they don't want me in the way.'

'For fear of spoiling her chances with your fatal beauty?' said Léonie.

'Good Lord, no. But men bore Isabel frightfully, and we get a lot of fun out of ragging her wretched *prétendants*. When we're together, we get much better ideas. Last Christmas there was a man quite dumb with admiration for Isabel, and he was awfully rich and appropriate and all that, but she couldn't stand him. So she made him eat some chocolates, though he didn't want to in the least, and we'd filled all the chocolates with cascara. He never came back.'

Rosario withdrew her arm from Clare's.

'What barbarians you English are.'

'But he was awful, Rosario, really he was. As red as a radish and as stupid as a bull. Not in the least like . . .' She paused and bit her lip. 'No, I can't tell you that.'

'A love affair in the holidays, I suppose,' said Léonie with an air of ineffable boredom. 'Really, Clare, you're too primitive.'

'Not a love affair at all,' said Clare, crossly. 'I just happened to meet a rather interesting Prussian painter at the art school, that's all. We used to read Heine together and once we actually had a glass of beer at a café. He was terribly intelligent, and there was none of that nonsense of treating one like a schoolgirl.'

'You'd better get him out of your mind,' advised Léonie, 'because there's certainly going to be a war with Germany within the next year or two. I was in Berlin and Vienna in August, and there's a lot of talk about it. So your precious artist will get conscripted and one of your hearty brothers will probably put a bullet through his cropped head.'

'I love to hear little Léo talking about what goes on behind the scenes in diplomacy,' sneered Clare, trying not very successfully to ger her own back.

But Rosario flew to Léonie's defence.

'She knows a lot,' she insisted in her soft, fierce voice. 'Papa has the greatest respect for her mind. He says she should have been a man.'

'I like old men best,' said Léonie simply. 'They are so restful.

And they often forget one is there after they have patted one's head, and go on talking, and one overhears the most interesting things.'

'If there were a war with Germany,' said Nanda suddenly, 'you would be an enemy, wouldn't you, Léo?'

'I'm not sure,' mused Léonie. 'It depends whether I went in with my German relations or my French ones. In the Franco-Prussian war I had a great-uncle on each side.'

'Your father's German, anyhow,' persisted Clare.

'Hoch der Kaiser. Nationality is all rot, anyhow,' said Léonie.

'How can you say that?' flamed Rosario. 'I would rather be dead than be anything but Spanish. And however madly in love with anyone I might be, I wouldn't marry him unless he were Spanish to the backbone.'

'What did you do with your holidays, beautiful savage?' asked Léonie.

'We were in Biarritz nearly all the time. It was very gay and amusing. There was a dance for Elita given by my aunt De Las Rojas, and I was not supposed to be going because I am not properly out yet. But the King himself saw me at a polo match in the afternoon, and asked Papa as a special favour that I should come.'

'And did you dance with the King?' said Clare, touching her sleeve. 'I wish I could have seen you.'

'Yes, I danced with him. But I had no time to get a proper frock, and so I had to wear an old pink chiffon that is very *jeune fille*. But Elita looked wonderful. Papa was pleased, but my aunt was angry. She said: "Why, the child's actually *made up*."'

'And what did the King say?' asked Nanda.

'My aunt told me that he said Elita was a great beauty, but that he preferred the little wild Palencia.'

'Meaning you?' smiled Clare.

'Yes,' admitted Rosario with complete simplicity.

'Then you might be Queen of Spain one day, darling?'

Rosario turned a thunderous blue and black gaze on Clare.

'How can you be so utterly disloyal and . . . and so utterly vulgar?' she flashed. Without another word, she swung round, tossing her great golden plume of hair, and strode away angrily, arms crossed and head thrust forward.

Suddenly bold, Nanda caught Clare's wrist.

'Don't go after her,' she begged. Léonie had already sauntered off, whistling '*Die Wacht am Rhein*' with an air of masculine indifference.

'But I must go,' whispered Clare, her nostrils quivering and her eyes blind and bright as a hare's. 'Must go,' she insisted, wrenching away from Nanda.

'I wish you'd be a little proud sometimes, Clare,' said Nanda, in a small, cold, even voice.

But Clare, staggering a little on her high bronze heels, was already running towards the corner where Rosario had disappeared.

The term began peacefully enough. There was the usual reshuffling of classes and a distribution of rewards at which Nanda was agreeably surprised by being awarded a green ribbon. Much elated, she wrote home to her parents.

'I'm awfully glad, but I really didn't expect it. The school and the nuns vote for it, you know. Of course, the others tease me about it a good deal, and so does Mother Percival. I've been moved up, but she is still taking our class. I'm an Angel now, too. We've got four congregations, you know, Holy Child, St Aloysius, Angels and Children of Mary. You wear your medal on white ribbon on feast days and there is a sort of secret meeting on Sunday evenings with Mother Radcliffe, and you have a book of rules that only other Angels may read. Léonie's uncle has given her a horse and a violin. She has got the violin here, but she is very angry that she can't have the horse too. She is going to play in the hockey match against the Five Wounds at Southsea, and we are all going to do penances all day so that we may win. Our table is going to put salt instead of sugar on the stewed fruit. I wonder if the Southsea children will do the same. Do pray hard that Clare may become a Catholic. I know she wants to really. I think she looks prettier than ever since she came back from Germany; most people look ugly with freckles, but hers suit her. I've never seen anyone with such bright eyes, either; they're brown, but if you look very closely they have little green rays like chips of emerald in them. Léo has given me an ivory card-case; it's Turkish, I think, all inlaid with lined with sandalwood which smells heavenly. I don't suppose I shall ever actually want a card-case, but it is lovely to have. There is a rumour that a cardinal is coming some time this term. I hope it's true, because it will mean a play and a holiday.'

The next day, in the middle of a French lesson, a blue ribbon put her head officiously round the door and said: 'Please, Mother, Nanda Grey is to see Mother Radcliffe at once.'

With a palpitating heart, Nanda tore off her apron and fidgeted in her pocket for her gloves.

'Here, take mine,' whispered Léonie, holding out a seedy pair, 'and don't look so terrified. She can't hang you.'

But this scarcely comforted Nanda as she stood knocking at Mother Radcliffe's door. As she knocked she feverishly but unsuccessfully examined her conscience for some misdeed. At last, after about half an hour, as it seemed to her, a cold sweet voice called: 'Come in.'

But when she entered, Mother Radcliffe did not look up. She went on entering figures in a beautiful square, upright hand in a large notebook. When she reached the end of the column, she went back and very carefully crossed all the tails of the sevens.

Nanda's heart was bumping so hard against her ribs that she thought Mother Radcliffe must hear it. T calm herself, she began to make an inventory of the room. One red carpet, one table covered with green serge, faded; one crucifix, no, two crucifixes; one portrait of Mother Guillemin; one portrait of Leo XIII; one statue of Our Lady of Lourdes; two chairs. Mother Radcliffe looked up suddenly and seemed to notice Nanda for the first time. Having noticed her, she looked at her with a polite, but increasing interest. She took off her glasses, polished them and replaced them, fixing her gaze, not on Nanda's face, but somewhere about her collar. At last, with a sudden smile, as if at last she recognized her, she said:

'Ah, Nanda Grey. Yes, I sent for you, Nanda, did I not? Sit down, child, and don't fidget so.'

Nanda sat down on the edge of a chair. Mother Radcliffe's smile was wiped out suddenly as it had appeared. She stared at Nanda with a stern and puzzled air.

'Well, and what have you to say for yourself?'

'Please, Mother, I don't know why you wanted to see me,' Nanda muttered.

'No?' said Mother Radcliffe very mildly.

With extreme deliberation, she opened a large file and extracted a sheet of notepaper. Nanda recognized her own handwriting.

'Perhaps you can guess now?' hazarded the nun

'Did I forget to leave the envelope open?' suggested Nanda hopefully.

Mother Radcliffe made a little face at the letter as if it gave off an unpleasant smell. 'No, you left it open,' she admitted, 'though I should not have been surprised had you wished to close it. Surely you realize, my dear, that the tone of this letter is not at all what we expect to find in the correspondence of a child of the Five Wounds?'

'Is it . . . is it the grammar?' asked Nanda in a parched voice.

'No. The grammar is slipshod enough. But it is the whole spirit of the contents to which I am objecting.'

Mother Radcliffe peered again at the letter through her large, clear glasses. The glasses were steel-rimmed, and Nanda observed that they had been neatly mended with a bandage of black thread. Then she looked very thoughtfully at Nanda.

'You know quite well that the school rule does not approve of particular friendships. They are against charity, to begin with, and they lead moreover, to dangerous and unhealthy indulgence of feeling. I do not think your father and mother will share your rather morbid interest in Clare Rockingham's appearance. Chips of emerald. Really, Nanda. Aren't you rather ashamed at the sheer silliness of it?'

Nanda looked at her shoes.

'Yes, I suppose so,' she muttered.

'Talking of green things,' said Mother Radcliffe very blandly. 'What about that ribbon you are wearing? I suppose you don't want by any chance to lose that particular chip of emerald, do you?'

'No, Mother.'

'Your father will be so pleased to know about it. You tell him in this unfortunate letter, I observe, but I have already written to him about it. So that if you lost it, he would be very disappointed indeed, would he not?'

'Yes, Mother,' said Nanda. She was calming down now that she knew the worst, and beginning to feel bored and restless. Why, oh why, at Lippington, couldn't they go straight to a point and have done with it?

'Your father is a convert, is he not? Conversion is a great grace, but the Catholic outlook, Catholic breeding, shall we say, does not come in one generation, or even two, or three. So I suppose I must overlook this extraordinary lapse in your case, Nanda. Of course, I shall destroy this wretched letter; at least, I shall not send it. You will write another letter home during your midday recreation. And I hope that in future I shall see you about more with friends of your own age. There are girls such as Marjorie Appleyard and Monica Owen who are about your equals in years and in station of life. I think you would do well to cultivate their society. You may go.'

With a very stiff curtsy, Nanda turned to the door. But instead of dropping her eyes, she looked very straight at Mother Radcliffe. The nun threw back her head and gave the merest ghost of a smile.

'You are very fond of your own way, aren't you, Nanda?'

'Yes, I suppose so, Mother.'

'And do you know that no character is any good in this world unless that will has been broken completely? Broken and re-set in God's own way. I don't think your will has been quite broken, my dear child, do you?'

Although Nanda did not lose her green ribbon as a result of this interview, she was considerably shaken by it. For a time, she actually avoided Clare, and in spite of Léo's mockery, cultivated the society of Marjorie and Monica. The experiment was not a great success, for Marjorie and Nanda bored each other even more disastrously than they had three years ago, while the unexpected attention warmed Monica's dim friendliness into an embarrassing devotion. All the same, it did something to allay suspicion, and a severe bout of teasing by Mother Percival which had begun the very day after Nanda's talk with the Mistress of Discipline died down after a week into an occasional mild sarcasm. As in the Jesuit Order, every child was under constant observation, and the results of this observation were made known by secret weekly reports to Mother Radcliffe and the Superior. But how detailed such reports could be, covering not only the broad outlines of a character, but the minutest physical peculiarities and nervous habits, Nanda did not realize until she saw Mother Radcliffe play the famous Key Game. In the afternoon of some minor holiday, Mother Radcliffe summoned the whole Senior School into St Stanislas Kostka, the assembly room. In her hands she held an ordinary door key. 'I am going,' she announced, 'to play a rather unusual game which is played here from time to time, and which we call the Mistress of Discipline's game. There are about eighty of you here; all except the new ones, fairly well known to me. Better known, perhaps, than you realize. I shall go out of the room for a few minutes, and the head of the school, Rose Maclean, will give this key to anyone she chooses. No one is to speak while this is being done, and no names are to be spoken. Rose may keep the key herself if she likes. I think you will all trust me sufficiently not to think of Rose as a kind of conjuror's accomplice. She may give it to anyone in this room, but I ask her not to give it to any child who is actually new this term. When I come in again, you will all remain in complete silence while I try to discover, without asking any questions, which of you is hiding the key. When I think I know, I shall not say any name, but I shall give you indications by which you will all know whether or not I have guessed right.'

She left the room and Rose, after a little thought, gave the key to Rosario de Palencia, who put it in her pocket. As Mother Radcliffe re-entered, every child composed her face into an unnatural blankness. The nun walked slowly down the rows of seated figures, peering into each face, skimming over some and gazing for nearly a minute at others. In front of Nanda she stopped for a long time, and, although she had not the key, Nanda felt herself blush guiltily. At Rosario she gave only a swift glance. After about a quarter of an hour of nervous tension, Mother Radcliffe returned to her table, and the whole school relaxed with a flutter of relief. Staring straight ahead of her, Mother Radcliffe began dreamily: 'We have been at Lippington, I think for some years. We have not any ribbon, though we are a Child of Mary, yet we are one of those personalities which are known to the whole school. We are not English; we come from a country where most of the inhabitants are dark, yet we have fair hair and do not conform to the usual habit of wearing that hair in a plait. We are courteous, but we are very proud, and perhaps we are rather passionate as well. We love the arts, especially music, and we have no great aptitude for mathematics. We are perhaps a little old for our age and have been out in the world more than an English girl of our age, which is about seventeen. Some months ago we suffered a great loss, a loss which we feel more than we admit.' But she was interrupted by the muffled clapping of eighty gloved hands. She smiled, as Rosario whipped the key out of her pocket and waved it triumphantly.

Three more times Mother Radcliffe performed her strange trick, but at the suggestion of a fourth attempt, she shook her head. 'This game is rather a strain,' she said, 'and I think we will not have any more thought-reading today.' As she gave the signal for the gathering to break up, Nanda noticed that she looked pinched and whiter than usual, while the hand holding the signal trembled.

'My dear, isn't it too uncanny?' shrieked Clare to Léonie, as the school, chattering rather hysterically, ran out to the playgrounds.

'Rather beastly, I think,' growled Léonie. 'I hate that sort of spiritual showing-off. If we had dossiers of the community as they have of us, I dare say we could bring off this Sherlock Holmes business just as successfully.'

'Yes? But how did she do it? I watched Rosario's face the whole time and she never blinked an eyelid.'

'She probably noticed you, my dear Watson,' said Léonie. 'There's a rational explanation of most miracles.'

Nanda, who was passing, caught the last words, and exclaimed:

'Don't you believe in miracles, Léo?'

'Not entirely, my child. But I'm willing to enter into the spirit of them. Like all the old men who bellow that they believe in fairies when Tinkerbell is at her last gasp.'

'But you wrote such a lovely and convincing one for your Christmas story,' protested Nanda.

'I like the Catholic way of looking at things,' said Léo. 'Any way of looking at life is a fairy story, and I prefer mine with lots of improbable embellishments. I think angels and devils are much more amusing than microbes and Mr Wells's noble scientists.'

'But you're a pagan,' asserted Clare in a shocked voice.

'So are hundreds of practising Catholics. I could tell you things about the Renaissance Popes that would make your hair stand on end.'

'I'm beginning to think that there's something to be said for being a Protestant after all,' said Clare.

'Oh, no, Clare,' Nanda assured her, horrified at seeing the prospective convert wavering. 'Don't you see it's just another proof that the Church really is divine and inspired? Any other institution would have been done for centuries ago with so much corruption in individual members. There really is something that keeps it going in spite of all that, and the gates of hell don't prevail in spite of all sorts of horrors.'

'Go it, Nanda,' mocked Léonie. 'No one like a convert for getting up the subject good and strong. Yet I wouldn't mind betting that twenty years from now she's a red-hot, fool-proof rationalist while I'm a model Catholic mother with my children all festooned with scapulars and a pious sodality meeting every afternoon in my drawing-room.'

She made a face and sauntered away, leaving the other two together for the first time for many weeks.

'One never sees you these days, infant,' began Clare at once. 'Are you afraid of being contaminated by poor heretics?'

'Of course not,' said Nanda uncomfortably, 'but Mother Percival is always herding us together to play hockey or something, and we hardly ever get a chance to speak to the other divisions.'

'But even on holidays one never sees anything of you,' persisted Clare. 'I believe you've lost interest in me and don't care whether I ever become a Catholic or not.'

'Oh, but I do,' protested Nanda. 'I want you to awfully.

Really, Clare. Only there's nothing any of us can do but pray for you.'

'Aren't you all kind?' said Clare sarcastically. 'I suppose the truth is we're a little puffed up now we've got a green ribbon.'

'Don't be a beast,' Nanda flared. 'You know that's got nothing whatever to do with it. Anyway, I'm pretty sure to lose it soon.'

Clare changed her tone.

'I'm so awfully unhappy,' she said softly, screwing up her bright eyes. 'I don't suppose you can understand at your age. Besides, I don't believe fair people can really understand sorrow at any age.'

Deeply offended, Nanda assured her that she understood every variety of suffering with the greatest sympathy.

'Really, I do, Clare,' she said, nodding very sagely. 'I can't show it because I haven't got the right sort of face. And if you knew how I loathed being fair and having idiotic dimples, you'd realize that there's quite a lot of suffering in that. It's as bad as being deformed, almost,' she added gloomily.

Clare began to crow with laughter.

'You're adorable, baby,' she cried.

But Nanda was by no means soothed. She edged away with great dignity as Clare attempted to tweak her ear. There was silence for a minute, then Clare said sadly:

'I don't really think of you as a baby at all. It's only because you look such a child. You understand things wonderfully, you know. Poetry and all that. And some of your essays and things are really beautiful . . . more beautiful than you know. I often think that you must be one of those twice-born people. Your soul's so much older than your body.'

Nanda softened visibly.

'Oh, nonsense, Clare,' she said in a pleased voice.

'But I'm not only thinking of mental suffering,' went on Clare, 'though goodness knows I have enough of that. It's physical suffering too. I get the most frightful headaches.'

'Well, why not see Mother Regan about them?' suggested Nanda helpfully.

'She wouldn't understand,' Clare assured her. 'I have spoken about them, but the fool doctor here says he can't find anything the matter. I'll just have to bear them, I suppose. Perhaps they'll help me to get converted. But I've got a queer feeling that they're a kind of warning. Perhaps I won't live long. Don't look so sad, darling. What does it matter, anyway? But I'd like to die a Catholic.'

Nanda capitulated, but she was glad when the bell announced the end of the brief recreation, and of this rather embarrassing talk. But she forgot about Clare and her sorrows at the sight of Monica Owen, weeping loudly, being dragged towards the house by Mother Percival. As she passed Nanda, Monica managed to gasp out:

'Something frightful's happened. Pray for me.'

For two or three days no one knew exactly what had happened to the unlucky Monica, but it was clearly something very serious. She appeared at no classes and her place was vacant in the refectory. When the others went into the chapel she was brought in by a lay-sister after everyone else and placed in a bench by herself at the back. As they filed out they could see her blank, pale face, almost unrecognizable from much crying, and speculate as to what her awful crime could be. Nanda was extremely worried. Although Monica was rather a nuisance, she had come to look upon her as a protége, and she was genuinely sorry for her. She felt, too, that Monica was rather shabbily treated by the nuns, who made no secret of the fact that her father was a struggling doctor in a provincial town, and that her family could not afford the full fees at Lippington. True, they very rarely alluded to this openly, but they found a hundred ways of humiliating Monica. She was never given new lesson-books but had to be content with shabby copies blotted and torn by a former owner. Her uniform, too, had been made over from an elder sister's and shone lamentably at shoulders and elbows, while her gloves were darned at every finger. When the rest of the school was fitted out with new white dresses for feast days, Monica was forced to go on wearing her old nun's-veiling, yellow with age and of an antique and conspicuous pattern. Her seat was always the worst in every class, and she was grudged her very pencils and india-rubbers. Not very intelligent by nature, as Mother Frances had long ago discovered in her Junior School days, she had become duller still under this treatment.

All her interest was concentrated in her passion for drawing dogs, and after some years of constant practice, she really did draw dogs with uncanny skill. And she was not allowed a sketch-book, she was forced to draw her mastiffs and terriers in the margin of her already battered lesson-books, a practice which kept her in almost constant hot water. But Monica, tearful and yielding in everything else, was obstinate in this. Every notebook was decorated with drawings of dogs of every age and in every attitude.

Many of Monica's dogs had oddly human faces. Nanda had laughed at a King Charles spaniel that bore a remarkable resemblance to Marjorie Appleyard, a collie with a distinct look of Clare, and a Saluki with Elita de Palencia's dark eyes and languid grace.

Out of various rumours about Monica's disgrace, Nanda at last sorted out one that had the air of authenticity. A notebook had been found in Monica's desk bearing the inscription, 'European History'. Instead of containing notes on the Holy Roman Empire, it was decorated with pictures of dogs, each dog a recognizable caricature of some member of the community. Nanda made many enquiries before she was finally convinced this was the true explanation. Satisfied that it was, she took great pains to discover what Monica's punishment was likely to be. But here she met with wise head-shakings and gloomy prophecies. Some people went as far as to say that Monica had committed blasphemy in ridiculing the Brides of Christ, and one and all agreed that she would almost certainly be expelled. Nanda was so horrified at this that she went to Rose Maclean, the red-cheeked, amiable girl who had succeeded Madeleine as head of the school.

'Is it true that Monica Owen is going to be expelled?' she asked outright.

'I don't think that concerns any of us,' said Rose uncomfortably.

'It certainly does if it's true,' insisted Nanda angrily.

'Well, you'd better ask Mother Radcliffe,' said Rose with a nervous giggle. 'No doubt she's longing to take you into her confidence.'

But Rose's mild sarcasm was lost on Nanda.

'I'll go this very minute,' she said, white with rage. Two minutes later she was knocking at Mother Radcliffe's door. Summoned in, she found Mother Radcliffe busy writing letters.

'What is it, Nanda?' said the nun rather irritably. 'I don't think I sent for you, did I?'

'No, Mother,' said Nanda very quietly, though her knees were shaking with excitement.

'Then what is it? Be quick, please. I am very busy, as you see.'

Anger and a hot sense of injustice had given Nanda a most unusual courage.

'It's about Monica Owen. Is she really going to be expelled?' she blurted out.

Mother Radcliffe dropped her pen with surprise.

'Really, Nanda, what a very odd question. I don't think that concerns you, does it? Is Monica another of these wonderful friends of yours?'

It was on the tip of Nanda's tongue to remind Mother Radcliffe of what she had said at their last interview, but she bit back the obvious retort. Still filled with her unnatural courage, she said in a cold and unreasonable voice:

'Because if you *are* going to, it's horribly unfair. Whatever Monica's done, she's been punished enough already. You know she's not quite like other people. She's not very clever, I mean. And people have always been rather unfair to her and laughed at her. There isn't an ounce of harm in Monica, everyone knows that. And if she is expelled, she's going to have a perfectly beastly time at home. She's got a very strict father and a stepmother who isn't any too nice to her in the ordinary way.'

During this speech, Mother Radcliffe looked at Nanda with a blank amazement. If a cat had begun to talk, she could hardly have seemed more astonished. When Nanda stopped there was a strained silence, during which Mother Radcliffe's face slowly assumed an expression of sternness and distaste.

'Very interesting,' she said at last. 'I have not often been told my duty quite so clearly by a child of your age. Invaluable as your advice is, I am afraid I do not see my way to taking it. There are some things which are no doubt permitted in the high schools to which your Protestant friends are accustomed but they are not permitted at Lippington. Monica Owen has done something which cannot possibly be overlooked.'

But even this did not deter Nanda.

'Monica hasn't spoken to a soul for three days,' she said passionately. 'She's been shut up in the retreat house all this time and only allowed into the chapel. She looks half dead with sheer misery. It's too much punishment for anyone. I thought Catholics were supposed to be charitable. Can't some of us go and see her just for five minutes . . . three minutes even?' she implored.

Mother Radcliffe picked up her pen, dipped it in the inkpot and began a new paragraph in her letter. Without looking up, she said:

'There is no question of that. Monica Owen was expelled from this house two hours ago.'

Chapter Nine

The expulsion of Monica left a definite mark on Nanda. A small core of rebelliousness which had been growing secretly for four years seemed to have hardened inside her. Outwardly her conduct was perfectly respectable; she no longer giggled or talked at forbidden times, she worked fairly hard and generally comported herself as a green ribbon should. But she delighted in asking awkward questions in the Christian Doctrine class and smiled with the complacent cynicism of thirteen when her mistress was temporarily flustered. Once she plunged into deeper waters than she knew and without understanding the implications of her remark brought a violent blush to Mother Percival's prim cheek.

Mother Percival was explaining the circumstances which could make a marriage invalid. If a couple did not conform to certain regulations, they might be man and wife according to the law of the country, but their marriage would not be recognized by the Church.

'You mean to say that people might *think* they were properly married, but they mightn't be married at all?' asked Nanda.

'Exactly.'

'Then how could they tell?' asked Marjorie Appleyard.

Without giving Mother Percival time to answer Nanda called out briskly.

'It's quite simple, isn't it, Mother? If they had some children they would know they were properly married, and if they didn't they wouldn't have been. Only married people can have children, can they?'

Nanda made this remarkable observation in all innocence, and for once she did not mean to be impertinent. But Mother Percival turned as red as a peony, and answered in a voice faint with horror.

'Really, Nanda, this is hardly a subject for discussion. No modest girl should have the remotest interest in the why or wherefore of such things. God gives children to whom He pleases and it is not for us to question his decisions. Marjorie, will you please give me a brief account of the origin of the Sacrament of Penance.'

Nanda's rebelliousness, such as it was, was directed entirely against the Lippington methods. Her faith in the Catholic Church was not affected in the least. If anything, it became more robust. She went to Communion every morning and never again experienced the strange dryness and emptiness of her first approach. Outwardly, she was less emotional about her religion, and no longer lighted innumerable candles to St Anthony, nor wrote *Ad Majorem Dei Gloriam* on the flyleaf of her lesson-books. The flowery ecstacies of the Garden of the Soul no longer satisfied her; she preferred the colder, more solid prayers of St Augustine and St Thomas Aquinas. But only very rarely and by extreme concentration could she ever obtain from any religious exercise the pure delight that poetry or music aroused without the least effort on her part. Quite sincerely, she tried to make religion the centre of her life, but to do so required constant watchfulness and direction of her will. She tried to persuade herself that her love of beauty was connected with God (how many pious and applauded essays she had written on 'The Message of Beethoven', 'The Message of Fra Angelico', 'Whither was Browning Tending?', 'Art, the Handmaid of Religion'), but some small, clear, irritating voice assured her

that it was an independent growth. At other times, she forced
herself to remember what she had so often heard, that conscious
emotion was no part of religion, that it was a grace which God
occasionally conferred but far more often withheld. Yet when
she read the lives of the saints it seemed clear to her that their
feeling at the thought of God was of the same kind as her own
extreme delight when Léonie read Blake aloud, or Rosario sang
Wolf. She was, of course, beginning to write herself and was
alternately puffed up and disgusted by what she produced. For
the most part, she wrote laboured little lyrics about spring and
the sea, with a tardy reference to God in the last verse, and
elaborate fairy-tales with saints for princes and devils for
dragons. But now she was projecting something far more
ambitious, nothing less than a full-length novel. The idea
fascinated and alarmed her; she knew that religion must play a
large part in it, but feared that too much piety would conflict
with a really exciting plot. So she decided to describe a brilliant,
wicked, worldly society, preferably composed of painters,
musicians and peers, and to let all her characters be sensationally
converted in the last chapter. She had already made several
sketches for this great work, including one of Bohemian life, the
material for which she had gathered during a half-hour's visit to
the Café Royal, where Mr Grey, rather surprisingly, used to play
dominoes every Sunday night. But at thirteen, Nanda had not
entirely decided where her talents lay. When the novel, scribbled
in bed by the dim light of a low burning gas-jet outside her
cubicle, went badly, as it usually did, she would turn to
playwriting, only to realise, as the second act petered out
halfway through, that she would never write anything half as
good as Léonie's *Death of Socrates*. Often she thought she would
like to be a painter, and, encouraged by Clare, who drew
remarkably well, she would turn out weak little landscapes of
flat country with two or three poplar trees grouped against acres
of sky. However, the ultramarine in her paint-box gave out so
early in each term that she usually fell back on music. Apart from
the regular hour each day, she would spend her free study in the
piano cells, playing Chopin's nocturnes with tremendous
expression and more pedal than accuracy. But the sight of
Léonie making appalling faces at her through the window had

severely shaken her confidence and lately her musical activities had taken the form of listening admiringly while Léo drummed out Bach fugues with great sternness and precision. In the background, of course, there was acting. At Lippington, as at most convent schools, there were plays and tableaux and dramatic recitations every term, and after a small success as an English Martyr or Prince Arthur or Alice in Wonderland, Nanda was usually ready to abandon all her other pursuits for the stage.

All through this present autumn term there had been rumours of a cardinal's visit and a play of hitherto unheard-of elaboration and splendour. A new wing, containing an ambitious theatre-room had just been completed, and the cardinal had promised to open it.

Twice his visit had been announced and postponed, but, towards the end of November, a notice was put up saying that His Eminence would definitely arrive on 15 December.

The whole school was in a ferment of excitement to know what play could be considered worthy of such an honour. There were old favourites which had been acted year after year: *Thomas à Becket, Antigone, Joan of Arc, The Ugly Duckling* and *The Rose and the Ring*. Last year there had been a spectacular presentation of King Arthur's Knights in a mild Lippington version which left out all references to Guinevere, and Nanda and Léonie had swaggered terrifically in cardboard armour and horsehair plumes. But, immensely successful as it had been, no one felt that King Arthur was equal to such an occasion as this. But when, at last, it was announced that *The Vision of Dante* was to be performed, everyone agreed that Mother Castello, the community's star producer, had risen magnificently to the occasion.

At the first recreation after the notice had appeared, there was no talk of anything but the great question of casting. Even Mother Percival's breezy sarcasm could not keep alive a listless game of hockey and the children broke up into groups of earnest debaters. All the possible Beatrices assumed expressions of extreme spirituality, and when startled out of their dream, exclaimed modestly: 'Oh, I couldn't. Mother Castello would never choose me. I expect I'll just be one of the lost souls or noises off.'

Léonie, having heard this remark for the seventh time, observed:

'We'll need a good many damned, if we're going to stick to the book. And there are some very ingenious tortures. We'll have to hire a batch of heretics from outside.'

'Well, here's one all ready,' said Clare winningly.

'There's an excellent torture for you,' Léonie told her. 'You get shut in a fiery tomb for all eternity. The lid's off now, but after the day of judgement they shut it down and never take it off again.'

'I think Catholics have some horrible ideas,' shuddered Clare.

'Oh, well, Dante isn't dogma,' Léonie grinned.

'That's one blessing,' said Clare.

'All the same,' admitted Léonie, 'everyone agrees that he really drew it pretty mild. The early fathers thought of lots more revolting things than Dante ever did.'

'I sometimes wonder,' Clare said, 'how Catholics can bear the thought of anyone, however wicked, being in a hell like that.'

'Ah,' said Léonie, 'we've got you very neatly there. It's only a dogma that hell exists; it isn't a dogma that there's anybody in it.'

Clare smiled.

'It sounds awfully like *Alice in Wonderland*.'

'It is. Very,' admitted Léonie.

'I do hope I'm in the play,' Nanda broke in. 'I don't honestly care what I am, but I do love rehearsals and things. And both of you and Rosario are sure to be in it.'

'I don't know about me,' said Clare; 'but, of course, Rosario will be Beatrice. No one could look at her and hesitate. I wish they'd let me have a shot at Dante, but obviously, Léonie ought to play that. She's got the right voice and the right sort of noble head, and everything. If I can't be Dante, I'd like to be Paolo, and listen, wouldn't Nanda make a rather good Francesca?'

None of the three had noticed Mother Percival moving quietly up behind them, and they all started as she slid between Clare and Nanda and observed coldly:

'Those are names I never expected to hear mentioned in this school. No Christian woman, let alone a Catholic, who has any pretensions to decency, would sully her mind with such an episode as that.'

She gave Nanda a penetrating look and moved away. 'So much for our greatest Catholic poet,' said Léonie, wrinkling her handsome nose.

'I remember now,' said Clare. 'The Upper First are doing Dante this term in Cary's translation, and the whole of the fourth canto has been cut out of their books.'

In a few days, the casting was known, and private disappointments were lost in public surprise. Contrary to everybody's expectations, Léonie was to play Beatrice and Rosario Dante. Clare was content to be Virgil, and Nanda delighted with the small part of Matilda of Tuscany. After recent events, she was delighted to be allowed to play anything so agreeable, for she had quite expected to be fobbed off with one of the prophets in paradise. Even plays at Lippington were apt to be run on disciplinary lines; parts which called for an attractive appearance were usually played by the most meek and mortified children of the school, while anyone suspected of thinking herself pretty was fairly sure to be cast for a hermit with prodigious wrinkles and a long beard.

Once the play was in rehearsal there were no more murmurs about the choice of Léo and Rosario for their respective parts. Rosario, to whom all languages came easily, spoke Italian particularly well, and her first reading proved that she would be an admirable Dante. All her softness dropped from her; she was grave, stern and passionate. Léonie, on the other hand, seemed to have borrowed all Rosario's former grace. No one had ever supposed that Léo, with her untidiness, her slouch, her masculine gestures and her bitter tongue, could be so delicate and moving a Beatrice. Her voice, usually hoarse and rough, took on the clear ring it had when she sang, as she spoke her lines. Even at rehearsals, standing on a sugar-box, with a lank lock drooping over her magnificent forehead and one hand tucked in her crumpled apron, she was impressive and beautiful. Mother Castello was in raptures. Her black eyes glittered with tears in her wizened, bilious little face, as she clapped energetically and cried: '*Bene, molto bene, fanciulla mia.*'

The rest of the cast by no means lived up to this high level.

Marjorie Appleyard wept regularly whenever she had to rehearse the ghostly embrace of Dante and Casella. Ten or twelve times, Mother Castello would make her go through it, but never with any success.

'But, Marjoree,' she would scream, 'Casella is a spirit . . . a spirit, not a great, clumsy human being. And when he cannot embrace Dante he should look sad and puzzled, not imbecile as if he had just dropped a cricket ball. Have you no feeling at all for poetry? *Ancora una volta.*'

Nanda fared a little better, but felt horribly self-conscious picking imaginary flowers among the benches which represented the earthly paradise, while Clare's Virgil, apart from being far too young and eager, was not too severely criticized, except when she gazed with such fond admiration at Dante that she forgot her cues.

The awkward stiffness of Anglo-Saxon gestures distressed Mother Castello so much that, after the first week, she begged that for the remainder of the time the play should be rehearsed in costume on the stage. Lights and dresses and scenery certainly did a good deal to loosen the agonized self-consciousness of the actresses, and to Nanda at least, the illusion of another world was complete. The new stage was equipped with machinery she had never dreamed of; there were trap-doors and spotlights, and even wires from which nervous but complacent angels could be suspended. The home-made dresses of spangles and sateen glistened magically under the coloured lights, and the dullest people looked suddenly beautiful.

Nanda, in blue and rose, felt every inch a duchess, and gathered her calico flowers with a quite convincing grace, while Rosario, in her scarlet mantle with her hair hidden under the peaked headdress, was the image of a young Dante who had never looked on hell. There was, indeed, no hell in the Lippington version of the *Divina Commedia*. It began with the meeting of Dante and Virgil outside the fatal gates, and proceeded to scenes in purgatory and paradise. Nanda's own part was so small that she had plenty of time to watch from the wings, following every movement till her eyes ached and whispering the lines till she knew everyone else's as well as her own. She loved the scene where the souls in purgatory dressed in thin grey draperies, glided in their boat, singing '*In exitu Israel de Egypto.*' It did not worry her in the least that the boat creaked rather than glided, and that the holy souls disembarked on to rocks of canvas-covered packing-cases. She was deeply impressed by the tableau of the Celestial Rose at the end, with the blessed in white sateen grouped gracefully and uncomfortably in the clouds round Our Lady. But the most wonderful moment of the play for her was when Beatrice appeared in her gilded car drawn by gryphons, and Léonie, pale, radiant and transfigured in her green cloak and flame-coloured dress, spoke her first words to Dante. Clare, who had just made her exit, would join her in the wings, and hand-in-hand, silent with ecstasy, they would listen to Léonie, saying gravely and sorrowfully:

> '*Dante, perchè Virgilio se ne vada*
> *Non pianger anco, non pianger ancora;*
> *Chè pianger ti convien per altra spada,*'

to the great moment when she lifted her veil and her voice rang out triumphantly:

> '*Guardaci ben; ben sem, ben sem Beatrice.*'

About a week before the cardinal was due to arrive, Mother Radcliffe announced her intention of being present at one of these dress-rehearsals. She sat alone in the large auditorium, a tall, inexpressive, black-and-white presence, betraying no emotion, but occasionally making notes by the light of a small electric torch. The children were nervous, but, rather surprisingly, played far better than usual. The excitement of a new audience, even an audience of one, keyed them up to act with more variety and less restraint. The stage mechanics, too, surpassed themselves, and the boat sailed on realistically, Beatrice's chariot appeared without the least hitch, and the lights glowed and dimmed in complete accord with Mother Castello's loudly whispered directions. But the real glory of the evening lay with Dante and Beatrice themselves. Rosario and Léonie shone like the sun and moon in some element of their own. They were no longer young girls, Nanda thought, in her lair in the wings, but the very spirits of poetry. When the curtain fell on Dante standing with uplifted arms, the sound of the last lines was too much for Nanda's pent-up feelings.

At the words:

'L'amor che move il sole e l'altre stelle'

her blood seemed to turn and run backwards through her veins, and she burst into tears. Throwing off Clare's consoling hand, she jumped up and ran blindly, stumbling over scenery, towards the door at the back of the stage that led to the main school building. Her one thought was to get away, to be by herself. The corridors were mercifully empty, and she ran panting and sobbing through doors and round corners, until she was in the deserted vestibule of Our Lady of Aberdeen. Here she flung herself on the prie-dieu, buried her head in her hands, and gave herself up entirely to convulsive tears. Her whole attitude was that of a penitent in the throes of remorse, she sobbed as if her heart would break, but her tears had nothing to do with sorrow or repentance. On the contrary, she felt blissfully happy, and the weeping she could not check was no more than a hysterical relief. How long she knelt there she did not know, but it seemed to her at least an hour. She was still sobbing, but more quietly and mechanically, when she felt a hand on her shoulder.

'Nanda, my dear child,' said the voice of Mother Percival. 'Whatever is the matter?'

'Nothing,' choked Nanda without looking up.

'But one does not cry for nothing,' insisted Mother Percival. 'Look at me.'

Very reluctantly, Nanda raised her head.

'But, my good child, your face is all swollen. Why, you've hardly any eyes left. You really must tell me what is the matter.'

Nanda hesitated. After all, why was she crying? Did she really know? She could hardly say it was because Dante was so beautiful. She forced an unnecessary sob to gain time.

'Come now. I insist on knowing,' said Mother Percival with her old asperity.

Desperately, Nanda groped for some respectable reason. At last she whispered:

'My . . . my mother's awfully ill.'

To her great relief, this was accepted. Mrs Grey was known vaguely to be 'delicate' and actually did spend a considerable time in nursing homes.

But as Mother Percival shepherded her up to the dormitory, with soothing promises of prayers and crumbs of advice on the duty of resignation, Nanda thought she looked at her rather oddly.

The next day's rehearsal was as flat as might be expected. It was made flatter still by the absence of Léonie, who had been called away to Mother Radcliffe immediately after lunch. Her part was read by Marjorie Appleyard, who had been given the understudy because there seemed not the least chance of her ever having to perform. Everyone knew that nothing short of death would keep Léonie away on the actual night. Nanda had been surprised and a little amused to see how much Léonie, usually so bored and casual, cared about the play. She was glad Léo could not hear Marjorie in her stolid British Italian, mangling the verse she loved so passionately. Faced with such a Beatrice, Rosario lost half her fire and recited her part in the most perfunctory way. Even Mother Castello seemed sad and indifferent, and only pulled Marjorie up when she ruined a line beyond recognition. There was something more in the air, Nanda felt, than the mere staleness of reaction; something gloomy, even ominous. Rosario looked sullen; Clare bit her lip as if to keep back a secret; a group was whispering warily in a corner. When the rehearsal broke up, there was none of the usual lingering chatter; the children dispersed quickly, almost guiltily, as if they had been doing something forbidden.

In the passage outside Mother Radcliffe's door, Nanda caught sight of Léonie. Running up to her, she pulled her by the sleeve, but Léonie swerved away and turned her head towards the wall, muttering: 'For God's sake, leave me alone.' She did not, however, turn quite quickly enough and Nanda saw enough of her face to know that she had been crying. Horrified, Nanda ran on as quickly as she could, without a backward glance at her friend. Never before had anyone seen Léonie cry.

During the geometry class that followed, Nanda could think of nothing but this episode. When the short evening recreation came, she plunged with unusual fervour into one of the dismal indoor ball games and strenuously avoided Léonie, who was leaning up against the parallel bars with an air of extreme boredom. But this time it was Léo who took the initiative. As the centre of the squealing game shifted to the other side of the room, she beckoned to Nanda, who promptly forgot all about her duties as goalkeeper and dashed to her friend's side.

'Forget all about this afternoon,' said Léonie in her hoarsest voice. 'I was so furious that I'd have pulled all the feathers out of an archangel if I'd met one at that moment.'

Her eyes were tearless, though the lids still showed red, and her face even paler than usual. The vein in the centre of her forehead that always swelled when she was excited, stood out like a blue cord.

Nanda suffered at the sight of this strained, exposed face as she once had at the sight of Léonie's ugly hands.

So she looked at her own shoes as she said:

'Oh, shut up, Léo. I understand.'

'I thought you'd like to know what'd happened. It'll be all over the place anyhow, tomorrow. I've been chucked out of the play.' Nanda gasped and stared at Léonie, whose face had relaxed now into its old amused expression, so that she could look at her without embarrassment.

'Nonsense,' she said dizzily. 'I simply don't believe it.'

'It's true, anyhow.'

'But, why on earth? You were so frightfully good. Everyone said so. You were simply marvellous.'

'Ah, but, my child,' said Léo in a pious snuffle. 'Didn't you observe that I enjoyed myself? Didn't you observe that I took a wilful and sensuous pleasure in the performance? Had that pleasure anything to do with the glory of God or the honour of this sactified school? No, my child, it hadn't.'

'Surely they can't take away your part just because you liked playing it?'

'Good heavens, girl, haven't you been here long enough to know that it is the perfect Radcliffian reason? Have you forgotten that we are not here to acquire vain accomplishment but to form our characters? And don't you realize that there's nothing worse of the Catholic character than to do something it really enjoys? Oh, Mother Radcliffe was excessively affable. She even said I played Beatrice remarkably well, except that perhaps I emphasized the earthly side a *leetle* too much. For Beatrice, my dear child, was not the ghost of a woman whom Dante had loved in the human way, but the spirit of divine wisdom.'

'Oh, I'm sick of all this beastly cant,' burst out Nanda. 'Why can't we for once do something for its own sake, instead of tacking everything on to our eternal salvation. One can't even get dressed or have a bath or eat one's bacon and eggs without keeping an eye on eternity. I'm prepared to be as devout as you like, if I can only have a little time to myself.'

'Steady on,' growled Léonie. 'Sir Percival's got her steely eye on you.'

But Nanda could not be checked. She stumbled and blundered on, talking much louder than she realized.

'It's impossible to think about God and Religion every minute of one's day. However fond one is of people, one doesn't think of them all the time. Even one's best friends. When I got so excited about the play the other night it hadn't anything to do with you or Rosario or God or anything. It was just the thing itself. I don't want poetry and pictures and things to be messages from God. I don't mind their being that as well, if you like, but not only that. Oh, I can't explain. I want them to be complete in themselves.'

Mother Percival walked up to them.

'How often have I told you, Nanda,' she remarked, 'that you are not to stand about talking in twos at recreation? Will you kindly go outside with Marjorie Appleyard for a game of clumps?'

With the disappearance of Léonie from the cast of Dante, the play lost nearly all its life. Mother Castello coached Marjorie by the hour and did indeed manage to improve her accent, but failed entirely to infuse any spark of warmth or beauty into her performance. Rosario was too good an artist to speak her lines any less admirably than before, but the strange electricity that had flashed out that other night in her scenes with Beatrice never returned. At the end of the three weeks, everyone was heartily sick of the play and only longing for it to be decently buried and forgotten.

The cardinal did at last appear, and was received with due splendour. Every corridor was garlanded and hung with Japanese lanterns; the children went about for three whole days in their best white uniforms and the chapel blazed like a ballroom with hundreds of candles. The cardinal moved freely about the school, attended by his secretaries and Reverend Mother, and at any corner Nanda was liable to meet his scarlet-robed figure. As she swept a nervous curtsy and kissed the huge amethyst on his finger, his handsome, peevish old face would nod to her and murmur a vague blessing.

The performance of the play on the third afternoon went off as well as could be expected. Marjorie looked as pretty as a muscial comedy princess and delivered her lines in a weak, fluttering little voice. The cardinal sat throughout with his great chin resting on his scarlet bosom, and showed not the slightest trace of emotion. A special distribution of prizes and ribbons followed the performance. Baskets of wreaths were placed in front of him, and he roused himself sufficiently to place one on the head of each white-frocked winner. Nanda won a special prize for English and returned to her place with a large yellow calf copy of *Ancient Catholic Homes of Scotland* (which she had already received for geography the previous summer) and a crown of paper roses set askew on her fair hair. The glittering, tiresome day crawled slowly to its end with a blast of trumpets playing Handel's water music as the cardinal left the building, and the children, once more in their old blue dresses, filed into a supper that was at once an anticlimax and a relief.

There was no recreation that night, and they went straight from the refectory to the chapel. The cardinal's emblazoned chair was gone, the red carpet had been rolled away, and the altar too was back in its sober, everyday dress. The dimness, lit only by the two sanctuary lamps and a stray candle or two, was welcome to Nanda's eyes, tired by the pomp and glare of the last three days. Half asleep, she mumbled the response to the night prayers and made no effort to fight her distractions. In front of her knelt Léonie and Rosario with stern, peaceful faces; across the aisle she could see Clare with her head buried in her gloved hands. From the shaking of her shoulders, she knew that she was giving way to one of her fits of weeping. There had been a good deal of weeping during the last week at Lippington, she reflected. Everyone seemed a little excited and overwrought. She would be glad when the term was over.

Chapter Ten

Nanda's father was so delighted about her green ribbon that the Christmas holidays passed even more agreeably than usual. There were extra treats, including a party with a conjurer, a visit to *The Blue Bird*, a concert and an afternoon at the Wallace Collection. Much as Nanda enjoyed these festivities, a little guilt was mingled with her pleasure. In her heart of hearts she realized that she held that green ribbon on very precarious terms. What would her father say if he knew of some of her recent interviews with Mother Radcliffe? She soothed her conscience, however, by making a fervent mental promise to behave irreproachably when she returned to school.

During these three weeks, Nanda and her father lived in a state of blissful companionship. Mrs Grey was away at Bournemouth recovering from one of her mysterious indispositions, and the spate of private pupils which at all other times engulfed Mr Grey's leisure, had shrunk to a mere trickle round about Christmas. Tea with cream buns to the sound of female quartets sobbing out the Indian Love Lyrics was as rare a treat to him as to Nanda, and there was a gay air of truancy about all their expeditions. To her great delight, her father had begun to treat her as a grown-up person. He dressed for dinner in her honour, asked her permission before he lit his pipe, and bought her pink carnations on the great gala nights when they dined out at a restaurant. For still further proof that he considered her a responsible being, he actually asked her advice in an important decision about her own future.

They dined at home that night; Nanda in last summer's white

muslin and blue bows, and her father in his scrupulously brushed, green-black dinner jacket. Instead of going up to the drawing-room afterwards, he invited her into his study.

The study still had certain awful associations for Nanda. All family discussions, all upbraidings about over-spent pocket money and unsatisfactory reports, took place within its book-lined walls. A stale, but rather pleasant smell of tobacco pervaded every fold of its shabby serge curtains and green plush chairs; she could not open a book without inhaling the fumes of long dead pipes. The small space above the bookcases was papered with faded red and hung with photographs of Athens, while the shelves themselves were filled with volumes in the ugly bindings peculiar to classical works and commentaries. Among the rows of dull reds and liquorice browns stood out a cheerful regiment of fresh green-backed files. These were labelled in Mr Grey's neat, upright hand: 'Greek Prose', 'Greek Unseens', 'Tripos', 'Greats', 'Matric', and so on. Only four of these had any interest for Nanda; three containing the notes for Mr Grey's important, but not yet written, pamphlet on the Catalogue of Ships in the Iliad, a work for which she had a most daughterly and ignorant reverence, and the fourth which bore the mysterious title *Haec Olim*. This last was a mine of fascinating records. It was stuffed to the brim with yellowed photographs of dead or dispersed Cambridge undergraduates of the early 'nineties; menus of huge, long-eaten dinners, a lock of her mother's hair, a tie of an obscure college club, and her own first letter to her father. She had spent many pleasant, stuffy Sunday evenings with its contents spread out before her, inventing stories about the stiff, elegant young men and tracing her father through successive incarnations, from a small boy in braided pantalettes to a young man in his third year at Emmanuel, surprisingly arrayed in a tiny bowler hat, a coat with the shortest possible lapels and an extremely fanciful waistcoat.

'I haven't looked at *Haec Olim* for years, Daddy,' she exclaimed, catching sight of its reassuring back.

'No, my dear?' he smiled. 'Well, it's old, faded, musty stuff. It's time we added something to it. When you leave Lippington, we'll put that green ribbon in with the rest.'

'I'm afraid it'll be the last ribbon I'll ever get,' said Nanda.

Her father gave her a quick look over the top of his spectacles. 'Why do you say that?'

'Well, I somehow cannot imagine myself as a blue ribbon. I don't believe if I stayed at Lippington till I was twenty they'd ever take me seriously enough for that.'

'I see no reason why you should not have a blue ribbon one day . . . if you stayed on at the convent. It's about that I wanted to talk to you.'

Nanda must have looked surprised, for Mr Grey added hastily: 'Now, my dear, don't be alarmed. Nothing's been decided. Nothing at all. And nothing shall be decided without your full consent.'

'You mean you want me to leave Lippington?' She was conscious that her voice sounded far more sad and quavery than she meant it to. All the same, the idea was a severe shock.

'Not immediately. No, no. As I told you, I haven't decided anything at all. I wanted to know what you felt about it.'

'But where would I go?' she asked helplessly.

'I've thought all that out, of course. But it's the merest suggestion. It's only your present and future happiness I have at heart, my dear.'

Nanda had a horrible feeling that she was going to cry, but she managed to say in her coolest, grown-up voice: 'What was your idea, Daddy?'

'Ever since I became a Catholic, I wanted more than anything that you should go to the Five Wounds and have a real knowledge in your Faith. I wanted you to have a real Catholic background of the kind I can't give you at home. Now, if I had been a rich man, and if I hadn't felt that at some time you must have a training that would enable you to earn your own living, nothing would have pleased me better than that you should stay on at Lippington till you were eighteen.'

'But I won't even be fourteen until the spring.'

'I know, my dear. But you'll soon be of an age to take examinations such as the Cambridge Senior. And though I think the nuns teach you remarkably well, they don't profess to coach girls for exams. Have you ever thought what you would like to do when you're grown-up?'

'No, not really,' said Nanda gloomily. The breath of cold

reality affected her like an east wind so that she actually shivered in her muslin frock.

'If you'll take my advice, you'll go in for teaching. I think you have all the right gifts for it, and with training, above all with a really good degree, I think you'd make a success. I could help you a good deal, you know.'

'Oh, yes, I know, Daddy,' she agreed tonelessly.

'So I had thought perhaps of your leaving the convent, say at the end of next summer. Then you could go to a really good High School and start working for your exams in real earnest. The longer you leave it, the harder it will be. I'm afraid the nuns have the haziest ideas of teaching Latin. And your mathematics are practically non-existent. Of course, your music is excellent and so are your languages and your literature. But what, after all, *are* literature and music?'

To her dismay, Nanda could keep back tears no longer. Three weeks ago, she had been bored and restless at Lippington, silently mutinous under its discipline, sick to death of its routine. Now, at the mere notion of leaving, she was overwhelmed with a passionate affection for the place. However much she might grumble and criticize, her roots were there. It was not only the possible loss of Clare and Léonie that horrified her. Day by day, for the last four years, she had been adapting herself to the Lippington standard, absorbing the Lippington atmosphere. Even now, in the shock of the revelation of her dependence, she did not realize how thoroughly Lippington had done its work. But she felt blindly she could only live in that rare, intense element; the bluff, breezy air of that 'really good High School' would kill her.

Mr Grey, alarmed and distressed at this unexpected outburst, patted her head and muttered:

'There, there, Nanda. Don't cry like that.'

Nanda recovered herself a little, and he went on: 'I'd no idea Lippington meant so much to you.'

'Nor had I,' sobbed Nanda. 'I'm furious with myself for being so silly.'

She was indeed furious with herself. She had, moreover, the oddest sense of having been tricked, betrayed. Her own nature saw the sense of her father's suggestion, even wanted to fall in with it. Yet here was some force she had never reckoned with bursting up in her mind, taking possession of her, driving her to protest with a violence she did not consciously feel.

'Listen, Nanda,' said Mr Grey comfortingly, 'we won't talk about it any more. And please dry your eyes and stop crying, my dear little girl.'

He pushed a large, clean handkerchief, that reminded Nanda of a nun's, into her limp hand. She blew her nose vigorously.

'I'm quite all right now,' she said with difficulty. 'Please let's go on talking.'

'I only wanted to know how you felt about it,' he said, sucking at his dead pipe. The familiar whistling noise did much to calm Nanda's nerves, and she even managed, with a watery smile, to hand him a matchbox.

'Thank you, my dear,' he said gravely. Then, applying himself to the relighting of his pipe, he added: 'Once upon a time I used to wish I had a son. But a daughter's a much better thing to have.'

He did not look at Nanda, but she saw that his hands were shaking so that it took even more matches than usual to get the pipe going again.

'I had thought that, having been at the convent for four of the most receptive years of your life, the Catholic impression was now strong enough in you not to be effaced, and that it would do you no harm to make a change. But I see you don't want it, so we'll forget all about it. I'm very glad indeed to know that you're so happy at Lippington. And I'm very pleased with your record there, both for work and conduct. I hope you'll go on as you've begun. If you do that, I shall always be glad that we went by your wishes and not by my own in this.'

'I'll try, Daddy,' said Nanda uncomfortably.

'Just one more thing, my dear. I hate even to mention it, but I think you ought to know. I'm not very well off, and these nursing homes and doctors' bills for your mother have been a great drain. Lippington is an expensive school, but they are always willing to make concessions to Catholics who cannot afford the full fees. They have been very kind to me, but if you are to go on there, I shall have to ask them to be kinder still.'

'Oh, Daddy, I never realized that,' Nanda burst out, appalled. Thoughts of Monica Owen and the hundred tiny humiliations which had preceded her final catastrophe rushed through her head.

'If things are like that,' she went on eagerly, 'please forget all about my silliness tonight. I'll leave Lippington tomorrow, if you like. Really, Daddy, I will. I'd rather.'

But her father shook his head, smiling.

'Nonsense, my dear. It's very generous of you, but I'm not going to let you sacrifice yourself like that. I've no doubt something can be managed. There's only one thing I would like to ask you, but I'm sure it will have occurred to you already. If you do stay on at Lippington on those terms, you must go on doing as well, even better, if possible, than you have done. That's the best way you can show your appreciation of what the nuns are doing for you.'

Nanda nodded her head in silence. The clock on the mantelpiece, a reproduction of the Acropolis in black and green marble, struck ten.

'Good heavens,' exclaimed Mr Grey, 'it's hours past your bedtime, my child. Up you go at once, and for goodness' sake, don't tell your mother I kept you up so late.'

He held her for longer than usual as she kissed him good night, smoothing back her hair from her forehead, and looking into her eyes.

'I'm very proud of my daughter,' he said. 'We've always been the best of friends, haven't we?'

'Yes, Daddy.'

'And we always shall be, shan't we? I've never believed all those dreary people who say that fathers and children can never see each other's point of view.'

'It's nonsense, isn't it, Daddy?' she laughed, waving a last good night to him from the door.

In the hall she found a letter addressed to her. The envelope was thick and white, the stamp accurately placed, the writing familiar to her in a hundred exercise-book corrections. It was from Mother Percival.

Nanda sped upstairs to her room, her heart thumping with curiosity and misgiving. Why should Mother Percival write to her? She had never in her life received a letter from a nun. Tearing open the envelope, she read the following:

'My dear Nanda,

'I daresay you will be surprised at receiving a letter from your class mistress while you are on your holiday, and thoughts of Lippington and lessons are probably the last things in your mind.

'All the same, it is not a bad thing that you should sometimes pause and look at yourself, not in the flattering mirror of young and perhaps not very wise friends, but in the eyes of one who, though your sincere well-wisher, is not so blind to your faults.

'I am purposely sending you this letter so that you will receive it a few days before the re-opening of classes in the hopes that you may be able to spare a few minutes from a doubtless continual round of holiday gaieties to meditate on its contents. I am not so optimistic as to suppose a child so independent as yourself will see fit to act on its advice at once, but I believe that one day you may be grateful for it.

'Now, my dear Nanda, God has seen fit to give you certain talents. He has given every human being on this earth talents of one kind or another, and I should like to remind you that the mere possession of a gift is no merit. It is the use you make of that gift which counts. Nor is there any superiority in possessing one kind of talent rather than another. It is a hundred times better to knit a pair of socks humbly for the glory of God than to write the finest poem or symphony for mere self-glorification. In fact, every talent carries its own responsibilities and its own temptations.

'It has struck me rather forcibly of late, from the tone of your essays and your conversation, that you are in danger of forgetting these important facts. A school is a little microcosm (I wonder if you understand that long word; if not, your father, with his knowledge of Greek, will explain it to you) of the great world outside. As a child behaves in her school days, so she will behave through life. Prizes are unimportant. In after life it is not the prize-winners, but those who have built up their characters by obedience and self-denial who make their influence felt for good.

'And I cannot help feeling, my dear Nanda, that you are

not building up your character as you should; I notice that you choose your friends rather for such superficial attributes as cleverness and humour and even for the still more unworthy and frivolous reasons of mere "good looks" and a social position above your own. Remember that the healthiest friendships are those between people who share the same background.

'These may seem hard words, but they are spoken in a spirit of sincere interest in your welfare. I do not mind hurting your vanity, but I do not want to hurt your feelings. Schoolgirls are notoriously uncritical and in the world you may find that Nanda Grey does not seem the clever, fascinating little person she appears to a small circle at Lippington.

'Well, I have lectured you enough, and I have enough faith in your honesty and good sense to hope you will take this in the spirit it was written. I shall be glad to see you back here next week. I think you will be interested in the new geography lessons we are to have next term. Mary Zulecca, an old child of the Five Wounds, who has been doing some splendid missionary work in Central Africa, has consented to give us three lantern lectures on the Congo.

'Remember me in your prayers as I remember you in mine.

'Yours in the charity of the Five Wounds,

'MARGARET PERCIVAL.'

Nanda read this letter three times before she thoroughly mastered its contents. Then she tore it into very small pieces, put it in the grate and set fire to it with a match. She felt hurt and outraged, as if someone had struck her in the face. The world that five minutes before had been so warm, had turned unfriendly. Even the room that had been inviolably hers until now was polluted. There was no privacy anywhere. Why, oh why, hadn't she taken her chance and escaped from Lippington while there was yet time? She sat on the edge of her bed, clenching and unclenching her cold hands, and muttering to herself: 'Unjust. Unjust.'

Looking up, she caught sight of her face in the old, smeared glass. It looked pale and blank and ugly under the silly bows.

Creeping closer to examine it, she remembered the letter again, hastily put out the light, and undressed in the dark.

She was very silent at breakfast the next morning. Never had she been so grateful for her father's unobserving eye. He evidently noticed nothing odd in her strained face and unbrushed hair.

For several minutes they sat without speaking, while Mr Grey read the paper and Nanda cut her uneaten toast into smaller and still smaller cubes.

At last, reaching out mechanically for another cup of tea, her father said:

'Here's something that will interest you, my dear. You remember that Lady Moira Palliser, who entered your convent some years ago?'

Nanda gave him a toneless 'Yes.'

'Well, her father, the Earl of Kilmorden, died at Christmas, and she is now the Countess in her own right. It says that against her own wishes, but in obedience to the commands of her superiors, she is now returning to the world. They say it is her duty to go back and administer her estates. I think that shows great wisdom on their part, though I expect it is a great sorrow to her.'

'She certainly wanted awfully to be a nun,' assented Nanda, a spark of life returning to her voice.

'I think it puts your Order in a most excellent light,' said Mr Grey heartily. 'It's a magnificent reply to all the people who accuse Catholics of being grasping.'

'I suppose it does,' Nanda agreed reluctantly, 'but she'll feel like a fish out of water in the world after all these years. You can't get away from Lippington just by growing your hair and putting on ordinary clothes.'

Her father looked at her with an air of slight annoyance and returned to his paper. He did not speak again until he was leaving the room. At the door he paused and said a little coldly:

'You didn't happen to notice if there were any letters in the hall when you went up to bed last night?'

'Were you expecting one?' she asked innocently.

'Yes. As a matter of fact, I was.'

'No, there weren't any letters at all, Daddy,' said Nanda, bending over her plate, and slicing an infinitesimal corner off one of her cubes of toast.

It was the first direct lie she had ever told him.

Chapter Eleven

Never had Nanda returned to school so unwillingly as she did at the beginning of her fifth Lent term. Certainly, she had not enjoyed the last days of the Christmas vacation, soured as they were by the taste of Mother Percival's charitable advice, but they had at least not brought her face to face with the adviser. She did her best to postpone the hateful day, but without success. A promising cold, which she had tried hard to foster into pneumonia, betrayed her hopes by vanishing completely on the very morning of the re-opening of classes, so that there was nothing for it but to pack her trunk and get ready. As it was, she dawdled so long over the process that she kept the cab waiting for twenty minutes and quite wore out her father's patience. Their drive together to Lippington was strained and almost silent, but Nanda wished it would last for ever. However, by some perversity, the cabman whipped up his old horse into the briskest of trots and, long before she had had time to compose herself, they were at the convent door.

To her surprise and discomfiture, Mother Percival herself was waiting at the portress's lodge. As Mr Grey hastily kissed Nanda goodbye, the nun smiled at them with unusual friendliness. Nanda loitered a little in the corridor, expecting to be called back, but Mother Percival gave no sign, so she hastened along to the changing-room with a slightly easier mind.

Léonie and Rosario had not yet arrived, but she found Clare and was comforted by the eagerness of her welcome.

'But you're not looking a bit well, infant,' Clare said in her warm, quick voice. 'Are you ill or is something worrying you?'

'A bit. But I want to forget about it. Let's talk about you instead.'

'I'm so glad to be back,' said Clare with a gusty sigh. 'I've had the most miserable holiday. My family were terribly difficult about letting me come back at all.'

'Because of . . .' Nanda hesitated.

'Because of the Catholic business? Yes. They just can't understand that anyone should want a different religion from theirs. They've tried every argument from tears to threatening to cut me off entirely, but it's no good. Sooner or later I've got to be a Catholic. I know it quite clearly now.'

'Did you tell them you had really made up your mind?'

'No. I begged for just a little more time to think it over. After all, nothing definite's been done. I'm not even having instruction or anything. The nuns won't take any responsibility about that.'

'It's funny,' mused Nanda. 'People always imagine that tight-lipped nuns and wily Jesuits stand at street corners trying to entice people into becoming Catholics, whereas in actual fact they're rather discouraging if you do want to get converted.'

'I know,' agreed Clare. 'I think that's why I managed to get back for just one more term. My father came up and had a long talk with Reverend Mother, and came away almost convinced that she, at any rate, would rather I stayed as I was.'

'I wonder what she said.'

'For one thing that I was much too young to know my own mind. Such nonsense. Why, I shall be eighteen in the autumn. And another thing that simply infuriated me . . . that girls often get ideas of that kind into their heads and then they meet someone and get married and forget all about it.'

'What did your father say to that?'

'Well, he said it might be a crazy religion, but there were some damn sensible women in convents, so I might as well stay here till Easter and then he'd give me a season in London to get all these schoolgirl fads out of my head.'

'So you were very meek and grateful and all that?'

'Yes, But I was simply boiling inside. And nothing, absolutely *nothing* can change my conviction about Catholicism now. Reverend Mother and the whole lot of them can just wait and see.'

Nanda frowned and bit her lip.

'I wonder why you want to be a Catholic so very much? Do you remember how you used to laugh when I told you about indulgences and purgatory and things? I must have been an awful little prig in those days.'

Clare leant back and clasped her knee in her thin, over-sensitive hands.

'I may have laughed, but I never, never thought you a prig, infant. Secretly, I was terribly impressed. You looked such a baby, but you talked away so earnestly and used such long words, and so obviously understood it all and believed it all that I felt that there must be a tremendous amount in your religion. And it was just the same with Léo and Rosario and all the rest of you. You might joke about miracles and so on, but you had some wonderful secret, a real security. I was desperately curious about it. So I read everything I could lay hands on – the catechism, lives of the saints, anything. I've still got those retreat notes you copied out for me years ago. And sometimes I'd think it was all wonderful and at other times I'd be repelled by the whole idea. But it's just been slowly growing on me . . . the fact that I've got to be a Catholic or nothing.'

'I see,' nodded Nanda wisely. There was a moment's silence, and she stole a glance at Clare's face. Something about its bright, ecstatic eyes and half-open mouth reminded her of Theresa Leighton and touched her with a faint discomfort.

'If you really feel like that,' she added in her most business-like voice, 'you'll certainly get what you want, whatever happens. I'll pray for you all I know how.'

Clare started and bent her wild, dreaming face towards Nanda. She was so pale with emotion that her freckles showed almost black.

'Darling, darling,' she whispered quickly, and gave Nanda's hand a sudden squeeze.

Nanda jumped up. The room had been emptying as they talked, and they were now alone except for a snivelling new child who was changing into her uniform.

'Heavens, I forgot. I simply must take my home clothes up to the linen room before supper. See you at recreation, Clare.'

The next day, Léo and Rosario returned. They had been spending their holidays in Paris, and the Channel boat had been delayed by a storm. Léonie appeared during the early morning preparation, when talking was strictly forbidden, but she waved violently to Nanda and went through a masterly pantomime of sea-sickness and slow recovery.

In the brief mid-morning break, when the children were supposed to run briskly round the garden, she strolled up to Nanda and seized her by the pigtail.

'Don't paw the ground like that, as if you were going to break into a fiery canter. Aren't you glad to see your childhood's friend?'

'Jolly glad,' said Nanda, 'but the Percival's got her stop-watch out and she's timing me.'

'Nonsense,' said Léonie comfortably. 'Let me tell you just how it was. You were just running at full speed when you saw Léonie de Wesseldorf, Mother, and Léonie felt rather meta-grobolized and dispericraniated after her dreadful crossing yesterday, and you sat down beside her and said: "Léonie, my old friend and trusted confidante, can I do anything for you?" And Léonie said: "Let us sit down on this rustic bench for ten minutes until the agony is somewhat abated, and then I shall be sufficiently recovered to be able to enjoy one of your incomparable geography lessons, Mother."'

Nanda laughed. 'You're just the same as ever, Léo.'

'Well, why not?'

'I don't know. There's been something queer about these Christmas holidays. They've only lasted three weeks, yet I feel like a sort of Rip Van Winkle coming back after years and years.'

'And you expected to find me in a bath-chair surrounded by troops of grandchildren?'

'Idiot,' said Nanda. She scraped the gravel with the toe of her shoe and added with a sigh: 'I suppose you're horribly rich and all that, aren't you, Léo?'

'Horribly,' assented Léonie with a grimace.

'I was afraid so,' Nanda said gloomily.

'Why worry about it? You're not going to preach me a sermon on the appalling effects of riches on the character, are you?'

Nanda grinned but did not answer.

'Seriously, my dear, what are you getting at?' asked Léonie.

'Well, I've just realized that in three or four years we'll all be growing up and leaving school, and I'll probably never see any of you again.'

'Why on earth not?'

'Oh, you'll see it all perfectly well if you'll just think a minute. I shall probably be teaching a howling mob of children and you'll be married to a duke, and I'll be lucky if I occasionally see a photograph of you in *The Tatler*.'

'I never heard such nonsense in the whole of my life,' said Léonie witheringly.

'It's true all the same,' Nanda protested.

'Oh, for God's sake, shut up,' Léonie broke out, with a ring of cold anger in her voice.

The bell rang for the end of the brief recreation and they moved towards the school, Léonie stalking ahead and Nanda deliberately hanging behind.

They seated themselves side by side in Mother Percival's classroom without exchanging a grimace or a whisper. Léonie began to arrange her books with elaborate care; Nanda stared moodily at the unrolled map of Africa. She felt Mother Percival's eye on her and was compelled after a few seconds to look up at the nun's face. To her surprise, instead of being disapproving, it seemed curiously softened and happy. The explanation came quickly.

Mother Percival clasped her hands on her desk, surveyed her class with a smile that suggested a shyness unusual to her usually straightforward, astringent nature, and said:

'I have some news for you which I wanted the Lower Third to be the first to hear. I shall be leaving you at the end of the week . . . leaving Lippington for some months.'

'I knew it. She's going to get her ring,' whispered Nanda's other neighbour triumphantly.

Nanda nodded absently. A wave of relief broke over her and washed away some of the barbs of that memorable letter. She was used to these sudden disappearances. After two years of novitiate and four of probation, the religious of the Five Wounds went to another house of the Order and made a six-months' retreat before professing their final vows and receiving the symbolic wedding-ring.

'I am going to Liège,' Mother Percival went on, 'and I think you will all know that I shall pray for each one of you while I am away. Mother Clement, who has recently arrived from one of our American houses, will take on my work, and I hope – I *know* – that you will all do your best to make things easy for her.'

Her voice shook, and Nanda almost fancied she saw a tear in the unemotional grey eyes. But before she could be quite sure, Mother Percival had turned to the map of Africa, tapped it smartly with her pointer, and asked in her usual brisk, frosty manner:

'Hilda, could you *now* point out, with some faint degree of accuracy, the course of the Zambesi river?'

The rest of the day passed uneventfully. So quickly did the children slip into the orderly routine of a day chequered into sections varying from an hour to ten minutes that the homes they had left only yesterday already seemed ineffably remote. The punctual bells regulated every movement to classroom, to playground, refectory or chapel. They smoothed away some of the discomfort and bewilderment that had roughened the surface of Nanda's life for the last week. Except for the tension between herself and Léonie, she was almost happy. She looked at Lippington through fresher eyes, and was ashamed of her many disloyalties. After all, where would she find a place like it? In its cold, clear atmosphere everything had a sharper outline than in the comfortable, shapeless, scrambling life outside. The scrubbed boards and whitened walls and shining brasses reminded her of a ship. As in a ship, too, one had the scantiest of personal belongings stowed away in the smallest possible space; one wore a uniform, one obeyed orders. The simile rather pleased her, and she pushed it further, wondering whether, however much she might grumble and rebel against life on board, she did not secretly despise mere landsmen.

Half past eight came, and night prayers in the chapel, where that mixed smell of incense and beeswax reminded her afresh of her first night at Lippington four years ago. Something in her softened, humble mood seemed to blow away the dust that had gathered on the familiar petitions she had repeated hundreds of times. They sounded as if newly improvised to fit her own needs. In the silence that followed, she found herself praying earnestly for friends and enemies alike, for Mother Percival and Léonie, above all for the conversion of Clare Rockingham. She was full of good resolutions. She would be kinder to stupid people and fierce only to her own vanity. She would break down that core of stubborn independence. She would think less of human friendships and more of Our Lady and the saints whom she had so neglected of late.

Outside the door, someone suddenly came abreast of her and thrust a piece of paper into her prayer-book. It was Léonie. But before Nanda had had time to do more than look astonished, she was gone again.

She was longing to look at the paper, but prudence warned her to wait until she was safe behind the curtains of her cubicle. There, in the faint glimmer from the gas-jet outside, she made out the well-known, cramped writing:

'You're an idiot but you are my best friend. So kindly shut up now and always.
'LÉONIE MAGDALENA HEDWIG DE WESSELDORF.'

Chapter Twelve

February was wet and misty, with fogs hanging over the lake and puddles lying in the sodden playground. As Lent drew nearer, spirits became more and more depressed. There was an outburst of apparent cheerfulness on the two Shrove-tide half holidays, but with the austerities of Ash Wednesday just ahead, the gaiety was decidedly forced.

On Shrove Monday it was the custom for the lay-sisters to have a whole holiday from their heavy work, and for the children to take their places in kitchen and pantry. They scrubbed the passages and swept the dormitories, laid the tables in the refectory and actually cooked the meals. A band of younger ones was told off to entertain the Sisters, and shouts of applause greeted the appearance of old Sister Richter, who ruled the school cloakrooms with a military fierceness, driving up and down the alleys in the donkey-cart accompanied by the entire Junior School.

Sister Richter was one of the Lippington 'characters,' a focal point for the 'My dear, *do* you remember's' of generations of old children. She was reported to be about ninety years old, and occasionally mixed past and present in her consciousness. Nanda and the rest had been delighted one day when she had scolded Mother Percival before a whole division for letting her pupils get their feet wet, and had ended up by saying: 'I'm ashamed of you, Miss Margaret. I'll report you for this, and you will for certain lose your exemption.'

She was very devout, and would often be discovered kneeling on a wooden work-box in the corner of the cloakroom, absorbed in prayer. But her devotions never interfered with her duties. She would leap up from her knees to pounce on any culprit who left a tap running or otherwise misdemeaned herself. 'Vot a vicked extraffagance, my tear,' she would mumble accusingly. 'It is kvite unnecessary to use so much soap. And that peautiful hot vater! You vill haf to account to the tear Lort for effery trop you haf vasted.'

It was so long since Sister Richter had entered that she could hardly remember her short life in the world. But she clung tenderly to the memory of her native village in Thuringia. If any German child came to the school, she would waylay her, and producing a faded picture postcard from her pocket, ask wistfully: 'Do you know this? It is Behrenwald, the most peautiful fillage in Ghermany. I was porn there.'

Léonie, who claimed actually to have visited Behrenwald, was her cherished favourite. Léonie might use hot water by the gallon, tear her towels to ribbons, or even use the precious soap for blowing bubbles; in Sister Richter's eyes she could do no wrong. Once, hearing her being scolded, she had planted herself in front of the mistress and declared: 'You are kvite wrong, Mother. Miss Léonie is a good child. She knows my peautiful Behrenwald.'

By Shrove Tuesday, the spirit of mortification had already set in. Several of the children voluntarily spent an extra half-hour in the chapel instead of playing hide and seek, to atone to the Blessed Sacrament for the sins committed during the carnival in

Spain and Italy. Others gave up sweets or story-books for the same reason. The last moments of the holidays leaked swiftly away in tepid gaieties, and half-depressed, half-relieved, the school braced itself for the six weeks of penance.

Nanda had always hated Ash Wednesday. It had the gloom of Good Friday without its noble sorrows. The day began with the distribution of the holy ashes. The children knelt in long rows at the Communion rails, while Father Robertson walked to and fro smudging a cross on each forehead murmuring: '*Mememto, Homo, quia pulvis es et in pulverem reverteris.*' Breakfast, eaten in complete silence, consisted of two thin slices of dry bread and a cup of tea without milk or sugar. The school kept the proper fast only on Good Friday, but the nuns, while going about their ordinary business, fasted every day except Sunday throughout Lent. They were allowed one good meal at midday, the only stipulation being that they might not eat both fish and meat; their supper consisted of a meagre collation of bread or cabbage. They abstained from milk and butter every day and from meat on Wednesdays and Fridays. But this was the least of their mortifications. Each member of the community had her private penances, spiritual and physical, at which Nanda could only guess. She remembered how horrified, yet impressed, she had been during her very first Lent at Lippington, when Mother Frances's sleeves had slipped back as she reached up to lift something from a high shelf, revealing small iron chains bound tightly round her arms. There were whispers of spiked belts and wire scourges, and when a mistress was sharper of tongue than usual during a class, the more charitable put it down to the fact that she was probably wearing a hair shirt that day.

However, the children were strongly discouraged from imitating such practices. Betka Winkenstahl was discovered wearing small pebbles in her shoes and forced to remove them before the whole school, and Vera Cooling-Brown was discouraged from drinking vinegar by being made to sit by herself in the middle of the refectory while a lay-sister plied her with cups of cocoa.

The spring term in all boarding schools is usually marked by the outbreak of infectious diseases. Two oppressive weeks of Lent had crawled by when a child, having sickened for a day or so, retired to the infirmary, and was later observed, wrapped in blankets, being wheeled along the passage that led to the isolation wing. Spirits revived magically. Epidemics were popular during a dull term. For the lucky victims they meant not merely the luxury of the infirmary, but a cheerful convalescence and a blissful quarantine free from regular lessons and restrictions.

'I hope to heaven it isn't only chicken-pox or German measles,' said Léonie to Nanda at the first opportunity. 'I'd rather on the whole it weren't whooping-cough, because it's such a barbaric disease. Anyhow, whatever it is, I'm determined to catch it.'

'Unless it's scarlet fever,' said Nanda cheerfully, 'in which case, it's hardly worth the trouble, because we'll all be sent home anyhow.'

It turned out to be measles, and to everyone's delight, three more cases were reported by the end of the week. The infirmarian was busy with disinfectants, gargles and liquorice powder, but the children were still busier trying to outwit her. Everyone with even a mild cold became an immediate object of interest and found herself surrounded by people anxious to be in contact with her and to borrow her possessions. In twenty-four hours, Léonie, who always got what she wanted, was going about with streaming eyes and a flushed face. Before she went up to the infirmary, she drew Nanda aside and croaked hoarsely:

'I've done it, my dear. Pains in the head and temperature rising every minute. Here is a precious legacy.'

She produced a slightly grey handkerchief. 'Perfectly clean,' she added, as she gave it to Nanda; 'it's only that colour because I did a bit of dusting with it. But it's been under my pillow all night, and with any luck, it should be swarming with germs by now.'

Whether or not the handkerchief had anything to do with it, Nanda shortly found herself in the isolation wing. By great good fortune, Clare and Rosario also developed measles a day or two later. All four had the disease mildly enough to make a quick recovery, and they were soon thoroughly enjoying themselves in the convalescent stage. Among the dozen or so of the other patients they formed a compact and almost inseparable group, and their number freed them from the grave reproach of 'going about in twos'.

Never had Nanda enjoyed so free a life at Lippington. The only nun who visited them was a kind old Irishwoman who had not taught in the school for some years; for the rest, they were under the charge of two nurses, both of whom appeared to be iron disciplinarians until Léonie had the happy thought of ordering huge propitiatory boxes of sweets for them from Charbonnel & Walker. After that, the four did more or less what they pleased. No one disputed their right to the shabby armchairs by the fire in the convalescent sitting-room, and they were often allowed to sit up unchaperoned long after the others had been packed off to bed.

Léonie managed to smuggle in books by the dozen; Rosario had her guitar; Clare conjured up biscuits and chocolates and Nanda put in several hours of work on her much-neglected novel.

'I wish we could live like this for ever,' sighed Clare one night, as she pulled the faded serge curtains closer to shut out the sound of the March wind and rain.

'Oh, so do I,' echoed Nanda. Léonie deep in the only really comfortable chair, with her legs flung ungracefully over its arm, merely grunted. Transferring a large caramel into one cheek, she said thickly:

'Sing something, Rosario.'

Rosario, who was kneeling by the fire, smiled and shook her head. She had been washing her hair, and the thick fleecy gold hung in showers round her shoulders. Clare reached out her hand and drew one of the shining strands through her fingers.

'I've never seen such hair,' she said. 'It's like a fairy princess's. Really, you're too lovely to live, darling.'

'Oh, *don't* be so silly,' said Rosario crossly, jerking her head away.

'And don't be so fierce,' laughed Clare. 'I only said you had wonderful hair. And such yards of it.'

'It's not as long as yours,' insisted Rosario.

'Oh, but it is. Miles longer. Just look,' said Clare. Her hands were busy with hairpins. In a minute the thick, doubled plait was unravelled and she shook down a great, coppery mane that reached nearly to her waist.

She leant her head against Rosario's and looked up with shining brown eyes at Nanda.

'Tell me, infant, aren't I right?'

Nanda frowned judicially.

'No, yours is longer, Clare. Quite two inches. But you do both look terribly beautiful tonight.'

Léonie swallowed her caramel, shut her book with a bang, and yawned.

'When you've quite finished your beauty competition, you might get on with that singing.'

'Oh, very well,' laughed Rosario. 'You always get your own way in the end.'

She took down her gaily beribboned guitar from the wall and seated herself on a heap of cushions. As she tested the strings, Clare cried excitedly:

'Let's put out the lamps. The fire's heaps bright enough.'

'What a one you are for the dramatic,' observed Léonie. 'If ever you have a young man, I don't suppose you'll ever let him kiss you unless the moon's out and there's a band playing *The Blue Danube* in the distance.'

Clare pulled Léonie's brief and untidy plait, but she put out the lights all the same. Then she flung herself on the hearthrug at Rosario's feet.

'*Now* we're ready,' she purred luxuriously. Rosario bent over her guitar. In the glow its belly had a ruddy shine. Her hair, as she continually tossed it back from her face, seemed to give off flakes of light, while Clare's red-brown head was frayed with gold at the edges. Nanda and Léonie drew back into the shadows; the latter huddled in her chair with her arms folded and her chin sunk on her chest.

Rosario strayed from song to song in her rich, soft voice that had none of the trailing languor of Elita's. She sang Spanish peasant songs and even love songs; she sang *The Rowan Tree* and *Funiculì, Funiculà*, in which the others joined guardedly in the chorus. At last she put down her guitar, shook back her hair, and said: 'That's enough.'

But Nanda and Clare begged for more. Rosario looked

doubtful; then smiled as if an idea had struck her. She tightened the pegs of her guitar, struck a chord, and began to play a little prelude. Léonie shifted in her chair, and Rosario said through the music: 'You don't mind, Léo?'

'No. Go on,' answered Léonie gruffly. Rosario leant over the guitar again and sang almost in a whisper:

> 'To a lovely myrtle bound
> Blossoms show'ring all around
> O, how sick and weary I
> Underneath my myrtle lie.
> Why should I be bound to thee,
> O my lovely myrtle tree?'

There was silence as she finished. After a minute she said:

'That's Léonie's setting, you know. I think it's most beautiful.'

'But it's exquisite,' burst out Clare, who could not hum the simplest tune.

'Did you really write the music, Léo?' asked Nanda with awe. She was deeply moved.

'Uhu,' grunted Léonie in her most forbidding tone. Then she jumped up, and in spite of Clare's cries of protest, turned on the lights. The four blinked at each other with shy, apologetic smiles, their eyes bright and sleepy, with the pupils shrunk to mere specks.

'You are a heartless brute,' said Clare. 'I was so beautifully happy and comfortable.'

'Well, go and be beautifully happy and comfortable in bed,' grinned Léonie.

'Nonsense,' Clare insisted. 'Come and sit down and be sensible. We've got heaps of time still. I'm not going to leave this fire till I'm dragged away by main force.'

Léonie rejoined the circle and they began to talk idly.

'I wonder where we shall all be in ten years' time?' began Clare romantically. It was one of her favourite themes.

'I shall be married,' said Rosario, quietly but definitely.

'Why so certain, darling?' asked Clare. Rosario shrugged her elegant shoulders.

'Why not? Elita is engaged already, and she has only been out six months. My relations have several people in mind for me already.'

'How can you be so matter-of-fact about it?' said Clare, shocked. 'You can't fall in love to order.'

'No, I know that.'

'And so you mean to go through your whole life without ever really falling in love?'

'That doesn't follow at all.'

'You mean, you'll fall in love with someone else after you've married your suitable person?'

'Of course not,' said Rosario with great dignity. 'Once I am married, I should never allow myself to do such a thing. It wouldn't be fair to my husband or my family. But I don't mean to marry until I am at least twenty-one. Until then, I consider I have a right to do as I please.'

'What would you do if you were madly in love, Rosario?' asked Clare.

Rosario smiled and looked straight in front of her with enormous blue eyes.

'I should sit on the very top of the Pyrenees and read poetry and play the guitar.'

'I don't suppose I shall ever marry,' said Clare, busy with her own future. 'But I shall be the most divine old maid, growing roses and things and driving about in a dog-cart and being the most marvellous aunt to all of your children. Of course, I'll be frightfully poor, because I'll be a Catholic and my family will have cut me off with an old bootlace.'

'I shall have exactly two children,' stated Léonie firmly, ignoring Clare's last remark. 'One male and one female, and both incredibly talented and incredibly bad-tempered.'

They all laughed and Clare said: 'What about Nanda? We've left her out of all this?'

Léonie gave Nanda a glance of brotherly affection.

'Nanda's a dark horse,' she declared.

Chapter Thirteen

All too soon, this slothful and delightful life came to an end. The school doctor arrived one day, inspected them, and told them that they might shortly return to school, since they were now perfectly well and there was no danger of their infecting the others. Léonie, as the first arrival, was the earliest to leave; it would be Nanda's turn next.

She spent her last two days in the isolation wing polishing up the fourth chapter of her novel. Surveying what she had written with as dispassionate an eye as possible, she decided that it really was rather good. Anyhow, it seemed to read remarkably like a real book. The heroine, who had 'geranium red lips and hair of finest spun gold and huge, limpid violet eyes', might almost stand comparison with some of Mr E. F. Benson's, whom she so greatly admired. In deference to her master, she also supplied her with a 'tiny, tip-tilted nose' and furnished her background with a splendour drawn from other works of fiction and occasional visits to the Trocadero. But most of her loving care had been lavished on the hero, who was, she flattered herself, an entirely original creation. To begin with, he was extremely ugly, with an ugliness 'redeemed only by a pair of brilliant and marvellously penetrating eyes'. He studied black magic and wrote poetry 'wrapped in a dressing-gown of yellow oriental silk, wrought with strange symbols'. In the end he was to reject the love of the violet-eyed heroine and to enter a Trappist monastery, but at this early stage Nanda was only concerned with the difficult business of making her characters as wicked as possible in order that their conversion might be the more spectacular. The hero 'frequented mysterious dens in Chinatown, from which he might be observed issuing in the early hours of the morning, still dazed with the fumes of strange narcotics'; the heroine's life was one giddy round of balls and flirtations. There was one moment where the heroine's other admirer, after having 'swooned with her in the languid ecstasies of a waltz' took her out on the balcony and 'pressed a kiss of burning passion on her scarlet mouth, a kiss which had some of the reckless intoxication of the music that throbbed out from the Hungarian band they could hear in the distance'.

Clare and Rosario, watching her alternately biting her pen and dashing it across the paper at breakneck speed, often begged her to show them what she was writing. But though she secretly longed for an audience, she always said sternly: 'No, you must wait till it's finished. The whole point's the *end*, you see.'

At last came the gloomy day of return to normal life, a day which Nanda faced as unwillingly as a walk in the east wind after an afternoon by the fire, and which even the prospect of rejoining Léonie could not brighten.

She was greeted carelessly and jealously by her classmates, for whom the rigours of Lent had had no mitigation.

'You're only just in time for Holy Week,' grumbled Marjorie Appleyard.

'Well, it's not *my* fault, is it?' said Nanda crossly.

'Of course, you didn't want to get measles, did you?' sneered Marjorie. 'And you didn't try to catch them? Oh no.'

And she bent virtuously over her exercise-book.

Léonie was more comforting. 'It's nice to see a human face again,' she said. 'One more day among these sheep and I'd have been bleating myself. By the way, I suppose you had to burn your manuscript?'

'What manuscript?'

'Why, your novel, or whatever it is. I had to make a complete bonfire of all my most cherished possessions.'

'Good Lord,' said Nanda. 'I forgot all about it. Nurse Marsh told us to, and I burnt letters and so on, but I forgot all about *that*.'

'Well, don't let them know, that's all.'

Holy Week arrived and proceeded on its majestic way. Each year, however much she might have wavered in her devotion or her unquestioning obedience, its slow, magnificent rituals impressed on her afresh the beauty and poetry of Catholicism. Each of the great days had its special drama. After Palm Sunday every statue was veiled with purple, the organ was silent, and the altar bell replaced by a harsh wooden clapper. On the evenings of Tuesday, Wednesday and Thursday, the children and the nuns sang the office of Tenebrae in the darkened chapel. She was profoundly moved by the lamenting psalms with the recurrent, urgent cry '*Jerusalem, Jerusalem, convertere ad dominum Deum tuum*.' At the end of each psalm, the sacristan nun extinguished one of the candles, until only one remained. This she took and placed behind the altar to symbolize the laying of Our Lord in the tomb. There was a brief silence; then a deep rumbling on the organ announced the resurrection; the candle was brought out from its hiding, and the office was over for the night.

Maundy Thursday came like a sad *Corpus Christi* with something funereal about the white flowers and lights round the Altar of Repose. The chapel, with all its lamps extinguished, and the door of the tabernacle opened wide was like an empty house. The Blessed Sacrament had been taken away; no one genuflected today before the deserted altar; even the holy water stoups were dry. The whole life of the Church had dwindled to its lowest pulse before the catastrophe of Good Friday.

The ordinary school routine on Holy Thursday served only as a background to the seven visits to the Holy Sepulchre, as they called the side-chapel where the host now reposed. At six o'clock came Tenebrae, the last and most sorrowful office of the *triduum*. Nanda noticed that the candles were being extinguished not by the usual sacristan nun, but by a postulant. At intervals her old fear of a vocation re-asserted itself so that the sight of any new aspirant always filled her with a certain discomfort. Supposing that one day one of those figures in ancient, borrowed skirts and dark flannel blouses should be herself? The chapel was too dim to make out the face of the newcomer, but she saw that she was tall and slender and moved with a rather awkward grace, as if her natural motion were swifter. But when she carried the last candle to its hiding place, its beam shone full on her face, and Nanda recognized Hilary O'Byrne.

In the short recreation after their silent meal, Nanda made straight for Léone.

'Did you see her . . . the new postulant?'

'Hilary O'Byrne? Of course. I knew all about that ages ago.'

'I suppose I'll never be a proper Catholic,' mused Nanda, 'but it does seem rather horrible, somehow. She was so gay and all that.'

'People who become nuns often are.'

'Do you think,' said Nanda romantically, 'that it was a sort of idea of atonement? I mean, because Moira Palliser wanted to be a nun and they made her go back to the world? Perhaps Hilary thought she ought to make up for it by being a nun, though she didn't want to?'

'Rubbish,' declared Léonie with great firmness. 'You don't even try to be a nun unless you're pretty convinced that you've got a vocation. You understand a lot of things, but you simply don't understand that specific Catholic something. I don't mean dogmas and all that. No one can trip you up on those. I can't explain in the least what I mean.'

'You might try, anyhow,' insisted Nanda.

'Well, I can just tell you the first example that occurs to me. It's nothing whatever to do with this. I had an old grandmother who lived in the country in France and spent most of her time going to mass and playing whist with the *curé* and doing endless knitting for the poor. Well, she died last year at the age of eighty or so. After she had received the Last Sacraments, she asked for her knitting. Her maid was rather shocked: '*Mais Madame la Marquise a été administrée,*' she exclaimed. '*Elle va mourir.*' To which my grandmother replied: '*Ma chère, ce n'est pas là une raison pour perdre son temps.*''

The nun in charge was looking at the clock. In a minute the bell would ring.

'Hi, quick . . . before we're plunged into twenty-four hours' silence,' said Léonie urgently. 'Lend me that novel of yours to look at.'

'But I can't,' demurred Nanda. 'It's nothing like finished. Besides, I haven't shown it to a soul.'

'I should hope not, if you haven't shown it to me.'

'I'd much rather not, Léo,' said Nanda.

Léonie fixed her with a cold, grey eye.

'Look here, are you my best friend or are you not?' she demanded.

Nanda gave in.

'Oh, very well. I'll give it to you when we get our veils for night prayers. But for heaven's sake don't let anybody see it — specially a nun.'

'Do you think I'm a congenital idiot?' asked Léonie acidly as the bell rang.

The children went to bed early that night to prepare for the long day of fasting and prayer on the morrow.

There was no early mass, but at half past seven they had a silent breakfast of dry bread and milkless tea. The entire morning was spent in the chapel for the Mass of the Presanctified and the Adoration of the Cross. No host is consecrated on Good Friday and the one the priest receives is that brought back from the altar of repose. The priest slowly unveiled the crucifix, and the whole school and the community approached one by one to kiss it, while two singers intoned the lamentations and responses of the *Improperia*. The long, chanted gospel of the passion and the longer prayers for the whole world tired Nanda more than usual, so that by the time the altar was being silently stripped of its few clothes she felt quite faint.

After their lunch of salt fish and bread and water, the children returned to the chapel to watch there in spirit with Christ on the cross until three o'clock. There is a tradition that any prayer made as the clock strikes three on Good Friday will be granted. Nanda had long decided what her petition that year should be. On the first stroke of the clock she whispered urgently: 'Whatever happens, dear Lord, please make Clare Rockingham a Catholic.'

After they returned from this devotion, the tension relaxed a little. Although there were no lessons and they were not permitted to talk or to play games, the children could read pious books, sew, or tidy their desks. Nanda's class went for a walk in silence round the garden. When they returned to the study-room, they were greeted by the sight of many raised desk-lids.

During their absence, Mother Radcliffe had made one of her periodical visitations to see whether all was in order. Those whose desks were untidy were left open as a reproach, and usually lost their exemptions. Both Nanda's and Léonie's were open, as they usually were on these occasions. Léonie, with a click of annoyance, began rummaging in hers, throwing up holy pictures, broken crystal rosaries, letters with foreign stamps, snapshots, and biscuit crumbs from its amazing confusion. After two or three minutes, she turned to Nanda, looking paler than usual, and whispered:

'My God – it's gone.'

'What's gone?' asked Nanda, also in a whisper.

'Your novel.'

Chapter Fourteen

Nanda had seldom passed a worse night than she did that Good Friday. In the false security of the isolation wing, she had written on and on in a holiday spirit, with no idea that the eye of anyone in authority might fall on her work. The kind old Irish nun had never asked questions about it. She had even encouraged Nanda as she sat writing, patting her shoulder and occasionally observing: '*Laborare est orare,* my dear,' or 'The pen is mightier than the sword.'

Nor, by the standards of the Mudie books that always lay about in the drawing-room at home, did her novel seem at all subversive. Certainly, it was rather 'strong', so far, but the magnificent repentances and renunciations of the end would only make it all the more striking as propaganda for the Faith.

But, as she lay in the dark, sobered and shivering, she remembered passage after passage which would require a good deal of explanation in any nun's eyes; in Mother Radcliffe's most of all. She remembered the scene last term over her mildly silly letter about Clare. This time, Mother Radcliffe would be ruthless. She discarded the comforting hope that the manuscript might not, after all, have been in Léonie's desk. Léo was untidy, but trustworthy. She would never have taken the risk of leaving it lying about. Nor could she console herself with the thought that any other nun could have made the inspection, for Mother Radcliffe had appeared later in the day and delivered a lecture to the whole Senior School on the appalling disorder she had discovered in the course of her review. She had felt herself flush every time the Mistress of Discipline's eye had rested on her, but the nun had given no sign. For the remainder of the evening she had started every time the door opened, expecting to be called to Mother Radcliffe's room. She had not even been able to talk to Léonie about the disaster, for the rule of the Good Friday silence prevented any speech. As they sat sewing after supper, Léonie would only make guarded grimaces of remorse and consolation to which Nanda had responded with the ghastliest of smiles.

Where was the wretched book now? Did Mother Radcliffe already know the worst? Or was it still lying unread on her table? She had wild ideas of creeping down in her nightgown and abstracting the manuscript, but luckily, common sense told her that this would only aggravate her offence. True, the manuscript was not signed. But Mother Radcliffe knew the handwriting of every child in the school. There was nothing, absolutely nothing she could do.

Daylight came and she dressed herself slowly and miserably. Her head was aching and her eyes stung as if they were full of sand. At breakfast, she could only swallow a cup of milk. The bread and butter stuck in her throat. How was she ever going to get through the two and a half hour service in this agony of suspense? Should she rush now, uninvited, into Mother Radcliffe's room, and implore her to let her know the worst? Anything, anything would be better than this maddening uncertainty.

Half a dozen times during breakfast she was on the point of asking for permission to leave the refectory. Half a dozen times the opportunity slipped by. At last, the bell rang for grace and it was too late to do anything.

Never had the ceremonies of Holy Saturday seemed so interminable. In other years they had been her favourites in the whole year's liturgy. They had once been celebrated at the very first dawning of Easter Sunday, and their whole tone was that of renewal and rejoicing. Even today her spirits flickered up a little when the priest brought in the newly-struck fire, and the paschal candle, with its five grains of incense symbolizing the embalmed wounds of Christ, was solemnly kindled. But they flagged again during the twelve long prophecies, and her mind strayed back to Mother Radcliffe and her wretched book. She tried to calm her nerves and drive away the nagging distractions by following the service in her missal, but she could neither hear the words not control her weary eyes. However hard she tried to restrain them, they were always at least a page ahead of the priest, so that the prayers seemed to crawl with ant-like slowness. The blessing of the font might have been an entire High mass; the petitions of the Litany of the Saints droned on unendingly. At last, the moment to which she had always looked forward approached. Today, she only welcomed it because it brought the end of the office nearer. The purple veils were torn from the statues; the bells that had been silent for a week rang out all together; the organ pealed, and the priest, dressed now in the white vestment, intoned the first 'Alleluia'. Every other year, her heart had magically lightened at the sound of that 'Alleluia', but today she felt no response. Her only thoughts were: 'Has Mother Radcliffe read that book yet? What is she going to do when she has?'

An hour later the children, their chatter for once unchecked, ran noisily out into the garden. Everyone was already infected with the Easter spirit. The sun was out. Lent was over. tomorrow would be Easter Sunday, and the last day of term. They rushed up and down the alleys like mad things, jumping over benches, pretending to give each other the kiss of peace and shouting: 'Alleluia, Alleluia.'

But Nanda only stayed there for a minute. Under cover of the noise, she slipped back into the house and tore off coat and apron and goloshes. As she did so, the sight of her green ribbon struck her as such a mockery that she nearly took that off as well. She would certainly lose it in a few hours' time. However, until she was officially deprived of it, she must go on wearing the wretched decoration.

Hastily smoothing her hair and pulling on her gloves, she presented herself outside the Mistress of Discipline's door. As she knocked, her knees trembled and she felt so violently sick that she was sure she was going to faint. Hardly waiting for the nun's 'Come in,' she wrenched the handle and almost fell into the room. The mild, spectacled face of Mother Bidford, the secretary, looked up from the desk with an air of surprise.

'Well, my child?'

'I want to speak to – Will Mother Radcliffe be back soon?' Nanda stammered.

'No, my child. She will not be in the school all day. Is there anything I can do for you? It's Nanda Grey, isn't it?'

'No, it's all right, thank you, Mother,' muttered Nanda and dashed from the room.

There was nothing for it but to rejoin the others in the garden. The fresh, bright air revived her a little. To her relief, she saw Léonie on the terrace. The latter waved to her, but approached slowly, hiding something under her coat.

'I saw you go in, and thought I'd hang about,' said Léonie. 'Here, drink this.'

She produced a half-empty glass of milk with the strained smile of an amateur conjuror producing a rabbit.

'Some of it got spilt, I'm afraid. A great, clean-limbed hockey-playing blue ribbon cannoned into me. But there's a bit left.'

Nanda drank it gratefully. 'Well, any news?' asked Léonie, throwing the empty glass into a laurel bush. 'I'll never forgive myself to my dying day about this business,' she added gloomily.

'You don't think there's any hope of its turning up?' said Nanda faintly.

'No. I know it was in my desk, folded up in a French exercise-book. That's gone, too. She must have been on the search for something. I believe that inspection was just a blind.'

'It's just possible,' admitted Nanda. 'But what's she going to *do* about it? It's this hanging about not knowing that I can't stand.'

'If she's any sense, she'll take the whole thing as a joke, make a few scathing remarks, and that'll be the end. But you never know with nuns.'

'There were some pretty awful things in it,' said Nanda uncomforted.

'Yes, but nothing blasphemous or seditious or even anti-Lippington. That's what flicks them on the raw. Besides, anyone with half an eye could see it was written by a perfect sucking-dove of innocence.'

Nanda's vanity was far too deflated to resent the slight on the brilliant worldliness of those four chapters. Suddenly she began to laugh.

'It's pretty good irony, isn't it?' she said bitterly.

'What is, poor old devil?' asked Léonie, putting her hand on her shoulder.

'I've just remembered it's my birthday tomorrow.'

The rest of the day passed without a sign.

Nanda mechanically darned stockings, went to the chapel, ate meals which tasted of sawdust, played rounders and read the life of St Francis of Sales, until it was time to go to bed. To her surprise, she slept soundly and dreamlessly until the rising bell. She woke with her nerves a little soothed. Had she, after all, been working herself up into a state about nothing? She was further reassured when Mother Radcliffe appeared in the refectory as was customary on Easter Sunday, and handed each child a coloured egg. Nanda received the same cheerful smile as the others, and Mother Radcliffe even added: 'It's your birthday, isn't it? Many happy returns.' Perhaps things were not so bad after all.

But her misgivings awoke again as the afternoon approached. Her parents were coming to see her, she knew. Would Mother Radcliffe say anything to them?

Three o'clock came and she sat pretending to read in the study-room, fidgeting and jumping to her feet every time the parlour sister appeared at the door. Child after child was called away to see her friends or relations, but no summons came for Nanda. Impatience grew to foreboding, then to alarm. Her parents usually arrived most punctually at three. On her birthday, of all days, they would hardly be late without warning her. Half past three came; four o'clock; a quarter past. At half past four the bell rang, and Nanda went into the refectory to face the ghastly travesty of a birthday tea-party.

On the centre table stood her cake, with its fourteen candles, and the places of the six friends whom she was allowed to invite laid with crackers. Clare, Léonie and Rosario, with the three younger nonentities whom she had asked for prudence's sake, were waiting for her. She sat down absent-mindedly and had to be reminded by Rosario that she had not said grace. Léonie gave her a swift look, and seeing that she was dull and preoccupied, took the load of entertaining off her hands. She pulled crackers right and left, made the most outrageous jokes, until Clare's loud crows and the flattering giggles of the nonentities nearly made the nun in charge ring for silence.

'Why, Nanda,' said Rosario kindly, 'you've forgotten to light your candles.'

Someone produced a taper, and with a trembling hand, Nanda clumsily lit the nearest three. The taper went out, and no one offered her a match. She could see from their surprised faces that something was wrong. Looking round, she saw Mother Radcliffe standing behind her. She was not smiling now.

'I'm afraid you will have to leave your guests to finish the party without you,' she said gently. 'I want to speak to you.'

Too stricken to say goodbye to the others, she followed Mother Radcliffe out into the passage.

'Your parents are here to see you,' she said, still gently. 'You will find them, not in the school parlour, but in the little community one. For reasons which you will understand presently, I thought it would be better to see them undisturbed.'

Nanda's knees shook so that she could hardly walk. She was paralysed with terror and apprehension. In a few minutes, she would know the worst. Something in Mother Radcliffe's look told her that the worst was very bad indeed.

Chapter Fifteen

Her father and mother were sitting at a plush-covered table in an austere and unfamiliar little room. They did not rise to greet her, though she heard her mother whisper: 'After all, John, it *is* her birthday.' But her father shook his head. Never, during the worst scolding had she seen his face like this. It was stiff as a death-mask, with all the colour drained away to a uniform greyish yellow. Her mother, too, looked stern, but there was none of that inhuman coldness in her air, and she fidgeted with her handbag as if not altogether associating herself with the scene. There was silence for a minute or two; then her father spoke in an icy voice whose edge Nanda felt like a physical hurt.

'And what, may I ask, have you to say for yourself?'

'About . . . about what, Daddy?' she gasped, forcing her voice out with immense effort as one tries to scream in a nightmare.

'I would rather you did not use that name, if you please.'

She said nothing, but plaited the fringe of her green ribbon to try and calm herself.

'I have always believed in you and trusted you, Fernanda,' went on the icy voice, 'I even flattered myself that I knew something of your nature. In spite of many faults, I have always believed that fundamentally you were sweet and innocent – and good. Yesterday, if anyone had shown me the disgusting and vulgar filth that I have seen today in your own handwriting, I would have doubted my own eyes. Today, with the evidence I have from Mother Radcliffe, I am forced to believe that you wrote it, and wrote it deliberately.'

'But listen – listen,' Nanda almost shrieked. 'Let me explain.'

'I do not want any explanation. I do not propose to discuss anything so vile and so degrading as the whole subject.'

'John, really,' put in her mother weakly. But her father ignored the interruption.

'I want to ask you one question. Until two hours ago I – wrongly, no doubt – believed you to be truthful. Until that, too, is disproved, I shall continue to hope so. Did you write this entirely of your own accord, without help or suggestion from any other person?'

'Yes,' said Nanda, summoning up the dregs of her courage to look at him.

'No other girl bullied you into it?'

'No.'

Mr Grey brought his hand down with a thud on the table.

'Then I say that if a young girl's mind is such a sink of filth and impurity, I wish to God that I had never had a daughter.'

Nanda's last thread of self-control snapped. She burst into a storm of convulsive, almost tearless sobs that wrenched all her muscles and brought no relief. The whole world had fallen away and left her stranded in this one spot alone for ever and ever with her father and those awful words. She felt her mother touch her sleeve and shook her off, blindly, mechanically, hardly knowing that she was there.

Her father was speaking again, but though she heard him distinctly, in spite of her sobbing, the words made no impression. All her consciousness was withdrawn into one burning centre of pain and misery, and the sounds merely beat on a numbed outer skin.

He was saying that she must leave Lippington for ever the next day. That though she was not officially expelled, her dismissal had all the stigma of expulsion. That Mother Radcliffe had even suggested that she might be removed to another house of the Order, but that he had refused to take the responsibility. She must go to some Protestant school where she was completely unknown and where, though he and she and her mother could never forget the scandal and shame of the whole affair, it could at least be kept from becoming public.

He seemed to talk for hours. At intervals, her mother interposed with a 'But, John,' or 'I really can't help feeling – ' but he did not even answer.

In time, from utter exhaustion, Nanda's breathless sobbing became quieter. She even looked up and dimly noticed the albums on the table, and a kid-gloved hand still fidgeting with the clasp of a bag. Then her eye caught the sight of a brown paper parcel only half-hidden by her mother's muff. She guessed at once that it contained her birthday present. Another wave of misery poured over her. A little while before, one sentence of her father's had torn right through every protective covering and shamed her to the very marrow. If he had stripped her naked and beaten her, she would not have felt more utterly humiliated. Never, never, could things be the same. Never again would he believe in her. Never again could she love him in the old way. But now, the sight of the absurd birthday parcel suddenly showed her all the small human losses included in that one great loss. She wept wildly for all the dear, silly things that were gone for ever; the happy tea-times of the Christmas holidays, the talks in the study, the *Haec Olim* file to which she could never add her green ribbon.

In the midst of this fresh outburst, Mother Radcliffe came in. Nanda, too given up to misery to move, saw her father stand up and make a stiff bow. She heard Mother Radcliffe say:

'I think Nanda has learnt her lesson now,' and felt the nun's arm round her shoulders. She buried her face in her hands and seemed actually to lose consciousness for a little. Very far away, she heard people moving, heard someone whispering, heard a door shut. When at last she raised her head, she was alone with Mother Radcliffe. The nun sat down beside her and took her hands in her own cool, dry ones.

'There, my child,' she said over and over again in a soothing, almost hypnotic voice. 'There, my child.'

They sat thus for a long time, until Nanda's tears were almost spent and she was conscious of nothing but an aching head and a feeling of shivering sickness.

Presently the nun said, still in the same gentle measured voice:

'Those are good tears, Nanda. I have waited for them and prayed for them. You understand very little yet, my dear child, but one day you will understand the significance of all this.'

Nanda did not reply, and Mother Radcliffe went on:

'You are feeling that you have been unjustly treated – that no offence could deserve so great a punishment. Nanda, you must try and believe that all this is for your own good.'

But Nanda could only mutter with dry and swollen lips:

'Daddy – Daddy.'

The nun put her hand on her forehead.

'God asks very hard things from us,' she said, 'the sacrifice of what we love best and the sacrifice of our own wills. That is what it means to be a Christian. For years, I have been watching you, Nanda. I have seen you growing up, intelligent, warm-hearted, apparently everything a child should be. But I have watched something else growing in you, too – a hard little core of self-will and self-love. I told you once before that every will must be broken completely and re-set before it can be at one with God's will. And there is no other way. That is what true education, as we understand it here at Lippington, means. Real love is a hard taskmaster, and the love of God the hardest taskmaster of all. I am only acting as God's instrument in this. I had to break your will before your whole nature was deformed.'

Nanda glanced at the nun's face. It was pale and controlled as usual, yet lighted with an extraordinary, quiet exaltation.

'Many things must have happened to you here at Lippington which have seemed unkind, unjust even. Very few of those things happened by accident. I am speaking to you now as if you were a grown-up person. Yours is a nature with a great capacity for good and evil; you are gifted but wayward; obstinate, yet easily led. You have one quality which I think will help you through life. I believe you are fundamentally honest. But there was a quality you needed more. We tried to teach you easy ways, but today you have had to learn it by hard ones – the quality of humility.'

'Mother – Mother – won't you give me one more chance?' Nanda begged suddenly. Her eyes were dry now, as if the last drop of moisture had been scorched out of her body.

The nun appeared to think a minute. Then very kindly she said:

'No, my dear. You must take your penance. I am not going to talk about the wicked, foolish things you wrote. You have enough sense to see them now in their proper light. But there are many reasons why you should not stay here. For one thing, in some ways, we have no more to teach you. For another, I have a hundred other children to consider. There are some people, harmless in themselves, who can be a source of danger to others, as there are people healthy in themselves, who are what doctors call "germ carriers". But I want you always to think of yourself as one of us, as a child of the Five Wounds. Come back and see us often – write to us – pray for us, as we shall pray for you.'

'But my friends – Léo and all of them – ?' pleaded Nanda, and would have wept had she had a tear left.

'Give them up bravely, as part of your sacrifice. God will not forget. Remember, He never allows Himself to be outdone in generosity.'

'It's too much,' said Nanda quietly. 'I'm not a . . . not a very strong sort of person.'

The nun smiled and patted her hand. 'We shall see. God sends us strength as we need it. And sometimes He sends us consolation when we least expect it. For many months, you and all of us have prayed for something that seemed hopeless. This afternoon, Reverend Mother gave me a letter about which no one else, even the child it concerns, as yet knows anything. It is from Clare Rockingham's father, giving his consent for Clare to be received into the Catholic faith.'

A week ago it would have meant so much, but now Nanda hardly knew whether she were glad or not. She heard herself answer mechanically: 'How wonderful,' but no other words came.

Another long minute passed, then Mother Radcliffe said gently:

'It is seven o'clock, my dear child. I must leave you. Run and bathe your eyes before supper.'

But at this Nanda's tears started afresh.

'I can't possibly go into the refectory,' she sobbed.

'Very well, Nanda. Go up to the infirmary and ask Mother Regan to give you some supper there.'

'No . . . please . . . I couldn't eat anything.'

'I thought you were going to be obedient. Nanda,' said Mother Radcliffe, with her old firmness.

Nanda stood up.

'Very well, Mother,' she said firmly.

The nun smiled.

'That's right. Life's not all over at fourteen, my dear.'

She took Nanda's arm and led her out into the passage.

'Perhaps you'd like to pay a little visit to the Blessed Sacrament?'

Nanda did not answer, but let Mother Radcliffe guide her to the chapel door. She went in alone and, forgetting to take holy water or even to genuflect, knelt down heavily in the nearest bench. From the smaller chapel came the sound of the Junior School saying their night prayers.

Everything was the same – the smell of beeswax, the red lights of the sanctuary, the words that the children were whispering beyond the altar screen. But Nanda knew that whatever might happen in the future, nothing for her would ever be the same again.

The Lost
Traveller

To the memory of
HUGH KINGSMILL

'In the sojourning of this carnal life each man carries his own heart and every heart is closed to every other heart.'

St Augustine

Introduction

It is unusual for the publisher of a book to provide its preface. Antonia White wanted to write a new introduction to the three books – *The Lost Traveller, The Sugar House* and *Beyond the Glass* – which complete the story she began in her famous novel *Frost in May*. Now eighty years of age, and a novelist whose small output reflects the virulent writers' block which has constantly interrupted her writing life, she preferred to talk to me. For though separated by age, country of birth and nationality, we share a Catholic upbringing which has been a dominant influence on both our lives. What follows is based on a long conversation I had with Antonia White in December 1978, and on the many times we've talked since Virago first re-published *Frost in May* earlier that year.

'Personal novels,' wrote Elizabeth Bowen in a review of Antonia White's work, 'those which are obviously based on life, have their own advantages and hazards. But we have one "personal" novelist who has brought it off infallibly.' Antonia White turned fact into fiction in a quartet of novels based on her life from the ages of nine to twenty-three. 'My life is the raw material for the novels, but writing an autobiography and writing fiction are very different things.' This transformation of real life into an imagined work of art is perhaps her greatest skill as a novelist.

Antonia White was the only daughter of Cecil Botting, Senior Classics Master at St Paul's School, who became a Catholic at the age of thirty-five taking with him into the Church his wife and seven-year-old daughter, fictionalized as 'Nanda' in *Frost in May*. This novel is a brilliant portrait of Nanda's experiences in the enclosed world of a Catholic convent. First published in 1933, it was immediately recognized as a classic. Antonia White wrote what was to become the first two chapters of *Frost in May* when she was only sixteen, completing it sixteen years later, in 1931. At the time she was married to Tom Hopkinson, writer, journalist and later editor of *Picture Post*.

'I'd written one or two short stories, but really I wrote nothing until after my father's death in 1929. At the time I was doing a penitential stint in Harrods' Advertising Agency ... I'd been sacked from Crawfords in 1930 for not taking a passionate enough interest in advertising. One day I was looking through my desk and I came across this bundle of manuscript. Out of curiosity I began to read it and some of the things in it made me laugh. Tom asked me to read it to him, which I did, and then he said "You must finish it." Anyway Tom had appendicitis and we were very hard up, so I was working full time. But Tom insisted I finish a chapter every Saturday night. Somehow or other I managed to do it, and then Tom thought I should send it to the publisher – Cobden Sanderson – who'd liked my short stories. They wrote back saying it was too slight to be of interest to anyone. Several other people turned it down and then a woman I knew told me that Desmond Harmsworth had won some money in the Irish sweep and didn't know what to do with it ... so he started a publishing business and in fact I think *Frost in May* was the only thing he ever published ... it got wonderful reviews.'

Between 1933 and 1950 Antonia White wrote no more novels. She was divorced from Tom Hopkinson in 1938, worked in advertising, for newspapers, as a freelance journalist and then came the war. Throughout this period she suffered further attacks of the mental illness she first experienced in 1922. This madness Antonia White refers to as 'The Beast' – Henry James's 'Beast in the Jungle'. Its recurrence and a long period of psychoanalysis interrupted these years.

'I'd always wanted to write another novel, having done one, but then you see the 1930s were a very difficult time for me because I started going off my head again. After the war and the political work I did I was terribly hard up. Then Enid Starkey, whom I'd met during the war, suggested to Hamish Hamilton that I should have a shot at translating and they liked what I did. After that I got all these commissions and I was doing two or three a year but I was completely jammed up on anything of my own, though I kept on trying to write in spite of it. I always wanted to write another novel, and I wanted this time to do something more ambitious, what I thought would be a "proper" novel, not seen only through the eyes of one person as it is in *Frost in May*, but through the eyes of her father, her mother and even those old great aunts in the country. Then suddenly I could write again. The first one [*The Lost Traveller*] took the longest to write. I don't know how many years it took me, but I was amazed how I then managed to write the other two [*The Sugar House* and *Beyond the Glass*]. They came incredibly quickly.'

In 1950, seventeen years after the publication of *Frost in May*, *The Lost Traveller* was published. In it Antonia White changed the name of her heroine Nanda Grey to Clara Batchelor. 'Of course Clara is a continuation of Nanda. Nanda became Clara because my father had a great passion for Meredith and a particular passion for Clara Middleton (heroine of *The Egoist*). Everything that happened to Clara in *The Lost Traveller* is the sort of thing that happened to me, though many things are changed, many invented. I wanted *The Lost Traveller* to be a *real* novel – *Frost in May* was so much my own life. So I changed her name . . .' In every other respect this novel begins where *Frost in May* ends. It is a vivid account of adolescence, of the mutual relationships of father, mother and daughter as Clara grows to maturity and comes to grips with the adult world.

* * *

Two years later Antonia White continued Clara's story, in *The Sugar House*.

Carmen Callil, Virago, London, 1979

PART ONE

Chapter One

On every ordinary weekday in term-time, Claude Batchelor stepped out of his house at exactly twenty minutes past nine, slammed the door and set off at a furious pace in the direction of St Mark's School. People who lived in certain West Kensington streets timed their watches by the sturdy, immaculately dressed figure which hurried past their windows as punctually as a train. But on a certain Tuesday in March 1914 it was well after eleven when Claude Batchelor left his house. He shut the door softly behind him and stood hesitating on the steps as if he could not decide which way to go.

He was as carefully dressed and shaved as usual but his blue eyes were bloodshot and his clear skin dulled to a greyish yellow. His was one of those faces that suffering caricatures. The firm, fleshy features, Saxon in colouring, late Roman in cast, were trained to express humour and anger; under the stress of grief they merely looked dissipated.

For three years Claude had known that his father might die at any time. He had accustomed himself to say to his wife, 'We must realize that my father cannot live indefinitely' and even 'When my father dies, we might do so-and-so.' Now that his father was dead, he knew that never for one moment had the idea been real to him.

Certainly he had behaved as he had always intended to behave. Ever since the nurse had said 'Poor man, he really has gone now' and competently closed his father's eyes, Claude had done everything expected of him. For the past few hours he had been calming and directing with stoical efficiency, making neat lists of what must be done and who must be informed. Now, standing alone in front of the shrouded house, his will collapsed.

It cost him a huge effort to remind himself why he had come out and to order his legs to carry him in the right direction.

By the time he reached the post office he had recovered enough mechanical awareness to write out several telegrams. His small upright hand, the writing of a man who constantly uses Greek characters, was as lucid as usual but his mind was still clouded. When he came out into the street again, the spring sunshine seemed as unnatural as the electric light and drawn blinds he had left at home and people as remote as figures on a stage. North End Road was filling up with the miscellaneous crowd that took possession of it when the city men had gone to work and the two great schools drawn in their population. It was the hour when the young actresses, with smears of last night's make-up still on their eyelids, sauntered out to have their hair waved or to exercise their little dogs; when the old actors, pretending they were on their way to rehearsal, converged in the direction of the 'Three Kings'. Wives were doing their shopping, frowning over their kists and demanding that the joint or the whiting be sent 'in time for lunch, without fail, please'. Girls, newly grown-up and taking tiny selfconscious steps in tight skirts that clung to their black silk ankles were staring into drapers' windows or ordering cakes for their mother's bridge parties.

Perhaps because from now on there would be only women in his home he looked at the actors and the yellow-faced men retired from the East almost wistfully. Had his sense of fitness not been so strong, he would have crossed over to the 'Three Kings' and, leaning on a counter spotted with wet rings, unloaded his misery on a stranger. Instead he stood by the pillar-box, clutching his bundle of black-edged letters and staring. His jaw, which he had consciously thrust forward for so many years that it was now underhung, dropped open as it used to do when he was a boy. The blow had momentarily cracked the shell of Claude Batchelor the successful schoolmaster and exposed a long-forgotten Claude, dreamy, uncertain and awkward. Standing there on the pavement he lost for a time, as in childhood, the sense of separate existence. Nothing marked him off from the girl staring into the hatshop window, the man leering at her, the errand boy on the green bicycle, the old woman stuffing a cabbage into her string bag. He was so merged in them that he knew when head would turn or a foot falter. Suddenly he was touched by an old fear of which he had never spoken to anyone, the fear that one day he might lose all control of his mind. Against that there was only one weapon; his obstinate will. With all his might he called it into play, holding his breath as if forcing himself into a tight jacket. Then he shot his letters in the box, clenched his teeth and set off at his usual quick pace towards home.

Valetta Road was one of the older streets of West Kensington. Built of stucco and sparrow-coloured brick, it was modelled on the plan of more ambitious neighbourhoods but the houses were so narrow that they looked overloaded by their pillars and balconies. Along the tops of either row ran a balustrade decorated at intervals with spiked urns shaped like policemen's helmets. Each house owned a pillar and a half so that when occasionally a tenant repainted his stucco, it produced an odd piebald effect. No two façades were the same colour but showed greys, biscuits, ochres and hot browns in various stages of dinginess.

Sixteen years earlier, when Claude had come to live in Valetta Road, it had been one of the 'best' streets. Now, though it was going downhill and he could well afford to move, he stayed on from habit and a kind of loyalty. Several houses still had well-cleaned steps and shining brass and were inhabited by a single family. But, year by year, one or two more sank to the degradation of a blistered front door flanked by three or four bells with a buckled card beside each. In summer there appeared on the balconies of such houses people of whom the permanent inhabitants disapproved; young men who played banjoes, Indian students and girls who sat about in flowered kimonos drying their hair in the sun and calling 'Coo-ee' to their friends in the street.

Among the long-term tenants were men who worked in the city, doctors, army coaches and retired civil servants. The houses of all these were arranged, as if by agreement, on exactly the same pattern. The ground floor windows had curtains of heavy dark material, the first floor blue or rose brocade and white lace draperies and the second floor casement cloth or chintz. If the blinds of Number 18 had not been drawn, its curtains would have appeared perfectly correct except for those of the top floor bedroom. These were of pink satin and people who disapproved of Claude Batchelor's wife saw in them one more proof of her extravagance and oddness.

Usually the whole household knew when its master arrived home. Claude's key grated loudly in the lock, the door banged and the clatter of his stick, as he rammed it into the pottery stand, reverberated on every floor. But today he came in as noiselessly as he had gone out. Isabel, his wife, who was sewing in the darkened dining-room that opened off the hall, gave a little shriek when he appeared in the doorway.

'Claude! I didn't know you were in the house.'

'I'm sorry if I startled you.'

His voice, harsh with exhaustion, sounded angry rather than apologetic. The dimness was soothing to his eyes after the glare of the street. A single cone of light fell on the table where Isabel sat, removing a crimson feather from a black velvet hat; beyond its radius everything seemed blurred in fog. He remained in the shadow on the far side of the table, looking down at her.

'All the essential telegrams have gone,' he said. 'I shall send others as soon as we know the exact arrangements for the funeral.'

'So efficient even today,' she sighed. Then, more alertly, but without looking at him, she asked,

'What have you done about Clara?'

'I asked the Reverend Mother to send her home at once. Presumably she will arrive during the afternoon.'

Isabel raised her great eyes and stared at him.

'Oh.'

'Why that voice, my dear?'

'You never told me you'd decided.'

Her face, unlike his, was perfectly designed to express tragedy. Even when she was gay, the slight droop of her mouth and her large brown exposed eyes gave her an air of sadness. Her soft, stricken voice and the look that matched it accused him, as so often before, of being insensitive.

'I took it for granted you would want her to be there.'

'Poor little Clara,' she wailed. 'It seems so dreadful . . . a child at a funeral.'

'Nearly fifteen is hardly a child, surely.'

'Your mother's idea, I suppose.'

He showed that he was hurt by thrusting out his jaw and speaking in his classroom tone.

'As it happens, I did not consult my mother. I assumed . . . rashly it appears . . . that you would agree with me.'

Isabel made a few vague snips at her feather.

'Of course, if you've made up your mind, there's no point in my saying anything. Though how you can expose a little girl to all these horrors . . .'

'What exactly do you mean by horrors?'

She dropped her hands in her lap and shut her eyes.

'Really, Claude. Today of all days I didn't think you'd bully me.'

'Bully you? Oh, my God!' he said wearily.

'Or swear at me.' It was hardly more than a whisper. Her eyes remained closed.

He looked at her in silence. Once again she had defeated him. From his boyhood to this day his natural preference had always been for golden-haired women; plump, good-tempered and insipidly pretty. Yet the moment he had set eyes, twenty years ago, on a sallow, brown-haired girl whose beauty was only one degree removed from ugliness he had been fascinated, and fascinated he remained. The sickly light exposed her face to him now wan and lifeless. Her hair, carelessly done, hung limply, revealing the babyish, undeveloped forehead and eyebrows so faint as to be nearly invisible. The smooth arched eyelids were beginning to wrinkle; the perfect lips, pale today and slackly parted as if in sleep, showed teeth that were even but no longer white. The curves of cheek and jaw were still intact but the skin which had once had the satin texture of her arms now showed a roughened grain to which drifts of powder clung unevenly. He was reminded of a gardenia, just turning brown at the edges, its perfume intensified by the first touch of decay. His anger melted into resentful tenderness.

Feeling his eyes on her, she slowly opened her own and her soft high voice was no longer aggrieved as she lisped.

'What do I mean by horrors, dea'est? You've only to look around this room.'

The room was sombre enough at any time with its dark red walls and greenish-brown curtains. Today it was muffled in black draperies which blotted up the weak light. Black garments trailed everywhere over the chairs; even the mirror over the fireplace was swathed in a black shawl.

'When a family is in mourning, one expects this surely.'

'Not in all famiiies, Claude. My father insisted we weren't to wear black even at his funeral.'

'Your father, my dear, as you have repeatedly told me, was a highly unconventional man.'

'I don't see why we should have to go to the other extreme. I doubt if anyone draws the blinds down now except in the East End.'

'My mother would be upset if we didn't.'

'Your mother again. Of course, what I want counts for nothing in this house.'

'Isabel, be reasonable. Can't you just for once . . .?'

She ignored him.

'Your father would have agreed with me,' she persisted. 'He had all the right instincts, dear old man.'

Usually any praise of his father, however patronizing, softened Claude at once. However, he said nothing and, glancing at him, Isabel saw that his fact was set. She said coaxingly,

'I think it's a beautiful idea of yours to have him buried at Rookfield.'

'I'm glad you approve. I only hope that the sight of so many of my relatives won't be too much for you.'

She began to pluck once more at the feather with the uncertain movements of a woman who seldom uses her hands.

'Really, Claude, is it my fault if ugliness of any kind jars on me so dreadfully? I hope for her own sake that Clara isn't as sensitive as I am.'

'I'm quite certain she is not. As you often say, she takes after my family.'

Isabel pushed her hat away and stared into space.

'Father always thought I was born with a skin too few. I daresay it's literally true.'

'My dear, no one attempts to compete with you in the finer feelings. No doubt I myself was born with several skins too many.'

'Claude, how can you be so cruel and sarcastic today of all days? Don't you realize how all this brings things back to me? You seem to forget that I lost my father too. Oh, I know it's fifteen years ago. But it seems like yesterday.'

Once more she had beaten him. In sign of surrender he crossed the room and sat down beside her.

'I'm sorry, Isabel. I'm shockingly irritable this morning.'

She turned her eyes vaguely in his direction, looking at a point somewhere over his shoulder.

'I know it's dreadful for you, Claude. I can sympathize. But at least you were prepared.'

He said blankly,

'Oh yes. I was prepared.'

'I had no warning. We hadn't the faintest idea that he had a weak heart. Yet that morning when the telegram came I knew at once that it was Father. I've often wondered if I'm not a little psychic.'

'Very possibly.'

'You, Claude, at least still have a mother. Just think, I can't even remember mine. I was only three months old when she died.'

She had told him these things many times before in almost identical words. When she did so her eyes always became fixed and she spoke in a high faint monotone. With exasperated tenderness, he took her hand. She yielded it vaguely and the needle she was holding pricked his finger. At the sight of the blood she started and cried out too late,

'Oh, dea'est, be careful.'

She made a little grimace as he dabbed his bleeding finger. Then suddenly she smiled.

'Do you remember? When we were engaged. The pin in my belt. You were so furious because you thought it was untidy of me to have a pin in my belt at all. But the next day you sent me a poem in Latin all about the thorny rose.'

187

He did remember, as if from another life, Isabel with her hair in soft puffs and wearing a pink blouse, standing under a lilac tree in her father's garden.

'You had to translate it for me,' she went on. 'I was so proud of having a poem written to me in Latin and so ashamed not to be able to make out a single world except "Rosa". Such a foolish Belle. And then you did try to teach me Latin and had to give me up as hopeless. I've often wondered why, because my French is so good.'

'You can't teach when you're in love with your pupil.'

'Then I hope I was your only failure.'

He had to smile.

'Positively my only failure.'

'All the same, I expect you'd have been much happier if you'd married a female don or something.'

'Heaven forbid!'

'You and Clara between you sometimes make me feel a complete idiot. If one of your pupils sent Clara a love poem in Latin, she'd be able to understand every word, wouldn't she?'

His face stiffened again.

'If any of my pupils had the impertinence . . .' he began fiercely.

She interrupted,

'Yet you were just saying that she wasn't a child any more.'

'From that point of view, the longer we think of her as a child the better.'

'You needn't worry. I daresay you'll make Clara so learned that no young man will ever dare come near her.' She frowned. 'No one ever asked me if I wanted my pretty daughter turned into a blue-stocking.'

'The child has good brains. Why shouldn't she use them? Apart from the fact that she will almost certainly have to make her own living.'

'I still think it was overdoing it to make her puzzle over declensions and things when she was seven.'

'She enjoyed it.' His face cleared. 'Ah, at that age she was a joy to teach.'

'Isn't she now?' said Isabel innocently. 'She's always so desperately anxious to please you.'

Again he frowned.

'Hmm. I wonder. When she was younger, yes. But now . . . this last year or two . . . I wonder.'

'More than ever now, Claude. I'm in a very good position to judge.' She snapped her fingers. 'For ages I haven't counted *that* with Clara.'

He thrust his jaw forward.

'If I thought that were true, Isabel, I should have to speak to her. And in no uncertain terms.'

'Please don't, dearest. Certainly not today when she's just had such a shock. I daresay all clever daughters are critical of their Mammas at her age. Yet when I think how I used to long for a mother when I was beginning to grow up! But I wasn't a bit like Clara. I was such an absurd romantic little thing, living in a sort of fairytale world of my own.'

'I'm by no means satisfied with Clara myself,' said Claude. 'It seems to me that lately the child has become hard and self-centred.'

'Yet she was so sweet and affectionate when she was tiny, wasn't she? I can see her now in her big white bonnet, trotting along beside her grandfather, holding his hand and looking up at him so adoringly.'

'Ah,' he sighed. 'If we could go back to those years!'

She touched his hand lightly.

'Poor Claude. I was almost forgetting. I'm sure no one will miss him more than I shall.'

'He was so fond of you, Isabel.'

'Wasn't it touching, the way he took such an interest in my clothes and so on? He really had quite a flair for such things. It's strange when you think of . . .'

She broke off in time and he, knowing perfectly well what she had been about to say, made no comment. To cover it, she gave the feather a tug and it came away with a crackle of ripped stitches.

'There, now I've deliberately ruined his favourite hat. He would have been the first to see it's nothing without the feather.'

'I think he would have been touched by your sacrificing it.'

'What good can it do him, poor dear? I think there's something positively unChristian in all this gloomy attitude to death. After all, we *are* supposed to believe he's gone to a happier place.'

He half smiled.

'As Catholics, we usually expect a certain delay.'

'You mean purgatory and all that? I think purgatory's a wonderful idea. So consoling for people like me. And so logical when you come to think of it. All the same, in the east they wear flowers at funerals and make quite a festival of the whole thing.'

'I've no idea what they do in the east.'

Isabel stroked her cheek with the crimson feather and said dreamily, 'If I died first, you'd have to make all the arrangements for my funeral, wouldn't you, Claude?'

She ignored his 'Dear girl . . . for heaven's sake!' and went on:

'I should like everyone to wear their nicest clothes. And no funeral march. Just that Chopin nocturne I used to play you when we were engaged. And don't give me a tombstone. I should feel crushed under it. I'd like you to plant a rose bush and a cypress tree on my grave.'

'Will you kindly stop, Isabel.'

She looked at him with a childish wonder that might or might not have been simulated.

'I've always prayed,' he said, 'that you would outlive me.'

'Isn't that rather selfish, dearest? It's so much worse for the one who is left.'

'Of course it is selfish,' he said angrily, suddenly pulling her close to him.

There was a knock at the door and they quickly composed their faces and attitudes. Zillah the housemaid came in, carrying an enormous cardboard box. She wore her black afternoon uniform instead of her morning print and her handsome grey eyes were swollen.

'Mr Shapiro's chauffeur left this for you, sir.'

'Even the servants loved him,' Claude said when the girl had gone. 'Poor Zillah was in tears this morning.'

'Servants love deaths and funerals. Even a pretty girl like Zillah doesn't get much excitement in her life.'

Claude methodically untied the box. From layers of tissue paper, there emerged an immense wreath of lilies of the valley and mauve cattleyas.

'Oh, how exquisite,' said Isabel, staring greedily.

Claude's eyes filled.

'If only he could see them!'

'When we're alive,' said Isabel, 'no one thinks of sending us orchids. All the time he was ill, Becky Shapiro never sent him so much as a bunch of violets.'

'Really, it is too much. They shouldn't have done it.'

'Why? It's nothing to these rich Jews.'

'Plenty of rich Christians wouldn't even have thought of it,' he said sharply.

'The Shapiros owe it you. Look at all you've done for their little Izzy and their little Sam. All right, my dear, I admit it is nice of them. But I can never help smiling when I think of those boys, born over a fried fish shop, going to Oxford.'

'Is it any odder than my sending Clara to Mount Hilary? Why shouldn't the Shapiros want things for their children that they haven't had themselves?'

It was her turn to stiffen.

'You seem to forget,' she said coldly, 'that Clara is half a Maule. If my grandfather hadn't lost his money, if my father hadn't been eccentric and cut himself off from society . . .'

'Yes, yes, my dear,' he said hastily to avert what must inevitably come next; the maule coat of arms; the Lawrence portraits; the snuffbox presented by George III. 'No one realizes it better than I. And no one is gladder for Clara's sake.'

Easily propitiated, she smiled.

'It's the *only* trace,' she said. 'Your being so impressed by money and the Shapiro kind of vulgar success.'

'I like Shapiro for himself.'

'You always say he's very intelligent. He certainly plays an extraordinary game of bridge. But I can't get over that accent and those fingers.'

She stroked her nose appreciatively with her own impeccable hand. The nose too was impeccable; straight and thin, with finely incised nostrils.

'Such a pity about Clara's nose,' she said. 'You couldn't call it ugly but it has definitely spread a trifle.'

Her eyes wandered again to the flowers.

'Lovely, lovely things. Doesn't it seem criminal to think of them mouldering on a grave?'

He got up abruptly and moved towards the door.

'I must go, Isabel. There are still innumerable things to do.'

'All these ghastly formalities. They can't even let one die and be buried in peace. Will you be in to luncheon?'

'No. I shall get some lunch at my club.'

Her eyes were still on the flowers.

'If he had been alive, the very first thing he would have done would have been to give me one.'

'No doubt, my dear.'

She looked at him innocently.

'I think that eastern custom is a charming idea, don't you?'

'Eastern custom?' he asked in bewilderment.

'I told you just now, dearest. About wearing . . .'

'Goodbye, Isabel,' he said and left her. She heard him collecting his hat and stick in the hall and this time he did not leave the house noiselessly.

Chapter Two

Isabel waited till she heard the front door close. Then she took the scissors from her workbox and carefully snipped off two of the largest orchids from the wreath. Going over to the mirror, she lifted a corner of the black shawl. Finding it was still impossible to get a good view of herself, she pulled the shawl off altogether. She switched on the centre light and returned to the mirror. No sooner had she pinned the orchids to the shoulder of her dress than the door was stealthily pushed open and someone came in.

'Oh, it's you,' she said, swinging round. 'I do wish you wouldn't creep about so quietly.'

Old Mrs Batchelor advanced slowly into the room, having switched off the main light and closed the door as carefully as if she feared to waken a sleeper.

'I'm sorry, Isabel. I thought you would wish everything as quiet as possible today.'

'Please put that light on again.'

'I didn't mean any harm,' said Mrs Batchelor meekly. 'I was only thinking of Claude's purse.'

'I want it on, please.'

Mrs Batchelor turned on the light and stood hesitating by the door.

'Do come and sit down,' said Isabel.

'You're sure I shan't be in your way?'

'No, no. Is there anything you want? Shall I tell Zillah to get you a cup of tea?'

'No, thank you, dear. I wouldn't like to give the maids extra trouble.'

'That's not the point. Do you *want* some tea?'

'No, really, Isabel. I couldn't touch anything.'

Mrs Batchelor sat down in the hardest chair and dabbed her eyes.

'I'm afraid I shall be more of a burden than ever to you now that he's gone,' she sobbed.

'Oh, please try not to cry. You'll only tire yourself out. Do you mind if I just arrange your hair a little?'

It was only with great effort that Isabel could bring herself to touch her mother-in-law. After living in the same house with her for over ten years, the morning and evening kisses were still an ordeal. The very appearance of the old woman was an affront to her eyes. Ellen Batchelor was barely five feet high and cruelly misproportioned. Her large flattened head was dumped down on the narrowest of shoulders; her enormous stomach thrust forward in a solid mound below the tiny bust which she had compressed since her girlhood in iron stays. Her broad plump face was as white as lard and the irises of her dull brown eyes were rimmed, like onyx stones, with bluish white. She always wore a wig of rich deep chestnut curls, pulled so far forward that wisps of her own grey hair escaped at the back.

'There, that looks better,' said Isabel, settling the wig at its proper angle. 'I can't think, though, why you don't have a white one. It would be far more becoming. Claude thinks so too.'

'I had beautiful chestnut hair when I was a girl,' said Mrs

Batchelor. 'I know I've nothing to be vain about now. But poor Fred always admired my hair.'

'You could order a white one in time for the funeral. It's a very good moment to make the change, don't you think?'

Mrs Batchelor's violet lips began to tremble again.

'It would be so expensive. And somehow I don't feel inclined to think about hair at such a time. It's all very well for you, dear. You still have a husband to care how you look.'

She craned her head forward and peered at Isabel's orchids.

'Excuse me asking. But are those real blooms you're wearing?'

'My cattleyas? Yes, of course they're real.'

'You will pardon my remarking on them, won't you?'

Isabel said nothing.

The old woman glanced round nervously and, in doing so, caught sight of the wreath.

'Oh, what lovely flowers. They must have cost a fortune. Did Claude? Poor boy, he shouldn't have afforded them with all the other expenses.'

She went over and fumbled the orchids with her puffy, veined hands.

'Oh, please don't,' cried Isabel. 'You'll bruise them. If you want to know, they're from Claude's friends, the Shapiros.'

'How very kind of the Shap – Shapers . . . Oh, dear, I never can pronounce that name right. I must remember to thank them.'

'Claude will do that. They were sent to *him*.'

Mrs Batchelor sat down again. After a moment she said with timid boldness, 'I would like to ask a favour of you, Isabel.'

'What is it?'

'You've so much influence with Claude. He won't listen to me, I know. But I do wish he could be persuaded not to go to so much expense over the funeral.'

'He's quite definitely made up his mind. And you should know better than anyone what Claude is when his mind is made up.'

'All the same, I wish you'd try, dear,' Claude's mother went on with dull courage. 'If you could even get him to give up the idea of having the burial at Rookfield.'

'But why? It is a beautiful idea. What could be more appropriate? His father came from that part of the world. People should always be buried in those charming little country churchyards if there's any possible excuse. There's something so sordid and impersonal about these great hideous London cemeteries.'

'I don't deny that Rookfield is a pretty spot,' said Mrs Batchelor without enthusiasm, 'but all the same, Isabel . . .'

'I wish you'd say straight out what's on your mind.'

'Well, it's something one hardly cares to mention.'

'Oh, for goodness' sake, say it!'

With a great effort Mrs Batchelor approached the point.

'It's like this, Isabel. I know you don't think much of some of Claude's relations on his father's side. And I'm not saying for a minute they've got a position like Claude has. But some of them have done quite well in business. And they do notice things so. I'm sure you wouldn't want them to have any opportunity of looking down on Claude.'

'What on earth do you mean?'

'I don't know how to put it without you misunderstanding me. But my sisters, the little aunts, as you call them, they're very countrified. And Paget's Fold . . . it's hardly more than a cottage and not at all stylishly furnished. Then Cousin John Hoadley . . . he does speak so very broad.'

'I suppose you mean,' said Isabel, 'that you're ashamed of your relatives.'

'There, I was afraid you'd misunderstand me. It's only that I wouldn't wish anyone to feel embarrassed.'

'I've always found the aunts and John Hoadley perfectly charming.'

'I know, dear. It's always surprised me that you thought so much of them,' murmured Mrs Batchelor.

'But apparently, though they're good enough for me, they're not good enough for people like Sidney Gould and Horace Batchelor. Really, you have the strangest ideas.'

'Don't mistake my meaning, Isabel. You make allowances for their being simple people. But Horace Batchelor, he always was jealous of Claude from a boy and he judges everything by show.

He fancies himself a lot now that he's bought himself a motor-car and is so intimate with Sir Rex Popham.'

'Popham,' exclaimed Isabel, closing her eyes as if the name made her feel faint. 'You can hardly expect *me* to be impressed.'

But Mrs Batchelor stuck to her point with surprising obstinacy.

'Horace has never been to this house where everything's so nice. Now if the funeral were to take place in London . . .'

Isabel cut her short.

'I tell you Claude has made up his mind. And I entirely agree with him.'

Mrs Batchelor sighed and folded her hands in resignation.

'Then there's nothing more to be said.'

The old woman looked so meekly hopeless that Isabel said more gently, 'He really is right, you know. There are some things you don't quite understand.'

'No. I daresay not.'

'Just as some people have no ear for music or can never pronounce a foreign language.'

'We all know you have a great many advantages, dear. You could have looked much higher than Claude.'

Isabel was silent.

'Still you couldn't have a truer, kinder husband,' the old woman went on. 'I hope you'll never find yourself placed as I am, all alone in the world.'

'You can't say you're alone while you have Claude.'

'Yes, indeed, Isabel. I know I should be thankful. But poor Fred and I . . . we were together nearly fifty years.' Her onyx eyes filled again. 'I can't get used to the idea that he's gone.'

The fat face under the wig was that of a stupid child who has been cruelly used. Isabel tried to feel pity for her mother-in-law. But she could only feel sorry for the situation, not for the person.

'Do lean back and be comfortable,' she said, putting a footstool under Mrs Batchelor's feet. 'I'm sure Claude would like you to have a glass of sherry.'

'No, really, please. Is Claude gone out?'

'Yes.'

'Poor Claude. It all falls on him. And he feels this so much, though he doesn't show it. He did so worship his father, ever since he was a little boy.'

'He was certainly a wonderful son.'

'To both of us, Isabel. No one will ever know all Claude's unselfishness. In the bad times when we had the shop and things went wrong, not through any fault of Fred's . . .'

'I know, I know,' said Isabel, trying desperately to be patient. Mrs Batchelor blew her nose.

'I know you don't like my mentioning the shop. But trouble does bring things back so.'

'I wish you could stop thinking once and for all about those awful times.'

'Claude says he wants me to stay on here just the same. But I shouldn't want to be a burden.'

Isabel was silent a moment. Then she said very amiably, 'Have you ever thought of going to live at Paget's Fold? It's so lovely and peaceful down there. And it would be so nice for you to be with your sisters.'

But Mrs Batchelor's obstinacy returned.

'Somehow I never did seem to care for the country. And I don't think it's good for my rheumatism. I've always thought Paget's Fold was damp.'

'The aunts never complain.'

'I daresay you get used to it if you've lived there all your life. And then Sophy and Leah have got very set in their own ways. I doubt if they'd really want me.'

'Oh well, it was only a suggestion. Of course if you don't want to go . . .'

'I'm not in the habit of consulting my own wishes. May I ask if Claude has mentioned such a thing?'

'We haven't discussed it.'

'Oh dear,' said Mrs Batchelor, tearful again, 'how much better if it had been me that had been taken.'

Isabel began to put her needles and cottons very carefully back in her workbox.

'I suppose most women want to die before their husbands,' she said in a neutral voice. There was a pause during which Mrs Batchelor sniffed and composed her trembling face.

'You've been doing a lot of sewing, I see. Mourning makes so much work, doesn't it?'

'I think the whole idea of mourning is horrible,' said Isabel. 'I was saying so to Claude just now. I shall wear black till after the funeral and not a day longer.'

'I know you have very modern ideas, Isabel. Yet I seem to remember that when the King died in 1910, you wore black for quite a long time.'

'That was court mourning. There are still one or two things my family expect me to do. Perhaps you have forgotten that my grandfather had a post at court.'

Mrs Batchelor was silent, but not because she had forgotten about Isabel's grandfather.

'In my day things were different,' she said. 'We went into deep black even for quite distant relations. Someone in my family or Fred's was always going so after I was thirty I took to wearing black always. My looks had gone by then and it saved the dyeing.'

Isabel shuddered.

'How horribly depressing. Didn't Mr Batchelor object?'

'He didn't altogether like it but he was glad of any little money I could save. He tried to comfort me by saying I looked slimmer in black.'

'Poor Mrs Batchelor. Of course black is kinder to some figures,' said Isabel, unconsciously running her hands over her own beautiful body. 'Personally I look my worst in it. It doesn't suit my skin.'

'It's wonderful how you've kept your youthful figure, my dear. Of course you didn't have to be on your feet directly after your confinements as I did.'

'For heaven's sake,' Isabel burst out, 'aren't there enough ghastly things at the moment without remembering all that?'

'I'm sorry, Isabel. I didn't mean to say anything to grieve you.'

'Birth and death! One's as crude and horrible as the other!'

The old woman looked frightened.

'You say such strange things sometimes, Isabel. I don't always follow you.'

'Claude's father would have understood. He hated ugliness of all kinds.'

'Yes, indeed, so he did. Poor Fred,' Mrs Batchelor sighed. 'You remember we had to get rid of one of the nurses because he objected to her teeth. And what a handsome man he was. I've even heard you say, Isabel, how distinguished he looked. Ah, all the girls were in love with him when he was young. I never expected him to choose me, even though there was the little bit of money. Still, I suppose not everyone was willing to marry a deaf man.'

'He couldn't have had a more devoted wife,' said Isabel politely.

'I certainly studied to please him. But then in my day women took it for granted they should give way to their husbands.'

'Didn't that make the men rather selfish?'

'I'm sure I don't know, dear. Certainly Fred didn't pay me all the attentions Claude still pays you after all these years. Ah, you're lucky in your husband, Isabel. No doubt it's natural for a mother to think so but it isn't only me that says it.'

'I who say it,' said Isabel absently.

'I beg your pardon. I often wish for Claude's sake I'd had more education. But we thought it enough for a woman to be able to cook and sew and run her husband's house economically.'

'My mother,' said Isabel, stifling a yawn, 'spoke four languages perfectly and couldn't so much as boil an egg.'

She stood up, gathered up her hat and her workbox and moved towards the door.

'Forgive me. I must go and arrange about Clara's room.'

Mr Batchelor's dull eyes brightened.

'Then dear little Clara *is* coming home for the funeral.'

'That's what you wanted, isn't it?' said Isabel smoothly.

'It wasn't for me to say. Her Daddy wished it, I know. But I thought perhaps you . . .' Suddenly she noticed something and broke off.

'Isabel,' she said in a frightened voice, 'the shawl. It's fallen off the looking-glass. And I'd made sure I'd put it up so it couldn't.'

'I took it off, if you want to know.'

'But, dear, surely you know it brings bad luck to the whole family. A looking-glass uncovered when there's a corpse in the house.'

Isabel's suppressed rage broke out at last. Her face turned dead white and her nostrils quivered as she said in a voice of fury, 'This is beyond anything. I am not to look in a mirror for three days because of some absurd peasant superstition. Am I mistress of this house or am I something rather less than a housemaid? Yes, go and whine about me to Claude. As if I cared!'

She swept a heap of clothes off a chair and flung out of the room.

Mrs Batchelor's face, at first terror-stricken, assumed a look of patient malice. As soon as she was sure Isabel had gone upstairs, she went over to the fireplace and, with clumsy movements of her short arms, replaced the black shawl over the glass.

Chapter Three

For the next few hours, Claude had no time to think of his grief. Yet all the time he was interviewing registrars and undertakers, ordering flowers or writing letters at his club, he was preparing for the moment when he would have to feel its full weight. One commission he left to the last and, just as the sunny, windy spring afternoon was beginning to fade, he presented himself at the door in the bleak façade of Oratory House.

It was nearly eight years since he had taken the decisive step of his life and become a Catholic. His colleagues at St Mark's had been amused, dismayed or bewildered. None of them had thought of him as a man likely to go through any kind of spiritual crisis; he had seemed, at thirty-five, too comfortably settled in his profession, his opinions and his general way of life. Till then, like most of the other masters he had professed a tolerant agnosticism, talked rather daringly in the Common Room and lived blamelessly. From the point of view of his career his conversion was sheer insanity. He had already been approached with offers of headmasterships by two or three minor public schools and the governors of St Mark's had their eye on him as a possible successor to Doctor Cavell. As a Catholic he could never hope to be more than an Assistant Master for the rest of his days.

There had been no question of his having to leave St Mark's; he was far too valuable an asset. He was a good classical scholar, he was popular and presentable and, above all, he had a genius for coaching. Year by year scholarships and exhibitions were won by Marcians who had seemed the most unlikely material till they had passed through 'Batchelor's mill'. Doctor Cavell had dealt with the matter with great diplomacy. As a clergyman of the Church of England, he had mildly, but firmly, deplored Claude's step. As a headmaster, he decided that it was now safe to offer him a rise of only fifty pounds instead of the hundred he had been contemplating.

Claude's conversion had seemed at the time sudden and even dramatic. It was in fact neither. Ever since Cambridge, where, to his mother's puzzled distress, he had given up all religion, he had been fascinated by the Roman Church. It had fascinated him then by the very things which gave it such a sinister aura in the eyes of his family. Intoxicated with Wilde and Pater, it had glittered for him with decadent splendours. He had occasionally gone to High Mass with a sense of delicious daring and had even read a paper to a College Society in which he had connected it with the Eleusinian Mysteries. It was not till he was well over thirty and had long ago abandoned this romantic attitude that he came to study it seriously. One of his favourite old pupils became a Catholic and induced Claude to come with him to a course of sermons by a Jesuit who was simply concerned to show the reasonableness of his Church's doctrine. Claude was impressed. He made up his mind to go into the whole subject but he did not, as his friend had hoped, ask for an interview with the Jesuit. It was not till three years later that he decided to put himself under instruction.

Night after night during those three years he had sat in his smoky study in Valetta Road after his last pupil had gone; a glass of whisky at his elbow and books of theology and controversy littered about his desk. As a boy, without any outside encouragement, he had set himself to master Greek and algebra. With the same patience he now set himself to tackle the Christian religion. He compared the claims of Lutheran, Calvinist, Anglican and Catholic as carefully as he had once studied the arguments for and against the unity of Homer.

Gradually it became clear to him that if he were to be a Christian at all, nothing would satisfy him but the Catholic Church. If its first premisses were granted . . . and he could find no positive grounds for not granting them . . . there seemed to be no flaw in its deductions. His mind was delighted by the subtle interrelation of its doctrines; he saw that nothing could be changed or mutilated without altering the delicate balance of the whole body. More and more it appeared to him as a living organism that had grown and was still growing according to a mysterious inner law. It was this principle of life that most impressed him, surviving and renewing itself through so many centuries in spite of weakness, corruption and greed. If, as it claimed, the source of that life was divine, then the Church had the right to speak with the scandalizing authority and he had no choice but to submit. Yet still he continued to hesitate.

The prospect of spoiling his career hardly weighed with him. If this was the truth about the nature of things, he must accept it and act upon it, whatever the consequences. Yet suppose that some day he should be convinced that, after all, it was not the truth? He knew himself well enough to realize that if he committed himself, it would be for life. All his loyalties had originally been based on convictions. Sometimes the convictions had wavered or vanished, but the loyalty had always remained. In becoming a Catholic he would be involving other people. Isabel, who would never have come to such a decision on her own, was willing to follow him. Catholicism seemed to her a poetical and aristocratic religion. Nothing would have induced her to wrestle with historical or doctrinal problems but she had already gone so far as to buy herself a crystal rosary and a black lace mantilla. There was the still more acute problem of Clara who was still under seven. The whole responsibility of 'bringing them over' rested on him.

There were grounds enough to make him hesitate, but the real cause of his delay went deeper. His mind was satisfied but his heart remained cold. He felt nothing that could be called a religious impulse; no craving for God, no awakening of faith. And so for months he had stayed suspended, tired with his years of collating evidence, convinced in his reason but impotent to act.

One Sunday evening he went alone to Benediction in the French church in Soho. Although he now knew its meaning, the service no longer impressed him as it had done in his Cambridge days. Usually insensitive to details, he was annoyed by the perfunctory movements of the fat, blue-jowled priest who gabbled the Latin in a strong Marseilles accent. In front of him knelt two old Italian women in black, stinking woollen shawls and the whole church reeked of stale incense and garlic. Bored and distracted, he became acutely aware of a girl beside him, a sallow, sullenly handsome girl in a suit which fitted her so closely that it seemed to be worn next to the skin. When she slowly peeled off her white kid gloves, the ringless hands against the dark stuff gave him the sense of deliberately exposed nakedness. Mixed with the smell of benzine from the gloves came the smell of sandalwood soap. She repelled and disturbed him; unable to attend to the droning of the rosary his mind fastened on her. With her deep-lidded eyes and pale lips she had a look of Isabel and he guessed that the body under the severe suit would have the same fluid softness. Suddenly, without warning, the demons of his imagination leapt on her, stripping her, using her with a cold brutality of lust. He was not looking at her, but, as if she had guessed his thoughts, he felt her shift further away from him.

The service came to an end. An acolyte put out the candles one by one till only the red sanctuary lamp burnt on the altar. The Italian women shuffled out in their felt slippers; he stood up mechanically to let the girl pass him; he heard her high heels tapping down the aisle. The last footsteps died away; the door creaked to; he was alone in the empty church.

For half an hour he knelt in a rigidity of despair that was like death, not attempting to pray, unable even to think. Then, very gradually, a faint warmth began to penetrate his numbness. He relaxed a trifle, unclenched his clasped hands and noticed that the knuckles were white. Slowly the faint thawing warmth grew in his heart as if someone, far away down a long passage, were bringing a light. He stared at the sanctuary lamp as if its red bead of flame were the one point of contact with the world of sanity and hope. Then he became aware, not with his mind or his sense but with some faculty never awakened before, of an intense personal presence in the church. Words formed themselves so clearly in his brain that it was as if someone had spoken. They were words he had read a hundred times in the Gospel without attaching more than the most general meaning to them. 'I am the way and the truth and the life.' Now they broke on him like an illumination. It was as if the living Christ offered Himself here and now for his acceptance or refusal. Christ was the key that could unlock his prison of frozen isolation and the key was his for a single act of faith. He buried his face in his hands, muttering over and over again, 'Lord, I believe, help Thou mine unbelief.'

His moment of experience had quickly passed but he had had no more doubts or hesitations. The next day he asked for a priest to instruct him and six months later he was received into the Church. Isabel was conditionally baptized with him and Clara a few weeks after. Since then he had behaved with a steadiness unusual in converts, showing no fanatical fervour in his early days and no relaxing when the novelty had worn off. His religion had profoundly influenced his habits and opinions, he was minutely faithful to all its observances but never again had he experienced that direct touch on his soul.

Neither of his parents had followed his example. Even his mother's blind adoration would not carry her as far as that though, after his conversion, she took to going to a very high church. His father had regarded religion as entirely a matter of nationality. Claude's step had seemed to him as peculiar as if he had decided to become a naturalized Italian. In vain his son had reminded him that, up to the time of Henry VIII, England had been Catholic. Frederick Batchelor had merely reiterated, 'All Roman Catholics are foreigners. I can't see why the Church of England isn't good enough for you. I don't hold with these foreign religions and never shall.'

In spite of his misery, Claude could not help smiling as he rang the bell of the presbytery to think how violently his father would have disapproved of his errand. For he had come to ask a priest to say Masses for the repose of his soul.

He was shown into a gloomy parlour furnished with a table, two straw-seated chairs, a prie-dieu, some Arundel prints and a 'Spy' caricature of Cardinal Newman. It reminded him inevitably of the still gloomier parlour at Farm Street, furnished on the same pattern, where, eight years ago, he used to go for his weekly instructions.

After a long wait, an old Oratorian father appeared. Claude explained, with the shyness he had never been able to shake off in the presence of priests, that, as his father had not been a Catholic, he presumed Masses could not be said for him by name but only for his own 'intention'.

'Oh no. We can mention his name. But they cannot be actual Requiem Masses, you understand. Are you by any chance a convert, Mr . . .?'

'Batchelor. Yes, Father.'

'Forgive me for asking,' said the old man kindly. 'I am a convert myself. I know how one feels at such times. My own father was an Anglican clergyman. When he died I kept thinking, "Here am I, a priest, and I could not give him the Last Sacraments." But I remember him every day in my mass.'

Claude felt his throat contract. He could only nod and take the warm, shrivelled hand the old priest held out.

'There is nothing I can say to comfort you,' said the other, 'except what you know already, that every man who sincerely follows what lights God gives him belongs to the soul of the Church.'

'I don't think my father ever asked himself questions. He was a very simple man.'

'Well, we know what Our Lord said about children.'

After a few minutes' talk, Claude asked if he could go into the church.

They walked down a gloomy stone passage and entered the Oratory by a side door. After the austere parlour, the great ornate church with its coloured marbles, its silver lamps and its mounds of lighted candles seemed almost theatrical. He felt exposed and ill-at-ease as, having made a stiff genuflection, he stood fidgeting with his hat and muttering some kind of thanks in a whisper to the priest. The other replied in exactly the same voice he had used in the parlour. This and the way he came into the church, as if merely passing from one room of a house to another, gave Claude a peculiar reassurance. Here was a man whose life was all of one piece. Their conversation had lasted only a few minutes, he had been offered in words no more than pious commonplaces, yet when the old man left him, the ,reassurance lingered like a track of warmth in the air.

Walking slowly down the church, looking for an empty side-chapel, he came to the bare black and white altar of Our Lady of Sorrows. There he knelt down, put his face in his hands and at once broke into the painful choking tears of a man who has almost forgotten how to weep. After a time he no longer attempted to control them; they rose, collected and fell in a regular rhythm as blood wells from a wound. For the wound was deep, deeper than anyone he knew realized. No one else would weep like that for Frederick Batchelor. For three years he had been hardly more than a living doll and most of his life he had been a total failure. But he had been the one person whom Claude had loved without asking for any return.

It was an incurable love for it had been born in disillusion. Until a certain summer afternoon not long after Claude's eighth birthday, he had merely admired his father as a powerful, all-wise being. Even his deafness had seemed a splendid and mysterious attribute, giving something oracular to his irrelevent replies to a small boy's questions. On that particular afternoon he had been sitting under the counter of his father's shop and playing his favourite game of pretending that he owned it. He could not see the customers but he knew them by their voices and amused himself by guessing what each had come to buy. His father seemed even more deaf than usual that day; he moved uncertainly, often knocking a tin or a bottle off its shelf. The customers too seemed to be behaving oddly; never had he heard so many complaints and impatient raps on the counter. Even his father's voice sounded strange. Not only was he talking a great deal and laughing when there seemed nothing particular to laugh at, but he was running all his words together just as Claude himself did when excited. Suddenly an indignant woman left the shop, slamming the door behind her so that the bell rang like an alarm; then he heard young Goatcher the assistant and Harry the errand boy giggling together and muttering something he could not catch. The next moment there came a heavy thud and the boys stopped giggling. Claude jumped up and peered over the counter. His father was lying full-length on the floor, his eyes closed and his face ashy. Claude was too frightened to say anything. When his mother came fussing in from the parlour behind the shop, he crouched down again in his hiding place. Harry and Goatcher carried his father through into the parlour while Mrs Batchelor mounted guard over the street-door. When they came back, he heard her say 'It's a kind of attack your master has sometimes. I daresay the heat has been too much for him.'

Claude had guessed from her voice that she did not believe what she said and from the way Goatcher answered 'There's no denying it's a hot day' that he did not believe it either. No one talked of sending for a doctor. When his mother had gone, Goatcher and the errand boy began to talk.

'What she ought to have said was 'It's a thirsty day'', eh?'

''Taint no business of yourn, young Harry.'

'Reckon it's most people's business. I warn't born yesterday, Bert Goatcher. Everyone round here knows what old Batchelor's trouble is. Long before I come into this shop, I knew all about it.'

'Well, there's no call to screech so. The Missus 'ull hear you.'

'Why don't she do what my mother does to my Dad Saturday nights? Puts him out in the yard and turns the pump on him, that's what she does.'

'It's like this, Harry,' said Goatcher patronizingly. 'Mr Batchelor, he's a poor, feeble sort of chap. Can't hold a tiddly drop no more than a woman hardly.'

Harry snorted.

'Proper drunk he was, eh? My Dad'll laugh outway when I tell him.'

Claude had listened, shocked and fascinated. He could only grasp that his father was in the habit of doing something that gave people like Goatcher and Harry the right to jeer at him. At last he jumped up and shouted, 'I heard you . . . I heard every word.'

'Little pitchers has long ears,' sneered Harry.

'You shouldn't dare . . . you've no right,' Claude spluttered.

'And you ain't got no right to spy on your elders and betters, Claudie,' said Goatcher.

'You wait . . . you just wait,' Claude was nearly choking with rage and misery. 'No one's going to laugh at my father. When I'm grown up, I'll show you, I will.'

'Go it, Claudie,' mocked Harry.

Goatcher gave him a cuff. 'Leave the kid be. Claudie, you run along to your Ma.'

Still muttering, 'I'll show you,' Claude had run, not to his mother but out into the garden. Up and down the lawn where he played his endless solitary games of croquet, the blue ball against the red, he had stumped with his eyes screwed up to keep the tears back and his hands clenched in the pockets of his home-made jacket. It was a blazing June day and he had never again been able to smell sweet peas or the faint reek of manure from a strawberry bed without remembering that afternoon. He had not been angry that day or any day since with his father, only with anyone who dared to jeer at him. Pacing furiously up and down the tiny parched lawn, he made up his mind that he would show, not merely Harry and Goatcher but the whole world, that Claude Batchelor's father was not to be laughed at. He would grow up as soon as he possibly could; he would work very hard so that he could look after his father and make everyone respect him.

He had kept his promise. The business at Hamling went bankrupt. Claude won a scholarship to Dulwich and his father, in partnership with a brother, opened another grocer's shop in the neighbourhood or the school. By the time Claude was sixteen the second business had also failed. While still a schoolboy himself, he set up as a coach to younger or less bright ones. He was so successful that he was soon able to raise his fees a shilling to half-a-crown an hour.

After his second bankruptcy, Frederick Batchelor thankfully decided that he was not cut out for a business man. For some years he managed to get intermittent jobs in city offices. The exquisite copperplate writing which was his one accomplishment and the deafness which stopped him from wasting his employers' time in conversation made him an ideal copying clerk. But, after a few months in any firm, he would have one of his drinking spells, insult someone in authority and be dismissed.

As soon as Claude was established as a master at St Mark's, with a regular flow of private pupils, he had made his father give up all attempts to work. Long before he afforded himself any luxuries, even in the days when he had expected Isabel to dress on twenty pounds a year, it had been his joy to buy expensive things for Frederick Batchelor; silk socks, handmade shirts, good cigars to smoke after his Sunday lunch. No sooner had his father entered on this career of being spoilt and cherished than he gave up his drinking bouts. He thoroughly enjoyed an occasional glass of port or madeira but he never again touched spirits. Gradually he became exactly what Claude had always dreamt he should be, an extremely distinguished-looking old gentleman, known and respected throughout the neighbourhood. Tall and thin, with small bones and delicate hands, he had always seemed as out of place among the stocky, coarsely-built Batchelors as a crane in a flock of geese. As his hair grew white and his features still finer-drawn with age, the freakish elegance of his appearance became more and more marked. He and Isabel took a connoisseur's interest in each other's looks and clothes. His wife, who had grown plainer and heavier with every year of marriage, he had regarded as an ugly, but indispensable piece of furniture. He did not share her almost idolatrous devotion to their son. He was fond of Claude, he was grateful to him, but there had always been a cool detachment about his gratitude. The only person for whom Frederick Batchelor had really put himself out was his granddaughter Clara. He had stood up for her, right or wrong, against parents, nurses and all other authorities. She had revived in him the one passionate affection he had ever felt, which had been neither for Ellen nor Claude but for his first child, a girl, who had lived eighteen months and died the day before his son was born.

It was to Clara that Claude's thoughts turned first when his tears had spent themselves. Would she be able to understand anything of what he felt? He banished the thought as a distraction and, staring with dry, aching eyes at the picture of the Virgin over the sombre altar, he tried to pray for his father's soul. But he was too exhausted to pray. He was no longer even aware of his grief. Weariness gave him a counterfeit peace. Where his heart should have been, there was nothing but a cold empty space. He forced himself to recite set prayers for the dead, saying them as if for a stranger. While one part of his mind carefully spelt out the De Profundis, another hunted distractedly for something to fill that cold space under his ribs. Again and again it came back to the thought of Clara. How would he find her when he returned home? Would she be unhappy? Would unhappiness melt the ice that had so imperceptibly formed between them? Would she turn to him for comfort as she used to do when she was a child? His forced prayer petered out. Images began to compose and dissolve in his mind as they do on the edge of sleep. He saw Clara shaking back her fair hair, smiling up at him, slipping her arm through his as she used to do long ago on their walks. Innocent images, yet suddenly he forced himself to check them. There is a point at which a dream, while still sweet, becomes menacing. He made himself inhabit the cool, scentless black and white chapel, for, in another second, he might have been kneeling in a different church.

Chapter Four

Late in the afternoon, Clara arrived home. Isabel, whose quick ears had caught the first sound of the cab wheels, had slipped out of the room without warning Mrs Batchelor and was waiting in the hall.

'Darling,' she exclaimed gaily, throwing her arms round her daughter. 'How lovely to see something young and fresh.'

Clara, still clutching her luggage, stood stiffly in her mother's embrace. All through the long drive from the Convent she had been nerving herself to face a grief-stricken family. Relieved, but a trifle shocked, she could only say lamely, 'Hullo, Mummy.'

Then stooping down and fidgeting with her bag she muttered, 'Is Daddy very upset?'

'Yes, darling, of course. But don't let's think about all those sad things yet. Come along up to my room where we can talk properly. It's so wonderful to have you home.'

'Oughtn't I to see Daddy and Granny first?'

'Daddy is out,' said Isabel, adding untruthfully, 'Granny doesn't want to be disturbed.'

Whispering, 'Leave your luggage for Zillah,' she almost ran up the stairs, pushing the child in front of her. On the second landing, Clara stopped outside her grandfather's room.

'Is he there?'

'Yes, pet, but don't go in.'

'I know what dead people look like. I saw Mother Veronica at school.'

Isabel shuddered.

'Really. I didn't know nuns were so morbid.'

As she was hurrying Clara up the next flight, a plaintive voice called from the hall below, 'Is that little Clara?'

Isabel put her hand over Clara's mouth.

'There's no need to answer. You'll see her soon enough. I deserve to have you to myself for a moment after all I've been through.'

In Isabel's bedroom the blinds were not drawn. After the gloom of the rest of the house it looked wantonly bright. The last sunshine poured in like shafts of limelight, striking prismatic sparks from the litter of silver and cut glass on the dressing-table and showing up the worn places on the carpet. Isabel had modelled the room on a description of a French actress's boudoir that she had once read in a novel. Now the satin-striped paper was yellowish with age and its blue garlands unevenly bleached; the veneer on the imitation Sheraton had begun to blister and the pink satin curtains sagged from their rings. During the time that Isabel had coloured her daydreams with Loti and Lafcadio Hearne, she had put fans and kakemonos on the walls and an incense burner among the china shepherds on the chimney-piece. On a small table in a corner stood a crucifix festooned with a rosary, an empty holy-water stoup and a dusty strip of blessed palm. Near it was a prie-dieu over which was flung a négligée trimmed with matted swansdown. The windows were open, for Isabel believed in fresh air, but the room still smelt of scorched hair, camphor and Shem-el-Nessim.

Isabel, breathless from her climb, went straight to her dressing-table and considered herself in the mirror as if scanning the face of a beloved invalid. She seemed to have forgotten all about Clara as she plunged a puff in a bowl and shook it out so vigorously that a cloud of scented dust mingled with the motes in the sun-shaft. Between dabs at her face she said defiantly:

'If I want to have the blinds up, I shall *have* the blinds up. If anyone is shocked, they can *be* shocked. Anyhow, she can't climb four flights.'

Clara, who had taken up her stand by the bed, said nothing. She began to screw and unscrew one of the brass knobs of the bedstead. The huge bed with its black bars and polished rails was aggressively out of keeping with the rest of the room. It was an uncompromising middle-class late-Victorian bed, solid in workmanship and repulsive in design; planned to bear the weight of pregnancies, long illnesses and dead bodies.

Isabel wrenched herself from the mirror and faced Clara.

'Don't you think I'm perfectly right, darling?'

Clara blinked.

'Right about what?'

'Don't you ever listen to anything I say?'

'Sorry. I didn't realize you were talking to me. Yes, I expect so.'

'Why on earth don't you sit down instead of standing there like a stranger?'

Clara bit her lip and went on screwing and unscrewing the brass knob.

'I'd rather not. I've been sitting for hours in that cab.'

'I wish you wouldn't frown like that, darling. You'll ruin your nice forehead. Do you know you've got two quite definite lines over your nose already? And you're only fourteen.'

'Nearly fifteen,' Clara corrected her, still frowning.

Isabel gave a whimsical sigh.

'Imagine my having a daughter who's nearly grown-up . . . or thinks she is. But I'm not going to be one of those horrid mothers who are jealous of their daughter. I want you to be as pretty as possible.'

Clara blushed and made a face.

'It's no good, Mother. I'll never be pretty.'

'You could be if you'd take a little trouble.'

It was Clara's turn to sigh. The conversation was taking an all too familiar turn but she could think of nothing to say to deflect it.

'What's the matter, Clara?' Isabel asked impatiently. 'Is it Grandfather or what? Of course it's very sad for *us* but we ought really to be glad for him.'

'Yes, I expect so,' said Clara politely without raising her long fine eyelashes.

'It's quite right and natural you should be sorry. He adored you. But I assure you you don't feel it any more than we do.'

'Daddy will really mind most, won't he?'

'Yes, I daresay. It's such a dreadful thing to lose a parent. Of course I never knew my mother. She died when I was a tiny baby, poor thing. But I've felt the loss all my life. And I was only ten years older than you when my father did and I had no one. After all, Daddy still has Granny.'

'You were married, though, weren't you?'

'Ah, darling. But no one can ever replace a parent. You'll realize that yourself some day. A *long* time hence, let's hope.'

Clara became very intent on the knob.

'We shall both have to be very kind to poor Daddy, shan't we?'

Clara seemed not to have heard but she gave the knob such a violent twist that it came right off.

'Sorry. I can put it back.' She began to do so.

'That wretched bed. I wouldn't mind if you pulled the whole thing to bits. But it seems to be indestructible like all ugly things.'

'Granny and Grandfather gave it you for a wedding present, didn't they?'

'Of course they did. I've told you so a hundred times. It's got Granny's appalling taste written all over it. Really, darling, you seem very absent-minded today.'

Clara made a great effort and brought her mind into focus.

For the first time she opened her eyes wide and looked intelligently at her mother. The eyes were neither blue like Claude's nor brown like Isabel's, but a changeable grey flecked with hazel. When she opened them (she had a habit of keeping her lids half-closed) her whole face came to life.

'I suppose,' she said, 'that on the whole you'd really rather it was Granny who died.'

Isabel looked away. 'Clara . . . what a wicked thing to say. As if I'd wish anybody dead!'

'Still, if one had to choose,' said Clara undaunted, 'I've been thinking the same thing myself.'

'You naughty little thing.'

'Not that I've anything against Granny. But if someone had to . . .'

Isabel smiled.

'Well, darling, since you've said it. If someone had to . . .' She gave Clara a confiding look. 'It's very alarming sometimes to have an intelligent daughter. But sometimes it's rather nice. It's something we'd never dare to say to Daddy, isn't it? Though I shouldn't be surprised if he felt just the same.'

'Was it Daddy who wanted me to come home? Or everybody?'

'I didn't want it, darling. I longed to see you, of course, but if I'd had my way, you shouldn't have been let in for all this. Mothers understand some things better than fathers, don't you think? I've always said, in spite of everything, you were just as sensitive as I am.'

Clara was staring out of the window. She watched a pigeon flapping across the sky. The cement urns on the balustrade opposite were a rosy ochre in the late afternoon light.

'It's still missing,' she said suddenly.

'What? What's missing?'

'The urn that fell off last holidays. Don't they ever put them back?'

'Nothing is ever put back in this neighbourhood. West Kensington is going down and down. But of course I can't persuade Daddy to move There's a charming little house in Edwardes Square that I've got my eye on. Only there wouldn't be room for Granny. So that's out of the question. I *had* hoped

214

that now she would want to go and live at Paget's Fold with the aunts.'

'I don't think they'd get on very well, would they?' said Clara cautiously.

'They're her sisters. They're her own generation. Why should I have to put up with it all the best years of my life? Just think, Clara. Never to be able to have one's own way in the smallest thing. It's not as if I wanted much. A little white house with green shutters and window boxes and furnished as I like it instead of with their horrible old things.'

'Yes, it would be fun,' Clara agreed.

'I knew you'd understand. You've got my artistic tastes. The Batchelors haven't the faintest feeling for that kind of thing.'

Clara said with sudden anxiety, 'Will Daddy be home soon?'

'Not till dinner-time, I expect.'

'We should hear the door if he did, shouldn't we? Even up here?'

'Certainly. If he makes his usual clattering. But he's not at all like himself today. It's rather dreadful to see him.'

Clara turned white.

'What on earth am I to say to him?'

'Just be your nicest, most natural little self. You can be a very sweet Clara when you want to be.'

'I'd better go down and get washed and changed, hadn't I?'

'There's heaps of time. Why are you always so anxious to run away from me? All this time you've been standing there like a statue, obviously dying to get away. You haven't so much as taken off your hat and coat.'

Clara obediently pulled off her outdoor clothes and threw them on the bed. Her face was blank and set. The tight felt hat had flattened her hair and left a jagged red mark like a scar across her forehead. She stood there stiffly in her high-necked, long-skirted uniform dress of navy serge as if before a tribunal.

'Why on earth are you wearing your school uniform?' Isabel demanded.

'The nuns made me. That bright blue thing I went back in doesn't exactly look like mourning, does it?'

'That awful serge. It's dreary enough to wear at the funeral.'

'Oh, Mother. It's dark blue, not proper black.'

'I suppose Daddy will insist. Whatever *can* you wear?'

'There's my new best dress, the black velvet. Only we'd have to take off the red sash and the lace collar.'

'Ruining it, of course. Still, I've had to ruin my lovely hat from Cécile's.'

'I'll go and get it, shall I?' said Clara, brightening at the thought of even a brief escape. For the last few months it had been misery for her to be alone with either of her parents. It was all the worse because she had no idea why this was and Clara was always frightened by anything she could not explain. There seemed to be a new creature growing up inside her, something still unformed and skinless that could not bear to be exposed to the light. The thoughts that nourished this inner self were too sacred or too silly to be told to her father or mother and the mysterious creature was insistent, resenting interruption and demanding constant attention. When she heard her mother say 'All right, darling,' she gave a radiant smile of gratitude on behalf of the mysterious creature and almost danced out of the room.

No sooner had she gone than Isabel opened a drawer in her dressing-table and pulled out a paper-covered book from its hiding-place under a heap of crumpled underclothes. The book was called *The Diary of a Lost One*. On the cover was the picture of a man wearing evening clothes, an opera cloak, and the ribbon of an order, embracing a woman whose blue kimono had slipped off one bare shoulder. Quickly she found the page she had turned down and began to read. Immediately she was absorbed. She had read nearly a chapter of the cramped, broken print before she heard Clara's step on the stairs. In a flash another corner was turned down, the book slipped under the heap of underclothes and the drawer closed. When Clara came in with her dress her mother was sitting staring into space, her hands clasped in her lap.

'Sorry I was so long. I ran into Granny.'

'Were you long, pet?' said Isabel with her sad smile. 'I was thinking. I'm so used to sitting alone and thinking that I sometimes forget all about time.'

'It will be quite easy to alter,' said Clara brisky. She spoke more stoically than she felt. The black velvet dress meant a great deal to her; it was the first she had ever been allowed to choose for herself. For once she had enlisted her mother's support against her father. Claude had wanted her to have a childish blue cashmere. The old Clara would cheerfully have agreed but the mysterious creature had a craving for something grown-up and sophisticated and the mysterious creature was unscrupulous when it wanted something. The dress was cut almost like one of Isabel's, in a proper 1914 fashion, tight-fitting and short-sleeved with a frill of creamy lace at the neck and a vivid crimson sash. When Clara put it on, she felt at least nineteen and walked and spoke quite differently. In her bedroom she had even tried the effect with her plaits wound round her head, and, in a glass that did not show her legs, it seemed to her that she looked completely grown-up.

'The lace, the dash of colour, they're the making of it,' said Isabel with real concern. 'Poor Clara.'

Clara assured her carelessly that it didn't matter and she didn't mind. But, though nothing would have induced her to show it, she was glad of her mother's sympathy.

'You're my daughter in one thing, anyhow. You do like pretty clothes.'

'Most of us do at the convent,' said Clara, withdrawing again. 'I expect it comes of wearing ghastly uniforms all the time.'

'Take the horrid thing off and we'll try your frock on.'

'There's no point, is there? I've only got to unpick the trimmings.'

'I want to try the effect of a rather nice piece of black frilling I might let you have.'

'I'm sure it will do beautifully. There's no need to try the thing on.'

'Darling, you really are maddening, the way you argue over every tiny thing. You'd never dream of behaving like that with Daddy. Do as I tell you at once.'

Clara frowned and flushed as she began very slowly to unhook her high stiff collar.

'Absurd child. I believe you're shy of your own mother. It's these convent ideas I suppose. Nuns must have very peculiar minds.'

'It's nothing to do with the nuns,' said Clara uncomfortably. 'I'm sure to have a hole in my petticoat or something.'

She finished unhooking her uniform and stepped out of it in her white cotton petticoat and black woollen stockings. Isabel studied the immature body as if measuring it against her own finished curves. She herself was not tall, but she was so well-proportioned and held her head so high on her long neck that she appeared so. Neither was she slight. Her small bones were cushioned with flesh firm as just-ripened fruit. But her tapering wrists and ankles, and the light way she moved all helped to give an impression of slenderness.

There was no sign that the child standing there so stiffly, dangling her long frail arms would ever develop that sleek, harmonious shape. Though Clara was still thin, she was squarely-built, like her father, with broad shoulders and hips. The slender arms and legs were oddly matched with the heavier bones of the torso; she seemed to have the body of one person and the limbs of another. There were the same elements of lightness and heaviness in her face. Its contours, compared with Isabel's perfect oval, were carelessly drawn and her features contradicted each other. Her hair, brushed severely back, showed a high masculine forehead and small feminine ears. The modelling round the eyes was delicate but the dented obstinate chin and the blunt tip of the otherwise well-drawn nose seemed to have been added by a coarser hand. According to her mood, her face could look vivid, almost beautiful, or dull. The transformation was sometimes so sudden that in a moment not only the contours, but the size and colour of the eyes and even the texture of the skin would appear entirely different.

Now, as she stood exposed to her mother's critical stare, her body looked its most awkward and her face its most sullen and lifeless.

'You've grown,' Isabel said at last after surveying her daughter point by point. 'Just as well, perhaps. You'll need to be tall to carry off those hips and shoulders. Why, oh why, my pet, did you have to inherit the Batchelor torso? Thank goodness you've got decent arms and legs. You've got me to thank for those.'

Clara put up a slender, ill-kept hand and fidgeted with her

shoulder straps. Against the whiteness of her arms, the rough, reddened skin was as conspicuous as a glove.

'You must do something about your hands,' Isabel scolded. 'You can't have been using that lotion I gave you to take back to school.'

'Not allowed to,' said Clara with a gleam of a smile.

'Oh, these nuns . . . these nuns . . .' wailed Isabel, rolling her splendid eyes. 'And look at the dreadful way they do your hair. A noble brow is all very well but there are limits. Your hair's easily your best point.'

She pulled off the ribbons and untwisted the two thick plaits and drew the long rippling strands forward all about Clara's face and shoulders. The hair was thick and silky, almost pure gold in colour.

'Now you look more like my pretty child. But you'll deform your lower lip of you keep biting it like that. That petticoat needs letting out. You'll spoil your figure for life if you go on wearing it so tight across the chest.'

'I'll put the black dress on,' said Clara, blushing. She struggled ungracefully into it before her mother could make any more criticisms. When her head emerged, pink-cheeked and tangled, she looked an entirely different creature in spite of her red hands and heavy shoes and stockings. Against the black velvet sheath her arms and neck were very white and the mass of hair made her face seem small and soft.

'And people say clothes don't make a difference,' cried Isabel. 'Just come and look at yourself.'

Clara let her mother drag her to the long glass. She wanted to go on looking sulky but the dress would not let her. In spite of herself she smiled. She had an attractive, mischievous smile and a dimple in one cheek.

'Go on. Look at yourself,' insisted her mother.

Clara looked with pretended indifference but found she wanted to go on looking. The flushed girl in the glass with the loose, shining hair and the white neck was like a stranger.

'Of course it looks ridiculous with these shoes and stockings,' she said in a new grown-up voice.

'Thank goodness you're not *all* brains, my pet,' said Isabel kissing her. Clara accepted the kiss without flinching.

From downstairs came the faint crash of the front door. Clara froze like a scared rabbit.

'It's Daddy,' she said. All the life and colour had gone out of her face. She made for the door. 'I must fly. He might be coming up here.'

'Don't be so silly. Whatever does it matter?'

'I couldn't possibly let him see me like this. Not today.'

'Clara! Really, you're behaving as if you were out of your mind. Anyone would think you'd been doing something disgraceful.'

But Isabel found herself protesting to an empty room. She went out on to the landing and called angrily 'Clara'. There was no answer. In a burst of fury she took the girl's hat and coat and flung them after her down the stairs. Then she went back into the room and, having exchanged her usual questioning glance with her reflection, drew the curtains. She returned to the mirror again and sat for some moments, staring at herself and fingering the orchids on her dress. At last, with a sigh, she unpinned them, went over to the washstand and splashed some water into a glass. She took the orchids over to the little table in the corner and with a face half penitent, half mischievous, placed them in front of the crucifix.

Chapter Five

Soon after dinner, Isabel yawned and said she was too tired to stay up any longer. Old Mrs Batchelor had already gone to bed and the three others were sitting in Claude's study. Clara tried to make her escape at the same time but her father held her back.

'I won't keep you up long,' he said, as he closed the door behind Isabel and sat down again at his desk. He signed to her to take the armchair near him that her mother had left empty but Clara, appearing not to notice, went back to her corner. Barricaded from him by the two great desks that stood back to back and half-filled the room she felt safer.

'You'll forgive me if I just finish correcting this prose?'

'Of course, Daddy,' she said, thankful for the respite.

He nodded, shook some red drops from his fountain pen and went on ringing and underlining words in the exercise book before him. There was no sound but the ticking of the clock and the soft scratching of the nib. Clara sat rigidly in her corner between two bookshelves and wondered why she had not the courage to tiptoe over to the door and slip out. This was the moment she had been dreading ever since the arrival of the telegram. She was hardly yet able to feel sorry that her grandfather was dead. All her affection was overlaid with resentment at his having exposed her to this unbearable situation. She shut her eyes, trying hopelessly to persuade herself that the whole thing was a dream. She even prayed wildly for a miracle. She knew perfectly well that her crazy prayer would not be heard, yet, in spite of herself, she held her breath and strained her ears to catch some sound from her grandfather's room overhead; the impatient tap of his stick on the wall or his muffled cry of 'Ellen!' She still heard nothing but the clock and the metallic whisper of the pen.

When she opened her eyes again, the room, hazy with smoke, swam a little. Objects which she had known ever since she could remember seemed threatening, like things distorted in nightmare. The shelves filled with dingy bindings and black files, the dusty plaster casts of Plato and Athene, even the great faded plush armchair were all hostile. The smell of tobacco, ink and old leather which made up the permanent atmosphere of the study oppressed her like a drug. She felt her arms and legs growing thick and heavy and her eyes stiffening in their sockets. But why, she kept asking herself, should she be in such a state simply because she was alone with the person she cared for more than anyone in the world? Only a few months ago they had been companions and conspirators; her greatest delight had been to steal half an hour with him when her mother was not there. She had even wished that something terrible would happen to him so that she could prove how much she loved him. Now it had come and she felt nothing but terror and distaste. She glanced at his tired face, bent over the prose he was so methodically correcting. Why could she not get up this minute, go over and put her arms round him and say the perfect comforting words?

As if he felt the impact of her look, he stopped writing and raised his head. Then he screwed the cap on his pen and, with the gesture she knew so well, planted it upright in the bowl of lead shot in front of him.

'Come and sit over here, Clara.'

Reluctantly she moved into the great armchair that stood beside his desk. Its high padded sides hedged her in like a prisoner's dock; the light overhead poured mercilessly down on her face.

'You look white, my dear,' he said, considering her with kind, glazed eyes. 'This is a sad homecoming for you.'

'It's much worse for you,' she said in a high, artificial voice. To avoid his look, she stared straight ahead at the row of photographs on the mantelshelf. They stared back at her like the cardboard audience in a toy circus she had once had and their familiar faces seemed to have the same disquieting look of expectancy. They watched her with cynical interest, waiting for her to fall from the trapeze. The one that mocked her most was a photo of herself at seven which she had always hated Isabel, wearing flowing skirts and a great feathered hat, sat gracefully on a property balustrade and she herself stood beside her mother, stiff as a sentinel in her kindergarten gym tunic and an absurd hussar cap. The sight of that cap always embarrassed her though once she had been so proud of it that she had slept with it on her pillow. Now the stolid, glowering child, whose only trouble had been that she could never be a colonel of hussars, sneered at her from her security.

'Are you wondering where *his* photo is?' her father asked kindly. 'I know it's very weak of me. But just for a day or two I felt I couldn't bear it.'

His voice faltered. For a moment she feared that he was going to break down in front of her. Anger and reproaches she could bear but not that. Clutching the arms of the chair, she held her breath and began to count slowly as she always did when undergoing an ordeal. She knew she was expected to say something but no words would come. Why couldn't he understand without being told that there was nothing she would not do, cut her hair off, hold her hand in the fire, if it would give him any comfort? Why couldn't he realize that the one impossible thing was to speak?

The whirr of the clock striking half past nine gave her a scrap of courage. Time was still moving on, however slowly. At some point it must release her. She glanced at her father; he was apparently absorbed in stuffing tobacco into his pipe. He pressed the shreds down firmly with his short white fingers, using, as he always did when he handled things, a little more force than was necessary.

'Your mother,' he said, after the long pause, clearing his throat, 'your mother does not agree with me.'

'What about, Daddy?'

'That you are old enough to be with us all just now. She thinks it would have been better to leave you at the convent. What's your own opinion?'

'Of course I'd rather have come,' she lied.

'I hope you like the idea of his being buried in Sussex.'

'Oh, yes, I think it's a very nice idea.' She was lying again. Ever since she had heard it discussed at dinner, she had been hating the thought that the funeral was to be associated with Paget's Fold, the one place she connected only with happiness. Worse still was the thought of a slow, fifty-mile drive, sitting in silence, watching his miserable face.

'After all, he was a Sussex man. The churchyard at Rookfield is full of his and your grandmother's people. It seems only right for him to be with them.'

'Yes, of course. How will the aunts manage with all those people?'

He eyed her a trifle severely.

'They will rise to the occasion as they always do. You know how wonderfully unselfish they are. They seem to take a real pleasure in putting themselves out for other people.'

'Yes, don't they?' she said almost brightly. She went on to ask some perfunctory questions about the arrangements, hardly listening to the answers. What was it he had really kept her back for? Soon she could feel that her careless questions were beginning to irritate him. Perhaps it would be a good thing to let him get angry with her. After all, she was used to that. When he was annoyed, he spared her no more than his other pupils. She had been through plenty of bad moments of that kind in this very room and she could bear those. She whispered to herself '*un mauvais quart d'heure*', unaware that her lips were moving, though she felt a muscle twitch in her cheek and put up her hand to hide a silly, nervous smile.

'Were you going to say something, Clara?'

'No, Daddy, really.'

Try as she would, she could not control her face. She knew it had taken on the expression he most disliked, with her eyelids drooped and her lips, in the effort to keep from trembling, set in a superior smile.

'You were looking at the clock. Perhaps you would like to go to bed.'

Not daring to say 'Yes' she shook her head.

He sucked at his pipe.

'I'm inclined to think your mother was right after all when she said you were too young to understand the meaning of death.'

Caught off her guad, Clara said contemptuously, 'As if Mother knew everything about me.'

'That is not the tone to use when you speak of your mother.'

He drew fiercely at his pipe. When he spoke again he had mastered his annoyance.

'I was thoughtless enough at your age, heaven knows. And long after. But it wasn't till today that I realized how bitterly one regrets the things one might have done for a person and didn't do.'

'But you were always so good to Grandfather,' she said warily. 'Everyone said so. He was always saying so himself.'

'Never good enough. Never good enough.' He sighed. 'My dear child, if I only knew how to spare you that kind of remorse.'

She made a great effort to meet him.

'It's so difficult sometimes,' she said, speaking almost naturally, 'to know what other people *do* want.'

He re-lit his pipe.

'It's usually obvious enough if one takes the trouble. I don't want to give the impression that your mother has been complaining. Far from it. But couldn't you make a little more effort?'

Clara froze again.

'I'll write oftener from school if you like.'

'I know she would like you to be rather more affectionate in your manner towards her. She is devoted to you and often, I am sure, she feels lonely. I have so little time to give her. You're old enough now to be a real companion for her.'

Was it possible he had kept her back only to talk on the old theme of her behaviour to her mother? In her relief she said warmly, 'I *will* try to be nicer.'

'There's another thing, Clara. Your grandmother. Life is going to be difficult for her now.'

Without stopping to think, she said, 'Because of Mummy, do you mean?'

He frowned.

'I certainly meant nothing of the kind. That was a singularly uncalled-for remark.'

'Sorry.'

'Granny had never had much to make her happy. Now she is a widow, there isn't much for her to live for. She's so pathetically grateful for every half-hour you spend with her.'

Clara began to long more than ever for the day when she could get back to school. Though the discipline was strict and every minute of her time parcelled out and supervised, she felt free there. In the enforced silences of the convent day the mysterious creature could breathe and grow. At home, to be silent was taken for a sign that one was sulking. However full, however empty one's mind, one was expected endlessly to be making conversation. Forgetting everything but herself for the moment she said out loud:

'It must be rather a blessing sometimes to be deaf.'

He glared at her.

'That would be an extremely impertinent remark at the best of times. But with my father lying dead . . .'

'Oh,' she broke in, appalled, 'I'd forgotten about Grandfather's being deaf. Truly I wasn't thinking about Grandfather. Or Granny either.'

Claude's nostrils expanded with anger.

'Apparently not. Or about anything that I have been saying to you tonight. You seem to be incapable of thinking of anyone but yourself.'

'Oh, Daddy, please, I didn't mean it.'

'You had better go to bed, Clara. I apologize for having kept you up.'

She tried to speak but her lips began to quiver uncontrollably. Without warning, she suddenly burst into loud childish sobs. For some moments she cried so convulsively that she did not hear him come over to her or feel his hand on her hair.

'Clara, my dear little girl,' he said in a shy, gentle voice, 'Clara, my dear.'

She let him soothe her but she would not rest against his shoulder. She sat rigid, fumbling for her handkerchief, as wary as an animal that submits to fondling from fear.

'Don't cry any more.' He smiled wanly. 'Or should I say do cry? They say it helps.'

She blew her nose violently and rubbed her fist over her eyes. Her forehead was covered with red blotches and her eyelids swollen as if they had been stung by wasps. Clara had never been able to weep otherwise than awkwardly and explosively.

'I *hate* crying,' she gasped.

'Don't be ashamed of your feelings, my dear. They're right and natural. You were really fond of him, weren't you?'

She groaned inwardly. How could he imagine she was crying about her grandfather? There was nothing to do but nod her head and mutter, 'Awfully fond.'

He sat down once more at his desk. Taking one of the three pens from the bowl in front of him he began mechanically to jab it in and out of the shot.

'He was a remarkable man,' he said softly. 'Too delicate in all his tastes and instincts for the kind of life he was born to. When I was a little boy I used to think of him as a prince in disguise.'

Clara's tears were locked back now. She could trust herself not to break out again. But she was beaten and could now only play for favour.

'I've only seen a prince once. Hedwig von Eisenspach's father. He was awfully disappointing. Very short and fat. Grandfather looked as they ought to look.'

She was vile, she told herself, seeing her father's face brighten. She had said nothing about some quality in the little fat man which made her grandfather's brittle handsomeness and his famous 'manners' show up as mere gimcrack.

'It pleased him so much,' said Claude, 'to think you should be at school with a real princess. Often I can hardly believe it myself when I think of my own childhood.'

'She's not a bit exciting really. Oh, I know what you mean. It seems queer to me too. Everyone's awfully nice to me but I know I don't really belong.'

She looked at him anxiously, wondering if, once again, she had said the wrong thing.

'Perhaps I made a mistake,' he said thoughtfully. 'Perhaps I should never have sent you to a school where the other children have such a much more impressive background. Ever since we became Catholics, it was my dream to send you to Mount Hilary. But was it fair? I should be very much distressed if you came in any way to look down on *his* people. Or your grandmother's.'

'I'm awfully fond of the aunts and Uncle John Hoadley. And Blaze. Oh, lots of them,' she said evasively.

'I'm counting on you to be your nicest, most natural self on Thursday. With everyone, even Aunt Louie and Cousin Horace. I don't deny I find those two a little trying, myself.'

'Am I usually so awful with them?' sighed Clara, deflated by the image of that nicest, most natural self she could never recognize well enough to impersonate.

'No, of course not. I just wanted to ask you to make a special effort . . for *his* sake. Thursday will be a particularly trying day for your mother. You know how sensitive she is. So many things jar on her.'

'I do understand,' she said, realizing that he was appealing to her. 'I'll make an extra special effort.'

In spite of herself, she could not help yawning.

'You seem very tired.' It sounded like an accusation.

Swallowing another yawn she brought out bravely, 'Was there something special you wanted to say to me, Daddy?'

'As a matter of fact there was. But, as you seem so sleepy, perhaps we'd better leave it. It was just an idea I had.'

'Please do tell me.'

It was his turn to be embarrassed.

'I didn't quite like to suggest it even to your mother. You see, on religious matters, you're my authority. You are being trained in Catholic ways as neither your mother nor myself were able to be.'

Clara waited apprehensively. Only last year she had still been quite unselfconscious with him about religion. Lately in the holidays she had tried to avoid going to church alone with him. Religion had become part of her most secret life; it was deeply concerned with one aspect of the mysterious creature.

'And how happy it makes me,' he went on, 'to know that you are being so well grounded in the Faith. I don't know when I've felt so grateful, so deeply impressed as on the day of your First Communion. If ever I were to suffer from doubts, I think it would be enough to remember the look on your face that morning.'

'What did you want to ask me, Daddy?' she said stolidly.

'Even though he wasn't a Catholic, would there be any objection to reciting the Office of the Dead for him?'

'Oh no. I can't see any reason why you shouldn't.' Her voice was quite cheerful with relief. Whatever it was she had feared was not going to happen after all. She had worked herself up into a panic for nothing. She stood up. 'Do you mind if I say good-night, now, Daddy darling?'

He looked disappointed.

'Not, of course, if you're too tired. But my idea was that the two of us should go up and say it together . . . beside him.'

She was so horrified that she could only echo blankly, 'Say it together beside him?'

'Isn't that what you did at the convent when your Mother Veronica died?'

How could she explain the difference? She thought of the noble impersonality of that office chanted by the whole community in the chapel and she pictured the two o them kneeling in the cramped space by her grandfather's great bed. They would share a book; they would mutter the psalms self-consciously and stumble over the responses. She had a cruel impulse to cry out 'You have no sense of fitness.'

'Well, Clara, what do you say?'

She could only stare at him beseechingly.

'What is it, my dear? Are you afraid? He looks so peaceful,

there is nothing frightening. But the last thing I want to do is to harrow your feelings.'

Her look of desperation was almost impudent as she said, 'No, of course I'm not afraid.'

He stood up, pulled open a drawer and took out a black-bound book. Then, drawing her arm through his, he said, 'Thank you, my dear. We'll go up at once, shall we?'

Chapter Six

Old Mrs Batchelor's two sisters, the Misses Sayers, did not attend the funeral. They stayed behind at Paget's Fold to put the last touches to the cold luncheon which had taken them two days of anxious work to prepare. Cooking over oil burners in their dark stone-flagged kitchen, they had baked hams, roasted chickens and strained jellies till they were nearly worn out. It was the responsibility rather than the work that had tired them. They felt that Claude had conferred a great honour on them and had custard been burnt or piecrust heavy, Miss Leah and Miss Sophy would have blamed themselves all the rest of their lives.

Though the old ladies were sixty-eight and sixty-seven respectively and had lived at Paget's Fold since they were born, they never forgot that the house was not their own. Ellen had made it over to Claude on his twenty-first birthday and they looked on themselves simply as his caretakers. As he would not hear of their paying rent, they went to endless trouble to save him money on repairs. If a pane broke or a door came off its hinges, Miss Sophy got out her grandfather's old tools (he had been the village carpenter in the eighteen-thirties) and mended it according to the directions in 'Enquire Within Upon Everything'. Their joint income was about forty pounds a year but, sooner than accept the help Claude was only too willing to give them, they made a little extra money by teaching and dressmaking. Miss Leah, the elder, taught spelling and arithmetic to the children of the vicarage and the bigger farms;

Miss Sophy made dresses for the women for miles around. Her knack of fitting even the clumsiest figure and the beautiful finish of her work (her stitching was as neat and firm as a Frenchwoman's) kept up the demand in spite of the alluring readymades to be bought in Horsham and Brighton. Farmers driving in to Steyning market from other parishes would drop their womenfolk at Paget's Fold to plan or try on their new clothes. The dresses took her many evenings of hard work, for she was busy in house and garden all day, but, even for the most elaborate, she refused to charge more than five shillings. She and Leah could therefore never relax from the minute economy they had practised ever since they could remember. Their economy had nothing dreary about it for they had long ago turned it into an ingenious game.

They managed to find a use for the humblest and most unpromising objects. Old cotton reels were painted and converted into blind-cord tassels; corrugated paper was cut into strips, varnished and stuck round the walls as a dado or made into frames for pictures cut from the Christmas annuals. Even a cork had possibilities; fitted with a crochet jacket it became a decorative wasp-crusher. If Claude sent his aunts a box of chocolates, the chocolates themselves (eaten at the rate of two a day) were only part of the treasures they found in it. Each piece of tinfoil was carefully smoothed out to be used later to adorn a mirror-frame or hair-tidy; the paper shavings were kept for packing flowers, the ribbon trimmed their hats or tied back their lace curtains and the box itself did duty for years.

Leah, the elder, was thin, tense and earnest. She loved to store her mind with pellets of information from old encyclopaedias and magazines. In looks she was quite unlike either of her sisters. Her face, worn down almost to the bone, was narrow and well-shaped; her eyes, set in deep, shadowed sockets, were large and still bright and she had beautiful hair of a colour between flaxen and silver. Even when she was wearing her shabbiest working clothes and her garden clogs, she managed to preserve an air of frail elegance. When she was not looking anxious or disapproving, she had a charming faintly mischievous expression which was apt to mislead people into thinking that she had a great sense of humour. They soon found that the point of every joke had to be carefully explained to her and that she usually found it either cruel or ill-bred.

Miss Sophy, on the contrary, was plump, lively, quick-tempered and fond of a joke, good or bad. She thought Leah a paragon of learning and greatly admired her though she pretended to despise 'bookishness'. She read a great deal herself but in a way she never dared to own to Leah. Her one delicious indulgence was to retire to the bedroom they had shared since they were children, take a novelette and bury herself, till she was interrupted, in the loves of dukes and mill girls and the sins of high society.

Now and then the two old sisters pecked each other. Sophy would scold Leah for her didactic slowness and Leah Sophy for her frivolity but these birdlike scuffles did not affect their content with each other. They had become like a devoted, long-married couple, more amused than disturbed by their differences and resigned to the fact that neither could share the other's most passionate interest.

As the passing bell sounded, now clear, now muffled, carried on the gusts of the March wind from the church half a mile away, Miss Leah sighed.

'You should have gone to the service, Leah,' said Miss Sophy. 'I could have managed perfectly well by myself.'

'I don't deny I should have liked to go. But I couldn't leave you single-handed.'

'Two hands are better than four sometimes. I know you meant kindly, Leah, but you've been absent-minded all morning.'

'I'm sorry about the jelly glass,' said Miss Leah with dignity. 'I forgot how rapidly glass expands and that if the expansion occurs unevenly . . .'

'You poured the jelly in too hot, dear,' said Sophy briskly.

'No doubt I was careless, Sophy. Yet little accidents like that always make me think that a genius might have made them the occasion of some great discovery. If James Watt's mother had not let the kettle overboil . . .'

'I know. I know. We might never have had railways. A good thing too. Look at all the poor people who get killed because of them. I don't believe God meant us to go prying and peering into everything.'

'God would not have given us the faculty of discovery, surely, if He had not intended us to use it,' said Leah with mild severity.

'You clever ones have an answer for everything,' retorted Sophy. She was shocked to find herself scrapping with Leah on such a morning but she was tired and nervous. 'What about Adam and Eve? They wanted to know more than was good for them and look at the result of that.'

'Sophy, dear, I don't think we should let ourselves get involved in argument just now, do you?'

'Very well, Leah. Though you always say that when I'm getting the best of it.' Sophy put her head on one side, like a listening bird. 'Hark! The bell's stopped ringing.'

'It stopped many minutes ago,' asserted Leah.

'No. Only a moment. Your hearing isn't what it was.'

'My hearing is still excellent, Sophy,' said Leah, nettled for the first time. Sophy smiled but the smile vanished immediately and her faded, violet-blue eyes turned moist.

'Poor Fred,' she said softly. 'Sometimes when the wind was in the south like it is today he could just make out the sound of the church bells. Oh, the wickedness of that schoolmaster. Fancy boxing a little boy's ears so hard as to make him deaf for life.'

Her round face, crumpled yet glossy like a yellow apple that has only just begun to shrivel, was streaked with indignant pink.

'I am sure he never meant to do such dreadful harm. One has occasionally to punish children, boys especially. I myself . . .'

'Nonsense, Leah. As if you'd ever done more than rap their knuckles with a pencil.'

Miss Leah sighed. 'I daresay I have often hit harder than I should. I have no right to judge.'

'And it's not only the deafness that man will have to answer for,' said Miss Sophy, roused as she always was by any injustice: 'Who knows but what Fred's little weakness may have come from that? Think how cut off he must have felt. I wouldn't like to be that schoolmaster in the next world.'

Miss Leah sighed again. After a moment she said timidly, 'Sophy, if you meant what you said just now . . . that you can do the little finishing touches without me . . . would you mind if I went up to our room and read the burial service to myself?'

'You couldn't do anything better. Go along, dear.'

When she had gone, Sophy slipped back into the pantry, lifted the huge trifle from the cool brick floor where it had been standing all night and began decorating it with almonds and angelica. They had made just such a trifle for Fred and Ellen's wedding. She could see Ellen now with her plump narrow shoulders emerging from the frilled white petticoat and smell the hair-oil and the hot tongs on the chestnut ringlets as her sister bent down, stabbed a finger in the cream and licked it.

'Oh, you greedy,' Sophy muttered, just as if Ellen were still standing beside her. She had made Ellen's wedding dress; even at twenty that figure had been a problem to fit. Leah had been the pretty one, slender and white skinned, with big grey eyes and silky flaxen hair, yet no one had ever come near making her an offer. Sophy had often wondered why. Perhaps it was because she looked so delicate (their father had died young of consumption) and men did not want a sickly wife; perhaps merely because she frightened them with her air of aloofness and her bookish talk. Ellen was the only one who had determined to get a husband and succeeded. No doubt the tiny property had helped. Paget's Fold belonged to her and she owned fields and cottages that brought in about a hundred a year; she had flirted confidently till the day she set eyes on Fred Batchelor, the handsomest young man any of them had ever seen. How plain, how dull, how crushed she had become after all these years of marriage. When they were girls, Ellen had been bold and jolly, always giggling and tossing her chestnut ringlets, endlessly in trouble with Mamma over her behaviour with young men. She read the poems of Byron in secret; she got love-letters from the most unsuitable people; she made Leah and Sophy blush with her speculations about marriage and childbirth. Now not a trace of the old Ellen was left. Coarseness and liveliness alike had vanished with her flushed cheeks and bouncing curls, leaving a dreary pasty-faced old woman in a brown wig. In their childhood, Leah had been the one with the daring imagination. It was she who had planned their wildest escapades and practical jokes. Sophy could see her now, thin and long-legged, fearless as a gipsy, with her red cloak flying and her arms and legs always covered with bruises and scratches. She had become her present serious self almost overnight when she was fifteen, after Papa's death. Nothing remained of that other Leah but the faint mischievous expression that puzzled people so much. Carefully arranging the angelica in a lattice pattern (it had been circles for the wedding and, you never knew, Ellen might remember), Sophy realized that she had changed as much as her sisters. For, as a child, she had been quiet, shy and dull, tagging mutely after the others, not understanding their jokes and games, happiest sitting alone in her little chair with a picture book or a kitten. Now of all three she was the liveliest, hating to sit still, longing for someone to share her sense of fun, gay with people she knew though the old fits of shyness and melancholy often caught her in the company of strangers. Oddest of all, she had become the one to whom Leah and Ellen deferred on practical matters. Characteristically she put this down to her own faulty nature and often scolded herself about it. 'It can only be because you're so obstinate,' she told herself. 'If Leah weren't so unworldly and Ellen so meek, they'd never give way as they do.'

The trifle was ready and she carried it carefully to its place of honour on the sideboard. Paget's Fold had been built for a small farmhouse and the room they used for meals and all ordinary purposes had once been a large, stone-flagged kitchen. The front door, shielded by a threefold screen pasted all over with scraps, opened straight into it, as did also the doors to the stairs, the tiny dim green parlour, the dark kitchen that had been bakehouse and washhouse and the brick-floored pantry that still looked and smelt like a dairy. In spite of the draughts that eddied through these five old ill-fitting doors, the main room was as cosy as years of loving accumulation could make it. Layer on layer of wallpaper padded the walls till they were soft to the touch though the hardness of the stone floor could still be felt under the rag and patchwork rugs that almost covered the faded carpet Isabel had discarded ten years ago as too shabby for Valetta Road. Every chair had a flat plush cushion tied on with tapes to conceal its bareness; the old sofa was heaped with cushions stuffed with feathers laboriously collected from the green outside. Miss Sophy, straightening spoons and knives for the last time looked around it with affectionate pride. There was not an object in it which she did not love, from the pot of musk on the bamboo table in front of the hermetically sealed window to the spotty steel engraving of the execution of Strafford that hung over the sideboard. But at the thought of the strange eyes that would be soon looking and criticizing, her shyness returned. She was seized with a panicky desire to run away and avoid the whole thing. Then she reminded herself that Isabel and Clara would be there and her courage came back. They were her special favourites; Isabel even more than Clara now that the child was growing up so quickly. Claude's wife seemed like one of the heroines of her paper-backed novels come to life and Isabel repaid her devotion with an uncritical tenderness she showed to no one else. Isabel would support her and snub those loud-voiced Batchelor relatives who were 'rising' in the world and inclined to treat herself and Leah as figures of fun.

She glanced at the old grandfather clock; its dial, duck-egg green with age and covered with fine cracks, showed that it was nearly one. At any moment now the funeral party might return. The clock was still a person to her as it had been when she was a child; its heavy resonant tick sounded through the house like the beat of a heart. Last Monday night, without warning, one of the great leaden weights had dropped with a crash that woke both herself and Leah. She had brushed aside Leah's 'scientific' explanations; she was convinced that the clock had stopped at the very moment of Fred's death. Had it not stopped in the same mysterious way the night their mother died and only a little while before they heard the news that poor Bertie Hoadley, the good-looking cousin who had disgraced himself and been packed off to the colonies, had fallen over the ship's side and been drowned? As the hand jumped, she was oppressed by the thought that for the next two hours or more she would be imprisoned in a room filling with the fumes of wine, smoke and human beings. Recklessly she trotted into the kitchen, pulled on her heavy wooden clogs and slipped out through the back door into the garden.

She pattered up the wet brick path like a little hoofed animal, sniffing the sweet air. It had rained earlier in the morning and bright drops shook down from the trees n to her face and hair. This was the time of year she loved most, the middle of March.

After weeks of heavy snow, the wind had shifted suddenly; the thaw had run quickly, followed by two days of sunny, languid spring weather. Trees and hedges budded almost while you watched them though tufts of snow still lingered on the withered hemlocks in the ditches and in sheltered pockets on the roof. Clouds, in fleecy puffs or beaten out into long thin rifts, floated in a sky washed the purest, most transparent blue; high up a lark bubbled and just above her head a pair of thrushes flew busily to and fro, collecting twigs for their nest in the great walnut tree. She looked with a gardener's practical delight for every sign of green shoot or swelling bud. Her crocuses were out under the old apple tree; there was still a patch of snowdrops by the kitchen garden hedge. Forgetful of her best black skirt and the damp earth, she knelt down to touch them, the wind blowing her soft scanty hair, that she had pinned up so carefully for the occasion, into wild wisps. She picked a few snowdrops for Isabel, admiring their untarnished whiteness and delicate green scallops. Isabel loved flowers and, better still, she looked at them, which was more than most people did. In the summer holidays Sophy always ran out into the garden before breakfast to pick a rose or a pansy or a sprig of lemon thyme to lay on Isabel's plate. She was searching in her pocket for a wisp of bast to tie up her bunch when she realized that she was wearing, not her working skirt but her best, and that she had forgotten all about the funeral. Perhaps at this very moment, they were treading down the raw earth on the grave of a man she had known for nearly fifty years and had once been timidly inclined to love. She was shocked at herself. But, out here with the wind blowing and the wet grass shining, try as she would, she could not focus her mind on death. It was almost the first good gardening day of the year; she ached to grub about the beds and plan her spring sowing. Why should that be more disrespectful to Fred's memory than to sit interminably in a stuffy room watching Fred's odious nephew Horace overeat himself and listening to Louie's spiteful, jocular complaints? Gardening was out of the question, but, holding her snowdrops as carefully as if they were butterflies, she could not resst taking one more turn round the beloved half-acre. It was a rebellious act for Leah must by now have finished her Service and be hunting for her in every room.

She skirted the big oblong vegetable patch, bordered with currant and gooseberry bushes, and came down the path by the thatched shed against whose wall grew an espaliered nectarine and two or three pears. Pushing through the gap between the drenched laurels and a clipped hedge of arbor vitae she stepped on to the mossy lawn at the far end of which stood the walnut tree. Her mother had planted it when she was a little girl, nearly ninety years ago, and now, from a trunk like a triple pillar, it swelled out into a vast semi-circle of lichenous branches and twigs. Every year the leaves grew a little scantier but still each summer it formed a huge symmetrical cloud of green so that the house could be identified more than a mile away by the walnut tree, the biggest in the parish. She could not bear to think, that, however slowly, it was beginning to decay. Every winter now the gales split off dry branches and the common in front of the house was littered with broken twigs. Sophy rarely prayed for anything for herself but she often prayed that she would die before the tree had to be cut down. Paget's Fold would never be the same without it. It was a person to her just as the clock was a person; the spirit of the garden as the other was the spirit of the house. As she passed under it, she patted its trunk and tore away a strip of the choking ivy as a mother might tuck back a lock of child's hair. Beyond the walnut tree, some broken brick steps under a tangle of lilac and laburnum led to the two uneven strips of green in front of the house. A brick path divided them running from the gate in the iron palings that fenced them off from the common to the rickety wooden porch that was hardly more than a prop for the jasmine and French honeysuckle that climbed all over it. Beyond the gate, so old and loosely hung that the cows often pushed it open and walked into the front garden, the common, dotted with gorse bushes, sloped down to the main road and the scummy pond with its ring of elms. Paget's Green was large enough to give ample space to two farmhouses and half a dozen cottages and to pasture innumerable geese, cows and old horses. At all times of the year it was strewn with feathers; there was old Mrs Goatcher even now filling her apron with them. Miss Sophy had meant to slip past the house to her flower garden and the tiny orchard but, catching sight of Leah's profile at an upper window, she decided it would be wiser to move back to the gate and pretend to look down the road for the funeral party.

Her eyes fixed themselves not on the road but on the downs of sallow green and purple-brown fields beyond the ridges. Nye Timber, the one high point in the smooth swell, took the light differently from the rest and seemed to her to be made of a different material, of fine pale sand instead of worn green velvet. Today it was just that pearly lilac that had made her call it, as a child, the Heavenly Mountain. So it seemed to her still. She could not imagine a heaven that was not furnished with all the things she loved on earth. It was the downs she pictured when she said 'I will lift up mine eyes unto the hills'. Yet, though she loved them, she found them a little remote and frightening. As always, after gazing at them, she glanced back over her shoulder, to look at the house. She loved it, down to its very defects and discomforts; it shocked her to realize if Leah were to die she would suffer less than if the two of them had to leave Paget's Fold. In front the old pink brickwork, meshed in beams, was almost hidden by creepers and climbing plants. The box tree was much too high; it grew right up to one of the bedroom windows, blotting out all the light from the parlour so that you sat in a green gloom that smelt like a damp wood. The ivy was too thick; people were always warning her that it would pull the bricks apart. Often indeed it drove long sprays right into the rooms, through the deep walls and all those layers of paper. But she hated to cut it back; there was nothing she disliked so much as a naked-looking house. She thought with annoyance of all the people about to intrude on the old house's privacy and as she did so, she heard the sound of an approaching motor. Hurrying in, she was met by an indignant Leah.

'Sophy, what can have possessed you? Quick, take off your pattens. Your hair's all awry. And look – you've a great splash of mud on your good skirt. Sophy dear, how *could* you? Whatever will Claude think?'

Chapter Seven

The funeral guests, crammed elbow to elbow round the small table, had automatically herded into family groups; the Batchelor connections at Claude's end and the Hoadleys at Miss Leah's.

Clara had managed to attach herself to the Hoadleys. She wanted to be as far away as possible from her father for she could not forget the horrible thing that had happened in the cemetery. As he had stepped forward to throw the earth on the coffin, he had burst into tears in front of all those people and stood with his shoulders heaving and his face buried in his hands until her mother had taken him by the arm and led him away. She could not help feeling shame as well as pity. It was bad enough that Horace Batchelor and Aunt Louie should have seen him cry. It was worse to remember how he had stumbled away, blindly clinging to her mother.

Now, out of the corner of her eye, she could see him forcing himself to eat while the aunts coaxed him like a sick child.

'Claude, do let me give you a little more pie. I daresay you had a very small breakfast.'

'No, really, thank you, Aunt Leah.'

'I trust you don't find the pastry heavy,' she said anxiously.

He managed to smile.

'I assure you it is delicious. No one ever made such pastry as you and Aunt Sophy. But today you've surpassed yourselves.'

His cousin Horace scooped up a huge mouthful of pie and, with his cheek still bulging, held out his plate.

'If Claude can't do justice to it, here's someone that can. And I wouldn't say no to a slice of ham while you're about it, Claude. Time someone made a breach in it. Unless you've got it on sale or return of course.'

'Ah, there's no one could carve like my poor Fred,' said Ellen Batchelor, as Claude cut the ham. She had had two glasses of sherry to revive her after the ordeal of the long drive and the funeral and was in a state of melancholy benevolence. 'It was a pleasure to watch him with a ham.'

'Sliced it a shade too thin for my taste,' said Horace. 'That's right, Claude. Give her a good old hack.'

'Such carvers as Frederick are born, not made,' said Leah. 'Though I'm sure Claude carves very well. That was your father's favourite knife, Claude. I'm afraid I could never put such a fine edge on it as he could.'

'If the provision trade was a matter of slicing ham, poor old Uncle might have made a pile,' said Horace.

There was an uncomfortable silence; a few people looked anxiously at Claude's mother. But old Mrs Batchelor's air was almost as remote as Isabel's.

'Wonderful, Fred was with his hands,' she said, as if she had not heard. Everyone, except Horace and Aunt Louie Batchelor, put down their knives and forks and murmured agreement. 'I daresay some of you have seen those walking sticks he used to make. Dogs' heads and so on to the life. And done with nothing but an ordinary penknife. Then think of his handwriting. Everyone said he would have made a wonderful writing master.'

'We have a beautiful specimen of his work upstairs,' said Miss Leah. 'You remember, Clara dear, in your bedroom?' Clara nodded. 'I often bring it down to show people and it has been greatly admired. The Lord's Prayer, with every petition written in a different script. Copperplate, Gothic, and what I believe is called Italiano. There was no style he could not copy.'

'Lucky he was honest, eh, Auntie?' said Horace.

Miss Leah stiffened her spine and seemed to grown an inch taller.

'Strictly speaking, Mr Batchelor, I am not your aunt. Your father, Mr Edgar Batchelor, was only a connection of ours by marriage.'

'Does that mean I could marry you if I hadn't got a better half already? And I would too, for the pastry alone.'

The blood rose under Miss Leah's transparent skin. Unutterably offended, she pinched her lips and looked down at her plate.

'Haha, she's blushing,' went on Horace, delighted to see that

Claude was frowning at him. 'Bet it isn't the first proposal she's had.'

'Horry, you shouldn't,' said his mother admiringly. 'He just can't help it,' she explained to the company. 'He's got such a sense of humour.' She was a small tight shrivelled old woman in an old-fashioned jet-trimmed bonnet tied under her chin. Her greedy black eyes and the way she held her head on one side made her look as if she were always guessing the price of something. 'After all, it doesn't always pay to put a long face on your troubles. Look where Horace has got with his jokes. Sir Rex has just promoted him chief sales manager, no less.'

'No call to let that out, Mother,' smirked Horace. 'You'll have me blushing too. Besides, it's still sub rosa, as you might say. Didn't know I was a Latin scholar, did you, Claudie?'

Claude raised his glass.

'Congratulations, Horace.'

'Thanks, old boy. I don't say I shan't miss being on the road at first. Free and easy life. Suits me. Lot of responsibility, this new job. Have to mind my p's and q's. Going to have a lady secretary too.' He dug his wife Ada in the ribs. 'Probably have to work late at the office while she's new to the job. *You* won't mind, will you, old girl?'

The anaemic wife smiled uneasily, revealing her pale gums.

'No, of course not, Horace.'

'There's a nice wife for you! Only too pleased to get her old man out of the way.'

Ada flushed. Claude came to her rescue.

'How is your little boy, Ada?'

Before she could answer, her mother-in-law exclaimed, 'A picture, isn't he, Horace? And the image of his dad. Just like Horry at his age, the things he comes out with.'

'Let's hope he'll be as successful,' said Claude.

'He'll have a better start in life,' said Aunt Louie ominously. 'Horace has got where he is by his own exertions. Through no fault of his own he had to start at the bottom of the ladder.'

Isabel shifted her chair and closed her eyes.

'I suppose,' said Claude, 'it's early days to think about a school for Georgie?'

'Trying to land one for the old firm, Claudie?' Horace shook his head. 'Nothing doing. Not even if you got him in wholesale. Sound commercial education and come into the business at sixteen. That's what I plan for Georgie.'

'No doubt you're right,' said Claude.

'And mark you, it's not a question of fees. It's a question of principle. Don't think I'm crabbing your old Eton and Harrod's, Claudie.' He raised his glass and took a long draught. 'A schoolmaster's got to live. No offence meant, but I doubt if you'd be worth more than three quid a week in business.'

Ellen's dull eyes brightened.

'I don't agree. Claude is so clever and so hard-working he'd have made a success of anything.'

'Come on, Auntie. I was only having a bit of fun. Didn't I say "no offence meant"?'

There was a moment's embarrassed silence. It was obvious that old Mrs Batchelor was not appeased. Ada plucked up courage to speak. She was a faded blonde who quirked her little finger as she handled her knife and glass.

'I'm sure,' she said in a shaking, ultra-ladylike voice, 'Horace would never wish to hurt anyone's feelings.'

She glanced nervously at him as she spoke. She could never forget that she had been only a shopgirl when he married her. Her life was an agony of apprehension that she would not be able to keep up with him as he pushed and elbowed his way towards the heights of the drapery world.

'Thanks, old lady, but I can speak up for myself.' He winked at Isabel who stared past him as if his chair were empty. He was determined to make her notice him.

'Pardon me, but that's a remarkably nice grown you're wearing. Paris model, I shouldn't wonder.'

'I bought it in London,' said Isabel from a great distance.

'Looks like Paree on you. It's the figure, no doubt.' He leaned over the table.

'Look here, Cousin Isabel, next time you want something pretty, you come along to Cousin Horace. I'm great pals with our gown buyers. Get you anything you want, straight from Paree, cost price . . .'

'Very kind of you, Horace,' interrupted Claude, 'but we couldn't think of putting you to so much trouble.'

'No trouble at all, old boy,' said Horace. 'Pleasure. Give me a ring any time and I'll take you down to the warehouse, Isabel.'

'Would you care for some trifle, Mr Batchelor?' said Miss Leah. 'It is made from our mother's special recipe.'

'Thanks, Miss Sayers, since I mustn't call you Auntie.'

When he tasted the trifle, he smacked his lips.

'Ah, I haven't had a tipsy-cake like this since I was a boy. You and me made ourselves sick on it once, Claudie. Remember?'

Miss Leah coughed with disapproval.

'We can both hold our drinks better now, eh, Claudie? Pretty good claret you've got here. Reminds me of some Sir Rex brings out when he's after a big order. Present from one of your Iky friends?'

'I bought a few dozen some years ago.'

'Glad you can afford it, Claude,' said the hollow voice of Sidney Gould, a distant relative of the Batchelors who kept a chemist's shop in Norwich. He was a cadaverous man of fifty-five with an expression of determined melancholy, like an undertaker's. His clothes too were like an undertaker's; a ready-made black suit and a dingy stiff collar of some synthetic material that could be sponged instead of laundered. He had been eating large quantities of food with slow concentration; intent on re-imbursing himself as far as possible for the fare from Norwich to London. If he ate sufficient, he would be able to save the price of his supper; if he ate too much or too quickly he would bring on his indigestion.

'I assure you I bought it very reasonably,' said Claude meekly. Once, in his hard-up days, he had borrowed fifty pounds from Gould and, though he had long ago repaid it, he had never been allowed to forget it.

'If you asked my advice,' said Gould gloomily, 'not that you'd take it if you did, you'd look on that wine as an investment. In ten years' time you'd make a very handsome profit on what you originally paid. However, it seems you can afford to be extravagant.'

'At my Edgar's funeral,' said Aunt Louie suddenly, 'there was no claret wine. Nor any other kind of wine either except some homemade cowslip. Ah, Ellen, you may be thankful you do not find yourself a widow in such case as I was.'

Two uneven red stains appeared on her yellow cheeks. She looked balefully at Ellen and added with meaning,

'And through no fault of my husband's.'

'I know what you refer to, Louie,' said Ellen with dignity. 'But I don't think we want to talk about all those bygone things today, do we?'

'Funerals jog the memory,' said Louie darkly. 'Very different for me the outlook was, the day *my* husband was laid to rest.'

'I know, Louie. It was a very difficult time for all. You forget my Fred lost everything too when the . . . er . . .' Mrs Batchelor caught Isabel's eye, 'the *business* failed.'

'Failed,' snorted Louie. 'It was killed stone-dead. If Fred had taken Edgar's advice . . .'

'Aunt Louie,' interposed Claude. 'We all know that my father had no head for business. It was a great pity he was ever persuaded to go into it.'

'A pity for others besides himself,' said Louie.

'I think it is out of place to refer to such subjects at all today,' said Miss Leah. 'If we must, would it not be better to remember that all the debts were fully and honourably discharged?'

Louie turned on her. The red stains spread like a blot and her eyes glittered under their granulated lids.

'Now there was a bit of high-falutin' nonsense if you like. They could have got away with six bob in the pound easy but for Claude's notions.' She shook her bonnet at her nephew. 'Oh, I know it came out of your pocket in the end. But if you wanted to throw money away, what about your own kith and kin? Charity begins at home, I say.'

'You'll never teach Claude the value of money any more than you'll teach a hen to swim,' said Sidney Gould. 'Miss Sophy, I wonder if you could oblige me with a glass of water?'

Sophy, glad of an excuse to leave the crowded room, the flushed and quarrelling faces, jumped up and disappeared into the pantry.

'In my business,' Gould went on, 'I allow myself exactly three pounds a week for board, lodging and incidentals. Everything over and above that goes back into the business or into my deposit account. Occasionally I invest a trifle. Not speculate, mark you. Invest.'

Miss Sophy dumped a glass of water in front of him.

'Much obliged, I'm sure. Excuse me, all.' He took a small cardboard box from his waistcoat pocket, selected a couple of pills with bony yellow fingers and swallowed them with a gulp of water. 'I have to be particularly careful with my dyspepsia.'

Isabel stood up and pushed back her chair.

'It's fearfully hot in here, Claude. I must have a breath of air.'

'Come and take a turn round the garden with me,' said Horace. 'I'm feeling a bit stuffed up myself.'

Isabel promptly sat down again. She laid the little bunch of snowdrops against her cheek and turned to Claude.

'Aren't they exquisite? Aunt Sophy picked them for me.'

'Charming, my dear.'

She tucked them in the neck of her dress.

'You usually prefer showier flowers, Isabel,' said old Mrs Batchelor meaningly.

'I love all flowers,' Isabel's voice was calm; 'especially the ones Aunt Sophy chooses for me.' She slipped her arm round the back of her neighbour's chair and touched Miss Sophy's shoulder.

'Everything's so late with the snow,' said Miss Sophy. 'I should have had some daffodils for your father's wreath, Claude, instead of having to make do with winter aconites. I did feel so sorry.'

'It was the nicest of all, your little yellow and white cross. Wasn't it, Claude?'

Claude looked at her with sad affection. He could forgive her many humiliations for her fondness for his two old aunts.

'Someone must have spent a pretty penny on that wreath of orchids and what d'you call 'ems,' said Horace. 'I meant to have a squint at the card.'

'It was a Mr and Mrs Shapiro . . . I think I've pronounced it right,' said Ellen proudly. It was her day and not even Isabel was going to put her down. 'Jewish people they are. Very rich. Claude teaches their son privately and they think the world of him.'

'Not by any chance Shapiro the big fur people?' asked Horace. His grin had vanished; his heavy face was alert and serious.

'As a matter of fact, yes,' said Claude.

Horace looked at him almost with respect. When he spoke, his voice was quite subdued.

'Look here, I say, Claude. Sending a wreath that size to Uncle's funeral. What, old Izzy himself? Of course I realize it's nothing to them as cash. Still, you must be on pretty good terms with them.'

'Mr Shapiro and his wife often come and play bridge with Claude and Isabel,' said Ellen triumphantly.

Horace sucked his teeth.

'H'm. They do, do they? I'm fond of a game of bridge myself. Ada's no earthly use of course. What I like is a real men's four.'

'The Shapiros always come together,' said Isabel firmly. 'We make a very good four.'

'I'd be the last to shove myself in where I wasn't wanted. All the same, I don't mind admitting I'd like to meet old Izzy in private life so to speak. Look here, Claude. I'll make you a proposition. I don't expect anyone to do something for nothing in this world. If someone were to put me in the way of meeting him, informally, you know, and anything came of it, I'd be very willing to give that person a bit of commish.'

Isabel bit her lip and Claude looked embarrassed. At last he said, 'I doubt if a business introduction from me would do you any good, Horace. Shapiro, like you, has the poorest opinion of my business abilities.'

'I'm not asking for a business introduction. I can send Popham's card up to him any day of the week. What I want is to meet him in a free-and-easy social way. Not a word of "bithneth".'

He hunched his shoulders and spread his hands like a third-rate comedian telling a Jewish story.

'I think it's the least you can do for Horace, Claude,' said Horace's mother. 'It ought to be a pleasure to you to oblige. For the sake of justice, if nothing else.'

Suddenly from the end of the table came the unexpected voice of Miss Leah. Her white face was flushed and she was quivering with nervous indignation. 'Mr Batchelor,' she said, confronting Horace like a moorhen facing up to a turkey cock, 'this is not my house and Claude must forgive me for interrupting. But I must

246

say I do not think this is the right moment to worry Claude with your private business affairs. And, Mrs Edgar, it is not respectful to poor Fred's memory to keep harping on the past. We all have our failings. I am sure none of us would wish them recalled on the day our friends carry us to the churchyard.'

Horace stared at her open-mouthed. He began to mumble something, thought better of it, poured himself out a glass of claret and turned away with a shrug. At a glance from him, his mother, who was obviously about to reply with considerable heat, compressed her lips and glowered at her plate. There was a moment's silence; then an awkward, half-hearted general conversation broke out. Under cover of it, old John Hoadley spoke for the first time.

'You said no more than was right, Cousin.'

Too shaken by her outburst to utter another word, Miss Leah could only give the old man a grateful look.

Even in his own home, John Hoadley's silence was proverbial. Among all these people he was so shy that he had hardly raised his eyes from the table. When he did so, it was to give a glance of intense sympathy at any face that seemed sad. Though he was just on seventy, his blue eyes were as those of his nineteen-year-old son Blaze who sat beside him. His wrinkled, sunburnt face in its frame of old-fashioned whiskers would have been insignificant but for those innocent, ageless eyes. Blaze had them too, as kindly but less calm, their blueness exaggerated by the violent red of his complexion. Sun and wind had permanently dyed the exposed parts of his fair skin to the colour of new brick; from his wheat-coloured hair to his collar he seemed to be one fiery blush. People often thought that 'Blaze' was a nickname given him on this account, but actually it was his real name. His mother, who was of French descent, had christened him after her grandfather Blaise Meunier but since she spoke no French and had never seen the name written, she spelt and pronounced it Blaze. Working in the fields, with his shirt rolled up over his splendid arms, Blaze had the charm of anyone at ease in his surroundings; today in his tight black coat whose sleeves shot back with every movement exposing his enormous red hands and wrists; with his hair plastered flat above his flaming face, he was the picture of awkward misery.

On either side of Clara sat two of his many elder sisters, both undeniably pretty in spite of their dowdy black dresses and work-roughened hands.

Protected on all sides by Hoadleys, Clara tried to ignore the conversation at the other end of the table. She saw the Horace Batchelors so seldom that she had not realized till today how awful they were. Every time Horace opened his mouth she burnt with shame. For the first time in her life she sympathized with her mother's snobbishness and even drew support from the Maule coat of arms. But she never dreamt of criticizing the Hoadleys; they were part of the enchanted summer holiday life which had no connection with London and Mount Hilary. She had known Throcking since she was four years old; some of her happiest memories were of trotting round the byres and fields with 'Uncle' John, helping to feed the calves and the chickens, wriggling through the heaped-up hay in the barns and being lifted on to the backs of the huge quiet horses. Inside a house John Hoadley always relapsed into silence but in his own fields and cattlesheds he answered all Clara's questions with careful deliberation, teaching her the difference between Shorthorns and Herefords and Friesians and explaining the merits of various breeds of poultry. Sometimes he would seem to forget that she was a child and advise her seriously never to buy a Jersey bull or to plough up a good piece of pasture and Clara, munching a piece of grass, would nod wisely. She was more flattered when John Hoadley said, 'Why, I reckon you've quite a good notion of stock, Clara' than by any of her mother's irritated praise of her 'cleverness'. Up at Throcking she was a different person, a person whom her mother and even her father would not have recognized. Sometimes she fancied she would like to be that simple and stolid person always. Looking at the faces of Horace and Aunt Louie and Sidney Gould, she felt a rush of affection for the Hoadleys. Blaze, in his tight Sunday suit, might be ludicrous; he could never be vulgar. She thought how good he was; how kind, how genuine. Even as a small boy he never bullied or showed off. He wasn't soft; he was stronger than any of the men on the farm and when he gave an order in his quiet, slow voice, it was obeyed at once. He knew and loved his job; he had no ambition to be anything else than a good farmer. Clara had always liked Blaze though, away from Throcking and Paget's Fold, she had hardly given him a thought. Now she glanced across at him and smiled, with a touch of self-satisfaction at being able to appreciate him. His eyes were already on her, but he did not smile back. No blush could have deepened that complexion yet she had the impression that he was embarrassed. Embarrassed in her turn, she looked past him into the dim greenish mirror of the sideboard. For a moment she did not recognize herself. All through the meal she had been so conscious of being the one child among the grown-ups that she was startled to find a reflection that did not look childish at all. Was it only the velvet frock that made her seem at least two years older and quite different? Even in the tarnished glass which dulled all colours, her hair shone and her skin was theatrically white against the black.

'Blaze,' she said petulantly, 'why do you look as if you didn't recognize me?' She wanted to establish some connection between this brillant person in the mirror and the Clara Blaze knew, an untidy child in a crumpled holland frock, with a shiny nose and scratched knees.

Blaze looked down at his plate.

'I recognize you all right, Clara,' he said with his Sussex drawl. 'It's just, well, reckon you've grown a lot since last summer. You're quite a young lady.'

'I'm *not* different,' she pleaded, half sincerely. 'Am I, Uncle John? Everyone looks older in black, don't they?'

The old man considered her gravely 'I'm sorry to have to see you in mourning, my dear. But what Blaze says is right. You're not a little lass any more.'

Suddenly she wanted to disown the girl in the glass.

'But I haven't changed. I know I'm older. But I still like the same things.'

'Come on, Clara,' mocked Violet. 'Would you still like Blaze to give you a ride in the wheelbarrow as he used to do?'

Clara sighed.

'I admit I'm old for that. Did Heather's calf come on all right after all, Uncle John? And did the landlord put up a new gate between Sweetacre and the Bottom?'

'Yes, that little heifer, Pansy we call her, she's a picture now. I was all for selling her, but Blaze, he said no, let me try my hand; and he brought her on wonderful. As to the gate, well, Mr Vernon he won't say yes and he won't say no in a manner of speaking.'

'Can I come up and see everything, quite soon in the summer holidays?'

'Why, you're always welcome, Clara. You know that,' said John Hoadley. 'But the time will soon be coming when you won't want to be spoiling your pretty clothes in a dirty old place like a farm.'

'Oh, how *can* you? You know I'll always love Throcking.'

Violet patted her hair. 'Same old Clara, eh?' The volume of Horace's talk was rising again and she spoke quietly so that her father and Blaze could not hear. 'You always were a quaint child. We could never understand how you took to it so, being brought up in London. Dad used to say you were more of a farmer's daughter than I ever was.'

'You do like the farm, don't you, Vi?'

'I don't stop to think whether I like it. I'm there and the work's got to be done.'

'Still, you must be awfully proud of your dairy. It's so lovely . . . just like Mrs Poyser's.'

'Who's Mrs Poyser? Someone at Bellhurst?'

'No, just someone in a book.'

Violet sighed.

'Sometimes I don't open a book for weeks on end. There's wonderfully little time for reading on a farm. You'd hate that, wouldn't you, Clara?'

Clara considered.

'I know one has to work awfully hard. And I've only seen Throcking in summer. All the same, I do sometimes wish . . .'

'You're luckier than you know,' said Violet. 'Think of the education you're getting. You're clever, we all know that. Only some girls never get the chance to find out whether they're clever or not.'

'I hadn't thought of that.'

'Look at me. Twenty-two and I don't know a quarter of the things you do. And you're not fifteen. It won't be long before you find your old country cousins very dull company.'

'Oh, Vi, I won't.'

'Don't tease her,' said the gentle Beatrice. 'You'll always keep a place for us, Clara, won't you?'

'Of course I will, Bee,' Clara's eyes were smarting childishly. 'Oh dear, everything's so horrid today. Everyone's different. I'm sure it's all because of those frightful people. Why don't they go? They don't belong here.'

'Hush, dear, they'll hear you,' said Violet. She added with a touch of mischief, 'They're much nearer relations to you than we are.'

'Did I hear you pining about education just now, Miss Hoadley?' broke in Horace Batchelor. 'If you ask my opinion as a man of the world, it's waste of time sending girls to school. There's only one thing a woman needs to learn and that's how to get a husband.'

'I suppose you'd allow us to be taught to read and write,' said Violet, flushing.

'No objection to that. Nor to a bit of figuring. Keep her accounts and read her love-letters, that's all a girl wants.'

'Claude isn't at all of your mind, Horace,' said Ellen Batchelor. 'He wants Clara to go to a university, just like he did.'

'Of all the crack-brained notions!' exclaimed Horace. 'What, a pretty kid like Clara stewing over a lot of rotten old books just when she ought to be having a bit of fun? You put your foot down, Clara. Don't let your Dad get away with it.'

'There's no question of forcing her,' said Claude coldly. 'It depends entirely on Clara herself.'

'I probably won't be good enough to get a scholarship, anyway,' Clara's voice was peevish.

'She will if she sets her mind to it,' said her grandmother. 'She's always top of her form at school.'

'Class,' muttered Clara under her breath.

'Chip of the old block, eh?' said Horace. 'Claude was always the brainy boy, wasn't he? Even in the old Young Gent's Academy days before he got a schol. to his classy public school. Didn't cut much of a figure out of lesson-hours, as I remember. Ever heard the saying, them that can *do*; them that can't, *teach*?'

Suddenly Clara lost all control of herself.

'You're always sneering at my father,' she burst out, her

cheeks flaming. 'It's simply beastly. I wish you'd stop.'

The whole table was suddenly silent. Everyone looked delighted, uncomfortable or shocked.

'Clara, whatever are you thinking of?' It was said in Claude's sternest voice. 'Apologize at once or leave the room.'

'I won't say I'm sorry, Daddy; I can't.'

'Ooh. Temper, temper!' mocked Horace, delighted. ''Pon my word, it suits you. My goodness, what a fine colour!'

Aunt Louie, equally delighted, snapped out,

'The impertinence! If you were a daughter of mine, Miss, I'd put you across my knee and spank you.'

Miss Leah cleared her throat unhappily.

'I'm sure Clara didn't mean . . .'

Aunt Louie cut across her.

'Nice manners, I *must* say. Is that what you learn from your princesses and duchesses at your Roman Catholic school?'

'Claude, the child was only . . .' began Isabel.

'Leave this to me, please,' he interrupted her. He turned an iron face to Clara. 'Did you hear what I said?'

'Yes, I did.' She tried to keep her voice from trembling. 'I'm going.' Her legs felt like paper but she managed to get up. Quickly and unsteadily she made for the nearest door and left the room.

Chapter Eight

In her blind haste, Clara had taken the door that led straight into the garden. After the stuffy room, the March wind struck like cold water on her face and half-bare arms. In a moment she was shivering in her velvet dress. It was impossible to go back and expose herself to all those staring faces and she dared not slip through the back door into the kitchen in case the old woman from the village who was coming to help with the washing-up had already arrived. She knew Mrs Twiner all too well; her disgrace would be known all over Rookfield by the evening and remembered and discussed for years.

Avoiding the windows, she ran round to the back of the house and up the overgrown path to the orchard and hid herself among the furthest trees. She was furious at having made such a fool of herself. Why couldn't she have had the sense to keep quiet? Nowadays it was always the same. When her father wanted her to speak, she was dumb. When she should have been silent, some imp prompted her to blurt out the wrong thing. This time, she muttered, angrily tearing strips of lichen from the bark of a tree, he really had been unfair. She had stood up for him and he had humiliated her. Her mother would never have done it quite in that way . . . *She* would probably have gone to the other extreme and done something embarrassing, such as calling her 'my loyal little daughter' or kissing her in front of everyone. But then she would never have attacked Cousin Horace on her mother's account. Supposing it had been her mother who had done the attacking? Probably her father would have been delighted. The scene in the churchyard came back to her. She thought jealously, 'I love him much more than *she* does.' If it had been her own funeral, would he have broken down and cried? It was very chilly in the orchard. If she got a cold and neglected it, it might turn to pheumonia. Then he'd be sorry. 'Darling child, it was all my fault. Can you ever forgive me?'

The minutes went by. A cloud came over the sun and the wind struck colder than ever. What should she do? She had wild thoughts of running away. She pictured herself stumbling on and on for miles and being picked up exhausted by the roadside, delirious perhaps, her velvet dress covered with dust. Common sense came to the rescue. She'd never get far in her thin best shoes; she would just be making herself ridiculous again. Why couldn't she have been more dignified? The girl in the glass would never have been rude in that shrill, clumsy way. She would merely have given Cousin Horace an ineffable look that would have silenced him. But the girl in the glass didn't exist any more. With her hair blown into tangles, her eyes watering and her nose turning blue with cold, Clara was just Clara again, an idiotic schoolgirl who had once again made an exhibition of herself.

A man's step sounded on the path behind the orchard hedge. Joy, terror and an impulse to run leapt up together. Just how angry would he be? Or was it possible he had come to forgive her. 'In front of all those people, dear, you understand, I had to pretend.' How gladly she would agree, and, entering into the conspiracy, apologize to Cousin Horace with the best grace in the world. The footsteps came nearer. She stood still, hiding her face against the apple tree. Close by her, the footsteps stopped. When she turned round she saw that the man was not her father but Blaze Hoadley.

'Clara,' he said in voice hoarse with shyness. 'Excuse me, won't you.'

She stared at his crimson face and thought she had never seen anyone who looked so kind. Did that mean good news?

'Have they sent you to fetch me?'

'No, I just slipped away on my own. You don't mind, do you, Clara?' He cleared his throat. 'I thought . . . well . . . fact is I was bit worried about you.'

'Awfully nice of you, Blaze. But I'm quite all right. Really I am.'

'It's a bitter wind. You must be cold out here with no coat on. Here, if you don't mind . . .'

Before she could object he had taken off his black jacket and wrapped it clumsily round her shoulders.

'No, Blaze, really.' She said it half-heartedly. The coat, warm from his body, was very comforting. 'But what about you?'

'Me?' he grinned. 'I need a bit of cooling off after that room.'

In his shirtsleeves and with the wind ruffling the unnatural smoothness of his hair, he was more like the Blaze of the farm.

'Now you look almost your old self,' she told him.

'Reckon you do too, Clara.'

Muffled in the big black coat, with her ribbon off and her hair whipped all over her face, it was no good trying to be dignified any more. She appealed to him, as in the days when she had torn her frock or lost her shoe scrambling about the farm.

'Blaze, what *am* I to do?'

'I'm sure your father didn't mean to speak so sharp,' he said soothingly. 'He's upset today and no wonder.'

'Yes, I *know*,' she wailed.

'Don't take it to heart so. Remember how fond he is of you. And proud as Punch, too. I daresay he didn't like seeing you giving way in front of that fellow. He can't bear to have you criticized. Mother's just the same with us. She flies out at us rather than anybody else shall.'

'But I only flew out because he was being so beastly about Daddy.'

'He asked for it all right. Don't fret yourself, Clara. It'll all smooth out.'

'Do *you* think I ought to go back and apologize?'

'It's not for me to judge. That'd mend it sooner than anything.'

'It's no good, Blaze. I can't. I'm *not* sorry.'

'Well, you know best. Dad and I always give in to Mother for the sake of peace. She's a bit unreasonable sometimes. But your father. He didn't act like himself today. I've never heard him speak anything but kindly to anyone.'

'Oh, but he can be absolutely ruthless, Blaze. You don't know him.'

'He couldn't be hard on *you* for long. No one could.' He looked at her ardently.

'Why do you say that, Blaze?'

He looked down at his thick black boots. When he spoke it was with an obvious effort.

'Well, Clara, when you were little, I thought you were the nicest kid I knew. Not to mention the prettiest. And now you've gone and changed into a young lady overnight. Only, you see, my ideas haven't changed, that's all.'

Clara did not know what to say. They were both relieved when a rabbit darted out a few yards from them and streaked away towards the field beyond the orchard.

'Oh, look, Blaze.'

'Wish I'd got my old gun. He's been at your Aunt Sophy's cabbages I shouldn't wonder.'

'I'm glad you haven't. I hate any animal being killed.'

'I don't hold with killing for killing's sake. But a farmer's got to keep the rabbits down. Terrible damage they do.'

'Yes, I know. And you're an awfully good shot.'

'Middling. Anyway, I always make sure they're finished off proper. I remember how upset you were years ago when we picked up one with a broken back.'

Clara winced.

'I've never forgotten that. Or Jerry the pig being killed.'

'Reckon there's a lot of things about farming that wouldn't suit you, for all you were saying just now in there.'

'Yes. I suppose so. But truly I'm not pretending when I say I love Throcking.'

'Maybe. Most kids like playing about on a farm.' He looked at her intently. 'But could you fancy yourself being content living all your life at Throcking or some such place?'

'How can I tell? I'm not likely to have the chance, am I? Sometimes, yes, Blaze, I do really think I could.'

'Hmm. I wonder.' His clear eyes under their reddened lids continued to search her face.

'Why do you look at me in that funny way?'

'Oh, nothing.' He stared at his boots again.

'Why, you're shivering, Blaze. Do have your coat back. I'm beautifully warm again.'

'Keep it on. I like seeing you in it,' he muttered.

'I must look awfully queer,' she said and giggled.

He raised his eyes.

'D'you know, that's the first time I've heard you laugh today.'

She became instantly gloomy.

'Oh, goodness, I'd forgotten. I certainly haven't got anything to laugh about at the moment.'

'I hate seeing you so put out, Clara. I wish I could say something to cheer you up. But I'm like Dad. Always got a knot in my tongue. Yet when you're not there, it's surprising how easy I talk to you.'

'I know *that* feeling,' Clara said with a wan smile.

Suddenly he stepped forward and, before she could move, put his arms round her and kissed her.

'There,' he said as he drew back. 'I know I oughtn't. But I just couldn't help it.'

Clara did not know whether she was pleased or angry. It was the first time a young man had kissed her. She could do nothing but stare at him in dismay. Blaze caught her two hands in his and held them tightly.

'Say you'll forgive me, Clara. I know I haven't the right. I never will have. I've lain awake at nights telling myself not to be such a fool. I thought I'd got more hold on myself. Forget all about it.'

Still he did not let go her hands. He lifted them up and pinned them against him so that she could feel the hard, warm flesh under his cotton shirt. She stood there awkwardly, not liking to draw away. It was not at all how she had imagined her first kiss. She was both moved and affronted. He was a ridiculous figure in his shirt and braces, with his hair half plastered down, half standing on end above his crimson face. But there was something in his expression that was not at all ridiculous.

'Oh, Blaze,' she said miserably. 'I *am* awfully fond of you.'

'I'd forgotten you were only a kid. You looked deceiving today. And I'm not a kid any more, Clara. I have the feelings a man has. It shan't ever happen again. Unless,' he broke off, looking down at her almost sternly.

'Unless?' she said, in spite of herself.

He shook his head. 'No. I've got that much sense left. Even if you ever . . . No, we've been bred to different ways and that's the end of it. But leave your hands be just this minute, Clara.'

They stood for some moments, searching each other's faces, their eyes watering in the wind. It was Blaze who moved first. With a curious dignity he bent his head, put her hands one after the other to his lips and gently let them go. In that one gesture, he seemed to grow up before her eyes. She realized the immense distance between them. He was at that moment a man, all that he would ever be. And she was nothing but a half-baked, pretentious little girl.

'That's all, Clara,' he said quietly. 'Only remember I'm your friend. If ever I can serve you in any way . . .'

'I'm your friend too, Blaze,' she said, feeling miserably inadequate.

'If you take my advice, you'll go back in and make it up with your Dad. Things only get worse if you put them off. I reckon I'll take a turn round the field.'

He took the coat she offered him, slung it over his shoulder and strode quickly away. She watched him jump the hedge and make off down the field without looking back, almost with a sense of grievance as if he had unkindly deserted her. Moving reluctantly towards the path she saw her father a few yards away standing perfectly still, watching her.

Her heart turned over. How long had he been there? What had he seen? She must have been too absorbed to hear his footsteps. She stumbled towards him on legs weak as a baby's.

'Oh, Daddy,' she stammered. 'You shouldn't have . . . I'm so sorry . . . I was just coming in to say . . .'

'Indeed,' he said coldly as she came up to him. 'Not on your own initiative, I think.'

He had heard Blaze's last words then. But how much else? He walked away and she followed meekly behind him down the path. The few yards through the orchard seemed interminable. At last he said over his shoulder,

'You'd better go in through the back door and do something to your hair before you go into the sitting-room. You're not fit to be seen.'

She could bear it no longer. Catching up with him and tugging at his sleeve, she burst out:

'Please, please, Daddy, don't be so angry. I am sorry, truly I am.'

He made a few steps as if he neither heard her nor felt her dragging at him. Then abruptly he turned, shook off her hand and looked at her. His face was pale and stern but, besides the anger which she expected, it had an expression she had never seen and could not read.

'Sorry for what, Clara?' he said sharply. There was an odd shrill note in his voice that reminded her of her mother.

She felt herself turn crimson.

'I'm sorry I was so rude to Mr Batchelor.'

'Oh, *that*.' He gave a half-smile that was like a grimace of pain. 'I had decided to overlook it. I came out here to tell you so. An ironic situation, don't you agree?'

She said nothing.

'I was idiot enough to imagine you might be unhappy,' he went on. 'I fancied I had been too harsh with you. There's no fool like a father.'

She looked at him wretchedly.

'I suppose you are going to tell me it is the first time?'

She nodded.

'If it is . . . which I doubt . . . you might perhaps have chosen a more suitable day, don't you think?'

This time he had gone too far. Suddenly his sarcasm ceased to wound her. She was still terrified but for the first time in her life, she felt almost equal to him.

'I didn't *choose*,' she said sullenly.

'Can I believe anything you say?' Angry as he was, he seemed to be almost pleading with her. 'There was a time when I would have trusted your word against anyone's. You were a truthful child.'

Clara said nothing.

An access of rage seemed to choke him. His face was distorted; his eyes narrowed as if the flesh round them was swelling and silting them up.

'You . . . you of all people. Kissing and giggling like a common servant girl. How that young oaf dared to touch you. The swine.'

'Blaze isn't a swine.' It took all her courage to say it.

She could no longer bear to look at him. The sun was still shining, a clump of daffodil buds nodded in the wind at her feet but a tainted mist seemed to have come over the spring day.

'He didn't mean . . . it wasn't his fault,' she muttered, hardly knowing what she was saying.

'Ah,' he gloated. 'There at least we have the truth. A young man doesn't . . . unless he is a scoundrel . . . if the girl doesn't lead him on. I've no right to blame Blaze Hoadley. You were fair game.'

She burst into tears.

'You're so cruel,' she sobbed. 'You never give me a chance to explain.'

'What excuse do you propose to make? I watched with my own eyes. If I did not interfere at once, it was because I wanted to make sure I was not suffering from hallucinations.'

He paused. After a moment he said, 'So I am cruel?' His voice was bitter but there was a hint of weariness and uncertainty in it. 'I thought you were an innocent child. Do you expect me to be pleased to find you are nothing of the kind?'

She turned away from him and hid her face against a tree. Enclosed in her misery, she was hardly any longer conscious of his presence. A very long time seemed to pass. At last, from a great distance she heard him say, as if to himself, 'I wanted one thing in my life to be perfect.'

When she dared to raise her head, he was gone. She saw his square black figure moving slowly down the path towards the house. His head, which he usually carried so stiffly erect, was sunk forward. She watched with stinging eyes till the black figure disappeared behind the angle of the wall. Bewildered and resentful as she was, there was one clear point in the confusion of her mind. Some part of herself seemed to have broken loose and to judge differently from the rest. Had he beaten her, the original Clara could not have felt more humiliated. But someone else . . . was it the girl in the glass? . . . had the strangest sense of triumph.

PART TWO

Chapter One

A few months after Frederick Batchelor's funeral, his daughter-in-law came very near to dying. Clara, at school, was merely told that her mother had had to undergo a serious operation and asked to pray for her. Half-way through the summer term, she received a letter from her father, saying that Isabel was out of danger and slowly recovering.

> 'This is my good news; now for the bad. We had always agreed that in the autumn of 1915 you should go to St Mark's Girls' School so that you could take your exams. But I fear that, owing to the expenses of your mother's illness, we shall have to make the change this coming September instead. So this, alas, will be your last term at Mount Hilary. I cannot possibly manage to afford another year for you at the convent. You will know how very distressed I am to have to take you away but your mother's life was in the balance and I had no alternative but to get the very best advice. She is still too weak to write but sends you her fondest love.
>
> > Ever your affectionate father,
> > C. F. B.'

When Clara first glanced through this letter in the refectory, she hardly took it in. During recreation she managed to slip away to her favourite hiding-place under the weeping ash. There she read it again slowly, absorbing the full shock. When she was at school, events at home always seemed remote and this illness of her mother's, with its atmosphere of secrecy, had hardly been real to her. Even now it was hard for her to believe that Isabel had been in danger of death. Only one thing in her father's letter struck home; the fact that she had to leave Mount Hilary in a few weeks' time. It was so overwhelming that she had no pity to spare for anyone but herself.

It was a still, softly-burning day in June and Mount Hilary was at its loveliest. From the cricket pitch came the lazy slap of bats and birdlike cries of 'Oh *played*, Theresa' and 'Well *held*, Adèle.' All the smells of summer were in the air, drifting from the limes in Community Alley, the drying hay in the paddock and the azaleas by the lake. Through the showering branches of the ash she had a glimpse of the water and an island of lilies. The Junior School were playing with the boat; she could hear splashes and the grind of the loose old row locks and shrill squeals from the bank – 'It's our trio next, Mother.' 'No, *honour*, Mother, it isn't. It's Philomena's.' Across the lower meadow passed a silent band of First Communicants in retreat, carrying flowers to decorate an altar for the Corpus Christi procession tomorrow. It was as if everything that most charmed her at Mount Hilary had been gathered together on this summer afternoon to remind her of what she had to lose.

If only she had known this was to be her last term, how she would have hoarded every minute. Now she had barely six weeks left. The careless voices from the pitch and the lakeside became an irritation. This time next year they would be calling 'I was *miles* inside the crease, Mother' or 'My pink ribbon's gone overboard.' Voices of people whose fathers did not have to worry about school fees; of people who would never be expected to earn their own living. Tears of self-pity rose in her eyes so that, when a figure pushed through the tent of boughs, she only saw a blur of striped cotton and black serge. When she had dashed away the tears with her fists, the blur resolved itself into her best friend, Nicole de Savigny.

'Hullo,' she said with relief, 'I was afraid it was a Child of Mary or something.'

'Almost as bad,' said Nicole, 'I've got a message.'

'Go back to Rec. I suppose? Well, I won't.'

'Neither will I. This is much more civilized.' Nicole flung herself on the grass, selected a blade with care and began to chew it, keeping her eyes averted from Clara's face. When Clara had had time to dab her eyes and blow her nose, she said:

'Mother Lovell wants you to go to her room after Rec. What is it? Bad news from home?'

'Well – yes.'

'Your mother's not worse?'

'No. She's going on quite well.'

Nicole, still chewing her grass-blade, looked at her thoughtfully. The light, filtering through the leaves that enclosed them like a tent made her flecked changeable eyes appear green –

'Rather I went?'

'For heaven's sake, *no*.'

'Good. I wanted an excuse to stay. Who but the English would waste this weather playing cricket? I wonder our sainted foundress didn't forbid it in the rules. Being French, I suppose she didn't legislate for barbarians.' Nicole pushed up the fringe from her damp forehead, '*Ciel*, it's hot.'

'She did legislate against fringes,' said Clara, smiling for the first time, 'I've always wondered how you managed to get away with yours.'

'Probably because my great-aunt gave the Order a house when they were on the rocks.'

Clara studied the handsome exposed forehead.

'You look ten times better without it.'

'Of course. It's entirely a matter of principle. I won't be browbeaten. This time next year, when you and I leave this prison-house I'll ceremonially cut it off. If you want a lock as a souvenir, I've got the perfect locket. Hearts, forget-me-nots, *ewige Freundschaft* . . .'

Clara broke in:

'I shan't be here next year. Not even next term.'

Nicole sat up.

'*Mon Dieu*, you haven't been expelled?'

'No. Just a sudden notion of my father's.'

'Well, he must give a reason.'

There was a pause during which Nicole sampled two or three more grass-stalks. Then Clara burst out:

'I wish there was no such thing as money.'

'Oh, it's *that*. Rotten luck. Haven't you any useful relatives?'

'Not one.'

'Quite sure? I thought everyone had.'

'Well, I haven't.'

Nicole shrugged her shoulders with an angry sigh.

'I wish he'd never sent me here,' said Clara miserably. 'This place isn't meant for people like me.'

'Don't blither.'

'I'm not blithering,' said Clara with unusual conviction. 'Look at you and me. Here we wear the same uniform, eat the same food . . .'

'Unfit for human consumption.'

'. . . but in the holidays we go back to different worlds.'

'I can do what I like with my money when I'm twenty-one. We might go to China. Or Africa. It would be amusing to go somewhere uncivilized, don't you agree?'

'I've never been on so much as a day trip to Boulogne,' said Clara bitterly. 'Anyway you won't be twenty-one for five whole years. And you know as well as I do what will happen. We'll keep up writing to each other for a bit. We might even go to a concert or a theatre now and then. And it'll end by our sometimes turning up at the same Old Children's meeting and giving each other a sheepish grin.'

'We live in a changing world, my child,' said Nicole piously. 'Now many of us here may live to see great upheavals and social landmarks swept away. Even in this world, how rash to trust to mere earthly fortune. Some of you here today, daughters of fond parents who hoped to shelter you from every worldly care, may even find yourself under the painful necessity of earning your daily bread. Should such be the case . . .'

'It's jolly well going to be the case with me. It's been rubbed into me ever since I can remember. When you step into your fortune I shall probably be deciding between the dazzling alternatives of being a schoolmistress or a clerk in the Post Office.'

'I may never step into it,' said Nicole placidly. 'Papa says there will definitely be a war between France and Germany in the next few years. If France were defeated, which Heaven forbid, I might be begging you to use your influence to get me a job as Mademoiselle in a broad-minded English boarding school.'

Clara laughed but Nicole's face suddenly became serious.

'You know,' she went on, chewing her grass-stalk, thoughtfully, 'it would be far better for me if I *had* to work for my living. I'm bone lazy. I work in this place because it annoys my vanity not to come out first and because if I didn't, I'd go melancholy mad from *ennui*. As soon as I've left, I shall just run to seed.'

Clara forgot her troubles for a moment.

'Nic, what nonsense,' she said with angry affection. 'You . . . with every talent in the world. You can't just waste it all. You won't.'

Nicole rolled over on her back and stared up at the sky through the branches, with narrowed eyes. Her thin sallow face, whose beauty was all in the modelling of the bones, never looked girlish; now it seemed to be that of a woman of thirty.

When she spoke at last, Clara was struck, as so often before, by the oddness of Nicole's voice, at once hoarse and musical. 'You speak like a very good singer with a very bad cold,' she had told her once.

'Oh yes,' Nicole said. 'There's practically nothing I couldn't do . . . if I wished to. But I shan't wish. People will always give me everything I want without my even having to ask for it. I'm the cat that will always find its saucer full of cream even though it might prefer skim milk.'

'You're awfully cynical,' said Clara admiringly. 'But you're right. You always will get what you want.'

Nicole sat up and grinned. She was sixteen again.

'Except, apparently in this case.'

Clara grinned in her turn.

'Skim milk? Thanks for the compliment.'

'The whole thing's ridiculous,' said Nicole, with unusual violence. 'How do they expect me to get through three whole terms without anyone to talk to?'

'Nicole, . . . do you *really* mind?' Clara ventured.

'Yes. I mind considerably,' said Nicole coolly.

Clara was too pleased to be delicate.

'But why?' she said recklessly.

Nicole merely yawned and glanced at a wrist-watch, which, like all her possessions, had something incongruous about it.

The watch itself was tiny and exquisite. Nicole wore it on a broad, battered strap obviously meant for a man.

'Five minutes before the bell. If you've got to face Mother Lovell, you'd better go in and tidy your hair and all that rot.'

They walked in silence past the cricket pitch and up the alley of limes to the terrace. Clara found herself staring at the familiar building as if she had never seen it before. In spite of the wings of grey Victorian Gothic that had been tacked on at right angles on either side, the original creamy stucco house with its pilasters and broad shallow bows kept its eighteenth-century elegance.

'I've never thought of Mount Hilary as a house before,' she said. 'It's always been just school. But the old part is really lovely.'

'Yes. Except for grisly associations, I wouldn't mind living in it.'

'You've got a château in France, lucky beast. It must be heavenly.'

'It's very agreeable to look at. But frightfully damp and the central heating never works.'

'I don't believe you appreciate anything you've got. Even your name. If I'd been born Clara d'Ellébeuse instead of Clara Batchelor . . .' She stopped and sighed.

Nicole's face became suddenly almost stern.

'*Viens toute nue, O Clara d'Ellébeuse*,' she said softly and critically. 'I wonder if it's really as good as we used to think it.'

'Oh, *surely*, Nic.' Clara was deeply disturbed. 'It's *magical*.'

'Well, just listen to this.

> *Je trône dans l'azur comme un sphinx incompris*
> *J'unis un coeur de neige à la blancheur des cygnes,*
> *Je hais le mouvement qui déplace les lignes*
> *Et jamais je ne pleurs et jamais je ne ris.*'

Clara gasped.

'Where did you find that? Who is it? Go on.'

'Baudelaire. I've just got on to him.'

A dark girl, carrying a great brass bell by its clapper ran past them, the ends of her blue ribbon streaming behind her.

'Oh damn. There goes Luz to ring for the end of Rec.,' said Clara, whipping off her apron. 'I must fly.'

Nicole shrugged her shoulders.

'We *would* be interrupted just when we were beginning to talk sense.'

A few minutes later, smooth-haired and wearing the dark cotton gloves required on formal occasions, Clara knocked on the door with the beautifully-written inscription 'Mistress General'. For once she was not nervous when she heard Mother Lovell's quiet voice say 'Come in.' She guessed why she was wanted: there was no reason to tremble or to examine her conscience. Nevertheless, from force of old associations, her knees were a little weak as she advanced into the room and made her curtsy.

Mother Lovell was sitting as usual, pen in hand, at a desk covered with piles of orderly papers. She laid down the pen, smiled and signed to Clara to sit on the only other chair in the small bare polished room. Then she put out a white, strong-looking hand and touched the tightly-clasped gloved ones.

'My poor Clara,' she said, considering her with an expression at once affectionate, pitying and a trifle amused. 'Yes . . . I think I know how you feel.'

Clara looked back miserably into the pale face framed in the crimped white bonnet. Mother Lovell must have been a beauty in her youth but, as with almost all the nuns, Clara could not imagine her face in any other setting. The jutting white bonnet which hid the profile and the black band which covered most of the forehead gave a peculiar definition to the features they left exposed. Even the plainest face took on a certain dignity under the coif but Mother Lovell with her pallor, her large eyes, her sweet mouth, a trifle compressed when she was not smiling, might have posed for the portrait of the ideal nun. Her other-worldly beauty was, however, anchored to earth by a pair of prosaic steel-rimmed spectacles, neatly mended at the bridge with cobbler's thread and the luminous eyes behind them could be uncomfortably shrewd.

'Yes, my dear. Yes indeed,' she said, smiling in sympathy and deprecation as if Clara had spoken. 'You don't have to tell me. But it is God's will. We must both remember that.'

'Yes, Mother,' said Clara shyly and without enthusiasm.

The nun folded her hands in her black sleeves and gazed kindly yet critically at her through the steel spectacles.

'It's such a shock,' said Clara, finding her tongue at last. 'I thought I had a whole year more.'

'I know, I know,' said Mother Lovell, with a kind of humorous despair, 'but what can we do, Clara? Your dear father wrote to Reverend Mother first. I had a long talk with her this morning.'

Clara flushed, guessing what they must have talked about.

'Try not to be too sensitive about that side of it, dear child,' said Mother Lovell. 'It might happen to anyone, you know. My sister, for example. Her husband is in the army, and the pay is *very* little for a large family. She had to take her two girls away from one of our houses and send them to a day school.'

'How rot – ' said Clara, trying to be interested in Mother Lovell's unknown nieces . . . 'I mean how sad for her.'

'Perhaps I'd better tell you what Reverend Mother said.' Again she patted the gloved hands clenched so tightly in Clara's lap. 'And you mustn't let it hurt your feelings. For, dear Clara, you are a little too sensitive.'

'Am I?' said Clara. 'At home they think that I'm awfully thick-skinned.'

The nun considered her shrewdly.

'You are very frightened, my dear, aren't you, of giving yourself away? Which isn't,' she tilted her head sideways again and spoke almost apologetically, 'quite the same thing as controlling one's feelings. But at fourteen . . . or is it fifteen now?'

'Yes, Mother. I've just had a birthday.'

'Of course. I should have remembered. Well . . . one doesn't expect people to be very proficient in that at fifteen. I remember than when I was fifteen I was all prickles inside and out.'

'Were you really, Mother?' said Clara, trying vainly to imagine Mother Lovell at fifteen.

'Yes, indeed,' the nun smiled. 'But we're here to talk about *you*. Now . . . and, again, I beg you not to have hurt feelings . . . Reverend Mother said that if you had been going to finish your whole education with us, she would most willingly have found means. You understand?'

'Oh yes,' said Clara, blushing again. 'That was awf . . . *most* kind of her.'

'*But* . . . as your dear father, for one reason and another, had decided that in any case you were to leave us in a year's time . . . well, you understand, Clara?'

'Oh yes, Mother,' said Clara, with a heart of lead. She was silent for a moment, then she broke out.

'I almost wish I'd never come here. I don't belong. And yet I'd come to feel as if I did.'

'Of course you belong. Our children are always our children . . . wherever they go. Don't forget that. You must come back and see us often, often.'

'Thank you, Mother.'

But Clara did not see herself coming back often. She would not be the right kind of 'Old Child'. The nuns would be very sweet, very tolerant but she would not belong like the others whose mothers and grandmothers had been to Mount Hilary and who would one day send their own children there as a matter of course. She thought of one girl who had left and taken a job on a provincial newspaper and who came back faithfully for prize-givings and reunions. The nuns always spoke of her as 'Poor Mary'. She did not want to become 'Poor Clara'.

'I hope,' said Mother Lovell, 'that you and I will be able to have many talks before the end of the term. We shall be very sad when that day comes. Still, from the point of view of prizes, I am sure you will leave in a blaze of glory. You've always done very well in work ever since you were in the Junior School. You've inherited your dear father's brains.'

'Sometimes I wish I hadn't.'

'Clara, that is a foolish thing to say. We must not quarrel with what God chooses to give us. And he gave you a good understanding to be used in His service.' She shook her head a little. 'Oh, my dear, I wish we could have kept you a little longer. You are going out into such a very difficult world. Here you have had Catholic surroundings, Catholic friends.' She smiled. 'Don't think I fear for your faith in a Protestant school. You can be a pugnacious young person. Your very obstinacy may help you there.'

Clara blushed. She could never understand why people called her obstinate when to herself she seemed the most jelly-like and amorphous of creatures.

'No,' the nun went on, removing her spectacles and polishing them with an enormous handkerchief. 'I am thinking of later on; of a far subtler kind of attrition. It is so difficult for a convert's child. You have not had to make sacrifices for your faith as your father did. And you have not the deep-rooted habit which becomes almost instinct with children with generations of Catholic blood. I had hoped in this last year to drive your roots so much deeper into what can never fail . . . the very sources of our spiritual life.' She breathed on the glasses and frowned. 'You have done so well in your religious instruction. Our prize little apologist . . . the Canon was specially pleased with your papers. And yet . . . and yet . . . I feel as if we were sending you out on a long, rough stormy journey with a hat and an umbrella but no shoes.' She replaced her glasses and looked questioningly at Clara. 'Do you see at all what I mean?'

'Yes, I think I do. But I'm sure I'll always be a Catholic, Mother.'

Again the nun considered Clara with her head on one side. She seemed to be about to say something but did not. Clara, embarrassed, stared out of the window. Already the room, even Mother Lovell herself, seemed to belong to another life. The french windows, framed in stiff serge curtains and frosted half-way up, looked out on a dull yard at the back of the house. On the far side was a twisted yew equally dark in June or December. Only the blue sky, faintly ashen as if consuming in its own heat, indicated that it was summer. From the yard came the the slop and splash of water where the lay-sisters were washing the vegetables for supper in huge galvanized tubs. Six weeks. Forty-two more suppers.

'Your faith . . . my dear,' the nun's voice seemed to come from a distance, 'of course you will hold fast to that. And we shall all pray for you. But perhaps that wasn't quite what was in my mind.'

Suddenly she leant forward and took both Clara's hands.

'Ah, my dear child,' she said, her face radiant with affection. 'Be simple . . . be happy. Remember what St François de Sales said to Ste Jeanne de Chantal . . . "Do not turn in upon yourself . . . do not philosophize about your troubles. Go straight on." When you first came to us, you were such a happy child. Lately . . . you don't have to tell me . . . I have seen it from your expression . . . something has clouded all that. And it comes from inside you, nowhere else. I feel you are no longer simple with yourself – with others – with God.'

Clara longed to respond. 'Oh, Mother . . . if only . . .' she began.

Far away, the Community bell rang. Mother Lovell immediately dropped Clara's hands and stood up.

'I must go and say Office now. We will talk another time.'

Clara did not, after all, have her six weeks. There was an epidemic of scarlet fever and the school broke up early in an atmosphere of flurry. As Mother Lovell was one of the victims, their interrupted talk was never resumed. There was a maimed prize-giving with no bishop, no tableaux, no ceremonial white dresses and crowns of flowers, so that, though Clara had never received more prizes, she did not have her 'blaze of glory'. There was not even the comfort of a last walk with Nicole for Madame de Savigny descended suddenly and removed her daughter a day before the others. Nicole had only time to mutter 'Au revoir, ma chère. I'll write,' and to thrust into her hands a copy of *Les Fleurs du Mal* and a magnificent ivory card-case, slightly chipped, before she was hurried away.

Clara's last day at Mount Hilary was a dismal anti-climax. The nuns seemed too harrassed to remember that she was leaving. She did not even receive a summons from Reverend Mother for the ritual 'going out into the world' advice. Feeling forlorn and neglected, she slipped the Baudelaire into her pocket and set out to walk round the grounds and take a final farewell of the lime alleys, the lake and the shrines. But just as she was escaping, she was stopped by the nun in charge of the linen-room.

'Ah, the very child I was looking for,' said Mother Damaris. 'You have not handed in your white veil and your *tablier*, Clara.

Go and do so at once, will you? And don't forget to remove your number . . . neatly, mind.'

Sulky and aggrieved, she went back to the study-room and obeyed. She had come to regard the white veil, symbol of Sundays and feasts, and the faithful old black serge apron of working days, as her own property and had hoped to take them home as relics. As she unpicked her number, she was overwhelmed with self-pity. Nothing ever went right for her as it did for other people. She was always being cheated and disappointed and misunderstood. They might at least have made a little fuss of her on her very last day.

'I'm nobody . . . nobody at all,' she reflected, surveying the two detached bits of tape, 'not even a school number now.' Next term some unknown child would listen anxiously for 'forty-three' in lists of privileges or punishments. A year from now, when Nicole too had left, no one would even remember that 'forty-three' had once been Clara Batchelor.

Chapter Two

The cheerfully submissive letter Clara had written on Mother Lovell's advice must, she supposed, have been a success. Otherwise how could she account for the warmth with which her father welcomed her home? Since the day of her grandfather's funeral (neither of them had ever spoken of it) he had treated her with cold formality. Now he seemed not merely friendly, but strangely anxious to please her. He gave her money to buy clothes, told her to order a bookshelf for her prizes and even hinted at a special treat for the two of them when Isabel should be a little better.

Her mother still lay all day in bed with a nurse in attendance. When Clara first saw her face, shrunken and yellow between the two plaits that made her look like a girl suddenly aged, she was filled with remorse. She could not remember ever having loved her mother and what she felt now as mainly pity, but she tiptoed out of the room full of good resolutions.

Out of gratitude to her father, she spent more time than usual with old Mrs Batchelor. Nothing pleased him more than any attention to his mother and she could be sure that her virtue would be faithfully reported. Clara had never shared Isabel's loathing of the old lady. She was too used to her ugliness to feel it as a constant irritation and she had always found Mrs Batchelor the most reliable of allies. When she was little, her grandmother had defied Isabel's rules whenever she had the chance and Clara was still grateful for forbidden sweets and for hours spent in warm teashops when she was supposed to be having a brisk walk in the park. Now, though her grandmother bored her, she was easier in her company than in Isabel's. Mrs Batchelor's uncritical adoration was like a feather bed. At times it was stifling but, when Clara's vanity was chilled or bruised, she sank into it shamelessly. Sometimes, though she despised herself afterwards, she confided to her things she would not have dreamt of telling her mother. Such moments were intoxicating to the old lady. Her dull eyes shone and her heavy white face became almost animated. She responded with 'secrets' of her own, abortive flirtations of fifty years ago or malicious little tales of her parents' courtship.

Isabel's illness had been a great event for old Mrs Batchelor. Not only were illness and disaster of all kinds meat and drink to her but with her tyrant and rival out of the way, she blossomed into new confidence. Though she refused to take Isabel's place at the table, she ruled the house, paid the bills and ordered the food she liked. Mealtimes, without Isabel's sighs when she dropped gravy on her bodice or mishandled her knife, became pleasure instead of torture. Each week she presented a meticulous statement of her accounts and each week Claude said, 'Really, Mother, it is astonishing how far you make the housekeeping money go.'

Even in this new luxury of importance there was one thing she dared not do and that was have her tea in the drawing-room. She liked to invite Clara to a ceremonial tea in her own room and, on these occasions, she provided special cakes out of her own money.

'It gives me such a nice feeling of independence, dear,' she would say. 'When you're my age, if by any sad chance you're not well off, you'll realize how much that means.'

Isabel regarded Mrs Batchelor's room with such horror that she went into it as seldom as possible and never without wishing to burn every object in it. Into its small space were crammed all the pieces of furniture that old Mrs Batchelor had managed to save from the shabby homes of her married life. A vast double bed, even more hideous than the one she had given Claude and Isabel, occupied most of the floor; the walls were lined with rickety wardrobes, piles of dusty cardboard boxes, chests of drawers with missing handles, and tattered trunks only half concealed by faded bits of cretonne. Though there were two bathrooms in the house, Mrs Batchelor refused to part with a huge, marble-topped washstand on which there always stood, behind the ugly jug and basin, ranks of stained medicine bottles and a tumbler containing her spare set of false teeth. Even when the window was open, which it seldom was, the room retained its peculiar smell of gas, stale clothes, and camphor balls. Sometimes these dense permanent layers were thinly super-imposed with the scent of lavender water. But, instead of freshening the air, this merely gave it the peculiar sickliness of perfume on unwashed flesh.

Clara, like everyone but old Mrs Batchelor herself, found the smell oppressive, but she was inured to it almost from babyhood. She could even bring herself to smile and nod when her grandmother, on winter afternoons, drawing the plush curtains and turning the leaking gas fire full on, would say happily, 'Now we're really cosy, aren't we, dear?'

However, as it was July, she was spared the torment of the gas fire and, though she longed for the coolness of the airy drawing-room, she bore these intimate tea-parties tol-erably well. During the first of them her grandmother said reflectively:

'I don't expect Daddy ever told you – he is so thoughtful, he wouldn't want to upset you – how nearly we lost your dear mother.'

'He did in one letter. Till then I didn't realize she was as ill as all that.'

'Oh, very ill. Very ill indeed.'

Clara saw from her grandmother's secret, yet inviting look

that she would tell her all about it if pressed. But, for some reason, Cara decided not to press.

'Ah well,' said the old woman, disappointed, 'there are some things it's better for you not to know yet awhile. Something internal, your mother had. She was always delicate internally, you know.'

'Was she?' said Clara, uninterested.

'Yes, indeed. Though I've my ideas on that subject. But I keep them to myself as I keep many things. Still, how thankful we should be that she was spared. Your dear Daddy would have been broken-hearted.'

The idea of her mother's dying had never seriously occurred to Clara. Now, in the very effort of putting it out of her mind, she found herself toying with it. It was impossible not to think how much more peaceful life at Valetta Road was at the moment. Then she remembered that, if her mother had died, she would have had to face her father's misery.

'Yes,' she said sincerely. 'I don't think I could have borne *that*.'

'You do love your Daddy, don't you?' purred Mrs Batchelor. 'And how he does love you. Ah, I know how it feels to love an only child. I never forgot my dear baby Helen that I lost, but your father was everything to me. And one of these days his little girl will grow up and get married and leave him. I've often thought it was a pity you had no brothers or sisters. You'd have liked them, wouldn't you dear?'

'They might have been rather fun,' said Clara stolidly. Just how much she wanted them, brothers especially, was a secret too personal to be told to any member of her family.

'It's sad,' sighed Mrs Batchelor, 'but we mustn't blame anyone, must we? Though from the first I never did think she looked healthy. Such a sallow skin. No, she wasn't at all the type your Daddy admired as a rule. He always thought so much of pink cheeks and golden hair. Like yours, dear.'

'I hate them myself,' said Clara.

'You naughty little thing. Why it's the real English type of beauty. Now, Ada, Cousin Horace's wife . . . you'd never think it to see her now, poor thing . . . was quite a picture as a girl. Golden curls she had and quite a perfect complexion. I've been told someone wanted to paint her likeness for the Royal Academy. Still I must say your mother's worn better. But she's had a kind husband and an easy life.'

'It must be awful to be married to that man.'

Mrs Batchelor sighed and wagged her head:

'Ah, I daresay she often wishes things had turned out otherwise.'

'You're looking mysterious, Granny. Tell me all.'

'Well, if I do, dear, you must promise never to mention it.'

Clara pursed her lips and nodded, pretending an interest she was far from feeling.

'I'm afraid there's no denying your Daddy was a bit of a flirt in his day. Fancy, people used to say the same of your old Granny. You'd never think it now, would you?'

'I know you were a heart-breaker. Aunt Sophy's told me things. But I shan't give her away.'

'You mustn't believe all you hear,' said the old lady with a smile at once fatuous and touching. 'Well, as I was saying there was a time when your Daddy was quite sweet on Cousin Ada. Of course she wasn't married then. And she was very taken by him; no girl could have helped being. I know poor Horace had many a twinge of jealousy. There's no knowing what might have happened if your mother hadn't come along. But after he'd met Miss Isabel Maule, Daddy stopped having eyes for anyone else. I know Ada was more than a little upset. The funny thing was it seemed to make Horace all the keener to marry her. Men are very peculiar sometimes. I've an idea he's paid her out in all sorts of little ways. And of course, right from a little boy, he's been jealous of your Daddy.'

The horrible lunch party at Paget's Fold came back into Clara's mind with new significance. She realized for the first time that her father and mother had had a life before she existed and that all those dull relatives whom she could never imagine otherwise than middle-aged had once been young and capable of feeling.

She said thoughtfully:

'If Daddy *had* married Ada, I wouldn't have existed. At any rate I wouldn't have been the same person.'

'No doubt there's a Providence in these things,' said Mrs

Batchelor piously. 'I often say to myself, "at least there's dear little Clara".'

'I suppose no one ever understands really why any two people get married.'

Mrs Batchelor looked frightened.

'Oh, please don't misunderstand me, Clara. Don't get the idea that I would ever dream of criticizing your mother.' She raised her voice as if she thought Isabel might be listening at the door. 'I wish you could have seen your mother when she was young, dear. Really, she was a very striking-looking girl. Quite fascinating, many people thought.'

Clara smiled.

'Don't be so desperately charitable, Granny. We all know she's awful to you sometimes.'

'I daresay it's my fault. I'm sure I never mean to vex her. But every little thing does seem to aggravate her so.'

'I often think I was born with a skin too few,' quoted Clara.

'You naughty, naughty little girl,' said Mrs Batchelor comfortably. 'Well, we all have our faults. I often blame old Mr Maule. He really did spoil her shockingly. He was very strict with his other children, but he gave in to Belle, as he called her, in everything.'

'Her sisters must have been awfully jealous.'

'I don't know, I'm sure. If they were, they were too frightened of their father to show it. A really terrible temper old Mr Maule had. I've seen him threaten your poor Grandpa with a poker. Of course he didn't at all care for her marrying into a family that he considered so much beneath him. With her looks he'd hoped she'd marry a title or at least a very rich man.'

'I suppose she did have lots of admirers?'

'Oh certainly, dear, by all accounts. But she hadn't a penny you know. And, though it was a very old family and all that, her father couldn't afford for her to have what you call a society life. Besides he quarrelled with all his relations. There was only one Lord I ever heard of wanted to marry her and he was a wicked old man with one foot in the grave. I'll say to her credit she wouldn't have him.'

'I suppose she was awfully in love with Daddy.'

'Oh yes. I'm sure she was. In the nature of things it had to be a very long engagement. Four whole years. It must have been very trying to anyone of her impatient disposition.'

'Didn't Daddy get impatient too?'

'No doubt. She always expected so much attention. And your Daddy was working so hard. Many a time when he ought to have been resting, he'd go all that way down to Norwood to see her for an hour. And of course they had their ups and downs. It was wonderful how he put up with all her little tantrums. Often I thought he ought to have been firmer with her for her own sake but it wasn't for me to say. And as I was telling you just now, we ought to blame old Mr Maule rather than her. If she'd been the only one, he couldn't have spoilt her more.'

An old grievance flared up in Clara.

'People always say only children are spoilt.'

'I'm sure that's not true of you, dear,' said her grandmother. 'Quite the reverse.'

'They always say it though,' said Clara resentfully. 'I get absolutely sick of it at school. They just assume if you're an only child you're a kind of monster. Even if they don't think you're particularly spoilt, they assume you're bound to be queer in some way.'

'In my opinion you could have done with a bit more spoiling when you were little. Your grandfather thought the same. Many's the time your Daddy hasn't dared show how fond he was of you for fear of . . . well, I won't say it. I daresay you can guess what I mean.'

Without knowing why, Clara suddenly felt disgusted with herself. The room seemed to have become unbearably stuffy. She glanced at the clock and gave a false start of alarm.

'Heavens, I'd no idea it was so late. I've only just time to get up to Mudie's to change Mother's book.'

'You've plenty time for another éclair,' said Mrs Batchelor. 'I know how you love them. The clock's ten minutes fast. In any case, you've lots of time if you take a bus.'

'No, Granny, really. I've had far too many éclairs already. I'd better go and walk them off.'

She stood up and shook the crumbs from her skirt.

'Well, if you insist,' sighed the old woman. 'I daresay the walk will do you good. But you must be tired of going the same way every day to change your mother's library book. Daddy appreciates what a good girl you've been since Mother was ill. It's wonderful the number of books she gets through lying there, isn't it?'

'I don't blame her,' said Clara. 'I always long for new books when I'm in the infirmary. We have to make some ghastly saint's life last for days.'

'You're an unselfish little thing, aren't you? Just like your Daddy. Don't think for a minute I'm blaming your mother. I'm sure I like a good read myself when I've the time. Poor Mummy, she must miss her bridge parties. Though, even when she's well, she's a great reader, isn't she?'

'So am I,' said Clara, driven for some reason to defend her mother.

'Yes. But you haven't got household duties. I often wonder if your mother wouldn't be happier if she took some interest in household things. It doesn't seem natural, somehow, a woman spending so much time lying on a sofa and reading, the way she does. Still, it's not for me to criticize. At any rate you can't lose money while you're reading as you can at bridge.'

Clara kissed the cheek the old woman offered her. She had never noticed before how damp and flabby it was.

'Thank you for a really lovely tea, Granny,' she said, impelled suddenly to assume her best Mount Hilary manner. 'I've enjoyed myself *so* much.'

Her grandmother looked up at her admiringly, yet with a touch of fear.

'Dear me, how you're growing up. It comes over me with quite a shock that you're not just a little thing any more. But you'll always be Daddy's girl, won't you?'

In spite of the unusual peace at home, the days had never dragged so heavily for Clara as they did that July. She pined for Mount Hilary and woke up each brilliant morning longing for the sight of its trees and meadows and the sound of its bells. All the children she knew were still at their schools; even at weekends she dared not invite anyone to tea for fear of disturbing her mother's rest or the nurse's. Sickness brooded over the house, upsetting its routine. Rooms grew dusty and silver tarnished, for the two servants were tired and cross from overwork. The endless carrying of trays up five flights of stairs had made even the friendly Zillah sulky. Clara spent most of her time running errands in the baking streets or reading aimlessly in her bedroom. The one or two brief notes that came from Nicole only sharpened her feeling of isolation. Though Nicole was in London and only a mile or two away, she might, as far as Clara was concerned, have been on the other side of the world. She seemed to be immersed in dressmakers, dances and theatres. In a letter she wrote, 'I am seriously thinking of entering. It would at least save one from the boredom of having to have one's hair done and changing one's clothes three times a day. The only thing that seriously deters me is the thought of Community recreation. I could easily get used to a hair shirt but not to "cheerful, edifying impersonal conversations" twice a day with the same women.' In another she suggested that she should slip away from her chaperone and meet Clara 'in the National Gallery or the British Museum like a guilty couple in Henry James'. But Clara, struck with panic, had made the excuse that she could not leave her mother. In all their three years' friendship she had never met Nicole outside Mount Hilary. Though in one way she longed to see her again, it was not only shyness that made her refuse. Since she had come back home, a kind of inertia had settled on her. She felt dull and stupid; she no longer expected, hardly even wanted anything interesting to happen. Monotony came to have an oppressive charm. She almost dreaded any break in the chalk circle in which she found herself stuck like a hypnotized bird.

Chapter Three

One morning at breakfast her father said carelessly:

'Are you by any chance free on Thursday evening, Clara?'

As she had been in every evening since she came home, she answered, wondering:

'Yes, of course. Why?'

'Only that they've extended the Opera season and I've managed to get two rather good seats for *Tannhäuser* if you'd care to come.'

Realizing this must be the promised treat, she said excitedly: 'Care to? I'd *love* to. Do you really mean it?'

He beamed at her.

'Certainly I mean it. I always promised to take you to *Tannhäuser* when you were fifteen.'

'Daddy always keeps his promises,' purred old Mrs Batchelor. 'Fancy your going to the Opera at night like a grand lady, Clara. She must wear her best frock, mustn't she, Claude? Granny'll wash and iron it for you, dear.'

Clara saw that this was to be a great occasion. The only cloud was the fear that she might not rise to it and thus disappoint him once again. For *Tannhäuser* was his one musical passion. He never went to concerts and music for him was almost entirely an affair of associations. He was fond of Gilbert and Sullivan because he had first heard them at Cambridge and he was deeply moved by certain old German songs and Chopin nocturnes because Isabel had played and sung them during their courtship.

Larry O'Sullivan, his great friend at Emmanuel, had been an ardent Wagnerian and, under Larry's influence, he had gone so far as to buy all the scores. But, except for *Tannhäuser* which was kept in the piano stool and tattered from use, they had gathered dust for twenty years in the darkest corner of the study.

He had fallen in love with *Tannhäuser* at the first hearing and each time he heard it he fell more in love than ever. He never missed a performance if he could help it and he always returned in a state of extraordinary elation. Almost always he went alone, for Isabel had never been able to understand why anyone should wish to see a play or hear an opera more than once. On this subject he was proof against Isabel's jeers. If she went too far he jeered in turn at her beloved Ibsen and Maeterlinck.

'I've no patience with your chlorotic adulteresses and your Don Juans in goloshes,' he would say. 'I am prepared to tread the primrose path to the sound of flutes but not to limp to perdition to the wheeze of a harmonium.'

For years he had been preparing Clara for her solemn initiation. When she was a small child, he had told her the story over and over again and she had hardly learnt her scales before he gave her a piano arrangement of the score. Now that she could play reasonably well, he listened patiently to Beethoven and Mozart on condition that she would give him 'just a morsel of *Tannhäuser* for a *bonne bouche*'. Invariably, after this, he would say, 'Ah, my child, you don't know what pleasure that gives me.' and, once or twice, she had seen actual tears of happiness in his eyes.

Sometimes, if he had a pupil-free half-hour on a Sunday morning, he would go himself to the old yellow-keyed piano and thunderously vamp out the Pilgrim's March or even sing extracts in odd transpositions he had made to fit his pleasant, short-ranged tenor. All her life, Clara associated the Sunday mornings of her youth in London with High Mass at the Carmelites, the smell of a roasting joint and her father's voice solemnly chanting:

> 'The light of heaven o-hon the pi-hil-grim glow-eth
> In holy freedo-hom and pea-eace now he go-eth'

or crying with full-throated fervour:

> 'The wi-hi-hill I sing,
> Oh Goddess young and te-hender.'

'You are too young yet to appreciate all it means,' he had often told her. 'I don't think I did myself until I became a Catholic. Now *Tannhäuser* seems to me the perfect expression of the whole problem of good and evil.'

When the great night came, Clara dressed herself in her white muslin party frock and the soft pale blue cloak from Liberty's that Mrs Shapiro had sent her the Christmas before last. Her newly-washed hair, adorned with a blue bow, hung in a shining mass over her shoulders. When she went up to say goodbye to her mother, she felt almost guilty for being so young and fresh and healthy. Isabel, lying among crumpled pillows with her limp hair pushed back anyhow from a face yellow as wax, seemed to have no connection with the sleek beauty of a few months ago.

'Darling, how charming you look,' she said wistfully. 'The

picture of youth. I wish I could have a portrait of you, just as you are at this moment.'

From force of habit, and for once unreproved, Clara fiddled with one of the brass knobs of the bed.

'It's only my old white muslin,' she said awkwardly. 'It's a shame you can't come too. You really must hurry up and get better.'

'Sometimes I wonder if I ever shall,' Isabel sighed.

'Of course you will,' said Clara heartily. 'The doctor says you're going on splendidly.'

'Doctors don't know everything.' The great dark eyes stared hungrily. 'Still, it does me good to see you. I've always loved everything young and gay and pretty. Oh why is life so cruel to women? But I shouldn't talk like this when yours is only just beginning. Come and kiss me, pet.'

Clara did so. Isabel, always so fresh, so perfumed, now had a sickly smell.

'Like a flower you look and feel,' she said, stroking Clara's bare arm. 'What a lovely cool white skin.'

The faint invalid voice became stronger.

'Don't grow up too fast. Something tells me you'll be attractive to men, just as I was. And whatever you do, don't be in too much of a hurry to get married.'

Clara laughed.

'Oh, I'll most probably be an old maid.'

Her mother smiled wanly.

'I can't quite see you as that. Though perhaps they're happier. Marriage can be so dreadfully disillusioning if one is at all romantic.' She sighed. 'And I *was* romantic.'

Clara waited for the usual sequel; the story of how, the first Christmas after their marriage, her father had gone out to dinner with some old friends from Cambridge and come home drunk. But it did not come. Instead her mother said hurriedly, almost guiltily:

'Don't think I am saying anything against Daddy. No, no. He is far better than most of them. It is what men are in themselves or what marriage is. Call it nature if you like.' She looked intently at Clara. 'I wonder, darling, have you any idea of such things?'

Clara frowned and clutched the brass knob. Her idea of 'such things' was of the haziest. The nuns, naturally, never mentioned them and at Mount Hilary it was not the fashion to discuss them, even with one's most intimate friends. But lately she had been reading *Adam Bede* and *Tess of the d'Urbervilles* and these had raised a very puzzling question. Her mother was, however, the last person she was inclined to ask for the answer.

'Oh yes, of course,' she said off-handedly.

'Really dear? Do you mean to say you know *everything*? Somehow I never thought the nuns . . .'

'I think things out for myself,' said Clara grandly.

'You're so clever, pet,' said her mother. 'All the same . . . But perhaps modern girls are different.' She lay back and, relapsing into her invalid voice, went on:

'I knew nothing. Absolutely nothing. Never, never shall I forget the appalling shock, the dreadful disillusion. And when a woman has a child, she goes down to the gates of hell.'

'Clara,' sounded Claude's voice from downstairs. Never had interruption been more welcome.

'I must go, Mummy. You know he hates to be kept waiting.'

With a hasty kiss and 'have a good night' she made her escape. She went downstairs, feeling obscurely angry with her mother as if, in some way, she had spoilt the evening. But when she saw her father standing in the hall and looking up at her with an almost mischievous smile, as if they were fellow conspirators, all her sense of freshness and gaiety came back.

'Ah, I'm glad you're in white, my dear,' he greeted her. 'Nothing suits you so well.' From behind his back he produced a spray of pink carnations. 'And here is something to match your cheeks. I have even remembered a pin.'

'Oh, *thank* you, Daddy. You do look magnificent,' she said, pinning on her flowers and gazing at him with admiration. Evening clothes suited him; they set off his fairness and made him seem taller. Never, she thought, had she seen him looking so young and handsome.

She giggled with sheer happiness.

'I never thought I'd go to the Opera with you in your opera hat, I *do* feel grand.'

He offered his arm.

'Your carriage is waiting.'

To her amazement, it was no mere taxi but a hired car with a chauffeur in livery. A hired car was the very greatest of luxuries, associated only with the most solemn family feasts such as her parents' wedding anniversary. Never before had he ordered one just for Clara.

'Daddy, you *are* spoiling me,' she said, leaning back on the thick grey cushions.

'Ah well, I am spoiling myself too. Once in a while, I like to enjoy the illusion of being rich.'

She nodded, too excited to speak. The chains of street lamps slid by in the July dusk. She felt as if London were illuminated in their honour.

'Do you mind if I smoke?'

He had never asked her permission before.

'Of course. Or does one say, of course not?'

'I take it I may?' He took out a gold case, presented by a grateful pupil, which he hardly ever used. To see him smoking a cigarette instead of his eternal pipe added to the delightful strangeness of everything. Glancing at his face, shining with pleasure among the blue wreaths of smoke, it was impossible to realize that this was the father who had paralysed her with terror. Their last drive together in a hired car, those appalling journeys to and from her grandfather's funeral, seemed as unreal as someone else's nightmare. Hardly noticing what she was doing, she tucked her arm through his as she used to do when she was a child. For several minutes they drove in blissful silence. Then he turned his face to her.

'Happy? Not bored at the thought of an evening alone with your aged parent?'

'Fisher,' she mocked him. 'Shameless fisher. I won't bite. And how dare you say you're old?'

She meant it. For the first time it occurred to her that he was probably not so very old after all. Until then, all grown-ups had seemed to her much the same age. They did not grow older as one did oneself; they simply belonged to a different species of human being. Very old people, like her grandmother, were merely another kind of grown-up.

He squeezed her arm.

'I'm perfectly willing to forget the question of age if you are. In fact I'm only too willing to forget everything tonight. Let us ignore the fact that I am a beggarly usher. Let us spend too much and be monstrously irresponsible.'

'I hate responsibility,' said Clara recklessly. '*Carpe noctem*.'

'Precisely. *Lente, lente, currite notis equi*.'

'Oh, they don't run *lente* enough,' she breathed. 'Why do nice things go so fast? We're nearly there.'

It was the first time Clara had been inside Covent Garden. From their seats in the front row of the circle, the whole house opened before them like the interior of a vast gold and crimson shell. She had never imagined anything like the great tiers, the massed flowers and the blazing chandeliers. Each box was like a tiny limelit stage with its curtains parted to reveal dazzling creatures from another world. She was so entranced that she almost forgot she had come to hear *Tannhäuser* and her programme lay unopened on her lap.

'I wanted you to have a proper first impression,' he said, revelling in her dazed delight. 'When I'm alone, I often go in the "gods". But your first *Tannhäuser* must be something to remember.'

He had even brought opera-glasses which he directed for her from box to box, telling her names to which she barely listened. The pleasure of being able to turn the brilliant puppets at will into human beings was interest enough. It was fascinating to bring a face so close that she could watch the play of every feature; to guess what made a woman smile or suddenly unfold her fan.

'Oh, it's wonderful,' she said. 'It's like seeing hundreds of novels all coming to life at once.'

'Probably not a quarter of them have come for the music. You'll see how the boxes empty after the first act. But I love to see them. Heaven forbid that Covent Garden should ever be filled with Jaeger suits and djibbahs.'

'Amen,' said Clara fervently.

'All the same, if a duchess chattered during the first bars of the overture, I should have not the least hesitation in shooting her.' He took the glasses from her and swept them round the boxes.

'Ah, my dear, there is something you really must look at. Yes, there is no mistaking *her* – Lady Sybil Clavering – the Duke of Westmorland's younger daughter. The gold and white, the goddess type. A Greek nymph with the English dew on her. But it would take Meredith to describe her.'

Clara took the glasses and searched obediently for the famous beauty.

'Third box . . . on the left . . . wearing something soft, white and clinging as male novelists say. No, you are looking at the wrong box.'

She found Lady Sybil and said warmly: 'Oh yes, she really is lovely,' but in her search she had seen something far more interesting. After a decent interval, she switched the glasses back to the wrong box.

'Daddy, there's a girl I know there. I wasn't sure at first, but now I am.'

'Really? Who is that?'

'Nicole de Savigny.'

'Your great friend at the convent. How interesting. May I look? Certainly a remarkable face, my dear. Not perhaps what one would call pretty, but piquant, undeniably piquant. And is that extremely distinguished-looking woman her mother? The Comtesse de Savigny, I believe you said.'

'Yes, I think so. But I've only seen her in the parlour and in a hat.'

'Do you know the Comtesse at all?'

'Oh no. We don't talk to other people's parents unless we know them at home.'

She glanced at him, afraid she might have hurt his feelings. But the glasses masked his expression. She wished he would put them down. Suppose Nicole should see them staring at her?

'I fancy you told me the Comtesse de Savigny had been an ambassadress. I must say she looks the part.'

At last he put down the glasses.

'Like all the low-born, I have a passion for the aristocracy,' he said.

Clara was too fond of him tonight to wince.

'Darling Daddy, I wish I could make you a duke.'

'And destroy my passion? My dear, you are too young to appreciate the exquisite taste of discontent.' He laughed. 'I agree it would have to be a duke. I haven't the figure for an earl. But dukes are often short and bucolic.'

'*You're* not bucolic,' she said indignantly. 'Blaze Hoadley is, if you like.' She stopped and bit her tongue. Now she had wrecked everything. But to her amazement he merely smiled and said:

'Ah, your rustic swain. My Chloë should have a prettier Daphnis.'

Clara had no time to brood on the incomprehensibility of parents for already the lights were lowered. There was a hush; then the first grave chords of the overture sounded in the darkness. Her father gave a sigh of pleasure and leant back with closed eyes.

In spite of all his warnings she could not help being disconcerted that both Venus and Tannhäuser should be so elderly and so very fat. But the smell of scent and dust, the glimmer of white shirt fronts and creamy shoulders in the vast dim house, the sense of being present at some extraordinary ritual soon produced a kind of intoxication. She forgot everything and let herself drown in the sensuous, easy music.

When the lights went up, she and Claude blinked at each other as if waking from the same rapturous dream.

'Well?'

'Oh, *Daddy*!'

He patted her hand.

'Ah, my dear, I'm so glad. I hoped you would feel as I do. Certainly I've heard better Tannhäusers. But what does that matter? In heaven, no doubt, de Reszke will sing it for me. Meanwhile, imagination bridges the gap.'

He began to talk of the genius that could so perfectly express in music the conflict between the two sides of a man's nature.

'Every man,' he said, 'is both Wolfram and Tannhäuser. But women are different. They are either Venus or Elizabeth.'

Clara listened with parted lips and shining eyes, as he talked on. She felt she was being initiated into a new world and abandoned herself completely to this extraordinary, transformed father. She thought with his mind, heard with his ears, until both his talk and the music she had just heard seemed a revelation of something at once subtle, exciting and profound.

Suddenly, in mid-flight, he broke off.

'I had forgotten, for the moment, you were only a child.'

'Oh, *please* go on forgetting.'

He shook his head, smiling.

'Let us take a turn and have a look at the lions.'

Reluctantly she followed him out to the foyer. Brilliantly dressed women, gay as tropical birds against the magpie elegance of their escorts sauntered to and fro chattering, fanning themselves, staring through their lorgnettes. At close quarters Clara found them less glamorous than in the frames of their boxes. When her father left her to get her some lemonade, she leant rather disconsolately against the wall, bewildered by the hubbub of shrill and languid voices and the glitter of jewels and sequins. Never had she felt more of a stranger than among this chattering, parading crowd of people who all seemed to know each other. Suddenly a hand was laid on her arm and a familiar husky voice said:

'Well, are you going to cut me?'

'Nicole!'

'I've escaped. Half the German embassy has invaded our box and I can't stand Germans. What luck to find *you* here.'

In a sophisticated pink evening dress, with a pearl comb in her unnaturally tidy hair, Nicole looked five years older. However, she wore her fine feathers as carelessly as her school uniform. She had obviously been dressed by a maid but already wisps were straying from the elaborate coiffure, a hook had come undone and the camellias on her shoulder had a battered look. Her hands, manicured and artificially whitened, fidgeted in search of non-existent pockets and her silver-shod feet were planted in her usual masculine stance.

'I feel like a circus-horse on these occasions,' she said. 'I'm not the type that can appear in public, in white muslin with its hair down. You can, my dear Clara, most successfully. The perfect English *jeune fille*. Who are you with?'

'My father. But I've lost him for the moment.'

'If you find him, you must introduce me,' said Nicole. 'You know how I long to meet this *parent terrible* of yours. Did you come to *Die Meistersinger* last week?'

Clara blushed.

'It's the first time in my life that I've been to the Opera.'

'Pity you've chosen such a rotten night. I'm not mad on Wagner even at his best but *Tannhäuser* really ought to be prohibited. It's musically indecent. Thank goodness, we are going after the next act.'

'Don't say that to my father,' said Clara in agony. 'He adores it.' She had not the courage to say, 'I'm adoring it too.'

Nicole shrugged her shoulders.

'Oh well. Each man to his own poison. I wonder why the English have this passion for Wagner. I suppose because, like the Germans, they've never been properly civilized.'

Clara sketched a curtsy.

'*Merci bien.*'

'Idiot, I don't mean you. Besides, I've a German grandfather if it comes to that.'

As they talked, Nicole once or twice broke off to smile or wave her fan at an acquaintance.

'It's so strange, meeting you here,' sighed Clara. 'I suppose you know lots of these people.'

'Oh, one runs into them everywhere.'

'I don't.'

'Well, you don't miss much. Thank goodness we go to France the day after tomorrow.

'Lucky wretch. I wonder if I shall *ever* go abroad.'

'What's the matter, *mon vieux*? I seem to have a depressing effect on you. You have a hunted look as if you expected to be arrested any moment.'

Nicole had hit exactly on Clara's state of mind. She was in an agony in case her father would join them. How would he appear to Nicole's merciless eye?

'Fickle creature. I don't believe you are a bit glad to see your childhood's friend.'

Clara clasped her hands together in misery.

'Oh, I am, Nicole, I am. If only there weren't all these people. I feel so stupid and bewildered. If you knew how I'd missed you. It might be five years instead of five weeks.'

'Well, I did my best to lure you to an assignation,' Nicole smiled with faint malice. 'I presume your mother is better since you and your Papa are both here.'

'Oh, much better.' Clara could feel herself blushing.

'Otherwise,' said Nicole, prodding her with her fan, 'I might be tempted to think you were shunning me. Now I don't see much hope. I hardly get a second to breathe since *Maman* decided to drag me through the fag-end of the season. I suppose she thought I mightn't have another chance if there's a war.'

'A war? Do you really think there might be?'

'You seem very surprised. Don't any rumours reach you in your remote tower?'

In the distance Clara caught sight of her father working his way towards them through the crowd. Nicole followed her look.

'Is that your Papa? The fair one with the moustache? He's absurdly like you.'

'Is he?' said Clara, faintly.

'*Ma chère*, you've completely misled me. I expected a tyrant with beetling brows. He looks like a cross between a cherub and one of the later Roman Emperors, the mild ones. The chin's slightly intimidating I admit. I insist on being presented to him.'

He was only a few yards away when, to Clara's relief, a majestic woman bore down on Nicole.

'*Ah, te violà enfin, Nicole. Ta maman m'a envoyée te chercher. C'est même un peu fort ce que tu fais là Londres, les fillettes ne se promènent pas toutes seules à l'Opéra.*'

With a freezing glance at Clara, she clutched Nicole's arm.

'*Viens donc, ma belle.*'

Nicole shrugged her shoulders:

'*D'accord, ma tante. Mais permets d'abord que je présente une grande amie du Pensionnat, Clara Batchelor. Clara chérie, Madame la Marquise de Vuillaume Grandpré.*'

The aunt coldly inclined her head: '*Mademoiselle.*'

'*Connais pas ce nom là,*' she whispered audibly to her niece.

'*Au revoir, mon vieux.* I'll write to you from France,' said Nicole glancing back with a grimace and a wave of her fan as she moved off under escort.

'*Au revoir,* Nicole.'

With a sigh half sad, half relieved, Clara watched Nicole's rose-coloured dress disappear into the crowd. When she looked up her father was standing beside her with a radiant face.

'How charming of your friend to seek you out like that. I was watching you but didn't want to intrude.'

'But you should have, Daddy,' said Clara. 'Nicole was saying how much she wanted to meet you.'

She chattered on recklessly, as she sipped the lemonade he had brought, trying to make up to him for her cowardice. 'She kept on saying so. And she picked you out at once. She said we were exactly alike.'

He could not hide his pleasure.

'Come, come, my dear, that is hardly flattering to you, though extremely gratifying to me.'

'Oh . . . and she said you looked like a Roman Emperor.'

'Indeed. That, again, can hardly apply to you. But I must say I take it as a compliment. I almost regret that I did not come forward. I should have liked to meet this charming young person. But I got a peculiar pleasure from watching the two of you together. Will you be seeing her again in the next interval? Then, perhaps . . .'

'No, they're going after this act. Isn't it a shame?' she added a lie. 'Nicole is furious. But she has to go on to some embassy dance or other.'

'*Noblesse oblige*. What a price to pay, though, to miss the last act of *Tannhäuser*. Still, no doubt she has heard it often. I think you told me she was musical.'

'Oh yes. Tremendously.'

'And who was that rather alarming but extremely impressive lady to whom she introduced you. Not, I think, the Comtesse de Savigny.'

'No, an aunt of hers. The Marquise de . . . sorry I can't remember the name.'

'My dear, you give me glimpses of a brilliant world,' he said as they made their way back to their seats.

Clara roused herself loyally and put her hand on his sleeve.

'And who brought me to Covent Garden?'

'My child, I have no illusions about myself. But when I saw you just now with your friend, I could not help feeling proud. I have always cherished the fancy that one day, to quote the immortal Carter, "from the top of my bus I shall look down on your carriage".'

The second act was ruined for Clara. Try as she would, she could not help being aware of Nicole's presence. One half of her still shared her father's uncritical ecstasy; the other half was imagining Nicole's amused distaste. Over and over again her eyes strayed from the stage, searching the huge darkened house for a particular box. Not till the lights went up and she saw that it was already empty, could she settle down to enjoy herself again. During the third act she tucked her arm penitently into her father's and he gave it a little squeeze. Once or twice she glanced at him, fearing that she might have broken the bond between them, but each time his head turned at once to meet her look and, in the dimness, she could see that his expression was one of solemn rapture. To her relief, he smiled when the blossoming staff, laid across the convex mound of Tannhäuser's stomach, began to sway up and down like a see-saw.

'The sublime certainly has its ridiculous moments,' he said as they stood up to go. 'Personally I adore them. Opera wouldn't be opera without them.'

As he settled the blue cloak on her shoulders, he smiled mysteriously.

'Not too sleepy, I hope? Because I have a mild surprise for you.'

Clara opened her eyes very wide.

'Of *course* I'm not sleepy.'

'Then I suggest we go and have a little supper.'

Chapter Four

It was evident from his manner that he was taking her somewhere special, but Clara had been to few restaurants and the name he gave the chauffeur meant nothing to her. When they were ushered into a single room not very large and rather dim, she was at first disappointed. She had expected something with bright lights and a band. Here there were only a few tables, lit with shaded lamps, though she noticed that the people sitting at them looked extremely elegant.

The room was so quiet, the curtains so heavy and the lights so subdued that the place might have been designed to protect delicate creatures from glare and noise. She walked behind the waiter on tip-toe till she found that her feet made no sound on the thick carpet. She and her father seemed to be expected. The table to which they were led had a vase of Clara's favourite pink carnations and beside it stood a gold-necked bottle in a pail of ice. She returned from leaving her cloak in charge of an alarming Frenchwoman, feeling absurdly young and selfconscious in her white muslin. One or two men gave her a languid, faintly amused stare. To her relief their own table was in a corner and from her place she could see no one but her father.

'I took the risk of ordering our supper beforehand,' he said as she sat down. 'I hope I have guessed what you'd like. I thought you would prefer cold *consommé* to oysters. Though we can eat them safely here even when there is no "r" in the month. I propose to do so. Then a little salmon, with asparagus tips. Chicken, with a rather special cream sauce you get nowhere else, and *omelette surprise* for a sweet. Does that sound all right?'

'It sounds wonderful,' Clara murmured, her eye on the waiter who was busy with the gold-necked bottle. When the cork flew out with a soft explosion, she managed not to look surprised.

'Yes . . . a little champagne for Mademoiselle,' her father nodded. 'If you don't like it, Clara, no doubt François can find you something else.'

'Of course I like it,' she said grandly, though she had only had occasional sips at weddings and much preferred fizzy lemonade. The waiter filled their glasses and, to her comfort, disappeared.

'It's lovely and cold,' she said, sipping it carefully and trying not to make a face. '*Much* nicer than any I've had before.'

'I ordered it partly for your sake. Though I admit I have a weakness for champagne myself. Strictly speaking, *Tannhäuser* calls for one of the Rhine wines . . . "the silver harp and the stained legend". But you might be a shade too young for a still wine.'

To show that she could at least appreciate champagne, Clara took a large gulp and tried not to wish it were sweeter. But when she tasted her *consommé* there was no need to pretend. Never had she imagined mere soup could taste so delicious.

'I see you have the makings of a *gourmet*.'

'I certainly do love luxury and nice things,' she sighed happily. 'We're being wickedly luxurious tonight, aren't we?'

'Ah well,' he smiled. 'The old hack must get out of harness once in a while. I confess I should like to be able to do this a little more often.'

Watching his face, it was impossible to imagine that he could ever be other than genial and expansive.

'You're a different person without your harness,' she risked. 'Oh, I do wish you could be awfully rich.'

'Riches are bad for the soul. We all subscribe to that . . . in theory. Yet sometimes I wonder if it isn't just as bad for the soul to be endlessly worrying about how one's going to pay one's bills.'

'I'm sure it is,' said Clara enthusiastically.

'But let's forget bills for tonight. By rights every penny we are spending should be going into some doctor's or draper's or tax-collector's pocket. After all, should I enjoy all this so much without the lurking sense of guilt? The only way to overcome a temptation is to yield to it.'

Between mouthfuls of delicious salmon, Clara stared at him fascinated. Was this really her father, the slave of duty, the stern disciplinarian who scolded her when she overspent her pocket money?

'I don't often break out,' he said, half apologetically. He lifted his shoulders as if shaking off a weight and looked about him. 'I hope you like this place. I came here first when I was an undergraduate. It is always associated for me with poor Larry O'Sullivan.' He sipped his champagne with half-closed eyes. 'I haven't been here often since his death.'

'He was your great friend at Cambridge, wasn't he?'

'The greatest friend I ever had in my life. No one could ever take his place. He died in Egypt when he was only thirty-two.' He sighed. 'I wish you could have known him. There never was such charm.'

'I've always liked his face.'

Ever since she could remember, Larry O'Sullivan's photo had stood in the place of honour in the study; a young face with a witty mouth under a drooping moustache and deep-lidded eyes that looked both melancholy and amused.

'He was a romantic figure to me,' her father mused. 'It was not only his charm: everyone felt the spell of *that*. He stood for everything I never had and he had the gift of turning life into a fine art. He sighed. 'He took things lightly. I have never been able to do that.'

'Nicole does too.'

'Yes, as soon as I saw your friend, for some reason, my mind flashed back to Larry. The French and the Irish . . . they know instinctively how to live. Perhaps you and I are attracted by the same types. It is an odd thing perhaps but I have never brought your mother here. When we occasionally celebrate we go to the Carlton or the Savoy. Now and then, very seldom indeed, I come here alone.'

Clara's glass of champagne had produced a slight exhilaration. She and her father seemed to be floating together in some wonderful element, entirely detached from their daily life.

'Nineteen, I was,' he went on – 'only a few years older than you, Clara, when Larry and I had our first supper here. It was always he who took me, of course. I was very hard up in those days. I know it was a Friday for he didn't remember till after he'd eaten his *caneton pressé*. And then he said to old Moulinot . . . it was in the father's time of course . . . "*Votre caneton vaut bien un brin de purgatoire.*"'

Clara nodded.

'I can just imagine Nic saying that.'

'Catholics born, the two of them. He took that lightly like everything else. How amused he would have been at my conversion.' He pulled himself up and said with a touch of his old manner, 'No doubt it went deeper than he admitted. I'm sure he made a good end.'

'I wish I could have known you when you were nineteen,' Clara said, to lure him back.

'I suppose it is inconceivable to you that your parents were ever young.'

'Well, it *is* difficult,' she admitted. 'Of course I know from photos what you both looked like. I know you had curly hair and wore a coat with funny short lapels. Only I can't imagine knowing you . . . as I know Nicole for example.'

'As your father, I should certainly have forbidden you to know me in those days. At nineteen I was a cynical young atheist. No, my dear, I should have been a shockingly bad influence.'

'I can't believe you were anything but good *ever*,' she said, sincerely.

'Can't you, my dear? Perhaps it's a fortunate illusion.' He seemed about to say something more but stopped. Instead he looked at her intently for a moment and then sighed: 'Ah, Clara.'

'What is it, Daddy?'

'Nothing. I was toying with a wild notion I sometimes have.'

'Tell me.'

'Well, now and then, I try to fancy how it would be if you and I were not father and daughter.'

She took it up eagerly.

'Oh, I've often thought that too.'

His eyes grew bright.

'*Have* you? That's remarkably interesting.'

'Of course I don't mean I want anyone else for a father. But just that now and then . . .'

'We could forget,' he nodded. 'Exactly. Sometimes the idea is so vivid to me that it is almost like a memory. We meet, you and I, in a lonely tower. I don't know why a tower. And by some spell, we have forgotten our own identities. We talk without any self-consciousness.'

The waiters interrupted them, bringing the *omelette surprise*.

'No, don't wait. Eat it at once,' he smiled, as she paused, eager for him to go on. 'You'll find it a new experience, I think.'

'But it's magic,' she said, tasting the hot *soufflé* and the ice simultaneously. 'It's like something out of the *Arabian Nights*.'

'A paradoxical sweet. Like these absurd dreams of ours.'

Half-way through her enormous helping, Clara laid down her spoon.

'I *am* having a lovely time,' she said blissfully. 'If only those horses would stand still now, for ever.'

'Happiness is remarkably becoming to you, my dear. I don't think I've ever seen you look so pretty. My instinct was right when I named you Clara after my beloved Clara Middleton. But I forgot, you haven't yet read *The Egoist*. I wonder if you will ever share my passion for Meredith.'

'I did find the style difficult when I tried,' she said humbly. 'But I'm longing to try again now I'm older.'

'Larry always used to say that your true Meredithian loves the master, not in spite of his obscurities, but because of them. It was Larry, of course, who introduced me to Meredith, as he did to Pater and to Wilde. I never discovered anything on my own; everything came through Larry. Except the one, the most important of all. Odd that the Catholic faith should have been the one thing he never tried to communicate to me.' He seemed to have forgotten all about Clara and to be talking to himself. 'Well, perhaps, not so odd,' he said with a peculiar smile and added, 'It was a comfort to me that Wilde died a Catholic.' He pulled himself up and addressed Clara once more.

'Yes, my dear, I long for you to read *The Egoist*. If it won't make you vain to know how I see you in my imagination. You will find Larry's portrait in it too. In his last years he was Horace de Cray to the life. De Cray with a dash of Lord Henry Wootton.'

'Are you in it too,' she asked, rather shyly.

'Alas, no, my dear. I should like to be able to see myself in Vernon Whitford. But I could hardly be described as "Phoebus Apollo turned fasting friar". Perhaps I have a touch of Dr Middleton . . . and, I fear, more than a touch of Sir Willoughby.'

'That's the Egoist himself, isn't it?' asked Clara. 'But you're most frightfully unselfish.'

'Another of your charming illusions, my dear.'

He seemed to have withdrawn a little. Already she fancied she could see the shadow of tomorrow faintly clouding his face, though they talked eagerly about books and *Tannhäuser* while he sipped brandy and smoked a cigar. Gradually Clara became aware that the room had become almost silent and that she was sleepy. The waiter hovered discreetly.

'*Eheu, fugaces,*' her father sighed, putting out his cigar. Without looking at the bill, he shook out a little pile of sovereigns on to the plate.

'Wha-at?' she said, on a not-quite-suppressed yawn.

'*Eheu, fugaces*. Or, as the immortal Carter translates, "The oysters are eaten and put down in the bill."

They spoke little in the car as it hurried them back to West Kensington and ordinary life. By the yellow tiled umbrella stand, he kissed her goodnight, more lingeringly than he had done for many months, stroking her hair while she tried to tell him what a wonderful evening it had been. The dining-room clock struck half past one with a fretful ping. The afterglow vanished from his face.

'Hurry up to bed, Cinderella.' Then he added, almost with everyday sternness: 'Shut your door quietly so as not to wakxour mother.'

She tiptoed upstairs to a room that seemed to have shrunk since she had left it only a few hours ago. Never had the sallow, once-white furniture seemed so shabby, the Indian cotton bedspread so faded. She tore off the white frock, crumpled now, and flung her other clothes in a careless heap. But she rescued the wilted pink carnation and laid it on her pillow so that she could feel its petals against her cheek and smell its bruised sweetness in the dark.

PART THREE

Chapter One

St Mark's breaking-up day came at last. Clara, doing last-minute repairs to her cotton frocks, wondered if it were really possible that she and her parents would sleep that night at Paget's Fold.

There was a routine connected with the beginning of the summer holidays. Traditionally the whole family attended the prize-giving at St Mark's, leaving barely time for them to change before the taxi was hooting at the door and old Mrs Batchelor, helpfully getting in everyone's way, was assuring them they would miss the train. Traditionally, too, it was the hottest afternoon of the year and Claude's white forehead glistened as, wearing his hood and gown over his morning clothes, he sat with his perspiring colleagues on the dais behind the cups and calf-bound books. Clara had come to take a perverse pleasure in this ordeal. The stuffier the hall, the prosier the speeches, the longer the Greek play, the more she appreciated the dash home and the annual transformation of her father. He would slam into his dressing-room in a state of dramatic irritability and emerge ten minutes later in an old tweed suit and a faded Panama, wearing an expression of blissful calm.

This year Clara was let off 'Speechers' so that she could help her mother get dressed and packed. Though it was a boiling day, she was sorry to miss the ritual torment and envied her grandmother as she drove off with Claude, proud as a Queen Mother in her black satin mantle and parma violet toque.

In her mother's bedroom the pink curtains were drawn to keep out the July sun. Isabel, already dressed for the journey, lay back in a chair with her feet up, giving languid directions. In the fortnight since the *Tannhäuser* evening, she had almost recovered.

That fortnight had seemed endless to Clara and, now that the longed-for day had come, something took the edge off her joy. She had not been to Paget's Ford since the day of the funeral. Would the place ever be quite the same again?

'My little girl is looking pale,' said Isabel as Clara paused in her packing, sat back on her heels and sighed. 'I daresay she needs some good country air almost as much as I do.'

'I'll be glad to get away from London anyway.'

'Your voice sounds tired. You've been such a sweet child lately, doing things for Mother. I'd no idea you could be such a good little nurse.'

'Oh well, it was mainly trays and errands – anyone can do that.'

'But you moved so nice and quietly. I feel I never want to hear the crackle of a nurse's apron again. When I was so dreadfully ill, it nearly drove me mad. You know how sensitive I am at the best of times.'

'Yes.'

'You can't think what a difference it makes, having someone who cares for you to look after you instead of people who are just paid to do it. For I really believe you are fond of your silly mother, aren't you darling? Sometimes when I felt oh so, so weak and tired, I was tempted just to slip away out of it all. And then I'd say to myself, "There's Clara. I must think of Clara and be brave." You're glad I did, aren't you, pet?'

'Of course,' said Clara, vigorously resuming her packing. 'Shall I put in two pairs of walking shoes?'

'One will be plenty. I'm afraid I shall do very little walking this year. You don't know what it is to be left without a mother. I do.'

'One, then,' said Clara efficiently. 'The great thing is you're better now. You must take great care not to get ill again.'

'It's a comfort to hear you say that. You know, sometimes I used to think it was all for Daddy. But I do believe there's room in your heart for both of us.'

'Certainly,' said Clara, with a bright grin. 'There isn't room for another pin in this trunk, though.'

She shut the lid and sat on it.

'Careful, pet. You'll strain the hinge. You're quite a weight, aren't you? I was a sylph at your age. Much too thin and frail of course. They were afraid I might be consumptive.'

'I'm uninterestingly healthy, like the Batchelors,' said Clara. She wrote a label with extreme care. 'Now there's only your little last-minute case.'

'How beautifully you pack, darling. It always surprises me because you're so slapdash and untidy about most things. I suppose they taught you to do it so efficiently at the convent.'

'Mother Damaris – she was Mistress of the Linen Room – was a dragon. At least I'll never have to pack under her ruthless eye again.'

'I daresay you were sorry to leave in some ways.'

'Oh well, it had to come sooner or later.'

'I suppose you feel it was a little bit my fault. I'm sure I didn't want to be ill.'

'No, of course not.'

'You've got an accusing look. You do blame me,' Isabel's face contracted. She said with sudden fierceness: 'If you only knew, it's the Catholic Church you ought to blame.'

Clara stared.

'The Catholic Church?'

Her voice was so startled that Isabel looked alarmed.

'I shouldn't have said that, Clara. Forget all about it.'

'What *did* you mean?'

'Nothing, darling. At least nothing you could understand.'

'How do you know?' said Clara, piqued and curious. 'I'm not a complete idiot.'

'Far from it. But there's no point in your knowing yet. It would only upset you.'

'I'd be much more upset not knowing.'

'Oh dear,' said Isabel helplessly. 'It's so hard to be always on my guard. I'm so weak. My poor head gets confused. I don't know what Daddy would say. He'd be furious with me.' She seemed on the verge of tears.

'Don't get so upset, Mother,' said Clara soothingly. 'I won't breathe a word to him.'

Isabel said in a low, troubled voice:

'The Catholic Church is terribly unfair in some ways. Especially to women. Oh darling, I often think for your sake it would have been a good thing if Daddy had had his way and you'd been a boy.'

'*Did* Daddy wish that?' asked Clara.

'Not after you'd arrived,' said her mother hastily. 'And of course now he wouldn't change you for worlds. And I definitely wanted a baby girl. You know what they say. "Your son's your son till he takes a wife: your daughter's your daughter all your life."'

'I certainly wish I'd been a boy.'

The idea was so old and ingrained that she brought it out automatically. But, as she said the words, she remembered the *Tannhäuser* night and wondered if they were still true.

'Oh darling,' wailed Isabel. 'Doesn't your mother's pleasure count for anything?'

Clara did not answer, being too busy with a pain of her own. Had he never thought of her as anything but a substitute? She hastily filled the suitcase and snapped it to.

'There! All finished. Mind if I go now? I've got lots of my own odds and ends left.'

She had quite forgotten whatever it was she had wanted to know. Just as she was about to escape, Zillah came in with their tea.

'You've time for a cup of tea surely? You look as if you needed it after all that labour.'

For some minutes they ate and drank in silence. Isabel had a preoccupied air. At last she burst out:

'Well, if you absolutely insist on knowing, darling. And if you'll swear not to tell Daddy.'

Clara nodded.

'Have you ever thought you'd like to have little brothers or sisters?'

To her fury, Clara blushed. The question hit without warning on a sore spot. Ever since she could remember, she had privately longed and prayed for them; brothers especially. Her defences went up immediately, but behind them was a wild hope.

'I suppose so. In a vague sort of way.'

Almost in a whisper her mother said: 'You might have had three little sisters.'

Clara was so startled that she dropped all her armour.

'Mother! what do you mean *might*? What happened to them? Why wasn't I told?'

'Two were born dead, darling. The other poor little thing only lived twenty minutes. Such a lovely baby, too.'

Clara was breathless with the effort of trying to take it in.

'Three. I just can't believe it. Why ever didn't you say anything about it? All younger than me? But how can you be born dead? It doesn't make sense.'

It was Isabel's turn to look startled.

'But Clara . . . you told me only a little while ago . . . I thought you knew how children came . . .'

Clara tried to retrieve herself. She said with her most worldly air: 'Idiotic of me. I forgot for the moment. Quite usual, isn't it, being born dead? Saves a lot of trouble if you come to think of it.'

Her bluff succeeded so well that her mother sighed: 'What a hard matter-of-fact child you are sometimes. And all these years we've never told you for fear of upsetting you.'

'Tell me the whole thing. In detail. Did they have names?'

'Darling, how could they? You can't be baptized when you're dead.'

'Didn't the living one get baptized?'

'There was no time to get a priest.'

'Why ever didn't you do it yourself?'

'My *dear* Clara. I was dreadfully *ill*. I wasn't even conscious.'

'I do think someone might have thought of it. Now she's in limbo and she might have been in heaven. Why ever didn't Daddy?'

'He was much too worried about me to think of anything else. You really are the most extraordinary child. You haven't even given a thought to poor Mother. Just imagine going through all that three times – for nothing.'

She checked herself from asking 'All what?' and said: 'Sorry. Yes, it must have been rotten for you.'

'You're so young,' sighed her mother. 'I suppose I ought to be glad you can't even imagine it. I shall never forget what I suffered when you were born. I was so ill they daren't give me chloroform, even at the end. And of course the first is nearly always the worst. You might think of that sometimes, all that agony I went through, when you are inclined to look down on me for not being clever. You know how Daddy loves you. But he's never had to *prove* his love. A mother has to go down to the gates of hell for her child.'

It was the phrase she had used on the *Tannhäuser* night. What could it possibly mean? Clara's mind was wrestling with so many new and extraordinary ideas that she had to keep a firm hold on herself not to admit her ignorance and ask her mother to explain. She put out a feeler.

'I suppose it always hurts rather?'

'Such pain as you couldn't even imagine. It stands to reason when you think what has to happen before a baby can come into the world.'

A wild idea flashed into Clara's mind. '*Fructus ventri tui*' it said in the 'Hail Mary'. She had always supposed that 'womb' had no connection with the ordinary meaning of 'venter'. Was it possible that after all, they *were* connected? No, she must be losing her grip even to imagine such a thing. Completely out of her depth, she nodded sagely.

'Isn't it strange, isn't it terrible,' her mother went on, assuming her dream voice, 'that men can inflict such torments on us in the name of love? I'm sure if they had the children the world would come to an end. And the Catholic Church backs them up. Of course it's run by men.'

Clara risked asking: 'How does the Church come into it?'

'By making us have babies whether we want them or not. I should have thought your nuns would have told you that.'

'Married people, you mean?'

'Why, naturally, darling.'

Having children, then, was a matter of choice; the man's choice. 'Tess' had taught her that it was possible to have them without being married and that a child was somehow the result of 'love'. Now her mother seemed to be implying that a man in some way forced a woman to have a child because he 'loved' her and that it caused her extreme suffering. But if a man had only to decide to make his wife have a child, why did some married couples pray for years for one and sometimes not get it in the end? Clara gave it up and returned to the far more interesting question:

'My three sisters. How old would they be now?'

'The first poor little thing came when you were only four. Then one when you were eight and another when you were eleven. That was the one that might have lived.'

'She'd have been getting on for five now. I just can't take it in.'

'There might have been a fourth baby.'

'Oh *when*?' said Clara breathlessly.

'It wasn't due till December.'

'*Which* December? How on earth did you know?' She was too consumed with crazy hopes to be cautious.

'This coming December. But something went dreadfully wrong. That's why I so nearly died in June.'

'Boy or girl?' asked Clara in a choked voice.

'It was too early to be sure.'

Here was yet another mystery. Clara felt as if an invisible stifling cocoon were being woven all round her.

'Of course I ought never to have had another,' Isabel went on. 'The doctor warned Daddy I might die if I did. But even the best of men is selfish when it comes to *that*. Thank goodness now there can't be any more.'

'I bet that one was a boy,' said Clara. 'Oh well, I never really expected it.' She had turned very pale. 'I say, do you mind if I open the window? It's so awfully hot in here.'

'But the windows are open. Both of them. Come over here and give Mother a kiss and tell her you're sorry she's had such a dreadful time.'

'I expect you'd like some eau-de-Cologne on your forehead,' said Clara hastily. 'It really is too hot for words.'

She dabbed her mother's temples as if hoping the eau-de-Cologne would act as an emotional astringent. She knew she was behaving heartlessly and that her mother had suffered enough to be entitled to a little sympathy. But she felt resentful and cheated. Forgetting that she herself dreaded the slightest pain, she blamed Isabel for cowardice. She was convinced that it was in some way her mother's fault that those children hadn't lived. Why couldn't she have done this mysterious job of having a baby properly?

But when the three of them were settled in the taxi and she

saw her father's face beaming under his old Panama hat, her hostile mood vanished. Her mother, looking wan but gay, was humming to herself and Clara gave her an almost sisterly grin. The old spell had begun to work. By the time they reached Victoria they had slipped into their summer holiday parts.

At the station they went through another annual ritual. Claude bought the summer number of *Punch* for Clara, *Queer Stories from Truth* for Isabel and the latest Phillips Oppenheim for himself. They dined in the purple, white and green tiled restaurant and made their usual weak joke about the suffragette colours. Claude ordered a bottle of hock and Clara, feeling considerably older than last year, asked for cider instead of ginger beer.

'Another year nearer,' said Claude, lifting his glass to Isabel. It was his dream to add some rooms and another acre to Paget's Fold and retire there when he was sixty. In two hundred years his mother's family had managed to scrape together some forty scattered acres and half a dozen labourer's cottages. Always at this dinner he would talk imposingly about 'the tenants'. 'Haywood is pestering me for a new well,' he would say with a scowl which deceived no one. 'I suppose I'll have to do something for the old scoundrel' or 'I'm sorry Cruttenden has ploughed up the Six Berries. Never thought the fellow would be such a fool or I'd have had a clause put in his lease. One of the finest bits of pasture in West Sussex, John Hoadley tells me.'

Neither Clara nor her mother could resist him in his landlord mood. Even Isabel had not the heart to reproach him for spending far more than his tiny rents in repairs, bottles of port and tobacco for 'the tenants'. The two dropped their private quarrels and entered into his dream as if they were grown-ups playing with a child.

'Old Squire Batchelor,' said Clara. 'You'll have to keep an eye on him, Mother. He'll be chewing straws and talking about "they turmits" in no time.'

'Do you think he'll even forget his Greek and Latin, Clara? Or that he ever terrified poor pupils out of their wits?'

'He'll remember two or three tags from the Georgics. And mutter them in a broad Sussex accent as he scratches the pigs' backs.'

'Few people realize what a fundamentally lazy man I am, my dears. If I followed my own inclinations I should never work at all.'

'Dea'est, what a fib!' said Isabel. 'Why, even on his poor little holiday, we've never yet managed to stop him working, have we, Clara?'

'An hour or two of correspondence pupils doesn't count as work. I could correct Greek proses in my sleep and frequently do.'

'You know perfectly well you get restless after three days,' said Clara. 'Own up. What's it going to be this year? Last year it was Sanskrit. And the year before – let's see . . .'

'*Ich hebe meine rechte Bein*,' prompted Isabel.

'Of course. As if I could ever forget!'

'Alas, my dears, *I* have. Sanskrit, alas, will have to wait till I retire.' He sighed. 'You know, I really think I could manage Sanskrit.'

'At least no one could correct your accent,' said Isabel.

'Daddy, you *have* got something up your sleeve.'

'No, no. Really not. Unless you count a couple of books on archaeology which I shall almost certainly leave uncut. If they were only Oppenheims! But the great man only produces one a year.'

'How you can read that nonsense!' said Isabel. 'My Mudie books, that you despise so, do at least bear some resemblance to real life.'

'Precisely why I have no desire to read them. Oppenheim and Le Queux transport me into an ideal world where I should be only too happy to live.'

'He doesn't want to be a country squire at all,' said Clara. 'He wants to steal crown jewels in faultless evening dress.'

'I suppose it's all very far-fetched,' he said, wistfully. 'But there must be some little basis of fact. After all there are such things as secret agents. And an actual Archduke was murdered less than a month ago.'

He stared past Isabel and Clara with the slightly angry expression he wore when following his own thoughts.

'You know,' he said seriously. 'In real life, they probably

choose quite ordinary people for those jobs. People no one would suspect.'

'Mother, do you think he's a secret agent?'

'No such luck,' he sighed. 'Adventures will never come my way. And yet . . . and yet . . .'

'Break the vow of silence to the Crimson Arrow and tell us,' said Clara.

He smiled.

'It's so patently absurd I can laugh at it myself. I suppose everyone has ridiculous fancies sometimes.'

'Tell us.'

'Well, fantastic as it seems even to myself . . . if ever there comes an unexpected ring at the door late at night after my last pupil has gone I wonder if they have come.'

'And who are They?' urged Clara.

'Representatives of a foreign power, travelling incognito. They have observed a remarkable likeness between myself and the ruling prince of . . . nowhere important of course . . . some obscure little Germanic State. Circumstances make it advisable the prince should disappear for a time.'

'And they want you to impersonate him?'

'Well, frankly, yes.'

'At great personal danger?'

'There is a certain risk involved.'

Isabel smiled faintly.

'Dea'est, I never suspected you of being so romantic.'

'I'm sure you didn't, Isabel. Clara, let that be a warning to you. A woman can be married to a man for sixteen years and know nothing of his innermost life.'

'Women have their secrets too. Don't they, Clara?'

Clara ignored her mother's meaning glance and said:

'Perhaps you really will have an adventure one day. Why shouldn't you? People do.'

'Not people like me, my dear. I am the man to whom nothing sensational will ever happen.'

Isabel drummed on the table.

'I'm sure enough unpleasant things have happened to both of us,' she said.

'Yes, indeed, my dear,' he said, meekly.

'Claude, don't you think we ought to be getting to the train? I'm beginning to feel tired and I do want to be sure of a corner seat.'

Tonight they were travelling first class. They found an empty carriage and Isabel promptly put her feet up and closed her eyes. Claude was soon as deep in his Phillips Oppenheim as a priest in his breviary. By the time they were well out of London, Clara had finished her *Punch*. It was too dark to see the country and there was nothing to fall back on but her own thoughts. If those sisters had lived, they would have been in the carriage with them now. The youngest might have been asleep on her lap or asking to be told a story. But it was impossible to imagine them, to give them personalities or even names. Try as she would, she could only see three wax dolls in white coffins. She glanced across at her mother, lying with her feet up, fast asleep. The overhead light threw shadows under her eyes and on either side of her half-open mouth. She looked older than Clara had ever seen her and there was something frightened and reproachful in her expression. Had she told the truth when she said that men were cruel to the women they loved? Once more she studied her father's absorbed face. No one could be frightened of him tonight, yet how often in his presence she had felt a panic out of all proportion to anything, however harsh, he might have said or done. What was he really in himself? The brilliant, conscientious schoolmaster, driving himself far harder than any pupil? The genial dreamer of this evening? The bitter accuser in the orchard? The wonderful, yet faintly disquieting companion of the *Tannhäuser* night? Images of his face in yet other moods formed and dissolved in her mind to the rhythm of the wheels till her head grew heavy and her eyelids closed.

She did not wake till the door flew open, letting in a gale of delicious air and a broad Sussex voice shouting 'Rookfield.' She stumbled out, still half asleep, but as soon as she was perched on the driving seat beside Mr Joles, her eyes opened wide. It was one of the freshest, sharpest joys of the holidays, this short drive through the night with the horse's crupper rising and falling in the lamplight and hooves and wheels sounding unnaturally loud. Cool air streamed past her face, bringing drifts of sweet or pungent country smells, blowing away problems, awakening old delights. Soon she would make out the dark bulk of the walnut tree against a sky peppered with stars. In a few minutes they had pulled up at the foot of the green and there was Aunt Leah standing in the doorway with a lamp while Aunt Sophy fumbled with the catch of the gate.

Once again she walked up the uneven brick path and smelt the stocks and tobacco plants; once again Aunt Sophy said, as every year: 'You must be dreadfully tired and hungry,' and Aunt Leah: 'Your train was remarkably punctual.'

On the table stood the painted biscuit tins she had known from childhood, the decanter of Aunt Sophy's wine, the home-made cake, the pink glass dish of sandwiches, the mug of milk for herself, just as they had always stood. Once again the aunts hovered like parent-birds, refusing to eat themselves. Once again, Aunt Leah, after ceremonial coaxing, was induced to drink a thimbleful of wine and Aunt Sophy said: 'Mind you don't get intoxicated, Leah. It's stronger than anything they sell at the "Goat".'

The old clock in the shadows beyond their lamplit circle cleared its throat portentously, whirred, clicked and struck twelve. Aunt Leah said, as she had said last year, 'It is only eleven by the correct time. We haven't yet been able to get the strike mended.'

Clara sipped her milk and nibbled her biscuits in drowsy bliss. Nothing had changed. Here at least life was simple, secure and sweet. Nothing mattered any more. The summer holidays had begun.

Chapter Two

The feather bed was hot and Clara could not go to sleep at once. In the dark, some of her nagging thoughts returned. So much had happened since she had last slept in this room that she wondered if even Paget's Fold could charm her back to her childhood self. With a sudden fear that the room itself might have changed, she groped for a match to light her candle but the box was empty. She fell asleep at last and when she woke, the leaf shadows on the thin red blind brought back the old sense of innocence and safety.

One by one, as a released prisoner checks his restored possessions, she welcomed each familiar object. There was the lame dressing-table with its yellow muslin skirts, the hair-tidy trimmed with pearl buttons, the patchwork pincushion on which, as every year, Aunt Sophy had arranged the pins in a huge C. A spray of ivy still grew in through the layers of faded wallpaper, the texts lettered by her grandfather still reminded her that her body was the temple of the Holy Ghost and that she knew not the day or the hour. As always on holiday mornings, the room smelt of a fresh dampness suffused with lavender, fermenting apples and frying bacon. With a rush of happiness she jumped out of bed, washed in icy rainwater and knelt down to say her morning prayers in a passion of gratitude.

Her room opened off her parents' so that when she was dressed she had to rattle the string latch and wait till they called her to come through.

Claude and Isabel were still in bed. As she stooped to kiss her mother's pale cheek and his rosy, unshaven one, she noticed how white his skin was where the pyjama jacket hung open at the neck. At Valetta Road she had never once seen him in bed. At Paget's Fold it seemed the most natural thing in the world.

In a day or two, the holiday routine was established. Every morning Claude and Clara played croquet while Isabel sat in her deck chair, occasionally glancing up from her novel to watch them. The full-sized lawn Claude had laid down some years ago still gave him a thrill of pride. Every time he looked at it, he remembered the bumpy little plot at Hamling where he had played those endless tournaments against himself. Croquet was his only game and he set about it with a methodical ferocity. He had coached Clara till she was able to beat him now and then. Isabel had always refused to learn tactics and played recklessly with total disregard for her partner if she had one. Nevertheless, having a good eye and not being above mild cheating, she beat him nearly as often as Clara. When this happened, Clara was deeply shocked, not by her father's defeat, but by her mother's frivolous attitude. This year, with Isabel reduced to a mere spectator, she and her father were able to pit themselves against each other with strict science and impeccable honour. Nor were they in the least disturbed when Isabel mocked them.

'I wish you could see your faces,' she would say. 'Anyone would think you were fighting a duel to the death instead of playing a game, I'm sure croquet brings out the worst in your characters.'

Clara and her father would merely exchange a superior smile and whichever of them was addressing the ball would do so with an extra touch of spite.

Punctually at eleven, Aunt Sophy would trot out with a tray of glasses and homemade cakes. The aunts, who ate like birds, lived in perpetual fear that the Batchelors might be underfed. In spite of entreaties, they toiled all day in the dark kitchen, producing wonderful dishes they would never have dreamt of cooking for themselves. Aunt Sophy thought nothing of walking three miles to the market town on the hottest morning to buy special things for Isabel and they had denied themselves all the June strawberries in order to bottle them for tarts for Claude's holiday.

After lunch, therefore, it was impossible to do anything for some time but laze in the garden. Clara usually hid herself with a book in the fork of the walnut tree; a perch which had once been a perilous climb but which she could now reach in two swings. Later they would wander out over the fields. If the three went together, it was only for slow, short strolls because of Isabel. Clara had still not got over her surprise and irritation at her mother's love of the country. Her own, like her father's, was deep and inarticulate; she was shy of talking about it just as she was of religion. Isabel, however, kept up a stream of ecstatic chatter. In her high, light voice she raved about every tree and flower, taking immense pleasure in telling Claude their names which, like many country-bred people, he had never bothered to find out. She would sit happily for hours, messing up Clara's best paintbox to make sketches of cornfields and cottages which the aunts treasured as masterpieces. Clara could forgive her mother's childish vanity about her pictures which were so bad as to have a kind of fascination. What she found almost unbearable was her caring so effusively for a place to which she had no right of blood and for which Clara had a jealous love. 'She's got the whole of the rest of England to rave about,' she would tell herself. 'Why can't she leave Sussex . . . or at least this particular bit of it . . alone?'

Her father had the same possessive, patriotic feeling but, unlike Clara, he was enchanted by Isabel's raptures. He loved this corner of Sussex less because it was beautiful or familiar than because his family had been artisans or farmers in those parts for generations. A turnip field had magic for him if he could prove it had once belonged to an ancestor's smallholding. If they drove out to a strange village, the first thing he did was to search the graveyard for tombstones of Batchelors or Hoadleys or Sayerses. If he found none, however charming the place, he was politely restless till they returned to Paget's Fold. Every Sunday after tea he would say, a little sheepishly, 'Anyone care to walk round the estate with me?' Then, wet or fine, alone or in company, he would set off on a tour of his forty scattered acres. He spent blissful evenings peering at creased old ground-maps in the lamplight discussing with Aunt Leah how each patch of land had been acquired. He was delighted when Clara and Isabel called him 'the man of property'. 'It's all very trivial, my dears,' he would say, 'and well I know it. Still I must admit I love to feel I have my absurd little stake in the country. As long as I stick to that, I can call myself a Sussex yeoman.' Sometimes he reminded them, 'Claude Frederick Batchelor, yeoman of this county. That's what I want on my tombstone. And RIP of course. I hope it's not heretical to feel I could only rest in peace in Sussex soil.'

Those evenings had a peculiar charm for Clara. The aunts would be coaxed with difficulty to sit down and rest. Isabel would lie on the horsehair sofa under the engraving of Strafford on his way to execution and the other four would gather round the table under the yellow light of the oil lamp. On hot nights the smell of stocks and tobacco plants came in through the open window and Aunt Sophy kept jumping up to try and save the moths from scorching themselves to death. Isabel, who loved Aunt Sophy as much as she hated Mrs Batchelor, would lure her on to tell of all the happenings in the village since last summer; the extraordinary appearance of the post-mistress at the village concert or the fiasco of the stoolball club picnic. Aunt Leah, a little ashamed of these trivialities, would try, for Claude's sake, to raise the conversation to a higher level. She would bring out her choicest scraps of historical information or pass severe judgements on the modern world. Clara would try to entice both of them to tell old stories she heard year after year and never tired of: how in their childhood they 'did hear tell' of a wizard at Henfield who supped with the devil, how Aunt Leah had dressed up as a gipsy and deceived her own mother, how a young man had appeared to Aunt Sophy at the very moment he had died in India.

Listening, as if to music, to the ebb and flow of the four voices, Clara felt her whole self soften and expand. She glowed with affection for each one of them, even her mother. Enfolded, yet detached, she was conscious of her own life waiting round the corner; she was convinced that it would be rich and wonderful as theirs had never been. Every gesture, every shift of shadow as the faces swam in and out of the circle of light, quickened some faculty she hardly knew she possessed. The pendulum of the old clock beat like a leaden heart; the ribbons of smoke untwined from Isabel's cigarette; a luminous spot reflected from a wineglass shifted slowly down Aunt Leah's throat. And it was as if all these details were connected, that they were like the separate letters of a word in an unknown language and that, if only she could understand the word, she would understand everything.

Now and then she would do something which would have been unthinkable in Valetta Road: she would suddenly go over into a dark corner and begin to say poems out loud to them. She hardly knew why she did it, only that whatever they gave her, without knowing it, at those particular moments, had some connection with poetry and this was the only coin in which she never knew beforehand what she was going to say; usually it was Yeats or Crashaw or Francis Thompson. Sometimes, though she knew her mother was the only one could understand it, she was impelled to recite a poem of Ronsard's or Verlaine's. When she stopped, abruptly as she had begun, there was always a moment of silence. Then Aunt Leah would praise her memory and Aunt Sophy, wiping her glasses, would say, 'It's stupid of me, but poetry, even when I don't follow the sense, always makes me want to cry.' Isabel occasionally referred to the beauty of the actual poem, especially if it were a French one. More often she said: 'You look your best when you recite. It's extraordinary how your face lights up' or 'Really, you've got quite a dramatic gift. You get that from me. I always longed to go on the stage but of course Papa would have seen me dead first.' Claude seldom did more than utter a deep sigh and say, 'Thank you, my dear.' But Clara noticed that on such evenings he held her closer than usual when he kissed her goodnight. Once he said, 'You should have lived in the golden age, my dear. In Greece you would have been a rhapsodist.' Then he added sadly, stroking back her hair, 'But Wragge is in custody, Wragge is in custody.'

On wet days Clara loved to walk alone and bareheaded through the lanes that smelt of wild peppermint and here and there of a fox. She sang loudly and vaguely as she walked, mixing scraps of Latin hymns with old French and English songs, breaking off only when she saw someone approaching. Then she would frown as if deep in thought and stride on very fast, swinging her stick at the thistle clumps. Recalled like this, she realized she must have looked extremely silly, if not a trifle mad. And when she returned home, with her cheeks stung red from the rain and her hair hanging in damp corkscrews, her mother's comments were far from reassuring.

Rubbing her drenched curls at the mirror, Clara had to admit that Isabel was right. She did not look wild or elfin but merely bedraggled.

'Why can't I be thin and brown and have great mysterious dark eyes?' she would ask her reflection angrily. 'Can you imagine a poet looking like me? Or *at* me for that matter? Wood-browned pools and a beautiful name like Viola Meynell. It's not fair. I know I'd have understood him better than she did.'

Comforted by hot cocoa (the aunts always expected her to catch cold if she went out in the rain) it was easier to accept the fact that she did not look a 'faery's child' and even that Francis Thompson had died without meeting her. After all, she reflected, she must be very earthly or she wouldn't enjoy food so much. As to her hated name, there was just a possibility that she might not have to keep it all her life. How lucky that she had not had the least inclination to marry Blaze. Clara Hoadley would have been even worse. Though if one loved someone, one would not mind what their name was; she would have been only too happy to be Mrs Thompson or Mrs Keats.

Another wet day pleasure was dreaming over books she had known ever since she first learned to read. There were less than forty books at Paget's Fold; many of them belonged to her great-aunts' childhood and a few had been bought over a century ago. Some had been read and re-read till they were only held together with brown paper and glue. There were odd volumes of *Beeton's Annual* and *The Gentleman's Magazine*; forgotten novels with biblical titles like *Holden with the Cord and Shiloh*; and, what she liked best of all, the old 'improving' stories for children.

'I don't see why you care for those tales, Clara,' Aunt Sophy said. 'They must seem so dull and old-fashioned to you.'

But it was for that very reason Clara loved them. Her own childhood had always seemed a complete failure to her because there were no brothers and sisters to share it. One could not go on pretending for ever, all by oneself, that one was Lord Roberts or Joan of Arc. So she had often imagined herself a member of one of these 'book' families, a large early Victorian family where the girls wore tuckers and mittens and the boys round jackets and nankeen trousers. They had a high-principled papa, stern but kindly, and a gentle, frail mamma who spent much of her time on a sofa. There was also a governess, a pony cart and a faithful old cook. They lived in a large house in the country; the boys were always tumbling off apple trees or into ponds and being nursed or rescued by their devoted sisters to whom they were grateful ever after. Sometimes there were terrible misunderstandings, only cleared up by an illness which nearly or quite proved fatal. But in the main it was a blissful life of golden summers and sparkling winters, punctuated by visits of mercy to the sick and poor and the arrival of wonderful presents from an uncle in India. Whole tracts of Clara's life, though she had never admitted this even to Nicole, had been lived in the setting of *Ministering Children* and *Les Malheurs de Sophie*. She had only to smell the brown-spotted pages with the s's that looked like f's, to see the stiff engravings of cotton mills and little girls in toques and pelerines, to be back in that enchanted world.

But, from her letters to Nicole, no one could have guessed how much she loved Paget's Fold and everything connected with it. 'While you,' she wrote, 'are deciding between Paris and Madrid, I am balancing the giddy alternatives of a boring walk to Rookfield to buy a bar of chocolate or an equally boring walk to Bellhurst to buy a pair of shoelaces. On Sunday we shall be in a social whirl for the Vicar is coming to tea. My great-aunts will produce four kinds of homemade jam instead of two. Aunt Sophy will wear her ceremonial crochet collar and Aunt Leah will rub up her ecclesiastical history. My Papa will be painfully polite and my Mamma will either retire to bed or give him languorous soulful glances while eating chocolate cake in an abstracted, spiritual way peculiar to herself. Our dissipation may even go so far as to accompany the Vicar up to the churchyard in order to lay flowers on the graves of deceased relatives. If I don't seem much disturbed by your dark forebodings of war, it is because our local life is so dramatic that it absorbs all my attention. Only yesterday the gardener's wife was stung by a wasp and today there is a rumour (uncomfirmed) that the postman's cat has had a kitten with six toes.'

Clara hated herself for writing like this but the remembrance of Nicole's cynical smile compelled her to. There were a great many things which she naturally loved and enjoyed which withered at the mere thought of how they would appear to Nicole. Sometimes her conscience was tormented by this duplicity and sometimes she wondered if she hid it quite as successfully as she liked to think.

One thing had begun to disturb her at Paget's Fold and that was a real or imagined change in Aunt Sophy. During the last two summers she fancied that her favourite aunt had grown a trifle shy and even a trifle critical of her.

Long ago when Clara was very small and her parents went abroad in the summer holidays, she used to be sent down to Paget's Fold with old Mr and Mrs Batchelor. In those days she had had two people who could be relied on to spoil her: her grandfather and Aunt Sophy. Aunt Leah was severe with all young children on principle and her grandmother was less amenable when she was left in charge. It was Aunt Sophy who had smuggled in the nightlights she was never allowed at home, who let her eat sugar biscuits after she had cleaned her teeth and sat by her bed telling stories when the sun pouring through the thin red blinds made it impossible to go to sleeep. In those days Aunt Leah had seemed a forbidding figure. Clara quite dreaded the Sunday afternoon Scripture lessons in the tiny parlour that smelt of mildew and where the box tree that blotted out the window threw a greenish light on Aunt Leah's white face as she spoke of the destruction of Sodom and the face of the children who mocked Elisha. But it was impossible to imagine anyone more comforting and unexacting than Aunt Sophy with her cottage-loaf figure and withered apple face. When the strain of her own parents became too intense, Clara had often thought how delightful it would be if Cousin John Hoadley had been her father and Aunt Sophy her mother. Once when she was about six she had confided this idea to Aunt Sophy and a slow pink blush had run all over the old woman's face.

'I'm too old to be your mother, dear. Or anyone else's.'

'Why? Old people are much nicer to children. I like old people.'

'That's because they get soft and spoil them. Besides it's naughty to want any parents but your own,' said Aunt Sophy, trying to look severe.

'I don't care,' said Clara, snuggling up to Aunt Sophy, the only person she ever did snuggle up to spontaneously. 'Of course I couldn't have been your little girl unlesss you'd been married. Why ever didn't you?'

'Because no one asked me, I expect.'

'Then why didn't you ask someone?'

'Ladies don't ask gentlemen to marry them, dear.'

'I'm sure Mr Hoadley wouldn't have minded if you had. Then you could have had me and a lot of other children.'

She remembered that Aunt Sophy had given her a very queer look, as if this time she were really cross, but she had hugged her tighter than usual when she said 'goodnight'.

Even now that she was fifteen, Clara still liked Aunt Sophy to put her to bed; a thing she would never have allowed her mother to do. She towered now above the tiny old woman and 'being put to bed' merely meant gossip with her while she undressed. But something of their former ease had gone: there was a touch of constraint about Aunt Sophy's voice and manner.

'You're getting too clever for me, Clara. All this French and Latin and I don't know what. It makes me quite giddy. I never was clever, no more than your Granny. Leah was the one for brains.'

And however much Clara might hug her and tell her between kisses:

'You're my darling, sweet, one and only little Aunt Sophy,' a pucker of distrust remained on the old, childlike forehead.

It was no compensation to Clara that Aunt Leah had begun to treat her with new respect. She praised her for having done so well at school and, a mark of the highest favour, sometimes consulted her on a knotty point of history or geography. Clara did not like being ranged among the blue-stockings: still less did she like anything at Paget's Fold to change. It was part of the order of things that Aunt Leah should be a trifle disapproving and Aunt Sophy wholeheartedly admiring. Most disturbing of all, Aunt Sophy seemed to have transferred that uncritical allegiance to Isabel. However hard Clara tried to be humble, however sharply she scolded herself for undutiful feelings, she remained convinced that she was a better person than her mother. Yet, though she reminded herself that Aunt Sophy was a very ignorant as well as a very innocent old woman, this did not alter the fact that she was usually right in her judgements. Clara could not quite rid herself of the uncomfortable notion that however much she might bluff other people and even herself, she did not succeed in bluffing Aunt Sophy.

Chapter Three

It was several days before Clara was able to do what she loved best of all; spend a whole day by herself on the hills. In London or at Mount Hilary the memory of the downs often came up so sharply that her eyes filled with tears of longing. This summer it seemed that never before had she needed them so much.

She took as always the shortest and steepest way up the slippery chalk path through the bostel. Stumbling over gnarled roots of beeches she panted on without a rest till she reached the top. Once in the open, she flung herself down on the turf where the harebells trembled above the star-thistles and the sheep-droppings. The strong wind dried her forehead and blew her hair out like a flag as she drew in great greedy breaths of the smell of thyme and sea. Her eyes were greedy too as she stared, now at the green and ochre map of the weald hundreds of feet below, now at the distant gap in the hills which the sea closed with a wedge of blue haze.

But she could not bear to stay still for long. As soon as she had recovered her wind, she an over the springy turf like a dog let off its lead, jumping over gorse bushes and molehills for the pleasure of using her limbs. When she got to the dewpond by Chanctonbury Ring, she took off her shoes and stockings and lay flat on her back on the grass. In spite of the wind, it was a burning day. As the sun climbed, the air began to dance in streaks over the chalk as over a hot stove. The roaring wood behind her broke the force of the wind so that it merely flowed over her in soft eddies; the heat of air and soil seemed to pass right into her bones. She would have liked to take off her clothes and lie there naked on the top of the world. Underneath she could feel the solid earth; miles and miles of it, supporting her on its grass-furred back. She could almost imagine she felt its motion, the reliable earth that could be trusted not to fling her off into space: at that moment she did not want to be anything but a contented animal. She and the chalk-blue dancing over her bare ankles were made of the same stuff and would one day be part of this earth which had bred them both.

'Yes, really *Mother* Earth,' she thought. 'Mother of everything, not just human beings. And she doesn't expect love and gratitude.' It was a strangely comforting idea. Shyly she turned over and kissed the ground, whispering, 'Still, you know I *am* grateful.'

The next second, shyness turned to fear. She sat up abruptly. 'But that is how the pagans felt.' She reminded herself that the earth itself had been created by God. It wasn't wrong for pagans to make gods of sun and moon, corn and sea; they hadn't known about the real God. Long before she herself had known about God, her father had taught her about Artemis and Apollo; they had been as real to her as the angels and saints had since become. But now she was a Christian she had no right even to toy with those old beliefs. Penitently she tried to think of angels, of Our Blessed Lady, of Christ Himself, but they no longer seemed real. The wind in the trees sounded mocking. Long before the Romans came, there had been a temple where the Ring was now planted. It was her father who had told her that. Devout Catholic as he was, he loved any rumour of ancient rites or haunted stones. He had said how easily he could imagine the old gods walking on the hills. And often he quoted, with a look that she now connected with the *Tannhäuser* night:

> 'The pagan kingdom Wilfred found
> Dreams as it dwells apart.'

Suppose, it were true? Suppose there were something, old as the world, still potent in spite of Christianity? Was it possible there were pockets in the universe where the Christian God had no power? Fascinated and frightened by such thoughts, she got up and walked out of the orbit of the Ring on to the open stretch of down. Yet still she could not shake off these insistent fancies or temptations. What else could the legend of the Venusberg mean? Even in the Christian middle ages they must have half believed in the old gods. She had read that the Early Fathers spoke of them as devils. But she could see nothing diabolical about Artemis or Ceres or the wise Athene who watched over

Telemachus as Our Lady watched over Christian children. Her father not only loved Homer as passionately as in his unbelieving days but was enchanted by any story of the pagan gods still active in the modern word. Wherever he came across such a story, good, bad or indifferent, he made a point of Clara's reading it too. Was his faith so secure that he could afford to treat them as fairy-tales or did he secretly wish they were true?

Half a mile further on she sat down again in the shelter of some gorse bushes and took out her book, half hoping to find an answer there. It was the copy of Francis Thompson's poems her father had given her on the day of her First Communion. At that time he had not read them himself and he had no idea of what they were to mean to her. She had just glanced at the book on that day, memorable because, with all its beauty, there had been the strangest sense of something just missed. It had seemed incomprehensible. Yet she knew at once there was something there for her, if she could burrow through the forbidding surface. And she had burrowed. For more than three years she had immersed herself in the poems, forcing herself to understand the peculiar idiom, learning quantities of them by heart till they had become part of herself. Nothing could shake her devotion to Francis Thompson, even though Nicole assured her he was a third-rate poet and quoted disastrous lines. Under all the turgidity and the mannerisms she found a spirit that spoke to her own and offered a hope of reconciling poetry and religion.

Her sense that the two were mysteriously opposed was something she had never spoken of, even to Nicole, for no one seemed to be disturbed by it. The great conflict for which every sermon and instruction at Mount Hilary prepared them was that between belief and unbelief, between Christian standards of morality and those of 'the world'. Within limits, a love of poetry was encouraged, but poetry and all art were subservient to the law of 'edification'. Every now and then Clara was seized by the uncomfortable but compelling idea that art had its own laws. Nicole would, of course, have agreed with her but Nicole appeared to suffer from no religious scruples. It was impossible to imagine Nicole anything but a Catholic but Clara had never discovered what religion meant to her and she would not have dreamed of asking. Clara herself was quite convinced that she would never 'lose her faith'. She was prepared to find it extremely difficult to obey the commandments when she grew up and found herself in the world faced with all sorts of temptations whose nature had been only darkly hinted. She had been well warned too against the dangers of intellectual pride but, though she was inclined to criticize and question, she could not imagine setting up her private judgement against the teachings of the Church.

What had begun to disturb her was the sense of a realm into which she penetrated now and then quite involuntarily and whose existence did not seem to be officially recognized. And this realm, though it seemed to her to be connected sometimes with truth, sometimes with beauty, seemed to have no connection with morals. A poem might be the key to it or some lovely sight or sound but quite often she would suddenly find herself in it for no apparent reason, waiting to buy cakes in a stuffy shop or on those evenings at Paget's Fold listening to the aunts' gossip. During these experiences she was not aware of 'right' or 'wrong': the words simple did not apply. How could they, since during these brief moments she was not aware of herself at all except as a kind of sensitive film? If they came from God, why were they not accompanied by a rush of fervour and a desire to be better? And if from the devil, why did they not provoke her to wicked thoughts and rebelliousness? But they seemed to have no results; if they left any wish at all, it was a desire somehow to express them. They seemed to be nothing but a sudden intensification of life and she could not control them in any way. Often she had tried to induce them, but she could not deceive herself for long; there was all the difference between flapping one's arms and pretending to fly and really flying. Sometimes she had dared to hope that this was what Christ meant when He said: 'I came that you might have life and have it more abundantly.' But, since she had always been assured that this meant the supernatural life of grace, something abstract and mysterious which one believed by faith but did not feel, she put the idea away as blasphemous.

Today not even Francis Thompson could help her. She

ignored the pages that opened easily, pages marked by her grubby fingers as she had worked through poem after poem learning it by heart. How deeply he had comforted her once, seeing Apollo and Danaë as 'types' of Our Lord and Our Lady, but at this moment these identifications seemed merely mechanical 'conceits'. These ways were too well-worn: she needed something new. She went on till she came to *The Dread of Height* which she had always avoided because its motto was the text that most terrified her in the Gospel. 'If ye were blind ye should have no sin but now ye say: We see; your sin remaineth.' She forced herself to read the poem. It gave her none of the reassurance she longed for.

> 'Lower than man for I dreamed higher
> Thrust down by how much I aspire
> And damned with drink of immortality.'

There was the truth, cutting all her poses and fancies. What use to dream what it would be like to live in the pre-Christian era? For better or worse, without having sought for it like her father, she 'saw'. She was a baptized Catholic: she could plead neither blindness nor 'invincible ignorance'. Unfaithfulness might be pardoned in others; it was unforgivable in herself. The problem came down to one thing. Was she prepared to put her whole self at God's disposal?

In the retreat she had made every year since her First Communion there was a conference she dreaded far more than those on death, judgement or hell; the one on vocations. Only one vocation was meant: the call to be a nun. Just because the idea was so repugnant to her, she had a terror that God might ask it of her. And if she refused the call, however virtuous her life, she would be like the rich young man who had kept all the commandments but refused to follow Christ. She had never mentioned the subject to Mother Lovell for fear discussion should make the idea too real. She loved 'the world'; there was no doubt of that. The world meant her father, Paget's Fold, the country, freedom to read and say and eat and wear what she liked, freedom to choose her friends and even, as a faint possibility, marriage. Not with anyone like Blaze Hoadley, of course, but with some wonderful, unimaginable young man.

As she tormented herself with these thoughts, the wind came in a sudden gust, ruffling the pages of her book, as if to say: 'Stop all this nonsense. You are a young human creature and it is a summer day.' She realized she was very hungry and began to devour her sandwiches. Far away in the valley the spire of Parkminster monastery reared up, holding her eye in spite of herself. It reminded her inexorably of the scene in *The Conventionalists*, a book she loved and hated, where the young man is brought up by two priests on to these very downs so that he shall see that spire and ask what it signifies.

Clara knew all too well what it signified. There lived the austere Carthusians, toiling in their gardens and workshops, rising in the middle of the night for the long office in the cold chapel, scaling the heights of prayer and always, whatever they did, intent only on God. Once a week they broke their silence and went for a walk in community. They often passed by Paget's Fold in their white habits and straw hats, chattering and laughing like a flock of schoolboys. Her mother used to say, 'Poor things, it's quite pathetic how happy they seem. I suppose in that awful monotonous life, even a walk is a great adventure.'

Clara would think, contemptuously, how little Isabel understood their real adventure. Today she realized the contempt should be not for her mother but for herself. For if she was capable of seeing, however dimly, the point of such a life, it could only be because something in herself corresponded to it.

At last her mind was so weary that she could not think any more; there was nothing but a meaningless chatter in her head that she could not stop any more than the wind. She got up and walked on listlessly in the midday heat. Something had gone wrong with the day. The incessant flight of shadows over the turf tired her like her own thoughts. Everything seemed to have turned hostile to her; the wind that would not stop buffeting her, the sun that hurt her eyes, the very molehills over which she stumbled. The white glare of a chalkpit became a mocking grin; the flash of a windscreen in the valley a joke at her expense. For the first time, up on the hills, solitude became unbearable. If only there were someone to share it, she might recover her old delight. Suddenly and absurdly, she began to long for that unimaginable lover to appear. She had no idea what he would look like: she only knew that they would recognize each other at once. There would be no need to talk or explain; they would simply go on together hand in hand.

All day she had seen no one, not even a shepherd. Now, suddenly, as if summoned by her thought, a man's figure appeared in the distance, right in the track where she was walking. She could only make out that he was tall, wore no hat or coat, and swung along with easy strides. Her heart began to beat madly and her whole body seemed to melt. Quickly she smoothed her cotton frock and dabbed her forehead, hoping the sun and wind had not turned her face scarlet. She turned and stood still, gazing intently at the blue haze of the sea. Her hair must be in the wildest tangle; she could only trust that it was shining in the sun. She had to hold her pose of absorbed contemplation for what seemed an endless time but at last came the thump of footsteps and her knees began to shake so that she could hardly stand. Now, surely, she could allow herself to turn round. She gave a start, like a wild creature disturbed and faced whoever was approaching with her eyes set in a dreamy stare. She found herself looking into the cheerful red common face of a man about her father's age.

'Hullo, Missie,' said a voice to match the face. 'Nice day, eh?'

She answered, almost giggling: 'Gorgeous, absolutely gorgeous.'

'Bit on the hot side if you're footing it. Still there's a nice breeze.'

'Yes, lovely breeze,' she agreed fervently, though she was inwardly raging with shame.

'On holiday?'

'Oh yes. Yes, I am.'

'Did you happen to come up from Steyning?'

'Yes. I always do.'

'Started off from Findon I did this morning. Reckoning to get a bit of lunch in Steyning. Looks the best part of three miles by the map.'

'It's about that.'

'Long way before I can get a pint. I haven't half got a thirst on me. Spotted you quite a long way off, I did. You looked a bit peculiar standing there. Not lost your road or anything have you?'

'No, thank you,' said Clara distantly. 'I've known these hills since I was a child.'

'No offence meant. You're a big girl now, aren't you? Know how to take care of yourself, eh?'

Clara was speechless with anger.

'Bet your Dad told you not to speak to strangers, didn't he?' he said with an insufferable grin. 'Quite right, too. But you needn't mind me, my dear. I've got a girl about your age myself. Gwen her name is. Something your build, too. Fancies she's too old to get a spanking, but I don't see eye to eye with her on that. Well, so long.'

She muttered something and began to walk away very fast to put as much distance as possible between herself and the odious man. Her eyes kept filling with angry tears which the wind dried as soon as they gathered. 'Beastly. Everything's beastly,' she said out loud, kicking at loose bits of chalk. The day was utterly ruined. She took the first track and stumbled down into the valley. There was nothing she wanted now but to get back as fast as she could to Paget's Fold. When she got to the village, it was not yet three. Pride forbade her to go home yet. A day alone on the downs was a treat to be begged and planned for: she could never admit that it had been a failure. She wandered into the post office and bought herself a twopenny *Tim Pippin* and a copy of *Home Notes*. With these she whiled away an hour or two in a dismal little teashop. She had not enough money for an ice and spun out endless cups of strong, tepid tea till the proprietress began to look impatient. She dawdled home as slowly as possible, with intervals of sitting on gates, being careful to leave *Tim Pippin* and *Home Notes* in a ditch, though not before she had read every word down to advice on how to care for false teeth and get rid of superfluous hair.

When she got home Isabel said:

'You look a little tired, darling. Did you walk too far?'

'I'm never tired, Mother,' insisted Clara, tossing her chin and her hair. 'I suppose I've walked about eleven miles. But I'm not in the least tired.'

'How I envy you your energy,' said Isabel wistfully. 'I used to be such a good walker. I wonder if I'll ever be able to again. Was it lovely on the hills?'

'Oh yes,' said Clara stolidly. 'Windy. But ripping all the same. I had a perfectly marvellous day.'

Her father had a preoccupied expression, familiar at Valetta Road but disturbing at Paget's Fold. For a moment Clara wondered whether he might be angry with her. She could not remember having done anything to annoy him but the last few hours had left her with an inexplicable feeling of guilt. Timidly she went up to him and kissed him.

'You're not cross with me for having gone off all day, Daddy?'

He put his arm round her.

'Cross, my dear? Heaven forbid. Enjoy all you can while you can. It's been a solace thinking of you up there on the hills. I'm so glad we didn't hear before you left. It might have spoilt your day.'

'Hear what?' It could not be anything very dreadful for her mother looked perfectly calm.

'Germany has declared war on Russia. Mark you, that still does not necessarily mean we shall be drawn in. But there's no denying things are extremely serious.'

'I rather wish there would be a war,' said Clara. 'It might make life a bit more exciting. I suppose I'd be too young to nurse the wounded?'

'I sincerely hope so, my dear. If it *should* happen – let's trust it will all be over long before you've even left school.'

'It's such a bore being a girl. If I were a boy, I could go as a drummer or something.'

Isabel interrupted:

'For heaven's sake don't let's start talking about fighting and killing. There's enough pain and misery in the world already. Of course we shan't go to war, Clara. Your father and Aunt Leah have been working themselves up all day. But Aunt Sophy and I know better, don't we?'

'I'm sure those Germans wouldn't dare,' said Aunt Sophy. 'The old Queen would turn in her grave. I've always heard she thought very poorly of that Kaiser though he was her nephew.'

'Let's hope you and Isabel are right, Aunt.' He drew Clara closer and said beneath his breath: 'I know just how you feel, my dear.'

He kissed her with sudden vehemence, saying aloud: 'All the same, thank God you're not a boy.'

The next day was Sunday, a day she hated in London and loved at Paget's Fold. When she pulled up the red blind, the dew was rising in mists over the meadows. The air was cool with the recovered freshness that comes between one hot day and another; smoke stood up straight from the chimneys: not a leaf stirred in the heavy August plumage of the trees. Yesterday, with its tormenting thoughts and its miasma of uneasiness, dissolved like a bad dream before the reality of this perfect morning. Washing in cold rainwater and putting on her clean Sunday clothes, she felt life beginning again, new and unspoilt. She said her prayers with devotion; asking forgiveness for yesterday's wild thoughts; asking to be made simple and contented.

Sunday had its own ritual. Before the three of them set out on the drive to Mass, they always went to the tangled beds on the little lawn at the back and picked themselves buttonholes. It was Clara's turn to choose the flowers and today she decided on roses for everyone. She selected them with special care, a red one for her father, a tea-rose for her mother and a striped York and Lancaster for herself. As she offered the rose to her mother, she was suddenly struck by her appearance. A few days in the country had revived Isabel's looks; the shadows had nearly faded from under her great brown eyes and her skin looked creamy under the bloom of powder. She was wearing a fresh shantung suit and a little toque made entirely of hyacinths. Clara found herself looking at her as if she had not seen her for a long time, almost as if she had never seen her before.

'Why, Mother,' she said. 'You're a really beautiful woman. But *isn't* she, Daddy? Seriously. Quite as beautiful as any of the heroines in her old novels.'

'My dear,' said her father, beaming, 'have you never noticed it before? Unobservant as I am, it struck me the very first time I set eyes on her. Four . . . five . . . twenty years ago, Isabel.'

'I think I'm jolly lucky in my parents.'

Isabel said, almost absently: 'Darling child.' She raised her eyelids and let her soft dark stare wander up from the beds of asters and roses and the leaf-strewn lawn, to the lichened roof of the old house and the martins clipping across the summer blue.

'Oh, our lovely, peaceful Sunday mornings. And you two wanting a war. Suppose this were our very last.'

'Please God, no, my dear.'

She gave her most wayward smile. 'Please God! It always seems to me so queer what we think does please God. Why should God be more pleased at my going to a dark, chilly church and listening to orphan boys with adenoids singing Latin words they don't understand, than if I stayed in this sweet garden and admired the flowers he made and listened to the birds?'

'Now, now, my dear,' said Claude good-humouredly. 'We've been into all that.'

'I know you think me illogical,' said Isabel, pulling down her veil, 'but how do you know I don't think you illogical?'

For once Clara did not rush to back her father in this ancient fray. She merely observed: 'I can hear the fly.'

'Of course, my dear,' said Claude, 'if you don't feel up to going to church . . .'

'Oh, I'll certainly come,' said Isabel. 'I adore that pretty drive. I'm not going to miss it when it might be our very last. Tell Daddy not to worry, Clara. I'll think about roses instead of the orphans' adenoids.'

'Isabel, you are an incorrigible pagan.'

'Oh no,' she said very seriously. 'I truly believe in God. And Christ and the Holy Virgin. It's all so beautiful.'

'Of course it's beautiful,' said Claude. 'But it's something much more important than beautiful.'

'I don't believe there's anything more important than beauty.' She unfurled her parasol and began to step smoothly across the lawn. Claude and Clara followed her, exchanging indulgent glances. He murmured:

'*Vera incessu patuit dea.*'

Isabel stopped and swerved round. The pink lining of the sunshade threw a warm glow over her dress so that she was all rosy cream like the flower at her neck.

'That's Latin, isn't it, dearest? Is it a prayer or a curse?'

'Neither, my dear.'

'Then what does it mean? I'll make Clara tell me if you won't.'

'It means that twenty . . . even ten years ago . . . I might have allowed myself to agree with you.'

PART FOUR

Chapter One

In the autumn, the first of the war, Clara went to St Mark's Girls' School. After the convent, she found it impossible to take a secular school seriously. From the beginning she adopted an attitude of amused tolerance borrowed from Nicole de Savigny. At first this had been mainly bluff but, finding that the bluff worked, she threw herself wholeheartedly into the part of the privileged eccentric. At Mount Hilary she had been nervously anxious to conform. At St Mark's she did not care in the least for public opinion, with the result that in a few weeks she had established herself as one of the personalities of the Upper Sixth.

She was helped by a piece of pure luck. Games were taken seriously at St Mark's and she was outstandingly bad at them. Each new girl was allotted to one of the six Games Clubs but, through an oversight, Clara's name was left out of the lists. As she was careful not to mention this, she managed to spend the whole of her time at St Mark's without once playing hockey, cricket or netball though she was prudent enough to turn up at important matches. Gym, being done in forms, was unavoidable, but gym had not the peculiar sacredness of games and she managed to keep up her prestige by combining the roles of class clown and mistress baiter. Luckily the muscular young woman fresh from Bedford College was as nervous of Clara's bland impertinence as Clara herself was of the vaulting horse and the parallel bars, so the awful fact that she was a 'funk' was never discovered.

In her other classes her behaviour was mildly outrageous but just stopped short of the danger line. Within a fortnight the English mistress had christened her 'The Cat That Walked By Itself' and the name caught on in the Common Room. Wherever she had gone a little too far and had qualms about her report, she adopted a technique which never failed. She conveyed to the particular exasperated mistress the idea that she alone could subdue her. Then, for several days in that class, she would be so alert, so obedient, so anxious to please that the storm never came to a head.

At Mount Hilary, she had worked hard and been almost invariably top of her class: now she allowed herself the luxury of letting others pass her, knowing she was good for a spurt if things became critical. The wild variation of her weekly marks gave her a footing in the two most important sets, the Brainies and the Hearties. Since she obviously wasn't a Swat and could be relied on to provide entertainment in boring lessons, the Hearties forgave her for not playing games. The Brainies accepted her on account of her essays and her French. The third set, the Swats, loathed her but, as they were despised by the other two, this was a positive advantage.

Nothing like the Swats had existed at Mount Hilary. They had minds like filing cabinets, and they worked with the nervous intensity of sheep feeding before a thunderstorm. To them Sophocles and Shakespeare were merely the raw material of 'distinctions' and 'alphas': they gazed down long vistas of exams to the goal of a post in some school exactly like St Mark's. At times the sight of their shiny noses and the anxious eyes behind their pince-nez affected Clara like a *memento mori*. Was this what her father really wanted her to be like? The Brainies also intended to have careers but they were constantly changing their minds about them. At one moment someone would decide she was going to be a writer and the next an explorer or, if women ever got the vote, a member of parliament. Clara was on excellent terms with all the Brainies but never became a formal adherent. She had no desire to cut a figure in public life or raise the status of her sex; her dreaming of careers was confined to a hope that something would turn up to save her from teaching or the Civil Service. However, she had one real friend in the set, a plain, witty Jewess who was her only serious rival in essays and the Literary Society. Apart from Ruth Philips, Clara had one other real friend and this friend outraged both the Brainies and the Hearties. She was not a Swat; Swats were at least respectable.

She was not even a colourless neutral. She was quite frankly an Impossible and, to make matters worse, she was in a lower form.

Sooner or later Clara knew there was bound to be a storm over Patsy Cohen. Towards the end of her first term it broke. One afternoon during prep. four of the leading Hearties, Beatrice Wilson, Rosalind Forbes, Jean Mckay and 'Blackie' Buckfield suddenly set on her.

'Spinster, we've got a bone to pick with you.' They pulled her up from her desk and manoeuvred her into position with her back against the wall. Clara did not resist.

'Look here, we've been holding a council about you.'

'And we all agree that you're a bit queer.'

'Shut up, Blackie. We agreed she was all right *herself*.'

'I haven't finished, Roz. We agreed we could put up with *her*.'

'But not with some of your friends, Spin.' Clara was far from feeling as detached as she was trying to look. The four faces, respectively freckled, pale, rosy and sunburnt but all smelling indentically of cloakroom soap, were menacing. Instinct warned her that her only hope was to be bold. She leant negligently against the wall as if she had taken up the position of her own accord.

'Really?' she said mildly. 'I don't think I remember having asked you to put up with anyone. You say "some" so I suppose you mean several.'

'We mean one, and jolly well you know it,' said Blackie grimly. Her thick eyebrows almost met when she frowned. 'A Yid, if you want a clue.'

'Not Ruth, surely?' asked Clara, looking earnest and puzzled. 'I could have sworn that even you liked Ruth.'

'Of course, not Ruth,' said Rosalind. She was the prettiest of the four, with dark eyes and white teeth in a face the colour of a brown egg. 'Ruth's as decent as can be. And we've nothing against Yids as such, provided they behave themselves.'

'May I tell Ruth that? I'm sure it would be a great comfort to her.'

'Come off it, Batchelor,' said Blackie, lowering her head, with its dangling dark plaits, like a bull about to charge. 'Cheek the staff as much as you like but you'd better not try it on with *us*.'

'You see, old thing, you're a new girl,' explained Beatrice

Wilson. She was the most amiable of the Hearties, a full-bosomed sixteen with glazed fox-glove-pink cheeks. 'We've all been at St Mark's for simply years. We've sort of made a exception in your case. But we know what's done and what's not done.'

'And my particular sin? Is it one of commission or omission?' asked Clara in her catechism class manner.

'Haven't the foggiest what you mean,' said Blackie.

'Nor I what you mean,' said Clara. 'I wish one of you would come to the point.'

'You must be jolly dense if you can't guess,' sneered Jean Mackay. 'Go on, tell her, Blackie.'

Blackie cleared her throat.

'Well, for one thing, it's not done to go about with people in lower forms.'

'Is there a rule about it?' asked Clara meekly. 'I didn't know.'

'Of course not. It's just not done.'

'In my case it seems it is done.'

There was a simultaneous bellow from the herd. Clara looked as if she were trying to follow a difficult piece of reasoning.

'You mean if Patsy were in six instead of five you wouldn't object?'

'Good lord, are you balmy? Or only pretending to be?'

'I should jolly well think we should object.'

'*Patsy*! What a name for a Yid!'

'Jezebel it ought to be,' said Blackie in a burst of inspiration. 'Pretty good, what? She's one of the Chosen and she certainly paints her face.' Her sulkiness melted into giggles at her own wit. Everyone tittered except Clara, who said judicially:

'Not paints. Only powders.'

'Golly, that's bad enough,' said Rosalind.

'I swear she uses rouge or something ghastly,' insisted Blackie. 'I vote we get hold of her and give her a good scrub under the cold tap.'

'It's been done already,' said Clara. 'Incidentally it made the scrubber look rather silly.'

'Not you, I bet.'

'Oh, dear me, no.'

'Tell who.'

'I don't think it would be "done" to give her away,' said Clara, virtuously.

'Rot.'

'We'll make you.'

'All right. If you insist, it was Miss Silver.'

Miss Silver was the headmistress. There were cries of 'You're spoofing.'

'Honour bright. Miss Silver sent for Patsy and accused her of being rouged. Patsy said she wasn't. Miss Silver made her wash her face in front of her. But no pink came off. So Miss Silver had to apologize.'

'Utter swiz,' said Blackie. 'The Cohen made it all up, if you didn't.'

'I can produce written evidence. Mrs Cohen was rather annoyed and wrote to Miss Silver. They've preserved her reply; it's really a handsome tribute "I confess I was deceived by the somewhat unusual brilliance of your daughter's complexion." Patsy wants to have it framed.'

Blackie, slightly deflated, growled.

'Pity she mucks up the unusual brilliance with all that powder then.'

'Yes, isn't it?' said Clara eagerly. 'I'm always telling her so. I'll tell her you said so, may I?' She fixed her gaze absently on Blackie's shining nose. 'With such a skin as that, she really would look better without powder, wouldn't she? I can't think of *anyone* else who would, can you?'

'Filthy stuff,' snorted Jean Mackay who was rather proud of her freckles. 'Anyway her beastly powder's only the beginning.'

'She never turns up at matches.'

'She wears a pneumonia blouse with her gym tunic.'

'She's always losing her school hat. Probably thinks it doesn't suit her beauty.'

'She gives male Marcians the glad eye.'

All this, Clara admitted, was perfectly true. But what exactly did they want her to do about it? She rightly guessed that no one quite liked to put it into words.

'Very well,' she said boldly. 'I'll spare your delicate feelings and say it for you. If I don't drop Patsy, you'll drop me. Right. Go ahead and drop me then.'

Two faces were still menacing; two were puzzled.

'Can't you really see how ghastly she is?' asked Rosalind.

Clara brought up all her reserves of courage.

'Do you know,' she said slowly. 'I believe I've never really appreciated Patsy till this moment. She's much more amusing on the subject of all of you and, incidentally, considerably more charitable than you are about her. And at least she isn't a prig.'

There was silence. Then Blackie said in a choked voice:

'Have you the nerve to suggest *we're* prigs?'

Clara imitated Nicole's shrug and faint, ambiguous smile. Her heart was thumping and her knees were so weak that she was glad of the support of the wall. They were established school powers; they were in the same form and would move up with her every year. To have the four of them permanently allied against her would make the rest of her life at St Mark's extremely unpleasant.

Jean said almost in a whisper:

'You seriously mean you'd rather chuck us than Patricia Cohen?'

Clara noticed the change of emphasis.

'I never talked of "chucking" anybody. You four started all this silly business. Personally I think it's all very Angela Brazilish.'

This went home. Even the heartiest Hearties despised Angela Brazilishness. She followed it up boldly.

'I don't in the least mind being The Most Unpopular Girl in the Sixth,' she said, hoping they did not guess she would mind exceedingly, 'but I propose to continue being seen in public with Patsy. What are you going to do about it?'

The four pairs of eyes consulted each other but no one spoke.

'Perhaps you'd like to hold another council? I'll leave you to it if you'll let me get out.'

The four remained solidly shoulder to shoulder blocking her escape. It was Rosalind who found her tongue first.

'Look here, Spin, you're obviously as mad as a hatter. But I personally rather like the way you stick up for your ghastly Cohen. If she were a friend of mine – which of course, is impossible.'

'Q.E.D.'

'Don't try to be funny, Mackay. It doesn't suit you. Well, as I was saying, I'd probably do the same.'

Clara watched the four exchange looks and nudges. Blackie said rather sullenly:

'I gather the general feeling is that you chaps want it to be Pax then?'

'Is it Pax by you, Spin?' asked Rosalind. Her voice was almost anxious.

'Pax by all means.'

Clara had not really expected to win and the relief made her feel slightly light-headed. She risked a gesture. She drew a small battered box of *Poudre Nildé* from her pocket and dabbed her nose with a shaking hand.

'Forgive me. These emotional scenes are so trying.'

'You picked *that* up from the Cohen I suppose,' sneered Jean.

'Good lord. You'll be smoking next,' said Beatrice.

'At least smoking isn't *soppy*,' declared Blackie. 'I smoke a fag myself now and then.'

'Patsy doesn't approve of smoking,' said Clara, replacing the powder-box. 'Afraid it might spoil her teeth.'

Once again the silence became ominous. Clara cursed herself for a fool. As usual she had gone too far and spoilt everything. Then suddenly Rosalind giggled and one by one the others burst out laughing.

'Spin, you really are rather priceless. You're what La Frog calls "im-pay-able".'

'Dare you to flour your nozzle in French tomorrow.'

'Done,' said Clara. They did not know this needed no courage at all.

Beatrice looked at her watch.

'I say, you chaps. Fuller's is still open. Who could do with a Pineapple Guzzler?'

'Spiffing notion. Come on, Spin, we'll stand you treat.'

It was Clara's first victory over public opinion. It was also the first of many fights she was to have with various people, herself included, on the subject of Patsy Cohen.

Chapter Two

Unlike Ruth Philips, Pasty Cohen was not a deliberately chosen friend. Being in different forms, Patsy and Clara would probably have ignored each other but for a coincidence which Clara had not mentioned in her battle with the Hearties. The coincidence was that Patsy and her two sisters had once spent a few terms at Mount Hilary.

At the convent Clara had only known the Cohens by sight and collectively. The three exotic little Jewesses, Vera, Mavis and Patricia, had appeared half-way through a dull term and, for some reason, had promptly become school pets. They were hardly thought of as separate identities: they were simply 'the Cohens'. All three were unusually short and the eldest, Vera, unusually fat. They always went about together, hopping along on their thin legs (even Vera's were like sticks) and chirping in indentical shrill voices like three small birds.

Rigid school conventions were revised for the sake of the Cohens. They were all so good at mathematics that they had to do them with the highest class. With their thin legs dangling from chairs much too big for them, they looked like children, among grown-ups. Three pairs of bright eyes, small in Vera, middling in Mavis, enormous in Patricia: watched the blackboard like hawks: three high voices propounded problems which the unhappy nun could hardly grasp, let alone solve. Vera was a violinist who, at the age of twelve, had already given a recital and got excellent notices. Twice a week, a master with an international reputation came to give her a lesson, breaking one of Mount Hilary's strictest rules and upsetting school time-tables by insisting on three hours' practice. The Cohens were always getting 'permissions' sternly refused to others. They were constantly going out, dressed in identical pretty clothes, to dentists and oculists or being let off games or allowed to get up late. Throughout their brief career at the convent, they remained friendly, popular and completely unassimilated. One day, again in the middle of a term, they vanished as unexpectedly as they had appeared.

Clara had never given them another thought till one morning, as she was walking to St Mark's, she found a small figure trotting breathlessly beside her.

'You're Clara Batchelor, aren't you? I've been chasing you for days but you walk so fast. D'you remember me at Mount Hilary? I'm the youngest of the Cohens, Patsy.'

Under the Marcian straw boater, worn at an angle forbidden by Miss Silver, two enormous, brilliant eyes shone up at Clara between theatrically long lashes.

At first she could not believe that this dazzling little face could possibly belong to any of the Cohens whom she remembered collectively as sallow and beaky.

'Your hair's as gorgeous as ever,' Patsy chattered on. 'We used to be awfully jealous of it, being dark ourselves and not a natural curl between the three of us. In fact, except for growing, you haven't changed a bit. Would you have recognized me?'

The voice at least had not altered. It was the Cohen voice, shrill but musical. And the legs, though clothed in black silk instead of black cotton, were recognizably Cohen legs, preternaturally slim and very slightly bowed.

'Honestly I don't think I would. You've changed tremendously.'

'I hope so. Except that I've hardly grown at all. None of us have. People won't believe that Mavis and I are sixteen and seventeen. But they always think poor Vera's miles more than eighteen because she's as fat as ever. Marmee makes her wear black velvet for concerts and what with that and her playing, everyone thinks she must be positively ancient. Some beastly critic actually took her for twenty-eight. Wasn't it ghastly for her? Luckily she's not vain like me.'

Studying Patsy's transformed face as she hopped and twittered beside her, Clara thought she had every excuse to be vain. For Patsy now looked exactly like one of the flamboyantly pretty girls on magazine covers, the kind that subalterns were beginning to pin up in their dugouts. Her eyes were even bigger than Isabel's and did not quite match in colour: one had greenish glints in it and the other blue. The lashes of both lids were so long and dark that combined with the faint shadow under them, they made Patsy's eyes look as if they were very skilfully made up. Her cheeks were very pink and her neck so white that the chalk-white powder she used only showed up as a bloom on it. At the convent, she had worn a plate on her front teeth. She must have worn it to some effect for now they were as even as any advertised smile. But what fascinated Clara most was Patsy's mouth. Rouge might have accounted for her cheeks but not for her lips. Hitherto she had supposed that coral lips were an Elizabethan convention but Patsy's exactly matched the coral brooch she wore and had the same faint sheen. She searched the vivid face for any feature she could connect with the former Patsy and found it at last in her nose. It was less obtrusive now that the childish peakiness had gone, it was carefully powdered, it was more than atoned for by those amazing eyes but it was still definitely the Cohen nose.

'Forgive my staring at you,' said Clara, 'but you really have grown up quite astonishingly pretty.'

'No one ever thought I would,' said Patsy. 'Do you remember what a fright I was at the convent? All nose and eyes and rabbit's teeth. But Marmee's still the beauty of the family. You wait till you see her. Gracious, I forgot. I've been carrying a note round for days from Marmee to your mother asking if you may come to tea one Sunday. You will, won't you? Mavis and Vera are dying to see you again.'

For the rest of the way they exchanged memories of Mount Hilary. Clara was slightly disconcerted to find how different the place had appeared to non-Catholic eyes. To Patsy, it had simply seemed a rather amusingly old-fashioned school run by kindly eccentrics.

'I can't think why some of them shut themselves up like that,' she said artlessly. 'Quite a lot were definitely good-looking even in those hideous bonnets.'

But, in spite of Patsy's irreverence, it was like meeting a compatriot abroad to talk to someone who knew what was meant by 'exemptions' and 'wishings', who had eaten *goûter* under the limes and played *Cache* on feast days.

When Isabel read Mrs Cohen's invitation, her first remark was:

'Your friend Ruth Philips is Jewish too, isn't she? You seem to have inherited Daddy's passion for the Chosen Race.'

'I've never thought about it one way or the other,' said Clara. 'Anyway the Cohens weren't friends of mine at Mount Hilary.'

'I'm surprised they allowed Jewesses at the convent at all. The nuns were supposed to be so very exclusive. Especially as they're not even Catholics. I suppose money unlocks all doors these days.'

'I don't think they're sensationally rich,' said Clara. 'After all they live in West Kensington just as we do. I don't suppose there's much to choose between Garthwaite Crescent and Valetta Road.'

'Do you want to go to tea with these people, Clara? You realize I shall have to call on the mother if you do. I hope she's not another Becky Shapiro. I'm sure the name Cohen is on every other shop in the Commercial Road. But at least she doesn't write "Yours" with an apostrophe and there's nothing vulgar about her notepaper.'.

Clara who, up to now, had not cared whether she went or not, became suddenly determined.

'Yes, I do want to,' she said stubbornly.

'You'll have to ask Daddy. If this Mrs Cohen knew us she'd realize it was a pure formality asking *my* permission about anything that concerns you.'

'I'm sure he'll let me. In fact he'll probably insist on it. You know he likes me to keep up with anyone from Mount Hilary.'

They were so much back in the Valetta Road routine that Paget's Fold might never have existed. But Isabel had her revenge.

'Isn't it odd, Clara,' she said sweetly, 'that the very first girl from the convent who asks you to her own home should be some little Jewess you never even knew at Mount Hilary.'

Claude consented without difficulty. He merely added with a sigh: 'I can't help being sorry they're not Catholics. It distresses me that you have no Catholic friends. But you still correspond with that delightful de Savigny girl I hope?'

'Oh yes,' said Clara with a guilty thankfulness that he could not see her own letters. She added informatively: 'She's pulling every string to try and get herself sent out to some French hospital.'

'Precisely what I should expect of her. All the same I'm thankful I'm in no position to pull strings if you got such notions into your head. In any case she's older than you are. But if the war went on longer than we expected and if some day you desperately wanted to join her, I suppose I couldn't in decency object.'

'Oh, there's not a hope for an English girl unless she's at least twenty-one,' said Clara hastily. After the excitement of the first week she had completely lost interest in the war.

She went to the Cohens not only the next Sunday but the two following ones. Very soon it became such a habit to run over to Garthwaite Crescent when she had nothing special to do that her mother complained that she preferred it to her own home.

This was perfectly true though she could never say just what it was that gave the Cohen house its peculiar charm. Perhaps it was that, for the first time, she found herself completely at home in a family. Within a few weeks she had become an honorary daughter and sister. In her present mood, the fact that it was a family of girls was an extra attraction. As a small girl she had despised other small girls and her friends had all been boys. Even during her time at Mount Hilary she had been, without her parents' knowledge, the only female member of a secret gang of boys in the lower forms of St Mark's or the higher ones of its Preparatory School, Corinth House. For, though Clara loathed games and could not face ropes and parallel bars in cold blood, she could be reckless when excited. In a black mask, with a cap-pistol in her belt she would walk along walls by moonlight or climb through the windows of empty houses without a qualm. In the character of Burglaress Bill she could do things which would have been impossible to Clara Batchelor. But, ever since Blaze had kissed her in the orchard, roof prowling and mock burglaries had somehow lost their charm. She preferred to be thought of as a girl rather than 'almost as good as a boy'. Until she knew the Cohens she still had bursts of playing with soldiers and trains and she continued to take in *The Captain*. Within a few weeks of meeting Patsy, the neglected regiments were gathering dust in the toy box and *The Captain* had been replaced by *Nash's*.

Garthwaite Crescent was as different as possible from Valetta Road. For one thing all the Cohens openly and demonstratively adored each other; there were no undercurrents of jealousy and dislike. For another, its doors were open at all times to all comers. At Valetta Road there were bridge parties and dinner parties but no one ever came uninvited and both Claude and Isabel detested noise. Garthwaite Crescent was always in a state of commotion. Often the front door was left ajar all day and when Clara stepped across the sill she was greeted by an agreeable babel, usually composed of the twittering of Mavis and Patsy, Vera's violin, the yapping of the two Pekes and the hum of Mrs Cohen's sewing machine. The telephone was always ringing, people, often total strangers, were constantly arriving and lingering on to several meals, the girls were always dashing upstairs to change their clothes or dashing down again, half-dressed, to try out a new record or a dance step. In spite of all this, Clara found the atmosphere as restful as a warm bath. She soon decided that this was entirely due to Mrs Cohen.

As soon as she set eyes on Lilian Cohen, she completely lost her heart. For 'Marmee' was like the angel mother in the old story-books at Paget's Fold. Patsy had not exaggerated when she said she would never be half as pretty as her mother. She was tinier even than Patsy, but so perfectly in scale that one never thought of her as short. Compared with her dark-eyed, ivory beauty, Patsy was a poster beside a Chinese drawing. Everything about Mrs Cohen was delicate and finely articulated from her narrow feet to her small pale face, Spanish rather than Jewish in type.

She was never idle but she did everything with a fairy-like quickness and ease. She would dart from the drawing-room to the kitchen and cook an admirable meal in less time than it would take the average person to assemble the ingredients. She would leave the sewing-machine where she was 'flying up' a dress for one of her daughters to sight-read a difficult accompaniment for Vera without a trace of nervous flurry. Unlike most efficient people, she never made others feel guilty about their laziness; in fact she had an enchanting gift of managing to appear lazy herself. When her fingers were flying over the keyboard or sewing so fast that the needle seemed to move in a continuous streak, she seemed to watch them with amused detachment as if they were working without any effort of hers.

Her husband and her daughters were the very centre of her life but from them her affection spread out in all directions not only to their friends and their friends' friends but to every human being who came her way. The shyest boys and girls thawed in her presence; the boorish became amiable and the most conceited cheerfully made fools of themselves for the pleasure of making her laugh. Clara might have found the Cohens' mutual adoration oppressive had it not been so lighthearted. They were gay and affectionate rather than passionate. The girls quarrelled and made up again as spontaneously as a family of kittens; no smothered resentments thickened the air as they did in her own home. As soon as she stepped into the cream-coloured hall hung with African trophies, she seemed to be enfolded in warm brightness even on the dullest day. There was nothing remarkable about the house itself although white paint, airy curtains and quantities of flowers everywhere made it far more cheerful than Valetta Road. Yet to Clara it seemed to exist in another climate, as if the Cohens had imported some of the Jamaican sun along with the rocking-chairs and the wicker tables and Marmee's plaited workbaskets.

Clara was not alone in feeling the fascination of the Cohen home. Every Sunday flocks of boys and girls from the Royal College of Music where Vera now both studied and taught and from Mavis's ballet class invaded the house. Young officers on leave made it their headquarters and brought their friends; there was a constantly changing influx of friends from Jamaica coming over to join up; French and Belgian uniforms mingled with the British. They usually began with serious music but sooner or later someone would launch into wild improvisation or jazz and people would begin to dance. This was Mavis's moment. She had remained sallow and beaky but was clever enough not to try and compete with Patsy's looks. She wore vivid amusing clothes that made her look like a sophisticated gipsy and emphasized the fact that her figure was nearly as good as her mother's. But, well as Patsy danced, she often found herself deserted in mid-floor while her partner tried to snatch even one turn with Mavis. Sometimes they extemporized burlesque opera or ballets; sometimes they merely glided sedately to the gramophone. When everyone was exhausted, they would turn out the lights and sit round the fire while Clara told ghost stories. This was a popular turn, chiefly because it gave people the chance of holding hands in the dark. There was only coffee and ginger beer unless Mr Cohen was at home and then whisky was offered by him in person only to the senior young men. But nobody seemed to mind. Their own youth and the general atmosphere of the house kept them all in the wildest spirits. Nor would anyone have enjoyed themselves half as much if Marmee had not always been hovering in the background or foreground, conjuring up food, taking her turn at the piano or knitting socks for the young soldiers while she watched them dance. Sometimes they would persuade her to dance herself and, when she did, it was evident where Mavis got her talent. But after a few turns she would always slip out of her partner's arms and escape on some domestic pretext.

'I was much too fond of dancing as a girl,' she would tell them. 'I used to dance every night and all night. But I gave it up when I married because Julius didn't care for it.'

Once a tall young Canadian tried to stop her when she made her usual breakaway.

'I'm jolly well not going to let you go. You waltz better than anyone I've ever met, even Mavis. I could dance with you for ever.' And he lifted her up bodily like a child. 'You're as light as a feather. I'm going to keep you up here till you promise to finish this dance.'

'Put me down *at once* please,' she said with such a flash of her dark eyes that he meekly obeyed.

'People were much too fond of doing that in Kingstown,' she said when she was on the ground again. 'It became such a nuisance that once, I'm afraid, I lost my temper and hit a young man with my fan.'

In Valetta Road there were occasional storms over Clara's spending so much time at the Cohens'. Her father suspected, with reason, that she was doing the minimum of homework but, on the whole, he was glad that she should have friends of her own age. He frowned a good deal over Patsy's appearance, though he privately found it attractive, and was thunderous when Clara went too far in imitation. But he liked Patsy's easy good nature and reassured himself by saying that, with such a mother, there could not be much harm in the girl. She further appeased him by always being nice to old Mrs Batchelor, asking after her rheumatism and bringing her little presents. The person who never had a good word for Patsy was Isabel. She disliked Patsy at first sight and though she listened greedily to her flattery and accepted frequent offerings of flowers and scent, she was never really won over.

Almost every day Clara had to listen to some criticism of Patsy. She looked like a chorus-girl or 'something I couldn't even mention to you': she had ugly hands: her prettiness was only that of any little Whitechapel Jewess and would be gone by the time she was twenty. There were two themes on which Isabel played endless variations. 'I pity poor Mrs Cohen who is really beautiful and elegant and perfectly *comme il faut* for having a daughter with such appalling style' and 'I can't think what a girl as clever as you can see in that brainless little thing.'

Clara nevertheless became increasingly attached to Patsy. Vera and Mavis were far more intelligent but she never wanted to idle away hours alone with either of them as she did with Patsy. Even Mrs Cohen was amazed at their devotion to each other for Patsy seemed to prefer Clara to either of her sisters and the two sometimes had to reckon with twinges of jealousy in Mavis. She said once, laughing: 'Really you and Patsy might be twins. You seem to have only one mind between you. It's rather a pity that it doesn't seem to be Clara's.'

'Oh, Clara's given up trying to improve my mind. It's a hopeless job. But you must admit I've improved her looks.'

'I don't think they needed any improving. Patsy, you've got far too much powder on as usual. And if you insist on wearing such a very thin blouse, you shouldn't have a safety-pin in your camisole. You should keep her in order, Clara.'

At Mount Hilary, frivolity had been sternly suppressed. Clara was just at the age to respond ardently to Patsy's interest in everything the nuns had taught her to despise. She continued, nevertheless, to be coldly critical to Isabel on the score of worldly vanity.

The two girls spent hours in Patsy's bedroom, eating caramels while they tried on each other's clothes and experimented with startling new hair-styles. Patsy had inherited her mother's flair for dressmaking; she taught Clara to make blouses and trim hats. She also made her conscious of her underclothes. The first time Clara removed her frock Patsy exclaimed in horror:

'Clara, darling, you mustn't wear those beegledy cotton petticoats.'

'Beegledy' was a Cohen family word which applied to everything from a murder to a drooping hem.

'Why? No one sees them.'

'Well, I'm seeing one now. And don't you ever look at yourself in the glass when you're undressing? I'm always practising for when I get married. I should hate my husband to be disillusioned. I've even worked out a wonderful way of putting my curlers in in the dark. Lucky pig, you don't have to bother about them. I'll beg some bits of crêpe-de-Chine from Marmee and make you some Kirchner girl camisoles.'

When Clara, on her sixteenth birthday, was promoted to a small dress allowance, she spent it entirely under Patsy's direction, often acquiring things she dared not wear at home. The two were always sending for free samples of face-creams and powders and trying out shampoos with 'brightening rinses'. Once, for a whole week, Patsy was nearly as fair as Clara while Clara was almost orange and it was not till the fifth frantic washing that they reverted to their normal colours. They had crises of anxiety about their figures and took to drinking lemon juice and doing strenuous exercises while continuing to eat unlimited caramels. And they discussed endlessly and earnestly the appearance of every other girl they knew and the exact degree of her success with men as if they were trying to lay down basic principles for a philosophy of attractiveness.

There was, however, another side to Patsy which Clara found equally fascinating. Life prevented no abstract problems to her. She had a touching admiration for Clara's 'braininess' but regarded her as slightly demented. General ideas had not the faintest interest for Patsy; her mind was concrete and empirical. Art was simply a talent, like Vera's violin playing. What she played didn't matter, provided she did it well. Religion, like music, was a natural taste. Either it appealed to you or it didn't. Marmee was religious and Parpee didn't believe in anything and, as they were both perfect darlings, it couldn't be very important. Her ethics were equally pragmatical. She believed that everyone ought to enjoy themselves as much as possible. If something you enjoyed led to unpleasant consequences or seriously interfered with someone else's pleasure, then you did without it. Very early in their friendship she enlightened Clara's ignorance and was amazed at her first reaction of disgust.

'But why? What's there so awful about it? After all our own parents must have done it.'

Clara could not explain that, to her, this was precisely the most awful part. For several days, she felt so contemptuous of her father and mother that she could hardly bring herself to speak to them. Yet, to her surprise, she did not feel the same contempt for Mr and Mrs Cohen. What shocked her most was the confirmation of her terrified suspicion that she had once been a part of her mother. She thought she would not have minded quite so much if her mother had been Lilian Cohen.

'Well, I certainly hope I never have any children,' she said.

'But why?' Patsy's great eyes were open to their fullest extent. 'I wouldn't mind having twenty if I could keep my figure like Marmee. Of course one looks a sight before. But they say if the man loves you he doesn't mind.'

She studied herself in a long mirror.

'I shall look extra frightful because I'm so short.'

Suddenly she whipped off her frock.

'I'm going to see just how beegledy I *do* look,' she said, stuffing a pillow under her silk slip.

'My goodness, Clara, he *will* have to love me,' she said ruefully as she glanced sideways at her reflection. 'Considering it will probably be two pillows before the end. Now you try. You oughtn't to look quite so ghastly, being taller.'

But Clara refused.

'I've definitely made up my mind not to get married.'

'Try anyway. It might act as an awful warning in case you ever felt yourself slipping.'

But Clara remained obdurate.

'I agree it would be much more fun just to go on flirting for ever,' said Patsy, throwing away the pillow and pulling her scanty clothes tight so as to look her slimmest. 'Still don't you think it would be awfully exciting to let oneself go and see what happened?'

'You *wouldn't*, would you, Patsy?' said Clara, scandalized.

'It's probably just as well Marmee keeps an eye on me. But sometimes I've felt a perfect beast, especially when it's someone sweet like Ronny or Colin and they're going back to the front.'

'You let them kiss you, I know. Do you think your mother has any idea how many of them have?'

'Kissing,' said Patsy, contemptuously. 'Really, Clara, one would think you lived in the moon.'

'You don't mean anyone's ever dared to suggest . . .'

'Goodness, they don't have to suggest. I honestly believe you don't know the first thing about men.'

'I was practically proposed to when I wasn't even fifteen,' said Clara, loftily.

'Don't look so offended, old thing. I don't mean for one sec. that you're not attractive to men. But I think they're a bit frightened of you. Perhaps it's your brains.'

'I sometimes think those famous brains are a myth,' said Clara. 'Or I have them in spasms. I'm sure I never give the least evidence of them here.'

'It isn't that you show off and snub people like Vera. But no matter how you act the giddy goat, everybody will always know. Don't ask me why. I expect men will always treat you differently from the way they treat me. There's something awfully "touch-me-not" about you.'

'Well, I *am* a Catholic, after all.'

'I bet that wouldn't stop them if *you* were different. I can't make you out sometimes. You like prinking almost as much as I do. And I've seen you flirt like anything in public. But I've not the faintest idea what happens when you're left alone with a man.'

'I jolly seldom am. I'd probably feel rather a fool. But, in public, it's just a sort of game. It's fun trying to intrigue someone new.'

'I believe you're just a cold-blooded fish. I'm glad I'm not a man. It would be pretty awful to fall in love with you.'

'Do you really think so?' said Clara, half flattered, half dismayed. 'Well, no one's in any danger at the moment. I've never been in love and I'm beginning to hope I never shall. I used to have romantic ideas about it but that was before I knew the facts. You've certainly cured me of my childish illusions.'

'I wish you could see your expression when you talk like that. No wonder men find you a bit alarming.'

'Have *you* ever been in love, Patsy?'

'I wish I knew for certain. I have the most lovely swoony feelings for at least six people, especially when I'm dancing with them. But I think there must be something more to it. I'd like to go to the limit with someone then p'raps I'd find out.'

'Patsy, you wouldn't *seriously*?'

'I definitely would if it weren't for Parpee and Marmee. They'd be frightfully upset if they found out.'

'I suppose it is different if you don't think it a sin.'

'Marmee would think it a sin all right. The funny thing is that Parpee's just as strict, if not stricter, though he thinks religion's all rot. Do you remember that nice old French nun who used to call us pagans? I jolly well wish I had been a pagan.'

'Pagan parents were just as strict. Look at what happened to Virginia.'

Patsy broke into a dance-step and singing 'Goodbye, Virginyer, I love the loveliness that's in yer'.

'What did happen to Virginia whoever she was?'

'Her father killed her to stop her from being seduced.'

'Do you think Parpee would go as far as that?' Patsy went on dancing.

'I love Virgin-yer's beautiful, beautiful eyes,' she sang, rolling her own at Clara. 'I love Virgin-yer's beautiful, beautiful skies. Anyway, if I ever did before I was married, I'd be jolly careful not to have a baby.'

'But people usually do, don't they?'

'Not if they don't want to.'

'They always have them in books. Look at Tess and Hetty Poyser. They certainly didn't *want* them.'

'You're always reading things written in the year dot. Women aren't such fools nowadays. Of course it's always a bit risky.'

Patsy stopped dancing to go into details, adding, 'Of course, Catholics aren't allowed to. I know that from my cousin Cita. She's a Catholic. All Marmee's Spanish relations are. That's how we got let into the convent.'

Something flashed into Clara's mind.

'I wonder if *that's* what my mother meant when she said . . .'

'What?'

'Oh, nothing. Show me that new step you were doing just now.'

Clara often wondered what Ruth Philips would have said had she heard this or any of her other typical conversations with Patsy.

No two girls could have been more unlike than Patsy and Ruth. Even the fact that they were both Jewish gave them nothing in common except their devotion to their families. As a family, the Philipses had no charm for Clara. Their house was far drearier and uglier than Valetta Road and she disliked Ruth's mother and older sister who had the knack of making her feel a thoroughly useless member of society. Ruth's mother had been headmistress of a board school before she married and the sister, Miriam, was studying social welfare. Both had a brisk, cheerful sarcastic manner which made Clara feel as if she were being scrubbed under the cold tap with medicated soap. Ruth herself was as plain as Patsy was pretty and made herself look considerably plainer than she need have done. Unlike the rest of her family she did not look in the least Jewish; she could have served as a model for an unflattering picture of the typical English schoolgirl. She was short, stocky and thick-ankled, with a round pink face and a button nose which shone as if it had been polished. Her clear lively grey eyes were obscured by round steel-rimmed spectacles which left a red furrow on her nose when she removed them and her brown hair had a dusty look and stuck out in uneven wisps. Even when she was not wearing a gym tunic, the unkindest of all garments for her dumpy body and stout legs, she favoured frocks of the same cruel cut, hanging limply from embroidered yokes. It was not that Ruth was indifferent to clothes. She chose the handwoven materials for her heather-coloured and sage-green and peat-brown djibbahs with the greatest care and regarded Clara as a reactionary slave to convention. She was always mocking at her high heels and pointing out the charm and comfort of her own sandals. But Ruth's mind was as agile as her body was clumsy and, though she had no idea of line or colour in her own clothes, she had the most critical eye for both in pictures.

The two had come to know each other long before Patsy had appeared on the scene. As the only Jewess and the only Catholic in the Sixth Form they had quarter of an hour alone every morning during School Prayers. Almost at once they discovered so many things to discuss that they made it a habit to walk home together. And even after the incursion of Patsy, the hour or two after afternoon school remained sacred to Ruth. Clara avoided Ruth's home as much as possible and Ruth, though she was approved of at Valetta Road, was more at her ease away from it. Clara's intimacy with Patsy had grown in the setting of Patsy's bedroom, among a litter of creams and powders and open drawers of tumbled silks and chiffons. Her real life with Ruth was a peripatetic one and its background was the grey and dull red streets of West Kensington.

On summer evenings and often in winter dusks they would spin out their walk for an hour or more. Even when, after pacing deep in talk up innumerable sidestreets, they found themselves back at Ruth's home, they usually started some fascinating new hare on the very doorstep. Then they would take 'just one more turn' up and down the grimy length of Smyrna Grove, losing count of the times they passed the house, until Mrs Philips called sharply from the window. They discussed art and literature, philosophy and religion; they made up satirical poems about school characters and gave cruel imitations of the staff. When either had written anything serious, she conveyed to the other that it was just possible that she might have it on her, but of course it was only the roughest draft and in no fit state to show. After pressing persuasion, the author would burrow in every pocket and, in the very last one, discover a scrap of paper. The scrap was always carelessly creased but there was never an erasure in what was written on it. Then the critic would gaze at the pavement with a concentrated frown while the author muttered the poem or the story very fast in a low fierce voice. Ruth would say:

'My God, that's good. It really does come off. I'm just wondering whether maybe you've slightly overdone the jewellery. D'you absolutely have to have chrysoprase and beryl in the same verse? By the way, just what colour *is* a chrysoprase?'

Clara, mindful of the second commandment, did not dare to say, 'My God' but swore to Ruth's genius by Homeric heroes. 'By Hector and Patroclus, you've done it again. It's as good as Dryden, it really is. I wouldn't touch a word except just conceivably to vary the rhyme in the last couplet.'

They had reached the same stage of mental intoxication; the fact that there was so much to read and see and to find out gave them a feeling of delicious vertigo. With Nicole, Clara had always been the follower who trailed some way behind the pioneer but with Ruth she marched side by side. At brief intervals, each in turn would discover the poem or the book or the picture which positively eclipsed all others. Oblivious of passers-by, they declaimed passages to each other or chanted them in unison as they paced the streets, their stiff straw hats askew and their satchels bumping on their backs. They had moods of noble indignation and burning idealism but Ruth's flickering wit saved them from solemnity. Her parodies and pastiches were so brilliant that Clara sometimes copied them out and sent them to Nicole. When, to Ruth's immense excitement, she won a prize in a *Saturday Westminster* competition, Clara was even more impressed by the fact that Nicole thought her entry *épatant*.

Till she knew Ruth, Clara had thought of a university as a dull prolonging of school. Soon they had both decided that their lives would not begin till they went to Cambridge. They were convinced the war would be over by the time they were ready to go up and they would be in at the dawn of a new world. All over England there must be people just like themselves, waiting to meet and set each other on fire. They vied with each other in drawing pictures of what Cambridge would be like and invented a place which was a combination of medieval Paris, Plato's

Academy and an eighteenth-century coffee-house. The dons in this dream city talked like Coleridge and Wilde and the undergraduates were all brilliant or fantastic.

There was no doubt that Clara delighted in Ruth's company nor that she admired and even liked her more than Patsy. All the same she continued to spend most of her spare time at Garthwaite Crescent. Often, with her eyes still lit up with wild enthusiasms and her brain humming with tremendous lines, she would rush home, put on her flightiest blouse and slip round to the Cohens' for supper. Then, her pleasure enhanced if anything by a faint sense of guilt, she would fritter away the rest of the evening gossiping with Patsy, practising the tango or strumming Delysia's latest songs.

Chapter Three

Claude's first impulse had been to throw up everything and enlist. Rejected as too old to serve abroad, he had to content himself with staying on at St Mark's and accepting a commission in the OTC.

His attitude towards his top form became increasingly humble. By 1916 enough of his old pupils had been killed to make him shudder every time a Second Lieutenant came to say goodbye. In spite of his fierce classroom manner, he had always been devoted to his boys. Now they became so many versions of the son he would never have.

The photographs on the mantelpiece, even those of his father and Larry O'Sullivan, were gradually displaced by smooth, moustached young faces staring self-consciously under peaked caps and Gorblimeys. The originals haunted the study when they were on leave. There was nothing he would not do for them, from filling them with his best brandy ('Priceless stuff, Sir. Wish you ran our Mess.') to lending them money ('There's a slight breeze at Cox's. Only temporary, of course.'). He came to dread the words 'Cheerio, Sir. See you next leave,' for over and over again there had been no next leave. The more attractive and promising the boy, the more likely he seemed to be killed. Pathetic little books, privately printed, began to appear on Claude's shelves among the classical texts and commentaries; 'J.M.L.'; 'Donald'; *Sed Miles*. Sometimes there would be a few poems or sketches by the dead boy: otherwise the contents varied little. There was the frontispiece showing him in uniform; the last holiday snapshot; a blurred head in a school group. Then came a loving memoir, his letter from the front, desperately cheerful; and lastly the inevitable note from his Colonel. John's men, Donald's men, Michael's men had been devoted to him; his courage and high spirits had been unfailing: his Commanding Officer felt his death as a personal loss.

Gradually Claude became so preoccupied with the fate of his pupils that he was almost indifferent to his family. Clara found it far easier to get her own way with him but he no longer seemed to want her intimacy. He rarely questioned her about her schoolwork and hardly ever mentioned her future. His sense of permanence had been too much shaken for him to imagine what kind of world she would have to live in when she grew up. He no longer had a cut-and-dried answer to every question. Often when others were defending convictions he had once firmly held, he would lean his head on his hand and sigh: 'I wonder . . . I wonder' or remain silent.

Grief and anxiety had deepened the lines on his face: his obstinately golden moustache was beginning to turn grey. Yet something of his youth had revived through his intense sympathy with his subalterns. They were enchanted that he, well on in his forties, should be a Second Lieutenant like themselves and never tired of teasing him about his military duties which he took with extreme earnestness. 'Is it true you went on parade wearing a bowler hat, Sir?' 'We hear you have your water-flask filled with whisky on route marches' – 'Got the long cam groove sorted out from the short cam groove yet, Sir? Wish I'd got you in my musketry class. I'd make you draw the parts of the rifle, on the blackboard and have my revenge for the parts of $\beta\alpha\lambda\lambda\omega$.' The drills and marches, a weary routine for his colleagues, were pure delight to Claude. They associated him, however absurdly, with the real thing.

For the first time since his marriage, he felt himself a man among men. Even Isabel lost much of her power over him and, for the moment, he was far less concerned about his one daughter than his twenty or thirty vicarious sons. If only he could have gone to the front with them, he would have been completely happy.

Old Mrs Batchelor had to admit that the war had greatly brightened her life. Never before had she been in such constant and flattering demand. Almost every day she attended a work party as a recognized authority on hospital shirts, sea-boot stockings and Balaclava helmets. She met other old ladies and soon came to know the details of innumerable family lives. The fact that she was the mother of 'that clever Mr Batchelor' gave her considerable prestige, for Claude was well known and highly respected. She always carried a photograph of him in uniform in her handbag and everyone agreed that with his keen eyes, firm jaw and clipped moustache he looked handsome and soldierly. At times she quite lost her air of crushed resignation and became decided, even slightly daring. She replaced the chestnut curls with a grey marcelled 'transformation' and trimmed her toques with aigrettes instead of purple pansies. Once she electrified Valetta Road by saying after dinner: 'Claude dear, do you know I'd quite like to try a cigarette? Old Lady Robinson tells me she smokes one now and then, only in her own home of course, and finds it most soothing.' And in spite of Isabel's amused looks and her own coughs, she had smoked it to the end.

Isabel, who had always detested sewing, avoided work-parties. To please Claude, she now and then put in an appearance at a Catholic one where there was no fear of meeting her mother-in-law. However, she and her friends ingeniously turned bridge into a patriotic duty by giving their winnings to the Red Cross. She also adopted a Lonely Soldier, organized drawing-room concerts in aid of various funds and became an ardent flag-seller. Quite often she allowed an admiring purchaser to give her lunch or tea and more than once she said to Clara:

'Really, darling if it weren't for Daddy . . . and of course for my being a Catholic . . . I could have the most extraordinary opportunities.'

Without affecting her directly, the war made Clara restless. Boys who had led the street gangs of her childhood were now leading men into battle: she could hardly open *The Tatler* without seeing pictures of girls from Mount Hilary only a few years older than herself standing beside soldier husbands on the steps of the Oratory or tending wounded 'somewhere in France'. Nicole was driving an ambulance; others were running canteens or acting as *chauffeuses* to generals. In gloomy moments she told herself that she was missing everything and felt that fate was very cruel not to have allowed her to be born a few years earlier.

She tried desperately to grow up as fast as possible but, in spite of all her efforts, the young soldiers she met at home or at the Cohens persisted in treating her as a child. She even went so far as to put up her hair on her sixteenth birthday, a step of which Patsy disapproved as much as her parents.

'Much better to stay an attractive flapper than a bad imitation of a grown-up,' said Patsy. 'I'm older than you and I'm jolly well going to keep mine down till it looks ridiculous. You're crazy, Clara. Your hair's your best point and now you'll have to wait till you're married for anyone to see it in all its glory again.'

Though Clara had an uncomfortable feeling that Patsy was right, and though doing her hair became a daily torment, she remained stubborn. But, even with the upswept hair and daring hats perched on it at a perilous angle, people still refused to treat her as if she were as sophisticated as she felt. Her old friends of the Burglaress Bill days regarded themselves as seasoned men of the world as soon as they got into uniform. Though they were well under twenty, they behaved as if they were giving a 'kid sister' a treat when they occasionally took her to theatres. They were never tired of telling her about the marvellous 'binges' they had had in night clubs or in chorus girls' flats. She even suspected that they took her out mainly to ensure that she should go on writing to them when they went back to the front. For if, as a leave-companion, her stock was low, as a correspondent it was high. The demand for her letters was enormous. They were passed round dug-outs and, quite often, total strangers would ask her to write to them. Sometimes one of her unknown correspondents would call at Valetta Road and ask Claude's permission to take her out. In his general benevolence towards all young soldiers, he usually gave it. But Clara found these occasions disappointing. She got sick of hearing 'I'd no idea you'd turn out to be so young. You write such topping letters, I thought you must be nineteen at least.' She got even more sick of endless confidences about 'peaches' they had danced with at Ciro's or the Four Hundred. 'Do you really think a chap like me has an earthly with a girl like that? She must have simply hundreds of johnnies hanging round her.' Nor was she comforted by being assured that she was 'an absolutely priceless kid' and would undoubtedly be 'simply fizzing' when she grew up. What deflated her most of all was their favourite compliment: 'You know, you're not a bit like other girls. You're so jolly understanding. What a topping sister you'd make.'

All the same Clara had to admit that it was only her vanity that was hurt. None of these young men, known or unknown, corresponded to the private image she still cherished. However much she derided, even to herself, the idea of marriage, she continued illogically to search each new face. Every time she was prevented from going to a party she was convinced that *he* might have been there. On her seventeenth birthday she was seized with something like panic in case *he* never appeared at all.

These hopes and fears were not confided to anyone. With Patsy she continued to pose as a cynical coquette and with Ruth as a free spirit. She and Ruth never discussed marriage except as an institution and they held strong views about it.

'If you and I are really going to do something about the independence of women,' Ruth would say, her spectacles flashing, 'we've jolly well got to begin at home. What's the use of our setting up as a pair of bright Atalantas if we're going to stoop to pick up wedding rings?'

Yet in the very moment of agreeing that they must spurn the temptation Clara hoped very much indeed that it would be offered.

With Patsy she was equally deceptive. Though she assured her that, to her, men were merely amusements and she had no intention of ever settling down, she was anxious to know just what Patsy thought of her. On the score of looks Patsy assured her she need not worry. 'You vary a lot but you've got lovely hair and a nice soft skin. Skin's *terribly* important with men, I find. And there are times when you really do look stunning.'

This was a great comfort to Clara who was often convinced that the reason the prince did not appear was because she was not pretty enough. Once, very carelessly, she asked Patsy whether she ever imagined an ideal husband.

After a moment's serious thought, Patsy said:

'I can't make people up. What would be the point if I could? When I want a hat, I don't imagine a hat. I go and buy the nicest one I can see. Naturally I'd like a husband as much like Parpee as possible.'

'Good heavens. I should have thought anyone would want to marry a man as unlike their father as possible.'

'The next best would be *your* father. I think Mr Batchelor's adorable. In fact, if he were a widower, I'd marry him tomorrow.'

'You wouldn't seriously?'

'I most certainly would. I like men older than myself. Forgive my saying so, but I don't believe your mother appreciates him one little bit. I'm sure I could make him terribly happy.'

Clara was so astounded and obscurely shocked that she could only laugh half-heartedly at the exquisite joke of having Patsy for a stepmother.

Since she had nobody at the front in love with her and was too young to be a nurse or a WAAC, Clara refused to take any interest in the progress of the war. No one at St Mark's could have guessed that she had once slept with a hussar cap on her pillow or taken a cavalry sabre to bed instead of a teddy-bear. She would never have admitted to Ruth, who inclined to pacifism, that she still occasionally cried over her tattered copy of *The Story of a Short Life* or that she knew half the Barrack Room Ballads by heart. Up to 1914 she had been a recognized military authority; boys had deferred to her on the subject of uniforms and regimental history. But the war she was living through bore no relation to *her* wars. There were no more scarlet and pipeclay, no more plumes and cuirasses, no pitched battles and, worst of all, no charges. Nor did any of the young soldiers she knew make the least effort to arouse her interest. The last thing they wanted to talk about was their life at the front. Even when she heard that one or other of them had been killed, it did not make the war more vivid to her. Though she remembered him in her prayers, she could never quite believe that he was dead.

Her indifference to the war effort became so marked that she was nearly branded as 'unpatriotic'. Since she could not tend wounded under heavy fire, the form's First Aid Class had no attraction. Her knitted contributions to the School Comforts fund became so meagre that the Hearties began to grow decidedly chilly. At one point she was very nearly sent to Coventry and only restored her prestige by putting in several Sundays of voluntary work at a munition factory. Her job was to sew the little bags which held the high explosive in the heart of a shell. The finest possible stitches were needed and here her convent training made it easy for her to excel the Hearties. The last time she had had to take such exquisitely minute stitches had been when she was making altar linen. As she sat sewing in a room that reeked of glue, listening to the factory girls yelling bawdy talk to each other above the clatter of the flanging machines, it was impossible not to think nostalgically of the workroom at Mount Hilary. Perhaps, at this very moment, children she had once known were sitting demurely, under the statue of St Anne teaching Our Lady embroidery, in a room that smelt of beeswax; stitching palls and corporals while a nun read aloud the life of a saint. Then she remembered ironically that sewing, even for the altar, was forbidden on Sunday.

It was two years since Clara had left Mount Hilary. She went down occasionally to see the nuns but at longer and longer intervals. Each time she was more reluctant to go and more anxious to get away as quickly as possible.

However carefully she prepared for these occasions, leaving her nose unpowdered and wearing her soberest clothes, she never achieved the right effect. A real 'Old Child' of Mount Hilary might be extremely elegant or extremely dowdy but in neither case were her clothes bought ready-made in Kensington High Street. And, though Clara left her wilder accessories at home, her wardrobe was so small that some detail was bound to betray Patsy's influence. It might be only a heel too high or a neck too low or a lingering trace of the wrong kind of scent but she knew that it 'placed' her.

There was the faintest chill in the nuns' welcoming smiles:

their eyes rested on her a shade too long as they stood talking to her with their bonnets inclined and their hands folded in their black sleeves. She felt the barb in certain phrases pronounced in the soft, disciplined voices: 'You look so grown-up: one would hardly have recognized you' or 'At least you have not succumbed to this dreadful new fashion of cutting the hair short.' They spoke with such commiseration of her having to leave Mount Hilary for what they persisted in calling 'this Protestant High School' that it was obvious they thought of her as a half-civilized savage who had relapsed into barbarism. 'But, after all,' the calm, pitying eyes seemed to say, 'what could we expect? A middle-class child and both parents converts. We must not judge too harshly.'

Educated themselves in convents or in their own homes, they had vague and alarming ideas about secular Girls' Schools. On Clara's first visit, Mother Lovell had said to her delicately, as they paced under the once-familiar limes:

'I suppose, my dear, you get some rather *rough* girls at your new school? And how it must go against the grain to have to put up your hand and say "Please, Teacher."'

'Oh, Mother, but we never do,' said Clara, stung more for her own pride than for the honour of St Mark's. 'And we call them mistress just as you do here.'

'Indeed?' Mother Lovell had sounded genuinely surprised. She added with a sigh: 'I suppose, with such very large classes, they find it impossible to keep discipline without at least the threat of corporal punishment. I always think it is such a mistake with girls. It tends to make the sensitive ones dishonest and only coarsens the more thick-skinned. I long to see it abolished in our own Catholic Elementary Schools.'

Clara was aghast. Did Mother Lovell really suppose that St Mark's was only one degree from a Board School? She wished she could confront her with Miss Silver, fine flower of Cheltenham and Girton, almost as stately in her gown as the nun in her habit. She had tried to reassure Mother Lovell, but the nun had not sounded altogether convinced. In fact her tone as she said 'Of course I don't doubt your word, my dear,' had reminded Clara irresistibly of Aunt Leah when corrected on a point of fact. And she had added with gentle insistence:

'All the same, you must find it different in many, many ways from Mount Hilary. Quite apart from its being . . . er . . . non-Catholic, the whole *tone* must be totally unlike ours.'

Clara had agreed, but she had soon given up trying to explain where the differences lay. She had discovered in this and other talks that, although the nuns were very ready to state their own ideas about her 'High School' they were much less ready to listen to hers. They had made up their minds on the subject and they preferred not to have them disturbed.

In two years at St Mark's, Clara still had not learnt how to manage her comparative freedom. The change from the convent discipline had been too violent. It was as if someone who had never been allowed to handle money had been given a hundred pounds to spend. In the enclosed world of Mount Hilary, every moment of her time was arranged for her; she was never on her own and never supposed to be alone with another child. It was only by subterfuge that she and Nicole had managed to snatch any private conversation. The liberty of St Mark's had been intoxicating at first but soon it became almost a burden. She felt compelled to fritter away her time simply because it was her own to squander. She missed the sharp distinction between home and school which had given a rhythm to her life. Often, when she would have actually preferred to be working, she would gossip, or linger in the cloakroom doing her hair, just because it was no longer punishable. Much of the charm of her endless tête-à-têtes with Ruth and Patsy came from the old ban on 'being in twos', and the hours she wasted experimenting with her appearance were partly accounted for by six years of wearing uniform and being forbidden to use a looking-glass. The other girls at St Mark's imposed a certain discipline on themselves but, though Clara frequently made good resolutions, she never kept them for long. She was so used to obeying other people that it was almost impossible to obey herself.

All this produced at times an uncomfortable sense of dissipation. She felt she was not so much growing up as expanding shapelessly in all directions. She read omnivorously, devouring but not absorbing; never going deep into anything for fear of missing something else till her head was a chaos of unrelated ideas. All the values that had seemed so clear at Mount

Hilary were becoming muddled. It was not that she doubted the truth of her religion but that it was becoming more and more difficult to make it a real part of her life. The nuns had prepared her to expect hostility and ridicule: what she found was indifference. People accepted her being a Catholic as they might have accepted her being a foreigner.

When she had first gone to St Mark's, she had rather enjoyed emphasizing her difference and had clung like an exile to some of Mount Hilary's customs. She had worn her medals outside her dress and kept a small statue of Our Lady on her desk. She had even dated her homework by the feasts of the Church until Ruth had taken to dating hers by the Jewish calendar and they were both asked to stop. Eventually the statue went because her High Church friends thought it irreverent, and the medals vanished inside her frock for worldly reasons. Soon, though she never missed her obligations and went to Confession and Communion at fairly regular intervals, she kept her Catholicism to herself.

The only person with whom she ever discussed religion was Ruth. The latter greatly admired Dante and St Francis and listened with interest to Clara's expositions of doctrine. But, though Ruth was sympathetic, nothing would have deterred her from her own Jewish observances which were mainly a matter of racial piety. For her own satisfaction she was trying to work out a synthetic religious philosophy based on Plato, Spinoza and Wordsworth. Ruth was so naturally good, so incapable of meanness or spite or dishonesty that Clara sometimes wondered whether orthodoxy were so important after all. Though she brushed the idea aside as a 'temptation against faith' it had an uncomfortable way of recurring. Ruth herself, Protestants like Mrs Cohen and the old aunts, even the Seventh Form atheist, Rhoda Delaine, were far more selfless, truthful and charitable than most of the Catholics she had known. Indeed, when she considered her vanity and duplicity and how little her beliefs influenced her behaviour, she began to wonder whether she might not be insensibly growing into a hypocrite.

Chapter Four

During the second summer of the war, old Mrs Batchelor said to Clara:

'There's one thing we've got to thank the Kaiser for. Have you noticed how much your mother's temper has improved lately? She doesn't get aggravated at every little thing as she used to.'

Clara had been too preoccupied with herself to notice any change in her mother. But, now her grandmother mentioned it, she decided it was true. It was quite a time since she had criticized even Patsy.

'No, she doesn't. But where does the Kaiser come in?'

'All this flagselling and so on. It's given her something to think about besides herself. She gives way to your Daddy more than what she used. You remember the fuss she used to make when he went off on his marches at weekends instead of keeping her company? I did think it a shame. He does enjoy them so and I'm sure the fresh air does him good. Now she quite encourages him to go. Would you believe it, I saw her with my own eyes polishing the buttons of his tunic?'

'Wonders will never cease,' said Clara. 'I'm afraid the war hasn't improved my character. Rather the reverse.'

'I'm sure there was no need for improvement, dear. You've always had a sweet nature. Thoughtful for others, like your Daddy.'

Some weeks before this conversation, Isabel had gone out on one of her flagselling expeditions. She always dressed with great care for these and set out in a spirit of adventure. Often the end of the afternoon found her tête-à-tête with a stranger in one of those dimly lit tea-rooms that were springing up in the neighbourhood of Piccadilly. Designed for officers on leave, the tables for two were set in alcoves and the waitresses did not appear until summoned. She never told the man her real name: he was no more than an audience before whom she acted different parts according to her mood. She hinted at romantic backgrounds and adopted a slightly foreign accent. Usually she impersonated her favourite heroines; by turns she would be Paula Tanqueray, Bella Donna, Nora or Mélissande. She would bewilder a simple business man by talking like Hedda Gabler or, having attracted a Frenchman by her languid, provocative look, behave like the Princess Lointaine.

One June day, when she had put on a new amber-coloured dress, the organizer asked if she would mind for once selling in Kensington High Street instead of the West End. She was on the point of saying she did not feel up to standing about, when the woman said:

'Forgive my saying so, Mrs Batchelor, but I don't think I've ever seen you look so lovely as you do in that yellow frock.'

Isabel could not help smiling. Her mirror had told her the same but it was pleasant to have it confirmed.

'The poor High Street did so badly for the Belgians,' sighed the organizer, 'I promised Lady Sisson that I would put our most attractive seller there for the Winter Comforts.'

After this, Isabel could hardly refuse to take the pitch outside Barker's. It was an exquisite day; she was in the mood for adventure and she fretted at being somewhere too near home to be either likely or safe for an interesting encounter. The morning passed slowly while she rattled her tin at crowds of shopping women. The few men about were so dull that she never once acceded to the request:

'I say, aren't you going to pin it on for me?'

After lunch in a stuffy teashop, she began to wonder how soon she could decently go home. As she stood hesitating, studying her reflection in a shop window and thinking how utterly wasted the day had been, she noticed a man's figure in profile reflected beside her own. The figure remained so still, with its head bent forward, that she suspected he was looking at her. She turned and met the intent gaze of a pair of blue eyes. At first sight she was dubious of the man himself. She could not quite place him. He was hatless and carelessly, even shabbily dressed; he had a sallow skin, untidy auburn hair and a reddish gold beard. The beard made it difficult to guess his age; he might be anything between twenty-eight and forty. He remained standing perfectly still, with his hands in his pockets, looking down at her from his considerable height with a faint smile and compelling eyes. The eyes were a smoky blue; at once tired and ardent. Their gaze confused her and she turned her own away.

'Ah, don't do that,' he said. 'I've waited so long for you to look at me, Mrs Batchelor.'

The voice had an unusual intonation but it reassured her. At least this man belonged to her own class.

'Do I know you then?' she said. 'I can't remember . . . I have a good memory for faces.'

He smiled.

'We haven't been introduced. But I have seen you four times.'

'And you know my name?'

'Only your surname. I found that out the first time.'

'And where was that?'

'At a concert at St Mark's School. You were in rose-red with two little silver wings in your hair. Do you remember?'

She smiled in her turn.

'That dreary concert. Yes, only too well.'

'You were the most beautiful person in the room. Also the only one who looked as bored as I had felt till that moment. I spent the rest of the evening looking at you and I assure you I wasn't bored at all.'

'Whatever induced you to go? You don't look like a parent.'

'Oh no, Madame. I am not a parent, at least as far as I know, and, if I were, I should certainly not be sending my son to an English Public School. I am a master.'

'You can't be. I know them all.'

'And I am not the type, you were going to add? I admit I am not the type. But with so many heroes at the front they have had to fill the gaps with what they could get. I am the temporary junior French master. My name is Callaghan.'

'That's Irish isn't it?'

'Certainly. But I had a French mother. And I have a French *prénom* . . . Reynaud.'

'Reynaud . . . what a charming name. I have some French blood myself.'

'I hoped that when I first saw you. Now, since I've heard you say Reynaud, you don't need to tell me.'

368

'It is so long since I've spoken French, I've almost forgotten it.'

'I would be very happy if you would let me refresh your memory.'

'I am sure you are an excellent schoolmaster, Monsieur Callaghan.'

'Oh . . . if you would only say Reynaud again.'

'Is that necessary? You've already said you were satisfied with my pronunciation.'

'I've had precious little to be satisfied with since I first set eyes on you. For three months I've had to content myself with glimpses of you in the street or through the window of a bus. I've speculated endlessly about what kind of woman you were. You always go about looking as if you were in a dream.'

'Do I look like that now?'

'You look as if it would be possible to arouse your curiosity.'

'Perhaps,' she said coldly, to hide the fact that she was childishly excited and a little frightened.

'I've made a tactical error, haven't I? Letting you know how passionately you've aroused mine? That's the Irish side of me, always butting his head into trouble and not content till he's made an arch fool of himself.'

Reassured, she smiled and asked, almost shyly: 'What is it you want to know so much?'

'Your name, first of all. You'd be amused if you knew how many times I've tried to christen you. Always French names. I can't imagine you as Joan or Gertrude or Marjorie.'

'What did you guess?'

'Mérode, Solange, Éliane, Isabelle.'

'Isabel was right,' she said, enchanted.

'Isabelle.' He drew it out syllable by syllable.

'I so much prefer it in French.'

An acid voice said at her elbow:

'Of course, if you're too *busy* to sell me a flag.'

She turned her attention to a woman who, after asking the price of every flag, decided on a penny one and demanded eleven coppers in change for her shilling.

'Won't a sixpence and five pennies do?'

'Certainly not. I need pennies for my gas meter.'

'This lady is not a machine for giving change,' said Callaghan. 'Hadn't you better take your shilling to the bank, Madam?'

'But I particularly want to have a flag. It is a disgrace how obstructive the flagsellers are.'

'Then permit me to present you with one.'

He dropped a shilling in Isabel's tin and pinned a flag on the woman's bosom.

She fluffed up her feathers but, seeing Callaghan's smile, she pursed her lips and walked indignantly away.

Isabel and Callaghan exchanged glances. She gave a sudden happy sigh.

'You'll ruin my reputation.'

'If only you'd let me. But what's happened to you? With that mischievous look on your face, you're all of a sudden a very young girl. Take off that look or take off that woman of the world hat. You can't wear both. They clash.'

'I'll keep my hat then,' she said. 'But oh, what a bore it is sometimes being *rangée*. I hate responsibility, don't you?'

'Loathe it. I've always been careful not to clutter myself up with any. Isn't it time we stopped getting in the way of all these worthy ladies and went for a walk in Kensington Gardens?'

'What about the Winter Comforts? I've hardly anything in my tin.'

'Naturally. How can you convince people of the need for winter comforts? They've only to look at you to know that it will be eternally summer.'

'Is it Reynaud or Callaghan who says such charming things?'

'For once they speak in unison.'

For the rest of the afternoon they wandered about the Gardens or sat under the trees. Isabel was too happy to adopt any of her parts; too happy even to be critical of Callaghan's shabbiness or to mind when people stared at them. She had no idea why she should be so happy; it was as if she had discarded her ordinary life like a heavy coat. Sometimes they talked a great deal; sometimes they hardly spoke. Often they stood perfectly still and silent, looking at a flowering tree or a tramp asleep with a newspaper over his face. Things she had never even noticed became suddenly delightful or interesting. She could not say whether being with this man were like finding something new or rediscovering something forgotten.

They lingered for a long time in the Dutch Garden, staring, through one of the windows cut in the hazel leaves, at the trim bright beds and listening to the faint tinkle of water dropping from the leaden tanks.

'I'd like to see you at Versailles,' he said. 'You are made for a formal setting. Nature needs taming and pruning and civilizing before she's fit to come into your presence.'

'Don't be too sure,' said Isabel, tossing her head so that the mask of lacy shadow danced over her eyes. 'In some moods, I like nature wilder than you might think.'

His hand moved closer to hers on the bar of the scrolled iron gate. She was on the point of withdrawing her own but let it stay.

'But I love Versailles,' she went on dreamily. 'I had an ancestress at the court of Louis XVI. I should have adored that life. Those exquisite clothes and the balls by candlelight and the masquerades by moonlight.'

'And the *galanteries*?'

'Perhaps even the *galanteries*,' she said demurely. 'It would all have been exquisite and artificial, like a play.'

'I wouldn't quite do for the part of the curled Marquis pushing the lady in a flower-wreathed swing.'

He turned and faced her, smiling wryly in his beard. She could not help noticing that his shirt collar was dirty and there were buttons missing from his frayed coat.

'You haven't always been a schoolmaster, have you, Reynaud?'

'No. What would you like me to have been? Or what do you think I am?'

'I don't know,' she said, vaguely disturbed at having to fit him into everyday life. 'An artist, perhaps.'

He frowned.

'An artist? In England that means a painter, doesn't it? If one is under forty and has a beard, one paints pictures. I'm sorry to disillusion you, Isabelle. I'm not a painter. Nor am I flattered when I'm taken for one.'

A little hurt, she said softly: 'I'm sorry, Reynaud. You see I've never met anyone like you.'

He went on roughly, as if he had not heard her: 'My father painted pictures. Damn bad ones that hadn't even the merit of selling. He died of drink.'

'How horrible for you. And for your mother,' she said with a shudder.

'How expensive, you should have said.'

He looked suddenly bitter and remote, standing there gazing, not at her but at the neat bright water garden, with his beard stuck out at an angle and a shaft of sun showing up the stains on his coat.

'I write, if you want to know,' he said abruptly. 'In French, mainly. Criticism. I wrote poems when I was young like any other idiot. You wouldn't be interested. Now I've been collecting stuff on and off for years for a study of the Parnassiens. No doubt, like all women, you read nothing but novels.'

'I'm afraid I do read a great many novels,' she said meekly. 'But I am very fond of poetry. Don't you ever write poems now?'

'No, I've got too much sense. I know my limitations.'

'Are you sure you never will again?'

'You think falling in love might do the trick? Would you like me to write a poem so you could hang it like a charm on your bangle? Ah, my dear, I might be fathoms deep in love but you'll not find a pearl in a herring's guts unless he swallowed it ready made. You know no more how a poem's made than I know how your hat's confected.'

She said in a troubled voice:

'I know I'm a very silly woman. But don't let's speak of falling in love, even as a joke.'

'Ah, but I want to speak of it,' he said. His manner had changed again. He too sounded troubled. 'Or do I? I was very certain I did when I ran into you this afternoon. Now I'm not so sure.'

She said, childishly:

'I've disappointed you.'

'I wish to heaven you had.' He went on without looking at

her, 'I've been making it up in my mind, all these months, just the way it would go. You see, the Frenchman fell in love with you at the concert in a perfectly normal French manner. All through those chaste madrigals you could sing with propriety before a community of nuns, he was thinking how to contrive a meeting and what that meeting might lead to by the usual well-worn steps. I know the road. I could walk it blindfold. But during the last half-hour I've been in a panic in case the Irishman might be involved too. And that hasn't happened for a very long time.'

Her heart was beating painfully. She longed for him to have said: 'Never.' Controlling her voice with difficulty she asked: 'What was she like?'

'Irish, too. Just a typical good little Irish girl. I used to hang about church doors waiting to catch a glimpse of her coming out from Mass.'

'And what happened?'

'She became a nun.'

'How dreadful. I can't understand what makes women become nuns.'

'Can't you? I nearly became a priest myself. I had a pious mother.'

'. . . A priest?' she asked almost with horror.

'Don't worry. The Frenchman wouldn't hear of it. I doubt if I've been to Mass in six months.'

'Is the Irishman still in love with the girl who became a nun?'

'He's enough of an Irishman to keep his thoughts off a religious. Though it wasn't the Frenchman's kind of love. It was lay my sword at your feet and put your head on my shoulder and may not I nor any other creature ever hurt a hair of your darling head.'

For a second she felt the mortal touch of jealousy and shivered in spite of the heat.

'Perhaps it was as well she went into her convent. At least she was spared disillusion.'

'Och, she never had any illusions about me. If she looked at me at all it was only to tell me I was a fool. May you be spared the spectacle of an Irishman in love. I was always staring after her like a mooncalf and wanting to pull the stars out of the sky to pin up her shawl. You know the stuff . . .

'And crowd the enraptured quiet of the sky
With candles burning to your lonely face.'

'Oh don't laugh, don't laugh,' she said on a sharp note of pain. 'It's so beautiful. I can't bear it.'

'Why, Isabelle.' He looked at her half-tender, half-ironical.

She turned away, feeling tears come into her eyes. After a moment she said uncertainly:

'Did you write that . . . to her?'

'I'd say yes if it would make you look at me this moment. You've far more the face for burning candles to than she ever had. Why do you have to keep changing? Why can't you stay the languid lady that looked as if she'd played with fire so often that the smell of smoke bored her? The Frenchman liked that. He knew where he was.' Suddenly he took her face in his hands and turned it towards him. 'Why do you have great dark eyes with tears in them like a stag at bay? They cry when they turn and face the hunters. Did you know that? I saw it when I was a small boy in Ireland.'

She fought with all her strength to keep her face away from his and managed somehow to smile.

'It's worse when you smile. Now you look like a child trying to be brave.'

'Reynaud, let me go. Please. I implore you.'

'Very well.' He dropped his hands and thrust them back in his pockets.

They stood for a moment or two in silence, Isabel with her hands clenched on the gate, looking at the flowerbeds through a dancing haze.

She said at last: 'Let's go. Let's walk about. This garden is dangerous.'

They walked twice round the pond, hardly speaking. Then, suddenly tired at the same moment, they dropped on to two chairs and sat watching the children's sailing boats. Reynaud said:

'I've got Baudelaire's passion for ships. I can't see one without wanting to get on board and sail away heaven knows where. I'd like to put you on board a ship, Isabelle, just as you are, and carry you off.'

'Where to? *Au pays de Cythère*?' she risked. Out here in the open, among the children and nurses and young officers with their girls, she felt safer.

'Ah, we'd be sure to land there in the end. The Frenchman would see to that. But we might touch at another port for a while . . .

> 'Where beauty has no ebb, decay no flood
> But joy is wisdom, Time an endless song . . .

Just as well you don't know the last line.'

'Oh don't,' she said. 'It's everything I feel . . .'

'It seems I've struck the right note,' he said.

> 'Faeries, come take me out of this dull world
> For I would ride with you upon the wind
> Run on the top of the dishevelled tide
> And dance upon the mountains like a flame.'

'It's not fair to torment me,' she said. 'I used to have such wild dreams when I was a girl.'

'What's wrong with dreams?' He went on with melancholy mischief:

> 'Faeries, come take me out of this dull house,
> Let me have all the freedom I have lost.

For it is a dull house, isn't it? Own up now.'

'It's wicked of me even to think,' she said, wringing the gloves she could not remember having taken off. 'My husband loves me. He is a good man. The best of men. He's very clever. He's wrapped up in his work. And I love him. I do love him. It's not his fault I could never talk to him as I've talked to you this afternoon.'

'Are there children?'

'One – a daughter.'

'How old?'

'Sixteen. I was hardly older than that when I married.' She had told the lie so often that she had come to believe it.

'Is she like you?'

'No. Not in any way.'

'You should have had a daughter as beautiful as yourself.'

'I don't mean she's not pretty,' said Isabel loyally. 'She's a typical, fair English girl. She's very clever, like her father. She thinks I'm foolish and frivolous.'

'She sounds detestable.'

'No, no, she isn't. It's just that she's never suffered. She's a strange girl. Sometimes she recites poetry with such feeling and with such a look on her face that you'd think it meant something to her. But I don't believe she has any feelings at all. She's like Undine without a soul.'

'Don't let's talk about the tiresome chit. It's minutes since you gave me a thought or a look. Would you like to be run away with, Isabel?'

With an effort, she smiled.

'I've never considered the possibility.'

He looked at the small white sails on the pond and sang under his breath.

> *Dites, chère Isabelle.*
> *Où voulex-vous aller*
> *La voile ouvre son aile*
> *La brise va souffler.'*

'I expect the voyage would end in a shipwreck.'

'And though that's a singularly becoming hat, it's unsuitable for a long sea trip. If the wind carried it away I couldn't afford to buy you another. I couldn't at this moment even stand you a cup of tea unless we broke into the Winer Comforts box.'

'Was that your last shilling that you dropped in with such a *beau geste?*'

'The last, and not strictly speaking mine. Don't worry. There are more where that came from. Ushers don't get paid till the end of term you know. They're supposed to be decent citizens and have a hump to live on. It's simply that I haven't a hump so I have to use my wits.'

She felt a pang of distaste.

'Money is so sordid, isn't it?' she said. 'It can't buy anything worth having.'

'I don't agree, I have the Frenchman's respect for money. However, an Irishman can always borrow and the Frenchman sees to it that he gets the utmost value out of every *sou*.'

'Then it must have been the Irishman who wasted that shilling. I think it was that absurd gesture that made me like you.'

'That's what the Frenchman hoped. He had to make an impression somehow. You must admit the shilling paid a handsome dividend.'

'My flags,' she said suddenly. 'Whatever did I do with them?'

'Heaven knows. At least you've still got the cashbox.'

'Reynaud, I must go.'

'Ah, not yet, not yet,' he said, rising and catching her hands so that she had to drop the gilt bag and the tin she had carefully gathered up.

'Yes. Now, at once. I'd forgotten all about time. I have to go to the depôt . . . I have to be back to dinner.'

'And you've remembered you're Caesar's wife.'

'You're abominably unkind.'

'I'm abominably wretched. When can I see you again?'

She stood there pulling on her gloves and flushing like a girl.

'Oh, Reynaud. We can't. We mustn't. It's all so impossible.'

'Are you glad it's impossible?'

'It's not a fair question.'

'Could I make you love me or hate me? Or shall we leave well alone?'

'Oh leave it alone,' she said pitifully. 'Let's both forget.'

He stood up facing her.

'If I'd kissed you, you wouldn't forget so easily.'

'You've no right to talk like that. I have a husband. Oh, I'm not a good Catholic I know. I don't suppose I'm even a good woman. But I've never . . .'

'You're starving for love and understanding. I could make you so happy. It's not just presumption, Isabelle. There's a whole side of you that's never had a chance. I'm the only person that even cares about it.'

377

'Don't say any more. Let me go.'

He let her go in the end, watching her till she was out of sight. Then he began moodily throwing stones into the pond until half by accident, half by design, he capsized one of the toy yachts.

She was still trembling when she got to Valetta Road. It was with the greatest difficulty she swallowed a few morsels of her dinner and managed to reply when anyone spoke to her. But no one appeared to notice anything unusual.

It was one of the evenings when Clara happened to be in. After dinner the two of them sat in the drawing-room. Clara was finishing herself a dress which meant that she was too absorbed to make conversation and kept running down to her bedroom to try it on. Isabel went to the piano and began to play. She always played erratically, with too much pedal and considerable sketchiness in the left hand. She tried the openings of several Chopin nocturnes she had played when she and Claude had been engaged but after a few bars her fingers dropped from the keys.

Clara, making one of her sudden exits, said cheerfully: 'Having a lovely strum, Mother? By the way, isn't it about time we had that old piano tuned?'

Suddenly her fingers found something she had almost forgotten she knew, a polonaise which she had learnt by heart at school. She was so absorbed that, when she struck the final chord, she was amazed to see Clara standing quite close to her.

'I say, you played that jolly well,' said Clara. 'I had to come back again and make sure it was really you.'

'You never think I can do anything, do you, Clara?'

'I didn't mean that. I've never heard you play it before, that's all. It's a brute, as I know from experience. Honestly, you play it nearly as well as Mrs Cohen. Her rhythm's better but you really put tremendous passion into it.'

'Thank you, Clara. A compliment from you *is* a compliment.'

'I really mean it. Play it again.'

'No. You make me self-conscious.'

'I'll go and listen from the bedroom.'

Isabel swung round on the piano stool.

'No pet. I'm not in the mood any more.'

'Sorry I broke the thread of inspiration. I must go and have another look at this skirt. I can't get the gathers right.'

'I'm afraid I'm useless at dressmaking. You should have gone round to the wonderful Cohens.'

'I would have, only the whole lot have gone to a concert.'

'I see. I thought perhaps you were staying at home of your own accord for once.'

'I often stay in. I was in last Tuesday. You were out that night playing bridge so you probably didn't know.'

'I very seldom go out in the evenings. I'm sorry I missed your being in. I hope you weren't lonely.'

'Oh no. I had plenty to do. I caught up a bit on my homework. Or are you being sarcastic?'

Isabel sighed.

'I suppose I ought to be glad you're fond of anyone, even Patsy Cohen. It shows you must have some affection in your nature.'

'I don't think I'm so stony-hearted as you make out. I'm very fond of Ruth too. And Nicole, of course, though I'll probably never see her again.'

Clara watched her mother's face; the conversation seemed to be heading towards familiar rocks. She was about to escape when Isabel unexpectedly smiled.

'Perhaps one of these days it will be a young man. You're growing up so fast; it's difficult to realize.'

'Oh, there are quite a lot of young men I like too. But I'm not in love or likely to be.'

'I thought the same when I was sixteen. But perhaps there's some young man in love with you and you don't even know it.'

This was an interesting thought. Clara stopped glancing towards the door and sat down.

'Is that an idea? Or are you hinting at something definite?'

'Queer things happen, Clara. You'd be astonished. Perhaps there's some young man who hangs about, just on the chance of getting a glimpse of you. For example, he might wait outside the church just to see you come out from Mass.'

Clara thought carefully, but could not remember having noticed anyone. She decided she would look the very next

Sunday. Her mother certainly had a rather peculiar look this evening. What did it mean?

'You're rather mysterious, Mummy. Have you got a secret or something?'

'Perhaps I have.'

'Tell.'

'Oh no. You are the last person I should tell.'

'Does it affect me?'

'If it stopped being a secret, it might affect you more than you think.'

'This is most intriguing. I do think you might tell.'

Her mother shook her head, turned back to the piano and idly played the first bars of a prelude.

'Oh well, if you insist on being an oyster, I'd better go back and wrestle with that dress.'

'Yes, perhaps you'd better, darling.'

As Clara moved, this time rather reluctantly, towards the door, her mother said, without turning her head, 'Oh, Clara, something I wanted to ask you.'

'Yes?'

'You know so much poetry. I wonder if you can tell me where this line comes from. I saw it quoted somewhere or other.

'With candles burning to your lonely face.'

'It's Yeats. "The Land of Heart's Desire".'

'It's very beautiful, isn't it?'

'I used to think it marvellous. That's when I had my Celtic Twilight period and was crazy about Yeats and Synge and all that Irish stuff. Cathleen ni Houlihan; the good people, Helen with a golden nosegay in her shawl. I was quite drunk with it. So was Ruth. Now I think it's all rather tush.'

Chapter Five

For the next few weeks, day and night, Isabel lived in a feverish, blissful dream. She went over and over again every moment of the afternoon in the Gardens with Callaghan. She even wrote down everything she could remember of it in a locked notebook, disguising it as a dialogue between 'The Poet' and 'The Lady'. She bought a copy of Yeats' poems and read 'The Land of Heart's Desire' every night before she went to sleep. A few days after their meeting she had a letter from him, an impasssioned letter in French, imploring her to meet him again. After a struggle with herself, she wrote gently refusing. But she put the letter in the locked book and read it till she knew it by heart. Away from him, she could forget everything that had faintly jarred: he became the troubadour and she the imprisoned queen. Appeased by her secret happiness, she became unexacting and could even take pleasure in the happiness of others.

Clara's seventeeth birthday occurred a few days after her meeting with Callaghan. She had already given her a present but, on a sudden impulse, she went out and bought her an evening frock out of her own dress allowance.

Clara was surprised and touched. She also felt slightly guilty since she had not remembered her mother's birthday till she saw the packages on the table and had had to rush upstairs and hastily wrap up a little coral brooch which she hoped Isabel would not recognize.'

'Mummy, you really shouldn't have,' she said, shaking out the folds of apple-green taffetas. 'It must have cost the earth. You've already given me that lovely bottle of Chaminade.'

'Well, one isn't seventeen every day,' said Isabel smiling. 'Enjoy your youth while you have it, darling. You won't realize how precious it is till it's gone.'

There was a dinner party that night in Clara's honour and she was allowed to invite whom she liked. She asked Patsy and

Mavis and three young officers she had met at the Cohens. At her father's request a fourth was added, one of his favourite old pupils who was at a loose end on his last night of leave. On these rare occasions, Isabel was apt to be irritable especially if Patsy were invited. Sometimes she would sit looking bored and aloof: sometimes she would embarrass Clara by behaving as if she belonged to the younger generation and joining too enthusiastically in charades or dancing. pt tonight, ahthopgh Patsy flirted outrageously with Claude and the young men were too busy showing off to each other to pay her much attention, she behaved perfectly. For once Clara could not compare her unfavourably to Mrs Cohen. As she said goodnight, she gave her mother a spontaneous hug and said:

'I've had a simply marvellous birthday. You've been angelic. You really have. Do you know Tony Brinton said he didn't see how you could possibly be old enough to have a daughter of seventeen?'

Some weeks later Claude said to her:

'There's rather an odd bird among these temporary masters. He's a Catholic, though not a particularly good one, I believe. I've been wondering whether we ought to ask him to dinner. Would it amuse you to have someone to talk French to?'

Isabel felt all her blood rushing back to her heart and was thankful she was so pale by nature. She managed to ask carelessly:

'Why? Is he a Frenchman?'

'Only half. His name's Callaghan. Irish. But he teaches French and seems to have spent most of his life in France. I'd better warn you he's rather unpresentable. Has a beard and is decidedly careless about his clothes.'

'Hardly the usual type for St Mark's surely.'

'No. That's why I thought he might amuse you. You find most of my colleagues infernally dull, I know. Actually they were rather scandalized when Cavell took this chap on. I don't altogether approve of him myself, but there's no doubt he's intelligent and I have to admit I find him rather entertaining.'

'You talk as if you saw a good deal of him.'

'Actually, during the last few weeks, I have. He always seems to be in the Common Room at the same time as myself. He's rather *mal vu* by the others and seems to have taken rather a fancy to me. Now and then I've stood him a drink. He's obviously very hard up, poor fellow and I thought it might be a kindness to have him here for a meal. But that's entirely up to you, my dear.'

Isabel felt slightly giddy. She had honestly done her best not to see Reynaud again. If Claude deliberately threw him in her way, she was not to blame.

'You look dubious. Don't if you don't want to.'

'I'm only thinking, dearest.'

She tried to imagine Reynaud sitting at their dinner table under the eyes of Claude and Clara and Mrs Batchelor. Clara would either be distantly polite or eager to show off her knowledge of French poetry. He would sit on her own right. They would have to pretend they had never met before, yet it would be impossible for them not to exchange an intimate look. She would feel treacherous and guilty. To see him like that, in the setting of her everyday family life, would be to rub the bloom off her secret.

To gain time she said: 'Is there a Mrs Callaghan we should have to ask too?'

'I discovered not. I didn't want to inflict an unknown quantity of a wife on you.'

'I don't want to be horrid, dearest. But wouldn't it be better if you took him out by yourself to a restaurant? It really is getting very difficult to manage food nowadays. If we're going to ask any of the staff here, it really should be the Slaters. We've owed them a dinner for ages.'

'H'm, yes. We can't kill two birds with one stone because Slater loathes the sight of Callaghan. I daresay you're right, my dear. I'll take Callaghan out for a bachelor evening some time. In any case, he's a man's man and probably ill at ease with women.'

There was mischief in Isabel's smile as she said: 'From your description, I've no doubt you're right.' But though she smiled, her heart was in a tumult. She had deliberately thrown away her chance but it was torment to think that Claude and not herself should spend a whole evening with him.

The very next morning, as she was shopping with Clara, she saw him on the other side of North End Road. If she had been alone, she would not have had the strength not to go across and speak to him. As it was, hoping he had not seen her, she hustled Clara into a shop and surreptitiously watched his tall, bearded figure till it was out of sight.

A few nights later, Claude's ten o'clock pupil put him off and he came up to bed earlier than usual. Even at that time he half-expected to find her asleep, for when she was doing nothing special she went to her room soon after dinner. But the light was on by her bed and she was sitting up reading. She looked up with a start as he came in.

'What's the matter, Claude? Why have you come up so early? Are you ill? You look terribly white.'

He sat down heavily on the end of her bed.

'No, no. I'm not ill. Only bad news again.'

'Another boy killed?'

'Yes. Raymond Harrison. He was at Clara's birthday party, you remember. One of the very best.'

'How terrible. When did you hear?'

'Just now. His young brother John was coming to me tonight. He rang up. Naturally he wants to be with his mother.'

'Oh Claude. I'm so sorry. What a wicked, wicked waste of young lives it all is.'

He leant his head on his hand with a weary gesture.

'Sometimes I feel ashamed to walk the earth, Isabel. They die so that useless fellows like me can go on rotting in comfort.'

'Claude, you mustn't say such dreadful things. How can you call yourself useless?'

He said nothing but closed his eyes and shook his head slowly, as if it were a great weight.

'You feel it so much each time it happens,' she said gently.

'Not enough. Not enough. One comes to take it as a matter of course.'

'You were particularly fond of this Harrison boy, weren't you?'

'Yes.' He sighed and repeated, 'One of the very best.'

'I remember thinking what a good-looking young man he was.'

'Yes, indeed. He had the makings of a first-rate classical scholar. He could have done all that I long ago gave up dreaming of doing.'

She said softly: 'Because you married?'

He managed to smile.

'Ah no, my dear. I hadn't the stuff in me. I know that now. But I have just enough to know the real thing when I see it. And I know enough to have got him started on the right lines.'

'Perhaps some day you'll find another like him.'

'No. Not like Raymond. There aren't more than two or three like him in a century. It was my dream that, if I could never be a real scholar myself, I might nurse one up. Then I could have said my *Nunc dimittis* in peace.'

'You thought once that Clara . . .'

'Yes. When she was a child. She showed real promise. But she lost interest long ago. I doubt if women can ever do it. Melian Stawell, Jane Harrison . . . admirable up to a point . . . but there's always something lacking . . . either the imaginative sweep or the mental muscle. You don't get the real right thing in women any more than you find pearls in herrings.'

Isabel's mind, which had begun to drift, became suddenly alert.

'Pearls in herrings. That's a clever metaphor.'

'Not my own. That man Callaghan said something of the kind the other day. We were discussing Greek poetry.'

'Poetry!'

'Yes, my dear. I'm not occupied entirely with "'ὅτε's' measurements". Though I often feel as if I were.'

She sighed and leant back on her pillows. In the light of the shaded lamp, with her eyes velvety and her acorn brown hair tumbled on her neck, she looked very young.

'That poor boy. I know it's very sad that he was so clever. But I keep thinking of everything in life he's missed. Perhaps already there was a girl who loved him.'

He leant his head on his hand again and said slowly: 'Yes, you're right. Hundreds of them. Killed before they had begun to live. Why should I feel the loss of one more than another? I've had the best of life. If I could give up the rest of mine just to save one, even the dullest little bank clerk, even an utter ne'er-do-well.'

'Oh, Claude, you mustn't talk like that. Think of all the good you do. All the people who need you.' She paused and added almost guiltily, 'Think of me.'

He looked at her wearily. 'Do you need me, Isabel?'

She lowered her eyes. The book still lay open on her lap and they caught a line. She read out:

'Oh, you are the great doorpost of this house.'

'What is that, my dear? It sounds like the translation of a line from one of the tragedies.'

'No, it's by an Irish poet. Yeats. He's still alive.'

'Ireland and Greece. Interesting. I've always felt there was a connection. I was saying so the other day to Callaghan and he agreed.'

She asked, wondering if her face looked strange:

'You seem to discuss a great many things with this Callaghan.'

'Yes, I suppose I do. Things I've hardly given a thought to since Cambridge. Maybe because he's Irish. Though on the outside he's as unlike as possible, there's something about him that puts me in mind of poor Larry O'Sullivan. But if there'd been a war and Larry had been Callaghan's age, he'd have got himself into it by hook or by crook. Of course Callaghan doesn't have to go. His father saw to it that he was born in Ireland so he can't be called up in France like his predecessor De Caux. And he's the kind of Irishman that loathes England. All the same, a rolling stone like that. You'd think he would have gone for the fun of it.'

'Perhaps he doesn't think anything worth fighting for.'

'Perhaps. It's the only thing I've got against him.'

Silence fell between them. Surreptitiously she closed the book of Yeats's poems and laid it on the table beside her bed. But his tired eyes followed her movement.

'The great doorpost,' he began, and broke off choked by a sudden sob. The next moment he was kneeling beside her with his head buried on her knees.

'Oh Isabel, Isabel. Without you I should be the loneliest man on earth.'

Chapter Six

One morning in the summer holidays that followed her seventeenth birthday, Clara woke very early. The term had left her with a sense of dissatisfaction though she had done far better than she deserved in the first part of Higher Local. In a day or two they would be going to Paget's Fold. She decided that down there she would pull herself together and try to bring her life into some sort of focus.

It was still only half past six when she had lain thinking for a long time without coming to any conclusion. On an impulse, she got up and went to early Mass; it was months since she had done so on an ordinary weekday. She made her Communion with a touch of her old fervour and walked home through quiet sunlit back-streets with a sense of freshness and peace she had almost forgotten. It took her back to Mount Hilary and, as she turned into Valetta Road, she decided she would go that very afternoon and see Mother Lovell.

The nun, as always, was delighted to see her. Standing in the red-tiled passage that always smelt faintly of incense, feeling the scratch of the starched bonnet against her cheek, she felt a rush of homesickness for Mount Hilary. All the children had gone; the grounds were empty except for an occasional nun walking with bent head saying her rosary or a lay-sister weeding a bed. It was a golden, windless afternoon; the reflection of the trees in the lake never stirred; there was no sound but rooks cawing and the chapel bell striking the quarters.

They paced down the alleys and round the playing fields, passing the stretch of grass with the weeping ash where, in another life, she had cried over her father's letter.

'It's so long since you came to see us,' said Mother Lovell. 'I was beginning to fear you'd given us up. I should . . . we all should . . . be very sad if that happened.'

Clara was about to make the usual excuses but decided to be frank.

'The fact is, Mother, I feel rather shy about coming back.'

'There's no special reason for that, is there, Clara?'

'No. I don't think so. It's just that now I lead such a totally different kind of life.'

'All the more reason for keeping in touch with us.'

Clara was silent.

'There's nothing on your mind, is there, child? I know the world is a difficult place for a Catholic girl. From what I hear, it is still more difficult since the war. You're still living at home?'

'Oh yes, Mother.'

'So many of our Old Children are doing war-work that takes them away from their families. I'm sure they do it in splendid spirit, yet I can't believe it's good for girls to be uprooted and have to mix with all and sundry.'

'I've still got a whole year more at school.'

'Ah, that Protestant school. How I wish we could have kept you with us. You must feel so isolated there. But thank God you have your home and that wonderful father of yours. Your mother is a Catholic too, isn't she? Home must be doubly precious to you now.'

Clara kicked a pebble.

'Nobody at St Mark's bothers about my being a Catholic. They think everyone has a right to their own religious opinions.'

'There's a certain danger in that attitude, Clara. You must be extra careful yourself not to get into loose ways of thinking. Never forget that the Faith can never be a matter of opinion; it is God's revealed truth.'

'Yes, of course, Mother.'

'Sometimes we need to be able to show others the logical base of our faith. Father Lamb has been telling us about some wonderful sermons another Jesuit, Father Coster, has been preaching at Farm Street. Have you heard any of them?'

'I've been working on Sundays lately,' said Clara. 'In a munition factory.'

'My dear Clara, is that necessary? I hope you don't miss Mass.'

'Oh no, Mother. I go very early.'

'Do you sometimes manage to get to Mass and Communion on weekdays?'

'Oh yes. I went this morning,' said Clara, feeling a hypocrite but assuring herself she really would go more often.

'Ah, I'm so glad,' said Mother Lovell, with real joy in her voice. 'As long as you are faithful to Mass and the sacraments, there's nothing to fear. I've heard such troubling things lately since this dreadful war; children of our own, girls from the best of Catholic homes.' She sighed and shook her head. They walked some steps in silence. Now and then a leaf from a lime tree dropped slowly at their feet or a pigeon called 'Rouk . . . Rouk' in the boughs.

As if her thought had travelled a long way in the interval, Mother Lovell went on:

'I often think of all that dear father of yours gave up in this world for the Faith. God must have had His own designs in taking you away from us just at that moment. Things often look so wrong to us until we get a hint of God's purpose and then we see that they were most exquisitely right.'

She stopped in her walk and turned her beautiful pale face to Clara, patting her arm. In the sunlight a few lines showed deeper than Clara had ever seen them and the keen eyes behind the glasses were a little weary.

'Mother, you look tired,' said Clara. With a sudden warmth of affection, she saw the nun for the first time as a human being with worries of her own. 'Have you been overworking this term?'

'No, no, of course not. Things have been difficult for the whole Community: the war affects us even here. We have more children than ever and not enough teaching nuns. And Mother Provincial has made herself ill with anxiety over all the problems the War has created in the Order. It may be a long time before we can re-establish contact with our houses on the Continent. That means heavy burdens for years to come on the English Province. I've been acting as her Secretary so I know her difficulties.'

'That means you've been doing all the work,' said Clara accusingly. 'What's more, I believe you've been ill yourself.'

'Nonsense, my dear. The merest indisposition. Mother Infirmarian is so anxious to exercise her charity that she puts us to bed on the slightest excuse.'

This was so far from true that Clara had to laugh.

'I am a pig,' she said ruefully. 'I haven't come to see you or even written for months.'

'Dear child, if you gave no sign for twenty years, it would make no difference,' said Mother Lovell gently. 'All the same, it is rather wonderful your coming today. I pray very much for you always. But this morning as I was making my thanksgiving, Our Lord put you so vividly into my mind.' She took both Clara's hands. 'Shall we sit down for a little?'

They sat on a bench, looking through a gap in the trees across to where a statue showed white among dark bushes on the far side of the lake.

'This is one of my favourite spots,' she said. 'I often come and make my meditation here, looking across at Our Lady of the Lake. Often it brings to my mind those lines of William Blake's:

> Though calm and warm were the waters wide
> I could not get to the other side.

But of course we *can* get to the other side. And Our Lady is watching over us and waiting for us there.'

She sat very still, her hands folded in her exquisitely darned black sleeves.

'I took a very important decision in my life, sitting on this very bench,' she said. 'One summer afternoon a very long time ago. Yes, a very long time, for I was not much older than you, Clara. I was a Mount Hilary child, you know.'

'Yes, Mother,' said Clara quietly, guessing what the decision had been.

'What a pity it is,' said the nun, reverting to her practical voice, 'that you can never come down for a retreat. I don't think anything helps one so much as a retreat. We all need now and then to be alone with God and our own souls. Especially in the world where there is so much noise all round us we can hardly hear God's voice. Perhaps, when you leave school next year?'

'I'm afraid I wouldn't be able to manage the summer one. It would still be term time,' said Clara hastily.

'We often have one for the Old Children in November,' said the nun. 'Have you thought at all what you are going to do when you do leave? I suppose you will take up teaching like your father.'

'I don't really know. If I can get a scholarship I might go to Cambridge.'

'Ah yes, indeed. They expect very high qualifications now, don't they? With all this new mania for examinations, though Reverend Mother doesn't approve of it at all, she is seriously considering opening a house of studies in Oxford or Cambridge after the war, so that some of the novices can try for degrees.' She sighed: 'I'm afraid that just at the moment we have not any very suitable ones. And of course, if any of our own children wished to go to the University it would be so nice for them to be there instead of at one of those non-Catholic colleges,' she smiled, 'I think we shall have to open a house of studies specially for your benefit, Clara.'

Clara laughed hoping her face did no betray that, even as a joke, the idea appalled her. Yet sitting here beside Mother Lovell, hearing a language she had half forgotten, watching a smiling lay-sister pass by, her blue apron full of vegetables, how remote seemed her own and Ruth's secular dreams. She stared at the toes of her shoes. They were patent leather ones, cracking already and dusty from their walk. She suddenly perceived how tawdry they were and wondered how she could have let Patsy induce her to buy them. Just as for months Mount Hilary had seemed dim and unreal, so now did West Kensington. Without knowing why, she sighed.

'Clara, my dear, you don't seem happy. Is there anything I can do or say that might help?'

'I'm not unhappy exactly. But everything's so confusing sometimes.'

'Do you feel you've lost your way a little?'

'Perhaps. Things seemed much simpler when I was here. But then I was only a child.'

'Is it that you feel you are approaching a turning point in your life and don't know which road to take?'

'Nothing so definite, really. I don't think much about the future. I suppose I'm just vaguely dissatisfied with the present. Yet I've no earthly reason to be discontented.'

'No earthly reason perhaps. Only God sometimes has reasons

for making us discontented. Do you remember St Augustine . . . "our hearts are restless till they rest in Thee".'

Clara sighed again, this time to try and throw off a strange sense of constriction. The long-forgotten words touched something in her which had been numbed; she felt a pang that was both aching joy and blind terror.

She said nothing. The nun laid her hand, with a touch light as a leaf, on Clara's.

'Pray a great deal, my dear. And I will pray too, more than ever. There is only one way for all of us, in or out of the world, the way of God's will. Will you come and see me again soon?'

'Yes, Mother.' She was suddenly nervous and remembered with relief that they were going away. 'When I come back from Sussex. Not for a month or more, I'm afraid.'

'I'm glad you're going to the country. It's the best place to "make one's soul". God is everywhere, of course, but it's easier for us to *feel* He is there when we are quiet and close to nature.'

Clara's mind went back to that day on the hills just on two years ago. Fighting down an unreasonable, mounting panic, she said rather coldly:

'I shall be glad to be in the country again. But there's nothing the matter with me, Mother. Doesn't everyone get silly moods at my age?'

'Yes, of course, my dear.' The nun stood up. 'I must be going in. I have to take the Novices' French reading. Poor Mother Duplessis is ill and there's no one else available at the moment.'

As they walked towards the great creamy stucco house, mellow in the waning July sun, Clara asked dutifully:

'Are there a lot of novices now?'

'Only five at the moment, alas. But we have a new postulant. You'll remember her. Winifred Cruickshank.'

'Winty,' exclaimed Clara. 'Why she's the very last person I thought would enter. If it had been May, I wouldn't have been in the least surprised.'

'God has a way of choosing the unexpected ones,' said the nun. 'At home we were always certain that it would be my sister Theresa. No one ever suspected I would . . . myself least of all.'

When they reached the door, Mother Lovell said: 'I've just five minutes. Shall we spend them with Our Lord in the chapel.'

But Clara's panic had reached such a pitch that she had to escape at once. She pretended she had only just noticed the clock.

'Oh Mother,' she blurted out, 'I'd have loved to. But look at the time. I promised my mother . . . if I don't catch the half past five bus, I'll be terribly late . . .'

Smiling a little sadly, the nun let her go.

'Of course I understand. I'll just come down to the lodge with you.'

Once more they passed together down the red tiled corridor, pausing for a moment by the statue of the Sacred Heart. Clara could not pray: she merely stared at the flame of the red lamp almost invisible in the sunlight. Once again she smelt the incense and the beeswax and felt the nun's bonnet scratch her cheek as she kissed her goodbye. The portress came out of her cubbyhole to open the grilled door. 'Goodbye, Miss Clara dear. Don't let it be so long before we see you again.'

When the bolts had grated behind her, Clara remained standing on the steps, hesitating. Was it relief she felt or a sense of banishment? For no reason, her eyes filled with tears. She blew her nose violently. Then, tightening her lips and fishing out her puff, she defiantly powdered her face on the very threshold of the convent.

PART FIVE

Chapter One

'What do you think of this, Claude?' said Isabel, taking a letter from her gilt mesh bag and handing it across the dinner-table.

For once they were dining alone. It was the end of August; old Mrs Batchelor had gone down to Paget's Fold and Isabel, for reasons of her own, had come back with Claude at the end of his three weeks.

He glanced at it: 'But it's written to Clara.'

'Yes. It should have been written to me.'

'Do you know this Catherine Lyons?'

'She's one of the pious spinsters at the Catholic workparty. A friend of that Mother Lovell Clara goes to see now and then. Full of good works and immensely well connected.'

He read the letter and passed it back.

'I'm afraid I can't help the lady. If Clara can't suggest a young Catholic governess to look after this boy, I'm sure I can't.'

'I told you she oughtn't to have written to Clara direct. Of course Clara's got the idea that she'd like to go herself.'

He said irritably: 'I won't hear of it. She can't leave St Mark's for another year. She's still got to take the second part of Higher Local.'

'She was sure you'd say no. I expect the thought of ten pounds a term went to her head.'

'Then she'd better forget it.'

'Yes, dearest.'

'She must write to Miss Lyons at once and say how sorry she is she knows no one suitable. Incidentally, where is Clara tonight?'

'Where she always is. At the Cohens'.'

'She seems to live there.'

'Yes. Isn't it a pity she hasn't some other friends besides that common little Patsy?'

'I've nothing against Patsy in herself. Nor against the plain one, the Philips girl. But I wish to goodness she knew some Catholics.'

'She still hears now and then from Nicole de Savigny. But she never sees her.'

His face clouded. After a moment he said: 'This governess idea is preposterous. All the same, the letter's a thorn in my conscience. It makes me realize how cut off from any Catholic life Clara's been since she left the convent.'

'Yes. It really seems an awful pity.'

He gave her a suspicious look; she was usually indifferent on this subject. She lit a cigarette.

'I'll tell Clara you said no. She'll be disappointed but not surprised.'

'Surely you agree with me, Isabel?'

'Certainly it would be rather absurd for her to be just a governess. After all you've spent on her education.'

'Of all the miserable, dependent jobs . . .'

'You must admit this case is rather different. Miss Lyons particularly says they want a girl who can be treated like one of the family. Obviously she's suggested Clara herself to Lady Cressett.'

'I'm afraid I can't follow the leaps of the feminine mind.'

'It's perfectly simple. I believe the whole idea came from Mother Lovell. She's devoted to Clara and wants to do her a good turn.'

'Mother Lovell? That hadn't occurred to me.'

'She still takes a great interest in Clara, you know.'

'Yes, indeed. She has written to me once or twice. I have an enormous respect for her.'

'It's nice that Clara's kept up with her, isn't it?' Isabel puffed at her cigarette: 'After all, it isn't as if you'd definitely decided on Clara's future. Or that she herself had.'

He frowned. 'I know I've been very remiss. But the future has become so hard to envisage. We've always assumed she should try for Cambridge next year.'

'Yet only a few weeks ago, you were saying you didn't think she was cut out for that kind of career.'

'She'll never be a scholar. I don't see why she shouldn't be a very passable schoolmistress. But she must get her degree.'

'Couldn't she go on working for her exam, at this place, Maryhall?'

'Possibly. But this whole notion is so extraordinary to me, I should have to give it a lot of thought. And I seem to find it remarkably hard to think these days.'

He leant his head on his hand. She waited a moment before asking softly: 'Don't you think Clara could do with a complete change of atmosphere? Haven't you noticed how restless and discontented she's been lately?'

'I'm afraid I'm not very observant. Anyhow she'll have a change next year if she goes up to Cambridge.'

'Girls are marrying in their teens these days. Suppose she married the first young man who came along . . . just from boredom.'

'*Marry*? Why she's only a schoolgirl.' His face stiffened. 'Isabel! You don't mean there's something behind all this. Some reason why you want to get the girl away?'

'A young man? Good heavens no!'

'Thank God! For one ghastly moment I thought . . .'

'*What*, Claude?'

He passed his hand over his forehead.

'Forgive me. Such appalling things happen these days.'

Isabel laughed.

'Really, dearest! What about the leaps of the masculine mind?'

'I can't see anything to laugh at.'

'Not even at the idea of hiding one's shame in the bosom of a virtuous Catholic family?'

Claude stared at her.

'You're talking very strangely, my dear. You were always so, how shall I say? So ultra-sensitive. One hardly dared . . . Have you changed like everything else?'

'Have I changed?' She did not look at him but spoke as if asking herself the question. Stubbing out her cigarette, she said:

'You do want Clara to marry some day, don't you?'

'Yes, yes, of course,' he said hastily. 'Provided it's the right type. And, I most sincerely hope, a Catholic.'

Isabel glanced at the letter again.

'It's only for six months, Miss Lyons says. Till the boy goes to Downside. She says that Maryhall is a lovely house and there are some charming Catholic families in the neighbourhood. Obviously she means Lady Cressett would take her about.'

'You realize I should have to pay next term's fees?'

'They're nothing compared to Mount Hilary's. Do you remember how we had to pinch and scrape because you were so anxious to send her to the convent? She's losing the charming manners she learnt there, all that indefinable *cachet*. It seems such a pity. But you can't blame Clara if West Kensington doesn't provide friends of the Mount Hilary type.'

He frowned and sighed. Zillah came in to announce his nine o'clock pupil. 'I'll think about it,' he said as he prepared to go into his study. 'I can't adapt myself quickly to sudden changes.'

Isabel went up to the drawing-room. She opened a book and shut it. She went to the piano, played the opening of two or three pieces idly and inaccurately, then got up and walked about the room, changing the places of ornaments. The restlessness that had come over her at Paget's Fold had pursued her back to London. It was no longer a delight to her to be left alone with her thoughts. She wished Clara were there; she would have welcomed anyone to distract her from her own imagination, even old Mrs Batchelor.

As she moved uncertainly about the room, picking up a vase or a silver box and trying it in a new position, she asked herself why she had been trying to persuade Claude to let Clara go to Maryhall. She had not meant to do more than raise the topic; she had not even been in favour of her going till they had begun to talk. She was surprised herself at the ingenious arguments she had found herself using. Was it that she wanted to be rid of Clara for a time? Or was it that she so urgently wanted a change in her own life that Clara must have it in her stead?

Change, change; how the word kept recurring. Could she have answered Claude's question? Something had happened to her at Paget's Fold. She had taken away with her the dream of the troubadour and the imprisoned queen. But down there the

397

appeasing magic had not worked. She had discovered that it was intolerable not to be in the same place as Reynaud Callaghan. And now that she was back in London she could not resume the dream that annihilated time and space and brought them together in a fairy world. Never yet in her life had she desired a man. She had had romantic attachments and greedy private fancies. In a burst of self contempt she had burnt *The Diary of a Lost One* when *The Land of Heart's Desire* became her secret reading. But since she had come home, this too had failed her. Every day, every night she became more and more painfully aware of an aching for Reynaud's human presence.

Chapter Two

Clara arrived at Maryhall on a perfect day in late September. All through the journey to Worcester she hugged the idea of a new life beginning. She had already spent a day with Lady Cressett and Charles and fallen in love with them and the house. The only cloud was that she had promised her father to go on working for her exam; she would like to have started fresh, with no obligation to the past.

Patsy had said: 'You're crazy and I shall miss you horribly, you beegledy thing. But I swear you'll be back long before Christmas. You'll be bored to tears. Nobody in his senses spends his leave in the country.'

Parting from Ruth had been less painless.

'Does this mean you've absolutely given up the idea of Cambridge, Spin?'

'I've told you. Daddy still wants me to try for a scholarship.'

'But you're not keen any more?'

'Oh Ruth, I don't know. In six months I daresay I will be again.'

It was unusual for Ruth to show anger but she flushed and said sullenly: 'After all our plans. I suppose you think it's freedom, being governess to some plutocrat's beastly brat.'

'You're always talking about experiencing as many sides of

life as possible,' said Clara, angry too. 'At least I'm doing something instead of just talking about it.'

'Living dangerously on ten pounds a term and all found.'

'As good as living dangerously in a prefect's hatband and being president of the Lit. Soc.'

'We seem to be having a vulgar brawl. We've avoided that up to now.'

'Sorry, Ruth. I thought you'd understand.'

'Idiot.' There were actually tears in Ruth's eyes behind the round spectacles. 'I'd go to any lengths to stop you going.'

'I'm so awful, if you only knew.'

'I know all right,' said Ruth with her wry smile. 'Cat that walked by itself. Critical Clara, the cynic of the Seventh.

'Just for a bundle of Bradburys she left us,
Just for a title to ram down my throat.'

'Go on, Sea-Green Incorruptible. Righteous Ruth the ruthless rhymer!'

'I believe at heart you're utterly conventional.'

'I've begun to suspect it myself. Goodbye, free spirit.'

'Goodbye, Jane Eyre.'

At Worcester, Charles came galloping up the platform to meet her. He was a remarkably handsome small boy with bright dark eyes and a high colour. His manner was even more excitable than she remembered. 'He's highly strung,' Lady Cressett had explained. 'And, I'm afraid, since his father's been at the front, more than a little spoilt.'

'Your train's late,' he said, snatching off his tweed cap. 'Five minutes and forty-three seconds. It's got a Bear Engine. Did you know?'

He danced along beside her.

'I found the platform from the indicator. I didn't ask anyone. Nan didn't want me to meet you: she said Milburn was quite enough. But Mummy said I could. We bust a tyre. I helped Milburn jack up the car. So you see without me we'd have been late. Sucks to Nan.'

When they got to the car, he said importantly:

'Miss Batchelor's luggage had better go on the rack. You can take that little case by you in front. I shall sit in the back now Miss Batchelor's come.'

'Very good, Master Charles.'

All through the drive he chattered at the top of his voice. Clara listened in a contented daze, watching the sallow sunlit fields and the distant flashes of the Severn through the autumn-coloured trees.

'Miss Batchelor's a funny name for a girl, isn't it?'

'They called me Spin at my last school. Short for Spinster.'

'Ha, ha. Rather good. Can I call you Spin too?'

'That depends on your mother.'

'I can usually make Mummy do what I like. Daddy's much stricter. They've just made him a major. I wish they'd made him a colonel. Jim Coldfield's father's a colonel and Jim swanks about it like anything though he's only temporary. Look at that plane. It's a Sopwith pup. Milburn, it *is* a Sopwith Pup, isn't it? I told you so. I'm making a new model plane, Spin. You can help me finish it if you like. Nan's in a wax because I spilt glue on the table. I expect that's why she tried to stop me meeting you.'

'Nan's been with you since you were a baby, hasn't she?'

'Yes. Of course I'm much too old to have a nurse. Nan's supposed to see to the linen and be a kind of maid to Mummy now. But since I had pneumonia last year, she's taken to sleeping in my room again. I put up with it because she's quite useful when I have nightmares.'

'Do you have them often?'

'No, but they're whoppers when I do. I walk in my sleep sometimes too. I'm terrifically highly strung. It's awfully bad for me not to have my own way.' He spoke with extreme gravity as if he were an elderly invalid discussing his symptoms.

'What happens if you don't?'

'Well, sometimes I get frightfully excited and don't quite know what I'm doing. The doctor says it's a kind of brainstorm. Once Nan took away my best engine and locked it up and I jumped into the pond and I didn't know I'd done it till I found myself flopping about in the cold water.'

'Did Nan always let you do what you liked after that?'

'Well, not always, no. She has fits of being frightfully strict as if I were still a baby. Sometimes I have to put my foot down and tell Mummy. She's a perfect dragon about tidiness. I hope you're tidy. You'll get into awful rows with Nan if you're not.

She used to get fearfully cross with Miss Stephenson, my last governess, for leaving things lying about in the schoolroom.'

'I'm not terribly tidy, I'm afraid.'

'Never mind. I'll protect you. I didn't protect Miss Stephenson because I was bored with her and wanted her to go. I can usually get round Nan because she adores me. Unless she's in one of her regular right-down royal waxes.' He glanced at Milburn's old-soldierly back in its green livery and lowered his voice to a hoarse whisper.

'Mummy's sister, Aunt Monica, says she's a domestic tyrant and Mummy ought to get rid of her.' He added aloud, 'No one could possibly imagine Maryhall without Nan.'

Clara could not help feeling slightly apprehensive though Lady Cressett had forewarned her. During her visit a fortnight before, Nan had remained in the background. But she retained a sharp image of a small, thin woman with smooth red hair, a pale bony face and downcast sandy lashes. Lady Cressert had warned her too that Nan was apt to be jealous of anyone Charles liked. 'That didn't arise with poor Miss Stephenson, because Charles never took to her. He has taken to you, quite violently.'

They turned in by the lodge and the house came in sight round the curve of a drive bordered by yew hedges. Clara gave a happy sigh; the place was as perfect as she remembered it. Maryhall was a small Jacobean manor house of plum-coloured brick, built in the form of a hollow square enclosing a flagged courtyard. It stood on a slight swell with lawns dotted with clipped yews sloping gently away from a low-walled terrace. Beyond it rose a semi-circle of woods, their leaves bright as a pheasant's plumage in the sun, and far in the distance lay the blue mass of the Malvern hills. When the engine stopped, she could hear the cooing of the pigeons in the stable yard and the clap of their wings as they flew up from the cote. The door of the house opened and a collie burst out, barking frantically and hurling itself on Charles as he jumped out of the car.

'Down, Hero, down. Don't be such a silly ass.' The dog crouched on its haunches, grinning. 'Come on, give the lady a paw.'

The dog looked doubtfully from Charles to Clara; allowed himself to be patted but did not offer his paw.

'Fool dog,' said Charles angrily slapping Hero on the muzzle. 'Do as your master tells you. Give your paw, Sir.'

'You'll never train him like that,' his mother called from the doorway. 'Leave Hero in peace, and Miss Batchelor too. Miss Batchelor, you must be dying for your tea. Come along in and don't let yourself be bullied.'

Lady Cressett was a big, strongly-built woman of thirty-eight with a settled look that made her seem older. Charles had not inherited one feature from her pale, Flemish type of face with its long nose and large lustreless grey eyes. Her greying brown hair was piled up in a modified version of the pompadour that had been fashionable when she was a girl; it was arranged with the utmost neatness and skill but it made no concessions to vanity. Everything about Theresa Cressett was plain, good and built to last from her well-cut, well-pressed tweeds to the brogues that shone like chestnuts. Her person, like her house, gave the impression of being kept always in perfect repair. Clara, in a crimson velour coat that had seemed both smart and countrified when she had bought it, with her hair blown into wild tangles under a crimson tam o'shanter felt once again that she looked all wrong. But Lady Cressett smiled at her with her peculiarly attractive expression and Clara forgot to be self-conscious. She had been charmed the first day by that smile. It was at once shy and humorous and it conveyed that the person she found slightly ridiculous was Theresa Cressett.

'I ought to ask if you're tired after your journey,' she said as she took Clara's arm and led her upstairs. 'But you look so young and bonny it doesn't seem to make sense. I do hope you're not going to find life too dull here.'

'I've been counting the days till I came,' said Clara fervently. 'I've remembered everything. Even the smell of the house.'

'Dear me!' said Lady Cressett, 'I've never noticed. I hope it's agreeable.'

'Heavenly. Beeswax to begin with like Mount Hilary.'

'That must be my furniture. I get it from the Carmelites. I hope it doesn't smell like a convent.'

'Oh no. The rest's quite secular. Woodsmoke and some mixture of herbs, rosemary's one I think. And somewhere in the background the sense of a very delicious cake being baked in the oven.'

'Well, let's hope today's delicious cake is waiting for you on the tea-table.'

Charles came clattering up the shallow oak stairs behind them, swinging one of Clara's suitcases.

'Hurry up and come down and let's get tea over,' he shouted. 'You needn't bother to take your coat off. I've got heaps of things still to show you outside.'

At the top of the stairs Nan was waiting. She wore a spotless white silk blouse, a dark skirt and a tiny muslin apron. Her thin lips smiled quite pleasantly as she said:

'Good afternoon, Miss Batchelor. I hope you had a nice journey.'

But as Charles continued to shout and tug at Clara's sleeve, her smile vanished.

'Come and wash your hands at once and stop pestering Miss Batchelor,' she said sharply and seized him by the shoulder. He tried to escape but, though she was only a few inches taller, her thin wrists were strong and she marched him off down the passage.

'I've given you the little blue room you said you liked,' said Lady Cressett, opening a door.

Clara exclaimed with pleasure, wondering at the same moment why it should be called the blue room since there was nothing blue in it but the carpet and one bowl. The walls were white-washed between the irregular squares of dark oak, there was a patchwork quilt on the narrow old four-poster and the curtains at the casement windows were embroidered with many-coloured silk flowers, once bright, now faded.

'It's nice looking out over the hills, isn't it?'

Clara had been too busy mentally inhabiting the room to think about the view. She glanced through the two diamond paned windows to the distant line of the Malverns and said:

'They're higher, but they make me think of the downs.'

'Your people come from Sussex, don't they? I hope you're not going to think the Midlands "sodden and unkind".'

'How could I? I know in my bones I'm going to love this place.'

Left alone, Clara put her outdoor things in the wardrobe, determined to be as tidy as possible. The water in the copper jug, though tepid, was deliciously soft; the linen towel smelt of lavender. There was no time to re-do her hair. She stuck in a few pins and hoped for the best, hoping too that her covert skirt and hastily knitted jumper looked sufficiently countrified. From now on she was determined to be an entirely different person.

As she came out, Charles bounded at her and butted her with his newly-brushed head.

'Come on slow-coach. Tea, tea, tea.'

She had meant to make a dignified entrance but he rushed her helter-skelter down the slippery stairs, making such a clatter that Hero and Lady Cressett's Scotch terrier barked in excited sympathy.

The tea-table was drawn up by a log fire that burned pale and clear in the late sunlight. No one could have guessed it was the third autumn of the war. There were hot scones and girdle-cakes, homemade jams, shortbread and even a jug of cream.

'At least we can feed you properly,' said Lady Cressett. 'We get plenty from the farm even when the hospital's had first turn.'

Clara was hungry and was unable to stop herself from eating an enormous tea; the kind of tea she used to eat at Paget's Fold when she was a child.

'Thank goodness, you can eat,' said Lady Cressett. 'I was afraid you would be worrying about your figure.'

'I ought to be,' said Clara ruefully; 'If I go on like this, I won't have a figure to worry about.'

'Charles will give you plenty of exercise if you let him.'

Charles, for a boy of ten, ate surprisingly little. He kept pulling at Clara's sleeve.

'What's the matter, Charles? Can't you let Miss Batchelor have her tea in peace?'

'Women dawdle and chatter so over meals. The light's going fast and I've got lots of things I was to show Spin.'

'Spin?'

'Need I call her Miss Batchelor? They called her Spin at school. Short for Spinster, see?'

'I get the point, Charles. But Miss Batchelor mayn't like it.

They called me Porky at the Sacred Heart. I shouldn't like it at all if the name had stuck.'

'Porky! Porky!' yelled Charles. 'I shall call you Porky, Mother.'

'I rather think you won't, my son,' said Lady Cressett tranquilly and Charles subsided.

'I don't mind what he calls me if you don't,' said Clara.

'What about discipline? I must say I find it hard to call you Miss Batchelor myself. You look such a baby.'

'I do hate my surname so.'

'Why? It's such a nice old English name. But I'd rather call you Clara.'

'Oh, please do.'

'Can I call her Clara too?'

'Certainly not, Charles. At least not in lesson times. Otherwise she'll never be able to keep you in order. I hope your father's let you into lots of professional secrets, Clara.'

'Secrets, what about?'

'About how to make ruffianly little boys behave and learn their lessons, Charles. Clara's father is a very famous schoolmaster.'

'How boring. Why isn't he in the army like mine? Or a submarine commander? Or a . . .'

'That's enough, Charles. If you've finished your tea and Miss Batchelor's nice enough to let you drag her about, you'd better say your grace.'

'Namerfather,' began Charles hurriedly.

'Say it properly.'

He said it properly. His mother and Clara crossed themselves.

'You'll have dinner with me tonight, won't you, Clara?'

'Can't I stay up her first night?'

'No, you cannot. There's no chance of peaceful conversation with you around.'

Once out of the house, Charles rushed Clara from the stables to the paddock, from the walled garden to the keeper's lodge. She had seen most of the estate before but now he showed her everything as if it already belonged to him. Though half the men had gone to the war, nothing looked neglected. The turf was shaven, the hedges clipped, the cowstalls on the home farm freshly white-washed. The two old hunters were as carefully groomed as if they were just going to a meet. Everything suggested order and security; a life that moved to a regular rhythm. Clara drew deep breaths of the wonderful air, distinguishing the smells of burning leaves, turned earth, sweet drifts from late roses and the faint darkness that steamed from the river as the sun waned.

As they walked she rubbed a sprig of rosemary between her fingers and sniffed it.

'I suppose rosemary's for remembrance because it's got such an unforgettable smell. I'm sure I shall think of Maryhall every time I smell it.'

'We've got masses of it. Especially in the walled garden. I like it best as stuffing,' said Charles. 'What do you think of Maryhall, Spin? Not a bad little place as places go, eh?' His voice was so grown-up and proprietorial that Clara nearly laughed.

'I'd hardly call it small, Charles.'

'It's not a great show place like Crickleham. But the Hughes-Folletts have only rented it. Maryhall's been ours for hundreds of years. And this size is easier to keep up properly. Of course Mummy and I have had a fearful time keeping it apple-pie with Daddy away. He's most frightfully particular. So am I.' To prove it he shouted at a one-armed boy who was picking apples.

'I say, Johnson, there's a pane cracked in the little green-house. You'd better jolly well tell Baines to get it mended. The Major may be home on leave any day.'

'Very good, Master Charles.'

'I expect Archie will come over one day soon.'

'Who's Archie?'

'Archie Hughes-Follett. The people I told you about. He's jolly decent.'

'Your sort of age?'

'Oh, no. Quite old. Older than you even. He's in the Inns of Court, waiting to get his commission. But he's home on sick leave. He had an accident. Old Archie's always smashing himself up. Mummy sometimes asks men over to shoot. But old Archie finds shooting a bore. He prefers playing with me. He comes over entirely for me.'

'What do you play at?'

'Oh, frightfully good games. Spy and war mainly. We make them up. The grown-ups think Archie's rather a dud. His father did.'

'Did?'

'He was in the Scots Guards. He got killed early on.'

'Poor Archie.'

'He didn't mind much. He couldn't bear his father.'

'Oh. I suppose his mother minded?'

'Dunno. Anyway she's got Archie just as Mummy would have me. My father's in the Coldstream. My grandfather was too. I hope this war goes on long enough to *me* to get a commission. Of course Daddy'll want me to be in his regiment. But I want to be in the Flying Corps.'

'You can't get a commission till you're eighteen. Do you really want this war to go on eight more years?'

'Beastly long time to wait. I can't really remember much before I was four. And that's only six years. Practically my whole life. I s'pose it wouldn't let me off school, even.'

'Then you'll stand for a bit of peace, perhaps?'

'As long as they have another decent war when I'm grown up. With simply millions of planes fizzing about everywhere. And *enormous* bombs. Like the one I've invented that can blow up Worcester Cathedral in one bang.'

'I didn't know you invented bombs.'

'I invent everything,' said Charles superbly. 'It was me that invented tanks among other things. I could fly an aeroplane as easy as winking. I've got a chart with all the controls. Milburn lets me steer the car sometimes. I do it jolly well. And a joy-stick's a million times easier. Are you warlike, Spin?'

'I would be if I were a man.'

'War's dull for women. Mummy hates it. Of course Daddy's frightfully bucked to be doing some real fighting at last. I have to pray every night he won't be killed.'

'Then I'm sure he won't be,' Clara's mind strayed for a moment. This boy, Archie Hughes-Follett, was older than herself and his father had been killed in the war. His father must have been about the same age as her own.

'Oh yes, I hope not,' said Charles cheerfully. 'Of course lots of chaps' fathers do get killed. If he did and got the VC they'd give me his medal, wouldn't they? And I'd be Sir Charles. Though I suppose even then I wouldn't be allowed to do just as I liked till I was twenty-one.'

Clara decided not to be shocked.

'What is it you want to do most?'

'Have my own aeroplane, of course. The south paddock would do for a landing field. Actually I've fixed up a windsleeve already. I'll show you how to land, shall I?' He whirled round, making a noise like an engine and working an invisible joy-stick. 'You must keep her nose in the wind. Like this.' He frowned with concentration. 'Whoa, steady there. Ah, there she bumps.' He relaxed into a grin of triumph. 'Nearly pancaked. Were you windy?'

'Not really. Considering it was the first time I'd been up.'

'I'll take you up with me whenever you like. I daresay I could train you to be an observer.'

'I'd need a lot of practice in map-reading.' Remembering that she was now a governess, she added: 'We might plan some air-routes when we're doing geography.'

'Beastly old lessons. Still it would be better than exports and imports. I can learn things when I'm interested but I'm very easily bored.'

'Intelligent but lazy, your mother said.'

'Shut up, Spin. There's a grey squirrel.' He threw a stone and the squirrel vanished in a silver streak.

'Glad you missed him.'

'Just like a girl. We're supposed to wage war on grey squirrels.'

'I know. I'm glad all the same.'

'I wasn't aiming properly.' He indicated a gate into a field. 'That's the way we go to church when we don't take the car.'

'How far it is?'

'Half a mile by the fields. Longer by road. We only take the car on Sundays. But Mummy walks over to Mass nearly every day. She's awfully holy.'

'I thought she was. What about you?'

'Not at the moment. In fact Father Samson says he sometimes wonders if my baptism took properly. But I might suddenly decide to be a saint. Lots of the saints were naughty when they were young.'

'Do you think one can be a saint just by deciding to be?'

'I could. I can do absolutely anything if I want to.'

'Saints don't boast.'

'I haven't decided to be one yet. Two in the family's enough.'

'Two? Who's the other? Not Nan?'

'Of course not. She's not even a Catholic. I said *family*. Mother and Aunt Monica. They each say the other is. I don't see how Aunt Monica *could* be with that temper. Besides, she's a suffragette. She threw a rice pudding at Daddy once because he said something rude about suffragettes. Still she did try like anything to be a nun. But they wouldn't have her.'

'Why?'

'Mother says it's her headaches and Aunt Mon says it's her temper. *I* think it's her face. She's the ugliest woman you ever saw.'

Dusk was falling when they returned to the house. Nan called from a lighted upper window:

'Come in at once, Master Charles. Your bath's been ready this ten minutes.'

'Botheration,' said Charles, breaking into a trot. 'That probably means a wax. Calling me Master Charles usually does. P'raps you'd better not come and talk to me while I have my bath. When she's in a wax, it's wiser to let her have one to herself.'

'She doesn't still give you your bath, does she?'

'Not *give*. I let her be my lady-in-waiting. Actually it saves a lot of fag to have someone to scrub my back.'

Clara avoided Nan and slipped into her own room. Her bed had been turned down and on it lay the black velvet dress she had worn at her grandfather's funeral, converted by herself and Patsy into a semi-evening one. One of her two treasured pairs of Milanese stockings lay beside it: she noticed that a hole in one had been exquisitely darned and guessed that Nan must have done it. All her things had been unpacked and ranged in the great drawers they did not nearly fill. Nan must have done that too. She was filled with shame at the thought of Nan's pale disapproving eye examining her scanty and carelessly mended underclothes. Why had she not spent some of her father's cheque on snowy lawn instead of letting Patsy persuade her into that crimson coat? The old tweed one she wore at Paget's Fold would have looked much better up here. And why had she been such a fool as to slip in Patsy's parting gift, a jade green camisole with '*Dieu, que les hommes sont bêtes*' embroidered on it in black? There it lay, carefully folded, on the top of the lean pile. She had barely finished dressing when Charles's voice sounded imperatively from the night nursery.

'Spin . . . Spin!'

Hastily thrusting the jade camisole out of sight, she hurried up the passage and found his door ajar.

'Come and say goodnight to me,' he said. 'Nan's having her supper.'

He was sitting up in bed, his face glowing and his hair tousled from his bath. In his pyjamas he looked far more childish.

'Read to me till the gong goes.'

While she was finding the place he said:

'Have you got any brothers?'

'No, worse luck.'

'You seem to like boys' things.'

'I always played with soldiers instead of dolls. But I'm rotten at cricket and so on.'

'I don't like games except the ones I make up myself. I've got heaps of soldiers. Shall we have a battle tomorrow?'

'Certainly. Want me to read now?'

'No. Changed my mind. You know, I desperately want someone to play with. Archie's only on leave by accident and Miss Stephenson was much too old. It's a nuisance being an only child, isn't it?'

'It certainly is.'

'Rather fun if you were my sister, wouldn't it be?'

Clara nodded carelessly. She was thinking it would be the most delightful thing in the world. She looked at the firelight playing on the chequered walls, at the statue of Our Lady with its lamp and flowers and wondered how it felt to have such a childhood and to grow up with a definite place to fill.

'I wouldn't mind an older *sister* because I'd still have Maryhall and be Sir Charles. It might be better if I married you. You're not so frightfully old. Mummy's older than Daddy. She told me so. Yes. I might quite likely decide to marry you when I grow up.'

Clara laughed.

'I notice it's you who are to do all the deciding.'

He said in his most precocious voice: 'Nan says I shall be a very good catch.'

The gong sounded.

'I must go. Goodnight, Charles.'

'Aren't you going to kiss me?'

'Don't boys hate being kissed?'

'Oh, I'm used to it,' he said, with a provocative look.

She kissed a cheek that felt like a peach and smelt of Wright's coal tar soap. Suddenly he pulled her down and covered her face with wet, explosive kisses, giggling helplessly between each.

'Charles, you little beast, let me go. I've just done my hair.'

She extricated herself and he dived under the blankets, rolling one dark, brilliant eye at her.

'Oh my,' he choked, 'Lovey Dovey. Be-yootiful Spin. Goodnight. Sleep tight. Mind the fleas don't bite.'

'Goodnight, Charles Cressett,' said Clara severely.

Chapter Three

Clara and Lady Cressett dined by candlelight, waited on by a parlourmaid. Lady Cressett was also in black velvet, long-sleeved and just low enough to show that her plain face was set on a handsome neck. She wore a small string of perfectly matched pearls and pearl studs in the large lobes of her exposed ears. Her expression, mild as it was, was less placid than Clara had at first supposed. Occasionally her forehead puckered in a nervous twitch. During dinner they talked about Mount Hilary, which Lady Cressett knew well; then the conversation turned to farming. Clara tried to remember everything Cousin John and Blaze had told her – she wanted desperately to emphasize all the country side of her life. At one moment she feared she had overdone it for her hostess asked her if she was fond of riding.

But, mercifully, she added before Clara had time to answer:

'I'm afraid you won't get much chance here. My husband won't let anyone ride his hunters except himself and the groom. I don't ride myself, and I have to admit I'm thankful that Charles doesn't seem keen. It's foolish to be nervous, I know, but when one's a hen with one chick . . .'

They had their coffee in the drawing-room. Freed from the hovering parlourmaid, Clara relaxed and let her eyes wander at will. The panelled walls were painted a greyish-green touched here and there with gilding and each piece of furniture, old or new, had that inimitable air that comes from being acquired in the century it was made. The room was a whole; the modern chintzes did not quarrell with the lute-backed chairs and the tapestry screens because everything had been chosen by people of definite tastes for their own use or pleasure and no one had tried to impose a scheme on it. Though no two rooms could have been more unlike, Clara was reminded of the old aunts' extraordinary dining-room which had grown in the same haphazard way.

'Do you mind if I wander about?' she said when she had finished her coffee. 'There are so many things I want to look at.'

'Wander as much as you like. I love people to look at our things.'

Clara examined the miniatures on the walls, tracing Charles's dark eyes and high colour back through two centuries; now his eyes stared languorously under Byronic curls; now sparkled under a powdered wig.

'The Cressett type persists, doesn't it?' said his mother. She indicated one of the old portraits. 'That boy with the lace collar and the bird . . . he was a page at Charles the First's court. We sent Charles to a fancy dress ball last year dressed like that. He was the picture come to life. It was rather uncanny.'

'I love old things and family histories,' said Clara. 'I'd like to know the whole life of every single one of these people. People look so final and definite in pictures. I'd like to know how it felt to *be* them. Whether they woke up one person one day and someone quite different the next.'

She wandered about the room, stopping now and then to pick up something or ask where it came from. A painted spinet had belonged to an Italian Lady Cressett, a snuffbox had been a present from the Young Pretender, a breviary taken from the body of a guillotined priest had been left by a Marquise who had taken refuge at Maryhall during the terror. All the while she was contrasting these things with the traces of her own ancestors at Paget's Fold. In almost as many centuries they had left no more than some clumsy pieces of furniture, a few paper silhouettes cut by travelling pedlars, an inlaid workbox or two and a handful of worn silver spoons.

'I wish you could infect Charles with some of your passion for the past,' said Lady Cressett when Clara at last sat down again. 'He only cares about the future. And the future for him means aeroplanes, submarines and goodness knows what more mechanical means of destruction.'

'I suppose all small boys are like that. Even when they're lucky enough to have always lived in a house like this.'

'This house seems to fascinate you. I love it myself so much, I can't help being pleased.'

'I've never been in just this kind of house before. When I was little I used to dream about such places and pretend I lived in one.'

'Then you must look out for a nice young man who has one and marry him.'

'I can't imagine marrying anyone,' said Clara rather gloomily. 'I expect I'll be an old maid.'

Lady Cressett laughed.

'At seventeen there's still reasonable hope. And I can't say you look the old maid type to me.'

'I can't imagine even being in love. If I were, I'm sure the person wouldn't be in love with me.'

'Don't let that stop you from marrying him if he'll have you. I'm old-fashioned. I think all women should marry or be in convents and the sooner they can find a man or an Order to take them on, the better. People will tell you that the important thing is that your husband should adore *you*. But they're wrong.' Lady Cressett's forehead twitched. She changed the subject to planning Clara's day with Charles.

'You've got your own "homework" to do, haven't you? So you'll probably prefer to have your dinner in the schoolroom most nights so that you don't have to waste time changing and so on.'

Clara realized that this was an order. Her face must have fallen for Lady Cressett added at once:

'I hope you'll often manage to keep me company all the same. And you must always come down when Charles does or if there's anyone you specially like staying or coming over for dinner. I do so hope you won't be dull. All the young people seem to have gone to the wars,' she sighed. 'I feel so useless. There's nothing I can do but keep Maryhall going and roll bandages and knit socks. And I'm afraid I thank God every day that Charles is only a child. I know women who have sons as well as husbands out there.'

'You must be anxious all the time,' said Clara shyly.

'Yes. Especially these last weeks. I'm pretty sure things are bad where he is. I'm afraid we all hate the sight of the telegraph boy. We're so lucky, being Catholics. When I think of all those who haven't got that, I'm ashamed of myself.'

They were both silent. Then Lady Cressett said:

'Your parents must be missing you tonight, Clara.'

Clara realized guiltily that she had never given them a thought.

'I frankly dread Charles's going to Downside. An only child leaves such a hole in a house.'

'Perhaps the war will be over soon and you'll have your husband home.'

'Not for a long time, I think. And when the war's over, it won't be the world I knew. You're young enough to find change exciting.'

'When I was really young I never wanted anything to change. But ever since I left Mount Hilary, I've been restless. I suppose it's the war.'

'Or growing up. Did you like your Protestant school?'

'Yes and no. I felt rather a fish out of water.'

'Then we must put you back in the river again.'

'I don't seem to belong anywhere,' said Clara in a burst of frankness. 'I love this house. I know I'm going to be terribly happy here. But I shan't belong.'

Lady Cressett looked at her thoughtfully.

'You're what's called introspective, aren't you? You worry about things and analyse them. Why not take them as they come?'

'I'll try,' said Clara.

'I do so want you to feel at home here. There'll be snags of course. You mustn't let that son of mine tyrannize over you. He can be very unkind when he's in a bad mood. You're sensitive; one sees that in your eyes. And then there's Nan. She's difficult with strangers but she's a wonderful woman. She'd go to the stake for her loyalties. Remember that she's not a Catholic and try to make allowances for her.'

'I know she's devoted to you all.'

'Nan's very pious. But she's proud. She comes from Herefordshire where they're so proud they starch their stockings. We hope she'll be a Catholic one day. But my sister Monica says she'd be too proud to admit she'd been wrong before. So you'll just have to come out strong in charity and patience in your dealings with Nan.'

'I'm afraid I'm remarkably weak in both.'

'What a golden opportunity, as the nuns used to say when the porridge was burnt. But don't be a martyr and suffer in silence. Come to me if you have any trouble. You're the ruler of the schoolroom now and I'll back up your authority.' She stood up. 'High time we were both in bed, don't you think?' She patted Clara's cheek. 'God bless you and happy dreams.'

Sleepy as Clara was, she said her night prayers properly for the first time for weeks. As she lay on a pillow that smelt of lavender, listening to the faint creaks and rustling of the old house and breathing the sharp country air, the last two years seemed to drop away from her. God had given her another chance. A new life was beginning, clean and uncomplicated. And this time, she firmly assured herself, she was not going to make any mistakes.

Chapter Four

In one way, Clara's life at Maryhall turned out the reverse of what she had expected. She had thought it would be the beginning of being grown up; instead, week by week, she found herself slipping further back into childhood. She became so completely absorbed in Charles that she entered into his world as if she had been ten years old herself.

Finding that his birdlike mind could not attend to anything for long, she turned lessons into a game. She drew dragons and submarines and aeroplanes which had to be destroyed by good marks and, by making every subject a battle, she forced a little knowledge into his unwilling head. Some of her father's talent for teaching was in her blood. Sometimes, warmed by Lady Cressett's praise, she even wondered whether he had not been right in wanting her to take up teaching. Then she would remember the rigid figures of the mistresses at St Mark's, the plain, tired faces under hair that was either wildly untidy or scraped into a meagre bun, the high-collared blouses adorned with fountan pens and enamel brooches and hastily put the idea away. Even becoming a nun could hardly be worse than that.

Her real life with Charles began when lessons were over. All day long they played with the utmost seriousness. She learnt far more from him than he from her. He forced her to master the internal mechanism of submarines and locomotives. For days on end they lived in different characters, carrying on the impersonation even at meals. Sometimes Clara was Wing, the intrepid commander of a destroyer, sometimes Jenks the comic fireman of the Scottish Express, sometimes Golden Eagle, the wise but cautious old Indian chief, reluctantly admiring the exploits of Fox Tail, the disobedient young brave.

She surprised herself by the thoroughness with which she threw herself into these various parts. Very soon, like Charles himself, she came to resent ordinary life as an interruption. When Nan, on the stroke of half past six, would ruthlessly demolish a submarine made of chairs or sweep the deployed armies into the toybox, Clara had to make an effort not to give away the fact she was just as furious as the boy. Often on her lonely evenings in the schoolroom, instead of tackling her set books, she found herself thinking up some elaborate game for the next day or working out new strategies to defeat Charles in battle.

Milburn had built them a Robinson Crusoe hut of willow branches in one of the shrubberies and there the two of them spent hours as Indians, shipwrecked mariners or pirates. Every part of the grounds had a place in their secret geography. The copse was an equatorial forest, the paddock a landing field, the walled kitchen garden a harbour and the hollow rose garden that had once been a cockpit a shell crater.

Lady Cressett was amused and bewildered by Clara's enthusiasm for these childish games. Sometimes, on the night they dined together or as they walked over the misty fields to eary Mass, she tried to fathom it.

'Either you're a wonderful actress or some part of you really is ten.'

'I was rather elderly and precocious when I really was ten. I suppose it's all coming out now.'

'I simply can't realize that you never had any brothers.'

'Perhaps that's why I like small boys so much.'

'It's not much fun for the only child. I never realized how badly Charles needed a companion till you came.'

Clara was often on the verge of bringing out the never mentioned and never forgotten thing her mother had told her but never actually did so.

'You must marry early and have a large family while you're still young enough to play with them.'

'I like children. But I can't see any attraction in babies.'

'Can't you?' Lady Cressett sighed. 'I like them almost best when they're tiny. I should like to have had a succession of babies in the nursery. It's queer how the Lord sends them to those who don't want them and not to those who do. However, I assure you that babies turn into children in no time, if that's any comfort to you. It seems only yesterday since Charles was in long clothes.'

The weeks slipped by in a kind of dream. Clara was so absorbed in her life at Maryhall that it was only with the greatest difficulty that she could bring herself to answer her parents' letters or Patsy's wild, gossiping scrawls. Only her fear of her father, attenuated though it was by distance, made her do some part of the programme of work she had promised. She was much more conscious of Charles's displeasure than of anyone else's; there were moments when she realized that Charles had more power over her than even her father had ever had.

She had no illusions about the boy. She knew he was spoilt, lazy, selfish and tyrannical. But she loved him as she had never loved any creature before. He knew his power and used it. Whenever she looked like escaping, he had some trick to bring her into subjection again. Sometimes he would sulk with her for a day or two and fall back on Nan, deliberately excluding her. Nan, as she had been warned, was jealous and disapproving. None of Charles's former governesses had thrown themselves into his life in this peculiar way. Nor had Clara's good resolutions about tidiness lasted long; often she was as untidy as Charles himself and took Nan's scolding as if she had been another child. Sometimes Nan would try to restore Clara's lost dignity. She would mend and press her clothes, do her hair for her when she dined downstairs, emphasize the fact that she was a young lady of seventeen and not a tomboy of ten. Drooping her sandy lashes and covering her hatred with an appearance of respectful interest, she would ask Clara about her plans for the future. Clara knew well that Nan lived for the day she herself could not bear to think about, the day when she would have to leave Maryhall. Nan could afford to wait; she would always be part of their life. She would have her place there when Clara would be a fainter memory to Charles than Hero the collie.

When Clara was out of favour and she was in and the three of them sat in front of the schoolroom fire in the interval between Charles's bath and bed, she would pull the sleepy Charles on to her lap. Murmuring 'Nan's boy. Nan's own lamb,' she would look across at Clara with a smile of triumph and pity. But when the balance of Charles's favour dipped the other way, there were moments of bitter tension.

One night when Clara was just going to bed and had taken off her dress and let down her hair, there came an agonized cry from the night nursery.

'Spin . . . Spin . . . Sp-in!' The sobbing wail rose to a shriek.

Clara hesitated. Then she remembered that Nan had a cold and was not sleeping with Charles. She huddled on her dressing-gown and ran along the passage. When she put on the light, she saw Charles sitting up in bed with his face distorted with terror. His eyes were wide open but she realized that he was still fast asleep in the grip of his nightmare.

She put her arms round him, soothing him while he continued to rave. When he woke from the bad dream, he clung to her frantically and would not let her go. At last she got him quiet enough to promise to try to go to sleep on condition she stayed with him. She turned off the light so that there was only the weak glow of the dying fire and the red bead of the lamp in front of Our Lady's statue. She took his hot hand and began to talk softly to him, reminding him that he had a guardian angel, perhaps St Michael himself with his sword and armour, and telling him old legends of Our Lady she had heard from the nuns. Just when his eyes had closed again and his hand relaxed in hers, the door opened and Nan came in with a candle. She too was in her dressing-gown and her red hair hung in two plaits on either side of her thin white face.

'What are you doing in here, Miss Batchelor, keeping the boy awake? Do you know it's gone eleven o'clock?'

'Charles had a nightmare,' said Clara, keeping her temper. 'He called out so I came to see what was the matter.'

'I don't believe you,' muttered Nan. 'You came in here when my back was turned and frightened him with your silly stories. You ought to have more decency at your age.'

'Please, Nan,' whispered Clara. 'I've only just got him to sleep again.' But Charles, roused by their voices, was awake again.

'Go away, Nan,' he screamed. 'I had an awful dream and I called out for Spin. I called out for Spin, not you. I want Spin.'

Nan's white skin turned a ghastly yellow. The candle shook in her hand, sending waves of shadow over a face clenched in hatred.

'Very well, Master Charles,' she said very low, 'I will go away. I will go away and never come back.'

Charles looked so terrified that Clara rashly interposed: 'He doesn't know what he is saying. He didn't mean it, did you, Charles?'

'Yes, I did,' he said with nervous defiance.

'I must go back to bed now. And you must go back to sleep.' But he clung to her.

'Stay with me, Spin. Make Nan go away. Beastly old Nan.'

'You'll be sorry for this, Master Charles. And you'll be sorry too, Miss Batchelor. I shall have something to say to her Ladyship in the morning.'

Nan's eyes were glittering. 'It's a downright wicked sin. You worm your way in here. You work on that poor child's feelings. It's a shame and a disgrace. You're not fit, you've no right . . .' She continued to rave at Clara, her voice rising more shrilly at each sentence.

Charles stared, frightened and fascinated. Clara was trembling all over but she kept enough grip on herself to say nothing. To her relief, the door opened and Lady Cressett appeared. With her greying brown hair tied loosely back and her long blue robe she looked like a Flemish Madonna. At the sight of her Nan stopped short.

'What is the matter? Is Charles ill?'

Both Nan and Clara remained silent. She turned to Charles who begain to explain volubly.

'I see, darling,' she said quietly. 'Nan, I think you had better go to bed. You too, Clara. I'll stay with Charles for a little.'

Nan and Clara left the night nursery by opposite doors. Back in her room Clara was too shaken to go to bed, even to finish undressing. She sat huddled on the edge of a chair, feeling at once humiliated and exultant. Absurd ideas raced through her head. At one moment she imagined Nan's dismissal and Lady Cressett imploring herself to make her home indefinitely at Maryhall. At another she thought of leaving secretly next day and began to compose a letter of renunciation. When there came a soft tap at her door, she started guiltily. It was Lady Cressett.

'I saw your light on. May I come in for a moment?'

'Oh, please do.' She jumped up and offered Lady Cressett her chair.

'No, I won't sit down. Clara, my dear, you look quite ill.' She put her hand under Clara's chin and turned her face up. 'You mustn't be so upset. You're far too sensitive.'

'Am I?' said Clara wretchedly.

'I quite understand what happened. You don't know Nan's little ways as I do. She'll be all right tomorrow. I guarantee that. You do realize it's only because she's so devoted to Charles, don't you?'

'Yes.'

'You'll try to forgive her for being so rude to you?'

'I'll try. But she does hate me so.'

'No. That's an exaggeration. She sees that Charles is very fond of you and the two of you have things she can't share. She's bound to be a little jealous. If I blame anyone, I blame Charles.'

'I expect it was my fault,' said Clara childishly, her lip beginning to quiver. 'It always seems to be.'

'Listen, Clara, I don't blame you in the least, not in the very least for what happened tonight. But do you mind if I say something to you?'

Clara shook her head, unable to speak.

'You're very fond of Charles, aren't you?'

She nodded.

'It's very touching. And, as Charles's mother, I can't help being pleased. But for your own sake and perhaps even for Charles's . . . I wonder if you aren't even a little too fond.'

Clara flushed. A wave of heat ran over her, drying the threatened tears. Suddenly she found her tongue.

'Oh, please. It's not wrong, is it? It can't be. You don't know how completely selfish I've always been. I've had friends I've been fond of, yes. But this is the first time, the very first time in my whole life I've cared for anyone more than myself.'

Lady Cressett bent down and kissed her.

'You poor child. Of course it's not wrong. But just because you love the boy, don't always give in to him. I know how terribly hard it is to be firm with people one's fond of. I've given in myself and let myself spoil Charles. I don't know what his father will say when he comes home. Will you . . . how can I put it . . . be a little more on the grown-ups' side? Will you help me, Clara?'

Put like that, Clara could only say: 'I'll try. Truly I'll try.'

Lady Cressett patted her cheek.

'I know you will. You're so very young yourself, aren't you? Now go to bed and forget all about tonight.'

'Is Charles quite all right now?' she ventured.

'I left him sound asleep. He always sleeps like a top after one of these nightmares and wakes up extra rampageous.'

As she moved towards the door, Clara noticed that she was very pale and that her forehead kept twitching.

'You're terribly tired,' she said, penitently.

'We're both tired. Things look all out of proportion at this hour of the night. God bless you and sleep well. But don't spend all your love on that scamp Charles. Keep a little in reserve for later on.'

When she had gone, Clara went obediently to bed but it was a long time before she could get to sleep. In spite of all Lady Cressett's kindness she had a sense of uneasiness and foreboding. However gently, however tactfully, she felt she had been warned of some danger.

Chapter Five

During the days that followed Nan's explosion, Lady Cressett kept Clara more than usual in her own company. She took her to visit various houses or sent Charles into Worcester with Nan while Clara helped her in the garden or rolled bandages at the Red Cross Depôt.

One Saturday she said at breakfast: 'It's high time I took you over to Crickleham. It's our show place in these parts. We might run over this morning as you've no lessons.'

'Can I come too?' said Charles promptly.

'Certainly not. What about Father Samson and catechism?'

'Bother catechism. I haven't seen Archie for ages.'

'I was thinking of bringing Archie back to luncheon if he's well enough. But if you're going to be silly . . .'

'All right,' said Charles. 'There's nothing to see at Crickleham, Spin. Just a house and a lake and some boring old swans. It'd be all right if it belonged to them but they've only rented it. Why don't they buy a decent house of their own, Mummy?'

'I daresay Mrs Hughes-Follett will when her lease is up. They had a place of their own in Dorset but the Captain sold it because he wanted somewhere with fishing. They only took Crickleham while he looked round for something.'

'Well, he's looking round purgatory now. They can go where they like.'

'Yes, Charles.'

Crickleham was a perfect cream-coloured Palladian house like a glorified version of Mount Hilary set among dark trees and smooth lawns. Charles had mentioned the lake but not the shallow white bridge reflected in it nor the yew walks with statues in their bays nor the fountain copied from Versailles.

The inside was decorated with great richness and comfort, even with taste, but it had the impersonality of all houses that have been let furnished to a succession of tenants. The few possessions the Hughes-Folletts had brought with them, mainly the late Captain's fishing-rods and trophies, only emphasized the fact that it was not their real home.

Clara liked Mrs Hughes-Follett at sight. She was a plain woman who had the courage to dress admirably. Her figure, though tall and straight, was not remarkably good; there was nothing about her that could be called beautiful except her slim wrists and ankles. Yet she was the most elegant person Clara had ever seen. Like Lady Cressett she wore a tweed suit, a wool jumper, ribbed stockings and heavy brogues but, whereas Lady Cressett's, excellent as they were, merely suggested practical necessity, hers were a work of art.

Her son Archie was as unkempt and untidy as his mother was immaculate. When he came slouching into the room in the private's uniform of the Inns of Court, he looked like an enormous overgrown schoolboy dressed as a solider. His dark red hair had grown long during his illness and, with his tunic unbuttoned and his hands thrust in his pockets, he was a most unmilitary figure. Instead of boots he was wearing an old pair of tennis shoes with their laces untied.

'You must forgive Archie,' said his mother. 'He hasn't been

on his feet long. Not that you were ever a model for the *Tailor &
Cutter*, were you, old boy?'

As they walked round the grounds, Clara found herself paired
off with Archie. When they were first introduced he had glanced
at her with suspicion like a shy child being introduced to a
grown-up. Though he was well over six foot and, in spite of his
slouch, firmly built and muscular, his face had an unfinished
look. He had large, irregular features and deep-set dark blue
eyes whose expression reminded Clara at once of Blaze Hoadley
and Charles's dog Hero.

At first he was obviously so ill at ease that Clara thought it
kinder not to make conversation. She watched his mother's
figure moving some distance ahead of them along the yew walks
and marvelled that a grey tweed suit should look as right in this
setting as hoops and panniers. Archie not only looked
completely out of place but seemed quite unmoved by the
beauty of Crickleham. At intervals he removed one hand from
his pockets and jerked a thumb in one or other direction,
muttering:

'That's the belvedere over there,' or 'That's the maze. Too
easy to be much fun.'

At last Clara had to laugh.

'It must be an awful bore having to show people over this
park. I suppose you've done it hundreds of times.'

'You're right. Especially when Papa was alive. He expected
me to be a ruddy guide-book.'

'You needn't bother for me.'

'I say, d'you mean it?'

'Of course.'

'Don't think I'm being rude and all that?'

'Not in the least.'

He stopped in his stride and surveyed her. Then his brow
cleared and he let out a long whistle.

'You're the first sensible girl I've met. I thought, being
Charles's governess, you'd want all the historical details.' He
stared at her with growing interest. 'I must say I've never seen a
governess in the least like you. You know you're pretty enough
to be on the stage. In fact, you distinctly remind me of one of the
girls in *The Bing Boys*.'

This was evidently a high compliment and Clara was sorry to have to admit she had not seen *The Bing Boys*.

'What rotten luck. I've seen it six times. Couldn't you take a day off and buzz up to London with me and do a show?'

'Afraid not.'

'Shame. I don't care how often I see it. I simply can't decide which is the more priceless, old George Robey or old Alfred Lester. And the songs are absolutely top-holibus.' He began to sing:

> 'If you were the only girl in the world,
>   And I were the only boy-ee.'

'Oh, I know the song,' said Clara. 'We were always singing it in London. All the errand boys whistle it. What an awfully good voice you have.'

'Queer, isn't it?' said Archie simply. 'Can't think where I got it from. Mamma plays the piano marvellously but can only chirp like a sparrow and Papa hadn't a note of music in him.'

He sang on with great fervour, but obviously no personal reference:

> 'Nothing else would matter in the world today,
>   We could go on loving in the same old way.'

There was no doubt about the beauty of Archie's voice. It was a rich tenor with no quaver in it and a peculiar quality that suggested a stringed instrument.

'Do you ever sing any other kind of music? I heard a tenor at Covent Garden once singing *Tannhäuser*. I'm sure his voice wasn't half as good as yours.'

He gave her his suspicious look again.

'Classical music? I had enough of Mendelssohn and Bach and all that stuff when I was in the choir at Beaumont. I wouldn't half mind going into musical comedy. But I'm miles too tall. You've got to be able to do fancy dancing too. Papa would have had a fit. And even Mamma wouldn't exactly chortle with joy.'

They walked on a little way in silence while Archie

contemplated the flapping laces of his large and shabby tennis shoes. Suddenly he said very gloomily:

'I might have known you'd be brainy.'

Clara felt that, at all costs, she must dispel this gloom. It was impossible not to like Archie and, without knowing why, to be sorry for him.

'Charles is always talking about you,' she said. 'All our best ideas come from you. We haven't been able to think up a really good Schweinhund for days. And we need you terribly at the moment. The secret telegraph's broken down.'

He brightened at once.

'Wants a new battery probably. So you know about Schweinhund? D'you mean you actually play those kid games with Charles?'

'We do it all the time. They get so real that, even when Charles isn't there, I find myself going on with them in my head.'

'But this is absolutely priceless. A grown-up girl that doesn't think it's all bilge. Some governess! I've been in bed for weeks, you know. I'd have been bored stiff if I hadn't been able to think up some new stunts for Schweinhund.'

After that he talked as volubly as Charles himself. Suddenly he said:

'I'll show you a secret. I was saving it up for old Charles but I'll let you in on it first.'

He led her to a remote rock-garden. There among the boulders and the tiny cascades he had fixed up an elaborate miniature railway.

'All electric,' he said, proudly. 'These are the Alps.' His dazed, puzzled look had vanished and his face was alight. Running his trains, commanding Clara, he was no longer an overgrown schoolboy but a man. She played, as fascinated as Archie himself.

'Let's have an accident. The first on this line.'

The railway had become so real to Clara that when the locomotives crashed into each other and a tiny coach came uncoupled and toppled over a precipice eighteen inches deep, she felt a shock of horror.

Mrs Hughes-Follett's voice sounded in the distance.

'Archie! *Archie!*'

'Come on,' said Archie. 'Let's run for it. Quick. I don't want her to find it.' He seized Clara's hand and pulled her along with him as he ran.

When they reached the terrace where his mother ann Lady Cressett were standing, Clara was flushed and breathless.

'We thought you two must have got lost in the maze,' she said. 'Good gracious, Archie, what have you been doing? You've run the poor girl off her feet.'

She turned to Clara, smiling. 'And what have you been doing to my son, Miss Batchelor? He looks cheerful for the first time for weeks.'

Chapter Six

Archie came back to lunch at Maryhall that day and for the rest of his sick leave he was constantly appearing on his battered motor-bicycle. All Archie's possessions quickly acquired a battered look. Some part of his own person was usually bandaged or in sticking-plaster. From babyhood he had attracted accidents and misfortunes of all kinds or been the innocent cause of accidents to others. China and glass seemed to smash at his approach and his motor-bicycle, skilled driver as he was, was constantly charging him into walls or flinging him into ditches. The fact that he was convalescing at Crickleham was due to a grenade having exploded, through no fault of his, killing another man and quite severely wounding Archie himself.

Lady Cressett was fond of him and encouraged him to come over and make a third in Charles's and Clara's interminable games. Occasionally Charles would be jealous of the two older ones since he regarded each as his personal property. Occasionally Clara was nervous, in case Charles should try to imitate Archie's recklessness. But, luckily, Charles had an extreme dislike of hurting himself and was quite satisfied wiih warning them of the alarming things he was just about to do in plenty of time for one or two of them to stop him. Clara noticed that, though Archie did not care how much he bruised and scratched himself, he watched over Charles almost like an anxious mother. He was nearly as devoted to Charles as she was herself and it made a bond between them. Only once did she ever see him angry with the boy and that was when Charles, who had been in an abominable mood all the afternoon, burst out:

'You're always butting in on everything, Spin. Can't you see men sometimes want to be alone together?'

Archie had boxed his ears and said furiously:

'Shut up, you little bastard. Sorry, Clara. Apologize at once or I'll leave this very sec. and take Clara with me.'

Nevertheless she did sometimes leave them to play together, though she loved the absurd adventure games as much as ever and hated to lose a moment of them. Remembering the night of Nan's outburst, she would try to conciliate her enemy by offering to clear out the toy cupboard or even to darn Charles's socks. Sometimes her offers were grudgingly accepted; more often they were declined with frigid politeness. Once Clara nearly lost her own temper when Nan, in an unusually affable mood, said:

'I expect you'll be glad when Mr Hughes-Follett goes back to his regiment, Miss. He's put your nose out of joint, hasn't he?'

However, if she left them for more than half an hour, Archie always came in search of her. And on this particular occasion, when he burst into the schoolroom, crying: '*There* you are, you deserter! Come right back, will you? Charles and I can't carry on another sec. without you,' she could have hugged him. When he came over to say goodbye, he was as downcast as a boy going back to school. Clara and he and Charles wandered sadly about their old haunts, too low-spirited to play.

'If you ever get sent to the front, Archie,' said Charles, 'you'd better jolly well look out or you're sure to get yourself blown to smithereens.'

'I expect I'll get chipped about a bit. But it's never fatal with me. Mamma says I must have used up at least six lives already.'

'You won't be going yet?' asked Clara, anxiously.

'No fear. Got to get my commission first. If I ever do. You'd better pray for me, Clara. I haven't hope of another leave till I get the ruddy thing. Gosh, what a priceless one this has been. I loathe going away.'

Charles hung on his arm.

'P'raps I'll write to you, old man,' said Charles kindly. 'I don't absolutely swear, though. I find letters very exhausting, don't I, Spin? You see, I *have* to write to my father every Sunday.'

'I'd be jolly bucked, Charles. Don't worry about spelling and all that rot. Can't spell myself.'

It was getting late. Nan called for the third time from the house, this time so imperatively that Charles said, 'Damn' and slouched off with his best imitation of Archie.

'Walk down to the lodge with me, Clara,' he begged. 'I left the old bike there. The Major's as touchy as my late Papa on the subject of gravel.'

He walked so slowly, in his unwillingness to go, that Clara was afraid she would be late for dressing. Miss Catherine Lyons, to whom she owed her coming to Maryhall, had arrived during the afternoon and she was to dine downstairs. Looking up at the tall, disconsolate figure in the creased uniform she felt intensely sorry for him. His hair had been cut very short and his whole appearance suggested a convict rather than a soldier. Though the two were totally unlike, she could not help being reminded of Blaze in his Sunday suit.

'We shall miss you awfully, Archie,' she said.

'Truth and honour?' he asked gloomily.

'Truth and honour.'

'It's asking an awful lot. You wouldn't write to me now and then, would you?'

Clara had a faint pang, remembering all the young soldiers whose letters had remained unanswered since she came to Maryhall. But she assured Archie she would write. He brightened at once.

'That's really priceless of you. I'd be hugely bucked if I got a letter from you. Only don't expect a brainy reply, will you? I know you're frightfully brainy however much you like fooling about with Charles and me.'

'I'm beginning to think it's all nonsense about my brains. I did have some once but I think they've just vanished.'

'Theresa Cressett said you were working for a scholarship to Cambridge or something. So you must be pretty hot.'

'Cambridge,' she said and stopped. It came over her how completely she had changed in the last two months. She had forced herself to work a little on her set books but she had not, of her own accord, read anything but boys' adventure stories and books on ships and engines. 'Don't mention Cambridge.'

'Sorry, old thing. Have I dropped a brick?'

'I just can't imagine how I ever wanted to go there. I've completely lost interest in all that kind of thing.'

'So you don't want to be a female blue-stocking after all?' he said, eagerly.

'I definitely do not. I don't think I want to be anything. In fact, I hate thinking about the future at all.'

'So do I. My Papa was always heckling me about what I was going to do and all that. Thank God for the jolly old war. At least it saved me from having to make up my mind. Isn't it a bore having to grow up?'

'I used to want to grow up as fast as possible,' said Clara. 'Especially since the war. I felt as if I'd miss everything otherwise. But, since I've come up here, I don't care. What is there to grow up *for*.'

'Exactly,' he said. 'You and me and Charles. Why can't it go on for ever?'

'Do you hate being in the army, Archie?'

'Not really. Not this amateur sort of thing. I couldn't have stuck the regulars. I like some of the chaps I'm with and of course I like any kind of an old scrap. All the same it gets my goat, the idea of killing people. Especially since I saw – well, never mind.'

He had never referred to the accident on the parade ground before. Clara said gently:

'It must have been awful for you. And you nearly got killed yourself.'

'Why can't we have battles like ours where the dead get up and go off to a whacking great tea? Not that I'd mind being dead personally. Solve the problem of the old future once and for all.'

'Do you really feel like that?'

'Sometimes. Don't you?'

'I admit I don't like thinking about the future. It seems completely unreal.'

'What, you too?' he said eagerly. He stopped in his walk and turned to her. 'I suppose you think I'm a pretty rum sort of chap?'

'I never met anyone quite like you, no.'

He studied her with his puzzled dark blue eyes.

'If you ask me, Clara, we're both a bit queer. You're miles beyond me, of course, but neither of us seem to quite belong anywhere, if you see what I mean. Or to know where the hell we're going.'

She saw only too well and was not altogether pleased; there were times when, fond as she was of Archie, she wondered whether he might not be suffering from arrested development. Then he struck his forehead with his large, nicotine-stained hand.

'There are so many thoughts in here that can't get out,' he said. 'You don't know how lucky you are being able to express things.'

His face was so wretched that Clara forgot her hurt vanity.

'What sort of thoughts, Archie?'

'I think about you a lot, for one thing. Did you know that?'

She shook her head as they walked on.

'I've never had much use for girls. Nor they for me. Of course I take a chorus girl out for a binge now and then, like anyone else. And I like hearing backstage talk. But they expect you to get sentimental and give 'em a diamond wristwatch. I can stand for the wristwatch but not the billing and cooing.'

They were at the lodge at last.

'Goodbye, Archie. I must rush back or I'll be frightfully late.'

'Goodbye, Clara, old thing. You will write, won't you?'

She nodded and began to run back up the drive. A moment later she heard him running after her.

'I'm a giddy idiot,' he said, as he caught up with her. 'I forgot this. Whole point of my asking you to come all this way. I wanted to give you something.'

He thrust a small revolver into her hand. She knew it was one of his most treasured possessions.

'Archie . . . I couldn't possibly take it,' she panted, keeping up her run.

'I'll chuck it in the river if you won't. I want you to have it. Better not use it. No licence. Don't tell Charles. He'd be green with envy.'

'But you love it.'

'That's the point. Cheerio!'

He dashed away again and Clara dared not waste any more time by going after him. When she got back to the house she made sure it was not loaded. She wished he had not given it to her. It was too cherished a possession and she had an odd feeling that it committed her to something. Next time she saw him she would make him take it back. Meanwhile her one concern was to get dressed as quickly as possible. She thrust the revolver under a pile of underclothes and forgot all about it.

Chapter Seven

Miss Lyons stayed only for a long weekend and when she had gone Lady Cressett's sister, Miss Monica Underwood, came for a fortnight.

She was a vividly ugly woman, with no resemblance at all to her sister Theresa. Her skin was swarthy, her mouth crooked, her thick eyebrows almost met over her nose and the witchlike impression was increased by a mass of short wiry black hair standing up all round her head. She was as lively as Lady Cressett was calm and she gave several displays of her celebrated temper.

The explosions were violent and often comic, but they were quickly over and followed by such rueful kindness to the victim that it was almost a pleasure to be attacked by her. It was certainly a material advantage for she always gave the object of her rage a present. By the end of her short visit, Charles's toybox had received several handsome additions and Clara herself a pair of silk stockings. Father Samson brought on a storm by attacking Christabel Pankhurst. The next day Aunt Monica hurried over to confession in the pouring rain, armed with a box of cigars.

'I brought it in case of emergency,' she explained at the breakfast table. 'I knew sooner or later I'd fly out at a man. If your parish priest insists on talking politics, I'd better bring a whole set of vestments next time.'

But Aunt Monica's greatest 'occasion of sin' was Nan. She was constantly driven to fury by Nan's self-righteousness and by her treating Charles as if he were still a baby. 'I wish you'd get your animal instincts straightened out, woman,' she roared once. 'Are you trying to be that boy's mother or his wife?' Nan remained coldly dignified through these assaults. Miss Underwood, as one of the family, was privileged: she classed her tremendous tempers and her tremendous headaches together as signs of her being 'not quite right'.

Aunt Monica was more contrite when she lost her temper with Nan than with anyone else. 'She's a maddening female,' she said to Clara once, 'but what hell nurses must go through. A mother does at least get something. But a Nanny's lucky if her beloved baby remembers her enough to send her a Christmas card.'

During the second week one of her fearful headaches came on. For the best part of three days she lay in a darkened room in the furthest wing. Clara, accidentally passing her door, heard a sound that she never forgot coming from inside: a moaning that was unlike any human noise.

On the morning she got up again, Clara walked with her round the walled kitchen garden. It was a still, frosty day in late October. Clara picked a sprig of rosemary, breathed on the fine fur of crystals till they melted, and sniffed it as they walked. It reminded her of her first walk with Charles. She thought, as then, that she would never smell its fresh, sharp scent without remembering Maryhall.

Miss Underwood's face was still drawn from the pain and her swarthiness had a greyish cast. She kept stopping to take a deep breath of the keen air and shaking her head, as if to test that it was safe to move it again. As they passed along the wall nearest the stables, one of the hunters whinnied and she whinnied back.

'I like horses in their proper place,' she said. 'I can't say I care for them galloping behind my eyeballs.'

Clara asked timidly if nothing could be done about the headaches.

'I really don't know, my dear girl. At intervals my family drag me to some new doctor who has some new theory about them and some new cure that doesn't work. My own theory is that, for one reason or another, God wants me to have them.'

'Surely God couldn't be so cruel.'

'God isn't cruel,' said Miss Underwood with a strange look. 'We are.'

Clara said with a shudder: 'I don't know how you put up with such pain.'

'I don't put up with it. I swear like a trooper and think of the crown of thorns.'

'There's one thing that repels me in the lives of the saints. They talk as if they enjoyed suffering.'

'My dear girl, don't ask *me* what the saints mean. Presumably one would have to be one to understand what they're driving at.'

'I'm afraid I'm terrified of pain and suffering.'

'So was Our Lord.'

'Yes, but I'd run away. I know I would. I'm the most arrant coward.'

'Well, sooner or later it'll catch up with you. And the funny thing is that, sooner or later, you'll be extremely thankful that it did.'

'There, you see. You're talking just like the saints.'

'Rubbish,' said Miss Underwood so violently that Clara was afraid she was going to explode. They walked some yards in silence. But when she spoke again it was in a reasonable, almost apologetic voice.

'I suppose the whole problem's somehow connected with love. You dote on that nephew of mine, don't you? Say he broke his arm. You'd probably rather you felt the pain than he did. Which isn't saying you like pain *as* pain.'

'It's so much easier to imagine doing things for the love of human beings than for the love of God,' sighed Clara.

'D'you think so? I know it's in St John, loving one's brother whom one has seen, et cetera. Personally, I tend to dislike my neighbour on the least provocation and to tell him so. I wish I could be like Tess.'

'Lady Cressett's wonderful, isn't she?' said Clara. 'She really seems to love everyone. I know someone else who's got the same angelic nature.' She was thinking of Lilian Cohen.

'I assure you she didn't start life with an angelic nature,' said Miss Underwood. 'When we were children there wasn't a half-penny to choose between us. If I grabbed the poker, she grabbed the tongs.'

She pushed up her wiry hair and exposed an old scar on her left temple. 'That's a little memento of Tess's angelic nature. Now she's as calm as a mill-pond except for that nervous twitch. I call it the tombstone of her temper.'

'Do you mean she just fought and fought until she conquered it?'

'No. I think something else just grew until there was no room left for it. Call it grace. Call it the love of God. I'm no heologian. In my opinion, Tess is much more of a saint than a great many on the official list. And I do *not* say that because she trudges a mile to Mass every morning and plays Lady Bountiful to the parish.'

They walked a few steps in silence. Then Miss Underwood asked abruptly:

'Ever met Charles's father?'

'No. I know he's very handsome from his photographs. I suppose he's very charming, too.'

'All the Cressetts are charming when they want to be. But he doesn't waste much of his charm on Tess. He treats her like an efficient housekeeper and makes the hell of a fuss if she isn't efficient enough.'

'Lady Cressett's awfully fond of him, though, isn't she?' said Clara uncomfortably.

'Devoted to him. And to the boy. Humanly speaking she'd break her heart if anything happened to either of them.'

'Is Sir George fond of Charles?'

'Extremely. Charles is himself all over again. He was madly keen to have an heir. It's an old baronetcy and would die out otherwise. But if Charles had been a girl, heaven help us. Tess can't have any more, you see.'

Clara was deeply shocked.

'Can it mean so much to a person, the idea of a title going on?'

'George is a snob, of course. But he's got a tremendous feeling about this place. It's his one permanent passion. I'm sure his idea of heaven would be permission to haunt Maryhall. And the notion of Maryhall without a Cressett would be purgatory . . . or worse.'

Clara sighed.

'And I've always thought of them as such an ideally happy family.'

'So they are in a way. It's Tess who keeps the whole thing going.'

'She's always saying how happy her life is. And encouraging other people to get married.'

'Good people always assume everyone else is as good as they are.'

When Aunt Monica had gone, Clara had moments of acute depression. After that conversation in the kitchen garden, though she admired and liked Lady Cressett more than ever, some of the charm had gone from Maryhall. She had made great efforts to be more of a governess and less of a wild playmate, with the result that Charles complained that she was getting as bad as Miss Stephenson. On the days when he was bored or sulky, she was horrified to realize how dependent she had become on the affection of one small boy.

November was grey and stormy. Sometimes, at night, as she sat in the schoolroom, with the wind howling outside, she felt lonelier than she ever had in her whole life. She took to writing long letters to Ruth and Patsy and even to Archie Hughes-Follett.

Chapter Eight

Early in December the house was thrown into commotion by the news that Sir George was expecting leave. Preparations began at once: everything indoors and out was reviewed and put in still more perfect order. A few days later a telegram came and, for the first time, Lady Cressett's fingers did not shake as she opened it.

'He arrives in London tomorrow,' she said. 'He's got ten days. I'm to go and meet him and stay in town for a couple of days' shopping.'

In private she said to Clara: 'You'll have to keep an eye on Charles. He'll be wild with excitement. He's quite capable of ordering one of George's young trees to be cut down to make a bonfire for the hero's return.'

As if she guessed Clara's misgivings, she added:

'I know you can keep him in order. You've been much less of a fellow-conspirator lately.'

As soon as his mother had gone, Charles's spirits became irrepressible. After weeks of dampness, the weather had cleared to blue sky and east wind. Clara invented an energetic outdoor spy game to keep him amused till tea-time. It was a success and, as they walked back to the house, he tucked his arm under hers.

'You're a decent old Spin,' he said. 'Sorry I ragged you and said you were like Stevie. You aren't a bit.'

After tea he ordered her to read to him.

'Get Mummy's *Times*. I must be up in the battle news for Daddy.'

He curled up on the floor in front of the schoolroom fire while she read him the day's despatches. It was like their first happy weeks. Now and then she glanced down from her paper at the dark head resting against her knee. Once she ran her finger down the pencilled groove at the nape of his neck.

'I like it when you do that, Spin. It gives me a nice shiver.'

He begged so hard that she broke the rule she had imposed on herself since the scene with Nan and went to say goodnight to him in bed.

'You're OC now Mummy's away,' he said. 'She told me so. Only it's a secret. Nan, you know.'

She nodded.

'All right. Only you'll have to behave yourself.'

'Don't worry. I promise not to grease the backstairs. Heard from old Archie lately?'

'I had a letter this morning. He's got his commission.'

'Good egg. That means he'll get leave. Not that I'll have much time, with Daddy here. But why didn't he write and tell *me*?'

'Because you never wrote to him, I suppose.'

'It takes so long writing things down. Anyway nothing exciting's happened. I wish a German aeroplane would crash in the garden and I could take all the crew prisoners.'

'Perhaps it will.'

He looked at her mysteriously.

'Do you *know*?'

'No. Only guessing.'

'Perhaps you've guessed right. Perhaps it'll be tomorrow. In the kitchen garden.'

'What, have you intercepted a message?'

'Shan't say.' He lowered his voice. 'Anyway there's a brand new type of anti-aircraft gun concealed in the gooseberry bushes.'

'Your invention?'

'I stole the plans. Of course I improved them a lot. It works by compressed air, and . . .'

'Shut up. Schweinhund may be in the cupboard.'

She tiptoed over and opened it.

'All right, Sir. No one there.'

'Sucks to you. I knew he wasn't. I happen to know he's piloting this plane. He's in Berlin at this moment, probably getting blotto with the Kaiser.'

'Why didn't you tell me?'

'You don't tell me everything. You've been keeping up a secret correspondence with Archie. Is he sweethearting you, Spin?'

'Don't talk rot. Goodnight, Charles.'

'Tuck me in. I'm an orphan boy tonight.'

She did so. Charles rolled his eyes.

'Beloved Spin,' he groaned in a deep bass. 'Say thou wilt be mine.' Then he squeaked, 'My own darling Archibald, I will.'

'Shut up, idiot.'

'Fancy tucking up a lot of little Hughes-Folletts. All with big feet and carroty hair.'

'Good*night*, Charles.'

'Holy water, please. Must keep the devil away.'

She made the sign of the cross on his forehead as his mother always did.

'God bless you. Now really, truly and finally, goodnight.'

'Goodnight, Spin. For ever and ever, amen.'

That night Clara went to bed happier than she had been for a very long time.

Next day after lunch, she and Charles went down to the keeper's lodge to see a new litter of puppies.

'This one's Hero's child all right,' said Charles, picking up a black and white. 'It's the spitting image of him as a puppy.'

At that moment there was the chugging of a motor bicycle in the lane.

'It's old Archie,' shrieked Charles, dropping the puppy back in its basket. 'I'd know his engine anywhere.'

A moment later, Archie dismounted at the gates.

'Golly! Do I have to salute you?'

Archie was resplendent in Second Lieutenant's uniform. It was still too new for him to have reduced it to the usual state of his clothes, though there were already spots of oil on the slacks.

He inserted himself between the two and put a long arm round each.

'Gosh, it's good to see you chaps. I hared straight over to celebrate. Your father hasn't arrived yet, has he?'

'No. Mummy's in London with him. I'm in charge.'

'Good egg. Can we have tea in the schoolroom?'

'Of course. But it's ages to tea. I haven't worked off lunch yet. What shall we do?'

'What time's that German plane due, Sir?' asked Clara, speaking across to Charles.

'Jove, I nearly forgot. About three pip emma. We'd better dash to the kitchen garden and give that gun crew their orders.'

On their way to the kitchen garden, Archie said: 'They're beginning to use parachutes quite a bit. Wonder if the German blighters have got 'em.'

'If they try and use them, we'll shoot them down in the air. Good egg,' said Charles.

'I don't think that's fair . . .' Clara began.

'Rot, Spin. Don't be soppy. They'd do it to our chaps. What can we use for a parachute?'

'Umbrella?' suggested Archie.

'Spiffing,' Charles dashed off at top speed.

'Bring mine,' Clara shouted after him. 'Doesn't matter what happens to it.'

In a few minutes Charles was back, panting and brandishing Clara's umbrella.

For once, no one was working in the kitchen garden. Clara, mindful of her responsibility, insisted that the aeroplane crashes took place on the gravel paths and not on the beds. Time after time Archie, as the German crew, was successfully brought down by the secret weapon in the gooseberry bushes. After at least his tenth leap from the eight foot wall, grasping the open umbrella, he rolled over on the gravel, groaning 'Ach, mein leg, mein leg, it gebroken is. Verdammte Chute, nicht open gut.' This was a great success and after that he had to keep pretending to injure himself. Once he stayed crumpled up and motionless for so long that Clara was afraid he really had hurt himself. But when she bent over him he whipped out an imaginary revolver and shot her. 'Schweinhund that last word has, so. Hoch der Kaiser.'

Suddenly Charles shrieked, 'It's my turn, I'm going to do some jumps.'

'Not from that wall you're not,' said Clara, ceasing to be Wing the gunner. 'It's much too high.'

'Rot. Archie's done it thousands of times.'

'Archie's nearly as high as the wall.'

'Don't be governessy. Give us a leg up, Archie.'

'Nothing doing, old man, Clara's right. You might easily damage yourself.'

'Soppy Archie! Soppy Spin!' yelled Charles in a fury. 'Go and play Pa and Ma by your silly soppy selves. I'm jolly well going to jump. I will and I shall.'

Before they could stop him, he had dashed away with the umbrella to another path that ran from a door in the wall between stone copings. Behind the copings on either side were thick bushes of rosemary.

Clara gasped: 'Archie! For mercy's sake stop him.'

'Don't worry. He can't possibly get up on that wall.'

Neither of them had noticed that someone had left a ladder leaning against it just at the place Charles was making for. In a flash he had scrambled up, kicked the ladder away and was dancing on the parapet, brandishing the open umbrella.

Clara opened her mouth to call him but Archie clapped his hand over it.

'Shut up,' he whispered. 'You'll only make him do it. Bluff's the only hope. Stay where you are.'

He ran till he was only a few yards from Charles.

'Just a sec., old chap. Let me get up too. Must do it scientifically.'

'I know how! I know how!' bawled Charles, beside himself with excitement. 'Get out of my way.'

Before Archie was near enough to catch him, Charles clutched the umbrella with both hands and made a wild, sprawling jump. Clara saw Archie lurch forward to try and break his fall but he was too late. She heard a thud and saw the umbrella shoot away and land upside down on a rosemary bush. Now Archie blocked her view so that she could not see what had happened. He was bending down; then he fell on his knees and remained perfectly still. If they were still playing, why did neither of them speak? If Charles was hurt, why didn't he cry? He usually made a fuss over the slightest graze. Her knees began to tremble so much that she could hardly run the twenty yards to where they were.

Archie was crouching over the boy, hiding the top part of his body from her. All that she could see was Charles's bare legs and brown shoes sticking out wide apart on one side and on the other the open umbrella rocking very slightly to and fro on the bush.

As she came behind them, Archie just turned his head. His face was grey. He said thickly:

'Get back indoors. Phone for the doctor.'

She tried to push Archie away and look. But her strength was gone; she could only tug feebly at his tunic.

'Go *in*, will you? Get him to come at once.'

In a daze of terror she stumbled back to the house. There was no one in the hall where the telephone stood. She found the doctor's number, was told he was expected back shortly and left an incoherent message. Then she heard Nan moving in the passage upstairs. She could not face telling Nan yet that Charles had been hurt and tore out of the house again, running at top speed back to the kitchen garden. It was a long run and her knees were giving way; she had to stop and get her breath. The effort of breathing calmed her a little; she was able to think. Then she realized the whole thing had been a hoax. She walked on slowly with a huge sense of relief. By the time she reached the open door of the kitchen garden she had forgotten her fear and was furious with the two of them. She stopped and listened but there was no sound of voices or laughter.

She went into the garden. Far away to the right, in the path that led to the other door, the two figures were still in the position she had left them a quarter of an hour ago. As she hurried towards them Archie got up and came towards her. He grabbed her by both shoulders and turned her round so that she had her back to Charles.

'Is the doctor coming?'

She stared at him. She had forgotten the terrible look he had had. It was still there. Her mouth went dry.

'Then he really is hurt?'

'Clara, you've got to know. Hold on to yourself, dear. It's just as bad as it can be.'

'What do you mean?'

He said very quietly, 'He's dead, dear. Instantaneous. He didn't suffer.'

She heard nothing but the word 'dead' and felt an appalling sensation half pain, half nausea, between her shoulder blades. Then she turned cold and began to shake all over. She said, with her teeth chattering:

'It can't be. It's not possible. Un . . . unconscious. Let me look.'

She tried to break out of Archie's hold but he would not let her go and she was too weak to struggle.

'I know the difference,' he said. His face worked. 'Oh, Clara, it's all my bloody fault.'

The misery in his voice steadied her.

'But Archie, it's only a little drop. It's barely eight feet. It couldn't kill anyone.'

'His head caught against the stone. He broke his neck.'

'I don't believe it.'

This time she was stronger than he and before he could stop her she was kneeling beside the body. She saw it clearly but it had no more relation to Charles than a dummy dressed in his clothes. Her mind no longer took in anything at all.

From the house the gong sounded for tea.

Archie pulled her to her feet. She did not resist.

'Try and understand what I'm saying, dear. We must go in now. We must tell Nan.'

Part of her consciousness came back. She clung to him, almost screaming. 'Oh no, oh no!' She could not grasp that Charles was dead, but she realized that something fearful and irrevocable had happened.

'Try to remember. You phoned the doctor, didn't you?'

She made a great effort to close the gap that seemed to have opened in her head.

'The doctor? Yes. I phoned the doctor.'

'And he said he'd come?'

'Somebody said he would come. Yes, that's right. When he got back.'

Archie forced her to walk in the direction of the house, half pushing, half dragging her along beside him. He shut the door of the kitchen garden behind him, locked it and put the key in his pocket.

'Why did you do that?' she said, vaguely.

'Never mind.'

It seemed to Clara that they were not moving at all but that the house was steadily advancing towards them. Familiar things went by like a film; the cockpit where a few late roses bloomed,

443

clipped yews, the faded blue face of the stable clock. A sense of extreme lassitude came over her. She could hear Archie talking from very far away.

'I'm going to leave you outside while I go in and tell Nan. I've got to tell her first, see? It was my fault. She's got to understand it was my fault. I'll see you through, Clara. I won't leave you alone with her.'

The words meant nothing to her. Suddenly she stopped. She had caught sight of the willow hut in the shrubbery.

'Look, Archie.'

'What is it?'

'There's a notice on it.'

A piece of paper was pinned to the hut. On it was printed in huge crooked letters: BEWEAR.

'Oh, God, the poor kid,' said Archie.

'What does it mean?'

'We shan't ever know.'

PART SIX

Chapter One

Clara woke the next morning in a strange bed in a very large room. Her head felt empty yet heavy, as if it were full of some dense gas. She could not make out where she was nor how she came to be there. The curtains were drawn but there was enough light to distinguish chairs and mirrors and the rail at the foot of the bed.

There was a lamp by the bedside. After a long time her mind took in the idea that, if she were not dreaming, this lamp could be turned on. It was difficult to keep this idea in focus and still more difficult to communicate it to her hand but, after an interval, she managed to switch on the light. Then she lay back with closed eyes, exhausted by the effort. When she opened them again she saw a huge, luxurious room in which nothing seemed to have any connection with her. Over the bedrail hung a fur-trimmed dressing-gown; she herself was wearing a silk and lace nightdress which did not belong to her. At last, on a gilt-backed chair, she made out a pile of clothes, neatly folded, which she recognized as her own. With great difficulty, as one tries to piece together the fragments of a vanishing dream, she managed to clutch at some vague memories. She realized she must be at Crickleham and rested for a long time on the triumph of this discovery. Now she must try and find out why she was at Crickleham. The fog in her mind thinned a little. She remembered sitting in the sidecar of Archie's motor bicycle. Then, very slowly, the fog cleared, a patch at a time and each clearing revealed an image until at last the whole hideous dream was connected up; every detail vivid. But what puzzled her was that the dream ended with a fact; the fact that she had woken up in someone else's nightdress in this great, soft unfamiliar bed.

There was a tap at the door. She called 'Come in.' It was Mrs Hughes-Follett. Clara watched her move noiselessly across the thick carpet and seat herself on her bed. She said very gently:

'Have you been awake long, Clara? How do you feel?'

'My head feels so strange. How did I get here?'

'We put you to bed here last night. The doctor gave you something to make you sleep.'

'The doctor? Have I been ill?'

'No dear. You just needed a good rest. Don't try and think. Just relax. Could you manage a little breakfast? It's nearly eleven o'clock.'

'No, thank you. I'm not hungry.' Clara sat up and pressed her hands to her temples. 'Oh, please, do help me to remember. Why am I here?'

'You've had a very bad shock. You must just be quiet and take things easy. Don't force your mind.'

Clara shook her head.

'No, I must get it right. Nothing seems real. I can remember a horrible dream. Only it doesn't seem like a dream. What day is today?'

'Thursday.'

'Then yesterday was Wednesday. These things happened on a Wednesday. I went into the hall and rang up the doctor and they said: "Wednesday's his day at the Malvern hospital." Was that right?'

Mrs Hughes-Follett was very pale. She gave Clara a long, pitying look.

'Yes, dear. Quite right. But let it come gradually.'

'No, no. I must know. Everything.'

'Are you sure you feel strong enough?'

'I'm quite well. It's just my head. I can't get things clear. Please, please help me.'

'I will. You've got to be very brave. Archie brought you here last night from Maryhall. Can you remember that?'

'That was the sidecar. Yes. There's a blank after that.'

'You were worn out and no wonder. The doctor wanted you to come here and rest. The worst's over now, Clara. We're going to look after you for the next few days.'

Mrs Hughes-Follett took her hand.

'Clara. Don't strain it. But do you remember at all before Archie brought you over?'

The touch unlocked something in Clara's head. She said:

'Charles is dead. I must go and tell his mother.'

'Hush, dear. She knows.'

'Who told her?' said Clara wildly. 'I ought to have told her. I was left in charge. It was all my fault,' she began to sob.

'Cry, dear. It will do you good,' said the other, laying a cool hand on her forehead. Through her dry, tearless sobs she heard a soothing voice saying:

'It was a dreadful thing to happen. It wasn't your fault. Archie told me all about it. The little boy didn't suffer. It was a terrible shock for everyone.'

'I'm not fit to live,' moaned Clara. 'Oh, why wasn't I killed?'

'Hush, Clara. You mustn't talk like that. Try and be a little calmer. We all have something very difficult to bear some time in our lives. We're all very, very sorry for you. Lady Cressett wanted you to know that.'

'Lady Cressett? How can she ever forgive me?'

'She knows it wasn't your fault.'

Suddenly Clara remembered something. She said with horror: 'His father?'

'You won't have to see his father.'

'Have I seen him?'

'No, Clara.'

'What happened? Did I run away?'

'No, dear. Archie took you away. I know it's painful but would it help to tell me what you remember?'

'Yes, please.' Clara pushed her hair and rammed her knuckles into her temples, trying to force her mind into focus.

'The doctor came. Yes. And a policeman. I had to answer a lot of questions. First me and Archie. Then me alone. They wouldn't let me see Charles again.'

'No. When there's an accident like that, they have to take the person away.'

A vague, terrifying memory came back.

'Nan,' she said. 'Something about Nan.'

Mrs Hughes-Follett's voice was unnaturally calm.

'Yes, dear. Nan can't hurt you.'

'What did Nan do? She screamed. Then someone got hold of her. But she got away and ran upstairs.'

'Nan was beside herself. She didn't know what she was doing. Try and understand that.'

'It's getting clearer now. Somebody phoned to London. I wanted to stay, didn't I? I knew I ought to stay and tell his father and mother.'

'Yes, but the doctor said no and Archie brought you back here. I think you've remembered enough, dear.'

'No . . . there's a bit still missing. I must get it,' said Clara obstinately. Suddenly she was aware of a slight pain in her left wrist. She looked at it and saw it was bandaged.

'Why have I got a bandage on my wrist?'

'You hurt yourself. Just a little cut. Nothing to worry about.'

'Now . . . now I remember. I went up to my room. And Nan was there. In the big cupboard where my clothes are. She had a pair of scissors and she was cutting pieces out of my clothes. No. That must have been in the dream.'

'It wasn't a dream, Clara. Nan was hysterical. I tell you she didn't know what she was doing.'

Clara touched the bandage.

'Did she do this?'

'Yes. We must be thankful it was no worse. Luckily Archie came in in time.'

'Did he? I don't remember that. I just remember Nan and the scissors.'

'Don't think about it. She would have been horrified if she'd realized.'

'I don't blame her,' said Clara wearily.

She lay back and closed her eyes, suddenly limp and exhausted. Every piece of the puzzle fitted now. There was nothing left to do but to try, inch by inch, to admit the intolerable facts. Charles was dead. She had wrecked his mother's happiness; destroyed the whole beloved fabric of the life at Maryhall. It was inconceivable that she herself could go on living, waking up morning after morning, finding this load of grief and remorse still there. She knew she was still too numb even to begin to feel its full weight. On the very edge of her consciousness one more appalling thought began to take shape. Sooner or later, she would have to tell her father.

She said in a painful whisper: 'If only . . . only he had let Nan do it. How can I go on living?'

She heard Mrs Hughes-Follett say almost sharply: 'My dear girl. You mustn't talk like that. Hasn't there been enough suffering? Do you want to make more? Poor Archie has been through hell over this. Can't you give him one thought?'

Clara roused herself with an effort. She said with shame:

'Archie was so good to me. You don't know how good.' She began to cry weakly. The tears oozed under her closed lids and crawled down her cheeks. She felt the cool hand on her forehead again.

'There, there, Clara. Realize you're among friends. I want you to know that Archie is very, very fond of you. Will you let him come and talk to you when you're feeling a little more yourself?'

Chapter Two

Isabel was having her breakfast in bed, as usual, when Claude burst into the room without knocking. There was a letter in his hand and his face was mottled. Her heart began to beat violently. She had only one thought: 'Reynaud.'

'Read that,' he said, flinging the letter on to her tray. Then she saw that the writing was Clara's. She said:

'Why does she write from somewhere called Crickleham Park?'

'You'll see why,' he said grimly.

When she had read it, she said softly: 'Oh, the poor child. The poor, poor child.'

'The Cressett boy. Yes, horrible.'

'I meant Clara.'

'*Clara*? Good God!'

'But, Claude, think what she must have been through.'

'I've no sympathy to spare for Clara. I'm thinking of that boy's parents. It was her fault. She admits it.'

'Can't you see she was half out of her mind when she wrote this?'

'She must have been quite out of it to be so criminally careless. She was left in charge. She admits she let the boy play this idiotic game.'

'But Claude, you know what boys are. You know how she loved the child. I'm certain . . .'

'She wasn't engaged to love him. She was engaged to look after him.' His lips were white. 'I suppose you realize there will be an inquest. Clara will have to give evidence. By God, if I were the boy's father, I'd have her up for manslaughter.'

'Claude . . . how can you be so horribly unfair?'

'Unfair, am I?' he shouted. 'D'you expect me to like having my name dragged through the police courts? It may not be a name to boast of, but at least I've made it decent in my profession.'

'You talk as if she'd deliberately . . .'

'She failed in her duty. Her elementary duty. If after this she imagines that any fourth-rate school . . .'

'Oh, what does all that matter? Can't you spare one thought for the child's feelings?'

'When has she ever thought of mine? Or yours either, for that matter? If my daughter's publicly disgraced, I had better hand in my resignation. As for Clara, the best thing she can do is to change her name and be thankful if she's allowed to serve behind a counter.'

Never before had she seen him in such a state of uncontrollable fury. She fought down her repulsion and let him rave on. At last she said:

'Claude, aren't you letting your imagination run away with you? We don't even know that anyone *is* going to blame her.'

'She blames herself. She'd have wriggled out of any responsibility if she could. Therefore I blame her, too.'

'What can we do? Should I go up there and see her?'

'Most certainly not. I absolutely forbid you to do any such thing. I shall write to Clara. And I assure you it will be a letter she won't forget.'

'Claude, I implore you, no. Not till you've calmed down a little.'

'I shall write what I please and when I please,' he said loudly.
'I shall also write to Lady Cressett. They shall see one member of
this family has some sense of shame.'

'Then I shall write too. You can't stop me. I shall write as one
mother to another.'

'You seem to ignore the fact that the boy had a father. What
must he be feeling? His only son.'

'I'm not denying that it's terrible for his parents. But we know
the litle boy was spoilt and disobedient. His mother told Clara so
when she first went there. Was that Clara's fault?'

'She wasn't alone. You forget that. There was some young
man or other about. Instead of looking after the boy, she was
fooling about with *him*. As a result the boy breaks his neck. I ask
you, was that Clara's fault, or was it not?'

'I don't see how we can possibly tell till we know just what *did*
happen.'

'The whole thing's perfectly obvious to anyone who knows
Clara. The very day of my father's funeral I found her in the
orchard carrying on like a servant girl with Blaze Hoadley.'

'That old nonsense!' she said contemptuously.

'You find it nonsense, eh?' he said savagely. 'I should have
supposed . . .'

'I think you're being utterly cruel and unfair. I didn't think
you could be so heartless to your own child.'

'Heartless, am I? Because I have an elementary sense of
justice?' He hung over the brass bars of the bedstead like an
animal half out of its cage. She could not bear to look at his grey,
blotched face and stared instead at her breakfast tray, at the half-
eaten toast and the pale scum of milk on the cooling tea. A clock
struck a quarter past nine.

'I must go to school,' he said. 'I shall have more to say about
this disastrous business at lunch-time.'

She was filled with such horror of him that she could not
bring herself to say goodbye and he went out slamming the
door. Clara's pathetic, half-crazed letter still lay on the bed. She
read it again, handling the paper as if it were a bruised creature
that could be hurt. She had known these blind rages of Claude's
before, but she could not understand this one. She read Clara's
letter again. It was addressed to Claude alone; there was not a

single mention of herself in it. A keen pain ran through her. She thought how many times Clara had shut her out like this. Everything had always been for her father; her mother was lucky to have an occasional crumb. She wondered how Clara would have felt if she had overheard the conversation between her parents. She had been going to write her a tender letter. But a great rush of bitterness came over her, making her tremble. She got up and dressed in frantic haste. She did not know what she wanted to do. She sat down at her desk and tried to write. Twice she began: 'My darling little Clara,' with a hand that shook. But love and hate had reached a pitch where she was impotent. At one moment she saw Clara white and tearful as she must have been when she wrote to her father. At the next she saw the cold eyes and the small contemptuous smile and knew that any tenderness of hers would only make them more contemptuous. She had a bitter impulse to describe, word for word, her conversation with Claude: Clara should see who really cared for her when it came to a crisis. But would Clara believe her? And, if she did, would her daughter ever forgive her? Would she ever forgive herself?

She sat at the desk, lighting cigarettes and throwing them away half-smoked or nervously twisting her wedding-ring. In the end she wrote nothing but 'I'm so terribly sorry for you, darling, and long to have you home.' It was still only half past ten. She looked round the dreary dining-room. Never had she hated it more. She could not bear the thought of staying in the house; at any moment her mother-in-law would appear, trying to find out, as she always did, what had been in Clara's latest letter. She ran up to her room, put on her outdoor clothes and went out, with no idea of where to go or what she meant to do. It was cruelly cold; the wind buffeted her through her veil and swirled dead leaves and old newspapers round her ankles; her hands were icy in her muff. Tears formed in her eyes and dried again as she walked blindly, taking any turning at random. Suddenly she stopped, finding herself in a street she did not know. She looked at the name and saw it was the one where Callaghan lived. She could not remember the number of the house where he had rooms. Whichever it was, he would not be there now; he must have left for St Mark's an hour ago. There could be no danger in just walking past the houses; it was an obscure comfort to know that one of those shabby doors must be his.

She had not gone more than a few yards before a man came running down the steps of a house just ahead of her. Before she had time to cross over, she was face to face with him and the next moment she was weeping in his arms.

Chapter Three

Callaghan held her for a moment or two without speaking. Then he said: 'We can't stand here. You'd best come inside.'

He helped her up the steps. When he dropped her arm to fumble for his key, Isabel had to clutch the railing to keep herself upright.

'Put your muff up and hide your face,' he muttered. 'Every window in this house is full of eyes.'

He jabbed his key into the lock at last and almost pushed Isabel into a dark hall that smelt of oilcloth and stale cooking. Whispering to her to walk quietly, he led her along a passage and opened a door with a broken china handle.

'You'll have to forgive this. It's the only room I have,' he said as he shut them in together. 'Will I lock the door? Better not.' Raking some books off the only armchair he thrust Isabel into its sunken seat.

Then he knelt beside her and pushed up her veil. 'For God's sake will you stop crying and trembling and tell me what's the matter?' She was no longer weeping but her breath came in choking gasps so that she could not speak.

He clutched her shoulder, hurting her. 'Here . . . wait.'

He got to his feet and stumbled about the room, slamming open a cupboard and flinging a pile of papers off a desk.

'Praise be, there's a finger left.'

He came over to her with a smeared tumbler with some whisky in it.

'Drink this.'

The smell made her feel sick. She tried to push the glass away but he held it against her mouth.

'Oh, come on, now. It'll pull you round.'

She managed to swallow a mouthful: some spilled down her chin.

'No more,' she coughed. 'It's horrible. It burns.'

'Then I'll finish it. If I'm seeing phantoms, I'll keep up the illusion that you're sitting in my chair.'

He drank the rest in one gulp and sat down on the bed. The shock of the whisky brought Isabel's mind into focus. She became aware of the shabbily furnished room; of Callaghan, still in his overcoat, sitting on the unmade bed holding the empty tumbler; of the smell of whisky, dead cigarettes and unwashed sheets.

'I must go at once,' she said. 'I never meant to come here.'

'I believe you,' he said. 'But stay where you are. You're in no state to move.'

'I am better now,' she said, trying to keep her voice steady. 'I shouldn't be here. Nor should you. You must have been on your way to St Mark's.'

'To hell with St Mark's. I was late as it was. They're used to my not showing up. I've got the sack anyway.'

'Oh, Reynaud, I'm sorry.'

'I can't say that I am. It's strange to hear you speak my name again.'

Outside in the street she had not looked at his face. Now in the harsh light, smirched but not softened by the dirty window pane, she compared it with the one she remembered. It was sallower than ever; the lids of the heavy blue eyes were swollen and the whites yellowish. She was conscious of all the disorder of her own; she had studied it for too many years to need a mirror to tell her how it must appear in that cold glare. Yet she did not pull down her veil to hide her reddened eyes and the tracks of tears through the powder. Almost proudly, she exposed her ravaged face for him to see if he wished. But he was not looking at her. His eyes were wandering moodily about the room as if seeing it for the first or last time. She let her gaze follow his, searching for traces of Reynaud himself among the neutrality of the lodging-house furniture. At first she found them only in the French books scattered on chair and chest of drawers and heaped in crooked piles on the floor. He had not even bothered to take down the landlady's pictures – 'Wedded', 'The Bath of Psyche' and a faded photograph of the Taj Mahal in a frame full of empty sockets which had once been inlaid. Gradually she found other traces: a torn dressing-gown on the door, shoes in the fender, ties and collars dangling from an old gas bracket. Above the mantelpiece, littered with crushed cigarette packets, hair-brushes and empty bottles, two photographs were tacked on the wall with drawing pins. They had evidently been torn out of books; one she recognized as Verlaine; the other was a boy with tight lips and fine arrogant eyes. These eyes seemed to be looking at her with such contempt under the high forehead and dishevelled hair that she turned away to glance again at Callaghan.

Their silence had lasted several minutes. It was a relief to her that he showed no signs of breaking it. There was a kind of weary content in inhabiting this room with him. She turned her eyes slowly back to the wall above the mantelpiece as if to defy the fierce, dishevelled boy. Then she noticed a third, very small picture, pinned up askew behind one of the bottles. It was so dusty and curled at the edges that she could only make out the blotches of crude red. It might have been an old Christmas card. She wondered with a pang of jealousy why he kept it.

'Well, my dear, have you taken in my surroundings? It's not a place I'd have wished you to see. But what could I do when I find you wandering like a lost soul almost on my doorstep?'

She was calm now, as if the weight of her heart kept her steady. He looked across at her, questioning. She looked back, taking in his weary eyes, his air of shabbiness and dissipation; trying to read his expression in which she seemed to make out bewilderment, triumph and anger. They stared at each other for a long time till she dropped her aching lids. She had seen all she needed to see: she had no more illusions. Everything confirmed what she had suspected ever since her return from Paget's Fold four months ago. There was no humiliation, no misery she would not accept simply to be with Reynaud Callaghan.

She said, quietly and reasonably, as if she were giving evidence:

'I had no idea of coming here. I was walking without thinking where I was going. I didn't know I was in your street till I looked up and saw the name. Then I meant to turn back. But it was too late.'

'How did you come to be walking in any street on a morning like this? You're not the sort of a woman that wanders about in an east wind for the pleasure of it.'

'I had to get out of the house. Something rather horrible had happened.'

As she spoke, she felt as if she were lying. The scene with Claude had become so remote and unimportant that she could not remember the details. She looked down, confused, and saw the letter she had written to Clara in such a passion of tenderness sticking out of her bag. She realized that she had forgotten all about Clara's misery. Nothing mattered but the fact that she was here in this room with Callaghan.

He asked:

'A quarrel, do you mean? You and Claude?'

'He lost all control of himself. He was cruel and unjust.'

'And why was he so angry?'

'Because of a letter. He . . .'

Callaghan interrupted sharply:

'Something to do with you and me?'

'No.'

'Thank God for that. I was afraid maybe . . .'

'You needn't be afraid,' she said, sharp in turn.

'You know Claude and I see each other now and then?'

'Yes. He talks about you. He admires you.'

'The more fool he. I had a morbid fancy to make his acquaintance. I came almost to like him. He's by no means so dull a dog as I once hoped. And he's a decent man, a generous man.'

Isabel said bitterly:

'He was neither decent nor generous this morning.'

'What man is when he's enraged with a woman?'

'Even with his own daughter?'

'A daughter's worse than a wife. You can't work off your rage by making love with her.'

'What an appalling thing to say.'

'I'm sorry. I forgot you had romantic notions about human beings.'

She sat silent and wounded.

'I've a genius for hurting you, haven't I, Isabel?'

She said very low:

'It doesn't matter.'

He sighed and frowned.

'I've a terrible head on me this morning. I can't think straight. What were you saying about a daughter? I didn't know you had one.'

'I told you I had. I told you that day.'

'Maybe you did. It's not the kind of thing I'd remember.' He stared into the empty tumbler and threw it on the floor. 'I'm sorry, my dear. I can't concentrate on anything, even you, without a drink. And they're not open yet.'

He lit a cigarette and began to smoke in quick, nervous puffs.

'I'd better go,' said Isabel, making a weak movement towards her muff and handbag. Her lips had begun to quiver again.

He dropped his cigarette and stood up.

'No, no. I'm a swine, but don't leave me like that. And don't begin to weep again for I can't bear it.' He stood up and began to move towards her. 'Talk, talk, talk . . . that's all that you and I have ever done. What's the use of all this welter of words?'

She said: 'No . . . stay over there' with such agitation that he sank down on the bed again and looked at her with a trace of his old smile. He picked up his cigarette. He had lit it badly and it was drawing on one side only so that the ash fell on his coat collar. 'My dear, I'm beginning to wonder if you haven't a drop of Irish in you somewhere. You fall on a man's neck in the open street but you won't let him within range of you inside four walls. I'm almost suspecting it's the first time you've been in a man's room.'

'Yes.'

'I believe you. Yet that's not how you struck me the first time I set eyes on you. What kind of a woman are you?'

'How should I know? A bad one, I suppose.'

'It's ironical, you'll admit. Here we are, alone together for the first time – in a room like a pigstye – you looking like Niobe with her hat awry and me with the spleen and a hangover. Winter Comforts . . . d'you remember?'

She managed to smile.

'Of course.'

He turned his head away so that she saw it at just the angle she had seen it at a particular moment in the Dutch Garden. The reminder was so sharp that she could almost feel the sun on her neck and hear the drip of the lead tanks.

'Well, it's winter all right,' he said morosely. 'And precious little comfort I'm being to you.'

They looked at each other once more and Isabel had the strangest sense that they had been together for years. When she spoke again, it was almost with the practical anxiety of a wife –

'Reynaud, what's this about your leaving St Mark's?'

'They've chucked me out, that's all.'

'But why?'

'General behaviour prejudicial to discipline. In other words, drunk and disorderly.' He waved his cigarette stub at Verlaine. 'I'm no more cut out for an usher than he was.'

'Where will you go?'

'God knows. Out of this bloody country if possible. Ireland, maybe. I might even enlist. They give you free board and lodging. Not to mention burial.'

She clasped her hands.

'Oh, no . . . no.'

'Why not? You could divert some of those belly bands and Balaclavas to me. After all, they owe me a shillingsworth.'

'Have you no money at all?'

'My end of term salary will just about meet my arrears of rent and my chits at "The Three Kings". They may give me a term's money in lieu of notice. I doubt it.'

She said fiercely, 'If only I had anything of my own.'

'Why? Claude provides for you doesn't he?'

'Yes. But I have to ask for every penny.'

'Then be thankful you haven't a taste for whisky at twelve and six a bottle.'

'Are you deliberately trying to hurt me?'

He smiled at her.

'Aren't we merely discussing money in the abstract?'

'You know very well we're not.'

'What's on your mind, Isabel?'

She said, without looking at him:

'If there were anything in the world I could do. Anything at all.'

'Not just money?'

'Not just money,' she said in a dry voice.

He considered her long and closely.

'What do you mean? Or believe you mean?'

'Do I have to say it?'

He lowered his head and rested his chin on his hands.

'I'm no good to you, Isabel. You frighten me, as a young girl would. You look old today. The first time I've ever seen you do so. It only brings home to me how much of a child you are, how much I'd hurt you. I'd hate myself for hurting you and you for being hurt.'

'I'm prepared for that,' she said. 'I would deserve to be hurt. Clara wouldn't miss me. But Claude . . .'

'You're not seriously suggesting leaving Claude.'

'What else?' she said proudly. 'You don't think I'd consider it any other way?'

He stared at her.

'Leave all and follow me . . . Is that it? I don't know whether to laugh or weep. Have you any idea of what you'd be committing yourself to? Have you ever lived in a room like this? The two of us together, we'd be lucky to get as good. I ask you, have you ever so much as seen a man in drink?'

'Yes.'

'How long ago?'

She answered at once.

'Eighteen years.'

'And you were so revolted that you've never been able to forget it.'

'The man wasn't you.'

'Isabel, Isabel. You're crazy, but you're superb. You can thank your guardian angel that I was drunk myself last night and I'm feeling the consequences. Otherwise . . .' he snatched another cigarette and lit it. She noticed how his hand shook. 'But it wouldn't do, my dear, it wouldn't do. It wouldn't be an *embarquement poru Cythère* at all. It would be my father and mother all over again.'

She said quietly:

'At least there would be no children.'

'Are you telling me you've thought the whole thing out? In a moment I'll believe you came here deliberately . . . that your weeping and wandering were all play-acting. Is that it?'

'I thought nothing out. I've told you nothing but the truth.'

'I can't fathom you at all. I doubt if I could even if I had the use of my head. I called you crazy just now. Yet you speak as if you were in your right mind.'

'I am, Reynaud. Perhaps for the first time in my life.'

They exchanged a long, almost impersonal look. It was Callaghan who looked away first.

He said heavily:

'No, my dear, no. Go home and forget me.'

'Forget! That's an insult.'

'It wasn't meant so. I'm thinking of you.'

'Men always say that.'

'Och, let's not quarrel. I won't deny I'm thinking of myself too. But it's the truth that I'm concerned for you. If you knew me at all, you'd know the fact that I'm trying to be honest with you means more than a lot of sweet words about love. I'm in no mood even for the thought of love at this moment, as you can see. But tonight, when I've a little drink in me again, I'll be cursing myself for letting you go. For don't think I haven't wanted you all these months.'

Her heart turned over with misery. She drew a fierce gulp of breath like a drowning person coming to the surface. They sat for some moments in silence. Then, with an effort she had not believed herself capable of making, she stood up.

'I'm going now.'

He came slowly over to her and put both his hands on her shoulders. At that, her eyes which had been as dry as sand suddenly filled up and the tears ran down her cheeks without a sob.

'Oh, Isabel.'

He laid his unshaven cheek against her wet one. Then he lifted his head and looked into her streaming eyes. His face was blurred by her tears: she smelt the whisky on his breath as they exchanged their only kiss.

As they drew apart, she forced herself to smile at him.

'Don't do that,' he said roughly. 'It's worse by far than when you cry.' She saw that there were tears in his eyes.

'Ah, no . . . no,' she said and turned away her face to encounter the cold stare of the boy pinned up beside Verlaine. To avoid it, she glanced beyond, looking for something, anything to distract her from her pain. She was like someone slipping helplessly down a cliff face, impatient, now that hope was gone, for the final drop yet clutching at any cranny. Suddenly it became of enormous importance to know what was painted on the crumpled card behind the whisky bottle. She would never be in this room again. In a moment she would have lost her last chance to find out. Straining her eyes she saw that it was a tawdry holy picture of the Sacred Heart.

'Of all things – to find that *here*.'

He followed her look.

'Are you shocked?'

She did not dare admit that she was.

'I thought . . . you didn't believe in all that.'

'I'm Irish enough to go a long way before I'll put a holy picture in the dustbin.'

'It seems . . . well . . . superstitious to me. I suppose because I wasn't brought up a Catholic.'

'*Does* your faith mean anything to you, Isabel?'

'I'm a wretchedly bad Catholic. I know that. But it does mean something. It was one of the things I was prepared to give up.'

'Had it occurred to you it mightn't give you up? Do you think, just because you're a convert, you can drop it like a dress you're tired of? You're wrong, my girl.'

'Haven't you dropped it yourself?'

'I've dropped the practice all right. As to the rest . . . don't ask me. All I know for certain is that it would have been one more torment between us.'

He pulled her veil down over her face.

'Now go, my dear. We'll do no good by talking. I've not much resolution. There . . . now I'll think of you as having taken the veil.'

461

'I'm not like her – She was lucky. Did she give you that picture?'

'She did.'

Isabel said, with sudden hysteria:

'That's why you kept it. Nothing to do with religion. Oh, you are hateful.'

He said quietly:

'I'm more hateful to myself than I can ever be to you.'

'Reynaud, forgive me – I don't know any more what I'm saying.'

'Will you take the picture yourself? As a token?'

'No, no I couldn't!'

He smiled.

'Not even to relieve me of the responsibility of it? As you say, it's out of place.'

She shook her head.

'As you wish – Will you pray for me now and then if you've a mind to?'

She sighed.

'Is there nothing you don't mock at?'

He touched her shoulder.

'I'm not mocking at all. I believe you when you said you'd do anything in the world. Well, that's what I'm asking you. Will you do that?'

She looked into his eyes and nodded.

'If you want me to . . . But my prayers . . . what good could they do? Wouldn't they be almost . . . blasphemy?'

He gave her a strange, slow smile.

'I think not, my dear. I couldn't pray for myself even if I wanted to. I'm too proud. But you're humble. Did you know that? Now go.'

Chapter Four

All the way to St Mark's Claude's fury possessed him as completely as his grief had done on the day of his father's death. Every resentment he had ever felt against Clara surged up violently. It seemed to him that all her life she had done nothing but frustrate him. It came over him with force how much he had come to hope, without realizing it, from her going to Maryhall.

His first doubts had been dispelled by a letter from Mother Lovell praising his wisdom in allowing Clara to have some months in the 'ideal Catholic atmosphere' of the Cressetts. Her own letters had built up a picture for him of a way of life he could never know himself but which was everything he had wanted for her. Lady Cressett had written saying how fond she was of Clara and how she hoped that she would often come to Maryhall when she was no longer Charles's governess. He had begun to dream of her marrying some young Catholic squire and having a country house of her own. Since he could never have a son, he had begun to look forward to the idea of a grandson. Now Clara had disgraced herself and destroyed the whole fabric of his dream. If Charles Cressett had been that grandson, he could hardly have felt more bitterly towards her.

When he arrived at the school, he was shaking all over. He could not control himself: he was in terror of how he might behave in front of his form. His rages in the classroom were merely for dramatic effect; none of his pupils had seen the real thing. During school prayers he went into the cloakroom and splashed his head and wrists with cold water to try and sober himself. He was calmer, but still trembling, as he snatched his gown from the peg and walked up the stone passage adorned with dusty plaster casts. Apollo and Antinoüs, Caesar and Socrates stared at him from blind sockets. The familiar smell of the school; ink, chalk, men's old clothes and mildewed books soothed him a little. By the time he turned the handle of his form-room door and heard the muffled stamping as the boys stood up, he had mastered himself. That morning he gave his lessons with unusual patience.

Back in the Common Room his anger began to throb again. Someone said to him: 'That rotter Callaghan hasn't turned up again this morning. I had to take Lower French. I hear Cavell's sacking him at the end of term. High time too.' Callaghan's absence was an added irritation. As he hung up his gown, it struck him that Callaghan was the only person whose company he could have endured that morning.

He walked home slowly for once, loathing the prospect of Valetta Road. If it had not been unprecedented, he would have lunched out. He was actually on the point of telephoning when he remembered that he must take a firm line with Isabel. After their conversation in the bedroom he could no longer trust her. He was filled with bitterness against her, too. She had not even attempted to see his point of view; he would force her to realize what he was suffering.

When he got home, he was exasperated to find that she had not yet come in. His mother, for once, was lunching out. There was no one to sympathize with him; no one on whom to vent his anger.

Zillah, seeing his thunderous face, said:

'I'll bring your lunch up at once, Sir. I'm sure the mistress won't be long.'

'Did she mention she was going to be late?'

'No, Sir. She went out very early, before Cook had time to give her the shopping list.'

'I'll wait.'

He waited twenty minutes. He almost forgot his fury with Clara in his new grievance against Isabel. Had she defied him and done something idiotic, such as going up to Worcester? The third time Zillah suggested bringing his lunch he spoke so roughly to her that she did not return. At last he heard the front door bell. The fact that Isabel must have forgotten her latchkey was a final, absurd irritation. He stamped down the passage, wrenched upon the door, tight-lipped with rage, to find himself glaring into the frightened eyes of Patsy Cohen.

'Mr Batchelor . . . I'm so terribly sorry . . . I didn't want to disturb you . . .'

'Who do you want to see, Patricia?'

'You,' she stammered. 'I'll come back later . . . I didn't want to interrupt your lunch.'

'I haven't begun my lunch. My wife has not returned yet. What do you want to see me about? Is it urgent?'

'Yes, but . . .'

He had never seen Patsy pale before. It entirely altered her appearance.

'You'd better come in,' he said harshly.

He hustled her along the passage into his study and shut the door.

'Sit down,' he commanded, almost pushing her into the great faded green armchair. She collapsed into it; her tiny body in the fur coat almost lost in its depths; her slim silk legs sticking out in front of her like a doll's.

'Well, what is it?'

She could not speak at first. She ran her tongue once or twice over her lips. Against her unusual pallor they looked brighter than ever. At last she brought out:

'It's Clara. We had a letter. We're so terribly sorry for you all.'

'Do you mean to say she's told you about this appalling business? I'm surprised she should be so anxious to spread the news.'

'She's so frightfully upset.'

He said grimly: 'So she should be.'

Patsy was trembling but she went on:

'I know how frightfully upset you must be too. But please, oh please don't be angry with her. She's so afraid you will be. She keeps saying it was her fault. But I'm sure it wasn't.'

'I'm afraid I disagree.'

'But her letter . . . Marmee said she'd never seen anything so pathetic. It was absolutely unlike Clara. You could hardly read the writing even. Surely you realize . . .'

'Realize what?'

'She just doesn't know what she's saying. The shock must have done something to her brain. She's got the most dreadful ideas. That she's disgraced you . . .'

'She has disgraced us all.'

'I'm sure it wasn't her fault,' wailed Patsy. 'I'm sure Mrs Batchelor knows it wasn't.'

'No doubt you mean well, Patricia. I should have had more respect for Clara if she hadn't sent you to get round me.'

'She didn't. She didn't.' Patsy was on the edge of tears. 'I came of my own accord. I wish I hadn't. I never dreamt . . . you were always so kind.'

'You flatter me,' he said, with a savage smile. He stood over her, with his hands in his pockets, glaring down at her. After a moment Patsy said in a shaky voice:

'I know you've had a fearful shock. I expect you're not yourself any more than she is. I'd better go.'

'No, stay, Patricia. There are one or two things I have to say on this subject.'

'Yes?'

'No doubt Clara has always described me as a brutal father?'

'Oh, *no*,' said Patsy, gripping the arms of the chair. 'Never. She adores you. Can't you see that's why she's in such a state? She just doesn't know how to face you. She feels you'll never trust her again.'

'She is perfectly right. As for this affection you speak of, I can't say I have seen many signs of it.'

'Clara finds it awfully hard to say what she feels.'

'Really? My own impression is that she feels remarkably little.'

'That's not true. I *know* it isn't. She's just one of those people who bottle everything up.'

'So you know my daughter better than I do?'

A little colour came into Patsy's cheeks.

'Perhaps I do in some ways. After all she's my best friend. She's just the opposite of me. I blurt everything out. I expect it's just because I'm shallow.'

He considered her, sitting there like some bright-eyed, smooth-furred animal.

'Shallow, are you, Patsy?'

He took a deep breath and said in a less bitter voice: 'I think you don't understand the situation. But you've stood up pluckily for your friend. Loyalty's a rare thing. I can never be quite indifferent to it, however mistaken.'

Patsy blinked away her tears.

'I know I'm a little fool. But I'm awfully fond of Clara. And I know you are too, whatever you say.'

He said nothing, but continued to stare at her. Her eyes, still wet, were more brilliant than ever and the long lashes had caked into points so that they seemed framed in soft black thorns. At last he gave her a wry smile.

'Men are rather partial to little fools when they happen to be remarkably pretty.'

She bit her coral-coloured lower lip that was a trifle swollen from crying, but did not answer.

'I'd like to ask you a question,' he went on.

She whispered: 'Yes?'

'You like men, don't you?'

'Yes, of course.'

'You'll probably get married one of these days. Suppose you had a son. And suppose that son were killed through someone's criminal carelessness. How would you feel then?'

'I'd feel awful of course. But I do believe I'd be a bit sorry for the person. Think what they'd be feeling.'

'I'm afraid I can only think of one thing at this moment: what that boy's parents must be going through.'

'You keep talking as if she'd done it deliberately.'

'Deliberately or not, what does it matter? The boy's dead.'

'It's awful I know. But surely, surely . . . Suppose it had been Clara herself.'

'Let's stick to facts,' he said, almost wearily. He shook his head and sighed. 'As if there weren't enough slaughter in your generation. This boy was young enough to have survived it.'

Patsy regained a little confidence.

'I expect I sounded rather heartless – I didn't mean to – It's just that one's got so used to people being killed suddenly.'

He considered her for some moments without speaking. His harsh expression relaxed but something in his face made her uneasy –

'Young men you know . . . friends of yours . . . have been killed, have they, Patsy?'

'Yes. Several.'

Again he considered her. When he spoke again his voice was low, almost confiding

'You said just now that you liked men. Evidently men like you, too. Are you kind to them . . . the boys who go out there?'

Nervous again, but in a different way, she drew herself further into the chair and asked:

'What do you mean?'

He said, still more softly:

'You know very well what I mean. Or do you think I am too old to understand or . . . or . . .'

Suddenly he swooped down and grasped one of her silken ankles, muttering in a thick voice:

'You're made to attract, aren't you? Made to make people forget?'

He fell on his knees and leant over her, his face close to hers.

'Please don't – *please*.'

'You're not frightened of me *now*, are you, Patsy?'

She wished frantically that he would be cold and angry again. His face was so near her own that it was out of focus. His breath, smelling of tobacco, came in gusts against her cheek. She drew as far back as she could, pressing her head against the chair so that a little fold formed under her soft chin.

He pulled her fur coat open and kissed her neck, almost groaning:

'So white, so soft.'

She was trying to push him away when she heard the front door open. In a moment he was on his feet again. His face was convulsed. She watched him force it back, with a fearful play of muscle, into a face that she could recognize.

'My wife,' he said.

He looked suddenly so old and unhappy that her revulsion turned to pity.

She whispered:

'I understand. I do understand. I won't remember.'

He turned to her blindly and seemed about to speak but said nothing. Instead, with an astonishingly swift movement he dropped on one knee and kissed her shoe. The next moment he was opening the door. She recovered herself enough to murmur: 'Clara. Promise you won't be too hard on Clara,' before he had gone. She heard light steps in the passage, then his voice, saying humbly:

'Ah, there you are, my dear. I was getting anxious.'

Even through her numbness, Isabel noticed the change in Claude's voice since she had last heard it. She stood in the dark hall waiting for him to question her. He merely asked solicitously if she had had anything to eat.

'I don't want anything – I'll go straight up to my room. I'm rather tired.'

'Can you wait one moment?' he implored. 'There's something I must say to you before I go back to school. It's almost time I left.'

He led her into the dining-room and shut the door. She stared at the bleak white tablecloth and the undisturbed knives and forks and said:

'You haven't had your lunch. Why?'

'Like you, I'm not hungry. But sit down. You look exhausted.'

'Can't we go into the study?'

'There's someone in there.'

Some constraint in his voice made her look at him for the first time.

'Claude – you look ill. You've not had any more bad news?'

'No, no, my dear. But it's about Clara that I wanted to speak.'

There was a sound of light footsteps in the passage: then the front door softly closed.

'Whoever it was has gone,' said Isabel. 'Do let's sit in the study. I really can't bear this room.'

He glanced at the black marble clock.

'I'm late as it is. This won't take a moment.'

Then he saw that she was shivering.

'What a brute I am. Come along: it's warmer in there.'

He took her into the study and seated her in the great green chair while he poked up the fire. Isabel, trying desperately to drag herself back to the present, said:

'This chair's warm. Do your pupils usually sit in it?'

Stooping over the fire, with his back to her, he answered:

'It wasn't a pupil. It was Patricia Cohen.'

'Whatever was she doing here?'

'She wanted to see me. She had had a letter from Clara.'

Isabel felt a stab of jealousy which brought back her old pain and made the present all too real. Far from obliterating the new one, it made it sharper still.

She said bitterly:

'So she could write to *Patsy*. But not a word to me.'

Claude turned and faced her, stammering:

'But my dear . . . my dear. That other letter . . . Obviously meant for both of us.'

'I read it. You forget that. I wasn't so much as mentioned.'

'The child didn't know what she was writing. You said so yourself – you said . . .'

'You didn't believe me, did you?' she broke in passionately. 'I was the one who tried to find excuses for Clara. You wouldn't listen. You were unjust . . . more than unjust . . . heartless. And now . . .'

'I know, Isabel,' he said wearily. 'You don't have to tell me. I realize it now. Can you ever forgive me?'

His face was so wrung with misery that she could not help pitying him. But standing over her, looking so abject, he filled her with distaste, almost contempt.

'This is rather a violent change, isn't it? Is Patsy Cohen responsible for it?'

He winced.

Isabel went on ruthlessly:

'Clara should be extremely grateful to Patsy. She's done what her own mother so utterly failed to do.'

'Isabel . . . please. I deserve every hard thing you can say . . . and more. Can't you accept the fact that I've seen that I was wrong and you were right?'

'It hardly seems to matter now.'

He sighed. 'Not to you perhaps. But it is going to matter to Clara.'

She said coldly: 'Did you write her that letter? The one you suggested this morning?'

'Thank God, no. Isabel . . . if you knew how I loathed myself.'

He sounded so wretched that she softened a little.

'Well, what do you propose to do?'

'I leave it all to you. I will go absolutely by what you say. One of us must write at once. Or should we send a telegram?'

'I wrote her a note,' said Isabel. Then she frowned and added as if to herself, 'Yes. I did post it after all.'

'Thank God, again. Oh, my dear, where would I be without you? Where would Clara be?'

'It won't mean anything to Clara,' she said. 'Naturally, I couldn't speak for you. So it won't mean anything at all.'

'I implore you . . . Isabel. If Clara realized what a father she has . . . I don't deserve to have a daughter – I don't deserve either of you.'

His face and voice were full of such despair that for the first time she felt guilty. She said slowly:

'You're being too hard on yourself. Don't people – sometimes – say things . . . do things . . . that no one would expect them to do? Things they didn't know they were capable of themselves?'

He muttered, 'Yes . . . yes, indeed.'

'Clara doesn't know. She won't ever know. So she can't be hurt.'

'You're too good to me.'

He leant forward and caught her hands, snatched them up as if to kiss them, then let them go. 'No. I'm not fit to touch you.'

She leant back in the chair, pushing her hat askew.

'I'm not good,' she said wearily. 'We'd better be practical, hadn't we? About Clara, I mean.'

He said humbly:

'Will you help me? I can see how worn out you are – that's all my fault too – But I have to get back to my grindstone . . . I shan't have a moment before the country post . . .'

'You want me to write another letter?'

'I hardly dare to ask you – But you would know how to put it . . . to say how sorry I am for what she's been through . . . that, of course, I'll write myself tonight.'

'Yes.' She stood up. 'I'll do it now. Then I must get some rest. I'm terribly tired. Zillah can post it.'

'My poor girl. You should never have gone out at all on a morning like this. I've been so full of my own concerns I've not so much as asked you where you have been all this time.'

'Nowhere in particular.'

He put his hands on her shoulders and she gave an involuntary slight start.

'You've been nearly driven out of your mind. How can you ever forgive me for all I've made you suffer?'

She forced herself to look at him and two pairs of tired eyes considered and questioned, each aware of something unspoken in the other.

Claude said at last:

'She will be all right. At that age . . . one can recover from what seems unendurable.'

She gave him the faintest smile . . . 'At that age – Yes.'

Suddenly, he took her in his arms.

'Oh, my dearest. I thought you would never smile at me again.'

Chapter Five

It was two days since Charles's death. Clara and Lady Cressett walked in silence along the border of the lake at Crickleham. There was neither sun nor wind: the air was damp and cold. By the water the bushes were knee-deep in fog; the statue of a nymph stood as if on a cloud among the dripping laurels. They seemed to be walking in a dream. Clara had no more tears; only utter desolation. She was no longer even afraid. Nothing mattered any more. It would have been a consolation to walk like this for ever, never to have to speak again.

'The boy is with God,' said his mother at last. The words came as a shock to Clara. She had not been able to comfort herself with the thought that Charles was in heaven.

'Yes,' she murmured. Then as the pain began once more to stir under the numbness, 'How can you even bear to speak to me?'

'Clara, you must stop blaming yourself. It couldn't have happened if it hadn't been God's will.'

'I can't believe that God *could* want . . .' she said. Her voice sounded loud as a blasphemy in the stillness.

'No. Everything that happens. Everything,' Lady Cressett's voice was dry from weariness. 'We don't understand. We don't see why. We can only pray.'

'I've tried to pray,' said Clara. 'I can't. Nothing seems real.'

They spoke at long intervals. Clara watched her own shoes moving over the gravel and the dead leaves.

'God wanted the boy,' Lady Cressett said. 'He took him while he was innocent.'

Clara noticed that for all her calm she could not bring herself to say Charles's name. She muttered:

'What you've been through . . . I daren't think. If only you'd be angry with me.'

'I have been angry,' said Lady Cressett. 'I couldn't control it . . . the feeling. I could only try not to will it. You weren't to blame. Or no more than the rest of us. When I was able to think of anything besides myself, I knew you must be suffering even more.' Clara glanced for the first time at her face. It was haggard and twitching and there were red veins in the eyeballs.

'You're so much too good to me,' she said wretchedly.

'You're very young. The first terrible thing that happens to us . . . we just don't understand it. Clara, I don't want to hurt you. But there are one or two things I feel I must try and say.'

'Yes,' said Clara, feeling her cowardly heart sink.

'Archie came to Maryhall last night as you know.'

'Yes.'

'Remember, I believe everything that Archie said. That's a very brave young man, Clara. I just want to know . . . it did happen as he said . . . didn't it? You tried to stop . . .'

'But so did Archie. So did Archie. If he's blamed himself, it's not true. We were both there.'

'Yes, he said that. But other people . . . you understand, Clara?'

'I don't care what they do. I wish they'd put me in prison.'

'There's no question of that, Clara. But, you must face it, they may say something harsh at the inquest. That will hurt. I know you don't deserve it. But Nan will be a witness. She has tried to convince his father. I am sure for your own sake you would rather not see Maryhall again just now. But in any case . . . my husband, well, you understand?'

'Yes,' said Clara, with dry lips.

'I packed your things. I've brought them with me in the car.'

'*You* packed them?'

'Yes. I know what Nan did. I don't listen to what she says. Can you forgive her, Clara?'

'Yes.'

'That is very good. You were always generous. But . . . and I'm afraid I have to say this . . . apt to be reckless sometimes. Perhaps you can guess what I found when I was packing your clothes. It was empty, yes. But it should never have been in your possession. Anyone in charge of a child . . .'

'Archie's revolver,' said Clara, almost in a whisper. 'I'd forgotten it. Truly, truly I never wanted to take it. I begged him not to give it me.'

'I'm sure you did. But you have enough influence over Archie to have been firm. If I hadn't been the one who found it and if it had come out at the inquest . . . well, I don't think I need say any more. It's with your other things. No one knows but the two of us.'

Clara broke out:

'Oh, why do you try to let me off? I deserve to be punished.'

'I am very fond of you, Clara. I know how you loved him. Then there are others who are fond of you, to be thought of. Your father and mother. And Archie.'

'Yes.'

'If you have heard how he spoke of you, how he stood up for you.'

'He was so good to me that day. I can't ever forget.'

'It's quite likely he saved your life, Clara. Nan must have been quite beside herself. She is very strong.'

'I almost wish she had killed me. I do wish it.'

For the first time there was anger in Lady Cressett's voice.

'That is wrong, Clara. But I'm sure you don't really mean it. You can't realize what you're saying. Think of Nan having to live all her life with *that* on her conscience.'

They walked in silence again. Then Clara said:

'Always the same. I think of no one but myself. Why should you, why should anyone care what happens to me?'

After a pause Lady Cressett said: 'Archie's not what one

would normally call a strong character. But all this, the really splendid way he came out, made me realize something.'

'What was that?'

'That if there were someone in his life he really cared for, he might be very different.'

Clara said hesitantly 'Yesterday he . . . he asked me to marry him. And I said no.'

'Was that because you couldn't think of anything like marriage just now? When these sad days are over . . . for we do get peace, Clara, even after what seems unbearable at the time . . . mightn't you think again?'

'Oh, I don't know, I don't know,' she sighed. 'I can't even imagine the future.'

'You must make an effort one day. It's hard now, I know. But I have thought about you so much. There's all your life ahead.'

Clara said in a choked voice: 'I would give it all up – all. Just to know that he . . . Oh, why couldn't it have been me?'

'I know, Clara, I know,' Lady Cressett spoke very quietly. 'But we have to go on living as long as God wishes us to. Our lives aren't our own to dispose of.'

'What ought I to do with mine?' said Clara, desperately. 'I've been utterly selfish, utterly useless. Always. There's something that haunts me, something I've always been terrified I ought to do. I've shut my ears. I was so afraid *that* was what God wanted.'

'Do you mean become a nun?'

'Yes. How did you know?'

'Wouldn't it be likely to be the first thing you'd think after a blow like this?'

'Then you see what I mean? What's the use of feeling sorry? I want to *prove* I'm sorry. I want to be punished.'

For the first time Lady Cressett smiled.

'The old Clara, all or nothing. Have you ever had the idea of becoming a nun before?'

'Yes. Because it was the one thing in the whole world I was most frightened of. So I thought God must want it.'

'Then you must have wrong ideas of God. God is not a harsh father, expecting us to do impossible things against the grain of our natures. Hard things, ah yes, often. But even those, out of love, not out of fear.'

Clara asked anxiously:

'Do you truly think I haven't a vocation? That I oughtn't to try?'

'Try by all means. But I don't think any Superior in her senses would take you if you tell her what you've just told me. As to having a vocation, of course you have one. We all have. Vocation is only a name for God's will for us. And so often it is nothing spectacular; just the ordinary duties of life as they come along. For most women, marriage.'

'I can't imagine marrying.'

'How often you've said that. All girls do.'

'Don't you see?' said Clara desperately. 'Less than ever now. I'm not fit.'

'You're being morbid. That's what I most feared. That you would turn in on yourself. Can't you see, Clara, that this is just another form of selfishness? God never sends us suffering, even the bitterest without a reason. Isn't he perhaps giving you a great opportunity now, the chance of really devoting yourself to making someone else happy?'

After a long pause, Clara asked: 'You think I should have said yes?'

'My dear, that's not for me to say. It is something for you to think about and pray about. All I know is that you and Archie have been brought together in a very strange and tragic way. Archie isn't a very happy person, as you know. There's so much latent good in him but he might so easily go to the bad. His mother worries herself sick about him sometimes. He's never cared for a girl before. The two of you might bring out the best in each other. There would be a home and children and best of all, the bond of both being Catholics. Don't think I'm trying to influence you, Clara. I've no right to do that. I'm only suggesting that you should weigh all this up very carefully and try to find out whether that might perhaps be God's way for you.'

When Lady Cressett had gone, Clara walked for another hour in the park thinking over this conversation. Yesterday, when Archie had asked her to marry him, she had been almost too dazed to take it in. All that she remembered sharply was the misery of his face when she had refused him. Yesterday there had been no past and no future; everything was blotted out by the huge fact that Charles was dead. She had written incoherent letters to her father and to Patsy; she could not remember a single sentence of either. But now, since she had seen Lady Cressett, the torn edges of her life had begun to come together again. It was at once a relief and a new suffering; the future stretched blankly ahead, thousands and thousands of days when she must get up, wash, dress, eat, fill up the day, go to bed. Suddenly she realized that by now her father must have got her letter. In less than a week she would be at home again. At the thought, her heart almost stopped. The thought of home was like going back to prison. Never again would he trust her, never again would she be allowed to escape. And she would be utterly alone. There would be no one who had ever seen Charles, no one who knew what she had felt and lived through the last two days. She wandered aimlessly along the misty alleys, losing herself, finding herself back at the tree or the stone bench she had passed a few minutes before. Soon she found she was completely lost. She stood hesitating not knowing which direction to take. Then, in the muffled silence, she heard a faint metallic clashing and whirring. She followed the sound and found herself in the rock garden where she had gone that first day at Crickleham with Archie. He was there, crouching over his miniature railway, absorbed and forlorn. He did not hear her at first; then, just as she was moving away, he looked up with a start, clutching a toy engine in each hand, and turned red.

'I say, old thing. What a swine you must think me. The fact is I just had to do something to take my mind off, well, everything.'

'I don't think you a swine at all,' she said. 'I know just how you feel.'

'You were absolutely right, Clara. Now you see just the sort of fool I am. I don't know how I ever dared,' he said, wretchedly. 'I suppose it was somehow thinking we were in it together that gave me the nerve. Just forget it.'

'Do you want me to?'

'Of course. I've been awake all night thinking what a bloody fool I was to think for one moment that you . . . Oh, Clara,' he threw the engines down and turned his tired, unhappy face away.

'Archie.'

'You don't need to do any explaining.'

'Archie, would it make a lot of difference to you if I'd said yes?'

'Oh God, don't torture a fellow. Difference!'

She went up to him, took his head in her hands and turned it towards her. At first he only stared at her blindly. Then, as he took in what she meant, she forgot everything else in the sight of his transfigured face. For the first time in her life, for one moment, she had made another person completely happy.

PART SEVEN

Chapter One

Clara travelled back to London the day after the inquest. It had
been even more horrible than she had feared. She had steeled
herself in advance for the questions she would be asked: the
comments that might be made. What no one had prepared her
for was the presence of Sir George Cressett. All through the
ordeal she had been aware, not of the inquisitive or sympathetic
eyes that kept glancing at her but of the pair that remained
steadily averted. In spite of herself, she was constantly
compelled to look at him, to verify each feature and to torment
herself with his appalling likeness to Charles.

As she sat in the train, trying to obey Mrs Hughes-Follett's
last words 'try and think only of the future, my dear', her still
dazed mind kept reverting to the day before. Archie had been
wonderful. If she were never to see him again, she would like to
remember him as he had stood up in the court, straighter than
she had ever seen him hold himself, going to such lengths to take
all the blame that at one point the Coroner had said drily: 'I
might almost suppose this young man is trying to get himself
indicted for manslaughter.' Yet, touched and grateful as she
was, all Archie's protectiveness had been no comfort to her. The
only thing that had given her the strength to get through
without breaking down were some words in her mother's
writing on a sheet of paper she kept clutched in one hand.
'Daddy sends you all his love and sympathy in your terrible
trouble darling. He will be writing himself tonight.'

She had that other letter with her now. It had arrived just
before she left Crickleham. Yet, oddly enough, it was that first
message in Isabel's writing that had meant the most. Perhaps
because the reassurance had come when she most needed it,

perhaps because all she had so desperately wanted to know was that he was not angry with her, his own letter, long and loving as it was, seemed almost as flat as the confirmation of a telegram.

Every station she passed seemed to put Charles's death further away in time as well as in space. The pain and horror were still there but they no longer made an impenetrable wall between her and ordinary life. As the train approached the outskirts of London, she began to think almost with pleasure of Valetta Road; even to imagine what it would be like to see Ruth and Patsy again. Then she realized that something, not the ache to which she was growing accustomed as one grows accustomed to the loss of a limb, was nagging her mind. How was her father going to take the news of her engagement? He must have got Mrs Hughes-Follett's letter by now. When Archie's mother had told her she was writing to her parents, Clara had hardly taken it in. She had been too dazed to connect her acceptance of Archie with anything that affected her father. Now she grasped that this might be an even worse shock to him than the other. Might it not seem one more proof of her utter heartlessness? He knew that Archie had been with her in the walled garden. He would suppose that they had been too occupied with each other to notice what Charles was doing. Suppose he were to remember the garden at Paget's Fold and his finding her with Blaze on the day of her grandfather's funeral.

The train was drawing into Paddington. She realized with horror that he might be on the platform to meet her. He had said he would, if he could get away from St Mark's in time. In a panic she pulled off the diamond ring Archie's mother had given him for her to wear and thrust it into her pocket.

As the train slowed down, she leapt up and looked out of the window, peering anxiously through the dusk. There were not many people waiting: she strained her eyes to pick out any man of her father's height and build. Then she saw her mother walking alone up the platform. Her relief was so great that she stumbled out of the still moving train and ran to her. In a moment she was in Isabel's arms, almost sobbing words she had never intended to say –

'Oh, Mummy . . . I'm so awfully glad it was you.'

In the business of dealing with her luggage, she had time to collect herself. Ashamed of her outburst, she sat stiffly beside Isabel in the taxi though she let her mother keep her arm through hers. They drove back to Valetta Road almost in silence. Isabel asked none of the questions she dreaded—she said little beyond how glad they were to have her home again.

There were two letters waiting for her in the hall, one from Ruth and the other from Patsy. She took them to her room, meaning to read them at once. But the sight of the room itself drove everything else out of her mind. How small and shabby it seemed after the rooms she had grown used to in the last months, yet how inexpressibly dear. There were her books and her few pictures, things for which she had once cared passionately and had now almost forgotten; there was the scratched desk where she had done her homework and even written poems. Without removing her hat and coat she began at once to pull open drawers and cupboards, identifying and rediscovering old possessions. In a few moments she was so much back in the past that she almost resented the few changes in the room; a chair in a different place, the new blue bedspread that had replaced the faded Indian cotton, even the vase of flowers on the dressing table. She had already reduced it to something like its old disorder when her mother tapped on the door saying:

'Your tea's getting cold, Clara. Come along. You must be starving.'

Tea was laid by a blazing fire in the drawing-room: a magnificent tea with all her favourite cakes. She had the oddest sense of having awakened from a very long nightmare. For a few minutes she ate and drank in silence. Presently her mother said:

'You know, darling, you look better already. You looked so terribly white and ill at the station.'

'I think I must be a little mad,' said Clara. 'All this . . . do you know what it keeps reminding me of?'

'What, pet?'

'Coming home from Mount Hilary for the Christmas holidays. The first tea at home after a bad term.'

Her mother smiled.

'At this moment, you don't look any older than you did at the convent. It's impossible to realize that . . .'

Clara interrupted, frowning:

'I just can't fit things together yet. Something seems to have got jammed in my head. It's as if I were two people and one of them had never left here at all.'

Isabel said gently:

'I know how you must feel. Don't try and think things out. Don't talk if you don't want to.'

Something unfamiliar in the way her mother spoke made Clara look at her. It struck her that Isabel seemed older. It brought home to her the fact that she had been away. Was she merely noticing lines and shadows that had been there before but which one only perceives on a familiar face after long absence? Isabel looked as if she had been ill or suffered some painful experience. Then she guessed that this must be connected with her own. And at once her nagging preoccupation returned. She asked abruptly:

'Will Daddy be home soon?'

'Not for another half-hour. He was so disappointed not to be able to get away in time to meet you.'

'Mother . . . there's something I must ask you before he comes back. Has he . . . have you both had a letter from Mrs Hughes-Follett?'

'Yes, darling. This morning.'

'And he's read it?'

'Of course. We both have. I didn't say anything about it on purpose. I thought you'd rather wait till Daddy was home to talk about it.'

'Is he angry?'

Isabel gave her a peculiar look and paused for a moment before answering:

'Angry? Why should you expect him to be angry? Naturally he was surprised. We both were. We hadn't been prepared for anything of the kind and you're so young.'

Clara gave a sigh of relief.

'I was afraid Archie would be one more nail in my coffin.'

Her mother smiled but her eyes remained troubled.

'Darling . . . what a very strange way to think of the young man you're going to marry.' Her face became serious again. 'I've thought about nothing else all day . . . trying to take in the idea that you're engaged . . . or want to be. It isn't just that you're so very young. But you never gave us the least hint in your letters. You hardly mentioned this . . . this Archie except as someone almost . . . well . . . absurd.'

'He's been anything but absurd the last few days,' said Clara defensively.

'Oh, my darling child,' Isabel exclaimed. 'I didn't mean to hurt you. I know how you hate showing your feelings. Forgive me . . . I've been tactless and stupid. But I can't help being bewildered – the idea's so very new and strange.'

'It's rather new and strange to me,' Clara said.

'Yes. Of course,' said Isabel almost absently. She seemed preoccupied with some worrying thought. At last she said hesitantly:

'You must know that I'm longing to hear all about it . . .about Archie, I mean. But not if you don't feel like it now.'

'What did Mrs Hughes-Follett's letter say?'

'It was a very charming letter. I'd show it you, only Daddy took it to St Mark's with him. She must be a very nice woman.'

'Yes. She was awfully kind to me. I stayed there, you know.'

'I know, darling.' As if fearful of coming too near the subject neither of them had mentioned, she asked at once what she looked like.

'She's not good-looking but she's always most exquisitely turned out and *soignée*. Just the exact opposite of Archie.'

'Ah . . . of course it's Archie I really want to hear about.'

But here Clara had no glib description ready. She said haltingly. 'Well . . . he's tall. He's got red hair. And he's frightfully good at mechanical things. I've told you already he's awfully untidy. Oh, yes . . . he's got a rather wonderful singing voice – Really good enough for opera.'

'Is he artistic, then? That should be right for you. You're so artistic yourself.'

For the first time since Charles's death, Clara laughed.

'Oh, Mummy – Archie artistic! You can't possibly know how funny that is.'

Isabel looked almost hurt but then she had to smile. Once Clara had begun to laugh, she could not stop at once.

'Well . . . the only thing that matters is that he should make you happy. It's so lovely to hear you laugh again.'

When Clara had recovered, she said:

'I'm no good at describing people. But Archie really is difficult. You see he doesn't seem in the least like anyone I've ever met.'

Her mother said hopefully:

'That's because you're in love with him.'

Clara frowned.

'But Archie *really* isn't like other people. Everyone admits it. Even his own mother.'

'She said he'd never shown signs of caring for anyone before. And that he was absolutely devoted to you. She seems very fond of you, Clara.'

'Yes. She seems frightfully pleased about the whole thing,' said Clara with such detachment that Isabel looked thoughtful. She said after a pause:

'It seemed to mean a good deal to Daddy . . . her being so obviously anxious to have you for her daughter-in-law. I was glad too . . . but it seemed perfectly natural to me.'

'I suppose . . . well, they are an awfully old Catholic family. One of the oldest. And Archie's the heir.'

'So is my family, the Maules, very old,' said Isabel with a touch of sharpness. 'And, like all old families, it must have been Catholic once.'

'I know, Mother, I know. Only I mean . . . those sort of people . . . well they all live in big country houses and so on. And the Hughes-Follett's are quite alarmingly rich.'

Isabel resumed her thoughtful look.

'All that, naturally, weighs with Daddy. Most of all, of course, the fact of their being Catholics.'

'You sound as if *you* didn't approve of something.'

'Don't misunderstand me, darling. Of course . . . I should be delighted if you made what's called a brilliant marriage. But you're such a child . . . not even eighteen. And his mother implies that you're thinking of getting married quite soon.'

'There's no point in waiting, is there? I should have thought the sooner the better. I've made up my mind.'

Isabel said almost harshly:

'Marriage isn't a thing to be rushed into, even these days. I know you'll say there's a war, that he'll be going to the front. But you've known each other such a short time. And marriage lasts for so long.'

'Not always, nowadays.'

'Clara . . . darling . . . don't even let yourself think about that.'

'I didn't mean it about us. Archie's got a charmed life.'

'Let's hope he has. But oh, darling, if you'd wait a little – if you'd be engaged even for a year.'

'I told you. I've made up my mind,' said Clara stiffly.

Isabel stiffened, too.

'You're as obstinate as your father. I suppose you realize that you're too young to marry without our consent.'

'Well, from what you say, it doesn't sound as if Daddy is going to object.'

Isabel lost her self-control. She said bitterly:

'It never seems to occur to you that you have two parents.'

But Clara was not attending. She had caught the click of her father's latchkey and was already half-way to the door.

Chapter Two

Claude had kept that evening clear of pupils and, after dinner, Isabel left him alone with Clara in the study. The subject of her engagement had been discussed between the three of them when he had returned from St Mark's. It seemed to Clara that it had gone almost too smoothly; there was something unnatural in the way he had glossed over all Isabel's hesitations. She found herself wishing that he would make some objection, however faint. She had never known him so compliant, so anxious to please her since she had returned home from Mount Hilary after that last summer term. Towards the end of the family conference, she and her mother had said almost nothing while he continued to talk about practical details with such enthusiasm that he might have been the person most deeply concerned in the whole affair.

'In all the circumstances . . . it would be better to have a very quiet wedding. You would wish that, wouldn't you? Of course you will have a Nuptial Mass. The Oratory is not our parish church but I should so much like you to be married there. There was a priest I met there once who impressed me so much. I wish I could remember his name. I should so much like him to marry you. But only, of course, if you and Archie have no preference of your own.'

To hear him talk of Archie only increased Clara's sense of unreality. She could not yet manage to connect Archie with her family or Crickleham with Valetta Road. She was almost appalled to see how much she had set in motion by a single gesture. He had asked her to put on her ring again.

'Even though their engagement will be private for the time being, I think she should wear it, don't you, Isabel? Certainly among the family. I will tell my mother not to broadcast the news just yet. But I may let Granny into the secret, mayn't I, Clara? It will give her such enormous pleasure. And, if I may say so, what a superb ring it is!'

At one point Clara had glanced at the heavy glittering stones that looked so out of place on her chapped, unmanicured hand and wished she had never seen them. For a moment they seemed nothing but an unwanted responsibility, like Archie's revolver.

Now that she was alone with her father for the first time since her return, Clara thought that he too looked older. Though his skin was still rosy and he held himself more stiffly upright than ever, there was an indefinable air of brittleness about him. She noticed too that, when he filled his pipe, he did so with slower, almost fumbling movements, unlike the quick ramming she remembered so well.

He turned to her with such a fond, happy face that she was obscurely disturbed.

'My dear . . . I hardly know what to say to you. To think that . . . after such tragedy . . . this should be the outcome.'

Once again she felt her old sense of inadequacy. She said lamely:

'You're really pleased about it then?'

'Pleased, my dear? Pleased is an understatement. This is one of the greatest moments in my life. I could almost say my *Nunc dimittis* – in perfect peace.'

She looked at him, a little frightened by the strange elation in his face and voice. He said more soberly:

'I know your mother thinks I am being rather rash . . . that I ought to insist on your waiting. And from every ordinary point of view, she would be perfectly right. But I cannot bring myself to look on this from the ordinary point of view. To me, it is like a dispensation . . . I might almost say a direct answer to prayer.'

She said faintly:

'It is all rather extraordinary, isn't it? I can't quite believe it myself.'

'It must be difficult, I know. The shock of happiness after the terrible trial you've been through. I . . . that is to say we, of course, have been so worried about you. Now you must think only of the future.'

Clara said nothing. She was trying to attach some meaning to the words 'shock of happiness'.

He pulled at his pipe, staring in front of him at the bookcase filled with black files. Those files had been there ever since Clara could remember. How often she had read their neat labels . . . 'Responsions', 'Little-Go', 'Fair Copies G.P.' and the mysterious one marked '*Haec Olim*' . . . as she sat anxiously beside him while he scored her proses in red ink.

'Do I seem heartless,' he said, 'to talk only of this? My dear . . . don't think I've forgotten the . . . other thing. I know how deeply you have reproached yourself. I know you must still be very much affected by it. Your mother felt that there was some reserve . . . that, even allowing for all you had been through . . .' He hesitated and cleared his throat. 'I said it was only . . . and it does you credit, my dear . . . that your own happiness was clouded by thinking of someone else's grief.'

Clara could only make an incoherent sound.

'Don't think I want to reopen that wound. But there's just one thing I want to tell you. I haven't told your mother yet. I don't quite know why.'

'What is it?'

'I had a letter from Lady Cressett this morning. A letter that touched me most profoundly. She must be a very wonderful woman . . . almost a saint.'

'Yes.'

'She could rejoice in your happiness . . . at a time like this. That made a very great impression on me. Perhaps you wonder . . . I am sure your mother did . . . why I asked so little about Archie. But I felt that if a woman like Lady Cressett who must know him very well . . . and who so obviously has a real affection for you . . . so evidently approves.'

Clara stared at her ring.

'She does very much want us to marry – yes.'

'But for that,' he said, 'I think I should have insisted on a much longer engagement. I could not have borne the idea that it might seem too sudden . . . even callous . . . to Lady Cressett. Now I see no reason why you should not be married, as you naturally want to be, before Archie goes to the front.'

'He thinks it will be about three months – less perhaps.'

'So soon?' He sighed. 'You are both such children.' He glanced involuntarily at the subalterns on the mantelpiece. 'Please God . . .'

Abruptly he stood and came over to her, clumsily smoothing back her hair.

'My dearest child,' he said. 'You've hardly so much as smiled this evening when you should have been so happy. Try and think of all the joy ahead. Such a wonderful new life beginning for you.'

His face was so tender and sorrowful that she forced herself to smile.

She said, speaking almost naturally:

'You know, Daddy . . . I can't imagine it properly. It's been so restful coming back to my old one. Just at the moment, I feel quite content with that.'

He kissed her.

'Oh, don't think I want to lose you. If you knew how I used to dread the very idea of your getting married.'

He sat down in the great green chair then half rose again.

'My dear . . . you should be sitting here. Whatever am I thinking of?'

'No, do relax for once, Daddy. Do you know, I've hardly ever seen you sitting in that chair.'

'I used to at Cambridge. Somehow I never seem to have had much time to since.'

'It's funny, isn't it? I might have gone to Cambridge myself.'

'Yes. I wanted that so much once. I had such ambitions for you.'

'I've always been a disappointment to you, haven't I, Daddy? I didn't mean to be, but . . .'

'My dear, never say that. If you knew how this surpasses all my wildest dreams for you.' His face lit up again with that almost frightening elation. 'To think that you are making a Catholic marriage – to think that there will be children growing up in a real Catholic atmosphere – all that, as converts, your mother and I could never give you. And the other aspects – I should be lying if I said they did not count.'

'I suppose we shall actually have money some day,' said Clara. 'It's seems very queer.'

He smiled.

'Very queer indeed to anyone in this family. I know money is not everything but there's no doubt it makes life very much easier. Yes . . . I can't deny I'm glad of that. Though I feel ashamed that you should have to go to your husband empty-handed or very nearly. But what delights me so much is that you should have the background I always longed for for you. You know my feudal temperament.'

She said hesitantly:

'I'm afraid Archie's not awfully feudal. He rather hates that sort of thing.'

'Then perhaps I shan't find him too alarming. But I expect it is just temporary with him. At his age, he is restive. Poor Larry was the same. But he reverted to type. I'm longing to meet my son-in-law.'

She said in sudden panic:

'We're not married yet.'

He looked at her ruefully.

'My dear . . . forgive me. I can't help anticipating. But it means so much to have something to look forward to. After all the tragedy, the devastation of this war . . . to have good news instead of bad. I'm getting old, Clara. And I find that makes one live in the future . . . not in the past as I had always supposed. In the future of others . . . that is.'

'Oh . . . Daddy . . . I can't bear you to talk like that.'

'Nonsense, my dear,' he said with his old smile. 'It's a very healthy sign.'

She said tentatively:

'You're not . . . ill or anything are you?'

'Certainly not. A little weary, that's all. I've overdone things a trifle lately. Who hasn't? My doctor wants me to cut down on pupils. And maybe . . . now that I know your life is so happily provided for . . . I might consider it.'

Suddenly, without the least idea she was going to, Clara began to cry. They were not violent tears but they brimmed over and crawled down her cheeks without her being able to stop them.

'My dear,' he said in consternation, 'whatever is the matter? Whatever have I said?'

She said unsteadily:

'I can't bear it when you talk like that.'

Misunderstanding, he said:

'I didn't mean to alarm you, my child. I assure you I am as sound as a bell. I assure you, nothing short of assassination is going to stop me from living to be a grandfather.'

But Clara's tears continued to run though she made violent efforts to check them. He leapt up from his chair and stood over her, with his hand on her shoulder.

'Clara,' he said at last, in a voice of such terror that she managed to control herself. 'You're not worried about anything else . . . You're not regretting anything?'

Through the blur of her tears she saw his face. Its expression was so like Archie's on that morning she had found him playing with his trains that once again nothing mattered except to wipe out that expression of blind misery.

She stood up beside him and threw her arms round his neck.

'Darling Daddy. Of course it's all right. Truly, truly it is.'

Pain and relief struggled in his face.

'You're certain my dear?'

She put a finger at each side of his mouth and pushed up the corners of his mouth.

'Smile! Oh please smile!'

He did so at last. Then he turned away, fished out his handkerchief and blew his nose violently. Clara did the same. She caught sight of their two heads in the smoke-dimmed mirror behind the rows of photographs. 'We're a pretty pair,' she said, with a hysterical bubble of laughter.

'Your mother will never forgive me,' he said. 'I should have seen that you were worn out. Goodnight, my dearest child and God bless you.'

'Goodnight, Daddy. And don't worry about anything ever again.'

They embraced stiffly, at arm's length, like acolytes giving each other the kiss of peace.

Chapter Three

The date of the wedding was provisionally fixed for the middle of March. As the days drew on towards it they seemed to Clara to gather speed till they ran together in one continuous streak. There was an interval of light during which she visited shops and dressmakers, opened parcels and, if Archie were on leave, went to a nightclub or a theatre; then an interval of dark, sometimes blank but more often filled with disturbing dreams. Most often they were of Charles, alive and nearly always in his most mocking mood. Occasionally she dreamt of the wedding. She could not get to the church in time or, when she arrived, another bride was walking up the aisle on her father's arm. Once she waited a long time at the altar but no bridegroom appeared; then she realized that Archie and her father were drinking champagne together at the restaurant they had gone to on the *Tannhäuser* night. Once . . . and this was the most painful dream of all . . . the bridegroom was not Archie but Charles. He was wearing the brown blazer and grey shorts he had worn in the kitchen garden. Horror and joy overwhelmed her. She cried out:

'Oh, Charles, I thought you were dead,' and was about to embrace him when he said, 'Don't touch me, Spin. Someone cut my head off and Nan sewed it on again. I have to wear Hero's collar to hide the join.'

One morning she woke up and realized that she was to be married in less than a month. What brought it home to her was the fact that Mrs Hughes-Follett was in London and was giving a dinner for her and Archie that night. The thought of this party, at which the bridesmaids and the best man were to be present, shocked her out of the state of blank light-headedness in which she had drifted for weeks. Up to now she had been almost detached from the girl who received congratulations, tried on dresses and wrote letters of thanks to total strangers. She saw Archie only at rare intervals and seeing him, if anything, increased her sense of unreality. He regarded the preparations for the wedding as a boring convention on which parents insisted and took no interest in concrete plans. It was enough for him that, once the war was over, he and Clara would be together always and be able to do as they liked without anyone interfering. Meanwhile he was so pathetically happy to be with her that she had nothing to do but let herself be adored. He asked nothing of her at all beyond accepting his devotion; even his love-making was confined to an occasional rough, but respectful, kiss or holding her closer than usual if they were dancing to a sentimental tune. He showered her with expensive and incongruous presents, ranging from a pearl necklace to a giant Meccano set. At first he had made desperate efforts to 'improve' himself, asking Clara to tell him books he 'ought' to read or suggesting they went to a serious play instead of a revue. But Clara preferred to adapt herself to Archie's tastes and found a certain pleasure in doing so. In his company she was spared any necessity of thinking and thinking was the last thing she wanted to do. Often their engagement seemed to her no more than one of their old make believes played in the setting of Ciro's and the Berkeley. Often indeed, when they were alone together, they dropped back into characters from the Schweinhund game, finding it a huge relief from having to think of things to say to each other.

One thing at least was almost painfully real: her father's

persistent and ecstatic happiness. He had taken Archie straight to his heart as 'one of the very best'. Things which he might have criticized in a boy of his own class he saw merely as charming foibles against the glamour of Archie's background. When Isabel once remarked that she did not think him nearly intelligent enough a husband for Clara, he insisted almost angrily that courage and kindheartedness were far more important than brains. He was fascinated by Archie's physical recklessness and his genius for understatement. He even seemed anxious in case Clara did not appreciate him enough. 'Archie may not be a brilliant talker,' he would say, 'but he's something far better. He's the kind that gets the VC and then apologizes for "stunting". I've dealt with young men all my life and I know the right thing when I see it. You're very lucky, my dear.' There were even moments when Clara was almost jealous of her father's affection for Archie which Archie whole-heartedly returned. She knew how much he had hated his own father but he was so devoted to Claude that he gave him almost as many presents as he gave Clara. Often he insisted on Claude's accompanying them to theatres and even nightclubs and the only concrete plan he seemed to have for the future was that Claude must retire and live with them. When Claude smilingly refused Archie would persist obstinately: 'What's the good of my beastly money, Sir, if you won't let me buy you out of that ghastly treadmill?'

The only breath of chill air in the warm, drugged atmosphere of approval in which Clara had lived ever since she returned to Valetta Road was her mother's attitude. Since that first evening, Isabel had never again suggested deferring the marriage. She remained strangely remote, dealing with the preparations efficiently but without enthusiasm. Archie was rather in awe of her: she was perfectly polite to him but there was no sympathy between them. Clara resented her mother's behaviour, not because she cared in the least what she thought or felt, but because it made her uneasy. There were times when it nearly provoked her to stop and think when all her instincts warned her that to do so might be dangerous.

This particular morning, however, she found herself nearer to thinking than she wanted to be. There was something uncomfortably definite about the idea of this dinner party tonight. It was as if she had been putting off learning a part in a play which she never imagined would be produced and found herself faced with the dress-rehearsal. She put off getting up as long as possible and dawdled in her bath till the water was cold, unable to face the day. When she was half-dressed, she wandered over to a shelf and began idly pulling out some of her old books. She stood for several minutes turning over the pages of her worn copy of Francis Thompson's *New Poems* and trying to find any connection between her present self and the Clara who had once cared so passionately for poetry when her eye caught the words 'The Dread of Height'. All at once she experienced a burning pang of shame and disappointment: she remembered the hot noonday on Chanctonbury Ring and the horrible man who had called her 'Missie'. The next minute she remembered all the absurd things she had been dreaming when she had first caught sight of a man's figure in the distance; her sense of loneliness and bewilderment, her sudden longing for a lover who would share her most private thoughts.

She flung the book away and snatched another at random without looking at the title. She let it fall open of its own accord and found herself reading:

> '*Je trône dans l'azur comme un sphinx incompris*
> *J'unis un cœur de neige à la blancheur des cygnes.*'

It was the Baudelaire Nicole had given her just before she left Mount Hilary. It was natural it should open there; she had learnt the poem by heart in those dready weeks of her mother's illness before that sense of blankness and unreality had descended on her. She shut the book and sat down on her unmade bed. Was she not in the same state of hypnotized lassitude at this moment? But there was nothing she could do. It was too late. She was like a person gliding with shipped oars towards a waterfall.

In spite of herself the poem continued to write itself out unfalteringly, line by line, in her head. She was almost frightened to find that she remembered it so clearly. Suppose that other things she had forgotten or tried to forget should resurrect themselves as vividly? To distract herself, she turned her mind to Nicole. They had not corresponded for months until lately she had written telling her that she was going to be married and Nicole had replied that her brother had known a small boy at Beaumont called Archie Hughes-Follett. 'He doesn't seem to remember you fiancé except in a surplice or in splints. He says he had an angelic treble and a fiendish capacity for getting into scrapes.' The thought of that letter gave Clara a faint comfort. By marrying Archie she would at least be able to move in Nicole's world; they would be able to meet, to visit each other's houses. Fond as she was of Ruth and Patsy, she had not tried to recapture their old intimacy since she returned to West Kensington. At best they had been poor substitutes for Nicole. She was seized with a passionate desire to see Nicole again and hear her husky voice. If she could see Nicole often, would it matter so very much that Archie would rather hear *The Bing Boys* ten times than *The Magic Flute* once? Then the faint comfort gave way to a new despair; she imagined how Archie would look to those critical green eyes and thanked heaven that she was in France and could not be invited to the party tonight.

The gong had gone long ago. By the time she was dressed and down in the dining-room her father had left for St Mark's and there was no one at the table but her grandmother. Isabel, as usual, was having breakfast in bed.

Mrs Batchelor greeted her with:

'I'm glad you've had a nice lie-in, dear. I expect you'll be up late with your grand party tonight. Quite an occasion, isn't it? It makes you realize that the wedding's quite close on us now.'

Clara let her chatter on while she sipped her half-cold tea. She had heard it so often before that she did not need to listen. Nearly every day since her grandmother had been told of the engagement she had listened to her marvelling at Clara's good fortune, at the impossibility of imagining her 'little girl' as a married lady, at Archie's being such a nice, unaffected boy 'not a bit what you might expect considering it's such a grand family and he might even come into a title one day, Lady Robinson says.'

But this morning, some unexpected words caught Clara's attention.

'You know, dear, I've just discovered such a peculiar coincidence.'

'What's that, Granny?'

'The date of the wedding. I do hope it's not unlucky. March fifteenth.'

'Why?'

'Well, dear, I don't suppose it would mean anything to you. In fact I'd almost forgotten it myself till I was looking at an old diary – but it's the anniversary of the day your poor grandfather died.'

Clara said nothing. Mrs Batchelor gave her an anxious glance and said hastily:

'Oh dear, I hope I haven't said anything to upset you. I'm sure I didn't mean to. After all, when you come to think of it, it's really very nice, isn't it? To think how sad we all were that year and how happy we shall be this.'

Clara still remained silent and her grandmother gave her an anxious look.

'Dear me, Clara, you don't look quite yourself this morning. Have I said the wrong thing again? You haven't had any bad news?'

'No. None.'

'I'm so relieved. I was so afraid for a moment that perhaps you'd heard that Archibald wasn't able to get leave after all and the wedding would have to be postponed.'

'I don't think there's the least likelihood of that, Granny,' said Clara, getting up and leaving the room rather abruptly.

The routine of things that had to be done carried her through the morning; she had an appointment with the hairdresser; one or two accessories had to be bought to go with the new dress she was to wear tonight. As she chose a pair of silver sandals, without first asking the price as she had done hitherto all her life, it struck her how easily she had acquired expensive tastes. Her father had been almost extravagantly generous with money for her trousseau. Occasionally she felt guilty, suspecting that he would have to drive himself harder than ever to recoup himself. But she salved her conscience by telling herself that this extravagance gave him pleasure, that very soon she would be off his hands for life and that, once she was married, she and Archie would find a way to make him accept money from them. For some reason the guilt was stronger than usual this morning and at the last moment she countermanded the sandals in favour of a cheaper pair. The assistant, who had been all smiles and flattery, froze at once. 'Of course, Mademoiselle sees that there is no comparison in *quality*. However . . . if Mademoiselle wishes.' There was such scorn in her voice, in the very set of her shoulders as she tied up the parcel that, for the first time, Clara realized what it would mean to be rich.

She lunched with Archie and his mother at the Hyde Park hotel where Mrs Hughes-Follett was staying for a few days and where the party was to be held that night. All through the meal Clara found it difficult to concentrate on Mrs Hughes-Follett's animated talk about the dinner and the wedding and several times missed her cues. Once, as she tried to improvise an answer to a question she had not heard, she saw her future mother-in-law looking at her anxiously.

'Clara, dear, are you sure you're quite well? You're looking very pale.'

Clara hastily assured her that she was perfectly well though a little tired.

'You've been overdoing things. There's always such a lot of running about and arranging, even for the simplest wedding.'

'I can't see why two people can't get spliced without all this fuss,' said Archie gloomily.

'Surely you can put up with a little fuss for once,' his mother said with a touch of sharpness. 'After all it's only a couple of bridesmaids and hardly anyone except the family and very close friends. After all one must have a congregation at a Nuptial Mass.' She said kindly to Clara:

'You'll find all the trouble has been well worth while when it comes to the day. It's such a tremendous ceremony, Clara. You said you'd never been to a Nuptial Mass, didn't you? That wonderful moment . . . I've never forgotten it . . . when the bride and bridegroom go right up on to the altar . . . The only time in her life a woman does.'

'Rot. Church chars do,' said Archie, 'and the pious old girls who arrange flowers.' The prospect of the party, which he regarded as waste of precious leave, had made him sulky as a schoolboy.

'It's not in the least the same thing.'

There was an uncomfortable silence. At last Clara managed to say:

'I do feel stupidly tired. I think I'll go home and lie down or I'll be a wreck this evening.'

'Very sensible, dear,' said Mrs Hughes-Follett with relief. '*No* . . . Archie . . . you can stay here and keep your old Ma company for once. If you go with Clara you'll only persuade her to rush off with you somewhere instead of resting. Just go and get her a taxi.'

'No, please,' Clara implored. 'I'd rather walk. I need some air.' It had suddenly become desperately important for her to be alone.

She got away at last, unaccompanied. She walked fast, with no idea of what she intended to do, along Knightsbridge and into Brompton Road. When she came to the Oratory, she stopped and surveyed it – its Romanesque dome and colonnades which called for sunlight and blue skies looked gloomy in the grey February afternoon. It was there that she and Archie were to be married in a few weeks' time. On an impulse she walked up the grimy steps, empty except for a cripple selling Catholic papers, and went in.

The great dim church was almost empty too; a few people, mostly women, were kneeling in prayer at side altars. But there was none of the peace and silence she had expected. Men in green livery were busy unrolling a red carpet and shifting benches with a noise of thunder. Clara knelt down at the back and began to pray automatically, as she did every time she entered a church, for Charles and his mother. But, though she buried her head in her hands, she could not concentrate. The shattering roar of benches being dragged over bare wood echoed back from the stone walls with a menacing sound. She looked up and saw two red velvet prie-dieu being placed right in front of the high altar. At the sight of them she suddenly realized the huge commitment of a Catholic marriage. She was not going to take part in a play but to do something irreparable. By accepting Archie for life there, in the presence of God, she was going to renounce all hope of ever finding her true love. It was as if, having worked out a smooth solution of a problem, she found she had misread the question. Panic seized her. She wanted to cry out: 'I didn't understand. Give me time! Give me time!'

She began to pray frantically for light and guidance, for some sign from heaven to show her what she might do.

A moment later, a hand fell on her shoulder. She raised her head from her hands and looked up wildly expecting she knew not what: a miraculous intervention, an angel. It was one of the green-liveried men, whispering loudly. 'Sorry to disturb you, Miss. We want to shift this bench.'

She moved quickly away, angry and hurt. It was as if God had deliberately mocked her misery. Her first impulse was to run straight out of the church. But where could she go? She could not face the thought of returning home or wandering aimlessly about the cold streets. She began to walk hesitantly up the side aisle, pausing at the chapels with their stands of guttering candles. The Sacred Heart and St Joseph, each had its sparse collection of praying figures. The third was Our Lady of Sorrows. Only one woman was kneeling there, motionless and almost invisible in the shadows, her face hidden in her gloved hands.

Clara approached the black and white marble altar almost on tiptoe. It had a forlorn and deserted look as if it were seldom used. There was an air of perpetual mourning about it as if it were devoted only to Requiem Masses. Above the altar was a sombre painting of Our Lady as Mater Dolorosa, indifferent enough, yet conveying an impression of almost inconsolable grief. As she stared at it, something seemed to calm the fever of her own troubles; she began to think remorsefully of Theresa Cressett.

Kneeling down on the hard bench in the centre of the chapel she prayed, not with fierce importunacy but humbly and soberly. She asked forgiveness for whatever share she might have had in Charles's death and for the grace to make true reparation for it, to accept whatever penance God sent and not, self-willed, to inflict her own. She implored Our Lady to console his mother and then, gradually detaching herself from her private griefs, widened her petition to include all bereaved mothers. For a little while she felt an extraordinary peace descend on her: she lost all sense of time and space, conscious only of a penitent joy in the renewal of her relation with Our Lady which she had neglected for so long. How simple life would be, she thought, if she could be always in this state of calm and humble recollection; she would be patient, kind, unselfish, strong. But even in the very occurrence of these thoughts, the spell was beginning to break. She had not enough of the habit of prayer to be able to keep herself at bay for more than a few moments. Already she was becoming aware of the discomfort of the hard wood against her silk-clad knees. The men had stopped moving the benches but sounds intruded themselves again; footsteps, resonant whispers, the dropping of coins in a box. With the return of normal consciousness, her old preoccupations surged up more violently than ever. Once more her mind was in utter confusion. She stretched out her clasped hands towards the altar, muttering under her breath, like a litany, 'What shall I do? Refuge of sinners, Comfort of the Afflicted, my darling Mother Mary, what shall I do?' But now the chapel seemed empty. It was as if Our Lady, whose presence she had felt for those seconds, had withdrawn, leaving only the mediocre painting of a woman with eyes upturned in grief. Clara put her hands over her face and began to cry, at first quietly, then uncontrollably, like a child. She felt someone take the place beside her on the double bench and shifted further away, without looking up. But the person moved closer to her. Presently she felt an arm round her shoulders and someone gently lowered her hands and drew her wet face against fur that smelt familiar. Clara let her head stay where it was, too exhausted to be surprised, while her mother's voice whispered:

'My darling child. My poor little girl.'

They stayed so awhile till Clara was calmer. As they drove back to Valetta Road, Isabel seemed disinclined to talk. It was Clara who kept saying with childish obstinacy:

'But how did you come to be in the Oratory, Mummy? That's what I can't make out.'

'I go there quite often,' said Isabel.

'You're not a bit the sort of person who drops into churʳʰ ˙ʰ at odd times,' Clara persisted almost peevishly. 'I'm sure you never used to.'

'No. I never used to.'

'Whenever did you take to doing it?'

'Oh . . . quite lately . . . a few months ago.'

'About the time I came home?'

Isabel answered in a muffled voice.

'I daresay. Yes . . . it was about that time. What a lot of questions!'

'Sorry. Just one more . . . However did you know *I* was there?'

'I was in that chapel when you came and knelt there.'

'I remember noticing someone. Of course I never thought of its being you. Otherwise . . .'

'Otherwise what?'

'Oh, nothing,' said Clara uncomfortably. 'Is that your usual haunt . . . Our Lady of Sorrows?'

'No. Actually it's the first time I've ever gone into that chapel. I usually go into the first little one on the left. The Sacred Heart.'

When they reached the house, Isabel, with unusual authority made Clara go and lie down on her bed. She moved quietly about the room, putting away Clara's outdoor clothes; then she drew a chair up close to her.

Finding herself alone with her mother in her own room, Clara was seized with a panic of embarrassment.

'You've been an angel,' she said, 'but I'm quite all right now. Do go and have some tea. You must be pining for it?'

'Do you want some, darling? If so . . .'

'No, really, thank you. I think I'll be sensible and try and get some sleep. There's this party . . . I'd almost forgotten it . . .'

'I'm afraid we must talk first, Clara dear.'

She knew it was inevitable but protested feebly: 'Not now.' Her mind was splitting up into disconnected strands. She fixed her aching eyes on the silver dress hanging over the chair. Only yesterday it had seemed of enormous importance: perhaps in a few hours it would seem so again. At one moment one was on one's knees imploring the grace to submit wholly to the will of God, however painful: the next one was in a rage because a hemline drooped a quarter of an inch. How did all these things fit together? What was important? What was real? She closed her eyes and said in a whisper:

'I must have been a bit hysterical.'

'Rubbish,' said Isabel so sharply that Clara's eyes sprang open again. 'Are we going to face facts or not? Because if not you may just as well go to sleep. You *have* been asleep, more or less, in any case, for the last three months.'

Clara had never heard her mother speak so incisively. She stared at her as if she were a stranger. Isabel said more gently:

'You don't really want to marry Archie, darling, do you?'

Clara gasped:

'But I *must*. How could I break it off now? It's far too late . . . Besides . . .'

'Do you love him or don't you?'

'Oh, Mummy . . . I don't know. Does it really matter very much?'

'Matter!' said Isabel with such scorn that Clara was almost frightened. She said defensively:

'You said yourself once that it was better not to have romantic feelings when one got married. Anyway I *am* very fond of Archie.'

'Yes. As you might be of a nice dog.'

Clara sat up on the bed. 'You've no right to say that. You're being horribly unjust. I know you hated Archie from the first.'

'I don't hate him,' her mother said quietly. 'I'm very grateful for all he did for you. I'm very touched by his pathetic devotion to you. But I've never for one moment thought he was the right husband for you.'

'Surely that's for me to say.'

'Certainly. If you loved him.'

'I wish you'd stop harping on that. Daddy thinks he's the right person. You know how terribly pleased Daddy is about it.'

'I know, darling,' Isabel spoke all the more softly as Clara's voice rose. 'And I know how difficult that makes it for you.'

Clara looked at her mother. She had never known her in this mood of gentle firmness. Even her face was subtly different, as familiar faces are in dreams. She said, almost pleading:

'Mummy, I couldn't. It would break Daddy's heart.'

'It would be a terrible disappointment to him, yes. But if he knew that you weren't happy . . .'

Clara clutched her temples. 'I've always disappointed him – always. You don't know. You don't understand. And now . . . for the very first time . . . no, Mummy, it's impossible.'

Her mother looked down and sighed. After a moment she said hesitantly:

'Clara . . . you're far too young to realize this. But you'll find one day that you can't make people you care for happy just by giving them what they imagine they want.'

'Imagine? But he *does* want it.'

'What Daddy wants is not this actual marriage but his idea of it.'

For the first time, Clara stopped to think.

'I wonder. You might be right. But Archie . . . Archie really would be unhappy.'

Her mother clasped her hands together: her face was sterner and older than Clara had ever seen it.

'Unhappy? If you and Archie get married, Clara, the best for both of you would be that he should go straight to the front and get killed.'

Clara leapt up, furious.

'How dare you! Of all the wicked, vile things to say. I used to think you were soft and sentimental. I believed you were fond of me. I used to feel guilty because I wasn't fond of you. Now I see you're as hard as nails. I don't believe you've ever cared for anyone ever.'

'No?' Isabel had gone deathly white and the knuckles stood out on her clasped hands.

Clara sat down on the bed and burst into nervous sobs. Between them she said frantically.

'You're right . . . I'm not fit . . . No one ought to have anything to do with me . . . I just destroy all the people I care for. No one should be fond of me ever.'

Once again she felt Isabel's arm round her shoulders.

'Hush, my darling . . . it isn't true . . . it isn't true. You've tormented yourself about Charles haven't you?' She spoke on quietly, almost hypnotically through Clara's convulsive sobbing. 'You thought you could somehow make up for it . . .

forget it. My pet . . . the only way we can make up is by bearing our own unhappiness.'

At last the sobs died down and Clara relaxed against her mother's shoulder. They stayed thus a long time. Then Isabel said:

'I had to be cruel, darling. I had to give you a shock that would make you wake up.'

Clara asked childishly:

'Why didn't you long ago?'

'How could I? I was so frightened for you . . . after all you'd been through. I thought that you might stay in your half-awake state all your life and it would be safer not to disturb you. But then . . . when I saw you in the chapel . . .'

Clara nestled up to her as she had not done since she was a small child.

'Mummy, was it me you've been praying for all these months?'

Isabel hesitated a moment before answering:

'Of course I've prayed for you. But for . . . well . . . other people too.'

Clara smiled.

'I should hope so. Selfish to the last, aren't I.'

Isabel hugged her.

'Mother . . . I've just remembered. This party tonight. What am I to do? I can't possibly go.'

'I'll telephone and say that you are ill. If I do it now . . . there will be time for Philippa to put the other people off.'

'Do you think she'll have any suspicion? Still, she did say I wasn't looking well at lunch.'

'I hope she does have suspicions. It will make it easier all round.'

Already Clara was beginning to realize what she was going to have to do. She even had a pang of childish disappointment at all the pleasant things she would have to give up. She said, despising herself for her cowardice:

'Mother . . . I don't know how I'm going to break it to Archie . . . You couldn't possibly . . .?'

'No, darling, I'm afraid that's something you'll have to do yourself. Shall I ask him to come round tonight?'

Clara sighed and set her teeth.

'Yes.'

'That's a brave child. I do know how hard it's going to be. But I'll manage all the horrid practical details for you.'

Clara looked at her mother with admiration.

'You know, you *have* changed. You never used to be like that . . . so . . . so definite and thinking things out.'

Isabel smiled.

'Well . . . people change. There's another thing I've been thinking about. I wondered . . . when this is over . . . if you'd like to go to Paget's Fold for a little?'

'Paget's Fold?' said Clara eagerly. 'Oh, I would. It's the one place where I feel I could bear to be at the moment. I never thought of it . . . yet the moment you said it I knew it was right. However did you know?'

'I suppose I went by my own feelings. It's not just that it's so peaceful there – or that the old aunts are so sweet. But things seem more real down there. One finds out what is important and what isn't.'

'I know just what you mean,' said Clara. She added naively: 'Isn't that odd? I never imagined you and I could ever feel the same about anything.'

'Very odd,' said Isabel with sweet irony.

Clara considered.

'You know . . . you are different. Even your face and your voice. I thought there was something different about you that day I came back from Maryhall.' It was the first time she had managed to bring out that word. She guessed that Isabel, with this new alarming, yet reassuring sharpness, had noticed it too.

'Why were you the only person who understood about Archie and me?'

Isabel smiled.

'I wonder.'

'It's so strange,' Clara sighed. 'It's as if I saw you for the first time as a real person.'

'Perhaps I wasn't real to anyone. Even to myself.'

'But that's just how I feel,' said Clara. 'How do people become real? Does one just change as one gets older? Or did something definite happen to you?'

Isabel did not answer at once. At last she said, very low: 'Something did happen. Yes.'

'I wish you'd tell me.'

She looked at her mother eagerly and Isabel met her look with a strange, transfiguring smile. It brought back all the beauty to her weary face and added something to it that Clara had never seen and could not fathom. Confronted with that smile she felt a raw and ignorant child. Her mother slowly shook her head:

'Not yet, Clara. Not for a long, long time. Perhaps never.'

Antonia White

FROST IN MAY (1)
Frost in May
The Lost Traveller

FROST IN MAY (2)
The Sugar House
Beyond the Glass

The **Frost in May** quartet consists of a series of novels about a Catholic girl growing up in the first decades of this century. The heroine's intense relationship with her father, and the all-pervading influence of the Catholic faith are their dominant themes.

Frost in May is a portrait of a child's life in the enclosed world of a Catholic convent.

In **The Lost Traveller**, Clara experiences the vagaries of adolescence against the background of a world at war.

In **The Sugar House**, Clara, now twenty-one, strives to come to terms with a doomed love and an equally doomed marriage. Her dream of life crumbles, and in **Beyond the Glass** Clara has a strange, passionate love affair which erodes her fragile sense of identity – the glass wall shatters and she descends into madness . . .

All four novels have been filmed for BBC TV

All are available in Fontana

Simone de Beauvoir

She Came to Stay   £1.50

The passionately eloquent and ironic novel she wrote as an act of revenge against the woman who so nearly destroyed her life with the philosopher Sartre. 'A writer whose tears for her characters freeze as they drop.' *Sunday Times*

Les Belles Images   £1.25

Her totally absorbing story of upper-class Parisian life. 'A brilliant sortie into Jet Set France.' *Daily Mirror*. 'As compulsively readable as it it is profound, serious and disturbing.' *Queen*

The Mandarins   £1.95

'A magnificent satire by the author of *The Second Sex*. *The Mandarins* gives us a brilliant survey of the post-war French intellectual . . . a dazzling panorama.' *New Statesman*. 'A superb document . . . a remarkable novel.' *Sunday Times*

The Woman Destroyed   £1.50

'Immensely intelligent, basically passionless stories about the decay of passion. Simone de Beauvoir shares, with other women novelists, the ability to write about emotion in terms of direct experience . . . The middle-aged women at the centre of the three stories in *The Woman Destroyed* all suffer agonisingly the pains of growing older and of being betrayed by husbands and children.' *Sunday Times*

FONTANA PAPERBACKS

Beryl Bainbridge

TWICE WINNER OF THE WHITBREAD AWARD

'A brilliantly talented writer.' *The Times*.
'It is a joy to find writers with the skill and observation of
Miss Bainbridge.' *Daily Mirror*.
'Alarming humour . . . a powerful talent.'
Sunday Telegraph

A Quiet Life   £1·50

The Dressmaker   £1·25

The Bottle Factory Outing   £1·25

Harriet Said . . .   £1·25

Injury Time   £1·50

Young Adolf   £1·25

Another Part of the Wood   £1·25

Winter Garden   £1·50

Fontana Paperbacks

Eric Ambler

A world of espionage and counter-espionage, of sudden violence and treacherous calm; of blackmailers, murderers, gun-runners—and none too virtuous heroes. This is the world of Eric Ambler. 'Unquestionably our best thriller writer.' *Graham Greene*. 'He is incapable of writing a dull paragraph.' *Sunday Times*. 'Eric Ambler is a master of his craft.' *Sunday Telegraph*.

Fontana Paperbacks

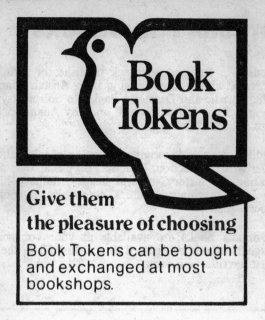

Fontana Paperbacks

Fontana is a leading paperback publisher of fiction and non-fiction, with authors ranging from Alistair MacLean, Agatha Christie and Desmond Bagley to Solzhenitsyn and Pasternak, from Gerald Durrell and Joy Adamson to the famous Modern Masters series.

In addition to a wide-ranging collection of internationally popular writers of fiction, Fontana also has an outstanding reputation for history, natural history, military history, psychology, psychiatry, politics, economics, religion and the social sciences.

All Fontana books are available at your bookshop or newsagent; or can be ordered direct. Just fill in the form and list the titles you want.

FONTANA BOOKS, Cash Sales Department, G.P.O. Box 29, Douglas, Isle of Man, British Isles. Please send purchase price, plus 8p per book. Customers outside the U.K. send purchase price, plus 10p per book. Cheque, postal or money order. No currency.

NAME (Block letters) _____

ADDRESS _____

_____

_____